greatest works of
Rudyard Kipling

I0739724

greatest works of
Rudyard Kipling

GREATEST WORKS OF RUDYARD KIPLING

ALL RIGHTS RESERVED. No part of this book may be reproduced in a retrieval system or transmitted in any form or by any means electronic, mechanical, photocopying, recording and or without permission of the publisher.

Published by

MAPLE PRESS PRIVATE LIMITED
office: A-63, Sector 58, Noida 201301, U.P., India
phone: +91 120 455 3581, 455 3583
email: info@maplepress.co.in
website: www.maplepress.co.in

ISBN: 978-93-80005-66-9

CONTENTS

THE JUNGLE BOOK

THE SECOND JUNGLE BOOK

JUST SO STORIES

THE EYES OF ASIA

THE STORY OF GADSBY

THE JUNGLE BOOK

MOWGLI'S BROTHERS

Now Rann the Kite brings home the night

That Mang the Bat sets free—

The herds are shut in byre and hut

For loosed till dawn are we.

This is the hour of pride and power,

Talon and tush and claw.

Oh, hear the call!—Good hunting all

That keep the Jungle Law!

Night-Song in the Jungle

It was seven o'clock of a very warm evening in the Seeonee hills when Father Wolf woke up from his day's rest, scratched himself, yawned, and spread out his paws one after the other to get rid of the sleepy feeling in their tips. Mother Wolf lay with her big gray nose dropped across her four tumbling, squealing cubs, and the moon shone into the mouth of the cave where they all lived. "Augrh!" said Father Wolf. "It is time to hunt again." He was going to spring down hill when a little shadow with a bushy tail crossed the threshold and whined: "Good luck go with you, O Chief of the Wolves. And good luck and strong white teeth go with noble children that they may never forget the hungry in this world."

It was the jackal—Tabaqui, the Dish-licker—and the wolves of India despise Tabaqui because he runs about making mischief, and telling tales, and eating rags and pieces of leather from the village rubbish-heaps. But they are afraid of him too, because Tabaqui, more than anyone else in the jungle, is apt to go mad, and then he forgets that he was ever afraid of anyone, and runs through the forest biting everything in his way. Even the tiger runs and hides when little Tabaqui goes mad, for madness is the most disgraceful thing that can overtake a wild creature. We call it hydrophobia, but they call it dewanee—the madness—and run.

"Enter, then, and look," said Father Wolf stiffly, "but there is no food here."

"For a wolf, no," said Tabaqui, "but for so mean a person as myself a dry bone is a good feast. Who are we, the Gidurlog [the jackal people], to pick and choose?" He scuttled to the back of the cave, where he found the bone of a buck with some meat on it, and sat cracking the end merrily.

"All thanks for this good meal," he said, licking his lips. "How beautiful are the noble children! How large are their eyes! And so young too! Indeed, indeed, I might have remembered that the children of kings are men from the beginning."

Now, Tabaqui knew as well as anyone else that there is nothing so unlucky as to compliment children to their faces. It pleased him to see Mother and Father Wolf look uncomfortable.

Tabaqui sat still, rejoicing in the mischief that he had made, and then he said spitefully:

"Shere Khan, the Big One, has shifted his hunting grounds. He will hunt among these hills for the next moon, so he has told me."

Shere Khan was the tiger who lived near the Waingunga River, twenty miles away.

"He has no right!" Father Wolf began angrily—"By the Law of the Jungle he has no right to change his quarters without due warning. He will frighten every head of game within ten miles, and I—I have to kill for two, these days."

"His mother did not call him Lungri [the Lame One] for nothing," said Mother Wolf quietly. "He has been lame in one foot from his birth. That is why he has only killed cattle. Now the villagers of the Waingunga are angry with him, and he has come here to make our villagers angry. They will scour the jungle for him when he is far away, and we and our children must run when the grass is set alight. Indeed, we are very grateful to Shere Khan!"

"Shall I tell him of your gratitude?" said Tabaqui.

"Out!" snapped Father Wolf. "Out and hunt with thy master. Thou hast done harm enough for one night."

"I go," said Tabaqui quietly. "Ye can hear Shere Khan below in the thickets. I might have saved myself the message."

Father Wolf listened, and below in the valley that ran down to a little river he heard the dry, angry, snarly, singsong whine of a tiger who has caught nothing and does not care if all the jungle knows it.

"The fool!" said Father Wolf. "To begin a night's work with that noise! Does he think that our buck are like his fat Waingunga bullocks?"

"H'sh. It is neither bullock nor buck he hunts to-night," said Mother Wolf. "It is Man."

The whine had changed to a sort of humming purr that seemed to come from every quarter of the compass. It was the noise that bewilders woodcutters and gypsies sleeping in the open, and makes them run sometimes into the very mouth of the tiger.

"Man!" said Father Wolf, showing all his white teeth. "Faugh! Are there not enough beetles and frogs in the tanks that he must eat Man, and on our ground too!"

The Law of the Jungle, which never orders anything without a reason, forbids every beast to eat Man except when he is killing to show his children how to kill, and then he must hunt outside the hunting grounds of his pack or tribe. The real reason for this is that man-killing means, sooner or later, the arrival of white men on elephants, with guns, and hundreds of brown men with gongs and rockets and torches. Then everybody in the jungle suffers. The reason the beasts give among themselves is that Man is the weakest and most defenseless of all living things, and it is unsportsmanlike to touch him. They say too—and it is true—that man-eaters become mangy, and lose their teeth.

The purr grew louder, and ended in the full-throated "Aaarh!" of the tiger's charge.

Then there was a howl—an untigerish howl—from Shere Khan. "He has missed," said Mother Wolf. "What is it?"

Father Wolf ran out a few paces and heard Shere Khan muttering and mumbling savagely as he tumbled about in the scrub.

"The fool has had no more sense than to jump at a woodcutter's campfire, and has burned his feet," said Father Wolf with a grunt. "Tabaqui is with him."

"Something is coming uphill," said Mother Wolf, twitching one ear. "Get ready."

The bushes rustled a little in the thicket, and Father Wolf dropped with his haunches under him, ready for his leap. Then, if you had been watching, you would have seen the most wonderful thing in the world—the wolf checked in mid-spring. He made his bound before he saw what it was he was jumping at, and then he tried to stop himself. The result was that he shot up straight into the air for four or five feet, landing almost where he left ground.

"Man!" he snapped. "A man's cub. Look!"

Directly in front of him, holding on by a low branch, stood a naked brown baby who could just walk—as soft and as dimpled a little atom as ever came to a wolf's cave at night. He looked up into Father Wolf's face, and laughed.

"Is that a man's cub?" said Mother Wolf. "I have never seen one. Bring it here."

A Wolf accustomed to moving his own cubs can, if necessary, mouth an egg without breaking it, and though Father Wolf's jaws closed right on the child's back not a tooth even scratched the skin as he laid it down among the cubs.

"How little! How naked, and—how bold!" said Mother Wolf softly. The baby was pushing his way between the cubs to get close to the warm hide. "Ahai! He is taking his meal with the others. And so this is a man's cub. Now, was there ever a wolf that could boast of a man's cub among her children?"

"I have heard now and again of such a thing, but never in our Pack or in my time," said Father Wolf. "He is altogether without hair, and I could kill him with a touch of my foot. But see, he looks up and is not afraid."

The moonlight was blocked out of the mouth of the cave, for Shere Khan's great square head and shoulders were thrust into the entrance. Tabaqui, behind him, was squeaking: "My lord, my lord, it went in here!"

"Shere Khan does us great honor," said Father Wolf, but his eyes were very angry. "What does Shere Khan need?"

"My quarry. A man's cub went this way," said Shere Khan. "Its parents have run off. Give it to me."

Shere Khan had jumped at a woodcutter's campfire, as Father Wolf had said, and was furious from the pain of his burned feet. But Father Wolf knew that the mouth of the cave was too narrow for a tiger to come in by. Even where he was, Shere Khan's shoulders and forepaws were cramped for want of room, as a man's would be if he tried to fight in a barrel.

"The Wolves are a free people," said Father Wolf. "They take orders from the Head of the Pack, and not from any striped cattle-killer. The man's cub is ours—to kill if we choose."

"Ye choose and ye do not choose! What talk is this of choosing? By the bull that I killed, am I to stand nosing into your dog's den for my fair dues? It is I, Shere Khan, who speak!"

The tiger's roar filled the cave with thunder. Mother Wolf shook herself clear of the cubs and sprang forward, her eyes, like two green moons in the darkness, facing the blazing eyes of Shere Khan.

"And it is I, Raksha [The Demon], who answers. The man's cub is mine, Lungri—mine to me! He shall not be killed. He shall live to run with the Pack and to hunt with the Pack; and in the end, look you, hunter of little naked cubs—frog-eater—fish-killer—he shall hunt thee! Now get hence, or by the Sambhur that I killed (I eat no starved cattle), back thou goest to thy mother, burned beast of the jungle, lamer than ever thou camest into the world! Go!"

Father Wolf looked on amazed. He had almost forgotten the days when he won Mother Wolf in fair fight from five other wolves, when she ran in the Pack and was not called The Demon for compliment's sake. Shere Khan might have faced Father Wolf, but he could not stand up against Mother Wolf, for he knew that where he was she had all the advantage of the ground, and would fight to the death. So he backed out of the cave mouth growling, and when he was clear he shouted:

"Each dog barks in his own yard! We will see what the Pack will say to this fostering of man-cubs. The cub is mine, and to my teeth he will come in the end, O bush-tailed thieves!"

Mother Wolf threw herself down panting among the cubs, and Father Wolf said to her gravely:

"Shere Khan speaks this much truth. The cub must be shown to the Pack. Wilt thou still keep him, Mother?"

"Keep him!" she gasped. "He came naked, by night, alone and very hungry; yet he was not afraid! Look, he has pushed one of my babes to one side already. And that lame butcher would have killed him and would have run off to the Waingunga while the villagers here hunted through all our lairs in revenge! Keep him? Assuredly I will keep him. Lie still, little frog. O thou Mowgli—for Mowgli the Frog I will call thee—the time will come when thou wilt hunt Shere Khan as he has hunted thee."

"But what will our Pack say?" said Father Wolf.

The Law of the Jungle lays down very clearly that any wolf may, when he marries, withdraw from the Pack he belongs to. But as soon as his cubs are old enough to stand on their feet he must bring them to the Pack Council, which is generally held once a month at full moon, in order that the other wolves may identify them. After that inspection the cubs are free to run where they please, and until they have killed their first buck no excuse is accepted if a grown wolf of the Pack kills one of them. The punishment is death where the murderer can be found; and if you think for a minute you will see that this must be so.

Father Wolf waited till his cubs could run a little, and then on the night of the Pack Meeting took them and Mowgli and Mother Wolf to the Council Rock—a hilltop covered with stones and boulders where a hundred wolves could hide. Akela, the great gray Lone Wolf, who led all the Pack by strength and cunning, lay out at full length on his rock, and below him sat forty or more wolves of every size and color, from badger-colored veterans who could handle a buck alone to young black three-year-olds who thought they could. The Lone Wolf had led them for a year now. He had fallen twice into a wolf trap in his youth, and once he had been beaten and left for dead; so he knew the manners and customs of men. There was very little talking at the Rock. The cubs tumbled over each other in the center of the circle where their mothers and fathers sat, and now and again a senior wolf would go quietly up to a cub, look at him carefully, and return to his place on noiseless feet. Sometimes a mother would push her cub far out into the moonlight to be sure that he had not been overlooked. Akela from his rock would cry: "Ye know the Law—ye know the Law. Look well, O Wolves!" And the anxious mothers would take up the call: "Look—look well, O Wolves!"

At last—and Mother Wolf's neck bristles lifted as the time came—Father Wolf pushed "Mowgli the Frog," as they called him, into the center, where he sat laughing and playing with some pebbles that glistened in the moonlight.

Akela never raised his head from his paws, but went on with the monotonous cry: "Look well!" A muffled roar came up from behind the rocks—the voice of Shere Khan crying: "The cub is mine. Give him to me. What have the Free People to do with a man's cub?" Akela never even twitched his ears. All he said was: "Look well, O Wolves! What have the Free People to do with the orders of any save the Free People? Look well!"

There was a chorus of deep growls, and a young wolf in his fourth year flung back Shere Khan's question to Akela: "What have the Free People to do with a man's cub?" Now, the Law of the Jungle lays down that if there is any dispute as to the right of a cub to be accepted by the Pack, he must be spoken for by at least two members of the Pack who are not his father and mother.

"Who speaks for this cub?" said Akela. "Among the Free People who speaks?" There was no answer and Mother Wolf got ready for what she knew would be her last fight, if things came to fighting.

Then the only other creature who is allowed at the Pack Council—Baloo, the sleepy brown bear who teaches the wolf cubs the Law of the Jungle: old Baloo, who can come and go where he pleases because he eats only nuts and roots and honey—rose upon his hind quarters and grunted.

"The man's cub—the man's cub?" he said. "I speak for the man's cub. There is no harm in a man's cub. I have no gift of words, but I speak the truth. Let him run with the Pack, and be entered with the others. I myself will teach him."

"We need yet another," said Akela. "Baloo has spoken, and he is our teacher for the young cubs. Who speaks besides Baloo?"

A black shadow dropped down into the circle. It was Bagheera the Black Panther, inky black all over, but with the panther markings showing up in certain lights like the pattern of watered silk. Everybody knew Bagheera, and nobody cared to cross his path; for he was as cunning as Tabaqui, as bold as the wild buffalo, and as reckless as the wounded elephant. But he had a voice as soft as wild honey dripping from a tree, and a skin softer than down.

"O Akela, and ye the Free People," he purred, "I have no right in your assembly, but the Law of the Jungle says that if there is a doubt which is not a killing matter in regard to a new cub, the life of that cub may be bought at a price. And the Law does not say who may or may not pay that price. Am I right?"

"Good! Good!" said the young wolves, who are always hungry. "Listen to Bagheera. The cub can be bought for a price. It is the Law."

"Knowing that I have no right to speak here, I ask your leave."

"Speak then," cried twenty voices.

"To kill a naked cub is shame. Besides, he may make better sport for you when he is grown. Baloo has spoken in his behalf. Now to Baloo's word I will add one bull, and a fat one, newly killed, not half a mile from here, if ye will accept the man's cub according to the Law. Is it difficult?"

There was a clamor of scores of voices, saying: "What matter? He will die in the winter rains. He will scorch in the sun. What harm can a naked frog do us? Let him run with the Pack. Where is the bull, Bagheera? Let him be accepted." And then came Akela's deep bay, crying: "Look well—look well, O Wolves!"

Mowgli was still deeply interested in the pebbles, and he did not notice when the wolves came and looked at him one by one. At last they all went down the hill for the dead bull, and only Akela, Bagheera, Baloo, and Mowgli's own wolves were left. Shere Khan roared still in the night, for he was very angry that Mowgli had not been handed over to him.

"Ay, roar well," said Bagheera, under his whiskers, "for the time will come when this naked thing will make thee roar to another tune, or I know nothing of man."

"It was well done," said Akela. "Men and their cubs are very wise. He may be a help in time."

"Truly, a help in time of need; for none can hope to lead the Pack forever," said Bagheera.

Akela said nothing. He was thinking of the time that comes to every leader of every pack when his strength goes from him and he gets feebler and feebler, till at last he is killed by the wolves and a new leader comes up—to be killed in his turn.

"Take him away," he said to Father Wolf, "and train him as befits one of the Free People."

And that is how Mowgli was entered into the Seeonee Wolf Pack for the price of a bull and on Baloo's good word.

Now you must be content to skip ten or eleven whole years, and only guess at all the wonderful life that Mowgli led among the wolves, because if it were written out it would fill ever so many books. He grew up with the cubs, though they, of course, were grown wolves almost before he was a child. And Father Wolf taught him his business, and the meaning of things in the jungle, till every rustle in the grass, every breath of the warm night air, every note of the owls above his head, every scratch of a bat's claws as it roosted for a while in a tree, and every splash of every little fish jumping in a pool meant just as much to him as the work of his office means to a business man. When he was not learning he sat out in the sun and slept, and ate and went to sleep again. When he felt dirty or hot he swam in the forest pools; and when he wanted honey (Baloo told him that honey and nuts were just as pleasant to eat as raw meat) he climbed up for it, and that Bagheera showed him how to do. Bagheera would lie out on a branch and call, "Come along, Little Brother," and at first Mowgli would cling like the sloth, but afterward he would fling himself through the branches almost as boldly as the gray ape. He took his place at the Council Rock, too, when the Pack met, and there he discovered that if he stared hard at any wolf, the wolf would be forced to drop his eyes, and so he used to stare for fun. At other times he would pick the long thorns out of the pads of his friends, for wolves suffer terribly from thorns and burs in their coats. He would go down the hillside into the cultivated lands by night, and look very curiously at the villagers in their huts, but he had a mistrust of men because Bagheera showed him a square box with a drop gate so cunningly hidden in the jungle that he nearly walked into it, and told him that it was a trap. He loved better than anything else to go with Bagheera into the dark warm heart of the forest, to sleep all through the drowsy day, and at night see how Bagheera did his killing. Bagheera killed right and left as he felt hungry, and so did Mowgli—with one exception. As soon as he was old enough to understand things, Bagheera told him that he must never touch cattle because he had been bought into the Pack at the price of a bull's life. "All the jungle is thine," said Bagheera, "and thou canst kill everything that thou art strong enough to kill; but for the sake of the bull that bought thee thou must never kill or eat any cattle young or old. That is the Law of the Jungle." Mowgli obeyed faithfully.

And he grew and grew strong as a boy must grow who does not know that he is learning any lessons, and who has nothing in the world to think of except things to eat.

Mother Wolf told him once or twice that Shere Khan was not a creature to be trusted, and that some day he must kill Shere Khan. But though a young wolf would have remembered that advice every hour, Mowgli forgot it because he was only a boy—though he would have called himself a wolf if he had been able to speak in any human tongue.

Shere Khan was always crossing his path in the jungle, for as Akela grew older and feebler the lame tiger had come to be great friends with the younger wolves of the Pack, who followed him for scraps, a thing Akela would never have allowed if he had dared to push his authority to the proper bounds. Then Shere Khan would flatter them and wonder that such fine young hunters were content to be led by a dying wolf and a man's cub. "They tell me," Shere Khan would say, "that at Council ye dare not look him between the eyes." And the young wolves would growl and bristle.

Bagheera, who had eyes and ears everywhere, knew something of this, and once or twice he told Mowgli in so many words that Shere Khan would kill him some day. Mowgli would laugh and answer: "I have the Pack and I have thee; and Baloo, though he is so lazy, might strike a blow or two for my sake. Why should I be afraid?"

It was one very warm day that a new notion came to Bagheera—born of something that he had heard. Perhaps Ikki the Porcupine had told him; but he said to Mowgli when they were deep in the jungle, as the boy lay with his head on

Bagheera's beautiful black skin, "Little Brother, how often have I told thee that Shere Khan is thy enemy?"

"As many times as there are nuts on that palm," said Mowgli, who, naturally, could not count. "What of it? I am sleepy, Bagheera, and Shere Khan is all long tail and loud talk—like Mao, the Peacock."

"But this is no time for sleeping. Baloo knows it; I know it; the Pack know it; and even the foolish, foolish deer know. Tabaqui has told thee too."

"Ho! ho!" said Mowgli. "Tabaqui came to me not long ago with some rude talk that I was a naked man's cub and not fit to dig pig-nuts. But I caught Tabaqui by the tail and swung him twice against a palm-tree to teach him better manners."

"That was foolishness, for though Tabaqui is a mischief-maker, he would have told thee of something that concerned thee closely. Open those eyes, Little Brother. Shere Khan dare not kill thee in the jungle. But remember, Akela is very old, and soon the day comes when he cannot kill his buck, and then he will be leader no more. Many of the wolves that looked thee over when thou wast brought to the Council first are old too, and the young wolves believe, as Shere Khan has taught them, that a man-cub has no place with the Pack. In a little time thou wilt be a man."

"And what is a man that he should not run with his brothers?" said Mowgli. "I was born in the jungle. I have obeyed the Law of the Jungle, and there is no wolf of ours from whose paws I have not pulled a thorn. Surely they are my brothers!"

Bagheera stretched himself at full length and half shut his eyes. "Little Brother," said he, "feel under my jaw."

Mowgli put up his strong brown hand, and just under

Bagheera's silky chin, where the giant rolling muscles were all hid by the glossy hair, he came upon a little bald spot.

"There is no one in the jungle that knows that I, Bagheera, carry that mark—the mark of the collar; and yet, Little Brother, I was born among men, and it was among men that my mother died—in the cages of the king's palace at Oodeypore. It was because of this that I paid the price for thee at the Council when thou wast a little naked cub. Yes, I too was born among men. I had never seen the jungle. They fed me behind bars from an iron pan till one night I felt that I was Bagheera— the Panther—and no man's plaything, and I broke the silly lock with one blow of my paw and came away. And because I had learned the ways of men, I became more terrible in the jungle than Shere Khan. Is it not so?"

"Yes," said Mowgli, "all the jungle fear Bagheera—all except Mowgli."

"Oh, thou art a man's cub," said the Black Panther very tenderly. "And even as I returned to my jungle, so thou must go back to men at last—to the men who are thy brothers—if thou art not killed in the Council."

"But why—but why should any wish to kill me?" said Mowgli.

"Look at me," said Bagheera. And Mowgli looked at him steadily between the eyes. The big panther turned his head away in half a minute.

"That is why," he said, shifting his paw on the leaves. "Not even I can look thee between the eyes, and I was born among men, and I love thee, Little Brother. The others they hate thee because their eyes cannot meet thine; because thou art wise; because thou hast pulled out thorns from their feet— because thou art a man."

"I did not know these things," said Mowgli sullenly, and he frowned under his heavy black eyebrows.

"What is the Law of the Jungle? Strike first and then give tongue. By thy very carelessness they know that thou art a man. But be wise. It is in my heart that when Akela misses his next kill—and at each hunt it costs him more to pin the buck—the Pack will turn against him and against thee. They will hold a jungle Council at the Rock, and then—and then— I have it!" said Bagheera, leaping up. "Go thou down quickly to the men's huts in the valley, and take some of the Red Flower which they grow there, so that when the time comes thou mayest have even a stronger friend than I or Baloo or those of the Pack that love thee. Get the Red Flower."

By Red Flower Bagheera meant fire, only no creature in the jungle will call fire by its proper name. Every beast lives in deadly fear of it, and invents a hundred ways of describing it.

"The Red Flower?" said Mowgli. "That grows outside their huts in the twilight. I will get some."

"There speaks the man's cub," said Bagheera proudly. "Remember that it grows in little pots. Get one swiftly, and keep it by thee for time of need."

"Good!" said Mowgli. "I go. But art thou sure, O my Bagheera"—he slipped his arm around the splendid neck and looked deep into the big eyes—"art thou sure that all this is Shere Khan's doing?"

"By the Broken Lock that freed me, I am sure, Little Brother."

"Then, by the Bull that bought me, I will pay Shere Khan full tale for this, and it may be a little over," said Mowgli, and he bounded away.

"That is a man. That is all a man," said Bagheera to himself, lying down again. "Oh, Shere Khan, never was a blacker hunting than that frog-hunt of thine ten years ago!"

Mowgli was far and far through the forest, running hard, and his heart was hot in him. He came to the cave as the evening mist rose, and drew breath, and looked down the valley. The cubs were out, but Mother Wolf, at the back of the cave, knew by his breathing that something was troubling her frog.

"What is it, Son?" she said.

"Some bat's chatter of Shere Khan," he called back. "I hunt among the plowed fields tonight," and he plunged downward through the bushes, to the stream at the bottom of the valley. There he checked, for he heard the yell of the Pack hunting, heard the bellow of a hunted Sambhur, and the snort as the buck turned at bay. Then there were wicked, bitter howls from the young wolves: "Akela! Akela! Let the Lone Wolf show his strength. Room for the leader of the Pack! Spring, Akela!"

The Lone Wolf must have sprung and missed his hold, for Mowgli heard the snap of his teeth and then a yelp as the Sambhur knocked him over with his forefoot.

He did not wait for anything more, but dashed on; and the yells grew fainter behind him as he ran into the croplands where the villagers lived.

"Bagheera spoke truth," he panted, as he nestled down in some cattle fodder by the window of a hut. "To-morrow is one day both for Akela and for me."

Then he pressed his face close to the window and watched the fire on the hearth. He saw the husbandman's wife get up and feed it in the night with black lumps. And when the morning came and the mists were all white and cold, he saw the man's child pick up a wicker pot plastered inside with earth, fill it with lumps of red-hot charcoal, put it under his blanket, and go out to tend the cows in the byre.

"Is that all?" said Mowgli. "If a cub can do it, there is nothing to fear." So he strode round the corner and met the boy, took the pot from his hand, and disappeared into the mist while the boy howled with fear.

"They are very like me," said Mowgli, blowing into the pot as he had seen the woman do. "This thing will die if I do not give it things to eat"; and he dropped twigs and dried bark on the red stuff. Halfway up the hill he met Bagheera with the morning dew shining like moonstones on his coat.

"Akela has missed," said the Panther. "They would have killed him last night, but they needed thee also. They were looking for thee on the hill."

"I was among the plowed lands. I am ready. See!" Mowgli held up the fire-pot.

"Good! Now, I have seen men thrust a dry branch into that stuff, and presently the Red Flower blossomed at the end of it. Art thou not afraid?"

"No. Why should I fear? I remember now—if it is not a dream—how, before I was a Wolf, I lay beside the Red Flower, and it was warm and pleasant."

All that day Mowgli sat in the cave tending his fire pot and dipping dry branches into it to see how they looked. He found a branch that satisfied him, and in the evening when Tabaqui came to the cave and told him rudely enough that he was wanted at the Council Rock, he laughed till Tabaqui ran away. Then Mowgli went to the Council, still laughing.

Akela the Lone Wolf lay by the side of his rock as a sign that the leadership of the Pack was open, and Shere Khan with his following of scrap-fed wolves walked to and fro openly being flattered. Bagheera lay close to Mowgli, and the fire pot was between Mowgli's knees. When they were all gathered together, Shere Khan began to speak—a thing he would never have dared to do when Akela was in his prime.

"He has no right," whispered Bagheera. "Say so. He is a dog's son. He will be frightened."

Mowgli sprang to his feet. "Free People," he cried, "does Shere Khan lead the Pack? What has a tiger to do with our leadership?"

"Seeing that the leadership is yet open, and being asked to speak—" Shere Khan began.

"By whom?" said Mowgli. "Are we all jackals, to fawn on this cattle butcher? The leadership of the Pack is with the Pack alone."

There were yells of "Silence, thou man's cub!" "Let him speak. He has kept our Law"; and at last the seniors of the Pack thundered: "Let the Dead Wolf speak." When a leader of the Pack has missed his kill, he is called the Dead Wolf as long as he lives, which is not long.

Akela raised his old head wearily:—

"Free People, and ye too, jackals of Shere Khan, for twelve seasons I have led ye to and from the kill, and in all that time not one has been trapped or maimed. Now I have missed my kill. Ye know how that plot was made. Ye know how ye brought me up to an untried buck to make my weakness known. It was cleverly done. Your right is to kill me here on the Council Rock, now. Therefore, I ask, who comes to make an end of the Lone Wolf? For it is my right, by the Law of the Jungle, that ye come one by one."

There was a long hush, for no single wolf cared to fight Akela to the death. Then Shere Khan roared: "Bah! What have we to do with this toothless fool? He is doomed to die! It is the man-cub who has lived too long. Free People, he was my meat from the first. Give him to me. I am weary of this man-wolf folly. He has troubled the jungle for ten seasons. Give me the man-cub, or I will hunt here always, and not give you one bone. He is a man, a man's child, and from the marrow of my bones I hate him!"

Then more than half the Pack yelled: "A man! A man! What has a man to do with us? Let him go to his own place."

"And turn all the people of the villages against us?" clamored Shere Khan.

"No, give him to me. He is a man, and none of us can look him between the eyes." Akela lifted his head again and said, "He has eaten our food. He has slept with us. He has driven game for us. He has broken no word of the Law of the Jungle."

"Also, I paid for him with a bull when he was accepted. The worth of a bull is little, but Bagheera's honor is something that he will perhaps fight for," said Bagheera in his gentlest voice.

"A bull paid ten years ago!" the Pack snarled. "What do we care for bones ten years old?"

"Or for a pledge?" said Bagheera, his white teeth bared under his lip. "Well are ye called the Free People!"

"No man's cub can run with the people of the jungle," howled Shere Khan.

"Give him to me!"

"He is our brother in all but blood," Akela went on, "and ye would kill him here! In truth, I have lived too long. Some of ye are eaters of cattle, and of others I have heard that, under Shere Khan's teaching, ye go by dark night and snatch children from the villager's doorstep. Therefore I know ye to be cowards, and it is to cowards I speak. It is certain that I must die, and my life is of no worth, or I would offer that in the man-cub's place. But for the sake of the Honor of the Pack,—a little matter that by being without a leader ye have forgotten,—I promise that if ye let the man-cub go to his own place, I will not, when my time comes to die, bare one tooth against ye. I will die without fighting. That will at least save the Pack three lives. More I cannot do; but if ye will, I can save ye the shame that comes of killing a brother against whom there is no fault—a brother spoken for and bought into the Pack according to the Law of the Jungle."

"He is a man—a man—a man!" snarled the Pack. And most of the wolves began to gather round Shere Khan, whose tail was beginning to switch.

"Now the business is in thy hands," said Bagheera to Mowgli. "We can do no more except fight."

Mowgli stood upright—the fire pot in his hands. Then he stretched out his arms, and yawned in the face of the Council; but he was furious with rage and sorrow, for, wolflike, the wolves had never told him how they hated him. "Listen you!" he cried. "There is no need for this dog's jabber. Ye have told me so often tonight that I am a man (and indeed I would have been a wolf with you to my life's end) that I feel your words are true. So I do not call ye my brothers any more, but sag [dogs], as a man should. What ye will do, and what ye will not do, is not yours to say. That matter is with me; and that we may see the matter more plainly, I, the man, have brought here a little of the Red Flower which ye, dogs, fear."

He flung the fire pot on the ground, and some of the red

coals lit a tuft of dried moss that flared up, as all the Council drew back in terror before the leaping flames.

Mowgli thrust his dead branch into the fire till the twigs lit and crackled, and whirled it above his head among the cowering wolves.

"Thou art the master," said Bagheera in an undertone. "Save Akela from the death. He was ever thy friend."

Akela, the grim old wolf who had never asked for mercy in his life, gave one piteous look at Mowgli as the boy stood all naked, his long black hair tossing over his shoulders in the light of the blazing branch that made the shadows jump and quiver.

"Good!" said Mowgli, staring round slowly. "I see that ye are dogs. I go from you to my own people—if they be my own people. The jungle is shut to me, and I must forget your talk and your companionship. But I will be more merciful than ye are. Because I was all but your brother in blood, I promise that when I am a man among men I will not betray ye to men as ye have betrayed me." He kicked the fire with his foot, and the sparks flew up. "There shall be no war between any of us in the Pack. But here is a debt to pay before I go." He strode forward to where Shere Khan sat blinking stupidly at the flames, and caught him by the tuft on his chin. Bagheera followed in case of accidents. "Up, dog!" Mowgli cried. "Up, when a man speaks, or I will set that coat ablaze!"

Shere Khan's ears lay flat back on his head, and he shut his eyes, for the blazing branch was very near.

"This cattle-killer said he would kill me in the Council because he had not killed me when I was a cub. Thus and thus, then, do we beat dogs when we are men. Stir a whisker, Lungri, and I ram the Red Flower down thy gullet!" He beat Shere Khan over the head with the branch, and the tiger whimpered and whined in an agony of fear.

"Pah! Singed jungle cat—go now! But remember when next I come to the Council Rock, as a man should come, it will be with Shere Khan's hide on my head. For the rest, Akela goes free to live as he pleases. Ye will not kill him, because that is not my will. Nor do I think that ye will sit here any longer, lolling out your tongues as though ye were somebodies, instead of dogs whom I drive out—thus! Go!" The fire was burning furiously at the end of the branch, and Mowgli struck right and left round the circle, and the wolves ran howling with the sparks burning their fur. At last there were only Akela, Bagheera, and perhaps ten wolves that had taken Mowgli's part. Then something began to hurt Mowgli inside him, as he had never been hurt in his life before, and he caught his breath and sobbed, and the tears ran down his face.

"What is it? What is it?" he said. "I do not wish to leave the jungle, and I do not know what this is. Am I dying, Bagheera?"

"No, Little Brother. That is only tears such as men use," said Bagheera. "Now I know thou art a man, and a man's cub no longer. The jungle is shut indeed to thee henceforward. Let them fall, Mowgli. They are only tears." So Mowgli sat and cried as though his heart would break; and he had never cried in all his life before.

"Now," he said, "I will go to men. But first I must say farewell to my mother." And he went to the cave where she lived with Father Wolf, and he cried on her coat, while the four cubs howled miserably.

"Ye will not forget me?" said Mowgli.

"Never while we can follow a trail," said the cubs. "Come to the foot of the hill when thou art a man, and we will talk to thee; and we will come into the croplands to play with thee by night."

"Come soon!" said Father Wolf. "Oh, wise little frog, come again soon; for we be old, thy mother and I."

"Come soon," said Mother Wolf, "little naked son of mine. For, listen, child of man, I loved thee more than ever I loved my cubs."

"I will surely come," said Mowgli. "And when I come it will be to lay out Shere Khan's hide upon the Council Rock. Do not forget me! Tell them in the jungle never to forget me!"

The dawn was beginning to break when Mowgli went down the hillside alone, to meet those mysterious things that are called men.

Hunting-Song of the Seeonee Pack

> *As the dawn was breaking the Sambhur belled*
> *Once, twice and again!*
> *And a doe leaped up, and a doe leaped up*
> *From the pond in the wood where the wild deer sup.*
> *This I, scouting alone, beheld,*
> *Once, twice and again!*
> *As the dawn was breaking the Sambhur belled*
> *Once, twice and again!*
> *And a wolf stole back, and a wolf stole back*
> *To carry the word to the waiting pack,*
> *And we sought and we found and we bayed on his track*
> *Once, twice and again!*
> *As the dawn was breaking the Wolf Pack yelled*
> *Once, twice and again!*
> *Feet in the jungle that leave no mark!*
> *Eyes that can see in the dark—the dark!*
> *Tongue—give tongue to it! Hark! O hark!*
> *Once, twice and again!*

KAA'S HUNTING

His spots are the joy of the Leopard: his horns are the Buffalo's pride. Be clean, for the strength of the hunter is known by the gloss of his hide. If ye find that the Bullock can toss you, or the heavy-browed Sambhur can gore; Ye need not stop work to inform us: we knew it ten seasons before. Oppress not the cubs of the stranger, but hail them as Sister and Brother, For though they are little and fubsy, it may be the Bear is their mother. "There is none like to me!" says the Cub in the pride of his earliest kill; But the jungle is large and the Cub he is small. Let him think and be still. Maxims of Baloo

All that is told here happened some time before Mowgli was turned out of the Seeonee Wolf Pack, or revenged himself on Shere Khan the tiger. It was in the days when Baloo was teaching him the Law of the Jungle. The big, serious, old brown bear was delighted to have so quick a pupil, for the young wolves will only learn as much of the Law of the Jungle as applies to their own pack and tribe, and run away as soon as they can repeat the Hunting Verse—"Feet that make no noise; eyes that can see in the dark; ears that can hear the winds in their lairs, and sharp white teeth, all these things are the marks of our brothers except Tabaqui the Jackal and the Hyaena whom we hate." But Mowgli, as a man-cub, had to learn a great deal more than this. Sometimes Bagheera the Black Panther would come lounging through the jungle to see how his pet was getting on, and would purr with his head against a tree while Mowgli recited the day's lesson to Baloo. The boy could climb almost as well as he could swim, and swim almost as well as he could run. So Baloo, the Teacher of the Law, taught him the Wood and Water Laws: how to tell a rotten branch from a sound one; how to speak politely to the wild bees when he came upon a hive of them fifty feet above ground; what to say to Mang the Bat when he disturbed him in the branches at midday; and how to warn the water-snakes in the pools before he splashed down among them. None of the Jungle People like being disturbed, and all are very ready to fly at an intruder. Then, too, Mowgli was taught the Strangers' Hunting Call, which must be repeated aloud till it is answered, whenever one of the Jungle-People hunts outside his own grounds. It means, translated, "Give me leave to hunt here because I am hungry." And the answer is, "Hunt then for food, but not for pleasure."

All this will show you how much Mowgli had to learn by heart, and he grew very tired of saying the same thing over a hundred times. But, as Baloo said to Bagheera, one day when Mowgli had been cuffed and run off in a temper, "A man's cub is a man's cub, and he must learn all the Law of the Jungle."

"But think how small he is," said the Black Panther, who would have spoiled Mowgli if he had had his own way. "How can his little head carry all thy long talk?"

"Is there anything in the jungle too little to be killed? No. That is why I teach him these things, and that is why I hit him, very softly, when he forgets."

"Softly! What dost thou know of softness, old Iron-feet?"

Bagheera grunted. "His face is all bruised today by thy—softness. Ugh."

"Better he should be bruised from head to foot by me who love him than that he should come to harm through ignorance," Baloo answered very earnestly. "I am now teaching him the Master Words of the Jungle that shall protect him with the birds and the Snake People, and all that hunt on four feet, except his own pack. He can now claim protection, if he will only remember the words, from all in the jungle. Is not that worth a little beating?"

"Well, look to it then that thou dost not kill the man-cub. He is no tree trunk to sharpen thy blunt claws upon. But what are those Master Words? I am more likely to give help than to ask it"—Bagheera stretched out one paw and admired the steel-blue, ripping-chisel talons at the end of it—"still I should like to know."

"I will call Mowgli and he shall say them—if he will. Come, Little Brother!"

"My head is ringing like a bee tree," said a sullen little voice over their heads, and Mowgli slid down a tree trunk very angry and indignant, adding as he reached the ground: "I come for Bagheera and not for thee, fat old Baloo!"

"That is all one to me," said Baloo, though he was hurt and grieved. "Tell Bagheera, then, the Master Words of the Jungle that I have taught thee this day."

"Master Words for which people?" said Mowgli, delighted to show off. "The jungle has many tongues. I know them all."

"A little thou knowest, but not much. See, O Bagheera, they never thank their teacher. Not one small wolfling has ever come back to thank old Baloo for his teachings. Say the word for the Hunting-People, then—great scholar."

"We be of one blood, ye and I," said Mowgli, giving the words the Bear accent which all the Hunting People use.

"Good. Now for the birds."

Mowgli repeated, with the Kite's whistle at the end of the sentence.

"Now for the Snake-People," said Bagheera.

The answer was a perfectly indescribable hiss, and Mowgli kicked up his feet behind, clapped his hands together to applaud himself, and jumped on to Bagheera's back, where he sat sideways, drumming with his heels on the glossy skin and making the worst faces he could think of at Baloo.

"There—there! That was worth a little bruise," said the brown bear tenderly. "Some day thou wilt remember me." Then he turned aside to tell Bagheera how he had begged the Master Words from Hathi the Wild Elephant, who knows all about these things, and how Hathi had taken Mowgli down to a pool to get the Snake Word from a water-snake, because Baloo could not pronounce it, and how Mowgli was now reasonably safe against all accidents in the jungle, because neither snake, bird, nor beast would hurt him.

"No one then is to be feared," Baloo wound up, patting his big furry stomach with pride.

"Except his own tribe," said Bagheera, under his breath; and then aloud to Mowgli, "Have a care for my ribs, Little Brother! What is all this dancing up and down?"

Mowgli had been trying to make himself heard by pulling at Bagheera's shoulder fur and kicking hard. When the two listened to him he was shouting at the top of his voice, "And so I shall have a tribe of my own, and lead them through the branches all day long."

"What is this new folly, little dreamer of dreams?" said Bagheera.

"Yes, and throw branches and dirt at old Baloo," Mowgli went on. "They have promised me this. Ah!"

"Whoof!" Baloo's big paw scooped Mowgli off Bagheera's back, and as the boy lay between the big fore-paws he could see the Bear was angry.

"Mowgli," said Baloo, "thou hast been talking with the Bandar-log—the Monkey People."

Mowgli looked at Bagheera to see if the Panther was angry too, and Bagheera's eyes were as hard as jade stones.

"Thou hast been with the Monkey People—the gray apes—the people without a law—the eaters of everything. That is great shame."

"When Baloo hurt my head," said Mowgli (he was still on his back), "I went away, and the gray apes came down from the trees and had pity on me. No one else cared." He snuffled a little.

"The pity of the Monkey People!" Baloo snorted. "The stillness of the mountain stream! The cool of the summer sun! And then, man-cub?"

"And then, and then, they gave me nuts and pleasant things to eat, and they—they carried me in their arms up to the top of the trees and said I was their blood brother except that I had no tail, and should be their leader some day."

"They have no leader," said Bagheera. "They lie. They have always lied."

"They were very kind and bade me come again. Why have I never been taken among the Monkey People? They stand on their feet as I do. They do not hit me with their hard paws.

They play all day. Let me get up! Bad Baloo, let me up! I will play with them again."

"Listen, man-cub," said the Bear, and his voice rumbled like thunder on a hot night. "I have taught thee all the Law of the Jungle for all the peoples of the jungle—except the Monkey-Folk who live in the trees. They have no law. They are outcasts. They have no speech of their own, but use the stolen words which they overhear when they listen, and peep, and wait up above in the branches. Their way is not our way. They are without leaders. They have no remembrance. They boast and chatter and pretend that they are a great people about to do great affairs in the jungle, but the falling of a nut turns their minds to laughter and all is forgotten. We of the jungle have no dealings with them. We do not drink where the monkeys drink; we do not go where the monkeys go; we do not hunt where they hunt; we do not die where they die. Hast thou ever heard me speak of the Bandar-log till today?"

"No," said Mowgli in a whisper, for the forest was very still now Baloo had finished.

"The Jungle-People put them out of their mouths and out of their minds. They are very many, evil, dirty, shameless, and they desire, if they have any fixed desire, to be noticed by the Jungle People. But we do not notice them even when they throw nuts and filth on our heads."

He had hardly spoken when a shower of nuts and twigs spattered down through the branches; and they could hear coughings and howlings and angry jumpings high up in the air among the thin branches.

"The Monkey-People are forbidden," said Baloo, "forbidden to the Jungle-People. Remember."

"Forbidden," said Bagheera, "but I still think Baloo should have warned thee against them."

"I—I? How was I to guess he would play with such dirt. The Monkey People! Faugh!"

A fresh shower came down on their heads and the two trotted away, taking Mowgli with them. What Baloo had said about the monkeys was perfectly true. They belonged to the tree-tops, and as beasts very seldom look up, there was no occasion for the monkeys and the Jungle-People to cross each other's path. But whenever they found a sick wolf, or a wounded tiger, or bear, the monkeys would torment him, and would throw sticks and nuts at any beast for fun and in the hope of being noticed. Then they would howl and shriek senseless songs, and invite the Jungle-People to climb up their trees and fight them, or would start furious battles over nothing among themselves, and leave the dead monkeys where the Jungle-People could see them. They were always just going to have a leader, and laws and customs of their own, but they never did, because their memories would not hold over from day to day, and so they compromised things by making up a saying, "What the Bandar-log think now the jungle will think later," and that comforted them a great deal. None of the beasts could reach them, but on the other hand none of the beasts would notice them, and that was why they were so pleased when Mowgli came to play with them, and they heard how angry Baloo was.

They never meant to do any more—the Bandar-log never mean anything at all; but one of them invented what seemed to him a brilliant idea, and he told all the others that Mowgli would be a useful person to keep in the tribe, because he could weave sticks together for protection from the wind; so, if they caught him, they could make him teach them. Of course

Mowgli, as a woodcutter's child, inherited all sorts of instincts, and used to make little huts of fallen branches without thinking how he came to do it. The Monkey-People, watching in the trees, considered his play most wonderful. This time, they said, they were really going to have a leader and become the wisest people in the jungle—so wise that everyone else would notice and envy them. Therefore they followed Baloo and Bagheera and Mowgli through the jungle very quietly till it was time for the midday nap, and Mowgli, who was very much ashamed of himself, slept between the Panther and the Bear, resolving to have no more to do with the Monkey People.

The next thing he remembered was feeling hands on his legs and arms—hard, strong, little hands—and then a swash of branches in his face, and then he was staring down through the swaying boughs as Baloo woke the jungle with his deep cries and Bagheera bounded up the trunk with every tooth bared. The Bandar-log howled with triumph and scuffled away to the upper branches where Bagheera dared not follow, shouting: "He has noticed us! Bagheera has noticed us. All the Jungle-People admire us for our skill and our cunning." Then they began their flight; and the flight of the Monkey-People through tree-land is one of the things nobody can describe. They have their regular roads and crossroads, up hills and down hills, all laid out from fifty to seventy or a hundred feet above ground, and by these they can travel even at night if necessary. Two of the strongest monkeys caught Mowgli under the arms and swung off with him through the treetops, twenty feet at a bound. Had they been alone they could have gone twice as fast, but the boy's weight held them back. Sick and giddy as Mowgli was he could not help enjoying the wild rush, though the glimpses of earth far down below frightened him, and the terrible check and jerk at the end of the swing over nothing but empty air brought his heart between his teeth. His escort would rush him up a tree till he felt the thinnest topmost branches crackle and bend under them, and then with a cough and a whoop would fling themselves into the air outward and downward, and bring up, hanging by their hands or their feet to the lower limbs of the next tree. Sometimes he could see for miles and miles across the still green jungle, as a man on the top of a mast can see for miles across the sea, and then the branches and leaves would lash him across the face, and he and his two guards would be almost down to earth again. So, bounding and crashing and whooping and yelling, the whole tribe of Bandar-log swept along the tree-roads with Mowgli their prisoner.

For a time he was afraid of being dropped. Then he grew angry but knew better than to struggle, and then he began to think. The first thing was to send back word to Baloo and Bagheera, for, at the pace the monkeys were going, he knew his friends would be left far behind. It was useless to look down, for he could only see the topsides of the branches, so he stared upward and saw, far away in the blue, Rann the Kite balancing and wheeling as he kept watch over the jungle waiting for things to die. Rann saw that the monkeys were carrying something, and dropped a few hundred yards to find out whether their load was good to eat. He whistled with surprise when he saw Mowgli being dragged up to a treetop and heard him give the Kite call for—"We be of one blood, thou and I." The waves of the branches closed over the boy, but Chil balanced away to the next tree in time to see the little brown face come up again. "Mark my trail!" Mowgli shouted. "Tell Baloo of the Seeonee Pack and Bagheera of the Council Rock."

"In whose name, Brother?" Rann had never seen Mowgli before, though of course he had heard of him.

"Mowgli, the Frog. Man-cub they call me! Mark my trail!"

The last words were shrieked as he was being swung through the air, but Rann nodded and rose up till he looked no bigger than a speck of dust, and there he hung, watching with his telescope eyes the swaying of the treetops as Mowgli's escort whirled along.

"They never go far," he said with a chuckle. "They never do what they set out to do. Always pecking at new things are the Bandar-log. This time, if I have any eye-sight, they have pecked down trouble for themselves, for Baloo is no fledgling and Bagheera can, as I know, kill more than goats."

So he rocked on his wings, his feet gathered up under him, and waited.

Meantime, Baloo and Bagheera were furious with rage and grief. Bagheera climbed as he had never climbed before, but the thin branches broke beneath his weight, and he slipped down, his claws full of bark.

"Why didst thou not warn the man-cub?" he roared to poor Baloo, who had set off at a clumsy trot in the hope of overtaking the monkeys. "What was the use of half slaying him with blows if thou didst not warn him?"

"Haste! O haste! We—we may catch them yet!" Baloo panted.

"At that speed! It would not tire a wounded cow. Teacher of the Law—cub-beater—a mile of that rolling to and fro would burst thee open. Sit still and think! Make a plan. This is no time for chasing. They may drop him if we follow too close."

"Arrula! Whoo! They may have dropped him already, being tired of carrying him. Who can trust the Bandar-log? Put dead bats on my head! Give me black bones to eat! Roll me into the hives of the wild bees that I may be stung to death, and bury me with the Hyaena, for I am most miserable of bears! Arulala! Wahooa! O Mowgli, Mowgli! Why did I not warn thee against the Monkey-Folk instead of breaking thy head? Now perhaps I may have knocked the day's lesson out of his mind, and he will be alone in the jungle without the Master Words."

Baloo clasped his paws over his ears and rolled to and fro moaning.

"At least he gave me all the Words correctly a little time ago," said Bagheera impatiently. "Baloo, thou hast neither memory nor respect. What would the jungle think if I, the Black Panther, curled myself up like Ikki the Porcupine, and howled?"

"What do I care what the jungle thinks? He may be dead by now."

"Unless and until they drop him from the branches in sport, or kill him out of idleness, I have no fear for the man-cub. He is wise and well taught, and above all he has the eyes that make the Jungle-People afraid. But (and it is a great evil) he is in the power of the Bandar-log, and they, because they live in trees, have no fear of any of our people." Bagheera licked one forepaw thoughtfully.

"Fool that I am! Oh, fat, brown, root-digging fool that I am," said Baloo, uncoiling himself with a jerk, "it is true what Hathi the Wild Elephant says: 'To each his own fear'; and they, the Bandar-log, fear Kaa the Rock Snake. He can climb as well as they can. He steals the young monkeys in the night.

The whisper of his name makes their wicked tails cold. Let us go to Kaa."

"What will he do for us? He is not of our tribe, being footless—and with most evil eyes," said Bagheera.

"He is very old and very cunning. Above all, he is always hungry," said Baloo hopefully. "Promise him many goats."

"He sleeps for a full month after he has once eaten. He may be asleep now, and even were he awake what if he would rather kill his own goats?" Bagheera, who did not know much about Kaa, was naturally suspicious.

"Then in that case, thou and I together, old hunter, might make him see reason." Here Baloo rubbed his faded brown shoulder against the Panther, and they went off to look for Kaa the Rock Python.

They found him stretched out on a warm ledge in the afternoon sun, admiring his beautiful new coat, for he had been in retirement for the last ten days changing his skin, and now he was very splendid—darting his big blunt-nosed head along the ground, and twisting the thirty feet of his body into fantastic knots and curves, and licking his lips as he thought of his dinner to come.

"He has not eaten," said Baloo, with a grunt of relief, as soon as he saw the beautifully mottled brown and yellow jacket. "Be careful, Bagheera! He is always a little blind after he has changed his skin, and very quick to strike."

Kaa was not a poison snake—in fact he rather despised the poison snakes as cowards—but his strength lay in his hug, and when he had once lapped his huge coils round anybody there was no more to be said. "Good hunting!" cried Baloo, sitting up on his haunches. Like all snakes of his breed Kaa was rather deaf, and did not hear the call at first. Then he curled up ready for any accident, his head lowered.

"Good hunting for us all," he answered. "Oho, Baloo, what dost thou do here? Good hunting, Bagheera. One of us at least needs food. Is there any news of game afoot? A doe now, or even a young buck? I am as empty as a dried well."

"We are hunting," said Baloo carelessly. He knew that you must not hurry Kaa. He is too big.

"Give me permission to come with you," said Kaa. "A blow more or less is nothing to thee, Bagheera or Baloo, but I—I have to wait and wait for days in a wood-path and climb half a night on the mere chance of a young ape. Psshaw! The branches are not what they were when I was young. Rotten twigs and dry boughs are they all."

"Maybe thy great weight has something to do with the matter," said Baloo.

"I am a fair length—a fair length," said Kaa with a little pride. "But for all that, it is the fault of this new-grown timber. I came very near to falling on my last hunt—very near indeed—and the noise of my slipping, for my tail was not tight wrapped around the tree, waked the Bandar-log, and they called me most evil names."

"Footless, yellow earth-worm," said Bagheera under his whiskers, as though he were trying to remember something.

"Sssss! Have they ever called me that?" said Kaa.

"Something of that kind it was that they shouted to us last moon, but we never noticed them. They will say anything— even that thou hast lost all thy teeth, and wilt not face anything bigger than a kid, because (they are indeed shameless, these Bandar-log)—because thou art afraid of the he-goat's horns," Bagheera went on sweetly.

Now a snake, especially a wary old python like Kaa, very seldom shows that he is angry, but Baloo and Bagheera could see the big swallowing muscles on either side of Kaa's throat ripple and bulge.

"The Bandar-log have shifted their grounds," he said quietly. "When I came up into the sun today I heard them whooping among the tree-tops."

"It—it is the Bandar-log that we follow now," said Baloo, but the words stuck in his throat, for that was the first time in his memory that one of the Jungle-People had owned to being interested in the doings of the monkeys.

"Beyond doubt then it is no small thing that takes two such hunters—leaders in their own jungle I am certain—on the trail of the Bandar-log," Kaa replied courteously, as he swelled with curiosity.

"Indeed," Baloo began, "I am no more than the old and sometimes very foolish Teacher of the Law to the Seeonee wolf-cubs, and Bagheera here—"

"Is Bagheera," said the Black Panther, and his jaws shut with a snap, for he did not believe in being humble. "The trouble is this, Kaa. Those nut-stealers and pickers of palm leaves have stolen away our man-cub of whom thou hast perhaps heard."

"I heard some news from Ikki (his quills make him presumptuous) of a man-thing that was entered into a wolf pack, but I did not believe. Ikki is full of stories half heard and very badly told."

"But it is true. He is such a man-cub as never was," said Baloo. "The best and wisest and boldest of man-cubs—my own pupil, who shall make the name of Baloo famous through all the jungles; and besides, I—we—love him, Kaa."

"Ts! Ts!" said Kaa, weaving his head to and fro. "I also have known what love is. There are tales I could tell that—"

"That need a clear night when we are all well fed to praise properly," said Bagheera quickly. "Our man-cub is in the hands of the Bandar-log now, and we know that of all the Jungle-People they fear Kaa alone."

"They fear me alone. They have good reason," said Kaa. "Chattering, foolish, vain—vain, foolish, and chattering, are the monkeys. But a man-thing in their hands is in no good luck. They grow tired of the nuts they pick, and throw them down. They carry a branch half a day, meaning to do great things with it, and then they snap it in two. That man-thing is not to be envied. They called me also—'yellow fish' was it not?"

"Worm—worm—earth-worm," said Bagheera, "as well as other things which I cannot now say for shame."

"We must remind them to speak well of their master. Aaa-ssp! We must help their wandering memories. Now, whither went they with the cub?"

"The jungle alone knows. Toward the sunset, I believe," said Baloo. "We had thought that thou wouldst know, Kaa."

"I? How? I take them when they come in my way, but I do not hunt the Bandar-log, or frogs—or green scum on a water-hole, for that matter."

"Up, Up! Up, Up! Hillo! Illo! Illo, look up, Baloo of the Seeonee Wolf Pack!"

Baloo looked up to see where the voice came from, and there was Rann the Kite, sweeping down with the sun shining on the upturned flanges of his wings. It was near Rann's bedtime, but he had ranged all over the jungle looking for the Bear and had missed him in the thick foliage.

"What is it?" said Baloo.

"I have seen Mowgli among the Bandar-log. He bade me tell you. I watched. The Bandar-log have taken him beyond the river to the monkey city—to the Cold Lairs. They may stay there for a night, or ten nights, or an hour. I have told the bats to watch through the dark time. That is my message. Good hunting, all you below!"

"Full gorge and a deep sleep to you, Rann," cried Bagheera. "I will remember thee in my next kill, and put aside the head for thee alone, O best of kites!"

"It is nothing. It is nothing. The boy held the Master Word. I could have done no less," and Rann circled up again to his roost.

"He has not forgotten to use his tongue," said Baloo with a chuckle of pride. "To think of one so young remembering the Master Word for the birds too while he was being pulled across trees!"

"It was most firmly driven into him," said Bagheera. "But I am proud of him, and now we must go to the Cold Lairs."

They all knew where that place was, but few of the Jungle People ever went there, because what they called the Cold Lairs was an old deserted city, lost and buried in the jungle, and beasts seldom use a place that men have once used. The wild boar will, but the hunting tribes do not. Besides, the monkeys lived there as much as they could be said to live anywhere, and no self-respecting animal would come within eyeshot of it except in times of drought, when the half-ruined tanks and reservoirs held a little water.

"It is half a night's journey—at full speed," said Bagheera, and Baloo looked very serious. "I will go as fast as I can," he said anxiously.

"We dare not wait for thee. Follow, Baloo. We must go on the quick-foot—Kaa and I."

"Feet or no feet, I can keep abreast of all thy four," said Kaa shortly. Baloo made one effort to hurry, but had to sit down panting, and so they left him to come on later, while Bagheera hurried forward, at the quick panther-canter. Kaa said nothing, but, strive as Bagheera might, the huge Rock-python held level with him. When they came to a hill stream, Bagheera gained, because he bounded across while Kaa swam, his head and two feet of his neck clearing the water, but on level ground Kaa made up the distance.

"By the Broken Lock that freed me," said Bagheera, when twilight had fallen, "thou art no slow goer!"

"I am hungry," said Kaa. "Besides, they called me speckled frog."

"Worm—earth-worm, and yellow to boot."

"All one. Let us go on," and Kaa seemed to pour himself along the ground, finding the shortest road with his steady eyes, and keeping to it.

In the Cold Lairs the Monkey-People were not thinking of Mowgli's friends at all. They had brought the boy to the Lost City, and were very much pleased with themselves for the time. Mowgli had never seen an Indian city before, and though this was almost a heap of ruins it seemed very wonderful and splendid. Some king had built it long ago on a little hill. You could still trace the stone causeways that led up to the ruined gates where the last splinters of wood hung to the worn, rusted hinges. Trees had grown into and out of the walls; the battlements were tumbled down and decayed, and wild creepers hung out of the windows of the towers on the walls in bushy hanging clumps.

A great roofless palace crowned the hill, and the marble of the courtyards and the fountains was split, and stained with red and green, and the very cobblestones in the courtyard where the king's elephants used to live had been thrust up and apart by grasses and young trees. From the palace you could see the rows and rows of roofless houses that made up the city looking like empty honeycombs filled with blackness; the shapeless block of stone that had been an idol in the square where four roads met; the pits and dimples at street corners where the public wells once stood, and the shattered domes of temples with wild figs sprouting on their sides. The monkeys called the place their city, and pretended to despise the Jungle-People because they lived in the forest. And yet they never knew what the buildings were made for nor how to use them. They would sit in circles on the hall of the king's council chamber, and scratch for fleas and pretend to be men; or they would run in and out of the roofless houses and collect pieces of plaster and old bricks in a corner, and forget where they had hidden them, and fight and cry in scuffling crowds, and then break off to play up and down the terraces of the king's garden, where they would shake the rose trees and the oranges in sport to see the fruit and flowers fall. They explored all the passages and dark tunnels in the palace and the hundreds of little dark rooms, but they never remembered what they had seen and what they had not; and so drifted about in ones and twos or crowds telling each other that they were doing as men did. They drank at the tanks and made the water all muddy, and then they fought over it, and then they would all rush together in mobs and shout: "There is no one in the jungle so wise and good and clever and strong and gentle as the Bandar-log." Then all would begin again till they grew tired of the city and went back to the tree-tops, hoping the Jungle-People would notice them.

Mowgli, who had been trained under the Law of the Jungle, did not like or understand this kind of life. The monkeys dragged him into the Cold Lairs late in the afternoon, and instead of going to sleep, as Mowgli would have done after a long journey, they joined hands and danced about and sang their foolish songs. One of the monkeys made a speech and told his companions that Mowgli's capture marked a new thing in the history of the Bandar-log, for Mowgli was going to show them how to weave sticks and canes together as a protection against rain and cold. Mowgli picked up some creepers and began to work them in and out, and the monkeys tried to imitate; but in a very few minutes they lost interest and began to pull their friends' tails or jump up and down on all fours, coughing.

"I wish to eat," said Mowgli. "I am a stranger in this part of the jungle. Bring me food, or give me leave to hunt here."

Twenty or thirty monkeys bounded away to bring him nuts and wild pawpaws. But they fell to fighting on the road, and it was too much trouble to go back with what was left of the fruit. Mowgli was sore and angry as well as hungry, and he roamed through the empty city giving the Strangers' Hunting Call from time to time, but no one answered him, and Mowgli felt that he had reached a very bad place indeed. "All that Baloo has said about the Bandar-log is true," he thought to himself. "They have no Law, no Hunting Call, and no leaders—nothing but foolish words and little picking thievish hands. So if I am starved or killed here, it will be all my own fault. But I must try to return to my own jungle. Baloo will surely beat me, but that is better than chasing silly rose leaves with the Bandar-log."

No sooner had he walked to the city wall than the monkeys pulled him back, telling him that he did not know how happy he was, and pinching him to make him grateful. He set his teeth and said nothing, but went with the shouting monkeys to a terrace above the red sandstone reservoirs that were half-full of rain water. There was a ruined summer-house of white marble in the center of the terrace, built for queens dead a hundred years ago. The domed roof had half fallen in and blocked up the underground passage from the palace by which the queens used to enter. But the walls were made of screens of marble tracery—beautiful milk-white fretwork, set with agates and cornelians and jasper and lapis lazuli, and as the moon came up behind the hill it shone through the open work, casting shadows on the ground like black velvet embroidery. Sore, sleepy, and hungry as he was, Mowgli could not help laughing when the Bandar-log began, twenty at a time, to tell him how great and wise and strong and gentle they were, and how foolish he was to wish to leave them. "We are great. We are free. We are wonderful. We are the most wonderful people in all the jungle! We all say so, and so it must be true," they shouted. "Now as you are a new listener and can carry our words back to the Jungle-People so that they may notice us in future, we will tell you all about our most excellent selves." Mowgli made no objection, and the monkeys gathered by hundreds and hundreds on the terrace to listen to their own speakers singing the praises of the Bandar-log, and whenever a speaker stopped for want of breath they would all shout together: "This is true; we all say so." Mowgli nodded and blinked, and said "Yes" when they asked him a question, and his head spun with the noise. "Tabaqui the Jackal must have bitten all these people," he said to himself, "and now they have madness. Certainly this is dewanee, the madness. Do they never go to sleep? Now there is a cloud coming to cover that moon. If it were only a big enough cloud I might try to run away in the darkness. But I am tired."

That same cloud was being watched by two good friends in the ruined ditch below the city wall, for Bagheera and Kaa, knowing well how dangerous the Monkey-People were in large numbers, did not wish to run any risks. The monkeys never fight unless they are a hundred to one, and few in the jungle care for those odds.

"I will go to the west wall," Kaa whispered, "and come down swiftly with the slope of the ground in my favor. They will not throw themselves upon my back in their hundreds, but—"

"I know it," said Bagheera. "Would that Baloo were here, but we must do what we can. When that cloud covers the moon I shall go to the terrace. They hold some sort of council there over the boy."

"Good hunting," said Kaa grimly, and glided away to the west wall. That happened to be the least ruined of any, and the big snake was delayed awhile before he could find a way up the stones. The cloud hid the moon, and as Mowgli wondered what would come next he heard Bagheera's light feet on the terrace. The Black Panther had raced up the slope almost without a sound and was striking—he knew better than to waste time in biting—right and left among the monkeys, who were seated round Mowgli in circles fifty and sixty deep. There was a howl of fright and rage, and then as Bagheera tripped on the rolling kicking bodies beneath him, a monkey shouted: "There is only one here! Kill him! Kill." A scuffling mass of monkeys, biting, scratching, tearing, and pulling, closed over Bagheera, while five or six laid hold of Mowgli, dragged him up the wall of the summerhouse and pushed him through the hole of the broken dome. A man-trained boy would have been badly bruised, for the fall was a good fifteen feet, but Mowgli fell as Baloo had taught him to fall, and landed on his feet.

"Stay there," shouted the monkeys, "till we have killed thy friends, and later we will play with thee—if the Poison-People leave thee alive."

"We be of one blood, ye and I," said Mowgli, quickly giving the Snake's Call. He could hear rustling and hissing in the rubbish all round him and gave the Call a second time, to make sure.

"Even ssso! Down hoods all!" said half a dozen low voices (every ruin in India becomes sooner or later a dwelling place of snakes, and the old summerhouse was alive with cobras). "Stand still, Little Brother, for thy feet may do us harm."

Mowgli stood as quietly as he could, peering through the open work and listening to the furious din of the fight round the Black Panther—the yells and chatterings and scufflings, and Bagheera's deep, hoarse cough as he backed and bucked and twisted and plunged under the heaps of his enemies. For the first time since he was born, Bagheera was fighting for his life.

"Baloo must be at hand; Bagheera would not have come alone," Mowgli thought. And then he called aloud: "To the tank, Bagheera. Roll to the water tanks. Roll and plunge! Get to the water!"

Bagheera heard, and the cry that told him Mowgli was safe gave him new courage. He worked his way desperately, inch by inch, straight for the reservoirs, halting in silence. Then from the ruined wall nearest the jungle rose up the rumbling war-shout of Baloo. The old Bear had done his best, but he could not come before. "Bagheera," he shouted, "I am here. I climb! I haste! Ahuwora! The stones slip under my feet! Wait my coming, O most infamous Bandar-log!" He panted up the terrace only to disappear to the head in a wave of monkeys, but he threw himself squarely on his haunches, and, spreading out his forepaws, hugged as many as he could hold, and then began to hit with a regular bat-bat-bat, like the flipping strokes of a paddle wheel. A crash and a splash told Mowgli that Bagheera had fought his way to the tank where the monkeys could not follow. The Panther lay gasping for breath, his head just out of the water, while the monkeys stood three deep on the red steps, dancing up and down with rage, ready to spring upon him from all sides if he came out to help Baloo. It was then that Bagheera lifted up his dripping chin, and in despair gave the Snake's Call for protection—"We be of one blood, ye and I"—for he believed that Kaa had turned tail at the last minute. Even Baloo, half smothered under the monkeys on the edge of the terrace, could not help chuckling as he heard the Black Panther asking for help.

Kaa had only just worked his way over the west wall, landing with a wrench that dislodged a coping stone into the ditch. He had no intention of losing any advantage of the ground, and coiled and uncoiled himself once or twice, to be sure that every foot of his long body was in working order. All that while the fight with Baloo went on, and the monkeys yelled in the tank round Bagheera, and Mang the Bat, flying to and fro, carried the news of the great battle over the jungle, till even Hathi the Wild Elephant trumpeted, and, far away, scattered bands of the Monkey-Folk woke and came leaping along the tree-roads to help their comrades in the Cold Lairs, and the noise of the fight roused all the day birds for miles round. Then Kaa came straight, quickly, and anxious to kill. The fighting strength of a python is in the driving blow of his head backed by all the strength and weight of his body. If you can imagine a lance, or a battering ram, or a hammer weighing nearly half a ton driven by a cool, quiet mind living in the handle of it, you can roughly imagine what Kaa was like when he fought. A python four or five feet long can knock a man down if he hits him fairly in the chest, and Kaa was thirty feet long, as you know. His first stroke was delivered into the heart of the crowd round Baloo. It was sent home with shut mouth in silence, and there was no need of a second. The monkeys scattered with cries of—"Kaa! It is Kaa! Run! Run!"

Generations of monkeys had been scared into good behavior by the stories their elders told them of Kaa, the night thief, who could slip along the branches as quietly as moss grows, and steal away the strongest monkey that ever lived; of old Kaa, who could make himself look so like a dead branch or a rotten stump that the wisest were deceived, till the branch caught them. Kaa was everything that the monkeys feared in the jungle, for none of them knew the limits of his power, none of them could look him in the face, and none had ever come alive out of his hug. And so they ran, stammering with terror, to the walls and the roofs of the houses, and Baloo drew a deep breath of relief. His fur was much thicker than Bagheera's, but he had suffered sorely in the fight. Then Kaa opened his mouth for the first time and spoke one long hissing word, and the far-away monkeys, hurrying to the defense of the Cold Lairs, stayed where they were, cowering, till the loaded branches bent and crackled under them. The monkeys on the walls and the empty houses stopped their cries, and in the stillness that fell upon the city Mowgli heard Bagheera shaking his wet sides as he came up from the tank. Then the clamor broke out again. The monkeys leaped higher up the walls. They clung around the necks of the big stone idols and shrieked as they skipped along the battlements, while Mowgli, dancing in the summerhouse, put his eye to the screenwork and hooted owl-fashion between his front teeth, to show his derision and contempt.

"Get the man-cub out of that trap; I can do no more," Bagheera gasped. "Let us take the man-cub and go. They may attack again."

"They will not move till I order them. Stay you sssso!" Kaa hissed, and the city was silent once more. "I could not come before, Brother, but I think I heard thee call"—this was to Bagheera.

"I—I may have cried out in the battle," Bagheera answered. "Baloo, art thou hurt?

"I am not sure that they did not pull me into a hundred little bearlings," said Baloo, gravely shaking one leg after the other. "Wow! I am sore. Kaa, we owe thee, I think, our lives— Bagheera and I."

"No matter. Where is the manling?"

"Here, in a trap. I cannot climb out," cried Mowgli. The curve of the broken dome was above his head.

"Take him away. He dances like Mao the Peacock. He will crush our young," said the cobras inside.

"Hah!" said Kaa with a chuckle, "he has friends everywhere, this manling. Stand back, manling. And hide you, O Poison People. I break down the wall."

Kaa looked carefully till he found a discolored crack in the marble tracery showing a weak spot, made two or three light taps with his head to get the distance, and then lifting up six feet of his body clear of the ground, sent home half a dozen full-power smashing blows, nose-first. The screen-work broke and fell away in a cloud of dust and rubbish, and Mowgli leaped through the opening and flung himself between Baloo and Bagheera—an arm around each big neck.

"Art thou hurt?" said Baloo, hugging him softly.

"I am sore, hungry, and not a little bruised. But, oh, they have handled ye grievously, my Brothers! Ye bleed."

"Others also," said Bagheera, licking his lips and looking at the monkey-dead on the terrace and round the tank.

"It is nothing, it is nothing, if thou art safe, oh, my pride of all little frogs!" whimpered Baloo.

"Of that we shall judge later," said Bagheera, in a dry voice that Mowgli did not at all like. "But here is Kaa to whom we owe the battle and thou owest thy life. Thank him according to our customs, Mowgli."

Mowgli turned and saw the great Python's head swaying a foot above his own.

"So this is the manling," said Kaa. "Very soft is his skin, and he is not unlike the Bandar-log. Have a care, manling, that I do not mistake thee for a monkey some twilight when I have newly changed my coat."

"We be one blood, thou and I," Mowgli answered. "I take my life from thee tonight. My kill shall be thy kill if ever thou art hungry, O Kaa."

"All thanks, Little Brother," said Kaa, though his eyes twinkled. "And what may so bold a hunter kill? I ask that I may follow when next he goes abroad."

"I kill nothing,—I am too little,—but I drive goats toward such as can use them. When thou art empty come to me and see if I speak the truth. I have some skill in these [he held out his hands], and if ever thou art in a trap, I may pay the debt which I owe to thee, to Bagheera, and to Baloo, here. Good hunting to ye all, my masters."

"Well said," growled Baloo, for Mowgli had returned

thanks very prettily. The Python dropped his head lightly for a minute on Mowgli's shoulder. "A brave heart and a courteous tongue," said he. "They shall carry thee far through the jungle, manling. But now go hence quickly with thy friends. Go and sleep, for the moon sets, and what follows it is not well that thou shouldst see."

The moon was sinking behind the hills and the lines of trembling monkeys huddled together on the walls and battlements looked like ragged shaky fringes of things. Baloo went down to the tank for a drink and Bagheera began to put his fur in order, as Kaa glided out into the center of the terrace and brought his jaws together with a ringing snap that drew all the monkeys' eyes upon him.

"The moon sets," he said. "Is there yet light enough to see?"

From the walls came a moan like the wind in the tree-tops—"We see, O Kaa."

"Good. Begins now the dance—the Dance of the Hunger of Kaa. Sit still and watch."

He turned twice or thrice in a big circle, weaving his head from right to left. Then he began making loops and figures of eight with his body, and soft, oozy triangles that melted into squares and five-sided figures, and coiled mounds, never resting, never hurrying, and never stopping his low humming song. It grew darker and darker, till at last the dragging, shifting coils disappeared, but they could hear the rustle of the scales.

Baloo and Bagheera stood still as stone, growling in their throats, their neck hair bristling, and Mowgli watched and wondered.

"Bandar-log," said the voice of Kaa at last, "can ye stir foot or hand without my order? Speak!"

"Without thy order we cannot stir foot or hand, O Kaa!"

"Good! Come all one pace nearer to me."

The lines of the monkeys swayed forward helplessly, and Baloo and Bagheera took one stiff step forward with them.

"Nearer!" hissed Kaa, and they all moved again.

Mowgli laid his hands on Baloo and Bagheera to get them away, and the two great beasts started as though they had been waked from a dream.

"Keep thy hand on my shoulder," Bagheera whispered. "Keep it there, or I must go back—must go back to Kaa. Aah!"

"It is only old Kaa making circles on the dust," said Mowgli. "Let us go." And the three slipped off through a gap in the walls to the jungle.

"Whoof!" said Baloo, when he stood under the still trees again. "Never more will I make an ally of Kaa," and he shook himself all over.

"He knows more than we," said Bagheera, trembling. "In a little time, had I stayed, I should have walked down his throat."

"Many will walk by that road before the moon rises again," said Baloo. "He will have good hunting—after his own fashion."

"But what was the meaning of it all?" said Mowgli, who did not know anything of a python's powers of fascination. "I saw no more than a big snake making foolish circles till the dark came. And his nose was all sore. Ho! Ho!"

"Mowgli," said Bagheera angrily, "his nose was sore on thy account, as my ears and sides and paws, and Baloo's neck and shoulders are bitten on thy account. Neither Baloo nor Bagheera will be able to hunt with pleasure for many days."

"It is nothing," said Baloo; "we have the man-cub again."

"True, but he has cost us heavily in time which might have been spent in good hunting, in wounds, in hair—I am half plucked along my back—and last of all, in honor. For, remember, Mowgli, I, who am the Black Panther, was forced to call upon Kaa for protection, and Baloo and I were both made stupid as little birds by the Hunger Dance. All this, man-cub, came of thy playing with the Bandar-log."

"True, it is true," said Mowgli sorrowfully. "I am an evil man-cub, and my stomach is sad in me."

"Mf! What says the Law of the Jungle, Baloo?"

Baloo did not wish to bring Mowgli into any more trouble, but he could not tamper with the Law, so he mumbled: "Sorrow never stays punishment. But remember, Bagheera, he is very little."

"I will remember. But he has done mischief, and blows must be dealt now. Mowgli, hast thou anything to say?"

"Nothing. I did wrong. Baloo and thou are wounded. It is just."

Bagheera gave him half a dozen love-taps from a panther's point of view (they would hardly have waked one of his own cubs), but for a seven-year-old boy they amounted to as severe a beating as you could wish to avoid. When it was all over Mowgli sneezed, and picked himself up without a word.

"Now," said Bagheera, "jump on my back, Little Brother, and we will go home."

One of the beauties of Jungle Law is that punishment settles all scores. There is no nagging afterward.

Mowgli laid his head down on Bagheera's back and slept so deeply that he never waked when he was put down in the home-cave.

                    Rudyard Kipling

Road-Song of the Bandar-Log
Here we go in a flung festoon,
Half-way up to the jealous moon!
Don't you envy our pranceful bands?
Don't you wish you had extra hands?
Wouldn't you like if your tails were—so—
Curved in the shape of a Cupid's bow?
Now you're angry, but—never mind,
Brother, thy tail hangs down behind!
Here we sit in a branchy row,
Thinking of beautiful things we know;
Dreaming of deeds that we mean to do,
All complete, in a minute or two—
Something noble and wise and good,
Done by merely wishing we could.
We've forgotten, but—never mind,
Brother, thy tail hangs down behind
All the talk we ever have heard
Uttered by bat or beast or bird—
Hide or fin or scale or feather—
Jabber it quickly and all together!
Excellent! Wonderful! Once again!
Now we are talking just like men!
Let's pretend we are ... never mind,
Brother, thy tail hangs down behind!
This is the way of the Monkey-kind.

Then join our leaping lines that scumfish through the pines,
That rocket by where, light and high, the wild grape swings.
By the rubbish in our wake, and the noble noise we make,
Be sure, be sure, we're going to do some splendid things!

"TIGER! TIGER!"

What of the hunting, hunter bold?
Brother, the watch was long and cold.
What of the quarry ye went to kill?
Brother, he crops in the jungle still.
Where is the power that made your pride?
Brother, it ebbs from my flank and side.
Where is the haste that ye hurry by?
Brother, I go to my lair—to die.

Now we must go back to the first tale. When Mowgli left the wolf's cave after the fight with the Pack at the Council Rock, he went down to the plowed lands where the villagers lived, but he would not stop there because it was too near to the jungle, and he knew that he had made at least one bad enemy at the Council. So he hurried on, keeping to the rough road that ran down the valley, and followed it at a steady jog-trot for nearly twenty miles, till he came to a country that he did not know. The valley opened out into a great plain dotted over with rocks and cut up by ravines. At one end stood a little village, and at the other the thick jungle came down in a sweep to the grazing-grounds, and stopped there as though it had been cut off with a hoe. All over the plain, cattle and buffaloes were grazing, and when the little boys in charge of the herds saw Mowgli they shouted and ran away, and the yellow pariah dogs that hang about every Indian village barked. Mowgli walked on, for he was feeling hungry, and when he came to the village gate he saw the big thorn-bush that was drawn up before the gate at twilight, pushed to one side.

"Umph!" he said, for he had come across more than one such barricade in his night rambles after things to eat. "So men are afraid of the People of the Jungle here also." He sat down by the gate, and when a man came out he stood up, opened his mouth, and pointed down it to show that he wanted food. The man stared, and ran back up the one street of the village shouting for the priest, who was a big, fat man dressed in white, with a red and yellow mark on his forehead. The priest came to the gate, and with him at least a hundred people, who stared and talked and shouted and pointed at Mowgli.

"They have no manners, these Men Folk," said Mowgli to himself. "Only the gray ape would behave as they do." So he threw back his long hair and frowned at the crowd.

"What is there to be afraid of?" said the priest. "Look at the marks on his arms and legs. They are the bites of wolves. He is but a wolf-child run away from the jungle."

Of course, in playing together, the cubs had often nipped Mowgli harder than they intended, and there were white scars all over his arms and legs. But he would have been the last person in the world to call these bites, for he knew what real biting meant.

"Arre! Arre!" said two or three women together. "To be

bitten by wolves, poor child! He is a handsome boy. He has eyes like red fire. By my honor, Messua, he is not unlike thy boy that was taken by the tiger."

"Let me look," said a woman with heavy copper rings on her wrists and ankles, and she peered at Mowgli under the palm of her hand. "Indeed he is not. He is thinner, but he has the very look of my boy."

The priest was a clever man, and he knew that Messua was wife to the richest villager in the place. So he looked up at the sky for a minute and said solemnly: "What the jungle has taken the jungle has restored. Take the boy into thy house, my sister, and forget not to honor the priest who sees so far into the lives of men."

"By the Bull that bought me," said Mowgli to himself, "but all this talking is like another looking-over by the Pack! Well, if I am a man, a man I must become."

The crowd parted as the woman beckoned Mowgli to her hut, where there was a red lacquered bedstead, a great earthen grain chest with funny raised patterns on it, half a dozen copper cooking pots, an image of a Hindu god in a little alcove, and on the wall a real looking glass, such as they sell at the country fairs.

She gave him a long drink of milk and some bread, and then she laid her hand on his head and looked into his eyes; for she thought perhaps that he might be her real son come back from the jungle where the tiger had taken him. So she said, "Nathoo, O Nathoo!" Mowgli did not show that he knew the name. "Dost thou not remember the day when I gave thee thy new shoes?" She touched his foot, and it was almost as hard as horn. "No," she said sorrowfully, "those feet have never worn shoes, but thou art very like my Nathoo, and thou shalt be my son."

Mowgli was uneasy, because he had never been under a roof before. But as he looked at the thatch, he saw that he could tear it out any time if he wanted to get away, and that the window had no fastenings. "What is the good of a man," he said to himself at last, "if he does not understand man's talk? Now I am as silly and dumb as a man would be with us in the jungle. I must speak their talk."

It was not for fun that he had learned while he was with the wolves to imitate the challenge of bucks in the jungle and the grunt of the little wild pig. So, as soon as Messua pronounced a word Mowgli would imitate it almost perfectly, and before dark he had learned the names of many things in the hut.

There was a difficulty at bedtime, because Mowgli would not sleep under anything that looked so like a panther trap as that hut, and when they shut the door he went through the window. "Give him his will," said Messua's husband. "Remember he can never till now have slept on a bed. If he is indeed sent in the place of our son he will not run away."

So Mowgli stretched himself in some long, clean grass at the edge of the field, but before he had closed his eyes a soft gray nose poked him under the chin.

"Phew!" said Gray Brother (he was the eldest of Mother Wolf's cubs). "This is a poor reward for following thee twenty miles. Thou smellest of wood smoke and cattle—altogether like a man already. Wake, Little Brother; I bring news."

"Are all well in the jungle?" said Mowgli, hugging him.

"All except the wolves that were burned with the Red Flower. Now, listen. Shere Khan has gone away to hunt far off till his coat grows again, for he is badly singed. When he returns he swears that he will lay thy bones in the Waingunga."

"There are two words to that. I also have made a little promise. But news is always good. I am tired to-night,—very tired with new things, Gray Brother,—but bring me the news always."

"Thou wilt not forget that thou art a wolf? Men will not make thee forget?" said Gray Brother anxiously.

"Never. I will always remember that I love thee and all in our cave. But also I will always remember that I have been cast out of the Pack."

"And that thou mayest be cast out of another pack. Men are only men, Little Brother, and their talk is like the talk of frogs in a pond. When I come down here again, I will wait for thee in the bamboos at the edge of the grazing-ground."

For three months after that night Mowgli hardly ever left the village gate, he was so busy learning the ways and customs of men. First he had to wear a cloth round him, which annoyed him horribly; and then he had to learn about money, which he did not in the least understand, and about plowing, of which he did not see the use. Then the little children in the village made him very angry. Luckily, the Law of the Jungle had taught him to keep his temper, for in the jungle life and food depend on keeping your temper; but when they made fun of him because he would not play games or fly kites, or because he mispronounced some word, only the knowledge that it was unsportsmanlike to kill little naked cubs kept him from picking them up and breaking them in two.

He did not know his own strength in the least. In the jungle he knew he was weak compared with the beasts, but in the village people said that he was as strong as a bull.

And Mowgli had not the faintest idea of the difference that caste makes between man and man. When the potter's donkey slipped in the clay pit, Mowgli hauled it out by the tail, and helped to stack the pots for their journey to the market at Khanhiwara. That was very shocking, too, for the potter is a low-caste man, and his donkey is worse. When the priest scolded him, Mowgli threatened to put him on the donkey too, and the priest told Messua's husband that Mowgli had better be set to work as soon as possible; and the village head-man told Mowgli that he would have to go out with the buffaloes next day, and herd them while they grazed. No one was more pleased than Mowgli; and that night, because he had been appointed a servant of the village, as it were, he went off to a circle that met every evening on a masonry platform under a great fig-tree. It was the village club, and the head-man and the watchman and the barber, who knew all the gossip of the village, and old Buldeo, the village hunter, who had a Tower musket, met and smoked. The monkeys sat and talked in the upper branches, and there was a hole under the platform where a cobra lived, and he had his little platter of milk every night because he was sacred; and the old men sat around the tree and talked, and pulled at the big huqas (the water-pipes) till far into the night. They told wonderful tales of gods and men and ghosts; and Buldeo told even more wonderful ones of the ways of beasts in the jungle, till the eyes of the children sitting outside the circle bulged out of their heads. Most of the tales were about animals, for the jungle was always at their door. The deer and the wild pig grubbed up their crops, and now and again the tiger carried off a man at twilight, within sight of the village gates.

Mowgli, who naturally knew something about what they were talking of, had to cover his face not to show that he was laughing, while Buldeo, the Tower musket across his knees, climbed on from one wonderful story to another, and Mowgli's shoulders shook.

Buldeo was explaining how the tiger that had carried away Messua's son was a ghost-tiger, and his body was inhabited by the ghost of a wicked, old money-lender, who had died some years ago. "And I know that this is true," he said, "because Purun Dass always limped from the blow that he got in a riot when his account books were burned, and the tiger that I speak of he limps, too, for the tracks of his pads are unequal."

"True, true, that must be the truth," said the gray-beards, nodding together.

"Are all these tales such cobwebs and moon talk?" said Mowgli. "That tiger limps because he was born lame, as everyone knows. To talk of the soul of a money-lender in a beast that never had the courage of a jackal is child's talk."

Buldeo was speechless with surprise for a moment, and the head-man stared.

"Oho! It is the jungle brat, is it?" said Buldeo. "If thou art so wise, better bring his hide to Khanhiwara, for the Government has set a hundred rupees on his life. Better still, talk not when thy elders speak."

Mowgli rose to go. "All the evening I have lain here listening," he called back over his shoulder, "and, except once or twice, Buldeo has not said one word of truth concerning the jungle, which is at his very doors. How, then, shall I believe the tales of ghosts and gods and goblins which he says he has seen?"

"It is full time that boy went to herding," said the head-man, while Buldeo puffed and snorted at Mowgli's impertinence.

The custom of most Indian villages is for a few boys to take the cattle and buffaloes out to graze in the early morning, and bring them back at night. The very cattle that would trample a white man to death allow themselves to be banged and bullied and shouted at by children that hardly come up to their noses. So long as the boys keep with the herds they are safe, for not even the tiger will charge a mob of cattle. But if they straggle to pick flowers or hunt lizards, they are sometimes carried off. Mowgli went through the village street in the dawn, sitting on the back of Rama, the great herd bull. The slaty-blue buffaloes, with their long, backward-sweeping horns and savage eyes, rose out their byres, one by one, and followed him, and Mowgli made it very clear to the children with him that he was the master. He beat the buffaloes with a long, polished bamboo, and told Kamya, one of the boys, to graze the cattle by themselves, while he went on with the buffaloes, and to be very careful not to stray away from the herd.

An Indian grazing ground is all rocks and scrub and tussocks and little ravines, among which the herds scatter and disappear. The buffaloes generally keep to the pools and muddy places, where they lie wallowing or basking in the warm mud for hours. Mowgli drove them on to the edge of the plain where the Waingunga came out of the jungle; then he dropped from Rama's neck, trotted off to a bamboo clump, and found Gray Brother. "Ah," said Gray Brother, "I have waited here very many days. What is the meaning of this cattle-herding work?"

"It is an order," said Mowgli. "I am a village herd for a while. What news of Shere Khan?"

"He has come back to this country, and has waited here a long time for thee. Now he has gone off again, for the game is scarce. But he means to kill thee."

"Very good," said Mowgli. "So long as he is away do thou or one of the four brothers sit on that rock, so that I can see thee as I come out of the village. When he comes back wait for me in the ravine by the dhak tree in the center of the plain. We need not walk into Shere Khan's mouth."

Then Mowgli picked out a shady place, and lay down and slept while the buffaloes grazed round him. Herding in India is one of the laziest things in the world. The cattle move and crunch, and lie down, and move on again, and they do not even low. They only grunt, and the buffaloes very seldom say anything, but get down into the muddy pools one after another, and work their way into the mud till only their noses and staring china-blue eyes show above the surface, and then they lie like logs. The sun makes the rocks dance in the heat, and the herd children hear one kite (never any more) whistling almost out of sight overhead, and they know that if they died, or a cow died, that kite would sweep down, and the next kite miles away would see him drop and follow, and the next, and the next, and almost before they were dead there would be a score of hungry kites come out of nowhere. Then they sleep and wake and sleep again, and weave little baskets of dried grass and put grasshoppers in them; or catch two praying mantises and make them fight; or string a necklace of red and black jungle nuts; or watch a lizard basking on a rock, or a snake hunting a frog near the wallows. Then they sing long, long songs with odd native quavers at the end of them, and the day seems longer than most people's whole lives, and perhaps they make a mud castle with mud figures of men and horses and buffaloes, and put reeds into the men's hands, and pretend that they are kings and the figures are their armies, or that they are gods to be worshiped. Then evening comes and the children call, and the buffaloes lumber up out of the sticky mud with noises like gunshots going off one after the other, and they all string across the gray plain back to the twinkling village lights.

Day after day Mowgli would lead the buffaloes out to their wallows, and day after day he would see Gray Brother's back a mile and a half away across the plain (so he knew that Shere Khan had not come back), and day after day he would lie on the grass listening to the noises round him, and dreaming of old days in the jungle. If Shere Khan had made a false step with his lame paw up in the jungles by the Waingunga, Mowgli would have heard him in those long, still mornings.

At last a day came when he did not see Gray Brother at the signal place, and he laughed and headed the buffaloes for the ravine by the dhk tree, which was all covered with golden-red flowers. There sat Gray Brother, every bristle on his back lifted.

"He has hidden for a month to throw thee off thy guard. He crossed the ranges last night with Tabaqui, hot-foot on thy trail," said the Wolf, panting.

Mowgli frowned. "I am not afraid of Shere Khan, but Tabaqui is very cunning."

"Have no fear," said Gray Brother, licking his lips a little. "I met Tabaqui in the dawn. Now he is telling all his wisdom to the kites, but he told me everything before I broke his back. Shere Khan's plan is to wait for thee at the village gate this evening—for thee and for no one else. He is lying up now, in the big dry ravine of the Waingunga."

"Has he eaten today, or does he hunt empty?" said Mowgli, for the answer meant life and death to him.

"He killed at dawn,—a pig,—and he has drunk too. Remember, Shere Khan could never fast, even for the sake of revenge."

"Oh! Fool, fool! What a cub's cub it is! Eaten and drunk too, and he thinks that I shall wait till he has slept! Now, where does he lie up? If there were but ten of us we might pull him down as he lies. These buffaloes will not charge unless they wind him, and I cannot speak their language. Can we get behind his track so that they may smell it?"

"He swam far down the Waingunga to cut that off," said Gray Brother.

"Tabaqui told him that, I know. He would never have thought of it alone." Mowgli stood with his finger in his mouth, thinking. "The big ravine of the Waingunga. That opens out on the plain not half a mile from here. I can take the herd round through the jungle to the head of the ravine and then sweep down—but he would slink out at the foot. We must block that end. Gray Brother, canst thou cut the herd in two for me?"

"Not I, perhaps—but I have brought a wise helper." Gray Brother trotted off and dropped into a hole. Then there lifted up a huge gray head that Mowgli knew well, and the hot air was filled with the most desolate cry of all the jungle—the hunting howl of a wolf at midday.

"Akela! Akela!" said Mowgli, clapping his hands. "I might have known that thou wouldst not forget me. We have a big work in hand. Cut the herd in two, Akela. Keep the cows and calves together, and the bulls and the plow buffaloes by themselves."

The two wolves ran, ladies'-chain fashion, in and out of the herd, which snorted and threw up its head, and separated into two clumps. In one, the cow-buffaloes stood with their calves in the center, and glared and pawed, ready, if a wolf would only stay still, to charge down and trample the life out of him. In the other, the bulls and the young bulls snorted and stamped, but though they looked more imposing they were much less dangerous, for they had no calves to protect. No six men could have divided the herd so neatly.

"What orders!" panted Akela. "They are trying to join again."

Mowgli slipped on to Rama's back. "Drive the bulls away to the left, Akela. Gray Brother, when we are gone, hold the cows together, and drive them into the foot of the ravine."

"How far?" said Gray Brother, panting and snapping.

"Till the sides are higher than Shere Khan can jump," shouted Mowgli. "Keep them there till we come down." The bulls swept off as Akela bayed, and Gray Brother stopped in front of the cows. They charged down on him, and he ran just before them to the foot of the ravine, as Akela drove the bulls far to the left.

"Well done! Another charge and they are fairly started. Careful, now—careful, Akela. A snap too much and the bulls will charge. Hujah! This is wilder work than driving black-buck. Didst thou think these creatures could move so swiftly?" Mowgli called.

"I have—have hunted these too in my time," gasped Akela in the dust. "Shall I turn them into the jungle?"

"Ay! Turn. Swiftly turn them! Rama is mad with rage. Oh, if I could only tell him what I need of him to-day."

The bulls were turned, to the right this time, and crashed into the standing thicket. The other herd children, watching with the cattle half a mile away, hurried to the village as fast as their legs could carry them, crying that the buffaloes had gone mad and run away.

But Mowgli's plan was simple enough. All he wanted to do was to make a big circle uphill and get at the head of the ravine, and then take the bulls down it and catch Shere Khan between the bulls and the cows; for he knew that after a meal and a full drink Shere Khan would not be in any condition to fight or to clamber up the sides of the ravine. He was soothing the buffaloes now by voice, and Akela had dropped far to the rear, only whimpering once or twice to hurry the rear-guard. It was a long, long circle, for they did not wish to get too near the ravine and give Shere Khan warning. At last Mowgli rounded up the bewildered herd at the head of the ravine on a grassy patch that sloped steeply down to the ravine itself. From that height you could see across the tops of the trees down to the plain below; but what Mowgli looked at was the sides of the ravine, and he saw with a great deal of satisfaction that they ran nearly straight up and down, while the vines and creepers that hung over them would give no foothold to a tiger who wanted to get out.

"Let them breathe, Akela," he said, holding up his hand. "They have not winded him yet. Let them breathe. I must tell Shere Khan who comes. We have him in the trap."

He put his hands to his mouth and shouted down the ravine—it was almost like shouting down a tunnel—and the echoes jumped from rock to rock.

After a long time there came back the drawling, sleepy snarl of a full-fed tiger just wakened.

"Who calls?" said Shere Khan, and a splendid peacock fluttered up out of the ravine screeching.

"I, Mowgli. Cattle thief, it is time to come to the Council Rock! Down—hurry them down, Akela! Down, Rama, down!"

The herd paused for an instant at the edge of the slope,

but Akela gave tongue in the full hunting-yell, and they pitched over one after the other, just as steamers shoot rapids, the sand and stones spurting up round them. Once started, there was no chance of stopping, and before they were fairly in the bed of the ravine Rama winded Shere Khan and bellowed.

"Ha! Ha!" said Mowgli, on his back. "Now thou knowest!" and the torrent of black horns, foaming muzzles, and staring eyes whirled down the ravine just as boulders go down in floodtime; the weaker buffaloes being shouldered out to the sides of the ravine where they tore through the creepers. They knew what the business was before them—the terrible charge of the buffalo herd against which no tiger can hope to stand. Shere Khan heard the thunder of their hoofs, picked himself up, and lumbered down the ravine, looking from side to side for some way of escape, but the walls of the ravine were straight and he had to hold on, heavy with his dinner and his drink, willing to do anything rather than fight. The herd splashed through the pool he had just left, bellowing till the narrow cut rang. Mowgli heard an answering bellow from the foot of the ravine, saw Shere Khan turn (the tiger knew if the worst came to the worst it was better to meet the bulls than the cows with their calves), and then Rama tripped, stumbled, and went on again over something soft, and, with the bulls at his heels, crashed full into the other herd, while the weaker buffaloes were lifted clean off their feet by the shock of the meeting. That charge carried both herds out into the plain, goring and stamping and snorting. Mowgli watched his time, and slipped off Rama's neck, laying about him right and left with his stick.

"Quick, Akela! Break them up. Scatter them, or they will be fighting one another. Drive them away, Akela. Hai, Rama! Hai, hai, hai! my children. Softly now, softly! It is all over."

Akela and Gray Brother ran to and fro nipping the

buffaloes' legs, and though the herd wheeled once to charge up the ravine again, Mowgli managed to turn Rama, and the others followed him to the wallows.

Shere Khan needed no more trampling. He was dead, and the kites were coming for him already.

"Brothers, that was a dog's death," said Mowgli, feeling for the knife he always carried in a sheath round his neck now that he lived with men. "But he would never have shown fight. His hide will look well on the Council Rock. We must get to work swiftly."

A boy trained among men would never have dreamed of skinning a ten-foot tiger alone, but Mowgli knew better than anyone else how an animal's skin is fitted on, and how it can be taken off. But it was hard work, and Mowgli slashed and tore and grunted for an hour, while the wolves lolled out their tongues, or came forward and tugged as he ordered them. Presently a hand fell on his shoulder, and looking up he saw Buldeo with the Tower musket. The children had told the village about the buffalo stampede, and Buldeo went out angrily, only too anxious to correct Mowgli for not taking better care of the herd. The wolves dropped out of sight as soon as they saw the man coming.

"What is this folly?" said Buldeo angrily. "To think that thou canst skin a tiger! Where did the buffaloes kill him? It is the Lame Tiger too, and there is a hundred rupees on his head. Well, well, we will overlook thy letting the herd run off, and perhaps I will give thee one of the rupees of the reward when I have taken the skin to Khanhiwara." He fumbled in his waist cloth for flint and steel, and stooped down to singe Shere Khan's whiskers. Most native hunters always singe a tiger's whiskers to prevent his ghost from haunting them.

"Hum!" said Mowgli, half to himself as he ripped back the skin of a forepaw. "So thou wilt take the hide to Khanhiwara for the reward, and perhaps give me one rupee? Now it is in my mind that I need the skin for my own use. Heh! Old man, take away that fire!"

"What talk is this to the chief hunter of the village? Thy luck and the stupidity of thy buffaloes have helped thee to this kill. The tiger has just fed, or he would have gone twenty miles by this time. Thou canst not even skin him properly, little beggar brat, and forsooth I, Buldeo, must be told not to singe his whiskers. Mowgli, I will not give thee one anna of the reward, but only a very big beating. Leave the carcass!"

"By the Bull that bought me," said Mowgli, who was trying to get at the shoulder, "must I stay babbling to an old ape all noon? Here, Akela, this man plagues me."

Buldeo, who was still stooping over Shere Khan's head, found himself sprawling on the grass, with a gray wolf standing over him, while Mowgli went on skinning as though he were alone in all India.

"Ye-es," he said, between his teeth. "Thou art altogether right, Buldeo. Thou wilt never give me one anna of the reward. There is an old war between this lame tiger and myself—a very old war, and—I have won."

To do Buldeo justice, if he had been ten years younger he would have taken his chance with Akela had he met the wolf in the woods, but a wolf who obeyed the orders of this boy who had private wars with man-eating tigers was not a common animal. It was sorcery, magic of the worst kind, thought Buldeo, and he wondered whether the amulet round his neck would protect him. He lay as still as still, expecting every minute to see Mowgli turn into a tiger too.

"Maharaj! Great King," he said at last in a husky whisper.

"Yes," said Mowgli, without turning his head, chuckling a little.

"I am an old man. I did not know that thou wast anything more than a herdsboy. May I rise up and go away, or will thy servant tear me to pieces?"

"Go, and peace go with thee. Only, another time do not meddle with my game. Let him go, Akela."

Buldeo hobbled away to the village as fast as he could, looking back over his shoulder in case Mowgli should change into something terrible. When he got to the village he told a tale of magic and enchantment and sorcery that made the priest look very grave.

Mowgli went on with his work, but it was nearly twilight before he and the wolves had drawn the great gay skin clear of the body.

"Now we must hide this and take the buffaloes home! Help me to herd them, Akela."

The herd rounded up in the misty twilight, and when they got near the village Mowgli saw lights, and heard the conches and bells in the temple blowing and banging. Half the village seemed to be waiting for him by the gate. "That is because I have killed Shere Khan," he said to himself. But a shower of stones whistled about his ears, and the villagers shouted: "Sorcerer! Wolf's brat! Jungle demon! Go away! Get hence quickly or the priest will turn thee into a wolf again. Shoot, Buldeo, shoot!"

The old Tower musket went off with a bang, and a young buffalo bellowed in pain.

"More sorcery!" shouted the villagers. "He can turn bullets. Buldeo, that was thy buffalo."

"Now what is this?" said Mowgli, bewildered, as the stones flew thicker.

"They are not unlike the Pack, these brothers of thine," said Akela, sitting down composedly. "It is in my head that, if bullets mean anything, they would cast thee out."

"Wolf! Wolf's cub! Go away!" shouted the priest, waving a sprig of the sacred tulsi plant.

"Again? Last time it was because I was a man. This time it is because I am a wolf. Let us go, Akela."

A woman—it was Messua—ran across to the herd, and cried: "Oh, my son, my son! They say thou art a sorcerer who can turn himself into a beast at will. I do not believe, but go away or they will kill thee. Buldeo says thou art a wizard, but I know thou hast avenged Nathoo's death."

"Come back, Messua!" shouted the crowd. "Come back, or we will stone thee."

Mowgli laughed a little short ugly laugh, for a stone had hit him in the mouth. "Run back, Messua. This is one of the foolish tales they tell under the big tree at dusk. I have at least paid for thy son's life. Farewell; and run quickly, for I shall send the herd in more swiftly than their brickbats. I am no wizard, Messua. Farewell!"

"Now, once more, Akela," he cried. "Bring the herd in."

The buffaloes were anxious enough to get to the village. They hardly needed Akela's yell, but charged through the gate like a whirlwind, scattering the crowd right and left.

"Keep count!" shouted Mowgli scornfully. "It may be that I have stolen one of them. Keep count, for I will do your herding no more. Fare you well, children of men, and thank Messua that I do not come in with my wolves and hunt you up and down your street."

He turned on his heel and walked away with the Lone Wolf, and as he looked up at the stars he felt happy. "No more sleeping in traps for me, Akela. Let us get Shere Khan's skin and go away. No, we will not hurt the village, for Messua was kind to me."

When the moon rose over the plain, making it look all milky, the horrified villagers saw Mowgli, with two wolves at his heels and a bundle on his head, trotting across at the steady wolf's trot that eats up the long miles like fire. Then they banged the temple bells and blew the conches louder than ever. And Messua cried, and Buldeo embroidered the story of his adventures in the jungle, till he ended by saying that Akela stood up on his hind legs and talked like a man.

The moon was just going down when Mowgli and the two wolves came to the hill of the Council Rock, and they stopped at Mother Wolf's cave.

"They have cast me out from the Man-Pack, Mother," shouted Mowgli, "but I come with the hide of Shere Khan to keep my word."

Mother Wolf walked stiffly from the cave with the cubs behind her, and her eyes glowed as she saw the skin.

"I told him on that day, when he crammed his head and shoulders into this cave, hunting for thy life, Little Frog—I told him that the hunter would be the hunted. It is well done."

"Little Brother, it is well done," said a deep voice in the thicket. "We were lonely in the jungle without thee, and Bagheera came running to Mowgli's bare feet. They clambered up the Council Rock together, and Mowgli spread the skin out on the flat stone where Akela used to sit, and pegged it down with four slivers of bamboo, and Akela lay down upon it, and called the old call to the Council, 'Look—

look well, O Wolves,' exactly as he had called when Mowgli was first brought there."

Ever since Akela had been deposed, the Pack had been without a leader, hunting and fighting at their own pleasure. But they answered the call from habit; and some of them were lame from the traps they had fallen into, and some limped from shot wounds, and some were mangy from eating bad food, and many were missing. But they came to the Council Rock, all that were left of them, and saw Shere Khan's striped hide on the rock, and the huge claws dangling at the end of the empty dangling feet. It was then that Mowgli made up a song that came up into his throat all by itself, and he shouted it aloud, leaping up and down on the rattling skin, and beating time with his heels till he had no more breath left, while Gray Brother and Akela howled between the verses.

"Look well, O Wolves. Have I kept my word?" said Mowgli. And the wolves bayed "Yes," and one tattered wolf howled:

"Lead us again, O Akela. Lead us again, O Man-cub, for we be sick of this lawlessness, and we would be the Free People once more."

"Nay," purred Bagheera, "that may not be. When ye are full-fed, the madness may come upon you again. Not for nothing are ye called the Free People. Ye fought for freedom, and it is yours. Eat it, O Wolves."

"Man-Pack and Wolf-Pack have cast me out," said Mowgli. "Now I will hunt alone in the jungle."

"And we will hunt with thee," said the four cubs.

So Mowgli went away and hunted with the four cubs in the jungle from that day on. But he was not always alone, because, years afterward, he became a man and married.

But that is a story for grown-ups.

THE WHITE SEAL

Oh! hush thee, my baby, the night is behind us,
And black are the waters that sparkled so green.
The moon, o'er the combers, looks downward to find us
At rest in the hollows that rustle between.
Where billow meets billow, then soft be thy pillow,
Ah, weary wee flipperling, curl at thy ease!
The storm shall not wake thee, nor shark overtake thee,
Asleep in the arms of the slow-swinging seas!

Seal Lullaby

All these things happened several years ago at a place called Novastoshnah, or North East Point, on the Island of St. Paul, away and away in the Bering Sea. Limmershin, the Winter Wren, told me the tale when he was blown on to the rigging of a steamer going to Japan, and I took him down into my cabin and warmed and fed him for a couple of days till he was fit to fly back to St. Paul's again. Limmershin is a very quaint little bird, but he knows how to tell the truth.

Nobody comes to Novastoshnah except on business, and the only people who have regular business there are the seals.

They come in the summer months by hundreds and hundreds of thousands out of the cold gray sea. For Novastoshnah Beach has the finest accommodation for seals of any place in all the world.

Sea Catch knew that, and every spring would swim from whatever place he happened to be in—would swim like a torpedo-boat straight for Novastoshnah and spend a month fighting with his companions for a good place on the rocks, as close to the sea as possible. Sea Catch was fifteen years old, a huge gray fur seal with almost a mane on his shoulders, and long, wicked dog teeth. When he heaved himself up on his front flippers he stood more than four feet clear of the ground, and his weight, if anyone had been bold enough to weigh him, was nearly seven hundred pounds. He was scarred all over with the marks of savage fights, but he was always ready for just one fight more. He would put his head on one side, as though he were afraid to look his enemy in the face; then he would shoot it out like lightning, and when the big teeth were firmly fixed on the other seal's neck, the other seal might get away if he could, but Sea Catch would not help him.

Yet Sea Catch never chased a beaten seal, for that was against the Rules of the Beach. He only wanted room by the sea for his nursery. But as there were forty or fifty thousand other seals hunting for the same thing each spring, the whistling, bellowing, roaring, and blowing on the beach was something frightful.

From a little hill called Hutchinson's Hill, you could look over three and a half miles of ground covered with fighting seals; and the surf was dotted all over with the heads of seals hurrying to land and begin their share of the fighting. They fought in the breakers, they fought in the sand, and they fought on the smooth-worn basalt rocks of the nurseries, for they were just as stupid and unaccommodating as men. Their wives never came to the island until late in May or early in June, for they did not care to be torn to pieces; and the young two-, three-, and four-year-old seals who had not begun housekeeping went inland about half a mile through the ranks of the fighters and played about on the sand dunes in droves and legions, and rubbed off every single green thing that grew. They were called the holluschickie—the bachelors—and there were perhaps two or three hundred thousand of them at Novastoshnah alone.

Sea Catch had just finished his forty-fifth fight one spring when Matkah, his soft, sleek, gentle-eyed wife, came up out of the sea, and he caught her by the scruff of the neck and dumped her down on his reservation, saying gruffly: "Late as usual. Where have you been?"

It was not the fashion for Sea Catch to eat anything during the four months he stayed on the beaches, and so his temper was generally bad. Matkah knew better than to answer back. She looked round and cooed: "How thoughtful of you. You've taken the old place again."

"I should think I had," said Sea Catch. "Look at me!"

He was scratched and bleeding in twenty places; one eye was almost out, and his sides were torn to ribbons.

"Oh, you men, you men!" Matkah said, fanning herself with her hind flipper. "Why can't you be sensible and settle your places quietly? You look as though you had been fighting with the Killer Whale."

"I haven't been doing anything but fight since the middle of May. The beach is disgracefully crowded this season. I've met at least a hundred seals from Lukannon Beach, house hunting. Why can't people stay where they belong?"

"I've often thought we should be much happier if we hauled out at Otter Island instead of this crowded place," said Matkah.

"Bah! Only the holluschickie go to Otter Island. If we went there they would say we were afraid. We must preserve appearances, my dear."

Sea Catch sunk his head proudly between his fat shoulders and pretended to go to sleep for a few minutes, but all the time he was keeping a sharp lookout for a fight. Now that all the seals and their wives were on the land, you could hear their clamor miles out to sea above the loudest gales. At the lowest counting there were over a million seals on the beach—old seals, mother seals, tiny babies, and holluschickie, fighting, scuffling, bleating, crawling, and playing together—going down to the sea and coming up from it in gangs and regiments, lying over every foot of ground as far as the eye could reach, and skirmishing about in brigades through the fog. It is nearly always foggy at Novastoshnah, except when the sun comes out and makes everything look all pearly and rainbow-colored for a little while.

Kotick, Matkah's baby, was born in the middle of that confusion, and he was all head and shoulders, with pale, watery blue eyes, as tiny seals must be, but there was something about his coat that made his mother look at him very closely.

"Sea Catch," she said, at last, "our baby's going to be white!"

"Empty clam-shells and dry seaweed!" snorted Sea Catch. "There never has been such a thing in the world as a white seal."

"I can't help that," said Matkah; "there's going to be now." And she sang the low, crooning seal song that all the mother seals sing to their babies:

> *You mustn't swim till you're six weeks old,*
> *Or your head will be sunk by your heels;*

And summer gales and Killer Whales
Are bad for baby seals.
Are bad for baby seals, dear rat,
As bad as bad can be;
But splash and grow strong,
And you can't be wrong.
Child of the Open Sea!

Of course the little fellow did not understand the words at first. He paddled and scrambled about by his mother's side, and learned to scuffle out of the way when his father was fighting with another seal, and the two rolled and roared up and down the slippery rocks. Matkah used to go to sea to get things to eat, and the baby was fed only once in two days, but then he ate all he could and throve upon it.

The first thing he did was to crawl inland, and there he met tens of thousands of babies of his own age, and they played together like puppies, went to sleep on the clean sand, and played again. The old people in the nurseries took no notice of them, and the holluschickie kept to their own grounds, and the babies had a beautiful playtime.

When Matkah came back from her deep-sea fishing she would go straight to their playground and call as a sheep calls for a lamb, and wait until she heard Kotick bleat. Then she would take the straightest of straight lines in his direction, striking out with her fore flippers and knocking the youngsters head over heels right and left. There were always a few hundred mothers hunting for their children through the playgrounds, and the babies were kept lively. But, as Matkah told Kotick, "So long as you don't lie in muddy water and get mange, or rub the hard sand into a cut or scratch, and so long as you never go swimming when there is a heavy sea, nothing will hurt you here."

Little seals can no more swim than little children, but they are unhappy till they learn. The first time that Kotick went down to the sea a wave carried him out beyond his depth, and his big head sank and his little hind flippers flew up exactly as his mother had told him in the song, and if the next wave had not thrown him back again he would have drowned.

After that, he learned to lie in a beach pool and let the wash of the waves just cover him and lift him up while he paddled, but he always kept his eye open for big waves that might hurt. He was two weeks learning to use his flippers; and all that while he floundered in and out of the water, and coughed and grunted and crawled up the beach and took catnaps on the sand, and went back again, until at last he found that he truly belonged to the water.

Then you can imagine the times that he had with his companions, ducking under the rollers; or coming in on top of a comber and landing with a swash and a splutter as the big wave went whirling far up the beach; or standing up on his tail and scratching his head as the old people did; or playing "I'm the King of the Castle" on slippery, weedy rocks that just stuck out of the wash. Now and then he would see a thin fin, like a big shark's fin, drifting along close to shore, and he knew that that was the Killer Whale, the Grampus, who eats young seals when he can get them; and Kotick would head for the beach like an arrow, and the fin would jig off slowly, as if it were looking for nothing at all.

Late in October the seals began to leave St. Paul's for the deep sea, by families and tribes, and there was no more fighting over the nurseries, and the holluschickie played anywhere they liked. "Next year," said Matkah to Kotick, "you will be a holluschickie; but this year you must learn how to catch fish."

They set out together across the Pacific, and Matkah showed Kotick how to sleep on his back with his flippers tucked down by his side and his little nose just out of the water. No cradle is so comfortable as the long, rocking swell of the Pacific. When Kotick felt his skin tingle all over, Matkah told him he was learning the "feel of the water," and that tingly, prickly feelings meant bad weather coming, and he must swim hard and get away.

"In a little time," she said, "you'll know where to swim to, but just now we'll follow Sea Pig, the Porpoise, for he is very wise." A school of porpoises were ducking and tearing through the water, and little Kotick followed them as fast as he could. "How do you know where to go to?" he panted. The leader of the school rolled his white eye and ducked under. "My tail tingles, youngster," he said. "That means there's a gale behind me. Come along! When you're south of the Sticky Water [he meant the Equator] and your tail tingles, that means there's a gale in front of you and you must head north. Come along! The water feels bad here."

This was one of very many things that Kotick learned, and he was always learning. Matkah taught him to follow the cod and the halibut along the under-sea banks and wrench the rockling out of his hole among the weeds; how to skirt the wrecks lying a hundred fathoms below water and dart like a rifle bullet in at one porthole and out at another as the fishes ran; how to dance on the top of the waves when the lightning was racing all over the sky, and wave his flipper politely to the stumpy-tailed Albatross and the Man-of-war Hawk as they went down the wind; how to jump three or four feet clear of the water like a dolphin, flippers close to the side and tail curved; to leave the flying fish alone because they are all bony; to take the shoulder-piece out of a cod at full speed ten fathoms deep, and never to stop and look at a boat or a ship, but particularly a row-boat. At the end of six months what Kotick did not know about deep-sea fishing was not worth the knowing. And all that time he never set flipper on dry ground.

One day, however, as he was lying half asleep in the warm water somewhere off the Island of Juan Fernandez, he felt faint and lazy all over, just as human people do when the spring is in their legs, and he remembered the good firm beaches of Novastoshnah seven thousand miles away, the games his companions played, the smell of the seaweed, the seal roar, and the fighting. That very minute he turned north, swimming steadily, and as he went on he met scores of his mates, all bound for the same place, and they said: "Greeting, Kotick! This year we are all holluschickie, and we can dance the Fire-dance in the breakers off Lukannon and play on the new grass. But where did you get that coat?"

Kotick's fur was almost pure white now, and though he felt very proud of it, he only said, "Swim quickly! My bones are aching for the land." And so they all came to the beaches where they had been born, and heard the old seals, their fathers, fighting in the rolling mist.

That night Kotick danced the Fire-dance with the yearling seals. The sea is full of fire on summer nights all the way down from Novastoshnah to Lukannon, and each seal leaves a wake like burning oil behind him and a flaming flash when he jumps, and the waves break in great phosphorescent streaks and swirls. Then they went inland to the holluschickie grounds and rolled up and down in the new wild wheat and told stories of what they had done while they had been at sea. They talked about the Pacific as boys would talk about a wood that they had been nutting in, and if anyone had understood them he could have gone away and made such a chart of that ocean as never was. The three- and four-year-old holluschickie romped down from Hutchinson's Hill crying: "Out of the way, youngsters! The sea is deep and you don't know all that's in it yet. Wait till you've rounded the Horn. Hi, you yearling, where did you get that white coat?"

"I didn't get it," said Kotick. "It grew." And just as he was going to roll the speaker over, a couple of black-haired men with flat red faces came from behind a sand dune, and Kotick, who had never seen a man before, coughed and lowered his head. The holluschickie just bundled off a few yards and sat staring stupidly. The men were no less than Kerick Booterin, the chief of the seal-hunters on the island, and Patalamon, his son. They came from the little village not half a mile from the sea nurseries, and they were deciding what seals they would drive up to the killing pens—for the seals were driven just like sheep—to be turned into seal-skin jackets later on.

"Ho!" said Patalamon. "Look! There's a white seal!"

Kerick Booterin turned nearly white under his oil and smoke, for he was an Aleut, and Aleuts are not clean people. Then he began to mutter a prayer. "Don't touch him, Patalamon. There has never been a white seal since—since I was born. Perhaps it is old Zaharrof's ghost. He was lost last year in the big gale."

"I'm not going near him," said Patalamon. "He's unlucky. Do you really think he is old Zaharrof come back? I owe him for some gulls' eggs."

"Don't look at him," said Kerick. "Head off that drove of four-year-olds. The men ought to skin two hundred to-day, but it's the beginning of the season and they are new to the work. A hundred will do. Quick!"

Patalamon rattled a pair of seal's shoulder bones in front

of a herd of holluschickie and they stopped dead, puffing and blowing. Then he stepped near and the seals began to move, and Kerick headed them inland, and they never tried to get back to their companions. Hundreds and hundreds of thousands of seals watched them being driven, but they went on playing just the same. Kotick was the only one who asked questions, and none of his companions could tell him anything, except that the men always drove seals in that way for six weeks or two months of every year.

"I am going to follow," he said, and his eyes nearly popped out of his head as he shuffled along in the wake of the herd.

"The white seal is coming after us," cried Patalamon. "That's the first time a seal has ever come to the killing-grounds alone."

"Hsh! Don't look behind you," said Kerick. "It is Zaharrof's ghost! I must speak to the priest about this."

The distance to the killing-grounds was only half a mile, but it took an hour to cover, because if the seals went too fast Kerick knew that they would get heated and then their fur would come off in patches when they were skinned. So they went on very slowly, past Sea Lion's Neck, past Webster House, till they came to the Salt House just beyond the sight of the seals on the beach. Kotick followed, panting and wondering. He thought that he was at the world's end, but the roar of the seal nurseries behind him sounded as loud as the roar of a train in a tunnel. Then Kerick sat down on the moss and pulled out a heavy pewter watch and let the drove cool off for thirty minutes, and Kotick could hear the fog-dew dripping off the brim of his cap. Then ten or twelve men, each with an iron-bound club three or four feet long, came up, and Kerick pointed out one or two of the drove that were bitten by their companions or too hot, and the men kicked those aside with their heavy boots made of the skin of a walrus's throat, and then Kerick said, "Let go!" and then the men clubbed the seals on the head as fast as they could.

Ten minutes later little Kotick did not recognize his friends any more, for their skins were ripped off from the nose to the hind flippers, whipped off and thrown down on the ground in a pile. That was enough for Kotick. He turned and galloped (a seal can gallop very swiftly for a short time) back to the sea; his little new mustache bristling with horror. At Sea Lion's Neck, where the great sea lions sit on the edge of the surf, he flung himself flipper-overhead into the cool water and rocked there, gasping miserably. "What's here?" said a sea lion gruffly, for as a rule the sea lions keep themselves to themselves.

"Scoochnie! Ochen scoochnie!" ("I'm lonesome, very lonesome!") said Kotick. "They're killing all the holluschickie on all the beaches!"

The Sea Lion turned his head inshore. "Nonsense!" he said. "Your friends are making as much noise as ever. You must have seen old Kerick polishing off a drove. He's done that for thirty years."

"It's horrible," said Kotick, backing water as a wave went over him, and steadying himself with a screw stroke of his flippers that brought him all standing within three inches of a jagged edge of rock.

"Well done for a yearling!" said the Sea Lion, who could appreciate good swimming. "I suppose it is rather awful from your way of looking at it, but if you seals will come here year after year, of course the men get to know of it, and unless you can find an island where no men ever come you will always be driven."

"Isn't there any such island?" began Kotick.

"I've followed the poltoos [the halibut] for twenty years, and I can't say I've found it yet. But look here—you seem to have a fondness for talking to your betters—suppose you go to Walrus Islet and talk to Sea Vitch. He may know something. Don't flounce off like that. It's a six-mile swim, and if I were you I should haul out and take a nap first, little one."

Kotick thought that that was good advice, so he swam round to his own beach, hauled out, and slept for half an hour, twitching all over, as seals will. Then he headed straight for Walrus Islet, a little low sheet of rocky island almost due northeast from Novastoshnah, all ledges and rock and gulls' nests, where the walrus herded by themselves.

He landed close to old Sea Vitch—the big, ugly, bloated, pimpled, fat-necked, long-tusked walrus of the North Pacific, who has no manners except when he is asleep—as he was then, with his hind flippers half in and half out of the surf.

"Wake up!" barked Kotick, for the gulls were making a great noise.

"Hah! Ho! Hmph! What's that?" said Sea Vitch, and he struck the next walrus a blow with his tusks and waked him up, and the next struck the next, and so on till they were all awake and staring in every direction but the right one.

"Hi! It's me," said Kotick, bobbing in the surf and looking like a little white slug.

"Well! May I be—skinned!" said Sea Vitch, and they all looked at Kotick as you can fancy a club full of drowsy old gentlemen would look at a little boy. Kotick did not care to hear any more about skinning just then; he had seen enough of it. So he called out: "Isn't there any place for seals to go where men don't ever come?"

"Go and find out," said Sea Vitch, shutting his eyes. "Run away. We're busy here."

Kotick made his dolphin-jump in the air and shouted as loud as he could: "Clam-eater! Clam-eater!" He knew that Sea Vitch never caught a fish in his life but always rooted for clams and seaweed; though he pretended to be a very terrible person. Naturally the Chickies and the Gooverooskies and the Epatkas—the Burgomaster Gulls and the Kittiwakes and the Puffins, who are always looking for a chance to be rude, took up the cry, and—so Limmershin told me—for nearly five minutes you could not have heard a gun fired on Walrus Islet. All the population was yelling and screaming "Clam-eater! Stareek [old man]!" while Sea Vitch rolled from side to side grunting and coughing.

"Now will you tell?" said Kotick, all out of breath.

"Go and ask Sea Cow," said Sea Vitch. "If he is living still, he'll be able to tell you."

"How shall I know Sea Cow when I meet him?" said Kotick, sheering off.

"He's the only thing in the sea uglier than Sea Vitch," screamed a Burgomaster gull, wheeling under Sea Vitch's nose. "Uglier, and with worse manners! Stareek!"

Kotick swam back to Novastoshnah, leaving the gulls to scream. There he found that no one sympathized with him in his little attempt to discover a quiet place for the seals. They told him that men had always driven the holluschickie—it was part of the day's work—and that if he did not like to see ugly things he should not have gone to the killing grounds. But none of the other seals had seen the killing, and that made the difference between him and his friends. Besides, Kotick was a white seal.

"What you must do," said old Sea Catch, after he had heard his son's adventures, "is to grow up and be a big seal like your father, and have a nursery on the beach, and then they will leave you alone. In another five years you ought to be able to fight for yourself." Even gentle Matkah, his mother, said: "You will never be able to stop the killing. Go and play in the sea, Kotick." And Kotick went off and danced the Fire-dance with a very heavy little heart.

That autumn he left the beach as soon as he could, and set off alone because of a notion in his bullet-head. He was going to find Sea Cow, if there was such a person in the sea, and he was going to find a quiet island with good firm beaches for seals to live on, where men could not get at them. So he explored and explored by himself from the North to the South Pacific, swimming as much as three hundred miles in a day and a night. He met with more adventures than can be told, and narrowly escaped being caught by the Basking Shark, and the Spotted Shark, and the Hammerhead, and he met all the untrustworthy ruffians that loaf up and down the seas, and the heavy polite fish, and the scarlet spotted scallops that are moored in one place for hundreds of years, and grow very proud of it; but he never met Sea Cow, and he never found an island that he could fancy.

If the beach was good and hard, with a slope behind it for seals to play on, there was always the smoke of a whaler on the horizon, boiling down blubber, and Kotick knew what that meant. Or else he could see that seals had once visited the island and been killed off, and Kotick knew that where men had come once they would come again.

He picked up with an old stumpy-tailed albatross, who told him that Kerguelen Island was the very place for peace and quiet, and when Kotick went down there he was all but smashed to pieces against some wicked black cliffs in a heavy sleet-storm with lightning and thunder. Yet as he pulled out against the gale he could see that even there had once been a seal nursery. And it was so in all the other islands that he visited.

Limmershin gave a long list of them, for he said that Kotick spent five seasons exploring, with a four months' rest each year at Novastoshnah, when the holluschickie used to make fun of him and his imaginary islands. He went to the Gallapagos, a horrid dry place on the Equator, where he was nearly baked to death; he went to the Georgia Islands, the Orkneys, Emerald Island, Little Nightingale Island, Gough's Island, Bouvet's Island, the Crossets, and even to a little speck of an island south of the Cape of Good Hope. But everywhere the People of the Sea told him the same things. Seals had come to those islands once upon a time, but men had killed them all off. Even when he swam thousands of miles out of the Pacific and got to a place called Cape Corrientes (that was when he was coming back from Gough's Island), he found a few hundred mangy seals on a rock and they told him that men came there too.

That nearly broke his heart, and he headed round the Horn back to his own beaches; and on his way north he hauled out on an island full of green trees, where he found an old, old seal who was dying, and Kotick caught fish for him and told him all his sorrows. "Now," said Kotick, "I am going back to Novastoshnah, and if I am driven to the killing-pens with the holluschickie I shall not care."

The old seal said, "Try once more. I am the last of the Lost Rookery of Masafuera, and in the days when men killed us by the hundred thousand there was a story on the beaches that some day a white seal would come out of the North and lead the seal people to a quiet place. I am old, and I shall never live to see that day, but others will. Try once more."

And Kotick curled up his mustache (it was a beauty) and said, "I am the only white seal that has ever been born on the beaches, and I am the only seal, black or white, who ever thought of looking for new islands."

This cheered him immensely; and when he came back to Novastoshnah that summer, Matkah, his mother, begged him to marry and settle down, for he was no longer a holluschick but a full-grown sea-catch, with a curly white mane on his shoulders, as heavy, as big, and as fierce as his father. "Give me another season," he said. "Remember, Mother, it is always the seventh wave that goes farthest up the beach."

Curiously enough, there was another seal who thought that she would put off marrying till the next year, and Kotick danced the Fire-dance with her all down Lukannon Beach the night before he set off on his last exploration. This time he went westward, because he had fallen on the trail of a great shoal of halibut, and he needed at least one hundred pounds of fish a day to keep him in good condition. He chased them till he was tired, and then he curled himself up and went to sleep on the hollows of the ground swell that sets in to Copper Island. He knew the coast perfectly well, so about midnight, when he felt himself gently bumped on a weed-bed, he said, "Hm, tide's running strong tonight," and turning over under water opened his eyes slowly and stretched. Then he jumped like a cat, for he saw huge things nosing about in the shoal water and browsing on the heavy fringes of the weeds.

"By the Great Combers of Magellan!" he said, beneath his mustache. "Who in the Deep Sea are these people?"

They were like no walrus, sea lion, seal, bear, whale, shark, fish, squid, or scallop that Kotick had ever seen before. They were between twenty and thirty feet long, and they had no hind flippers, but a shovel-like tail that looked as if it had been whittled out of wet leather. Their heads were the most foolish-looking things you ever saw, and they balanced on the ends of their tails in deep water when they weren't grazing, bowing solemnly to each other and waving their front flippers as a fat man waves his arm.

"Ahem!" said Kotick. "Good sport, gentlemen?" The big things answered by bowing and waving their flippers like the Frog Footman. When they began feeding again Kotick saw that their upper lip was split into two pieces that they could twitch apart about a foot and bring together again with a whole bushel of seaweed between the splits. They tucked the stuff into their mouths and chumped solemnly.

"Messy style of feeding, that," said Kotick. They bowed again, and Kotick began to lose his temper. "Very good," he said. "If you do happen to have an extra joint in your front flipper you needn't show off so. I see you bow gracefully, but I should like to know your names." The split lips moved and twitched; and the glassy green eyes stared, but they did not speak.

"Well!" said Kotick. "You're the only people I've ever met uglier than Sea Vitch—and with worse manners."

Then he remembered in a flash what the Burgomaster gull had screamed to him when he was a little yearling at Walrus Islet, and he tumbled backward in the water, for he knew that he had found Sea Cow at last.

The sea cows went on schlooping and grazing and chumping in the weed, and Kotick asked them questions in every language that he had picked up in his travels; and the Sea People talk nearly as many languages as human beings. But the sea cows did not answer because Sea Cow cannot talk. He has only six bones in his neck where he ought to have seven, and they say under the sea that that prevents him from speaking even to his companions. But, as you know, he has an extra joint in his foreflipper, and by waving it up and down and about he makes what answers to a sort of clumsy telegraphic code.

By daylight Kotick's mane was standing on end and his temper was gone where the dead crabs go. Then the Sea Cow began to travel northward very slowly, stopping to hold absurd bowing councils from time to time, and Kotick followed them, saying to himself, "People who are such idiots as these are would have been killed long ago if they hadn't found out some safe island. And what is good enough for the Sea Cow is good enough for the Sea Catch. All the same, I wish they'd hurry."

It was weary work for Kotick. The herd never went more than forty or fifty miles a day, and stopped to feed at night, and kept close to the shore all the time; while Kotick swam round them, and over them, and under them, but he could not hurry them up one-half mile. As they went farther north they held a bowing council every few hours, and Kotick nearly bit off his mustache with impatience till he saw that they were following up a warm current of water, and then he respected them more.

One night they sank through the shiny water—sank like stones—and for the first time since he had known them began to swim quickly. Kotick followed, and the pace astonished him, for he never dreamed that Sea Cow was anything of a swimmer. They headed for a cliff by the shore—a cliff that ran down into deep water, and plunged into a dark hole at the foot of it, twenty fathoms under the sea. It was a long, long swim, and Kotick badly wanted fresh air before he was out of the dark tunnel they led him through.

"My wig!" he said, when he rose, gasping and puffing, into open water at the farther end. "It was a long dive, but it was worth it."

The sea cows had separated and were browsing lazily along the edges of the finest beaches that Kotick had ever seen. There were long stretches of smooth-worn rock running for miles, exactly fitted to make seal-nurseries, and there were play-grounds of hard sand sloping inland behind them, and there were rollers for seals to dance in, and long grass to roll in, and sand dunes to climb up and down, and, best of all, Kotick knew by the feel of the water, which never deceives a true sea catch, that no men had ever come there.

The first thing he did was to assure himself that the fishing was good, and then he swam along the beaches and counted up the delightful low sandy islands half hidden in the beautiful rolling fog. Away to the northward, out to sea, ran a line of bars and shoals and rocks that would never let a ship come within six miles of the beach, and between the islands and the mainland was a stretch of deep water that ran up to the perpendicular cliffs, and somewhere below the cliffs was the mouth of the tunnel.

"It's Novastoshnah over again, but ten times better," said Kotick. "Sea Cow must be wiser than I thought. Men can't come down the cliffs, even if there were any men; and the shoals to seaward would knock a ship to splinters. If any place in the sea is safe, this is it."

He began to think of the seal he had left behind him, but though he was in a hurry to go back to Novastoshnah, he thoroughly explored the new country, so that he would be able to answer all questions.

Then he dived and made sure of the mouth of the tunnel,

and raced through to the southward. No one but a sea cow or a seal would have dreamed of there being such a place, and when he looked back at the cliffs even Kotick could hardly believe that he had been under them.

He was six days going home, though he was not swimming slowly; and when he hauled out just above Sea Lion's Neck the first person he met was the seal who had been waiting for him, and she saw by the look in his eyes that he had found his island at last.

But the holluschickie and Sea Catch, his father, and all the other seals laughed at him when he told them what he had discovered, and a young seal about his own age said, "This is all very well, Kotick, but you can't come from no one knows where and order us off like this. Remember we've been fighting for our nurseries, and that's a thing you never did. You preferred prowling about in the sea."

The other seals laughed at this, and the young seal began twisting his head from side to side. He had just married that year, and was making a great fuss about it.

"I've no nursery to fight for," said Kotick. "I only want to show you all a place where you will be safe. What's the use of fighting?"\

"Oh, if you're trying to back out, of course I've no more to say," said the young seal with an ugly chuckle.

"Will you come with me if I win?" said Kotick. And a green light came into his eye, for he was very angry at having to fight at all.

"Very good," said the young seal carelessly. "If you win, I'll come."

He had no time to change his mind, for Kotick's head was out and his teeth sunk in the blubber of the young seal's neck. Then he threw himself back on his haunches and hauled his enemy down the beach, shook him, and knocked him over. Then Kotick roared to the seals: "I've done my best for you these five seasons past. I've found you the island where you'll be safe, but unless your heads are dragged off your silly necks you won't believe. I'm going to teach you now. Look out for yourselves!"

Limmershin told me that never in his life—and Limmershin sees ten thousand big seals fighting every year—never in all his little life did he see anything like Kotick's charge into the nurseries. He flung himself at the biggest sea catch he could find, caught him by the throat, choked him and bumped him and banged him till he grunted for mercy, and then threw him aside and attacked the next. You see, Kotick had never fasted for four months as the big seals did every year, and his deep-sea swimming trips kept him in perfect condition, and, best of all, he had never fought before. His curly white mane stood up with rage, and his eyes flamed, and his big dog teeth glistened, and he was splendid to look at. Old Sea Catch, his father, saw him tearing past, hauling the grizzled old seals about as though they had been halibut, and upsetting the young bachelors in all directions; and Sea Catch gave a roar and shouted: "He may be a fool, but he is the best fighter on the beaches! Don't tackle your father, my son! He's with you!"

Kotick roared in answer, and old Sea Catch waddled in with his mustache on end, blowing like a locomotive, while Matkah and the seal that was going to marry Kotick cowered down and admired their men-folk. It was a gorgeous fight, for the two fought as long as there was a seal that dared lift up his head, and when there were none they paraded grandly up and down the beach side by side, bellowing.

At night, just as the Northern Lights were winking and

flashing through the fog, Kotick climbed a bare rock and looked down on the scattered nurseries and the torn and bleeding seals. "Now," he said, "I've taught you your lesson."

"My wig!" said old Sea Catch, boosting himself up stiffly, for he was fearfully mauled. "The Killer Whale himself could not have cut them up worse. Son, I'm proud of you, and what's more, I'll come with you to your island—if there is such a place."

"Hear you, fat pigs of the sea. Who comes with me to the Sea Cow's tunnel? Answer, or I shall teach you again," roared Kotick.

There was a murmur like the ripple of the tide all up and down the beaches. "We will come," said thousands of tired voices. "We will follow Kotick, the White Seal."

Then Kotick dropped his head between his shoulders and shut his eyes proudly. He was not a white seal any more, but red from head to tail. All the same he would have scorned to look at or touch one of his wounds.

A week later he and his army (nearly ten thousand holluschickie and old seals) went away north to the Sea Cow's tunnel, Kotick leading them, and the seals that stayed at Novastoshnah called them idiots. But next spring, when they all met off the fishing banks of the Pacific, Kotick's seals told such tales of the new beaches beyond Sea Cow's tunnel that more and more seals left Novastoshnah. Of course it was not all done at once, for the seals are not very clever, and they need a long time to turn things over in their minds, but year after year more seals went away from Novastoshnah, and Lukannon, and the other nurseries, to the quiet, sheltered beaches where Kotick sits all the summer through, getting bigger and fatter and stronger each year, while the holluschickie play around him, in that sea where no man comes.

"RIKKI-TIKKI-TAVI"

At the hole where he went in
Red-Eye called to Wrinkle-Skin.
Hear what little Red-Eye saith:
"Nag, come up and dance with death!"
Eye to eye and head to head,
(Keep the measure, Nag.)
This shall end when one is dead;
(At thy pleasure, Nag.)
Turn for turn and twist for twist—
(Run and hide thee, Nag.)
Hah! The hooded Death has missed!
(Woe betide thee, Nag!)

This is the story of the great war that Rikki-tikki-tavi fought single-handed, through the bath-rooms of the big bungalow in Segowlee cantonment. Darzee, the Tailorbird, helped him, and Chuchundra, the musk-rat, who never comes out into the middle of the floor, but always creeps round by the wall, gave him advice, but Rikki-tikki did the real fighting.

He was a mongoose, rather like a little cat in his fur and his tail, but quite like a weasel in his head and his habits. His eyes and the end of his restless nose were pink. He could scratch himself anywhere he pleased with any leg, front or back, that he chose to use. He could fluff up his tail till it looked like a bottle brush, and his war cry as he scuttled through the long grass was: "Rikk-tikk-tikki-tikki-tchk!"

One day, a high summer flood washed him out of the burrow where he lived with his father and mother, and carried him, kicking and clucking, down a roadside ditch. He found a little wisp of grass floating there, and clung to it till he lost his senses. When he revived, he was lying in the hot sun on the middle of a garden path, very draggled indeed, and a small boy was saying, "Here's a dead mongoose. Let's have a funeral."

"No," said his mother, "let's take him in and dry him. Perhaps he isn't really dead."

They took him into the house, and a big man picked him up between his finger and thumb and said he was not dead but half choked. So they wrapped him in cotton wool, and warmed him over a little fire, and he opened his eyes and sneezed.

"Now," said the big man (he was an Englishman who had just moved into the bungalow), "don't frighten him, and we'll see what he'll do."

It is the hardest thing in the world to frighten a mongoose, because he is eaten up from nose to tail with curiosity. The motto of all the mongoose family is "Run and find out," and Rikki-tikki was a true mongoose. He looked at the cotton wool, decided that it was not good to eat, ran all round the table, sat up and put his fur in order, scratched himself, and jumped on the small boy's shoulder.

"Don't be frightened, Teddy," said his father. "That's his way of making friends."

"Ouch! He's tickling under my chin," said Teddy.

Rikki-tikki looked down between the boy's collar and neck, snuffed at his ear, and climbed down to the floor, where he sat rubbing his nose.

"Good gracious," said Teddy's mother, "and that's a wild creature! I suppose he's so tame because we've been kind to him."

"All mongooses are like that," said her husband. "If Teddy doesn't pick him up by the tail, or try to put him in a cage, he'll run in and out of the house all day long. Let's give him something to eat."

They gave him a little piece of raw meat. Rikki-tikki liked it immensely, and when it was finished he went out into the veranda and sat in the sunshine and fluffed up his fur to make it dry to the roots. Then he felt better.

"There are more things to find out about in this house," he said to himself, "than all my family could find out in all their lives. I shall certainly stay and find out."

He spent all that day roaming over the house. He nearly drowned himself in the bath-tubs, put his nose into the ink on a writing table, and burned it on the end of the big man's cigar, for he climbed up in the big man's lap to see how writing was done. At nightfall he ran into Teddy's nursery to watch how kerosene lamps were lighted, and when Teddy went to bed Rikki-tikki climbed up too. But he was a restless companion, because he had to get up and attend to every noise all through the night, and find out what made it. Teddy's mother and father came in, the last thing, to look at their boy, and Rikki-tikki was awake on the pillow. "I don't like that," said Teddy's mother. "He may bite the child." "He'll do no such thing," said the father. "Teddy's safer with that little beast than if he had a bloodhound to watch him. If a snake came into the nursery now—"

But Teddy's mother wouldn't think of anything so awful.

Early in the morning Rikki-tikki came to early breakfast in the veranda riding on Teddy's shoulder, and they gave him banana and some boiled egg. He sat on all their laps one after the other, because every well-brought-up mongoose always hopes to be a house mongoose some day and have rooms to run about in; and Rikki-tikki's mother (she used to live in the general's house at Segowlee) had carefully told Rikki what to do if ever he came across white men.

Then Rikki-tikki went out into the garden to see what was to be seen. It was a large garden, only half cultivated, with bushes, as big as summer-houses, of Marshal Niel roses, lime and orange trees, clumps of bamboos, and thickets of high grass. Rikki-tikki licked his lips. "This is a splendid hunting-ground," he said, and his tail grew bottle-brushy at the thought of it, and he scuttled up and down the garden, snuffing here and there till he heard very sorrowful voices in a thorn-bush.

It was Darzee, the Tailorbird, and his wife. They had made a beautiful nest by pulling two big leaves together and stitching them up the edges with fibers, and had filled the hollow with cotton and downy fluff. The nest swayed to and fro, as they sat on the rim and cried.

"What is the matter?" asked Rikki-tikki.

"We are very miserable," said Darzee. "One of our babies fell out of the nest yesterday and Nag ate him."

"H'm!" said Rikki-tikki, "that is very sad—but I am a stranger here. Who is Nag?"

Darzee and his wife only cowered down in the nest without answering, for from the thick grass at the foot of the bush there came a low hiss—a horrid cold sound that made Rikki-tikki jump back two clear feet. Then inch by inch out of the grass rose up the head and spread hood of Nag, the big black cobra, and he was five feet long from tongue to tail. When he had lifted one-third of himself clear of the ground, he stayed balancing to and fro exactly as a dandelion tuft balances in the wind, and he looked at Rikki-tikki with the wicked snake's eyes that never change their expression, whatever the snake may be thinking of.

"Who is Nag?" said he. "I am Nag. The great God Brahm put his mark upon all our people, when the first cobra spread his hood to keep the sun off Brahm as he slept. Look, and be afraid!"

He spread out his hood more than ever, and Rikki-tikki saw the spectacle-mark on the back of it that looks exactly like the eye part of a hook-and-eye fastening. He was afraid for the minute, but it is impossible for a mongoose to stay frightened for any length of time, and though Rikki-tikki had never met a live cobra before, his mother had fed him on dead ones, and he knew that all a grown mongoose's business in life was to fight and eat snakes. Nag knew that too and, at the bottom of his cold heart, he was afraid.

"Well," said Rikki-tikki, and his tail began to fluff up again, "marks or no marks, do you think it is right for you to eat fledglings out of a nest?"

Nag was thinking to himself, and watching the least little movement in the grass behind Rikki-tikki. He knew that mongooses in the garden meant death sooner or later for him and his family, but he wanted to get Rikki-tikki off his guard. So he dropped his head a little, and put it on one side.

"Let us talk," he said. "You eat eggs. Why should not I eat birds?"

"Behind you! Look behind you!" sang Darzee.

Rikki-tikki knew better than to waste time in staring. He jumped up in the air as high as he could go, and just under him whizzed by the head of Nagaina, Nag's wicked wife. She had crept up behind him as he was talking, to make an end of him. He heard her savage hiss as the stroke missed. He came down almost across her back, and if he had been an old mongoose he would have known that then was the time to break her back with one bite; but he was afraid of the terrible lashing return stroke of the cobra. He bit, indeed, but did not bite long enough, and he jumped clear of the whisking tail, leaving Nagaina torn and angry.

"Wicked, wicked Darzee!" said Nag, lashing up as high as he could reach toward the nest in the thorn-bush. But Darzee had built it out of reach of snakes, and it only swayed to and fro.

Rikki-tikki felt his eyes growing red and hot (when a mongoose's eyes grow red, he is angry), and he sat back on his tail and hind legs like a little kangaroo, and looked all round him, and chattered with rage. But Nag and Nagaina had disappeared into the grass. When a snake misses its stroke, it never says anything or gives any sign of what it means to do next. Rikki-tikki did not care to follow them, for he did not feel sure that he could manage two snakes at once. So he trotted off to the gravel path near the house, and sat down to think. It was a serious matter for him.

If you read the old books of natural history, you will find they say that when the mongoose fights the snake and happens to get bitten, he runs off and eats some herb that cures him. That is not true. The victory is only a matter of quickness of eye and quickness of foot—snake's blow against mongoose's jump—and as no eye can follow the motion of a snake's head when it strikes, this makes things much more wonderful than any magic herb. Rikki-tikki knew he was a young mongoose, and it made him all the more pleased to think that he had managed to escape a blow from behind. It gave him confidence in himself, and when Teddy came running down the path, Rikki-tikki was ready to be petted.

But just as Teddy was stooping, something wriggled a little in the dust, and a tiny voice said: "Be careful. I am Death!" It was Karait, the dusty brown snakeling that lies for choice on the dusty earth; and his bite is as dangerous as the cobra's. But he is so small that nobody thinks of him, and so he does the more harm to people.

Rikki-tikki's eyes grew red again, and he danced up to Karait with the peculiar rocking, swaying motion that he had inherited from his family. It looks very funny, but it is so perfectly balanced a gait that you can fly off from it at any angle you please, and in dealing with snakes this is an advantage. If Rikki-tikki had only known, he was doing a much more dangerous thing than fighting Nag, for Karait is so small, and can turn so quickly, that unless Rikki bit him close to the back of the head, he would get the return stroke in his eye or his lip. But Rikki did not know. His eyes were all red, and he rocked back and forth, looking for a good place to hold. Karait struck out. Rikki jumped sideways and tried to run in, but the wicked little dusty gray head lashed within a fraction of his shoulder, and he had to jump over the body, and the head followed his heels close.

Teddy shouted to the house: "Oh, look here! Our mongoose is killing a snake." And Rikki-tikki heard a scream from Teddy's mother. His father ran out with a stick, but by the time he came up, Karait had lunged out once too far, and Rikki-tikki had sprung, jumped on the snake's back, dropped his head far between his forelegs, bitten as high up the back as he could get hold, and rolled away. That bite paralyzed Karait, and Rikki-tikki was just going to eat him up from the tail, after the custom of his family at dinner, when he remembered that a full meal makes a slow mongoose, and if he wanted all his strength and quickness ready, he must keep himself thin.

He went away for a dust bath under the castor-oil bushes, while Teddy's father beat the dead Karait. "What is the use of that?" thought Rikki-tikki. "I have settled it all;" and then Teddy's mother picked him up from the dust and hugged him, crying that he had saved Teddy from death, and Teddy's father said that he was a providence, and Teddy looked on with big scared eyes. Rikki-tikki was rather amused at all the fuss, which, of course, he did not understand. Teddy's mother might just as well have petted Teddy for playing in the dust. Rikki was thoroughly enjoying himself.

That night at dinner, walking to and fro among the wine-glasses on the table, he might have stuffed himself three times over with nice things. But he remembered Nag and Nagaina, and though it was very pleasant to be patted and petted by Teddy's mother, and to sit on Teddy's shoulder, his eyes would get red from time to time, and he would go off into his long war cry of "Rikk-tikk-tikki-tikki-tchk!"

Teddy carried him off to bed, and insisted on Rikki-tikki sleeping under his chin. Rikki-tikki was too well bred to bite or scratch, but as soon as Teddy was asleep he went off for his nightly walk round the house, and in the dark he ran up against Chuchundra, the musk-rat, creeping around by the wall. Chuchundra is a broken-hearted little beast. He whimpers and cheeps all the night, trying to make up his mind to run into the middle of the room. But he never gets there.

"Don't kill me," said Chuchundra, almost weeping. "Rikki-tikki, don't kill me!"

"Do you think a snake-killer kills muskrats?" said Rikki-tikki scornfully.

"Those who kill snakes get killed by snakes," said Chuchundra, more sorrowfully than ever. "And how am I to be sure that Nag won't mistake me for you some dark night?"

"There's not the least danger," said Rikki-tikki. "But Nag is in the garden, and I know you don't go there."

"My cousin Chua, the rat, told me—" said Chuchundra, and then he stopped.

"Told you what?"

"H'sh! Nag is everywhere, Rikki-tikki. You should have talked to Chua in the garden."

"I didn't—so you must tell me. Quick, Chuchundra, or I'll bite you!"

Chuchundra sat down and cried till the tears rolled off his whiskers. "I am a very poor man," he sobbed. "I never had spirit enough to run out into the middle of the room. H'sh! I mustn't tell you anything. Can't you hear, Rikki-tikki?"

Rikki-tikki listened. The house was as still as still, but he thought he could just catch the faintest scratch-scratch in the world—a noise as faint as that of a wasp walking on a window-pane—the dry scratch of a snake's scales on brick-work.

"That's Nag or Nagaina," he said to himself, "and he is crawling into the bath-room sluice. You're right, Chuchundra; I should have talked to Chua."

He stole off to Teddy's bath-room, but there was nothing there, and then to Teddy's mother's bathroom. At the bottom of the smooth plaster wall there was a brick pulled out to make a sluice for the bath water, and as Rikki-tikki stole in by the masonry curb where the bath is put, he heard

Nag and Nagaina whispering together outside in the moonlight.

"When the house is emptied of people," said Nagaina to her husband, "he will have to go away, and then the garden will be our own again. Go in quietly, and remember that the big man who killed Karait is the first one to bite. Then come out and tell me, and we will hunt for Rikki-tikki together."

"But are you sure that there is anything to be gained by killing the people?" said Nag.

"Everything. When there were no people in the bungalow, did we have any mongoose in the garden? So long as the bungalow is empty, we are king and queen of the garden; and remember that as soon as our eggs in the melon bed hatch (as they may tomorrow), our children will need room and quiet."

"I had not thought of that," said Nag. "I will go, but there is no need that we should hunt for Rikki-tikki afterward. I will kill the big man and his wife, and the child if I can, and come away quietly. Then the bungalow will be empty, and Rikki-tikki will go."

Rikki-tikki tingled all over with rage and hatred at this, and then Nag's head came through the sluice, and his five feet of cold body followed it. Angry as he was, Rikki-tikki was very frightened as he saw the size of the big cobra. Nag coiled himself up, raised his head, and looked into the bathroom in the dark, and Rikki could see his eyes glitter.

"Now, if I kill him here, Nagaina will know; and if I fight him on the open floor, the odds are in his favor. What am I to do?" said Rikki-tikki-tavi.

Nag waved to and fro, and then Rikki-tikki heard him drinking from the biggest water-jar that was used to fill the bath. "That is good," said the snake. "Now, when Karait was killed, the big man had a stick. He may have that stick still, but when he comes in to bathe in the morning he will not have a stick. I shall wait here till he comes. Nagaina—do you hear me?—I shall wait here in the cool till daytime."

There was no answer from outside, so Rikki-tikki knew Nagaina had gone away. Nag coiled himself down, coil by coil, round the bulge at the bottom of the water jar, and Rikki-tikki stayed still as death. After an hour he began to move, muscle by muscle, toward the jar. Nag was asleep, and Rikki-tikki looked at his big back, wondering which would be the best place for a good hold. "If I don't break his back at the first jump," said Rikki, "he can still fight. And if he fights—O Rikki!" He looked at the thickness of the neck below the hood, but that was too much for him; and a bite near the tail would only make Nag savage.

"It must be the head'" he said at last; "the head above the hood. And, when I am once there, I must not let go."

Then he jumped. The head was lying a little clear of the water jar, under the curve of it; and, as his teeth met, Rikki braced his back against the bulge of the red earthenware to hold down the head. This gave him just one second's purchase, and he made the most of it. Then he was battered to and fro as a rat is shaken by a dog—to and fro on the floor, up and down, and around in great circles, but his eyes were red and he held on as the body cart-whipped over the floor, upsetting the tin dipper and the soap dish and the flesh brush, and banged against the tin side of the bath. As he held he closed his jaws tighter and tighter, for he made sure he would be banged to death, and, for the honor of his family, he preferred to be found with his teeth locked. He was dizzy, aching, and felt shaken to pieces when something went off like a thunderclap just behind him. A hot wind knocked him senseless and red fire singed his fur. The big man had been wakened by the noise, and had fired both barrels of a shotgun into Nag just behind the hood.

Rikki-tikki held on with his eyes shut, for now he was quite sure he was dead. But the head did not move, and the big man picked him up and said, "It's the mongoose again, Alice. The little chap has saved our lives now."

Then Teddy's mother came in with a very white face, and saw what was left of Nag, and Rikki-tikki dragged himself to Teddy's bedroom and spent half the rest of the night shaking himself tenderly to find out whether he really was broken into forty pieces, as he fancied.

When morning came he was very stiff, but well pleased with his doings. "Now I have Nagaina to settle with, and she will be worse than five Nags, and there's no knowing when the eggs she spoke of will hatch. Goodness! I must go and see Darzee," he said.

Without waiting for breakfast, Rikki-tikki ran to the thornbush where Darzee was singing a song of triumph at the top of his voice. The news of Nag's death was all over the garden, for the sweeper had thrown the body on the rubbish-heap.

"Oh, you stupid tuft of feathers!" said Rikki-tikki angrily. "Is this the time to sing?"

"Nag is dead—is dead—is dead!" sang Darzee. "The valiant Rikki-tikki caught him by the head and held fast. The big man brought the bang-stick, and Nag fell in two pieces! He will never eat my babies again."

"All that's true enough. But where's Nagaina?" said Rikki-tikki, looking carefully round him.

"Nagaina came to the bathroom sluice and called for Nag,"

Darzee went on, "and Nag came out on the end of a stick—the sweeper picked him up on the end of a stick and threw him upon the rubbish heap. Let us sing about the great, the red-eyed Rikki-tikki!" And Darzee filled his throat and sang.

"If I could get up to your nest, I'd roll your babies out!" said Rikki-tikki. "You don't know when to do the right thing at the right time. You're safe enough in your nest there, but it's war for me down here. Stop singing a minute, Darzee."

"For the great, the beautiful Rikki-tikki's sake I will stop," said Darzee. "What is it, O Killer of the terrible Nag?"

"Where is Nagaina, for the third time?"

"On the rubbish heap by the stables, mourning for Nag. Great is Rikki-tikki with the white teeth."

"Bother my white teeth! Have you ever heard where she keeps her eggs?"

"In the melon bed, on the end nearest the wall, where the sun strikes nearly all day. She hid them there weeks ago."

"And you never thought it worth while to tell me? The end nearest the wall, you said?"

"Rikki-tikki, you are not going to eat her eggs?"

"Not eat exactly; no. Darzee, if you have a grain of sense you will fly off to the stables and pretend that your wing is broken, and let Nagaina chase you away to this bush. I must get to the melon-bed, and if I went there now she'd see me."

Darzee was a feather-brained little fellow who could never hold more than one idea at a time in his head. And just because he knew that Nagaina's children were born in eggs like his own, he didn't think at first that it was fair to kill them. But his wife was a sensible bird, and she knew that cobra's eggs meant young cobras later on. So she flew off from the nest, and left Darzee to keep the babies warm, and continue his song about the death of Nag. Darzee was very like a man in some ways.

She fluttered in front of Nagaina by the rubbish heap and cried out, "Oh, my wing is broken! The boy in the house threw a stone at me and broke it." Then she fluttered more desperately than ever.

Nagaina lifted up her head and hissed, "You warned Rikki-tikki when I would have killed him. Indeed and truly, you've chosen a bad place to be lame in." And she moved toward Darzee's wife, slipping along over the dust.

"The boy broke it with a stone!" shrieked Darzee's wife.

"Well! It may be some consolation to you when you're dead to know that I shall settle accounts with the boy. My husband lies on the rubbish heap this morning, but before night the boy in the house will lie very still. What is the use of running away? I am sure to catch you. Little fool, look at me!"

Darzee's wife knew better than to do that, for a bird who looks at a snake's eyes gets so frightened that she cannot move. Darzee's wife fluttered on, piping sorrowfully, and never leaving the ground, and Nagaina quickened her pace.

Rikki-tikki heard them going up the path from the stables, and he raced for the end of the melon patch near the wall. There, in the warm litter above the melons, very cunningly hidden, he found twenty-five eggs, about the size of a bantam's eggs, but with whitish skin instead of shell.

"I was not a day too soon," he said, for he could see the baby cobras curled up inside the skin, and he knew that the minute they were hatched they could each kill a man or a mongoose. He bit off the tops of the eggs as fast as he could, taking care to crush the young cobras, and turned over the litter from time to time to see whether he had missed any. At last there were only three eggs left, and Rikki-tikki began to chuckle to himself, when he heard Darzee's wife screaming:

"Rikki-tikki, I led Nagaina toward the house, and she has gone into the veranda, and—oh, come quickly—she means killing!"

Rikki-tikki smashed two eggs, and tumbled backward down the melon-bed with the third egg in his mouth, and scuttled to the veranda as hard as he could put foot to the ground. Teddy and his mother and father were there at early breakfast, but Rikki-tikki saw that they were not eating anything. They sat stone-still, and their faces were white. Nagaina was coiled up on the matting by Teddy's chair, within easy striking distance of Teddy's bare leg, and she was swaying to and fro, singing a song of triumph.

"Son of the big man that killed Nag," she hissed, "stay still. I am not ready yet. Wait a little. Keep very still, all you three! If you move I strike, and if you do not move I strike. Oh, foolish people, who killed my Nag!"

Teddy's eyes were fixed on his father, and all his father could do was to whisper, "Sit still, Teddy. You mustn't move. Teddy, keep still."

Then Rikki-tikki came up and cried, "Turn round, Nagaina. Turn and fight!"

"All in good time," said she, without moving her eyes. "I will settle my account with you presently. Look at your friends, Rikki-tikki. They are still and white. They are afraid. They dare not move, and if you come a step nearer I strike."

"Look at your eggs," said Rikki-tikki, "in the melon bed near the wall. Go and look, Nagaina!"

The big snake turned half around, and saw the egg on the veranda. "Ah-h! Give it to me," she said.

Rikki-tikki put his paws one on each side of the egg, and his eyes were blood-red. "What price for a snake's egg? For a young cobra? For a young king cobra? For the last—the very last of the brood? The ants are eating all the others down by the melon bed."

Nagaina spun clear round, forgetting everything for the sake of the one egg. Rikki-tikki saw Teddy's father shoot out a big hand, catch Teddy by the shoulder, and drag him across the little table with the tea-cups, safe and out of reach of Nagaina.

"Tricked! Tricked! Tricked! Rikk-tck-tck!" chuckled Rikki-tikki. "The boy is safe, and it was I—I—I that caught Nag by the hood last night in the bathroom." Then he began to jump up and down, all four feet together, his head close to the floor. "He threw me to and fro, but he could not shake me off. He was dead before the big man blew him in two. I did it! Rikki-tikki-tck-tck! Come then, Nagaina. Come and fight with me. You shall not be a widow long."

Nagaina saw that she had lost her chance of killing Teddy, and the egg lay between Rikki-tikki's paws. "Give me the egg, Rikki-tikki. Give me the last of my eggs, and I will go away and never come back," she said, lowering her hood.

"Yes, you will go away, and you will never come back. For you will go to the rubbish heap with Nag. Fight, widow! The big man has gone for his gun! Fight!"

Rikki-tikki was bounding all round Nagaina, keeping just out of reach of her stroke, his little eyes like hot coals. Nagaina gathered herself together and flung out at him. Rikki-tikki jumped up and backward. Again and again and again she struck, and each time her head came with a whack on the matting of the veranda and she gathered herself together like a watch spring. Then Rikki-tikki danced in a circle to get behind her, and Nagaina spun round to keep her head to his head, so that the rustle of her tail on the matting sounded like dry leaves blown along by the wind.

He had forgotten the egg. It still lay on the veranda, and Nagaina came nearer and nearer to it, till at last, while Rikki-tikki was drawing breath, she caught it in her mouth, turned to the veranda steps, and flew like an arrow down the path, with Rikki-tikki behind her. When the cobra runs for her life, she goes like a whip-lash flicked across a horse's neck.

Rikki-tikki knew that he must catch her, or all the trouble would begin again. She headed straight for the long grass by the thorn-bush, and as he was running Rikki-tikki heard Darzee still singing his foolish little song of triumph. But Darzee's wife was wiser. She flew off her nest as Nagaina came along, and flapped her wings about Nagaina's head. If Darzee had helped they might have turned her, but Nagaina only lowered her hood and went on. Still, the instant's delay brought Rikki-tikki up to her, and as she plunged into the rat-hole where she and Nag used to live, his little white teeth were clenched on her tail, and he went down with her—and very few mongooses, however wise and old they may be, care to follow a cobra into its hole. It was dark in the hole; and Rikki-tikki never knew when it might open out and give Nagaina room to turn and strike at him. He held on savagely, and stuck out his feet to act as brakes on the dark slope of the hot, moist earth.

Then the grass by the mouth of the hole stopped waving, and Darzee said, "It is all over with Rikki-tikki! We must sing his death song. Valiant Rikki-tikki is dead! For Nagaina will surely kill him underground."

So he sang a very mournful song that he made up on the spur of the minute, and just as he got to the most touching part, the grass quivered again, and Rikki-tikki, covered with dirt, dragged himself out of the hole leg by leg, licking his whiskers. Darzee stopped with a little shout. Rikki-tikki shook some of the dust out of his fur and sneezed. "It is all over," he said. "The widow will never come out again." And the red ants that live between the grass stems heard him, and began to troop down one after another to see if he had spoken the truth.

Rikki-tikki curled himself up in the grass and slept where he was—slept and slept till it was late in the afternoon, for he had done a hard day's work.

"Now," he said, when he awoke, "I will go back to the house. Tell the Coppersmith, Darzee, and he will tell the garden that Nagaina is dead."

The Coppersmith is a bird who makes a noise exactly like the beating of a little hammer on a copper pot; and the reason he is always making it is because he is the town crier to every Indian garden, and tells all the news to everybody who cares to listen. As Rikki-tikki went up the path, he heard his "attention" notes like a tiny dinner gong, and then the steady "Ding-dong-tock! Nag is dead—dong! Nagaina is dead! Ding-dong-tock!" That set all the birds in the garden singing, and the frogs croaking, for Nag and Nagaina used to eat frogs as well as little birds.

When Rikki got to the house, Teddy and Teddy's mother (she looked very white still, for she had been fainting) and Teddy's father came out and almost cried over him; and that night he ate all that was given him till he could eat no more, and went to bed on Teddy's shoulder, where Teddy's mother saw him when she came to look late at night.

"He saved our lives and Teddy's life," she said to her husband. "Just think, he saved all our lives."

Rikki-tikki woke up with a jump, for the mongooses are light sleepers.

"Oh, it's you," said he. "What are you bothering for? All the cobras are dead. And if they weren't, I'm here."

Rikki-tikki had a right to be proud of himself. But he did not grow too proud, and he kept that garden as a mongoose should keep it, with tooth and jump and spring and bite, till never a cobra dared show its head inside the walls.

TOOMAI OF THE ELEPHANTS

I will remember what I was, I am sick of rope and chain—
I will remember my old strength and all my forest affairs.
I will not sell my back to man for a bundle of sugar-cane:
I will go out to my own kind, and the wood-folk in their lairs.
I will go out until the day, until the morning break—
Out to the wind's untainted kiss, the water's clean caress;
I will forget my ankle-ring and snap my picket stake.
I will revisit my lost loves, and playmates masterless!

Kala Nag, which means Black Snake, had served the Indian Government in every way that an elephant could serve it for forty-seven years, and as he was fully twenty years old when he was caught, that makes him nearly seventy—a ripe age for an elephant. He remembered pushing, with a big leather pad on his forehead, at a gun stuck in deep mud, and that was before the Afghan War of 1842, and he had not then come to his full strength.

His mother Radha Pyari,—Radha the darling,—who had been caught in the same drive with Kala Nag, told him, before his little milk tusks had dropped out, that elephants who were afraid always got hurt. Kala Nag knew that that advice was good, for the first time that he saw a shell burst he backed, screaming, into a stand of piled rifles, and the bayonets pricked him in all his softest places. So, before he was twenty-five, he gave up being afraid, and so he was the best-loved and the best-looked-after elephant in the service of the Government of India. He had carried tents, twelve hundred pounds' weight of tents, on the march in Upper India. He had been hoisted into a ship at the end of a steam crane and taken for days across the water, and made to carry a mortar on his back in a strange and rocky country very far from India, and had seen the Emperor Theodore lying dead in Magdala, and had come back again in the steamer entitled, so the soldiers said, to the Abyssinian War medal. He had seen his fellow elephants die of cold and epilepsy and starvation and sunstroke up at a place called Ali Musjid, ten years later; and afterward he had been sent down thousands of miles south to haul and pile big balks of teak in the timberyards at Moulmein. There he had half killed an insubordinate young elephant who was shirking his fair share of work.

After that he was taken off timber-hauling, and employed, with a few score other elephants who were trained to the business, in helping to catch wild elephants among the Garo hills. Elephants are very strictly preserved by the Indian Government. There is one whole department which does nothing else but hunt them, and catch them, and break them in, and send them up and down the country as they are needed for work.

Kala Nag stood ten fair feet at the shoulders, and his tusks had been cut off short at five feet, and bound round the ends, to prevent them splitting, with bands of copper; but he could do more with those stumps than any untrained elephant could do with the real sharpened ones. When, after weeks and weeks of cautious driving of scattered elephants across the hills, the forty or fifty wild monsters were driven into the last stockade, and the big drop gate, made of tree trunks lashed together, jarred down behind them, Kala Nag, at the word of command, would go into that flaring, trumpeting pandemonium (generally at night, when the flicker of the torches made it difficult to judge distances), and, picking out the biggest and wildest tusker of the mob, would hammer him and hustle him into quiet while the men on the backs of the other elephants roped and tied the smaller ones.

There was nothing in the way of fighting that Kala Nag, the old wise Black Snake, did not know, for he had stood up more than once in his time to the charge of the wounded tiger, and, curling up his soft trunk to be out of harm's way, had knocked the springing brute sideways in mid-air with a quick sickle cut of his head, that he had invented all by himself; had knocked him over, and kneeled upon him with his huge knees till the life went out with a gasp and a howl, and there was only a fluffy striped thing on the ground for Kala Nag to pull by the tail.

"Yes," said Big Toomai, his driver, the son of Black Toomai who had taken him to Abyssinia, and grandson of Toomai of the Elephants who had seen him caught, "there is nothing that the Black Snake fears except me. He has seen three generations of us feed him and groom him, and he will live to see four."

"He is afraid of me also," said Little Toomai, standing up to his full height of four feet, with only one rag upon him. He was ten years old, the eldest son of Big Toomai, and, according to custom, he would take his father's place on Kala Nag's neck when he grew up, and would handle the heavy iron ankus, the elephant goad, that had been worn smooth by his father, and his grandfather, and his great-grandfather.

He knew what he was talking of; for he had been born under Kala Nag's shadow, had played with the end of his trunk before he could walk, had taken him down to water as soon as he could walk, and Kala Nag would no more have dreamed of disobeying his shrill little orders than he would have dreamed of killing him on that day when Big Toomai carried the little brown baby under Kala Nag's tusks, and told him to salute his master that was to be.

"Yes," said Little Toomai, "he is afraid of me," and he took long strides up to Kala Nag, called him a fat old pig, and made him lift up his feet one after the other.

"Wah!" said Little Toomai, "thou art a big elephant," and he wagged his fluffy head, quoting his father. "The Government may pay for elephants, but they belong to us mahouts. When thou art old, Kala Nag, there will come some rich rajah, and he will buy thee from the Government, on account of thy size and thy manners, and then thou wilt have nothing to do but to carry gold earrings in thy ears, and a gold howdah on thy back, and a red cloth covered with gold on thy sides, and walk at the head of the processions of the King. Then I shall sit on thy neck, O Kala Nag, with a silver ankus, and men will run before us with golden sticks, crying, 'Room for the King's elephant!' That will be good, Kala Nag, but not so good as this hunting in the jungles."

"Umph!" said Big Toomai. "Thou art a boy, and as wild as a buffalo-calf. This running up and down among the hills is not the best Government service. I am getting old, and I do not love wild elephants. Give me brick elephant lines, one stall to each elephant, and big stumps to tie them to safely, and flat, broad roads to exercise upon, instead of this come-and-go camping. Aha, the Cawnpore barracks were good. There was a bazaar close by, and only three hours' work a day."

Little Toomai remembered the Cawnpore elephant-lines and said nothing. He very much preferred the camp life, and hated those broad, flat roads, with the daily grubbing for grass in the forage reserve, and the long hours when there was nothing to do except to watch Kala Nag fidgeting in his pickets.

What Little Toomai liked was to scramble up bridle paths that only an elephant could take; the dip into the valley below; the glimpses of the wild elephants browsing miles away; the rush of the frightened pig and peacock under Kala Nag's feet; the blinding warm rains, when all the hills and valleys smoked; the beautiful misty mornings when nobody knew where they would camp that night; the steady, cautious drive of the wild elephants, and the mad rush and blaze and hullabaloo of the last night's drive, when the elephants poured into the stockade like boulders in a landslide, found that they could not get out, and flung themselves at the heavy posts only to be driven back by yells and flaring torches and volleys of blank cartridge.

Even a little boy could be of use there, and Toomai was as useful as three boys. He would get his torch and wave it, and yell with the best. But the really good time came when the driving out began, and the Keddah—that is, the stockade— looked like a picture of the end of the world, and men had to make signs to one another, because they could not hear themselves speak. Then Little Toomai would climb up to the top of one of the quivering stockade posts, his sun-bleached brown hair flying loose all over his shoulders, and he looking like a goblin in the torch-light. And as soon as there was a lull you could hear his high-pitched yells of encouragement to Kala Nag, above the trumpeting and crashing, and snapping of ropes, and groans of the tethered elephants. "Mael, mael, Kala Nag! (Go on, go on, Black Snake!) Dant do! (Give him the tusk!) Somalo! Somalo! (Careful, careful!) Maro! Mar! (Hit

him, hit him!) Mind the post! Arre! Arre! Hai! Yai! Kya-a-ah!"
he would shout, and the big fight between Kala Nag and the
wild elephant would sway to and fro across the Keddah, and
the old elephant catchers would wipe the sweat out of their
eyes, and find time to nod to Little Toomai wriggling with
joy on the top of the posts.

He did more than wriggle. One night he slid down from
the post and slipped in between the elephants and threw up
the loose end of a rope, which had dropped, to a driver who
was trying to get a purchase on the leg of a kicking young calf
(calves always give more trouble than full-grown animals).
Kala Nag saw him, caught him in his trunk, and handed him
up to Big Toomai, who slapped him then and there, and put
him back on the post.

Next morning he gave him a scolding and said, "Are not
good brick elephant lines and a little tent carrying enough,
that thou must needs go elephant catching on thy own account,
little worthless? Now those foolish hunters, whose pay is less
than my pay, have spoken to Petersen Sahib of the matter."
Little Toomai was frightened. He did not know much of white
men, but Petersen Sahib was the greatest white man in the
world to him. He was the head of all the Keddah operations—
the man who caught all the elephants for the Government of
India, and who knew more about the ways of elephants than
any living man.

"What—what will happen?" said Little Toomai.

"Happen! The worst that can happen. Petersen Sahib is a
madman. Else why should he go hunting these wild devils?
He may even require thee to be an elephant catcher, to sleep
anywhere in these fever-filled jungles, and at last to be
trampled to death in the Keddah. It is well that this nonsense

ends safely. Next week the catching is over, and we of the plains are sent back to our stations. Then we will march on smooth roads, and forget all this hunting. But, son, I am angry that thou shouldst meddle in the business that belongs to these dirty Assamese jungle folk. Kala Nag will obey none but me, so I must go with him into the Keddah, but he is only a fighting elephant, and he does not help to rope them. So I sit at my ease, as befits a mahout,—not a mere hunter,—a mahout, I say, and a man who gets a pension at the end of his service. Is the family of Toomai of the Elephants to be trodden underfoot in the dirt of a Keddah? Bad one! Wicked one! Worthless son! Go and wash Kala Nag and attend to his ears, and see that there are no thorns in his feet. Or else Petersen Sahib will surely catch thee and make thee a wild hunter—a follower of elephant's foot tracks, a jungle bear. Bah! Shame! Go!"

Little Toomai went off without saying a word, but he told Kala Nag all his grievances while he was examining his feet. "No matter," said Little Toomai, turning up the fringe of Kala Nag's huge right ear. "They have said my name to Petersen Sahib, and perhaps—and perhaps—and perhaps—who knows? Hai! That is a big thorn that I have pulled out!"

The next few days were spent in getting the elephants together, in walking the newly caught wild elephants up and down between a couple of tame ones to prevent them giving too much trouble on the downward march to the plains, and in taking stock of the blankets and ropes and things that had been worn out or lost in the forest.

Petersen Sahib came in on his clever she-elephant Pudmini; he had been paying off other camps among the hills, for the season was coming to an end, and there was a native clerk sitting at a table under a tree, to pay the drivers their wages. As each man was paid he went back to his elephant, and joined the line that stood ready to start. The catchers, and hunters, and beaters, the men of the regular Keddah, who stayed in the jungle year in and year out, sat on the backs of the elephants that belonged to Petersen Sahib's permanent force, or leaned against the trees with their guns across their arms, and made fun of the drivers who were going away, and laughed when the newly caught elephants broke the line and ran about.

Big Toomai went up to the clerk with Little Toomai behind him, and Machua Appa, the head tracker, said in an undertone to a friend of his, "There goes one piece of good elephant stuff at least. 'Tis a pity to send that young jungle-cock to molt in the plains."

Now Petersen Sahib had ears all over him, as a man must have who listens to the most silent of all living things—the wild elephant. He turned where he was lying all along on Pudmini's back and said, "What is that? I did not know of a man among the plains-drivers who had wit enough to rope even a dead elephant."

"This is not a man, but a boy. He went into the Keddah at the last drive, and threw Barmao there the rope, when we were trying to get that young calf with the blotch on his shoulder away from his mother."

Machua Appa pointed at Little Toomai, and Petersen Sahib looked, and Little Toomai bowed to the earth.

"He throw a rope? He is smaller than a picket-pin. Little one, what is thy name?" said Petersen Sahib.

Little Toomai was too frightened to speak, but Kala Nag was behind him, and Toomai made a sign with his hand, and the elephant caught him up in his trunk and held him level with Pudmini's forehead, in front of the great Petersen Sahib. Then Little Toomai covered his face with his hands, for he was only a child, and except where elephants were concerned, he was just as bashful as a child could be.

"Oho!" said Petersen Sahib, smiling underneath his mustache, "and why didst thou teach thy elephant that trick? Was it to help thee steal\ green corn from the roofs of the houses when the ears are put out to dry?"

"Not green corn, Protector of the Poor,—melons," said Little Toomai, and all the men sitting about broke into a roar of laughter. Most of them had taught their elephants that trick when they were boys. Little Toomai was hanging eight feet up in the air, and he wished very much that he were eight feet underground.

"He is Toomai, my son, Sahib," said Big Toomai, scowling. "He is a very bad boy, and he will end in a jail, Sahib."

"Of that I have my doubts," said Petersen Sahib. "A boy who can face a full Keddah at his age does not end in jails. See, little one, here are four annas to spend in sweetmeats because thou hast a little head under that great thatch of hair. In time thou mayest become a hunter too." Big Toomai scowled more than ever. "Remember, though, that Keddahs are not good for children to play in," Petersen Sahib went on.

"Must I never go there, Sahib?" asked Little Toomai with a big gasp.

"Yes." Petersen Sahib smiled again. "When thou hast seen the elephants dance. That is the proper time. Come to me when thou hast seen the elephants dance, and then I will let thee go into all the Keddahs."

There was another roar of laughter, for that is an old joke among elephant-catchers, and it means just never. There are great cleared flat places hidden away in the forests that are called elephants' ball-rooms, but even these are only found by accident, and no man has ever seen the elephants dance. When a driver boasts of his skill and bravery the other drivers say, "And when didst thou see the elephants dance?"

Kala Nag put Little Toomai down, and he bowed to the earth again and went away with his father, and gave the silver four-anna piece to his mother, who was nursing his baby brother, and they all were put up on Kala Nag's back, and the line of grunting, squealing elephants rolled down the hill path to the plains. It was a very lively march on account of the new elephants, who gave trouble at every ford, and needed coaxing or beating every other minute.

Big Toomai prodded Kala Nag spitefully, for he was very angry, but Little Toomai was too happy to speak. Petersen Sahib had noticed him, and given him money, so he felt as a private soldier would feel if he had been called out of the ranks and praised by his commander-in-chief.

"What did Petersen Sahib mean by the elephant dance?" he said, at last, softly to his mother.

Big Toomai heard him and grunted. "That thou shouldst never be one of these hill buffaloes of trackers. That was what he meant. Oh, you in front, what is blocking the way?"

An Assamese driver, two or three elephants ahead, turned round angrily, crying: "Bring up Kala Nag, and knock this youngster of mine into good behavior. Why should Petersen Sahib have chosen me to go down with you donkeys of the rice fields? Lay your beast alongside, Toomai, and let him prod with his tusks. By all the Gods of the Hills, these new elephants are possessed, or else they can smell their companions in the jungle." Kala Nag hit the new elephant in the ribs and knocked the wind out of him, as Big Toomai said, "We have swept the hills of wild elephants at the last catch. It is only your carelessness in driving. Must I keep order along the whole line?"

"Hear him!" said the other driver. "We have swept the hills! Ho! Ho! You are very wise, you plains people. Anyone but a mud-head who never saw the jungle would know that they know that the drives are ended for the season. Therefore all the wild elephants to-night will—but why should I waste wisdom on a river-turtle?"

"What will they do?" Little Toomai called out.

"Ohe, little one. Art thou there? Well, I will tell thee, for thou hast a cool head. They will dance, and it behooves thy father, who has swept all the hills of all the elephants, to double-chain his pickets to-night."

"What talk is this?" said Big Toomai. "For forty years, father and son, we have tended elephants, and we have never heard such moonshine about dances."

"Yes; but a plainsman who lives in a hut knows only the four walls of his hut. Well, leave thy elephants unshackled tonight and see what comes. As for their dancing, I have seen the place where—Bapree-bap! How many windings has the Dihang River? Here is another ford, and we must swim the calves. Stop still, you behind there."

And in this way, talking and wrangling and splashing through the rivers, they made their first march to a sort of receiving camp for the new elephants. But they lost their tempers long before they got there.

Then the elephants were chained by their hind legs to their big stumps of pickets, and extra ropes were fitted to the new elephants, and the fodder was piled before them, and the hill drivers went back to Petersen Sahib through the afternoon light, telling the plains drivers to be extra careful that night, and laughing when the plains drivers asked the reason.

Little Toomai attended to Kala Nag's supper, and as evening fell, wandered through the camp, unspeakably happy, in search of a tom-tom. When an Indian child's heart is full, he does not run about and make a noise in an irregular fashion. He sits down to a sort of revel all by himself. And Little Toomai had been spoken to by Petersen Sahib! If he had not found what he wanted, I believe he would have been ill. But the sweetmeat seller in the camp lent him a little tom-tom—a drum beaten with the flat of the hand—and he sat down, cross-legged, before Kala Nag as the stars began to come out, the tom-tom in his lap, and he thumped and he thumped and he thumped, and the more he thought of the great honor that had been done to him, the more he thumped, all alone among the elephant fodder. There was no tune and no words, but the thumping made him happy.

The new elephants strained at their ropes, and squealed and trumpeted from time to time, and he could hear his mother in the camp hut putting his small brother to sleep with an old, old song about the great God Shiv, who once told all the animals what they should eat. It is a very soothing lullaby, and the first verse says:

Shiv, who poured the harvest and made the winds to blow,
Sitting at the doorways of a day of long ago,
Gave to each his portion , food and toil and fate,
From the King upon the guddee to the Beggar at the gate.
All things made he—Shiva the Preserver.
Mahadeo! Mahadeo! He made all—
Thorn for the camel, fodder for the kine,
And mother's heart for sleepy head, O little son of mine!

Little Toomai came in with a joyous tunk-a-tunk at the

end of each verse, till he felt sleepy and stretched himself on the fodder at Kala Nag's side. At last the elephants began to lie down one after another as is their custom, till only Kala Nag at the right of the line was left standing up; and he rocked slowly from side to side, his ears put forward to listen to the night wind as it blew very slowly across the hills. The air was full of all the night noises that, taken together, make one big silence—the click of one bamboo stem against the other, the rustle of something alive in the undergrowth, the scratch and squawk of a half-waked bird (birds are awake in the night much more often than we imagine), and the fall of water ever so far away. Little Toomai slept for some time, and when he waked it was brilliant moonlight, and Kala Nag was still standing up with his ears cocked. Little Toomai turned, rustling in the fodder, and watched the curve of his big back against half the stars in heaven, and while he watched he heard, so far away that it sounded no more than a pinhole of noise pricked through the stillness, the "hoot-toot" of a wild elephant.

All the elephants in the lines jumped up as if they had been shot, and their grunts at last waked the sleeping mahouts, and they came out and drove in the picket pegs with big mallets, and tightened this rope and knotted that till all was quiet. One new elephant had nearly grubbed up his picket, and Big Toomai took off Kala Nag's leg chain and shackled that elephant fore-foot to hind-foot, but slipped a loop of grass string round Kala Nag's leg, and told him to remember that he was tied fast. He knew that he and his father and his grandfather had done the very same thing hundreds of times before. Kala Nag did not answer to the order by gurgling, as he usually did. He stood still, looking out across the moonlight, his head a little raised and his ears spread like fans, up to the great folds of the Garo hills.

"Tend to him if he grows restless in the night," said Big Toomai to Little Toomai, and he went into the hut and slept. Little Toomai was just going to sleep, too, when he heard the coir string snap with a little "tang," and Kala Nag rolled out of his pickets as slowly and as silently as a cloud rolls out of the mouth of a valley. Little Toomai pattered after him, barefooted, down the road in the moonlight, calling under his breath, "Kala Nag! Kala Nag! Take me with you, O Kala Nag!" The elephant turned, without a sound, took three strides back to the boy in the moonlight, put down his trunk, swung him up to his neck, and almost before Little Toomai had settled his knees, slipped into the forest.

There was one blast of furious trumpeting from the lines, and then the silence shut down on everything, and Kala Nag began to move. Sometimes a tuft of high grass washed along his sides as a wave washes along the sides of a ship, and sometimes a cluster of wild-pepper vines would scrape along his back, or a bamboo would creak where his shoulder touched it. But between those times he moved absolutely without any sound, drifting through the thick Garo forest as though it had been smoke. He was going uphill, but though Little Toomai watched the stars in the rifts of the trees, he could not tell in what direction.

Then Kala Nag reached the crest of the ascent and stopped for a minute, and Little Toomai could see the tops of the trees lying all speckled and furry under the moonlight for miles and miles, and the blue-white mist over the river in the hollow. Toomai leaned forward and looked, and he felt that the forest was awake below him—awake and alive and crowded. A big brown fruit-eating bat brushed past his ear; a porcupine's quills rattled in the thicket; and in the darkness between the tree stems he heard a hog-bear digging hard in the moist warm earth, and snuffing as it digged.

Then the branches closed over his head again, and Kala Nag began to go down into the valley—not quietly this time, but as a runaway gun goes down a steep bank—in one rush. The huge limbs moved as steadily as pistons, eight feet to each stride, and the wrinkled skin of the elbow points rustled. The undergrowth on either side of him ripped with a noise like torn canvas, and the saplings that he heaved away right and left with his shoulders sprang back again and banged him on the flank, and great trails of creepers, all matted together, hung from his tusks as he threw his head from side to side and plowed out his pathway. Then Little Toomai laid himself down close to the great neck lest a swinging bough should sweep him to the ground, and he wished that he were back in the lines again.

The grass began to get squashy, and Kala Nag's feet sucked and squelched as he put them down, and the night mist at the bottom of the valley chilled Little Toomai. There was a splash and a trample, and the rush of running water, and Kala Nag strode through the bed of a river, feeling his way at each step. Above the noise of the water, as it swirled round the elephant's legs, Little Toomai could hear more splashing and some trumpeting both upstream and down—great grunts and angry snortings, and all the mist about him seemed to be full of rolling, wavy shadows.

"Ai!" he said, half aloud, his teeth chattering. "The elephant-folk are out tonight. It is the dance, then!"

Kala Nag swashed out of the water, blew his trunk clear, and began another climb. But this time he was not alone, and he had not to make his path. That was made already, six feet wide, in front of him, where the bent jungle-grass was trying to recover itself and stand up. Many elephants must have gone that way only a few minutes before. Little Toomai looked back, and behind him a great wild tusker with his little pig's eyes glowing like hot coals was just lifting himself out of the misty river. Then the trees closed up again, and they went on and up, with trumpetings and crashings, and the sound of breaking branches on every side of them.

At last Kala Nag stood still between two tree-trunks at the very top of the hill. They were part of a circle of trees that grew round an irregular space of some three or four acres, and in all that space, as Little Toomai could see, the ground had been trampled down as hard as a brick floor. Some trees grew in the center of the clearing, but their bark was rubbed away, and the white wood beneath showed all shiny and polished in the patches of moonlight. There were creepers hanging from the upper branches, and the bells of the flowers of the creepers, great waxy white things like convolvuluses, hung down fast asleep. But within the limits of the clearing there was not a single blade of green—nothing but the trampled earth.

The moonlight showed it all iron gray, except where some elephants stood upon it, and their shadows were inky black. Little Toomai looked, holding his breath, with his eyes starting out of his head, and as he looked, more and more and more elephants swung out into the open from between the tree trunks. Little Toomai could only count up to ten, and he counted again and again on his fingers till he lost count of the tens, and his head began to swim. Outside the clearing he could hear them crashing in the undergrowth as they worked their way up the hillside, but as soon as they were within the circle of the tree trunks they moved like ghosts.

There were white-tusked wild males, with fallen leaves and nuts and twigs lying in the wrinkles of their necks and the folds of their ears; fat, slow-footed she-elephants, with restless, little pinky black calves only three or four feet high running under their stomachs; young elephants with their tusks just beginning to show, and very proud of them; lanky, scraggy old-maid elephants, with their hollow anxious faces, and trunks like rough bark; savage old bull elephants, scarred from shoulder to flank with great weals and cuts of bygone fights, and the caked dirt of their solitary mud baths dropping from their shoulders; and there was one with a broken tusk and the marks of the full-stroke, the terrible drawing scrape, of a tiger's claws on his side.

They were standing head to head, or walking to and fro across the ground in couples, or rocking and swaying all by themselves—scores and scores of elephants.

Toomai knew that so long as he lay still on Kala Nag's neck nothing would happen to him, for even in the rush and scramble of a Keddah drive a wild elephant does not reach up with his trunk and drag a man off the neck of a tame elephant. And these elephants were not thinking of men that night. Once they started and put their ears forward when they heard the chinking of a leg iron in the forest, but it was Pudmini, Petersen Sahib's pet elephant, her chain snapped short off, grunting, snuffling up the hillside. She must have broken her pickets and come straight from Petersen Sahib's camp; and Little Toomai saw another elephant, one that he did not know, with deep rope galls on his back and breast. He, too, must have run away from some camp in the hills about.

At last there was no sound of any more elephants moving in the forest, and Kala Nag rolled out from his station between the trees and went into the middle of the crowd, clucking and gurgling, and all the elephants began to talk in their own tongue, and to move about.

Still lying down, Little Toomai looked down upon scores and scores of broad backs, and wagging ears, and tossing trunks, and little rolling eyes. He heard the click of tusks as they crossed other tusks by accident, and the dry rustle of trunks twined together, and the chafing of enormous sides and shoulders in the crowd, and the incessant flick and hissh of the great tails. Then a cloud came over the moon, and he sat in black darkness. But the quiet, steady hustling and pushing and gurgling went on just the same. He knew that there were elephants all round Kala Nag, and that there was no chance of backing him out of the assembly; so he set his teeth and shivered. In a Keddah at least there was torchlight and shouting, but here he was all alone in the dark, and once a trunk came up and touched him on the knee.

Then an elephant trumpeted, and they all took it up for five or ten terrible seconds. The dew from the trees above spattered down like rain on the unseen backs, and a dull booming noise began, not very loud at first, and Little Toomai could not tell what it was. But it grew and grew, and Kala Nag lifted up one forefoot and then the other, and brought them down on the ground—one-two, one-two, as steadily as trip-hammers. The elephants were stamping all together now, and it sounded like a war drum beaten at the mouth of a cave. The dew fell from the trees till there was no more left to fall, and the booming went on, and the ground rocked and shivered, and Little Toomai put his hands up to his ears to shut out the sound. But it was all one gigantic jar that ran through him—this stamp of hundreds of heavy feet on the raw earth. Once or twice he could feel Kala Nag and all the others surge forward a few strides, and the thumping would change to the crushing sound of juicy green things being bruised, but in a minute or two the boom of feet on hard earth began again. A tree was creaking and groaning somewhere near him. He put out his arm and felt the bark, but Kala Nag moved forward, still tramping, and he could not tell where he was in the clearing. There was no sound from the elephants, except once, when two or three little calves squeaked together. Then he heard a thump and a shuffle, and the booming went on. It must have lasted fully two hours, and Little Toomai ached in every nerve, but he knew by the smell of the night air that the dawn was coming.

The morning broke in one sheet of pale yellow behind the green hills, and the booming stopped with the first ray, as though the light had been an order. Before Little Toomai had got the ringing out of his head, before even he had shifted his position, there was not an elephant in sight except Kala Nag, Pudmini, and the elephant with the rope-galls, and there was neither sign nor rustle nor whisper down the hillsides to show where the others had gone.

Little Toomai stared again and again. The clearing, as he remembered it, had grown in the night. More trees stood in the middle of it, but the undergrowth and the jungle grass at the sides had been rolled back. Little Toomai stared once more. Now he understood the trampling. The elephants had stamped out more room—had stamped the thick grass and juicy cane to trash, the trash into slivers, the slivers into tiny fibers, and the fibers into hard earth.

"Wah!" said Little Toomai, and his eyes were very heavy. "Kala Nag, my lord, let us keep by Pudmini and go to Petersen Sahib's camp, or I shall drop from thy neck."

The third elephant watched the two go away, snorted, wheeled round, and took his own path. He may have belonged to some little native king's establishment, fifty or sixty or a hundred miles away.

Two hours later, as Petersen Sahib was eating early breakfast, his elephants, who had been double chained that night, began to trumpet, and Pudmini, mired to the shoulders, with Kala Nag, very footsore, shambled into the camp. Little Toomai's face was gray and pinched, and his hair was full of leaves and drenched with dew, but he tried to salute Petersen Sahib, and cried faintly: "The dance—the elephant dance! I have seen it, and—I die!" As Kala Nag sat down, he slid off his neck in a dead faint.

But, since native children have no nerves worth speaking of, in two hours he was lying very contentedly in Petersen Sahib's hammock with Petersen Sahib's shooting-coat under his head, and a glass of warm milk, a little brandy, with a dash of quinine, inside of him, and while the old hairy, scarred hunters of the jungles sat three deep before him, looking at him as though he were a spirit, he told his tale in short words, as a child will, and wound up with:

"Now, if I lie in one word, send men to see, and they will find that the elephant folk have trampled down more room in their dance-room, and they will find ten and ten, and many times ten, tracks leading to that dance-room. They made more room with their feet. I have seen it. Kala Nag took me, and I saw. Also Kala Nag is very leg-weary!"

Little Toomai lay back and slept all through the long afternoon and into the twilight, and while he slept Petersen Sahib and Machua Appa followed the track of the two elephants for fifteen miles across the hills. Petersen Sahib had spent eighteen years in catching elephants, and he had only once before found such a dance-place. Machua Appa had no need to look twice at the clearing to see what had been done there, or to scratch with his toe in the packed, rammed earth.

"The child speaks truth," said he. "All this was done last night, and I have counted seventy tracks crossing the river. See, Sahib, where Pudmini's leg-iron cut the bark of that tree! Yes; she was there too."

They looked at one another and up and down, and they wondered. For the ways of elephants are beyond the wit of any man, black or white, to fathom.

"Forty years and five," said Machua Appa, "have I followed my lord, the elephant, but never have I heard that any child of man had seen what this child has seen. By all the Gods of the Hills, it is—what can we say?" and he shook his head.

When they got back to camp it was time for the evening meal. Petersen Sahib ate alone in his tent, but he gave orders that the camp should have two sheep and some fowls, as well as a double ration of flour and rice and salt, for he knew that there would be a feast.

Big Toomai had come up hotfoot from the camp in the plains to search for his son and his elephant, and now that he had found them he looked at them as though he were afraid of them both. And there was a feast by the blazing campfires in front of the lines of picketed elephants, and Little Toomai was the hero of it all. And the big brown elephant catchers, the trackers and drivers and ropers, and the men who know all the secrets of breaking the wildest elephants, passed him from one to the other, and they marked his forehead with blood from the breast of a newly killed jungle-cock, to show that he was a forester, initiated and free of all the jungles.

And at last, when the flames died down, and the red light of the logs made the elephants look as though they had been dipped in blood too, Machua Appa, the head of all the drivers of all the Keddahs—Machua Appa, Petersen Sahib's other self, who had never seen a made road in forty years: Machua Appa, who was so great that he had no other name than Machua Appa,—leaped to his feet, with Little Toomai held high in the air above his head, and shouted: "Listen, my brothers. Listen, too, you my lords in the lines there, for I, Machua Appa, am speaking! This little one shall no more be called Little Toomai, but Toomai of the Elephants, as his great-grandfather was called before him. What never man has seen he has seen through the long night, and the favor of the elephant-folk and of the Gods of the Jungles is with him. He shall become a great tracker. He shall become greater than I, even I, Machua Appa! He shall follow the new trail, and the stale trail, and the mixed trail, with a clear eye! He shall take no harm in the Keddah when he runs under their bellies to rope the wild tuskers; and if he slips before the feet of the charging bull elephant, the bull elephant shall know who he is and shall not crush him. Aihai! my lords in the chains,"—he whirled up the line of pickets—"here is the little one that has seen your dances in your hidden places,—the sight that never man saw! Give him honor, my lords! Salaam karo, my children. Make your salute to Toomai of the Elephants! Gunga Pershad, ahaa! Hira Guj, Birchi Guj, Kuttar Guj, ahaa! Pudmini,—thou hast seen him at the dance, and thou too, Kala Nag, my pearl among elephants!—ahaa! Together! To Toomai of the Elephants. Barrao!"

And at that last wild yell the whole line flung up their trunks till the tips touched their foreheads, and broke out into the full salute—the crashing trumpet-peal that only the Viceroy of India hears, the Salaamut of the Keddah.

But it was all for the sake of Little Toomai, who had seen what never man had seen before—the dance of the elephants at night and alone in the heart of the Garo hills!

Her Majesty's Servants

It had been raining heavily for one whole month—raining on a camp of thirty thousand men and thousands of camels, elephants, horses, bullocks, and mules all gathered together at a placc called Rawal Pindi, to be reviewed by the Viceroy of India. He was receiving a visit from the Amir of Afghanistan— a wild king of a very wild country. The Amir had brought with him for a bodyguard eight hundred men and horses who had never seen a camp or a locomotive before in their lives— savage men and savage horses from somewhere at the back of Central Asia. Every night a mob of these horses would be sure to break their heel ropes and stampede up and down the camp through the mud in the dark, or the camels would break loose and run about and fall over the ropes of the tents, and you can imagine how pleasant that was for men trying to go to sleep. My tent lay far away from the camel lines, and I thought it was safe. But one night a man popped his head in and shouted, "Get out, quick! They're coming! My tent's gone!"

I knew who "they" were, so I put on my boots and waterproof and scuttled out into the slush. Little Vixen, my fox terrier, went out through the other side; and then there was a roaring and a grunting and bubbling, and I saw the tent cave in, as the pole snapped, and begin to dance about like a mad ghost. A camel had blundered into it, and wet and angry as I was, I could not help laughing. Then I ran on, because I did not know how many camels might have got loose, and before long I was out of sight of the camp, plowing my way through the mud.

At last I fell over the tail-end of a gun, and by that knew I was somewhere near the artillery lines where the cannon were stacked at night. As I did not want to plowter about any more in the drizzle and the dark, I put my waterproof over the muzzle of one gun, and made a sort of wigwam with two or three rammers that I found, and lay along the tail of another gun, wondering where Vixen had got to, and where I might be.

Just as I was getting ready to go to sleep I heard a jingle of harness and a grunt, and a mule passed me shaking his wet ears. He belonged to a screw-gun battery, for I could hear the rattle of the straps and rings and chains and things on his saddle pad. The screw-guns are tiny little cannon made in two pieces, that are screwed together when the time comes to use them. They are taken up mountains, anywhere that a mule can find a road, and they are very useful for fighting in rocky country.

Behind the mule there was a camel, with his big soft feet squelching and slipping in the mud, and his neck bobbing to and fro like a strayed hen's. Luckily, I knew enough of beast language—not wild-beast language, but camp-beast language, of course—from the natives to know what he was saying.

He must have been the one that flopped into my tent, for he called to the mule, "What shall I do? Where shall I go? I have fought with a white thing that waved, and it took a stick and hit me on the neck." (That was my broken tent pole, and I was very glad to know it.) "Shall we run on?"

"Oh, it was you," said the mule, "you and your friends, that have been disturbing the camp? All right. You'll be beaten for this in the morning. But I may as well give you something on account now."

I heard the harness jingle as the mule backed and caught the camel two kicks in the ribs that rang like a drum. "Another time," he said, "you'll know better than to run through a mule battery at night, shouting 'Thieves and fire!' Sit down, and keep your silly neck quiet."

The camel doubled up camel-fashion, like a two-foot rule, and sat down whimpering. There was a regular beat of hoofs in the darkness, and a big troop-horse cantered up as steadily as though he were on parade, jumped a gun tail, and landed close to the mule.

"It's disgraceful," he said, blowing out his nostrils. "Those camels have racketed through our lines again—the third time this week. How's a horse to keep his condition if he isn't allowed to sleep. Who's here?"

"I'm the breech-piece mule of number two gun of the First Screw Battery," said the mule, "and the other's one of your friends. He's waked me up too. Who are you?"

"Number Fifteen, E troop, Ninth Lancers—Dick Cunliffe's horse. Stand over a little, there."

"Oh, beg your pardon," said the mule. "It's too dark to see much. Aren't these camels too sickening for anything? I walked out of my lines to get a little peace and quiet here."

"My lords," said the camel humbly, "we dreamed bad

dreams in the night, and we were very much afraid. I am only a baggage camel of the 39th Native Infantry, and I am not as brave as you are, my lords."

"Then why didn't you stay and carry baggage for the 39th Native Infantry, instead of running all round the camp?" said the mule.

"They were such very bad dreams," said the camel. "I am sorry. Listen! What is that? Shall we run on again?"

"Sit down," said the mule, "or you'll snap your long stick-legs between the guns." He cocked one ear and listened. "Bullocks!" he said. "Gun bullocks. On my word, you and your friends have waked the camp very thoroughly. It takes a good deal of prodding to put up a gun-bullock."

I heard a chain dragging along the ground, and a yoke of the great sulky white bullocks that drag the heavy siege guns when the elephants won't go any nearer to the firing, came shouldering along together. And almost stepping on the chain was another battery mule, calling wildly for "Billy."

"That's one of our recruits," said the old mule to the troop horse. "He's calling for me. Here, youngster, stop squealing. The dark never hurt anybody yet."

The gun-bullocks lay down together and began chewing the cud, but the young mule huddled close to Billy.

"Things!" he said. "Fearful and horrible, Billy! They came into our lines while we were asleep. D'you think they'll kill us?"

"I've a very great mind to give you a number-one kicking," said Billy. "The idea of a fourteen-hand mule with your training disgracing the battery before this gentleman!"

"Gently, gently!" said the troop-horse. "Remember they

are always like this to begin with. The first time I ever saw a man (it was in Australia when I was a three-year-old) I ran for half a day, and if I'd seen a camel, I should have been running still."

Nearly all our horses for the English cavalry are brought to India from Australia, and are broken in by the troopers themselves.

"True enough," said Billy. "Stop shaking, youngster. The first time they put the full harness with all its chains on my back I stood on my forelegs and kicked every bit of it off. I hadn't learned the real science of kicking then, but the battery said they had never seen anything like it."

"But this wasn't harness or anything that jingled," said the young mule. "You know I don't mind that now, Billy. It was Things like trees, and they fell up and down the lines and bubbled; and my head-rope broke, and I couldn't find my driver, and I couldn't find you, Billy, so I ran off with—with these gentlemen."

"H'm!" said Billy. "As soon as I heard the camels were loose I came away on my own account. When a battery—a screw-gun mule calls gun-bullocks gentlemen, he must be very badly shaken up. Who are you fellows on the ground there?"

The gun bullocks rolled their cuds, and answered both together: "The seventh yoke of the first gun of the Big Gun Battery. We were asleep when the camels came, but when we were trampled on we got up and walked away. It is better to lie quiet in the mud than to be disturbed on good bedding. We told your friend here that there was nothing to be afraid of, but he knew so much that he thought otherwise. Wah!"

They went on chewing.

"That comes of being afraid," said Billy. "You get laughed at by gun-bullocks. I hope you like it, young un."

The young mule's teeth snapped, and I heard him say something about not being afraid of any beefy old bullock in the world. But the bullocks only clicked their horns together and went on chewing.

"Now, don't be angry after you've been afraid. That's the worst kind of cowardice," said the troop-horse. "Anybody can be forgiven for being scared in the night, I think, if they see things they don't understand. We've broken out of our pickets, again and again, four hundred and fifty of us, just because a new recruit got to telling tales of whip snakes at home in Australia till we were scared to death of the loose ends of our head-ropes."

"That's all very well in camp," said Billy. "I'm not above stampeding myself, for the fun of the thing, when I haven't been out for a day or two. But what do you do on active service?"

"Oh, that's quite another set of new shoes," said the troop horse. "Dick Cunliffe's on my back then, and drives his knees into me, and all I have to do is to watch where I am putting my feet, and to keep my hind legs well under me, and be bridle-wise."

"What's bridle-wise?" said the young mule.

"By the Blue Gums of the Back Blocks," snorted the troop-horse, "do you mean to say that you aren't taught to be bridle-wise in your business? How can you do anything, unless you can spin round at once when the rein is pressed on your neck? It means life or death to your man, and of course that's life and death to you. Get round with your hind legs under you the instant you feel the rein on your neck. If you haven't room to swing round, rear up a little and come round on your hind legs. That's being bridle-wise."

"We aren't taught that way," said Billy the mule stiffly. "We're taught to obey the man at our head: step off when he says so, and step in when he says so. I suppose it comes to the same thing. Now, with all this fine fancy business and rearing, which must be very bad for your hocks, what do you do?"

"That depends," said the troop-horse. "Generally I have to go in among a lot of yelling, hairy men with knives—long shiny knives, worse than the farrier's knives—and I have to take care that Dick's boot is just touching the next man's boot without crushing it. I can see Dick's lance to the right of my right eye, and I know I'm safe. I shouldn't care to be the man or horse that stood up to Dick and me when we're in a hurry."

"Don't the knives hurt?" said the young mule.

"Well, I got one cut across the chest once, but that wasn't Dick's fault—"

"A lot I should have cared whose fault it was, if it hurt!" said the young mule.

"You must," said the troop horse. "If you don't trust your man, you may as well run away at once. That's what some of our horses do, and I don't blame them. As I was saying, it wasn't Dick's fault. The man was lying on the ground, and I stretched myself not to tread on him, and he slashed up at me. Next time I have to go over a man lying down I shall step on him—hard."

"H'm!" said Billy. "It sounds very foolish. Knives are dirty things at any time. The proper thing to do is to climb up a mountain with a well-balanced saddle, hang on by all four feet and your ears too, and creep and crawl and wriggle along, till you come out hundreds of feet above anyone else on a ledge where there's just room enough for your hoofs. Then you stand still and keep quiet—never ask a man to hold your head, young un—keep quiet while the guns are being put together, and then you watch the little poppy shells drop down into the tree-tops ever so far below."

"Don't you ever trip?" said the troop-horse.

"They say that when a mule trips you can split a hen's ear," said Billy. "Now and again perhaps a badly packed saddle will upset a mule, but it's very seldom. I wish I could show you our business. It's beautiful. Why, it took me three years to find out what the men were driving at. The science of the thing is never to show up against the sky line, because, if you do, you may get fired at. Remember that, young un. Always keep hidden as much as possible, even if you have to go a mile out of your way. I lead the battery when it comes to that sort of climbing."

"Fired at without the chance of running into the people who are firing!" said the troop-horse, thinking hard. "I couldn't stand that. I should want to charge—with Dick."

"Oh, no, you wouldn't. You know that as soon as the guns are in position they'll do all the charging. That's scientific and neat. But knives—pah!"

The baggage-camel had been bobbing his head to and fro for some time past, anxious to get a word in edgewise. Then I heard him say, as he cleared his throat, nervously:

"I—I—I have fought a little, but not in that climbing way or that running way."

"No. Now you mention it," said Billy, "you don't look as though you were made for climbing or running—much. Well, how was it, old Hay-bales?"

"The proper way," said the camel. "We all sat down—"

"Oh, my crupper and breastplate!" said the troop-horse under his breath. "Sat down!"

"We sat down—a hundred of us," the camel went on, "in a big square, and the men piled our packs and saddles, outside the square, and they fired over our backs, the men did, on all sides of the square."

"What sort of men? Any men that came along?" said the troop-horse. "They teach us in riding school to lie down and let our masters fire across us, but Dick Cunliffe is the only man I'd trust to do that. It tickles my girths, and, besides, I can't see with my head on the ground."

"What does it matter who fires across you?" said the camel. "There are plenty of men and plenty of other camels close by, and a great many clouds of smoke. I am not frightened then. I sit still and wait."

"And yet," said Billy, "you dream bad dreams and upset the camp at night. Well, well! Before I'd lie down, not to speak of sitting down, and let a man fire across me, my heels and his head would have something to say to each other. Did you ever hear anything so awful as that?"

There was a long silence, and then one of the gun bullocks lifted up his big head and said, "This is very foolish indeed. There is only one way of fighting."

"Oh, go on," said Billy. "Please don't mind me. I suppose you fellows fight standing on your tails?"

"Only one way," said the two together. (They must have been twins.) "This is that way. To put all twenty yoke of us to the big gun as soon as Two Tails trumpets." ("Two Tails" is camp slang for the elephant.) "What does Two Tails trumpet for?" said the young mule.

"To show that he is not going any nearer to the smoke on the other side. Two Tails is a great coward. Then we tug the big gun all together—Heya—Hullah! Heeyah! Hullah! We do not climb like cats nor run like calves. We go across the level plain, twenty yoke of us, till we are unyoked again, and we graze while the big guns talk across the plain to some town with mud walls, and pieces of the wall fall out, and the dust goes up as though many cattle were coming home."

"Oh! And you choose that time for grazing?" said the young mule.

"That time or any other. Eating is always good. We eat till we are yoked up again and tug the gun back to where Two Tails is waiting for it. Sometimes there are big guns in the city that speak back, and some of us are killed, and then there is all the more grazing for those that are left. This is Fate. None the less, Two Tails is a great coward. That is the proper way to fight. We are brothers from Hapur. Our father was a sacred bull of Shiva. We have spoken."

"Well, I've certainly learned something tonight," said the troop-horse. "Do you gentlemen of the screw-gun battery feel inclined to eat when you are being fired at with big guns, and Two Tails is behind you?"

"About as much as we feel inclined to sit down and let men sprawl all over us, or run into people with knives. I never heard such stuff. A mountain ledge, a well-balanced load, a driver you can trust to let you pick your own way, and I'm your mule. But—the other things—no!" said Billy, with a stamp of his foot.

"Of course," said the troop horse, "everyone is not made in the same way, and I can quite see that your family, on your father's side, would fail to understand a great many things."

"Never you mind my family on my father's side," said Billy angrily, for every mule hates to be reminded that his father was a donkey. "My father was a Southern gentleman, and he could pull down and bite and kick into rags every horse he came across. Remember that, you big brown Brumby!"

Brumby means wild horse without any breeding. Imagine the feelings of Sunol if a car-horse called her a "skate," and you can imagine how the Australian horse felt. I saw the white of his eye glitter in the dark.

"See here, you son of an imported Malaga jackass," he said between his teeth, "I'd have you know that I'm related on my mother's side to Carbine, winner of the Melbourne Cup, and where I come from we aren't accustomed to being ridden over roughshod by any parrot-mouthed, pig-headed mule in a pop-gun pea-shooter battery. Are you ready?"

"On your hind legs!" squealed Billy. They both reared up facing each other, and I was expecting a furious fight, when a gurgly, rumbly voice, called out of the darkness to the right— "Children, what are you fighting about there? Be quiet."

Both beasts dropped down with a snort of disgust, for neither horse nor mule can bear to listen to an elephant's voice.

"It's Two Tails!" said the troop-horse. "I can't stand him. A tail at each end isn't fair!"

"My feelings exactly," said Billy, crowding into the troop-horse for company. "We're very alike in some things."

"I suppose we've inherited them from our mothers," said the troop horse. "It's not worth quarreling about. Hi! Two Tails, are you tied up?"

"Yes," said Two Tails, with a laugh all up his trunk. "I'm picketed for the night. I've heard what you fellows have been saying. But don't be afraid. I'm not coming over."

The bullocks and the camel said, half aloud, "Afraid of

Two Tails—what nonsense!" And the bullocks went on, "We are sorry that you heard, but it is true. Two Tails, why are you afraid of the guns when they fire?"

"Well," said Two Tails, rubbing one hind leg against the other, exactly like a little boy saying a poem, "I don't quite know whether you'd understand."

"We don't, but we have to pull the guns," said the bullocks.

"I know it, and I know you are a good deal braver than you think you are. But it's different with me. My battery captain called me a Pachydermatous Anachronism the other day."

"That's another way of fighting, I suppose?" said Billy, who was recovering his spirits.

"You don't know what that means, of course, but I do. It means betwixt and between, and that is just where I am. I can see inside my head what will happen when a shell bursts, and you bullocks can't."

"I can," said the troop-horse. "At least a little bit. I try not to think about it."

"I can see more than you, and I do think about it. I know there's a great deal of me to take care of, and I know that nobody knows how to cure me when I'm sick. All they can do is to stop my driver's pay till I get well, and I can't trust my driver."

"Ah!" said the troop horse. "That explains it. I can trust Dick."

"You could put a whole regiment of Dicks on my back without making me feel any better. I know just enough to be uncomfortable, and not enough to go on in spite of it."

"We do not understand," said the bullocks.

"I know you don't. I'm not talking to you. You don't know what blood is."

"We do," said the bullocks. "It is red stuff that soaks into the ground and smells."

The troop-horse gave a kick and a bound and a snort.

"Don't talk of it," he said. "I can smell it now, just thinking of it. It makes me want to run—when I haven't Dick on my back."

"But it is not here," said the camel and the bullocks. "Why are you so stupid?"

"It's vile stuff," said Billy. "I don't want to run, but I don't want to talk about it."

"There you are!" said Two Tails, waving his tail to explain.

"Surely. Yes, we have been here all night," said the bullocks.

Two Tails stamped his foot till the iron ring on it jingled. "Oh, I'm not talking to you. You can't see inside your heads."

"No. We see out of our four eyes," said the bullocks. "We see straight in front of us."

"If I could do that and nothing else, you wouldn't be needed to pull the big guns at all. If I was like my captain—he can see things inside his head before the firing begins, and he shakes all over, but he knows too much to run away—if I was like him I could pull the guns. But if I were as wise as all that I should never be here. I should be a king in the forest, as I used to be, sleeping half the day and bathing when I liked. I haven't had a good bath for a month."

"That's all very fine," said Billy. "But giving a thing a long name doesn't make it any better."

"H'sh!" said the troop horse. "I think I understand what Two Tails means."

"You'll understand better in a minute," said Two Tails angrily. "Now you just explain to me why you don't like this!"

He began trumpeting furiously at the top of his trumpet.

"Stop that!" said Billy and the troop horse together, and I could hear them stamp and shiver. An elephant's trumpeting is always nasty, especially on a dark night.

"I shan't stop," said Two Tails. "Won't you explain that, please? Hhrrmph! Rrrt! Rrrmph! Rrrhha!" Then he stopped suddenly, and I heard a little whimper in the dark, and knew that Vixen had found me at last. She knew as well as I did that if there is one thing in the world the elephant is more afraid of than another it is a little barking dog. So she stopped to bully Two Tails in his pickets, and yapped round his big feet. Two Tails shuffled and squeaked. "Go away, little dog!" he said. "Don't snuff at my ankles, or I'll kick at you. Good little dog— nice little doggie, then! Go home, you yelping little beast! Oh, why doesn't someone take her away? She'll bite me in a minute."

"Seems to me," said Billy to the troop horse, "that our friend Two Tails is afraid of most things. Now, if I had a full meal for every dog I've kicked across the parade-ground I should be as fat as Two Tails nearly."

I whistled, and Vixen ran up to me, muddy all over, and licked my nose, and told me a long tale about hunting for me all through the camp. I never let her know that I understood beast talk, or she would have taken all sorts of liberties. So I buttoned her into the breast of my overcoat, and Two Tails shuffled and stamped and growled to himself.

"Extraordinary! Most extraordinary!" he said. "It runs in our family. Now, where has that nasty little beast gone to?"

I heard him feeling about with his trunk.

"We all seem to be affected in various ways," he went on,

blowing his nose. "Now, you gentlemen were alarmed, I believe, when I trumpeted."

"Not alarmed, exactly," said the troop-horse, "but it made me feel as though I had hornets where my saddle ought to be. Don't begin again."

"I'm frightened of a little dog, and the camel here is frightened by bad dreams in the night."

"It is very lucky for us that we haven't all got to fight in the same way," said the troop-horse.

"What I want to know," said the young mule, who had been quiet for a long time—"what I want to know is, why we have to fight at all."

"Because we're told to," said the troop-horse, with a snort of contempt.

"Orders," said Billy the mule, and his teeth snapped.

"Hukm hai!" (It is an order!), said the camel with a gurgle, and Two Tails and the bullocks repeated, "Hukm hai!"

"Yes, but who gives the orders?" said the recruit-mule.

"The man who walks at your head—Or sits on your back— Or holds the nose rope—Or twists your tail," said Billy and the troop-horse and the camel and the bullocks one after the other.

"But who gives them the orders?"

"Now you want to know too much, young un," said Billy, "and that is one way of getting kicked. All you have to do is to obey the man at your head and ask no questions."

"He's quite right," said Two Tails. "I can't always obey, because I'm betwixt and between. But Billy's right. Obey the man next to you who gives the order, or you'll stop all the battery, besides getting a thrashing."

The gun-bullocks got up to go. "Morning is coming," they said. "We will go back to our lines. It is true that we only see out of our eyes, and we are not very clever. But still, we are the only people to-night who have not been afraid. Good-night, you brave people."

Nobody answered, and the troop-horse said, to change the conversation, "Where's that little dog? A dog means a man somewhere about."

"Here I am," yapped Vixen, "under the gun tail with my man. You big, blundering beast of a camel you, you upset our tent. My man's very angry."

"Phew!" said the bullocks. "He must be white!"

"Of course he is," said Vixen. "Do you suppose I'm looked after by a black bullock-driver?"

"Huah! Ouach! Ugh!" said the bullocks. "Let us get away quickly."

They plunged forward in the mud, and managed somehow to run their yoke on the pole of an ammunition wagon, where it jammed.

"Now you have done it," said Billy calmly. "Don't struggle. You're hung up till daylight. What on earth's the matter?"

The bullocks went off into the long hissing snorts that Indian cattle give, and pushed and crowded and slued and stamped and slipped and nearly fell down in the mud, grunting savagely.

"You'll break your necks in a minute," said the troop-horse. "What's the matter with white men? I live with 'em."

"They—eat—us! Pull!" said the near bullock. The yoke snapped with a twang, and they lumbered off together.

I never knew before what made Indian cattle so scared of

Englishmen. We eat beef—a thing that no cattle-driver touches—and of course the cattle do not like it.

"May I be flogged with my own pad-chains! Who'd have thought of two big lumps like those losing their heads?" said Billy.

"Never mind. I'm going to look at this man. Most of the white men, I know, have things in their pockets," said the troop-horse.

"I'll leave you, then. I can't say I'm over-fond of 'em myself. Besides, white men who haven't a place to sleep in are more than likely to be thieves, and I've a good deal of Government property on my back. Come along, young un, and we'll go back to our lines. Good-night, Australia! See you on parade to-morrow, I suppose. Good-night, old Hay-bale!—try to control your feelings, won't you? Good-night, Two Tails! If you pass us on the ground tomorrow, don't trumpet. It spoils our formation."

Billy the Mule stumped off with the swaggering limp of an old campaigner, as the troop-horse's head came nuzzling into my breast, and I gave him biscuits, while Vixen, who is a most conceited little dog, told him fibs about the scores of horses that she and I kept.

"I'm coming to the parade to-morrow in my dog-cart," she said. "Where will you be?"

"On the left hand of the second squadron. I set the time for all my troop, little lady," he said politely. "Now I must go back to Dick. My tail's all muddy, and he'll have two hours' hard work dressing me for parade."

The big parade of all the thirty thousand men was held that afternoon, and Vixen and I had a good place close to the Viceroy and the Amir of Afghanistan, with high, big black hat of astrakhan wool and the great diamond star in the center. The first part of the review was all sunshine, and the regiments went by in wave upon wave of legs all moving together, and guns all in a line, till our eyes grew dizzy. Then the cavalry came up, to the beautiful cavalry canter of "Bonnie Dundee," and Vixen cocked her ear where she sat on the dog-cart. The second squadron of the Lancers shot by, and there was the troop-horse, with his tail like spun silk, his head pulled into his breast, one ear forward and one back, setting the time for all his squadron, his legs going as smoothly as waltz music. Then the big guns came by, and I saw Two Tails and two other elephants harnessed in line to a forty-pounder siege gun, while twenty yoke of oxen walked behind. The seventh pair had a new yoke, and they looked rather stiff and tired. Last came the screw guns, and Billy the mule carried himself as though he commanded all the troops, and his harness was oiled and polished till it winked. I gave a cheer all by myself for Billy the mule, but he never looked right or left.

The rain began to fall again, and for a while it was too misty to see what the troops were doing. They had made a big half circle across the plain, and were spreading out into a line. That line grew and grew and grew till it was three-quarters of a mile long from wing to wing—one solid wall of men, horses, and guns. Then it came on straight toward the Viceroy and the Amir, and as it got nearer the ground began to shake, like the deck of a steamer when the engines are going fast.

Unless you have been there you cannot imagine what a frightening effect this steady come-down of troops has on the spectators, even when they know it is only a review. I looked at the Amir. Up till then he had not shown the shadow of a sign of astonishment or anything else. But now his eyes began to get bigger and bigger, and he picked up the reins on his horse's neck and looked behind him. For a minute it seemed as though he were going to draw his sword and slash his way out through the English men and women in the carriages at the back. Then the advance stopped dead, the ground stood still, the whole line saluted, and thirty bands began to play all together. That was the end of the review, and the regiments went off to their camps in the rain, and an infantry band struck up with—

> *The animals went in two by two,*
> *Hurrah!*
> *The animals went in two by two,*
> *The elephant and the battery mul',*
> *and they all got into the Ark*
> *For to get out of the rain!*

Then I heard an old grizzled, long-haired Central Asian chief, who had come down with the Amir, asking questions of a native officer.

"Now," said he, "in what manner was this wonderful thing done?"

And the officer answered, "An order was given, and they obeyed."

"But are the beasts as wise as the men?" said the chief.

"They obey, as the men do. Mule, horse, elephant, or bullock, he obeys his driver, and the driver his sergeant, and the sergeant his lieutenant, and the lieutenant his captain, and the captain his major, and the major his colonel, and the colonel his brigadier commanding three regiments, and the brigadier the general, who obeys the Viceroy, who is the servant of the Empress. Thus it is done."

"Would it were so in Afghanistan!" said the chief, "for there we obey only our own wills."

"And for that reason," said the native officer, twirling his mustache, "your Amir whom you do not obey must come here and take orders from our Viceroy."

THE SECOND JUNGLE BOOKS

HOW FEAR CAME

The stream is shrunk--the pool is dry,
And we be comrades, thou and I;
With fevered jowl and dusty flank
Each jostling each along the bank;
And by one drouthy fear made still,
Forgoing thought of quest or kill.
Now 'neath his dam the fawn may see,
The lean Pack-wolf as cowed as he,
And the tall buck, unflinching, note
The fangs that tore his father's throat.
The pools are shrunk--the streams are dry,
And we be playmates, thou and I,
Till yonder cloud--Good Hunting!--loose
The rain that breaks our Water Truce.

The Law of the Jungle—which is by far the oldest law in the world—has arranged for almost every kind of accident that may befall the Jungle People, till now its code is as perfect as time and custom can make it. You will remember that Mowgli spent a great part of his life in the Seeonee Wolf-Pack, learning the Law from Baloo, the Brown Bear; and it was Baloo who told him, when the boy grew impatient at the constant orders, that the Law was like the Giant Creeper, because it dropped across every one's back and no one could escape. "When thou hast lived as long as I have, Little Brother, thou wilt see how all the Jungle obeys at least one Law. And that will be no pleasant sight," said Baloo.

This talk went in at one ear and out at the other, for a boy who spends his life eating and sleeping does not worry about anything till it actually stares him in the face. But, one year, Baloo's words came true, and Mowgli saw all the Jungle working under the Law.

It began when the winter Rains failed almost entirely, and Ikki, the Porcupine, meeting Mowgli in a bamboo-thicket, told him that the wild yams were drying up. Now everybody knows that Ikki is ridiculously fastidious in his choice of food, and will eat nothing but the very best and ripest. So Mowgli laughed and said, "What is that to me?"

"Not much NOW," said Ikki, rattling his quills in a stiff, uncomfortable way, "but later we shall see. Is there any more diving into the deep rock-pool below the Bee-Rocks, Little Brother?"

"No. The foolish water is going all away, and I do not wish to break my head," said Mowgli, who, in those days, was quite sure that he knew as much as any five of the Jungle People put together.

"That is thy loss. A small crack might let in some wisdom." Ikki ducked quickly to prevent Mowgli from pulling his nose-bristles, and Mowgli told Baloo what Ikki had said. Baloo looked very grave, and mumbled half to himself: "If I were alone I would change my hunting-grounds now, before the others began to think. And yet—hunting among strangers ends in fighting; and they might hurt the Man-cub. We must wait and see how the mohwa blooms."

That spring the mohwa tree, that Baloo was so fond of, never flowered. The greeny, cream-coloured, waxy blossoms were heat-killed before they were born, and only a few bad-smelling petals came down when he stood on his hind legs and shook the tree. Then, inch by inch, the untempered heat crept into the heart of the Jungle, turning it yellow, brown, and at last black. The green growths in the sides of the ravines burned up to broken wires and curled films of dead stuff; the hidden pools sank down and caked over, keeping the last least footmark on their edges as if it had been cast in iron; the juicy-stemmed creepers fell away from the trees they clung to and died at their feet; the bamboos withered, clanking when the hot winds blew, and the moss peeled off the rocks deep in the Jungle, till they were as bare and as hot as the quivering blue boulders in the bed of the stream.

The birds and the monkey-people went north early in the year, for they knew what was coming; and the deer and the wild pig broke far away to the perished fields of the villages, dying sometimes before the eyes of men too weak to kill them. Chil, the Kite, stayed and grew fat, for there was a great deal of carrion, and evening after evening he brought the news to the beasts, too weak to force their way to fresh hunting-grounds, that the sun was killing the Jungle for three days' flight in every direction.

Mowgli, who had never known what real hunger meant, fell back on stale honey, three years old, scraped out of deserted rock-hives—honey black as a sloe, and dusty with dried sugar. He hunted, too, for deep-boring grubs under the bark of the trees, and robbed the wasps of their new broods. All the game in the jungle was no more than skin and bone, and Bagheera could kill thrice in a night, and hardly get a full meal. But the want of water was the worst, for though the Jungle People drink seldom they must drink deep.

And the heat went on and on, and sucked up all the moisture, till at last the main channel of the Waingunga was the only stream that carried a trickle of water between its dead banks; and when Hathi, the wild elephant, who lives for a hundred years and more, saw a long, lean blue ridge of rock show dry in the very centre of the stream, he knew that he was looking at the Peace Rock, and then and there he lifted up his trunk and proclaimed the Water Truce, as his father before him had proclaimed it fifty years ago. The deer, wild pig, and buffalo took up the cry hoarsely; and Chil, the Kite, flew in great circles far and wide, whistling and shrieking the warning.

By the Law of the Jungle it is death to kill at the drinking-places when once the Water Truce has been declared. The reason of this is that drinking comes before eating. Every one in the Jungle can scramble along somehow when only game is scarce; but water is water, and when there is but one source of supply, all hunting stops while the Jungle People go there for their needs. In good seasons, when water was plentiful, those who came down to drink at the Waingunga—or anywhere else, for that matter—did so at the risk of their lives, and that risk made no small part of the fascination of the night's doings. To move down so cunningly that never a leaf stirred; to wade knee-deep in the roaring shallows that drown all noise from behind; to drink, looking backward over one shoulder, every muscle ready for the first desperate bound of keen terror; to roll on the sandy margin, and return, wet-muzzled and well plumped out, to the admiring herd, was a thing that all tall-antlered young bucks took a delight in, precisely because they knew that at any moment Bagheera or Shere Khan might leap upon them and bear them down. But now all that life-and-death fun was ended, and the Jungle People came up, starved and weary, to the shrunken river,—tiger, bear, deer, buffalo, and pig, all together,—drank the fouled waters, and hung above them, too exhausted to move off.

The deer and the pig had tramped all day in search of something better than dried bark and withered leaves. The buffaloes had found no wallows to be cool in, and no green crops to steal. The snakes had left the Jungle and come down to the river in the hope of finding a stray frog. They curled round wet stones, and never offered to strike when the nose of a rooting pig dislodged them. The river-turtles had long ago been killed by Bagheera, cleverest of hunters, and the fish had buried themselves deep in the dry mud. Only the Peace Rock lay across the shallows like a long snake, and the little tired ripples hissed as they dried on its hot side.

It was here that Mowgli came nightly for the cool and the companionship. The most hungry of his enemies would hardly have cared for the boy then, His naked hide made him seem more lean and wretched than any of his fellows. His hair was bleached to tow colour by the sun; his ribs stood out like the ribs of a basket, and the lumps on his knees and elbows, where he was used to track on all fours, gave his shrunken limbs the look of knotted grass-stems. But his eye, under his matted forelock, was cool and quiet, for Bagheera was his adviser in this time of trouble, and told him to go quietly, hunt slowly, and never, on any account, to lose his temper.

"It is an evil time," said the Black Panther, one furnace-hot evening, "but it will go if we can live till the end. Is thy stomach full, Man-cub?"

"There is stuff in my stomach, but I get no good of it. Think you, Bagheera, the Rains have forgotten us and will never come again?"

"Not I! We shall see the mohwa in blossom yet, and the little fawns all fat with new grass. Come down to the Peace Rock and hear the news. On my back, Little Brother."

"This is no time to carry weight. I can still stand alone, but—indeed we be no fatted bullocks, we two."

Bagheera looked along his ragged, dusty flank and whispered. "Last night I killed a bullock under the yoke. So low was I brought that I think I should not have dared to spring if he had been loose. WOU!"

Mowgli laughed. "Yes, we be great hunters now," said he. "I am very bold—to eat grubs," and the two came down together through the crackling undergrowth to the river-bank and the lace-work of shoals that ran out from it in every direction.

"The water cannot live long," said Baloo, joining them. "Look across. Yonder are trails like the roads of Man."

On the level plain of the farther bank the stiff jungle-grass had died standing, and, dying, had mummied. The beaten tracks of the deer and the pig, all heading toward the river, had striped that colourless plain with dusty gullies driven through the ten-foot grass, and, early as it was, each long avenue was full of first-comers hastening to the water. You could hear the does and fawns coughing in the snuff-like dust.

Up-stream, at the bend of the sluggish pool round the Peace Rock, and Warden of the Water Truce, stood Hathi, the wild elephant, with his sons, gaunt and gray in the moonlight, rocking to and fro—always rocking. Below him a little were the vanguard of the deer; below these, again, the pig and the wild buffalo; and on the opposite bank, where the tall trees came down to the water's edge, was the place set apart for the Eaters of Flesh—the tiger, the wolves, the panther, the bear, and the others.

"We are under one Law, indeed," said Bagheera, wading into the water and looking across at the lines of clicking horns and starting eyes where the deer and the pig pushed each other to and fro. "Good hunting, all you of my blood," he added, lying own at full length, one flank thrust out of the shallows; and then, between his teeth, "But for that which is the Law it would be VERY good hunting."

The quick-spread ears of the deer caught the last sentence, and a frightened whisper ran along the ranks. "The Truce! Remember the Truce!"

"Peace there, peace!" gurgled Hathi, the wild elephant. "The Truce holds, Bagheera. This is no time to talk of hunting."

"Who should know better than I?" Bagheera answered, rolling his yellow eyes up-stream. "I am an eater of turtles— a fisher of frogs. Ngaayah! Would I could get good from chewing branches!"

"WE wish so, very greatly," bleated a young fawn, who had only been born that spring, and did not at all like it. Wretched as the Jungle People were, even Hathi could not help chuckling; while Mowgli, lying on his elbows in the warm water, laughed aloud, and beat up the scum with his feet.

"Well spoken, little bud-horn," Bagheera purred. "When the Truce ends that shall be remembered in thy favour," and he looked keenly through the darkness to make sure of recognising the fawn again.

Gradually the talking spread up and down the drinking-places. One could hear the scuffling, snorting pig asking for more room; the buffaloes grunting among themselves as they lurched out across the sand-bars, and the deer telling pitiful stories of their long foot-sore wanderings in quest of food. Now and again they asked some question of the Eaters of Flesh across the river, but all the news was bad, and the roaring hot wind of the Jungle came and went between the rocks and the rattling branches, and scattered twigs, and dust on the water.

"The men-folk, too, they die beside their ploughs," said a young sambhur. "I passed three between sunset and night. They lay still, and their Bullocks with them. We also shall lie still in a little."

"The river has fallen since last night," said Baloo. "O Hathi, hast thou ever seen the like of this drought?"

"It will pass, it will pass," said Hathi, squirting water along his back and sides.

"We have one here that cannot endure long," said Baloo; and he looked toward the boy he loved.

"I?" said Mowgli indignantly, sitting up in the water. "I have no long fur to cover my bones, but—but if THY hide were taken off, Baloo——"

Hathi shook all over at the idea, and Baloo said severely:

"Man-cub, that is not seemly to tell a Teacher of the Law. Never have I been seen without my hide."

"Nay, I meant no harm, Baloo; but only that thou art, as it were, like the cocoanut in the husk, and I am the same cocoanut all naked. Now that brown husk of thine——" Mowgli was sitting cross-legged, and explaining things with his forefinger in his usual way, when Bagheera put out a paddy paw and pulled him over backward into the water.

"Worse and worse," said the Black Panther, as the boy rose spluttering. "First Baloo is to be skinned, and now he is a cocoanut. Be careful that he does not do what the ripe cocoanuts do."

"And what is that?" said Mowgli, off his guard for the minute, though that is one of the oldest catches in the Jungle.

"Break thy head," said Bagheera quietly, pulling him under again.

"It is not good to make a jest of thy teacher," said the bear, when Mowgli had been ducked for the third time.

"Not good! What would ye have? That naked thing running to and fro makes a monkey-jest of those who have once been good hunters, and pulls the best of us by the whiskers for sport." This was Shere Khan, the Lame Tiger, limping down to the water. He waited a little to enjoy the sensation he made among the deer on the opposite to lap, growling: "The jungle has become a whelping-ground for naked cubs now. Look at me, Man-cub!"

Mowgli looked—stared, rather—as insolently as he knew how, and in a minute Shere Khan turned away uneasily. "Man-cub this, and Man-cub that," he rumbled, going on with his drink, "the cub is neither man nor cub, or he would have been afraid. Next season I shall have to beg his leave for a drink. Augrh!"

"That may come, too," said Bagheera, looking him steadily between the eyes. "That may come, too—Faugh, Shere Khan!—what new shame hast thou brought here?"

The Lame Tiger had dipped his chin and jowl in the water, and dark, oily streaks were floating from it down-stream.

"Man!" said Shere Khan coolly, "I killed an hour since." He went on purring and growling to himself.

The line of beasts shook and wavered to and fro, and a whisper went up that grew to a cry. "Man! Man! He has killed Man!" Then all looked towards Hathi, the wild elephant, but he seemed not to hear. Hathi never does anything till the time comes, and that is one of the reasons why he lives so long.

"At such a season as this to kill Man! Was no other game afoot?" said Bagheera scornfully, drawing himself out of the tainted water, and shaking each paw, cat-fashion, as he did so.

"I killed for choice—not for food." The horrified whisper began again, and Hathi's watchful little white eye cocked itself in Shere Khan's direction. "For choice," Shere Khan drawled. "Now come I to drink and make me clean again. Is there any to forbid?"

Bagheera's back began to curve like a bamboo in a high wind, but Hathi lifted up his trunk and spoke quietly.

"Thy kill was from choice?" he asked; and when Hathi asks a question it is best to answer.

"Even so. It was my right and my Night. Thou knowest, O Hathi." Shere Khan spoke almost courteously.

"Yes, I know," Hathi answered; and, after a little silence, "Hast thou drunk thy fill?"

"For to-night, yes."

"Go, then. The river is to drink, and not to defile. None but the Lame Tiger would so have boasted of his right at this season when—when we suffer together—Man and Jungle People alike. Clean or unclean, get to thy lair, Shere Khan!"

The last words rang out like silver trumpets, and Hathi's three sons rolled forward half a pace, though there was no need. Shere Khan slunk away, not daring to growl, for he knew—what every one else knows—that when the last comes to the last, Hathi is the Master of the Jungle.

"What is this right Shere Khan speaks of?" Mowgli whispered in Bagheera's ear. "To kill Man is always, shameful. The Law says so. And yet Hathi says——"

"Ask him. I do not know, Little Brother. Right or no right, if Hathi had not spoken I would have taught that lame butcher his lesson. To come to the Peace Rock fresh from a kill of Man—and to boast of it—is a jackal's trick. Besides, he tainted the good water."

Mowgli waited for a minute to pick up his courage, because no one cared to address Hathi directly, and then he cried: "What is Shere Khan's right, O Hathi?" Both banks echoed his words, for all the People of the Jungle are intensely curious, and they had just seen something that none except Baloo, who looked very thoughtful, seemed to understand.

"It is an old tale," said Hathi; "a tale older than the Jungle. Keep silence along the banks and I will tell that tale."

There was a minute or two of pushing a shouldering among the pigs and the buffalo, and then the leaders of the herds grunted, one after another, "We wait," and Hathi strode forward, till he was nearly knee-deep in the pool by the Peace Rock. Lean and wrinkled and yellow-tusked though he was, he looked what the Jungle knew him to be—their master.

"Ye know, children," he began, "that of all things ye most fear Man;" and there was a mutter of agreement.

"This tale touches thee, Little Brother," said Bagheera to Mowgli.

"I? I am of the Pack—a hunter of the Free People," Mowgli answered. "What have I to do with Man?"

"And ye do not know why ye fear Man?" Hathi went on. "This is the reason. In the beginning of the Jungle, and none know when that was, we of the Jungle walked together, having no fear of one another. In those days there was no drought, and leaves and flowers and fruit grew on the same tree, and we ate nothing at all except leaves and flowers and grass and fruit and bark."

"I am glad I was not born in those days," said Bagheera. "Bark is only good to sharpen claws."

"And the Lord of the Jungle was Tha, the First of the

Elephants. He drew the Jungle out of deep waters with his trunk; and where he made furrows in the ground with his tusks, there the rivers ran; and where he struck with his foot, there rose ponds of good water; and when he blew through his trunk,—thus,—the trees fell. That was the manner in which the Jungle was made by Tha; and so the tale was told to me."

"It has not lost fat in the telling," Bagheera whispered, and Mowgli laughed behind his hand.

"In those days there was no corn or melons or pepper or sugar-cane, nor were there any little huts such as ye have all seen; and the Jungle People knew nothing of Man, but lived in the Jungle together, making one people. But presently they began to dispute over their food, though there was grazing enough for all. They were lazy. Each wished to eat where he lay, as sometimes we can do now when the spring rains are good. Tha, the First of the Elephants, was busy making new jungles and leading the rivers in their beds. He could not walk in all places; therefore he made the First of the Tigers the master and the judge of the Jungle, to whom the Jungle People should bring their disputes. In those days the First of the Tigers ate fruit and grass with the others. He was as large as I am, and he was very beautiful, in colour all over like the blossom of the yellow creeper. There was never stripe nor bar upon his hide in those good days when this the Jungle was new. All the Jungle People came before him without fear, and his word was the Law of all the Jungle. We were then, remember ye, one people.

"Yet upon a night there was a dispute between two bucks—a grazing-quarrel such as ye now settle with the horns and the fore-feet—and it is said that as the two spoke together before the First of the First of the Tigers lying among the flowers, a buck pushed him with his horns, and the First of the Tigers forgot that he was the master and judge of the Jungle, and, leaping upon that buck, broke his neck.

"Till that night never one of us had died, and the First of the Tigers, seeing what he had done, and being made foolish by the scent of the blood, ran away into the marshes of the North, and we of the Jungle, left without a judge, fell to fighting among ourselves; and Tha heard the noise of it and came back. Then some of us said this and some of us said that, but he saw the dead buck among the flowers, and asked who had killed, and we of the Jungle would not tell because the smell of the blood made us foolish. We ran to and fro in circles, capering and crying out and shaking our heads. Then Tha gave an order to the trees that hang low, and to the trailing creepers of the Jungle, that they should mark the killer of the buck so that he should know him again, and he said, 'Who will now be master of the Jungle People?' Then up leaped the Gray Ape who lives in the branches, and said, 'I will now be master of the Jungle.'"

At this Tha laughed, and said, "So be it," and went away very angry.

"Children, ye know the Gray Ape. He was then as he is now. At the first he made a wise face for himself, but in a little while he began to scratch and to leap up and down, and when Tha came back he found the Gray Ape hanging, head down, from a bough, mocking those who stood below; and they mocked him again. And so there was no Law in the Jungle—only foolish talk and senseless words.

"Then Tha called us all together and said: 'The first of your masters has brought Death into the Jungle, and the second Shame. Now it is time there was a Law, and a Law that ye must not break. Now ye shall know Fear, and when ye have found him ye shall know that he is your master, and the rest shall follow.' Then we of the jungle said, 'What is Fear?' And Tha said, 'Seek till ye find.' So we went up and down the Jungle seeking for Fear, and presently the buffaloes——"

"Ugh!" said Mysa, the leader of the buffaloes, from their sand-bank.

"Yes, Mysa, it was the buffaloes. They came back with the news that in a cave in the Jungle sat Fear, and that he had no hair, and went upon his hind legs. Then we of the Jungle followed the herd till we came to that cave, and Fear stood at the mouth of it, and he was, as the buffaloes had said, hairless, and he walked upon his hinder legs. When he saw us he cried out, and his voice filled us with the fear that we have now of that voice when we hear it, and we ran away, tramping upon and tearing each other because we were afraid. That night, so it was told to me, we of the Jungle did not lie down together as used to be our custom, but each tribe drew off by itself— the pig with the pig, the deer with the deer; horn to horn, hoof to hoof,—like keeping to like, and so lay shaking in the Jungle.

"Only the First of the Tigers was not with us, for he was still hidden in the marshes of the North, and when word was brought to him of the Thing we had seen in the cave, he said. 'I will go to this Thing and break his neck.' So he ran all the night till he came to the cave; but the trees and the creepers on his path, remembering the order that Tha had given, let down their branches and marked him as he ran, drawing their fingers across his back, his flank, his forehead, and his jowl. Wherever they touched him there was a mark and a stripe upon his yellow hide. AND THOSE STRIPES DO THIS CHILDREN WEAR TO THIS DAY! When he came to the cave, Fear, the Hairless One, put out his hand and called him

'The Striped One that comes by night,' and the First of the Tigers was afraid of the Hairless One, and ran back to the swamps howling."

Mowgli chuckled quietly here, his chin in the water.

"So loud did he howl that Tha heard him and said, 'What is the sorrow?' And the First of the Tigers, lifting up his muzzle to the new-made sky, which is now so old, said: 'Give me back my power, O Tha. I am made ashamed before all the Jungle, and I have run away from a Hairless One, and he has called me a shameful name.' 'And why?' said Tha. 'Because I am smeared with the mud of the marshes,' said the First of the Tigers. 'Swim, then, and roll on the wet grass, and if it be mud it will wash away,' said Tha; and the First of the Tigers swam, and rolled and rolled upon the grass, till the Jungle ran round and round before his eyes, but not one little bar upon all his hide was changed, and Tha, watching him, laughed. Then the First of the Tigers said: 'What have I done that this comes to me?' Tha said, 'Thou hast killed the buck, and thou hast let Death loose in the Jungle, and with Death has come Fear, so that the people of the Jungle are afraid one of the other, as thou art afraid of the Hairless One.' The First of the Tigers said, 'They will never fear me, for I knew them since the beginning.' Tha said, 'Go and see.' And the First of the Tigers ran to and fro, calling aloud to the deer and the pig and the sambhur and the porcupine and all the Jungle Peoples, and they all ran away from him who had been their judge, because they were afraid.

"Then the First of the Tigers came back, and his pride was broken in him, and, beating his head upon the ground, he tore up the earth with all his feet and said: 'Remember that I was once the Master of the Jungle. Do not forget me, O Tha! Let my children remember that I was once without shame or fear!' And Tha said: 'This much I will do, because thou and I together saw the Jungle made. For one night in each year it shall be as it was before the buck was killed—for thee and for thy children. In that one night, if ye meet the Hairless One—and his name is Man—ye shall not be afraid of him, but he shall be afraid of you, as though ye were judges of the Jungle and masters of all things. Show him mercy in that night of his fear, for thou hast known what Fear is.'

"Then the First of the Tigers answered, 'I am content'; but when next he drank he saw the black stripes upon his flank and his side, and he remembered the name that the Hairless One had given him, and he was angry. For a year he lived in the marshes waiting till Tha should keep his promise. And upon a night when the jackal of the Moon [the Evening Star] stood clear of the Jungle, he felt that his Night was upon him, and he went to that cave to meet the Hairless One. Then it happened as Tha promised, for the Hairless One fell down before him and lay along the ground, and the First of the Tigers struck him and broke his back, for he thought that there was but one such Thing in the Jungle, and that he had killed Fear. Then, nosing above the kill, he heard Tha coming down from the woods of the North, and presently the voice of the First of the Elephants, which is the voice that we hear now——"

The thunder was rolling up and down the dry, scarred hills, but it brought no rain—only heat—lightning that flickered along the ridges—and Hathi went on: "THAT was the voice he heard, and it said: 'Is this thy mercy?' The First of the Tigers licked his lips and said: 'What matter? I have killed Fear.' And Tha said: 'O blind and foolish! Thou hast untied the feet of Death, and he will follow thy trail till thou diest. Thou hast taught Man to kill!'

"The First of the Tigers, standing stiffly to his kill, said.

'He is as the buck was. There is no Fear. Now I will judge the Jungle Peoples once more.'

"And Tha said: 'Never again shall the Jungle Peoples come to thee. They shall never cross thy trail, nor sleep near thee, nor follow after thee, nor browse by thy lair. Only Fear shall follow thee, and with a blow that thou canst not see he shall bid thee wait his pleasure. He shall make the ground to open under thy feet, and the creeper to twist about thy neck, and the tree-trunks to grow together about thee higher than thou canst leap, and at the last he shall take thy hide to wrap his cubs when they are cold. Thou hast shown him no mercy, and none will he show thee.'

"The First of the Tigers was very bold, for his Night was still on him, and he said: 'The Promise of Tha is the Promise of Tha. He will not take away my Night?' And Tha said: 'The one Night is thine, as I have said, but there is a price to pay. Thou hast taught Man to kill, and he is no slow learner.'

"The First of the Tigers said: 'He is here under my foot, and his back is broken. Let the Jungle know I have killed Fear.'

"Then Tha laughed, and said: 'Thou hast killed one of many, but thou thyself shalt tell the Jungle—for thy Night is ended.'

"So the day came; and from the mouth of the cave went out another Hairless One, and he saw the kill in the path, and the First of the Tigers above it, and he took a pointed stick——"

"They throw a thing that cuts now," said Ikki, rustling down the bank; for Ikki was considered uncommonly good eating by the Gonds—they called him Ho-Igoo—and he knew something of the wicked little Gondee axe that whirls across a clearing like a dragon-fly.

"It was a pointed stick, such as they put in the foot of a pit-trap," said Hathi, "and throwing it, he struck the First of the Tigers deep in the flank. Thus it happened as Tha said, for the First of the Tigers ran howling up and down the Jungle till he tore out the stick, and all the Jungle knew that the Hairless One could strike from far off, and they feared more than before. So it came about that the First of the Tigers taught the Hairless One to kill—and ye know what harm that has since done to all our peoples—through the noose, and the pitfall, and the hidden trap, and the flying stick and the stinging fly that comes out of white smoke [Hathi meant the rifle], and the Red Flower that drives us into the open. Yet for one night in the year the Hairless One fears the Tiger, as Tha promised, and never has the Tiger given him cause to be less afraid. Where he finds him, there he kills him, remembering how the First of the Tigers was made ashamed. For the rest, Fear walks up and down the Jungle by day and by night."

"Ahi! Aoo!" said the deer, thinking of what it all meant to them.

"And only when there is one great Fear over all, as there is now, can we of the Jungle lay aside our little fears, and meet together in one place as we do now."

"For one night only does Man fear the Tiger?" said Mowgli.

"For one night only," said Hathi.

"But I—but we—but all the Jungle knows that Shere Khan kills Man twice and thrice in a moon."

"Even so. THEN he springs from behind and turns his head aside as he strikes, for he is full of fear. If Man looked at him he would run. But on his one Night he goes openly down to the village. He walks between the houses and thrusts his head into the doorway, and the men fall on their faces, and there he does his kill. One kill in that Night."

"Oh!" said Mowgli to himself, rolling over in the water. "NOW I see why it was Shere Khan bade me look at him! He got no good of it, for he could not hold his eyes steady, and—and I certainly did not fall down at his feet. But then I am not a man, being of the Free People."

"Umm!" said Bagheera deep in his furry throat. "Does the Tiger know his Night?"

"Never till the Jackal of the Moon stands clear of the evening mist. Sometimes it falls in the dry summer and sometimes in the wet rains—this one Night of the Tiger. But for the First of the Tigers, this would never have been, nor would any of us have known fear."

The deer grunted sorrowfully and Bagheera's lips curled in a wicked smile. "Do men know this—tale?" said he.

"None know it except the tigers, and we, the elephants—the children of Tha. Now ye by the pools have heard it, and I have spoken."

Hathi dipped his trunk into the water as a sign that he did not wish to talk.

"But—but—but," said Mowgli, turning to Baloo, "why did not the First of the Tigers continue to eat grass and leaves and trees? He did but break the buck's neck. He did not EAT. What led him to the hot meat?"

"The trees and the creepers marked him, Little Brother, and made him the striped thing that we see. Never again would he eat their fruit; but from that day he revenged himself upon the deer, and the others, the Eaters of Grass," said Baloo.

"Then THOU knowest the tale. Heh? Why have I never heard?"

"Because the Jungle is full of such tales. If I made a

beginning there would never be an end to them. Let go my ear, Little Brother."

THE LAW OF THE JUNGLE

Just to give you an idea of the immense variety of the Jungle Law, I have translated into verse (Baloo always recited them in a sort of sing-song) a few of the laws that apply to the wolves. There are, of course, hundreds and hundreds more, but these will do for specimens of the simpler rulings.

Now this is the Law of the Jungle--as old and as true as the
    sky;
And the Wolf that shall keep it may prosper, but the Wolf
    that shall break it must die.
As the creeper that girdles the tree-trunk the Law runneth
forward and back--
For the strength of the Pack is the Wolf, and the strength
    of the Wolf is the Pack.
Wash daily from nose-tip to tail-tip; drink deeply, but never
    too deep;
And remember the night is for hunting, and forget not the
    day is for sleep.
The jackal may follow the Tiger, but, Cub, when thy
    whiskers are grown,
Remember the Wolf is a hunter--go forth and get food of
    thine own.
Keep peace with the Lords of the Jungle--the Tiger, the
    Panther, the Bear;
And trouble not Hathi the Silent, and mock not the Boar
    in his lair.
When Pack meets with Pack in the Jungle, and neither will
    go from the trail,
Lie down till the leaders have spoken--it may be fair words
    shall prevail.

When ye fight with a Wolf of the Pack, ye must fight him
alone and afar,
Lest others take part in the quarrel, and the Pack be
diminished by war.
The Lair of the Wolf is his refuge, and where he has
made him his home,
Not even the Head Wolf may enter, not even the Council
may come.
The Lair of the Wolf is his refuge, but where he has
digged it too plain,
The Council shall send him a message, and so he shall
change it again.
If ye kill before midnight, be silent, and wake not the
woods with your bay,
Lest ye frighten the deer from the crops, and the brothers
go empty away.
Ye may kill for yourselves, and your mates, and your cubs
as they need, and ye can;
But kill not for pleasure of killing, and SEVEN TIMES
NEVER KILL MAN.
If ye plunder his Kill from a weaker, devour not all in
thy pride;
Pack-Right is the right of the meanest; so leave him the
head and the hide.
The Kill of the Pack is the meat of the Pack. Ye must
eat where it lies;
And no one may carry away of that meat to his lair, or he
dies.
The Kill of the Wolf is the meat of the Wolf. He may do
what he will,
But, till he has given permission, the Pack may not eat of
that Kill.

Cub-Right is the right of the Yearling. From all of his
  Pack he may claim
Full-gorge when the killer has eaten; and none mayrefuse
  him the same.
Lair-Right is the right of the Mother. From all of her year
  she may claim
One haunch of each kill for her litter, and none may deny
  her the same.
Cave-Right is the right of the Father--to hunt by himself
  for his own.
He is freed of all calls to the Pack; he is judged by the
  Council alone.
Because of his age and his cunning, because of his gripe
  and his paw,
In all that the Law leaveth open, the word of the Head
  Wolf is Law.
Now these are the Laws of the Jungle, and many and
  mighty are they;
But the head and the hoof of the Law and the haunch and
  the hump is--Obey!

THE MIRACLE OF PURUN BHAGAT

The night we felt the earth would move
  We stole and plucked him by the hand,
Because we loved him with the love
  That knows but cannot understand.

And when the roaring hillside broke,
  And all our world fell down in rain,
We saved him, we the Little Folk;
  But lo! he does not come again!

Mourn now, we saved him for the sake
Of such poor love as wild ones may.
Mourn ye! Our brother will not wake,
And his own kind drive us away!

Dirge of the Langurs.

Now this is the Law of the Jungle--as old and as true as the sky; And the Wolf that shall keep it may prosper, but the Wolf that shall break it must die. As the creeper that girdles the tree-trunk the Law runneth forward and back-- For the strength of the Pack is the Wolf, and the strength of the Wolf is the Pack.

Wash daily from nose-tip to tail-tip; drink deeply, but never too deep; And remember the night is for hunting, and forget not the day is for sleep. The jackal may follow the Tiger, but, Cub, when thy whiskers are grown, Remember the Wolf is a hunter--go forth and get food of thine own. Keep peace with the Lords of the Jungle--the Tiger, the Panther, the Bear; And trouble not Hathi the Silent, and mock not the Boar in his lair. When Pack meets with Pack in the Jungle, and neither will go from the trail, Lie down till the leaders have spoken-- it may be fair words shall prevail. When ye fight with a Wolf of the Pack, ye must fight him alone and afar, Lest others take part in the quarrel, and the Pack be diminished by war. The Lair of the Wolf is his refuge, and where he has made him his home, Not even the Head Wolf may enter, not even the Council may come. The Lair of the Wolf is his refuge, but where he has digged it too plain, The Council shall send him a message, and so he shall change it again. If ye kill before midnight, be silent, and wake not the woods with your bay, Lest ye frighten the deer from the crops, and the brothers go empty away. Ye may kill for yourselves, and your mates, and your cubs as they need, and ye can; But kill not for pleasure of killing, and SEVEN TIMES NEVER KILL MAN. If ye plunder his Kill from a weaker, devour not all in thy pride; Pack-Right is the right of the meanest; so leave him the head and the hide.

The Kill of the Pack is the meat of the Pack. Ye must eat where it lies; And no one may carry away of that meat to his lair, or he dies. The Kill of the Wolf is the meat of the Wolf. He may do what he will, But, till he has given permission, the Pack may not eat of that Kill. Cub-Right is the right of the Yearling. From all of his Pack he may claim Full-gorge when the killer has eaten; and none may refuse him the same. Lair-Right is the right of the Mother. From all of her year she may claim One haunch of each kill for her litter, and none may deny her the same. Cave-Right is the right of the Father--to hunt by himself for his own.

He is freed of all calls to the Pack; he is judged by the Council alone. Because of his age and his cunning, because of his gripe and his paw, In all that the Law leaveth open, the word of the Head Wolf is Law. Now these are the Laws of the Jungle, and many and mighty are they; But the head and the hoof of the Law and the haunch and the hump is--Obey!

THE MIRACLE OF PURUN BHAGAT

The night we felt the earth would move
We stole and plucked him by the hand,
Because we loved him with the love
That knows but cannot understand.
And when the roaring hillside broke,
And all our world fell down in rain,
We saved him, we the Little Folk;
But lo! he does not come again!
Mourn now, we saved him for the sake
Of such poor love as wild ones may.
Mourn ye! Our brother will not wake,
And his own kind drive us away!

Dirge of the Langurs.

There was once a man in India who was Prime Minister of one of the semi-independent native States in the north-western part of the country. He was a Brahmin, so high-caste that caste ceased to have any particular meaning for him; and his father had been an important official in the gay-coloured tag-rag and bobtail of an old-fashioned Hindu Court. But as Purun Dass grew up he felt that the old order of things was changing, and that if any one wished to get on in the world he must stand well with the English, and imitate all that the English believed to be good. At the same time a native official must keep his own master's favour. This was a difficult game, but the quiet, close-mouthed young Brahmin, helped by a good English education at a Bombay University, played it coolly, and rose, step by step, to be Prime Minister of the kingdom. That is to say, he held more real power than his master the Maharajah.

When the old king—who was suspicious of the English, their railways and telegraphs—died, Purun Dass stood high with his young successor, who had been tutored by an Englishman; and between them, though he always took care that his master should have the credit, they established schools for little girls, made roads, and started State dispensaries and shows of agricultural implements, and published a yearly blue-book on the "Moral and Material Progress of the State," and the Foreign Office and the Government of India were delighted. Very few native States take up English progress altogether, for they will not believe, as Purun Dass showed he did, that what was good for the Englishman must be twice as good for the Asiatic. The Prime Minister became the honoured friend of Viceroys, and Governors, and Lieutenant-Governors, and medical missionaries, and common missionaries, and hard-riding English officers who came to shoot in the State preserves, as well as of whole hosts of tourists who travelled up and down India in the cold weather, showing how things ought to be managed. In his spare time he would endow scholarships for the study of medicine and manufactures on strictly English lines, and write letters to the "Pioneer", the greatest Indian daily paper, explaining his master's aims and objects.

At last he went to England on a visit, and had to pay enormous sums to the priests when he came back; for even so high-caste a Brahmin as Purun Dass lost caste by crossing the black sea. In London he met and talked with every one worth knowing—men whose names go all over the world— and saw a great deal more than he said. He was given honorary degrees by learned universities, and he made speeches and talked of Hindu social reform to English ladies in evening dress, till all London cried, "This is the most fascinating man we have ever met at dinner since cloths were first laid."

When he returned to India there was a blaze of glory, for the Viceroy himself made a special visit to confer upon the Maharajah the Grand Cross of the Star of India—all diamonds and ribbons and enamel; and at the same ceremony, while the cannon boomed, Purun Dass was made a Knight Commander of the Order of the Indian Empire; so that his name stood Sir Purun Dass, K.C.I.E.

That evening, at dinner in the big Viceregal tent, he stood up with the badge and the collar of the Order on his breast, and replying to the toast of his master's health, made a speech few Englishmen could have bettered.

Next month, when the city had returned to its sun-baked quiet, he did a thing no Englishman would have dreamed of doing; for, so far as the world's affairs went, he died. The jewelled order of his knighthood went back to the Indian Government, and a new Prime Minister was appointed to the charge of affairs, and a great game of General Post began in all the subordinate appointments. The priests knew what had happened, and the people guessed; but India is the one place in the world where a man can do as he pleases and nobody asks why; and the fact that Dewan Sir Purun Dass, K.C.I.E., had resigned position, palace, and power, and taken up the begging-bowl and ochre-coloured dress of a Sunnyasi, or holy man, was considered nothing extraordinary. He had been, as the Old Law recommends, twenty years a youth, twenty years a fighter,—though he had never carried a weapon in his life,—and twenty years head of a household. He had used his wealth and his power for what he knew both to be worth; he had taken honour when it came his way; he had seen men and cities far and near, and men and cities had stood up and honoured him. Now he would let those things go, as a man drops the cloak he no longer needs.

Behind him, as he walked through the city gates, an antelope skin and brass-handled crutch under his arm, and a begging-bowl of polished brown coco-de-mer in his hand, barefoot, alone, with eyes cast on the ground—behind him they were firing salutes from the bastions in honour of his happy successor. Purun Dass nodded. All that life was ended; and he bore it no more ill-will or good-will than a man bears to a colourless dream of the night. He was a Sunnyasi—a houseless, wandering mendicant, depending on his neighbours for his daily bread; and so long as there is a morsel to divide in India, neither priest nor beggar starves. He had never in his life tasted meat, and very seldom eaten even fish. A five-pound note would have covered his personal expenses for food through any one of the many years in which he had been absolute master of millions of money. Even when he was being lionised in London he had held before him his dream of peace and quiet—the long, white, dusty Indian road, printed all over with bare feet, the incessant, slow-moving traffic, and the sharp-smelling wood smoke curling up under the fig-trees in the twilight, where the wayfarers sit at their evening meal.

When the time came to make that dream true the Prime Minister took the proper steps, and in three days you might more easily have found a bubble in the trough of the long Atlantic seas, than Purun Dass among the roving, gathering, separating millions of India.

At night his antelope skin was spread where the darkness overtook him—sometimes in a Sunnyasi monastery by the roadside; sometimes by a mud-pillar shrine of Kala Pir, where the Jogis, who are another misty division of holy men, would receive him as they do those who know what castes and divisions are worth; sometimes on the outskirts of a little Hindu village, where the children would steal up with the food their parents had prepared; and sometimes on the pitch of the bare grazing-grounds, where the flame of his stick fire waked the drowsy camels. It was all one to Purun Dass—or Purun Bhagat, as he called himself now. Earth, people, and food were all one. But unconsciously his feet drew him away northward and eastward; from the south to Rohtak; from Rohtak to Kurnool; from Kurnool to ruined Samanah, and then up-stream along the dried bed of the Gugger river that fills only when the rain falls in the hills, till one day he saw the far line of the great Himalayas.

Then Purun Bhagat smiled, for he remembered that his mother was of Rajput Brahmin birth, from Kulu way—a Hill-woman, always home-sick for the snows—and that the least touch of Hill blood draws a man in the end back to where he belongs.

"Yonder," said Purun Bhagat, breasting the lower slopes of the Sewaliks, where the cacti stand up like seven-branched candlesticks-"yonder I shall sit down and get knowledge"; and the cool wind of the Himalayas whistled about his ears as he trod the road that led to Simla.

The last time he had come that way it had been in state, with a clattering cavalry escort, to visit the gentlest and most affable of Viceroys; and the two had talked for an hour together about mutual friends in London, and what the Indian common folk really thought of things. This time Purun Bhagat paid no calls, but leaned on the rail of the Mall, watching that glorious view of the Plains spread out forty miles below, till a native Mohammedan policeman told him he was obstructing traffic; and Purun Bhagat salaamed reverently to the Law, because he knew the value of it, and was seeking for a Law of his own. Then he moved on, and slept that night in an empty hut at Chota Simla, which looks like the very last end of the earth, but it was only the beginning of his journey. He followed the Himalaya-Thibet road, the little ten-foot track that is blasted out of solid rock, or strutted out on timbers over gulfs a thousand feet deep; that dips into warm, wet, shut-in valleys, and climbs out across bare, grassy hill-shoulders where the sun strikes like a burning-glass; or turns through dripping, dark forests where the tree-ferns dress the trunks from head to heel, and the pheasant calls to his mate. And he met Thibetan herdsmen with their dogs and flocks of sheep, each sheep with a little bag of borax on his back, and wandering wood-cutters, and cloaked and blanketed Lamas from Thibet, coming into India on pilgrimage, and envoys of little solitary Hill-states, posting furiously on ring-streaked and piebald ponies, or the cavalcade of a Rajah paying a visit; or else for a long, clear day he would see nothing more than a black bear grunting and rooting below in the valley. When he first started, the roar of the world he had left still rang in his ears, as the roar of a tunnel rings long after the train has passed through; but when he had put the Mutteeanee Pass behind him that was all done, and Purun Bhagat was alone with himself, walking, wondering, and thinking, his eyes on the ground, and his thoughts with the clouds.

One evening he crossed the highest pass he had met till then—it had been a two-day's climb—and came out on a line of snow-peaks that banded all the horizon—mountains from fifteen to twenty thousand feet high, looking almost near enough to hit with a stone, though they were fifty or sixty miles away. The pass was crowned with dense, dark forest—deodar, walnut, wild cherry, wild olive, and wild pear, but mostly deodar, which is the Himalayan cedar; and under the shadow of the deodars stood a deserted shrine to Kali—who is Durga, who is Sitala, who is sometimes worshipped against the smallpox.

Purun Dass swept the stone floor clean, smiled at the grinning statue, made himself a little mud fireplace at the back of the shrine, spread his antelope skin on a bed of fresh pine-needles, tucked his bairagi—his brass-handled crutch—under his armpit, and sat down to rest.

Immediately below him the hillside fell away, clean and cleared for fifteen hundred feet, where a little village of stone-walled houses, with roofs of beaten earth, clung to the steep tilt. All round it the tiny terraced fields lay out like aprons of patchwork on the knees of the mountain, and cows no bigger than beetles grazed between the smooth stone circles of the threshing-floors. Looking across the valley, the eye was deceived by the size of things, and could not at first realise that what seemed to be low scrub, on the opposite mountain-flank, was in truth a forest of hundred-foot pines. Purun Bhagat saw an eagle swoop across the gigantic hollow, but the great bird dwindled to a dot ere it was half-way over. A few bands of scattered clouds strung up and down the valley, catching on a shoulder of the hills, or rising up and dying out when they were level with the head of the pass. And "Here shall I find peace," said Purun Bhagat.

Now, a Hill-man makes nothing of a few hundred feet up or down, and as soon as the villagers saw the smoke in the deserted shrine, the village priest climbed up the terraced hillside to welcome the stranger.

When he met Purun Bhagat's eyes—the eyes of a man used to control thousands—he bowed to the earth, took the begging-bowl without a word, and returned to the village, saying, "We have at last a holy man. Never have I seen such a man. He is of the Plains—but pale-coloured—a Brahmin of the Brahmins." Then all the housewives of the village said, "Think you he will stay with us?" and each did her best to cook the most savoury meal for the Bhagat. Hill-food is very simple, but with buckwheat and Indian corn, and rice and red pepper, and little fish out of the stream in the valley, and honey from the flue-like hives built in the stone walls, and dried apricots, and turmeric, and wild ginger, and bannocks of flour, a devout woman can make good things, and it was a full bowl that the priest carried to the Bhagat. Was he going to stay? asked the priest. Would he need a chela—a disciple—to beg for him? Had he a blanket against the cold weather? Was the food good?

Purun Bhagat ate, and thanked the giver. It was in his mind to stay. That was sufficient, said the priest. Let the begging-bowl be placed outside the shrine, in the hollow made by those two twisted roots, and daily should the Bhagat be fed; for the village felt honoured that such a man—he looked timidly into the Bhagat's face—should tarry among them.

That day saw the end of Purun Bhagat's wanderings. He had come to the place appointed for him—the silence and the space. After this, time stopped, and he, sitting at the mouth of the shrine, could not tell whether he were alive or dead; a man with control of his limbs, or a part of the hills, and the clouds, and the shifting rain and sunlight. He would repeat a

Name softly to himself a hundred hundred times, till, at each repetition, he seemed to move more and more out of his body, sweeping up to the doors of some tremendous discovery; but, just as the door was opening, his body would drag him back, and, with grief, he felt he was locked up again in the flesh and bones of Purun Bhagat.

Every morning the filled begging-bowl was laid silently in the crutch of the roots outside the shrine. Sometimes the priest brought it; sometimes a Ladakhi trader, lodging in the village, and anxious to get merit, trudged up the path; but, more often, it was the woman who had cooked the meal overnight; and she would murmur, hardly above her breath. "Speak for me before the gods, Bhagat. Speak for such a one, the wife of so-and-so!" Now and then some bold child would be allowed the honour, and Purun Bhagat would hear him drop the bowl and run as fast as his little legs could carry him, but the Bhagat never came down to the village. It was laid out like a map at his feet. He could see the evening gatherings, held on the circle of the threshing-floors, because that was the only level ground; could see the wonderful unnamed green of the young rice, the indigo blues of the Indian corn, the dock-like patches of buckwheat, and, in its season, the red bloom of the amaranth, whose tiny seeds, being neither grain nor pulse, make a food that can be lawfully eaten by Hindus in time of fasts.

When the year turned, the roofs of the huts were all little squares of purest gold, for it was on the roofs that they laid out their cobs of the corn to dry. Hiving and harvest, rice-sowing and husking, passed before his eyes, all embroidered down there on the many-sided plots of fields, and he thought of them all, and wondered what they all led to at the long last.

Even in populated India a man cannot a day sit still before the wild things run over him as though he were a rock; and in that wilderness very soon the wild things, who knew Kali's Shrine well, came back to look at the intruder. The langurs, the big gray-whiskered monkeys of the Himalayas, were, naturally, the first, for they are alive with curiosity; and when they had upset the begging-bowl, and rolled it round the floor, and tried their teeth on the brass-handled crutch, and made faces at the antelope skin, they decided that the human being who sat so still was harmless. At evening, they would leap down from the pines, and beg with their hands for things to eat, and then swing off in graceful curves. They liked the warmth of the fire, too, and huddled round it till Purun Bhagat had to push them aside to throw on more fuel; and in the morning, as often as not, he would find a furry ape sharing his blanket. All day long, one or other of the tribe would sit by his side, staring out at the snows, crooning and looking unspeakably wise and sorrowful.

After the monkeys came the barasingh, that big deer which is like our red deer, but stronger. He wished to rub off the velvet of his horns against the cold stones of Kali's statue, and stamped his feet when he saw the man at the shrine. But Purun Bhagat never moved, and, little by little, the royal stag edged up and nuzzled his shoulder. Purun Bhagat slid one cool hand along the hot antlers, and the touch soothed the fretted beast, who bowed his head, and Purun Bhagat very softly rubbed and ravelled off the velvet. Afterward, the barasingh brought his doe and fawn—gentle things that mumbled on the holy man's blanket—or would come alone at night, his eyes green in the fire-flicker, to take his share of fresh walnuts. At last, the musk-deer, the shyest and almost the smallest of the deerlets, came, too, her big rabbity ears erect; even brindled, silent mushick-nabha must needs find out what the light in the shrine meant, and drop out her mooselike nose into Purun Bhagat's lap, coming and going with the shadows of the fire. Purun Bhagat called them all "my brothers," and his low call of "Bhai! Bhai!" would draw them from the forest at noon if they were within ear shot. The Himalayan black bear, moody and suspicious—Sona, who has the V-shaped white mark under his chin—passed that way more than once; and since the Bhagat showed no fear, Sona showed no anger, but watched him, and came closer, and begged a share of the caresses, and a dole of bread or wild berries. Often, in the still dawns, when the Bhagat would climb to the very crest of the pass to watch the red day walking along the peaks of the snows, he would find Sona shuffling and grunting at his heels, thrusting, a curious fore-paw under fallen trunks, and bringing it away with a WHOOF of impatience; or his early steps would wake Sona where he lay curled up, and the great brute, rising erect, would think to fight, till he heard the Bhagat's voice and knew his best friend.

Nearly all hermits and holy men who live apart from the big cities have the reputation of being able to work miracles with the wild things, but all the miracle lies in keeping still, in never making a hasty movement, and, for a long time, at least, in never looking directly at a visitor. The villagers saw the outline of the barasingh stalking like a shadow through the dark forest behind the shrine; saw the minaul, the Himalayan pheasant, blazing in her best colours before Kali's statue; and the langurs on their haunches, inside, playing with the walnut shells. Some of the children, too, had heard Sona singing to himself, bear-fashion, behind the fallen rocks, and the Bhagat's reputation as miracle-worker stood firm.

Yet nothing was farther from his mind than miracles. He believed that all things were one big Miracle, and when a man knows that much he knows something to go upon. He knew for a certainty that there was nothing great and nothing little in this world: and day and night he strove to think out his way into the heart of things, back to the place whence his soul had come.

So thinking, his untrimmed hair fell down about his shoulders, the stone slab at the side of the antelope skin was dented into a little hole by the foot of his brass-handled crutch, and the place between the tree-trunks, where the begging-bowl rested day after day, sunk and wore into a hollow almost as smooth as the brown shell itself; and each beast knew his exact place at the fire. The fields changed their colours with the seasons; the threshing-floors filled and emptied, and filled again and again; and again and again, when winter came, the langurs frisked among the branches feathered with light snow, till the mother-monkeys brought their sad-eyed little babies up from the warmer valleys with the spring. There were few changes in the village. The priest was older, and many of the little children who used to come with the begging-dish sent their own children now; and when you asked of the villagers how long their holy man had lived in Kali's Shrine at the head of the pass, they answered, "Always."

Then came such summer rains as had not been known in the Hills for many seasons. Through three good months the valley was wrapped in cloud and soaking mist—steady, unrelenting downfall, breaking off into thunder-shower after thunder-shower. Kali's Shrine stood above the clouds, for the most part, and there was a whole month in which the Bhagat never caught a glimpse of his village. It was packed away under a white floor of cloud that swayed and shifted and rolled on itself and bulged upward, but never broke from its piers—the streaming flanks of the valley.

All that time he heard nothing but the sound of a million little waters, overhead from the trees, and underfoot along the ground, soaking through the pine-needles, dripping from the tongues of draggled fern, and spouting in newly-torn muddy channels down the slopes. Then the sun came out, and drew forth the good incense of the deodars and the rhododendrons, and that far-off, clean smell which the Hill people call "the smell of the snows." The hot sunshine lasted for a week, and then the rains gathered together for their last downpour, and the water fell in sheets that flayed off the skin of the ground and leaped back in mud. Purun Bhagat heaped his fire high that night, for he was sure his brothers would need warmth; but never a beast came to the shrine, though he called and called till he dropped asleep, wondering what had happened in the woods.

It was in the black heart of the night, the rain drumming like a thousand drums, that he was roused by a plucking at his blanket, and, stretching out, felt the little hand of a langur. "It is better here than in the trees," he said sleepily, loosening a fold of blanket; "take it and be warm." The monkey caught his hand and pulled hard. "Is it food, then?" said Purun Bhagat. "Wait awhile, and I will prepare some." As he kneeled to throw fuel on the fire the langur ran to the door of the shrine, crooned and ran back again, plucking at the man's knee.

"What is it? What is thy trouble, Brother?" said Purun Bhagat, for the langur's eyes were full of things that he could not tell. "Unless one of thy caste be in a trap—and none set traps here—I will not go into that weather. Look, Brother, even the barasingh comes for shelter!"

The deer's antlers clashed as he strode into the shrine, clashed against the grinning statue of Kali. He lowered them in Purun Bhagat's direction and stamped uneasily, hissing through his half-shut nostrils.

"Hai! Hai! Hai!" said the Bhagat, snapping his fingers, "Is THIS payment for a night's lodging?" But the deer pushed him toward the door, and as he did so Purun Bhagat heard the sound of something opening with a sigh, and saw two slabs of the floor draw away from each other, while the sticky earth below smacked its lips.

"Now I see," said Purun Bhagat. "No blame to my brothers that they did not sit by the fire to-night. The mountain is falling. And yet—why should I go?" His eye fell on the empty begging-bowl, and his face changed. "They have given me good food daily since—since I came, and, if I am not swift, to-morrow there will not be one mouth in the valley. Indeed, I must go and warn them below. Back there, Brother! Let me get to the fire."

The barasingh backed unwillingly as Purun Bhagat drove a pine torch deep into the flame, twirling it till it was well lit. "Ah! ye came to warn me," he said, rising. "Better than that we shall do; better than that. Out, now, and lend me thy neck, Brother, for I have but two feet."

He clutched the bristling withers of the barasingh with his right hand, held the torch away with his left, and stepped out of the shrine into the desperate night. There was no breath of wind, but the rain nearly drowned the flare as the great deer hurried down the slope, sliding on his haunches. As soon as they were clear of the forest more of the Bhagat's brothers joined them. He heard, though he could not see, the langurs pressing about him, and behind them the uhh! uhh! of Sona. The rain matted his long white hair into ropes; the water splashed beneath his bare feet, and his yellow robe clung to his frail old body, but he stepped down steadily, leaning against the barasingh. He was no longer a holy man, but Sir Purun Dass, K.C.I.E., Prime Minister of no small State, a man accustomed to command, going out to save life. Down the steep, plashy path they poured all together, the Bhagat and his brothers, down and down till the deer's feet clicked and stumbled on the wall of a threshing-floor, and he snorted because he smelt Man. Now they were at the head of the one crooked village street, and the Bhagat beat with his crutch on the barred windows of the blacksmith's house, as his torch blazed up in the shelter of the eaves. "Up and out!" cried Purun Bhagat; and he did not know his own voice, for it was years since he had spoken aloud to a man. "The hill falls! The hill is falling! Up and out, oh, you within!"

"It is our Bhagat," said the blacksmith's wife. "He stands among his beasts. Gather the little ones and give the call."

It ran from house to house, while the beasts, cramped in the narrow way, surged and huddled round the Bhagat, and Sona puffed impatiently.

The people hurried into the street—they were no more than seventy souls all told—and in the glare of the torches they saw their Bhagat holding back the terrified barasingh, while the monkeys plucked piteously at his skirts, and Sona sat on his haunches and roared.

"Across the valley and up the next hill!" shouted Purun Bhagat. "Leave none behind! We follow!"

Then the people ran as only Hill folk can run, for they knew that in a landslip you must climb for the highest ground across the valley. They fled, splashing through the little river at the bottom, and panted up the terraced fields on the far side, while the Bhagat and his brethren followed. Up and up the opposite mountain they climbed, calling to each other by name—the roll-call of the village—and at their heels toiled the big barasingh, weighted by the failing strength of Purun Bhagat. At last the deer stopped in the shadow of a deep pinewood, five hundred feet up the hillside. His instinct, that had warned him of the coming slide, told him he would be safe here.

Purun Bhagat dropped fainting by his side, for the chill of the rain and that fierce climb were killing him; but first he called to the scattered torches ahead, "Stay and count your numbers"; then, whispering to the deer as he saw the lights gather in a cluster: "Stay with me, Brother. Stay—till—I—go!"

There was a sigh in the air that grew to a mutter, and a mutter that grew to a roar, and a roar that passed all sense of hearing, and the hillside on which the villagers stood was hit in the darkness, and rocked to the blow. Then a note as steady, deep, and true as the deep C of the organ drowned everything for perhaps five minutes, while the very roots of the pines quivered to it. It died away, and the sound of the rain falling on miles of hard ground and grass changed to the muffled drum of water on soft earth. That told its own tale.

Never a villager—not even the priest—was bold enough to speak to the Bhagat who had saved their lives. They crouched under the pines and waited till the day. When it came they looked across the valley and saw that what had been forest, and terraced field, and track-threaded grazing-ground was one raw, red, fan-shaped smear, with a few trees flung head-down on the scarp. That red ran high up the hill of their refuge, damming back the little river, which had begun to spread into a brick-coloured lake. Of the village, of the road to the shrine, of the shrine itself, and the forest behind, there was no trace. For one mile in width and two thousand feet in sheer depth the mountain-side had come away bodily, planed clean from head to heel.

And the villagers, one by one, crept through the wood to pray before their Bhagat. They saw the barasingh standing over him, who fled when they came near, and they heard the langurs wailing in the branches, and Sona moaning up the hill; but their Bhagat was dead, sitting cross-legged, his back against a tree, his crutch under his armpit, and his face turned to the north-east.

The priest said: "Behold a miracle after a miracle, for in this very attitude must all Sunnyasis be buried! Therefore where he now is we will build the temple to our holy man."

They built the temple before a year was ended—a little stone-and-earth shrine—and they called the hill the Bhagat's hill, and they worship there with lights and flowers and offerings to this day. But they do not know that the saint of their worship is the late Sir Purun Dass, K.C.I.E., D.C.L., Ph.D., etc., once Prime Minister of the progressive and enlightened State of Mohiniwala, and honorary or corresponding member of more learned and scientific societies than will ever do any good in this world or the next.

A SONG OF KABIR

Oh, light was the world that he weighed in his hands!
Oh, heavy the tale of his fiefs and his lands!
He has gone from the guddee and put on the shroud,
And departed in guise of bairagi avowed!
Now the white road to Delhi is mat for his feet,
The sal and the kikar must guard him from heat;
His home is the camp, and the waste, and the crowd--
He is seeking the Way as bairagi avowed!
He has looked upon Man, and his eyeballs are clear
(There was One; there is One, and but One, saith Kabir);
The Red Mist of Doing has thinned to a cloud--
He has taken the Path for bairagi avowed!
To learn and discern of his brother the clod,
Of his brother the brute, and his brother the God.
He has gone from the council and put on the shroud
("Can ye hear?" saith Kabir), a bairagi avowed!

LETTING IN THE JUNGLE

Veil them, cover them, wall them round--
Blossom, and creeper, and weed--
Let us forget the sight and the sound,
The smell and the touch of the breed!
Fat black ash by the altar-stone,
Here is the white-foot rain,
And the does bring forth in the fields unsown,
And none shall affright them again;
And the blind walls crumble, unknown, o'erthrown
And none shall inhabit again!

You will remember that after Mowgli had pinned Shere Khan's hide to the Council Rock, he told as many as were left of the Seeonee Pack that henceforward he would hunt in the Jungle alone; and the four children of Mother and Father Wolf said that they would hunt with him. But it is not easy to change one's life all in a minute—particularly in the Jungle. The first thing Mowgli did, when the disorderly Pack had slunk off, was to go to the home-cave, and sleep for a day and a night. Then he told Mother Wolf and Father Wolf as much as they could understand of his adventures among men; and when he made the morning sun flicker up and down the blade of his skinning-knife,—the same he had skinned Shere Khan with,—they said he had learned something. Then Akela and Gray Brother had to explain their share of the great buffalo-drive in the ravine, and Baloo toiled up the hill to hear all about it, and Bagheera scratched himself all over with pure delight at the way in which Mowgli had managed his war.

It was long after sunrise, but no one dreamed of going to sleep, and from time to time, during the talk, Mother Wolf would throw up her head, and sniff a deep snuff of satisfaction as the wind brought her the smell of the tiger-skin on the Council Rock.

"But for Akela and Gray Brother here," Mowgli said, at the end, "I could have done nothing. Oh, mother, mother! if thou hadst seen the black herd-bulls pour down the ravine, or hurry through the gates when the Man-Pack flung stones at me!"

"I am glad I did not see that last," said Mother Wolf stiffly. "It is not MY custom to suffer my cubs to be driven to and fro like jackals. _I_ would have taken a price from the Man-Pack; but I would have spared the woman who gave thee the milk. Yes, I would have spared her alone."

"Peace, peace, Raksha!" said Father Wolf, lazily. "Our Frog has come back again—so wise that his own father must lick his feet; and what is a cut, more or less, on the head? Leave Men alone." Baloo and Bagheera both echoed: "Leave Men alone."

Mowgli, his head on Mother Wolf's side, smiled contentedly, and said that, for his own part, he never wished to see, or hear, or smell Man again.

"But what," said Akela, cocking one ear—"but what if men do not leave thee alone, Little Brother?"

"We be FIVE," said Gray Brother, looking round at the company, and snapping his jaws on the last word.

"We also might attend to that hunting," said Bagheera,

with a little switch-switch of his tail, looking at Baloo. "But why think of men now, Akela?"

"For this reason," the Lone Wolf answered: "when that yellow chief's hide was hung up on the rock, I went back along our trail to the village, stepping in my tracks, turning aside, and lying down, to make a mixed trail in case one should follow us. But when I had fouled the trail so that I myself hardly knew it again, Mang, the Bat, came hawking between the trees, and hung up above me." Said Mang, "The village of the Man-Pack, where they cast out the Man-cub, hums like a hornet's nest."

"It was a big stone that I threw," chuckled Mowgli, who had often amused himself by throwing ripe paw-paws into a hornet's nest, and racing off to the nearest pool before the hornets caught him.

"I asked of Mang what he had seen. He said that the Red Flower blossomed at the gate of the village, and men sat about it carrying guns. Now _I_ know, for I have good cause,"—Akela looked down at the old dry scars on his flank and side,—"that men do not carry guns for pleasure. Presently, Little Brother, a man with a gun follows our trail—if, indeed, he be not already on it."

"But why should he? Men have cast me out. What more do they need?" said Mowgli angrily.

"Thou art a man, Little Brother," Akela returned. "It is not for US, the Free Hunters, to tell thee what thy brethren do, or why."

He had just time to snatch up his paw as the skinning-knife cut deep into the ground below. Mowgli struck quicker than an average human eye could follow but Akela was a wolf; and even a dog, who is very far removed from the wild wolf, his ancestor, can be waked out of deep sleep by a cart-wheel touching his flank, and can spring away unharmed before that wheel comes on.

"Another time," Mowgli said quietly, returning the knife to its sheath, "speak of the Man-Pack and of Mowgli in TWO breaths—not one."

"Phff! That is a sharp tooth," said Akela, snuffing at the blade's cut in the earth, "but living with the Man-Pack has spoiled thine eye, Little Brother. I could have killed a buck while thou wast striking."

Bagheera sprang to his feet, thrust up his head as far as he could, sniffed, and stiffened through every curve in his body. Gray Brother followed his example quickly, keeping a little to his left to get the wind that was blowing from the right, while Akela bounded fifty yards up wind, and, half-crouching, stiffened too. Mowgli looked on enviously. He could smell things as very few human beings could, but he had never reached the hair-trigger-like sensitiveness of a Jungle nose; and his three months in the smoky village had set him back sadly. However, he dampened his finger, rubbed it on his nose, and stood erect to catch the upper scent, which, though it is the faintest, is the truest.

"Man!" Akela growled, dropping on his haunches.

"Buldeo!" said Mowgli, sitting down. "He follows our trail, and yonder is the sunlight on his gun. Look!"

It was no more than a splash of sunlight, for a fraction of a second, on the brass clamps of the old Tower musket, but nothing in the Jungle winks with just that flash, except when the clouds race over the sky. Then a piece of mica, or a little pool, or even a highly-polished leaf will flash like a heliograph. But that day was cloudless and still.

"I knew men would follow," said Akela triumphantly. "Not for nothing have I led the Pack."

The four cubs said nothing, but ran down hill on their bellies, melting into the thorn and under-brush as a mole melts into a lawn.

"Where go ye, and without word?" Mowgli called.

"H'sh! We roll his skull here before mid-day!" Gray Brother answered.

"Back! Back and wait! Man does not eat Man!" Mowgli shrieked.

"Who was a wolf but now? Who drove the knife at me for thinking he might be Man?" said Akela, as the four wolves turned back sullenly and dropped to heel.

"Am I to give reason for all I choose to, do?" said Mowgli furiously.

"That is Man! There speaks Man!" Bagheera muttered under his whiskers. "Even so did men talk round the King's cages at Oodeypore. We of the Jungle know that Man is wisest of all. If we trusted our ears we should know that of all things he is most foolish." Raising his voice, he added, "The Man-cub is right in this. Men hunt in packs. To kill one, unless we know what the others will do, is bad hunting. Come, let us see what this Man means toward us."

"We will not come," Gray Brother growled. "Hunt alone, Little Brother. WE know our own minds. The skull would have been ready to bring by now."

Mowgli had been looking from one to the other of his friends, his chest heaving and his eyes full of tears. He strode forward to the wolves, and, dropping on one knee, said: "Do I not know my mind? Look at me!"

They looked uneasily, and when their eyes wandered, he

called them back again and again, till their hair stood up all over their bodies, and they trembled in every limb, while Mowgli stared and stared.

"Now," said he, "of us five, which is leader?"

"Thou art leader, Little Brother," said Gray Brother, and he licked Mowgli's foot.

"Follow, then," said Mowgli, and the four followed at his heels with their tails between their legs.

"This comes of living with the Man-Pack," said Bagheera, slipping down after them. "There is more in the Jungle now than Jungle Law, Baloo."

The old bear said nothing, but he thought many things.

Mowgli cut across noiselessly through the Jungle, at right angles to Buldeo's path, till, parting the undergrowth, he saw the old man, his musket on his shoulder, running up the trail of overnight at a dog-trot.

You will remember that Mowgli had left the village with the heavy weight of Shere Khan's raw hide on his shoulders, while Akela and Gray Brother trotted behind, so that the triple trail was very clearly marked. Presently Buldeo came to where Akela, as you know, had gone back and mixed it all up. Then he sat down, and coughed and grunted, and made little casts round and about into the Jungle to pick it up again, and, all the time he could have thrown a stone over those who were watching him. No one can be so silent as a wolf when he does not care to be heard; and Mowgli, though the wolves thought he moved very clumsily, could come and go like a shadow. They ringed the old man as a school of porpoises ring a steamer at full speed, and as they ringed him they talked unconcernedly, for their speech began below the lowest end of the scale that untrained human beings can hear. [The other end is bounded by the high squeak of Mang, the Bat, which very many people cannot catch at all. From that note all the bird and bat and insect talk takes on.]

"This is better than any kill," said Gray Brother, as Buldeo stooped and peered and puffed. "He looks like a lost pig in the Jungles by the river. What does he say?" Buldeo was muttering savagely.

Mowgli translated. "He says that packs of wolves must have danced round me. He says that he never saw such a trail in his life. He says he is tired."

"He will be rested before he picks it up again," said Bagheera coolly, as he slipped round a tree-trunk, in the game of blindman's-buff that they were playing. "NOW, what does the lean thing do?"

"Eat or blow smoke out of his mouth. Men always play with their mouths," said Mowgli; and the silent trailers saw the old man fill and light and puff at a water-pipe, and they took good note of the smell of the tobacco, so as to be sure of Buldeo in the darkest night, if necessary.

Then a little knot of charcoal-burners came down the path, and naturally halted to speak to Buldeo, whose fame as a hunter reached for at least twenty miles round. They all sat down and smoked, and Bagheera and the others came up and watched while Buldeo began to tell the story of Mowgli, the Devil-child, from one end to another, with additions and inventions. How he himself had really killed Shere Khan; and how Mowgli had turned himself into a wolf, and fought with him all the afternoon, and changed into a boy again and bewitched Buldeo's rifle, so that the bullet turned the corner, when he pointed it at Mowgli, and killed one of Buldeo's own buffaloes; and how the village, knowing him to be the bravest hunter in Seeonee, had sent him out to kill this Devil-child. But meantime the village had got hold of Messua and her husband, who were undoubtedly the father and mother of this Devil-child, and had barricaded them in their own hut, and presently would torture them to make them confess they were witch and wizard, and then they would be burned to death.

"When?" said the charcoal-burners, because they would very much like to be present at the ceremony.

Buldeo said that nothing would be done till he returned, because the village wished him to kill the Jungle Boy first. After that they would dispose of Messua and her husband, and divide their lands and buffaloes among the village. Messua's husband had some remarkably fine buffaloes, too. It was an excellent thing to destroy wizards, Buldeo thought; and people who entertained Wolf-children out of the Jungle were clearly the worst kind of witches.

But, said the charcoal-burners, what would happen if the English heard of it? The English, they had heard, were a perfectly mad people, who would not let honest farmers kill witches in peace.

Why, said Buldeo, the head-m an of the village would report that Messua and her husband had died of snake-bite. THAT was all arranged, and the only thing now was to kill the Wolf-child. They did not happen to have seen anything of such a creature?

The charcoal-burners looked round cautiously, and thanked their stars they had not; but they had no doubt that so brave a man as Buldeo would find him if any one could. The sun was getting rather low, and they had an idea that they would push on to Buldeo's village and see that wicked witch. Buldeo said that, though it was his duty to kill the Devil-child, he could not think of letting a party of unarmed men go through the Jungle, which might produce the Wolf-demon at any minute, without his escort. He, therefore, would accompany them, and if the sorcerer's child appeared—well, he would show them how the best hunter in Seeonee dealt with such things. The Brahmin, he said, had given him a charm against the creature that made everything perfectly safe.

"What says he? What says he? What says he?" the wolves repeated every few minutes; and Mowgli translated until he came to the witch part of the story, which was a little beyond him, and then he said that the man and woman who had been so kind to him were trapped.

"Does Man trap Man?" said Bagheera.

"So he says. I cannot understand the talk. They are all mad together. What have Messua and her man to do with me that they should be put in a trap; and what is all this talk about the Red Flower? I must look to this. Whatever they would do to Messua they will not do till Buldeo returns. And so——" Mowgli thought hard, with his fingers playing round the haft of the skinning-knife, while Buldeo and the charcoal-burners went off very valiantly in single file.

"I go hot-foot back to the Man-Pack," Mowgli said at last.

"And those?" said Gray Brother, looking hungrily after the brown backs of the charcoal-burners.

"Sing them home," said Mowgli, with a grin; "I do not wish them to be at the village gates till it is dark. Can ye hold them?"

Gray Brother bared his white teeth in contempt. "We can head them round and round in circles like tethered goats—if I know Man."

"That I do not need. Sing to them a little, lest they be lonely on the road, and, Gray Brother, the song need not be of the sweetest. Go with them, Bagheera, and help make that song. When night is shut down, meet me by the village—Gray Brother knows the place."

"It is no light hunting to work for a Man-cub. When shall I sleep?" said Bagheera, yawning, though his eyes showed that he was delighted with the amusement. "Me to sing to naked men! But let us try."

He lowered his head so that the sound would travel, and cried a long, long, "Good hunting"—a midnight call in the afternoon, which was quite awful enough to begin with. Mowgli heard it rumble, and rise, and fall, and die off in a creepy sort of whine behind him, and laughed to himself as he ran through the Jungle. He could see the charcoal-burners huddled in a knot; old Buldeo's gun-barrel waving, like a banana-leaf, to every point of the compass at once. Then Gray Brother gave the Ya-la-hi! Yalaha! call for the buck-driving, when the Pack drives the nilghai, the big blue cow, before them, and it seemed to come from the very ends of the earth, nearer, and nearer, and nearer, till it ended in a shriek snapped off short. The other three answered, till even Mowgli could have vowed that the full Pack was in full cry, and then they all broke into the magnificent Morning-song in the Jungle, with every turn, and flourish, and grace-note that a deep-mouthed wolf of the Pack knows. This is a rough rendering of the song, but you must imagine what it sounds like when it breaks the afternoon hush of the Jungle:—

> *One moment past our bodies cast*
> *No shadow on the plain;*
> *Now clear and black they stride our track,*
> *And we run home again.*
> *In morning hush, each rock and bush*
> *Stands hard, and high, and raw:*

Then give the Call: "Good rest to all
That keep The Jungle Law!"
Now horn and pelt our peoples melt
In covert to abide;
Now, crouched and still, to cave and hill
Our Jungle Barons glide.
Now, stark and plain, Man's oxen strain,
That draw the new-yoked plough;
Now, stripped and dread, the dawn is red
Above the lit talao.
Ho! Get to lair! The sun's aflare
Behind the breathing grass:
And cracking through the young bamboo
The warning whispers pass.
By day made strange, the woods we range
With blinking eyes we scan;
While down the skies the wild duck cries
"The Day--the Day to Man!"
The dew is dried that drenched our hide
Or washed about our way;
And where we drank, the puddled bank
Is crisping into clay.
The traitor Dark gives up each mark
Of stretched or hooded claw;
Then hear the Call: "Good rest to all
That keep the Jungle Law!"

But no translation can give the effect of it, or the yelping
scorn the Four threw into every word of it, as they heard the
trees crash when the men hastily climbed up into the branches,
and Buldeo began repeating incantations and charms. Then
they lay down and slept, for, like all who live by their own
exertions, they were of a methodical cast of mind; and no one
can work well without sleep.

Meantime, Mowgli was putting the miles behind him, nine to the hour, swinging on, delighted to find himself so fit after all his cramped months among men. The one idea in his head was to get Messua and her husband out of the trap, whatever it was; for he had a natural mistrust of traps. Later on, he promised himself, he would pay his debts to the village at large.

It was at twilight when he saw the well-remembered grazing-grounds, and the dhak-tree where Gray Brother had waited for him on the morning that he killed Shere Khan. Angry as he was at the whole breed and community of Man, something jumped up in his throat and made him catch his breath when he looked at the village roofs. He noticed that every one had come in from the fields unusually early, and that, instead of getting to their evening cooking, they gathered in a crowd under the village tree, and chattered, and shouted.

"Men must always be making traps for men, or they are not content," said Mowgli. "Last night it was Mowgli—but that night seems many Rains ago. To-night it is Messua and her man. To-morrow, and for very many nights after, it will be Mowgli's turn again."

He crept along outside the wall till he came to Messua's hut, and looked through the window into the room. There lay Messua, gagged, and bound hand and foot, breathing hard, and groaning: her husband was tied to the gaily-painted bedstead. The door of the hut that opened into the street was shut fast, and three or four people were sitting with their backs to it.

Mowgli knew the manners and customs of the villagers very fairly. He argued that so long as they could eat, and talk, and smoke, they would not do anything else; but as soon as they had fed they would begin to be dangerous. Buldeo would be coming in before long, and if his escort had done its duty, Buldeo would have a very interesting tale to tell. So he went in through the window, and, stooping over the man and the woman, cut their thongs, pulling out the gags, and looked round the hut for some milk.

Messua was half wild with pain and fear (she had been beaten and stoned all the morning), and Mowgli put his hand over her mouth just in time to stop a scream. Her husband was only bewildered and angry, and sat picking dust and things out of his torn beard.

"I knew—I knew he would come," Messua sobbed at last. "Now do I KNOW that he is my son!" and she hugged Mowgli to her heart. Up to that time Mowgli had been perfectly steady, but now he began to tremble all over, and that surprised him immensely.

"Why are these thongs? Why have they tied thee?" he asked, after a pause.

"To be put to the death for making a son of thee—what else?" said the man sullenly. "Look! I bleed."

Messua said nothing, but it was at her wounds that Mowgli looked, and they heard him grit his teeth when he saw the blood.

"Whose work is this?" said he. "There is a price to pay."

"The work of all the village. I was too rich. I had too many cattle. THEREFORE she and I are witches, because we gave thee shelter."

"I do not understand. Let Messua tell the tale."

"I gave thee milk, Nathoo; dost thou remember?" Messua said timidly. "Because thou wast my son, whom the tiger took, and because I loved thee very dearly. They said that I was thy mother, the mother of a devil, and therefore worthy of death."

"And what is a devil?" said Mowgli. "Death I have seen."

The man looked up gloomily, but Messua laughed. "See!" she said to her husband, "I knew—I said that he was no sorcerer. He is my son—my son!"

"Son or sorcerer, what good will that do us?" the man answered. "We be as dead already."

"Yonder is the road to the Jungle"—Mowgli pointed through the window. "Your hands and feet are free. Go now."

"We do not know the Jungle, my son, as—as thou knowest," Messua began. "I do not think that I could walk far."

"And the men and women would be upon our backs and drag us here again," said the husband.

"H'm!" said Mowgli, and he tickled the palm of his hand with the tip of his skinning-knife; "I have no wish to do harm to any one of this village—YET. But I do not think they will stay thee. In a little while they will have much else to think upon. Ah!" he lifted his head and listened to shouting and trampling outside. "So they have let Buldeo come home at last?"

"He was sent out this morning to kill thee," Messua cried. "Didst thou meet him?"

"Yes—we—I met him. He has a tale to tell and while he is telling it there is time to do much. But first I will learn what they mean. Think where ye would go, and tell me when I come back."

He bounded through the window and ran along again outside the wall of the village till he came within ear-shot of the crowd round the peepul-tree. Buldeo was lying on the ground, coughing and groaning, and every one was asking him questions. His hair had fallen about his shoulders; his hands and legs were skinned from climbing up trees, and he could hardly speak, but he felt the importance of his position keenly. From time to time he said something about devils and singing devils, and magic enchantment, just to give the crowd a taste of what was coming. Then he called for water.

"Bah!" said Mowgli. "Chatter—chatter! Talk, talk! Men are blood-brothers of the Bandar-log. Now he must wash his mouth with water; now he must blow smoke; and when all that is done he has still his story to tell. They are very wise people—men. They will leave no one to guard Messua till their ears are stuffed with Buldeo's tales. And—I grow as lazy as they!"

He shook himself and glided back to the hut. Just as he was at the window he felt a touch on his foot.

"Mother," said he, for he knew that tongue well, "what dost THOU here?"

"I heard my children singing through the woods, and I followed the one I loved best. Little Frog, I have a desire to see that woman who gave thee milk," said Mother Wolf, all wet with the dew.

"They have bound and mean to kill her. I have cut those ties, and she goes with her man through the Jungle."

"I also will follow. I am old, but not yet toothless." Mother Wolf reared herself up on end, and looked through the window into the dark of the hut.

In a minute she dropped noiselessly, and all she said was: "I gave thee thy first milk; but Bagheera speaks truth: Man goes to Man at the last."

"Maybe," said Mowgli, with a very unpleasant look on his face; "but to-night I am very far from that trail. Wait here, but do not let her see."

"THOU wast never afraid of ME, Little Frog," said Mother Wolf, backing into the high grass, and blotting herself out, as she knew how.

"And now," said Mowgli cheerfully, as he swung into the hut again, "they are all sitting round Buldeo, who is saying that which did not happen. When his talk is finished, they say they will assuredly come here with the Red—with fire and burn you both. And then?"

"I have spoken to my man," said Messua. "Khanhiwara is thirty miles from here, but at Khanhiwara we may find the English—"

"And what Pack are they?" said Mowgli.

"I do not know. They be white, and it is said that they govern all the land, and do not suffer people to burn or beat each other without witnesses. If we can get thither to-night, we live. Otherwise we die."

"Live, then. No man passes the gates to-night. But what does HE do?" Messua's husband was on his hands and knees digging up the earth in one corner of the hut.

"It is his little money," said Messua. "We can take nothing else."

"Ah, yes. The stuff that passes from hand to hand and never grows warmer. Do they need it outside this place also?" said Mowgli.

The man stared angrily. "He is a fool, and no devil," he muttered. "With the money I can buy a horse. We are too bruised to walk far, and the village will follow us in an hour."

"I say they will NOT follow till I choose; but a horse is well thought of, for Messua is tired." Her husband stood up and knotted the last of the rupees into his waist-cloth. Mowgli helped Messua through the window, and the cool night air revived her, but the Jungle in the starlight looked very dark and terrible.

"Ye know the trail to Khanhiwara?" Mowgli whispered.

They nodded.

"Good. Remember, now, not to be afraid. And there is no need to go quickly. Only—only there may be some small singing in the Jungle behind you and before."

"Think you we would have risked a night in the Jungle through anything less than the fear of burning? It is better to be killed by beasts than by men," said Messua's husband; but Messua looked at Mowgli and smiled.

"I say," Mowgli went on, just as though he were Baloo repeating an old Jungle Law for the hundredth time to a foolish cub—"I say that not a tooth in the Jungle is bared against you; not a foot in the Jungle is lifted against you. Neither man nor beast shall stay you till you come within eye-shot of Khanhiwara. There will be a watch about you." He turned quickly to Messua, saying, "HE does not believe, but thou wilt believe?"

"Ay, surely, my son. Man, ghost, or wolf of the Jungle, I believe."

"HE will be afraid when he hears my people singing. Thou wilt know and understand. Go now, and slowly, for there is no need of any haste. The gates are shut."

Messua flung herself sobbing at Mowgli's feet, but he lifted her very quickly with a shiver. Then she hung about his neck and called him every name of blessing she could think of, but her husband looked enviously across his fields, and said: "IF we reach Khanhiwara, and I get the ear of the English, I will bring such a lawsuit against the Brahmin and old Buldeo and the others as shall eat the village to the bone. They shall pay me twice over for my crops untilled and my buffaloes unfed. I will have a great justice."

Mowgli laughed. "I do not know what justice is, but— come next Rains. and see what is left."

They went off toward the Jungle, and Mother Wolf leaped from her place of hiding.

"Follow!" said Mowgli; "and look to it that all the Jungle knows these two are safe. Give tongue a little. I would call Bagheera."

The long, low howl rose and fell, and Mowgli saw Messua's husband flinch and turn, half minded to run back to the hut.

"Go on," Mowgli called cheerfully. "I said there might be singing. That call will follow up to Khanhiwara. It is Favour of the Jungle."

Messua urged her husband forward, and the darkness shut down on them and Mother Wolf as Bagheera rose up almost under Mowgli's feet, trembling with delight of the night that drives the Jungle People wild.

"I am ashamed of thy brethren," he said, purring. "What? Did they not sing sweetly to Buldeo?" said Mowgli.

"Too well! Too well! They made even ME forget my pride, and, by the Broken Lock that freed me, I went singing through the Jungle as though I were out wooing in the spring! Didst thou not hear us?"

"I had other game afoot. Ask Buldeo if he liked the song. But where are the Four? I do not wish one of the Man-Pack to leave the gates to-night."

"What need of the Four, then?" said Bagheera, shifting from foot to foot, his eyes ablaze, and purring louder than ever. "I can hold them, Little Brother. Is it killing at last? The singing and the sight of the men climbing up the trees have made me very ready. Who is Man that we should care for him—the naked brown digger, the hairless and toothless, the eater of earth? I have followed him all day—at noon—in the white sunlight. I herded him as the wolves herd buck. I am

Bagheera! Bagheera! Bagheera! As I dance with my shadow, so danced I with those men. Look!" The great panther leaped as a kitten leaps at a dead leaf whirling overhead, struck left and right into the empty air, that sang under the strokes, landed noiselessly, and leaped again and again, while the half purr, half growl gathered head as steam rumbles in a boiler. "I am Bagheera—in the jungle—in the night, and my strength is in me. Who shall stay my stroke? Man-cub, with one blow of my paw I could beat thy head flat as a dead frog in the summer!"

"Strike, then!" said Mowgli, in the dialect of the village, NOT the talk of the Jungle, and the human words brought Bagheera to a full stop, flung back on haunches that quivered under him, his head just at the level of Mowgli's. Once more Mowgli stared, as he had stared at the rebellious cubs, full into the beryl-green eyes till the red glare behind their green went out like the light of a lighthouse shut off twenty miles across the sea; till the eyes dropped, and the big head with them—dropped lower and lower, and the red rasp of a tongue grated on Mowgli's instep.

"Brother—Brother—Brother!" the boy whispered, stroking steadily and lightly from the neck along the heaving back. "Be still, be still! It is the fault of the night, and no fault of thine."

"It was the smells of the night," said Bagheera penitently. "This air cries aloud to me. But how dost THOU know?"

Of course the air round an Indian village is full of all kinds of smells, and to any creature who does nearly all his thinking through his nose, smells are as maddening as music and drugs are to human beings. Mowgli gentled the panther for a few minutes longer, and he lay down like a cat before a fire, his paws tucked under his breast, and his eyes half shut.

"Thou art of the Jungle and NOT of the Jungle," he said

at last. "And I am only a black panther. But I love thee, Little Brother."

"They are very long at their talk under the tree," Mowgli said, without noticing the last sentence. "Buldeo must have told many tales. They should come soon to drag the woman and her man out of the trap and put them into the Red Flower. They will find that trap sprung. Ho! ho!"

"Nay, listen," said Bagheera. "The fever is out of my blood now. Let them find ME there! Few would leave their houses after meeting me. It is not the first time I have been in a cage; and I do not think they will tie ME with cords."

"Be wise, then," said Mowgli, laughing; for he was beginning to feel as reckless as the panther, who had glided into the hut.

"Pah!" Bagheera grunted. "This place is rank with Man, but here is just such a bed as they gave me to lie upon in the King's cages at Oodeypore. Now I lie down." Mowgli heard the strings of the cot crack under the great brute's weight. "By the Broken Lock that freed me, they will think they have caught big game! Come and sit beside me, Little Brother; we will give them 'good hunting' together!"

"No; I have another thought in my stomach. The Man-Pack shall not know what share I have in the sport. Make thine own hunt. I do not wish to see them."

"Be it so," said Bagheera. "Ah, now they come!"

The conference under the peepul-tree had been growing noisier and noisier, at the far end of the village. It broke in wild yells, and a rush up the street of men and women, waving clubs and bamboos and sickles and knives. Buldeo and the Brahmin were at the head of it, but the mob was close at their heels, and they cried, "The witch and the wizard! Let us see if hot coins will make them confess! Burn the hut over their heads! We will teach them to shelter wolf-devils! Nay, beat them first! Torches! More torches! Buldeo, heat the gun-barrels!"

Here was some little difficulty with the catch of the door. It had been very firmly fastened, but the crowd tore it away bodily, and the light of the torches streamed into the room where, stretched at full length on the bed, his paws crossed and lightly hung down over one end, black as the Pit, and terrible as a demon, was Bagheera. There was one half-minute of desperate silence, as the front ranks of the crowd clawed and tore their way back from the threshold, and in that minute Bagheera raised his head and yawned—elaborately, carefully, and ostentatiously—as he would yawn when he wished to insult an equal. The fringed lips drew back and up; the red tongue curled; the lower jaw dropped and dropped till you could see half-way down the hot gullet; and the gigantic dog-teeth stood clear to the pit of the gums till they rang together, upper and under, with the snick of steel-faced wards shooting home round the edges of a safe. Next instant the street was empty; Bagheera had leaped back through the window, and stood at Mowgli's side, while a yelling, screaming torrent scrambled and tumbled one over another in their panic haste to get to their own huts.

"They will not stir till day comes," said Bagheera quietly. "And now?"

The silence of the afternoon sleep seemed to have overtaken the village; but, as they listened, they could hear the sound of heavy grain-boxes being dragged over earthen floors and set down against doors. Bagheera was quite right; the village would not stir till daylight. Mowgli sat still, and thought, and his face grew darker and darker.

"What have I done?" said Bagheera, at last coming to his feet, fawning.

"Nothing but great good. Watch them now till the day. I sleep." Mowgli ran off into the Jungle, and dropped like a dead man across a rock, and slept and slept the day round, and the night back again.

When he waked, Bagheera was at his side, and there was a newly-killed buck at his feet. Bagheera watched curiously while Mowgli went to work with his skinning-knife, ate and drank, and turned over with his chin in his hands.

"The man and the woman are come safe within eye-shot of Khanhiwara," Bagheera said. "Thy lair mother sent the word back by Chil, the Kite. They found a horse before midnight of the night they were freed, and went very quickly. Is not that well?"

"That is well," said Mowgli.

"And thy Man-Pack in the village did not stir till the sun was high this morning. Then they ate their food and ran back quickly to their houses."

"Did they, by chance, see thee?"

"It may have been. I was rolling in the dust before the gate at dawn, and I may have made also some small song to myself. Now, Little Brother, there is nothing more to do. Come hunting with me and Baloo. He has new hives that he wishes to show, and we all desire thee back again as of old. Take off that look which makes even me afraid! The man and woman will not be put into the Red Flower, and all goes well in the Jungle. Is it not true? Let us forget the Man-Pack."

"They shall be forgotten in a little while. Where does Hathi feed to-night?"

"Where he chooses. Who can answer for the Silent One? But why? What is there Hathi can do which we cannot?"

"Bid him and his three sons come here to me."

"But, indeed, and truly, Little Brother, it is not—it is not seemly to say 'Come,' and 'Go,' to Hathi. Remember, he is the Master of the Jungle, and before the Man-Pack changed the look on thy face, he taught thee the Master-words of the Jungle."

"That is all one. I have a Master-word for him now. Bid him come to Mowgli, the Frog: and if he does not hear at first, bid him come because of the Sack of the Fields of Bhurtpore."

"The Sack of the Fields of Bhurtpore," Bagheera repeated two or three times to make sure. "I go. Hathi can but be angry at the worst, and I would give a moon's hunting to hear a Master-word that compels the Silent One."

He went away, leaving Mowgli stabbing furiously with his skinning-knife into the earth. Mowgli had never seen human blood in his life before till he had seen, and—what meant much more to him—smelled Messua's blood on the thongs that bound her. And Messua had been kind to him, and, so far as he knew anything about love, he loved Messua as completely as he hated the rest of mankind. But deeply as he loathed them, their talk, their cruelty, and their cowardice, not for anything the Jungle had to offer could he bring himself to take a human life, and have that terrible scent of blood back again in his nostrils. His plan was simpler, but much more thorough; and he laughed to himself when he thought that it was one of old Buldeo's tales told under the peepul-tree in the evening that had put the idea into his head.

"It WAS a Master-word," Bagheera whispered in his ear.

"They were feeding by the river, and they obeyed as though they were bullocks. Look where they come now!"

Hathi and his three sons had arrived, in their usual way, without a sound. The mud of the river was still fresh on their flanks, and Hathi was thoughtfully chewing the green stem of a young plantain-tree that he had gouged up with his tusks. But every line in his vast body showed to Bagheera, who could see things when he came across them, that it was not the Master of the Jungle speaking to a Man-cub, but one who was afraid coming before one who was not. His three sons rolled side by side, behind their father.

Mowgli hardly lifted his head as Hathi gave him "Good hunting." He kept him swinging and rocking, and shifting from one foot to another, for a long time before he spoke; and when he opened his mouth it was to Bagheera, not to the elephants.

"I will tell a tale that was told to me by the hunter ye hunted to-day," said Mowgli. "It concerns an elephant, old and wise, who fell into a trap, and the sharpened stake in the pit scarred him from a little above his heel to the crest of his shoulder, leaving a white mark." Mowgli threw out his hand, and as Hathi wheeled the moonlight showed a long white scar on his slaty side, as though he had been struck with a red-hot whip. "Men came to take him from the trap," Mowgli continued, "but he broke his ropes, for he was strong, and went away till his wound was healed. Then came he, angry, by night to the fields of those hunters. And I remember now that he had three sons. These things happened many, many Rains ago, and very far away—among the fields of Bhurtpore. What came to those fields at the next reaping, Hathi?"

"They were reaped by me and by my three sons," said Hathi.

"And to the ploughing that follows the reaping?" said Mowgli.

"There was no ploughing," said Hathi.

"And to the men that live by the green crops on the ground?" said Mowgli.

"They went away."

"And to the huts in which the men slept?" said Mowgli.

"We tore the roofs to pieces, and the Jungle swallowed up the walls," said Hathi.

"And what more?" said Mowgli.

"As much good ground as I can walk over in two nights from the east to the west, and from the north to the south as much as I can walk over in three nights, the Jungle took. We let in the Jungle upon five villages; and in those villages, and in their lands, the grazing-ground and the soft crop-grounds, there is not one man to-day who takes his food from the ground. That was the Sack of the Fields of Bhurtpore, which I and my three sons did; and now I ask, Man-cub, how the news of it came to thee?" said Hathi.

"A man told me, and now I see even Buldeo can speak truth. It was well done, Hathi with the white mark; but the second time it shall be done better, for the reason that there is a man to direct. Thou knowest the village of the Man-Pack that cast me out? They are idle, senseless, and cruel; they play with their mouths, and they do not kill the weaker for food, but for sport. When they are full-fed they would throw their own breed into the Red Flower. This I have seen. It is not well that they should live here any more. I hate them!"

"Kill, then," said the youngest of Hathi's three sons, picking up a tuft of grass, dusting it against his fore-legs, and throwing it away, while his little red eyes glanced furtively from side to side.

"What good are white bones to me?" Mowgli answered angrily. "Am I the cub of a wolf to play in the sun with a raw head? I have killed Shere Khan, and his hide rots on the Council Rock; but—but I do not know whither Shere Khan is gone, and my stomach is still empty. Now I will take that which I can see and touch. Let in the Jungle upon that village, Hathi!"

Bagheera shivered, and cowered down. He could understand, if the worst came to the worst, a quick rush down the village street, and a right and left blow into a crowd, or a crafty killing of men as they ploughed in the twilight; but this scheme for deliberately blotting out an entire village from the eyes of man and beast frightened him. Now he saw why Mowgli had sent for Hathi. No one but the long-lived elephant could plan and carry through such a war.

"Let them run as the men ran from the fields of Bhurtpore, till we have the rain-water for the only plough, and the noise of the rain on the thick leaves for the pattering of their spindles—till Bagheera and I lair in the house of the Brahmin, and the buck drink at the tank behind the temple! Let in the Jungle, Hathi!"

"But I—but we have no quarrel with them, and it needs the red rage of great pain ere we tear down the places where men sleep," said Hathi doubtfully.

"Are ye the only eaters of grass in the Jungle? Drive in your peoples. Let the deer and the pig and the nilghai look to it. Ye need never show a hand's-breadth of hide till the fields are naked. Let in the Jungle, Hathi!"

"There will be no killing? My tusks were red at the Sack of the Fields of Bhurtpore, and I would not wake that smell again."

"Nor I. I do not wish even their bones to lie on the clean earth. Let them go and find a fresh lair. They cannot stay here. I have seen and smelled the blood of the woman that gave me food—the woman whom they would have killed but for me. Only the smell of the new grass on their door-steps can take away that smell. It burns in my mouth. Let in the Jungle, Hathi!"

"Ah!" said Hathi. "So did the scar of the stake burn on my hide till we watched the villages die under in the spring growth. Now I see. Thy war shall be our war. We will let in the jungle!"

Mowgli had hardly time to catch his breath—he was shaking all over with rage and hate before the place where the elephants had stood was empty, and Bagheera was looking at him with terror.

"By the Broken Lock that freed me!" said the Black Panther at last. "Art THOU the naked thing I spoke for in the Pack when all was young? Master of the Jungle, when my strength goes, speak for me—speak for Baloo—speak for us all! We are cubs before thee! Snapped twigs under foot! Fawns that have lost their doe!"

The idea of Bagheera being a stray fawn upset Mowgli altogether, and he laughed and caught his breath, and sobbed and laughed again, till he had to jump into a pool to make himself stop. Then he swam round and round, ducking in and out of the bars of the moonlight like the frog, his namesake.

By this time Hathi and his three sons had turned, each to one point of the compass, and were striding silently down the valleys a mile away. They went on and on for two days' march—that is to say, a long sixty miles—through the Jungle; and every step they took, and every wave of their trunks, was known and noted and talked over by Mang and Chil and the

Monkey People and all the birds. Then they began to feed, and fed quietly for a week or so. Hathi and his sons are like Kaa, the Rock Python. They never hurry till they have to.

At the end of that time—and none knew who had started it—a rumour went through the Jungle that there was better food and water to be found in such and such a valley. The pig—who, of course, will go to the ends of the earth for a full meal—moved first by companies, scuffling over the rocks, and the deer followed, with the small wild foxes that live on the dead and dying of the herds; and the heavy-shouldered nilghai moved parallel with the deer, and the wild buffaloes of the swamps came after the nilghai. The least little thing would have turned the scattered, straggling droves that grazed and sauntered and drank and grazed again; but whenever there was an alarm some one would rise up and soothe them. At one time it would be Ikki the Porcupine, full of news of good feed just a little farther on; at another Mang would cry cheerily and flap down a glade to show it was all empty; or Baloo, his mouth full of roots, would shamble alongside a wavering line and half frighten, half romp it clumsily back to the proper road. Very many creatures broke back or ran away or lost interest, but very many were left to go forward. At the end of another ten days or so the situation was this. The deer and the pig and the nilghai were milling round and round in a circle of eight or ten miles radius, while the Eaters of Flesh skirmished round its edge. And the centre of that circle was the village, and round the village the crops were ripening, and in the crops sat men on what they call machans—platforms like pigeon-perches, made of sticks at the top of four poles— to scare away birds and other stealers. Then the deer were coaxed no more. The Eaters of Flesh were close behind them, and forced them forward and inward.

It was a dark night when Hathi and his three sons slipped down from the Jungle, and broke off the poles of the machans with their trunks; they fell as a snapped stalk of hemlock in bloom falls, and the men that tumbled from them heard the deep gurgling of the elephants in their ears. Then the vanguard of the bewildered armies of the deer broke down and flooded into the village grazing-grounds and the ploughed fields; and the sharp-hoofed, rooting wild pig came with them, and what the deer left the pig spoiled, and from time to time an alarm of wolves would shake the herds, and they would rush to and fro desperately, treading down the young barley, and cutting flat the banks of the irrigating channels. Before the dawn broke the pressure on the outside of the circle gave way at one point. The Eaters of Flesh had fallen back and left an open path to the south, and drove upon drove of buck fled along it. Others, who were bolder, lay up in the thickets to finish their meal next night.

But the work was practically done. When the villagers looked in the morning they saw their crops were lost. And that meant death if they did not get away, for they lived year in and year out as near to starvation as the Jungle was near to them. When the buffaloes were sent to graze the hungry brutes found that the deer had cleared the grazing-grounds, and so wandered into the Jungle and drifted off with their wild mates; and when twilight fell the three or four ponies that belonged to the village lay in their stables with their heads beaten in. Only Bagheera could have given those strokes, and only Bagheera would have thought of insolently dragging the last carcass to the open street.

The villagers had no heart to make fires in the fields that night, so Hathi and his three sons went gleaning among what was left; and where Hathi gleans there is no need to follow.

The men decided to live on their stored seed-corn until the rains had fallen, and then to take work as servants till they could catch up with the lost year; but as the grain-dealer was thinking of his well-filled crates of corn, and the prices he would levy at the sale of it, Hathi's sharp tusks were picking out the corner of his mud-house, and smashing open the big wicker chest, leeped with cow-dung, where the precious stuff lay.

When that last loss was discovered, it was the Brahmin's turn to speak. He had prayed to his own Gods without answer. It might be, he said, that, unconsciously, the village had offended some one of the Gods of the Jungle, for, beyond doubt, the Jungle was against them. So they sent for the head-man of the nearest tribe of wandering Gonds—little, wise, and very black hunters, living in the deep Jungle, whose fathers came of the oldest race in India—the aboriginal owners of the land. They made the Gond welcome with what they had, and he stood on one leg, his bow in his hand, and two or three poisoned arrows stuck through his top-knot, looking half afraid and half contemptuously at the anxious villagers and their ruined fields. They wished to know whether his Gods—the Old Gods—were angry with them and what sacrifices should be offered. The Gond said nothing, but picked up a trail of the Karela, the vine that bears the bitter wild gourd, and laced it to and fro across the temple door in the face of the staring red Hindu image. Then he pushed with his hand in the open air along the road to Khanhiwara, and went back to his Jungle, and watched the Jungle People drifting through it. He knew that when the Jungle moves only white men can hope to turn it aside.

There was no need to ask his meaning. The wild gourd would grow where they had worshipped their God, and the sooner they saved themselves the better.

But it is hard to tear a village from its moorings. They stayed on as long as any summer food was left to them, and they tried to gather nuts in the Jungle, but shadows with glaring eyes watched them, and rolled before them even at mid-day; and when they ran back afraid to their walls, on the tree-trunks they had passed not five minutes before the bark would be stripped and chiselled with the stroke of some great taloned paw. The more they kept to their village, the bolder grew the wild things that gambolled and bellowed on the grazing-grounds by the Waingunga. They had no time to patch and plaster the rear walls of the empty byres that backed on to the Jungle; the wild pig trampled them down, and the knotty-rooted vines hurried after and threw their elbows over the new-won ground, and the coarse grass bristled behind the vines like the lances of a goblin army following a retreat. The unmarried men ran away first, and carried the news far and near that the village was doomed. Who could fight, they said, against the Jungle, or the Gods of the Jungle, when the very village cobra had left his hole in the platform under the peepul-tree? So their little commerce with the outside world shrunk as the trodden paths across the open grew fewer and fainter. At last the nightly trumpetings of Hathi and his three sons ceased to trouble them; for they had no more to be robbed of. The crop on the ground and the seed in the ground had been taken. The outlying fields were already losing their shape, and it was time to throw themselves on the charity of the English at Khanhiwara.

Native fashion, they delayed their departure from one day to another till the first Rains caught them and the unmended roofs let in a flood, and the grazing-ground stood ankle deep, and all life came on with a rush after the heat of the summer. Then they waded out—men, women, and children—through the blinding hot rain of the morning, but turned naturally for one farewell look at their homes.

They heard, as the last burdened family filed through the gate, a crash of falling beams and thatch behind the walls. They saw a shiny, snaky black trunk lifted for an instant, scattering sodden thatch. It disappeared, and there was another crash, followed by a squeal. Hathi had been plucking off the roofs of the huts as you pluck water-lilies, and a rebounding beam had pricked him. He needed only this to unchain his full strength, for of all things in the Jungle the wild elephant enraged is the most wantonly destructive. He kicked backward at a mud wall that crumbled at the stroke, and, crumbling, melted to yellow mud under the torrent of rain. Then he wheeled and squealed, and tore through the narrow streets, leaning against the huts right and left, shivering the crazy doors, and crumpling up the caves; while his three sons raged behind as they had raged at the Sack of the Fields of Bhurtpore.

"The Jungle will swallow these shells," said a quiet voice in the wreckage. "It is the outer wall that must lie down," and Mowgli, with the rain sluicing over his bare shoulders and arms, leaped back from a wall that was settling like a tired buffalo.

"All in good time," panted Hathi. "Oh, but my tusks were red at Bhurtpore; To the outer wall, children! With the head! Together! Now!"

The four pushed side by side; the outer wall bulged, split, and fell, and the villagers, dumb with horror, saw the savage, clay-streaked heads of the wreckers in the ragged gap. Then they fled, houseless and foodless, down the valley, as their village, shredded and tossed and trampled, melted behind them.

A month later the place was a dimpled mound, covered with soft, green young stuff; and by the end of the Rains there

was the roaring jungle in full blast on the spot that had been
under plough not six months before.

MOWGLI'S SONG AGAINST PEOPLE

I will let loose against you the fleet-footed vines--
I will call in the Jungle to stamp out your lines!
The roofs shall fade before it,
The house-beams shall fall,
And the Karela, the bitter Karela,
Shall cover it all!
In the gates of these your councils my people shall sing,
In the doors of these your garners the Bat-folk shall cling;
And the snake shall be your watchman,
By a hearthstone unswept;
For the Karela, the bitter Karela,
Shall fruit where ye slept!
Ye shall not see my strikers; ye shall hear them and guess;
By night, before the moon-rise, I will send for my cess,
And the wolf shall be your herdsman
By a landmark removed,
For the Karela, the bitter Karela,
Shall seed where ye loved!
I will reap your fields before you at the hands of a host;
Ye shall glean behind my reapers, for the bread that is lost,
And the deer shall be your oxen
By a headland untilled,
For the Karela, the bitter Karela,
Shall leaf where ye build!
I have untied against you the club-footed vines,
I have sent in the Jungle to swamp out your lines.
The trees--the trees are on you!
The house-beams shall fall,
And the Karela, the bitter Karela,
Shall cover you all!

THE UNDERTAKERS

When ye say to Tabaqui, "My Brother!" when ye call
the Hyena to meat,

Ye may cry the Full Truce with Jacala--the Belly
that runs on four feet.

Jungle Law

"Respect the aged! O Companions of the River—respect the aged!"

Nothing could be seen on the broad reach of the river except a little fleet of square-sailed, wooden-pinned barges, loaded with building-stone, that had just come under the railway bridge, and were driving down-stream. They put their clumsy helms over to avoid the sand-bar made by the scour of the bridge-piers, and as they passed, three abreast, the horrible voice began again:

"O Brahmins of the River—respect the aged and infirm!"

A boatman turned where he sat on the gunwale, lifted up his hand, said something that was not a blessing, and the boats creaked on through the twilight. The broad Indian river, that looked more like a chain of little lakes than a stream, was as smooth as glass, reflecting the sandy-red sky in mid-channel, but splashed with patches of yellow and dusky purple near and under the low banks. Little creeks ran into the river in the wet season, but now their dry mouths hung clear above water-line. On the left shore, and almost under the railway bridge, stood a mud-and-brick and thatch-and-stick village, whose main street, full of cattle going back to their byres, ran straight to the river, and ended in a sort of rude brick pier-head, where people who wanted to wash could wade in step by step. That was the Ghaut of the village of Mugger-Ghaut.

Night was falling fast over the fields of lentils and rice and cotton in the low-lying ground yearly flooded by the river; over the reeds that fringed the elbow of the bend, and the tangled jungle of the grazing-grounds behind the still reeds. The parrots and crows, who had been chattering and shouting over their evening drink, had flown inland to roost, crossing the out-going battalions of the flying-foxes; and cloud upon cloud of water-birds came whistling and "honking" to the cover of the reed-beds. There were geese, barrel-headed and black-backed, teal, widgeon, mallard, and sheldrake, with curlews, and here and there a flamingo.

A lumbering Adjutant-crane brought up the rear, flying as though each slow stroke would be his last.

"Respect the aged! Brahmins of the River—respect the aged!"

The Adjutant half turned his head, sheered a little in the direction of the voice, and landed stiffly on the sand-bar below the bridge. Then you saw what a ruffianly brute he really was. His back view was immensely respectable, for he stood nearly six feet high, and looked rather like a very proper bald-headed parson. In front it was different, for his Ally Sloper-like head and neck had not a feather to them, and there was a horrible raw-skin pouch on his neck under his chin—a hold-all for the things his pick-axe beak might steal. His legs were long and thin and skinny, but he moved them delicately, and looked at them with pride as he preened down his ashy-gray tail-feathers, glanced over the smooth of his shoulder, and stiffened into "Stand at attention."

A mangy little Jackal, who had been yapping hungrily on a low bluff, cocked up his ears and tail, and scuttered across the shallows to join the Adjutant.

He was the lowest of his caste—not that the best of jackals are good for much, but this one was peculiarly low, being half a beggar, half a criminal—a cleaner-up of village rubbish-heaps, desperately timid or wildly bold, everlastingly hungry, and full of cunning that never did him any good.

"Ugh!" he said, shaking himself dolefully as he landed. "May the red mange destroy the dogs of this village! I have three bites for each flea upon me, and all because I looked— only looked, mark you—at an old shoe in a cow-byre. Can I eat mud?" He scratched himself under his left ear.

"I heard," said the Adjutant, in a voice like a blunt saw going through a thick board—"I HEARD there was a new-born puppy in that same shoe."

"To hear is one thing; to know is another," said the Jackal, who had a very fair knowledge of proverbs, picked up by listening to men round the village fires of an evening.

"Quite true. So, to make sure, I took care of that puppy while the dogs were busy elsewhere."

"They were VERY busy," said the Jackal. "Well, I must not go to the village hunting for scraps yet awhile. And so there truly was a blind puppy in that shoe?"

"It is here," said the Adjutant, squinting over his beak at his full pouch. "A small thing, but acceptable now that charity is dead in the world."

"Ahai! The world is iron in these days," wailed the Jackal. Then his restless eye caught the least possible ripple on the water, and he went on quickly: "Life is hard for us all, and I doubt not that even our excellent master, the Pride of the Ghaut and the Envy of the River——"

"A liar, a flatterer, and a Jackal were all hatched out of the same egg," said the Adjutant to nobody in particular; for he was rather a fine sort of a liar on his own account when he took the trouble.

"Yes, the Envy of the River," the Jackal repeated, raising his voice. "Even he, I doubt not, finds that since the bridge has been built good food is more scarce. But on the other hand, though I would by no means say this to his noble face, he is so wise and so virtuous—as I, alas I am not——"

"When the Jackal owns he is gray, how black must the Jackal be!" muttered the Adjutant. He could not see what was coming.

"That his food never fails, and in consequence——"

There was a soft grating sound, as though a boat had just touched in shoal water. The Jackal spun round quickly and faced (it is always best to face) the creature he had been talking about. It was a twenty-four-foot crocodile, cased in what looked like treble-riveted boiler-plate, studded and keeled and crested; the yellow points of his upper teeth just overhanging his beautifully fluted lower jaw. It was the blunt-nosed Mugger of Mugger-Ghaut, older than any man in the village, who had given his name to the village; the demon of the ford before the railway bridge, came—murderer, man-eater, and local fetish in one. He lay with his chin in the shallows, keeping his place by an almost invisible rippling of his tail, and well the Jackal knew that one stroke of that same tail in the water would carry the Mugger up the bank with the rush of a steam-engine.

"Auspiciously met, Protector of the Poor!" he fawned, backing at every word. "A delectable voice was heard, and we came in the hopes of sweet conversation. My tailless presumption, while waiting here, led me, indeed, to speak of thee. It is my hope that nothing was overheard."

Now the Jackal had spoken just to be listened to, for he knew flattery was the best way of getting things to eat, and the Mugger knew that the Jackal had spoken for this end, and the Jackal knew that the Mugger knew, and the Mugger knew that the Jackal knew that the Mugger knew, and so they were all very contented together.

The old brute pushed and panted and grunted up the bank, mumbling, "Respect the aged and infirm!" and all the time his little eyes burned like coals under the heavy, horny eyelids on the top of his triangular head, as he shoved his bloated barrel-body along between his crutched legs. Then he settled down, and, accustomed as the Jackal was to his ways, he could not help starting, for the hundredth time, when he saw how exactly the Mugger imitated a log adrift on the bar. He had even taken pains to lie at the exact angle a naturally stranded log would make with the water, having regard to the current of the season at the time and place. All this was only a matter of habit, of course, because the Mugger had come ashore for pleasure; but a crocodile is never quite full, and if the Jackal had been deceived by the likeness he would not have lived to philosophise over it.

"My child, I heard nothing," said the Mugger, shutting one eye. "The water was in my ears, and also I was faint with hunger. Since the railway bridge was built my people at my village have ceased to love me; and that is breaking my heart."

"Ah, shame!" said the Jackal. "So noble a heart, too! But men are all alike, to my mind."

"Nay, there are very great differences indeed," the Mugger answered gently. "Some are as lean as boat-poles. Others again are fat as young ja—dogs. Never would I causelessly revile men. They are of all fashions, but the long years have shown me that, one with another, they are very good. Men, women, and children—I have no fault to find with them. And remember, child, he who rebukes the World is rebuked by the World."

"Flattery is worse than an empty tin can in the belly. But that which we have just heard is wisdom," said the Adjutant, bringing down one foot.

"Consider, though, their ingratitude to this excellent one," began the Jackal tenderly.

"Nay, nay, not ingratitude!" the Mugger said. "They do not think for others; that is all. But I have noticed, lying at my station below the ford, that the stairs of the new bridge are cruelly hard to climb, both for old people and young children. The old, indeed, are not so worthy of consideration, but I am grieved—I am truly grieved—on account of the fat children. Still, I think, in a little while, when the newness of the bridge has worn away, we shall see my people's bare brown legs bravely splashing through the ford as before. Then the old Mugger will be honoured again."

"But surely I saw Marigold wreaths floating off the edge of the Ghaut only this noon," said the Adjutant.

Marigold wreaths are a sign of reverence all India over.

"An error—an error. It was the wife of the sweetmeat-seller. She loses her eyesight year by year, and cannot tell a log from me—the Mugger of the Ghaut. I saw the mistake when she threw the garland, for I was lying at the very foot of the Ghaut, and had she taken another step I might have shown her some little difference. Yet she meant well, and we must consider the spirit of the offering."

"What good are marigold wreaths when one is on the rubbish-heap?" said the Jackal, hunting for fleas, but keeping one wary eye on his Protector of the Poor.

"True, but they have not yet begun to make the rubbish-heap that shall carry ME. Five times have I seen the river draw back from the village and make new land at the foot of the street. Five times have I seen the village rebuilt on the banks, and I shall see it built yet five times more. I am no faithless, fish-hunting Gavial, I, at Kasi to-day and Prayag to-morrow, as the saying is, but the true and constant watcher of the ford. It is not for nothing, child, that the village bears my name, and 'he who watches long,' as the saying is, 'shall at last have his reward.'"

"_I_ have watched long—very long—nearly all my life, and my reward has been bites and blows," said the Jackal.

"Ho! ho! ho!" roared the Adjutant.

> *"In August was the Jackal born;*
> *The Rains fell in September;*
> *'Now such a fearful flood as this,'*
> *Says he, 'I can't remember!'"*

There is one very unpleasant peculiarity about the Adjutant. At uncertain times he suffers from acute attacks of the fidgets or cramp in his legs, and though he is more virtuous to behold than any of the cranes, who are all immensely respectable, he flies off into wild, cripple-stilt war-dances, half opening his wings and bobbing his bald head up and down; while for reasons best known to himself he is very careful to time his worst attacks with his nastiest remarks. At the last word of his song he came to attention again, ten times adjutaunter than before.

The Jackal winced, though he was full three seasons old, but you cannot resent an insult from a person with a beak a yard long, and the power of driving it like a javelin. The Adjutant was a most notorious coward, but the Jackal was worse.

"We must live before we can learn," said the Mugger, "and there is this to say: Little jackals are very common, child, but such a mugger as I am is not common. For all that, I am not proud, since pride is destruction; but take notice, it is Fate, and against his Fate no one who swims or walks or runs should say anything at all. I am well contented with Fate. With good luck, a keen eye, and the custom of considering whether a creek or a backwater has an outlet to it ere you ascend, much may be done."

"Once I heard that even the Protector of the Poor made a mistake," said the Jackal viciously.

"True; but there my Fate helped me. It was before I had come to my full growth—before the last famine but three (by the Right and Left of Gunga, how full used the streams to be in those days!). Yes, I was young and unthinking, and when the flood came, who so pleased as I? A little made me very happy then. The village was deep in flood, and I swam above the Ghaut and went far inland, up to the rice-fields, and they were deep in good mud. I remember also a pair of bracelets (glass they were, and troubled me not a little) that I found that evening. Yes, glass bracelets; and, if my memory serves me well, a shoe. I should have shaken off both shoes, but I was hungry. I learned better later. Yes. And so I fed and rested me; but when I was ready to go to the river again the flood had fallen, and I walked through the mud of the main street.

Who but I? Came out all my people, priests and women and children, and I looked upon them with benevolence. The mud is not a good place to fight in. Said a boatman, 'Get axes and kill him, for he is the Mugger of the ford.' 'Not so,' said the Brahmin. 'Look, he is driving the flood before him! He is the godling of the village.' Then they threw many flowers at me, and by happy thought one led a goat across the road."

"How good—how very good is goat!" said the Jackal.

"Hairy—too hairy, and when found in the water more than likely to hide a cross-shaped hook. But that goat I accepted, and went down to the Ghaut in great honour. Later, my Fate sent me the boatman who had desired to cut off my tail with an axe. His boat grounded upon an old shoal which you would not remember."

"We are not ALL jackals here," said the Adjutant. "Was it the shoal made where the stone-boats sank in the year of the great drouth—a long shoal that lasted three floods?"

"There were two," said the Mugger; "an upper and a lower shoal."

"Ay, I forgot. A channel divided them, and later dried up again," said the Adjutant, who prided himself on his memory.

"On the lower shoal my well-wisher's craft grounded. He was sleeping in the bows, and, half awake, leaped over to his waist—no, it was no more than to his knees—to push off. His empty boat went on and touched again below the next reach, as the river ran then. I followed, because I knew men would come out to drag it ashore."

"And did they do so?" said the Jackal, a little awe-stricken. This was hunting on a scale that impressed him.

"There and lower down they did. I went no farther, but that gave me three in one day—well-fed manjis (boatmen) all, and, except in the case of the last (then I was careless), never a cry to warn those on the bank."

"Ah, noble sport! But what cleverness and great judgment it requires!" said the Jackal.

"Not cleverness, child, but only thought. A little thought in life is like salt upon rice, as the boatmen say, and I have thought deeply always. The Gavial, my cousin, the fish-eater, has told me how hard it is for him to follow his fish, and how one fish differs from the other, and how he must know them all, both together and apart. I say that is wisdom; but, on the other hand, my cousin, the Gavial, lives among his people. MY people do not swim in companies, with their mouths out of the water, as Rewa does; nor do they constantly rise to the surface of the water, and turn over on their sides, like Mohoo and little Chapta; nor do they gather in shoals after flood, like Batchua and Chilwa."

"All are very good eating," said the Adjutant, clattering his beak.

"So my cousin says, and makes a great to-do over hunting them, but they do not climb the banks to escape his sharp nose. MY people are otherwise. Their life is on the land, in the houses, among the cattle. I must know what they do, and what they are about to do; and adding the tail to the trunk, as the saying is, I make up the whole elephant. Is there a green branch and an iron ring hanging over a doorway? The old Mugger knows that a boy has been born in that house, and must some day come down to the Ghaut to play. Is a maiden to be married? The old Mugger knows, for he sees the men carry gifts back and forth; and she, too, comes down to the Ghaut to bathe before her wedding, and—he is there. Has the river changed its channel, and made new land where there was only sand before? The Mugger knows."

"Now, of what use is that knowledge?" said the Jackal. "The river has shifted even in my little life." Indian rivers are nearly always moving about in their beds, and will shift, sometimes, as much as two or three miles in a season, drowning the fields on one bank, and spreading good silt on the other.

"There is no knowledge so useful," said the Mugger, "for new land means new quarrels. The Mugger knows. Oho! the Mugger knows. As soon as the water has drained off, he creeps up the little creeks that men think would not hide a dog, and there he waits. Presently comes a farmer saying he will plant cucumbers here, and melons there, in the new land that the river has given him. He feels the good mud with his bare toes. Anon comes another, saying he will put onions, and carrots, and sugar-cane in such and such places. They meet as boats adrift meet, and each rolls his eye at the other under the big blue turban. The old Mugger sees and hears. Each calls the other 'Brother,' and they go to mark out the boundaries of the new land. The Mugger hurries with them from point to point, shuffling very low through the mud. Now they begin to quarrel! Now they say hot words! Now they pull turbans! Now they lift up their lathis (clubs), and, at last, one falls backward into the mud, and the other runs away. When he comes back the dispute is settled, as the iron-bound bamboo of the loser witnesses. Yet they are not grateful to the Mugger. No, they cry 'Murder!' and their families fight with sticks, twenty a-side. My people are good people—upland Jats—Malwais of the Bet. They do not give blows for sport, and, when the fight is done, the old Mugger waits far down the river, out of sight of the village, behind the kikar-scrub yonder. Then come they down, my broad-shouldered Jats—eight or nine together under the stars, bearing the dead man upon a bed. They are old men with gray beards, and voices as deep as mine. They light a little fire—ah! how well I know that fire!—and they drink tobacco, and they nod their heads together forward in a ring, or sideways toward the dead man upon the bank. They say the English Law will come with a rope for this matter, and that such a man's family will be ashamed, because such a man must be hanged in the great square of the Jail. Then say the friends of the dead, 'Let him hang!' and the talk is all to do over again—once, twice, twenty times in the long night. Then says one, at last, 'The fight was a fair fight. Let us take blood-money, a little more than is offered by the slayer, and we will say no more about it.' Then do they haggle over the blood-money, for the dead was a strong man, leaving many sons. Yet before amratvela (sunrise) they put the fire to him a little, as the custom is, and the dead man comes to me, and HE says no more about it. Aha! my children, the Mugger knows—the Mugger knows—and my Malwah Jats are a good people!"

"They are too close—too narrow in the hand for my crop," croaked the Adjutant. "They waste not the polish on the cow's horn, as the saying is; and, again, who can glean after a Malwai?"

"Ah, I—glean—THEM," said the Mugger.

"Now, in Calcutta of the South, in the old days," the Adjutant went on, "everything was thrown into the streets, and we picked and chose. Those wore dainty seasons. But to-day they keep their streets as clean as the outside of an egg, and my people fly away. To be clean is one thing; to dust, sweep, and sprinkle seven times a day wearies the very Gods themselves."

"There was a down-country jackal had it from a brother, who told me, that in Calcutta of the South all the jackals were as fat as otters in the Rains," said the Jackal, his mouth watering at the bare thought of it.

"Ah, but the white-faces are there—the English, and they bring dogs from somewhere down the river in boats—big fat dogs—to keep those same jackals lean," said the Adjutant.

"They are, then, as hard-hearted as these people? I might have known. Neither earth, sky, nor water shows charity to a jackal. I saw the tents of a white-face last season, after the Rains, and I also took a new yellow bridle to eat. The white-faces do not dress their leather in the proper way. It made me very sick."

"That was better than my case," said the Adjutant. "When I was in my third season, a young and a bold bird, I went down to the river where the big boats come in. The boats of the English are thrice as big as this village."

"He has been as far as Delhi, and says all the people there walk on their heads," muttered the Jackal. The Mugger opened his left eye, and looked keenly at the Adjutant.

"It is true," the big bird insisted. "A liar only lies when he hopes to be believed. No one who had not seen those boats COULD believe this truth."

"THAT is more reasonable," said the Mugger. "And then?"

"From the insides of this boat they were taking out great pieces of white stuff, which, in a little while, turned to water. Much split off, and fell about on the shore, and the rest they swiftly put into a house with thick walls. But a boatman, who laughed, took a piece no larger than a small dog, and threw it to me. I—all my people—swallow without reflection, and that piece I swallowed as is our custom. Immediately I was afflicted with an excessive cold which, beginning in my crop, ran down to the extreme end of my toes, and deprived me even of speech, while the boatmen laughed at me. Never have I felt such cold. I danced in my grief and amazement till I could recover my breath and then I danced and cried out against the falseness of this world; and the boatmen derided me till they fell down. The chief wonder of the matter, setting aside that marvellous coldness, was that there was nothing at all in my crop when I had finished my lamentings!"

The Adjutant had done his very best to describe his feelings after swallowing a seven-pound lump of Wenham Lake ice, off an American ice-ship, in the days before Calcutta made her ice by machinery; but as he did not know what ice was, and as the Mugger and the Jackal knew rather less, the tale missed fire.

"Anything," said the Mugger, shutting his left eye again—"ANYTHING is possible that comes out of a boat thrice the size of Mugger-Ghaut. My village is not a small one."

There was a whistle overhead on the bridge, and the Delhi Mail slid across, all the carriages gleaming with light, and the shadows faithfully following along the river. It clanked away into the dark again; but the Mugger and the Jackal were so well used to it that they never turned their heads.

"Is that anything less wonderful than a boat thrice the size of Mugger-Ghaut?" said the bird, looking up.

"I saw that built, child. Stone by stone I saw the bridge-piers rise, and when the men fell off (they were wondrous sure-footed for the most part—but WHEN they fell) I was ready. After the first pier was made they never thought to look down the stream for the body to burn. There, again, I saved much trouble. There was nothing strange in the building of the bridge," said the Mugger.

"But that which goes across, pulling the roofed carts! That is strange," the Adjutant repeated. "It is, past any doubt, a new breed of bullock. Some day it will not be able to keep its foothold up yonder, and will fall as the men did. The old Mugger will then be ready."

The Jackal looked at the Adjutant and the Adjutant looked at the Jackal. If there was one thing they were more certain of than another, it was that the engine was everything in the wide world except a bullock. The Jackal had watched it time and again from the aloe hedges by the side of the line, and the Adjutant had seen engines since the first locomotive ran in India. But the Mugger had only looked up at the thing from below, where the brass dome seemed rather like a bullock's hump.

"M—yes, a new kind of bullock," the Mugger repeated ponderously, to make himself quite sure in his own mind; and "Certainly it is a bullock," said the Jackal.

"And again it might be——" began the Mugger pettishly.

"Certainly—most certainly," said the Jackal, without waiting for the other to finish.

"What?" said the Mugger angrily, for he could feel that the others knew more than he did. "What might it be? _I_ never finished my words. You said it was a bullock."

"It is anything the Protector of the Poor pleases. I am HIS servant—not the servant of the thing that crosses the river."

"Whatever it is, it is white-face work," said the Adjutant; "and for my own part, I would not lie out upon a place so near to it as this bar."

"You do not know the English as I do," said the Mugger. "There was a white-face here when the bridge was built, and he would take a boat in the evenings and shuffle with his feet on the bottom-boards, and whisper: 'Is he here? Is he there? Bring me my gun.' I could hear him before I could see him— each sound that he made—creaking and puffing and rattling his gun, up and down the river. As surely as I had picked up one of his workmen, and thus saved great expense in wood for the burning, so surely would he come down to the Ghaut, and shout in a loud voice that he would hunt me, and rid the river of me—the Mugger of Mugger-Ghaut! ME! Children, I have swum under the bottom of his boat for hour after hour, and heard him fire his gun at logs; and when I was well sure he was wearied, I have risen by his side and snapped my jaws in his face. When the bridge was finished he went away. All the English hunt in that fashion, except when they are hunted."

"Who hunts the white-faces?" yapped the Jackal excitedly.

"No one now, but I have hunted them in my time."

"I remember a little of that Hunting. I was young then," said the Adjutant, clattering his beak significantly.

"I was well established here. My village was being builded for the third time, as I remember, when my cousin, the Gavial, brought me word of rich waters above Benares. At first I would not go, for my cousin, who is a fish-eater, does not always know the good from the bad; but I heard my people talking in the evenings, and what they said made me certain."

"And what did they say?" the Jackal asked.

"They said enough to make me, the Mugger of Mugger-Ghaut, leave water and take to my feet. I went by night, using the littlest streams as they served me; but it was the beginning of the hot weather, and all streams were low. I crossed dusty roads; I went through tall grass; I climbed hills in the moonlight. Even rocks did I climb, children—consider this well. I crossed the tail of Sirhind, the waterless, before I could find the set of the little rivers that flow Gungaward. I was a month's journey from my own people and the river that I knew. That was very marvellous!"

"What food on the way?" said the Jackal, who kept his soul in his little stomach, and was not a bit impressed by the Mugger's land travels.

"That which I could find—COUSIN," said the Mugger slowly, dragging each word.

Now you do not call a man a cousin in India unless you think you can establish some kind of blood-relationship, and as it is only in old fairy-tales that the Mugger ever marries a jackal, the Jackal knew for what reason he had been suddenly lifted into the Mugger's family circle. If they had been alone he would not have cared, but the Adjutant's eyes twinkled with mirth at the ugly jest.

"Assuredly, Father, I might have known," said the Jackal. A mugger does not care to be called a father of jackals, and the Mugger of Mugger-Ghaut said as much—and a great deal more which there is no use in repeating here.

"The Protector of the Poor has claimed kinship. How can I remember the precise degree? Moreover, we eat the same food. He has said it," was the Jackal's reply.

That made matters rather worse, for what the Jackal hinted at was that the Mugger must have eaten his food on that land-march fresh and fresh every day, instead of keeping it by him till it was in a fit and proper condition, as every self-respecting mugger and most wild beasts do when they can. Indeed, one of the worst terms of contempt along the River-bed is "eater of fresh meat." It is nearly as bad as calling a man a cannibal.

"That food was eaten thirty seasons ago," said the Adjutant quietly. "If we talk for thirty seasons more it will never come back. Tell us, now, what happened when the good waters were reached after thy most wonderful land journey. If we listened to the howling of every jackal the business of the town would stop, as the saying is."

The Mugger must have been grateful for the interruption, because he went on, with a rush:

"By the Right and Left of Gunga! when I came there never did I see such waters!"

"Were they better, then, than the big flood of last season?" said the Jackal.

"Better! That flood was no more than comes every five years—a handful of drowned strangers, some chickens, and a dead bullock in muddy water with cross-currents. But the season I think of, the river was low, smooth, and even, and, as the Gavial had warned me, the dead English came down, touching each other. I got my girth in that season—my girth and my depth. From Agra, by Etawah and the broad waters by Allahabad——"

"Oh, the eddy that set under the walls of the fort at Allahabad!" said the Adjutant. "They came in there like widgeon to the reeds, and round and round they swung—thus!"

He went off into his horrible dance again, while the Jackal looked on enviously. He naturally could not remember the terrible year of the Mutiny they were talking about. The Mugger continued:

"Yes, by Allahabad one lay still in the slack-water and let twenty go by to pick one; and, above all, the English were not cumbered with jewellery and nose-rings and anklets as my women are nowadays. To delight in ornaments is to end with a rope for a necklace, as the saying is. All the muggers of all the rivers grew fat then, but it was my Fate to be fatter than them all. The news was that the English were being hunted into the rivers, and by the Right and Left of Gunga! we believed it was true. So far as I went south I believed it to be true; and I went down-stream beyond Monghyr and the tombs that look over the river."

"I know that place," said the Adjutant. "Since those days Monghyr is a lost city. Very few live there now."

"Thereafter I worked up-stream very slowly and lazily, and a little above Monghyr there came down a boatful of white-faces—alive! They were, as I remember, women, lying under a cloth spread over sticks, and crying aloud. There was never a gun fired at us, the watchers of the fords in those days. All the guns were busy elsewhere. We could hear them day and night inland, coming and going as the wind shifted. I rose up full before the boat, because I had never seen white-faces alive, though I knew them well—otherwise. A naked white child kneeled by the side of the boat, and, stooping over, must needs try to trail his hands in the river. It is a pretty thing to see how a child loves running water. I had fed that day, but there was yet a little unfilled space within me. Still, it was for sport and not for food that I rose at the child's hands. They were so clear a mark that I did not even look when I closed; but they were so small that though my jaws rang true—I am sure of that—the child drew them up swiftly, unhurt. They must have passed between tooth and tooth—those small white hands. I should have caught him cross-wise at the elbows; but, as I said, it was only for sport and desire to see new things that I rose at all. They cried out one after another in the boat, and presently I rose again to watch them. The boat was too heavy to push over. They were only women, but he who trusts a woman will walk on duckweed in a pool, as the saying is: and by the Right and Left of Gunga, that is truth!"

"Once a woman gave me some dried skin from a fish," said the Jackal. "I had hoped to get her baby, but horse-food is better than the kick of a horse, as the saying is. What did thy woman do?"

"She fired at me with a short gun of a kind I have never seen before or since. Five times, one after another" (the Mugger must have met with an old-fashioned revolver); "and I stayed open-mouthed and gaping, my head in the smoke. Never did I see such a thing. Five times, as swiftly as I wave my tail—thus!"

The Jackal, who had been growing more and more interested in the story, had just time to leap back as the huge tail swung by like a scythe.

"Not before the fifth shot," said the Mugger, as though he had never dreamed of stunning one of his listeners—"not before the fifth shot did I sink, and I rose in time to hear a boatman telling all those white women that I was most certainly dead. One bullet had gone under a neck-plate of mine. I know not if it is there still, for the reason I cannot turn my head. Look and see, child. It will show that my tale is true."

"I?" said the Jackal. "Shall an eater of old shoes, a bone-cracker, presume, to doubt the word of the Envy of the River? May my tail be bitten off by blind puppies if the shadow of such a thought has crossed my humble mind! The Protector of the Poor has condescended to inform me, his slave, that once in his life he has been wounded by a woman. That is sufficient, and I will tell the tale to all my children, asking for no proof."

"Over-much civility is sometimes no better than over-much discourtesy, for, as the saying is, one can choke a guest with curds. I do NOT desire that any children of thine should know that the Mugger of Mugger-Ghaut took his only wound from a woman. They will have much else to think of if they get their meat as miserably as does their father."

"It is forgotten long ago! It was never said! There never

was a white woman! There was no boat! Nothing whatever happened at all."

The Jackal waved his brush to show how completely everything was wiped out of his memory, and sat down with an air.

"Indeed, very many things happened," said the Mugger, beaten in his second attempt that night to get the better of his friend. (Neither bore malice, however. Eat and be eaten was fair law along the river, and the Jackal came in for his share of plunder when the Mugger had finished a meal.) "I left that boat and went up-stream, and, when I had reached Arrah and the back-waters behind it, there were no more dead English. The river was empty for a while. Then came one or two dead, in red coats, not English, but of one kind all— Hindus and Purbeeahs—then five and six abreast, and at last, from Arrah to the North beyond Agra, it was as though whole villages had walked into the water. They came out of little creeks one after another, as the logs come down in the Rains. When the river rose they rose also in companies from the shoals they had rested upon; and the falling flood dragged them with it across the fields and through the Jungle by the long hair. All night, too, going North, I heard the guns, and by day the shod feet of men crossing fords, and that noise which a heavy cart-wheel makes on sand under water; and every ripple brought more dead. At last even I was afraid, for I said: 'If this thing happen to men, how shall the Mugger of Mugger-Ghaut escape?' There were boats, too, that came up behind me without sails, burning continually, as the cotton-boats sometimes burn, but never sinking."

"Ah!" said the Adjutant. "Boats like those come to Calcutta of the South. They are tall and black, they beat up the water behind them with a tail, and they——"

"Are thrice as big as my village. MY boats were low and white; they beat up the water on either side of them and were no larger than the boats of one who speaks truth should be. They made me very afraid, and I left water and went back to this my river, hiding by day and walking by night, when I could not find little streams to help me. I came to my village again, but I did not hope to see any of my people there. Yet they were ploughing and sowing and reaping, and going to and fro in their fields, as quietly as their own cattle."

"Was there still good food in the river?" said the Jackal.

"More than I had any desire for. Even I—and I do not eat mud—even I was tired, and, as I remember, a little frightened of this constant coming down of the silent ones. I heard my people say in my village that all the English were dead; but those that came, face down, with the current were NOT English, as my people saw. Then my people said that it was best to say nothing at all, but to pay the tax and plough the land. After a long time the river cleared, and those that came down it had been clearly drowned by the floods, as I could well see; and though it was not so easy then to get food, I was heartily glad of it. A little killing here and there is no bad thing—but even the Mugger is sometimes satisfied, as the saying is."

"Marvellous! Most truly marvellous!" said the Jackal. "I am become fat through merely hearing about so much good eating. And afterward what, if it be permitted to ask, did the Protector of the Poor do?"

"I said to myself—and by the Right and Left of Gunga! I locked my jaws on that vow—I said I would never go roving any more. So I lived by the Ghaut, very close to my own people, and I watched over them year after year; and they loved me so much that they threw marigold wreaths at my head whenever they saw it lift. Yes, and my Fate has been very kind to me, and the river is good enough to respect my poor and infirm presence; only——"

"No one is all happy from his beak to his tail," said the Adjutant sympathetically. "What does the Mugger of Mugger-Ghaut need more?"

"That little white child which I did not get," said the Mugger, with a deep sigh. "He was very small, but I have not forgotten. I am old now, but before I die it is my desire to try one new thing. It is true they are a heavy-footed, noisy, and foolish people, and the sport would be small, but I remember the old days above Benares, and, if the child lives, he will remember still. It may be he goes up and down the bank of some river, telling how he once passed his hands between the teeth of the Mugger of Mugger-Ghaut, and lived to make a tale of it. My Fate has been very kind, but that plagues me sometimes in my dreams—the thought of the little white child in the bows of that boat." He yawned, and closed his jaws. "And now I will rest and think. Keep silent, my children, and respect the aged."

He turned stiffly, and shuffled to the top of the sand-bar, while the Jackal drew back with the Adjutant to the shelter of a tree stranded on the end nearest the railway bridge.

"That was a pleasant and profitable life," he grinned, looking up inquiringly at the bird who towered above him. "And not once, mark you, did he think fit to tell me where a morsel might have been left along the banks. Yet I have told HIM a hundred times of good things wallowing down-stream. How true is the saying, 'All the world forgets the Jackal and the Barber when the news has been told!' Now he is going to sleep! Arrh!"

"How can a jackal hunt with a Mugger?" said the Adjutant coolly. "Big thief and little thief; it is easy to say who gets the pickings."

The Jackal turned, whining impatiently, and was going to curl himself up under the tree-trunk, when suddenly he cowered, and looked up through the draggled branches at the bridge almost above his head.

"What now?" said the Adjutant, opening his wings uneasily.

"Wait till we see. The wind blows from us to them, but they are not looking for us—those two men."

"Men, is it? My office protects me. All India knows I am holy." The Adjutant, being a first-class scavenger, is allowed to go where he pleases, and so this one never flinched.

"I am not worth a blow from anything better than an old shoe," said the Jackal, and listened again. "Hark to that footfall!" he went on. "That was no country leather, but the shod foot of a white-face. Listen again! Iron hits iron up there! It is a gun! Friend, those heavy-footed, foolish English are coming to speak with the Mugger."

"Warn him, then. He was called Protector of the Poor by some one not unlike a starving Jackal but a little time ago."

"Let my cousin protect his own hide. He has told me again and again there is nothing to fear from the white-faces. They must be white-faces. Not a villager of Mugger-Ghaut would dare to come after him. See, I said it was a gun! Now, with good luck, we shall feed before daylight. He cannot hear well out of water, and—this time it is not a woman!"

A shiny barrel glittered for a minute in the moonlight on the girders. The Mugger was lying on the sand-bar as still as his own shadow, his fore-feet spread out a little, his head dropped between them, snoring like a—mugger.

A voice on the bridge whispered: "It's an odd shot—straight down almost—but as safe as houses. Better try behind the neck. Golly! what a brute! The villagers will be wild if he's shot, though. He's the deota [godling] of these parts."

"Don't care a rap," another voice answered; "he took about fifteen of my best coolies while the bridge was building, and it's time he was put a stop to. I've been after him in a boat for weeks. Stand by with the Martini as soon as I've given him both barrels of this."

"Mind the kick, then. A double four-bore's no joke."

"That's for him to decide. Here goes!"

There was a roar like the sound of a small cannon (the biggest sort of elephant-rifle is not very different from some artillery), and a double streak of flame, followed by the stinging crack of a Martini, whose long bullet makes nothing of a crocodile's plates. But the explosive bullets did the work. One of them struck just behind the Mugger's neck, a hand's-breadth to the left of the backbone, while the other burst a little lower down, at the beginning of the tail. In ninety-nine cases out of a hundred a mortally-wounded crocodile can scramble to deep water and get away; but the Mugger of Mugger-Ghaut was literally broken into three pieces. He hardly moved his head before the life went out of him, and he lay as flat as the Jackal.

"Thunder and lightning! Lightning and thunder!" said that miserable little beast. "Has the thing that pulls the covered carts over the bridge tumbled at last?"

"It is no more than a gun," said the Adjutant, though his very tail-feathers quivered. "Nothing more than a gun. He is certainly dead. Here come the white-faces."

The two Englishmen had hurried down from the bridge

and across to the sand-bar, where they stood admiring the length of the Mugger. Then a native with an axe cut off the big head, and four men dragged it across the spit.

"The last time that I had my hand in a Mugger's mouth," said one of the Englishmen, stooping down (he was the man who had built the bridge), "it was when I was about five years old—coming down the river by boat to Monghyr. I was a Mutiny baby, as they call it. Poor mother was in the boat, too, and she often told me how she fired dad's old pistol at the beast's head."

"Well, you've certainly had your revenge on the chief of the clan—even if the gun has made your nose bleed. Hi, you boatmen! Haul that head up the bank, and we'll boil it for the skull. The skin's too knocked about to keep. Come along to bed now. This was worth sitting up all night for, wasn't it?"

*****

Curiously enough, the Jackal and the Adjutant made the very same remark not three minutes after the men had left.1

A RIPPLE SONG

Once a ripple came to land
In the golden sunset burning--
Lapped against a maiden's hand,
By the ford returning.
Dainty foot and gentle breast--
Here, across, be glad and rest.
"Maiden, wait," the ripple saith.
"Wait awhile, for I am Death!"
"Where my lover calls I go--
Shame it were to treat him coldly--
'Twas a fish that circled so,
Turning over boldly."
Dainty foot and tender heart,

Wait the loaded ferry-cart.
"Wait, ah, wait!" the ripple saith;
"Maiden, wait, for I am Death!"
"When my lover calls I haste--
Dame Disdain was never wedded!"
Ripple-ripple round her waist,
Clear the current eddied.
Foolish heart and faithful hand,
Little feet that touched no land.
Far away the ripple sped,
Ripple--ripple--running red!

THE KING'S ANKUS

These are the Four that are never content, that have never
been filled since the Dews began--
Jacala's mouth, and the glut of the Kite, and the hands of the
Ape, and the Eyes of Man.

Jungle Saying.

Kaa, the big Rock Python, had changed his skin for perhaps the two-hundredth time since his birth; and Mowgli, who never forgot that he owed his life to Kaa for a night's work at Cold Lairs, which you may perhaps remember, went to congratulate him. Skin-changing always makes a snake moody and depressed till the new skin begins to shine and look beautiful. Kaa never made fun of Mowgli any more, but accepted him, as the other Jungle People did, for the Master of the Jungle, and brought him all the news that a python of his size would naturally hear. What Kaa did not know about the Middle Jungle, as they call it,—the life that runs close to the earth or under it, the boulder, burrow, and the tree-bole life,—might have been written upon the smallest of his scales.

That afternoon Mowgli was sitting in the circle of Kaa's great coils, fingering the flaked and broken old skin that lay all looped and twisted among the rocks just as Kaa had left it. Kaa had very courteously packed himself under Mowgli's broad, bare shoulders, so that the boy was really resting in a living arm-chair.

"Even to the scales of the eyes it is perfect," said Mowgli, under his breath, playing with the old skin. "Strange to see the covering of one's own head at one's own feet!"

"Ay, but I lack feet," said Kaa; "and since this is the custom of all my people, I do not find it strange. Does thy skin never feel old and harsh?"

"Then go I and wash, Flathead; but, it is true, in the great heats I have wished I could slough my skin without pain, and run skinless."

"I wash, and ALSO I take off my skin. How looks the new coat?"

Mowgli ran his hand down the diagonal checkerings of the immense back. "The Turtle is harder-backed, but not so gay," he said judgmatically. "The Frog, my name-bearer, is more gay, but not so hard. It is very beautiful to see—like the mottling in the mouth of a lily."

"It needs water. A new skin never comes to full colour before the first bath. Let us go bathe."

"I will carry thee," said Mowgli; and he stooped down, laughing, to lift the middle section of Kaa's great body, just where the barrel was thickest. A man might just, as well have tried to heave up a two-foot water-main; and Kaa lay still, puffing with quiet amusement. Then the regular evening game began—the Boy in the flush of his great strength, and the Python in his sumptuous new skin, standing up one against the other for a wrestling match—a trial of eye and strength. Of course, Kaa could have crushed a dozen Mowglis if he had let himself go; but he played carefully, and never loosed one-tenth of his power. Ever since Mowgli was strong enough to endure a little rough handling, Kaa had taught him this game, and it suppled his limbs as nothing else could. Sometimes Mowgli would stand lapped almost to his throat in Kaa's shifting coils, striving to get one arm free and catch him by the throat. Then Kaa would give way limply, and Mowgli, with both quick-moving feet, would try to cramp the purchase of that huge tail as it flung backward feeling for a rock or a stump. They would rock to and fro, head to head, each waiting for his chance, till the beautiful, statue-like group melted in a whirl of black-and-yellow coils and struggling legs and arms, to rise up again and again. "Now! now! now!" said Kaa, making feints with his head that even Mowgli's quick hand could not turn aside. "Look! I touch thee here, Little Brother! Here, and here! Are thy hands numb? Here again!"

The game always ended in one way—with a straight, driving blow of the head that knocked the boy over and over. Mowgli could never learn the guard for that lightning lunge, and, as Kaa said, there was not the least use in trying.

"Good hunting!" Kaa grunted at last; and Mowgli, as usual, was shot away half a dozen yards, gasping and laughing. He rose with his fingers full of grass, and followed Kaa to the wise snake's pet bathing-place—a deep, pitchy-black pool surrounded with rocks, and made interesting by sunken tree-stumps. The boy slipped in, Jungle-fashion, without a sound, and dived across; rose, too, without a sound, and turned on his back, his arms behind his head, watching the moon rising above the rocks, and breaking up her reflection in the water with his toes. Kaa's diamond-shaped head cut the pool like a razor, and came out to rest on Mowgli's shoulder. They lay still, soaking luxuriously in the cool water.

"It is VERY good," said Mowgli at last, sleepily. "Now, in the Man-Pack, at this hour, as I remember, they laid them down upon hard pieces of wood in the inside of a mud-trap, and, having carefully shut out all the clean winds, drew foul cloth over their heavy heads and made evil songs through their noses. It is better in the Jungle."

A hurrying cobra slipped down over a rock and drank, gave them "Good hunting!" and went away.

"Sssh!" said Kaa, as though he had suddenly remembered something. "So the Jungle gives thee all that thou hast ever desired, Little Brother?"

"Not all," said Mowgli, laughing; "else there would be a new and strong Shere Khan to kill once a moon. Now, I could kill with my own hands, asking no help of buffaloes. And also I have wished the sun to shine in the middle of the Rains, and the Rains to cover the sun in the deep of summer; and also I have never gone empty but I wished that I had killed a goat; and also I have never killed a goat but I wished it had been buck; nor buck but I wished it had been nilghai. But thus do we feel, all of us."

"Thou hast no other desire?" the big snake demanded.

"What more can I wish? I have the Jungle, and the favour of the Jungle! Is there more anywhere between sunrise and sunset?"

"Now, the Cobra said——" Kaa began. "What cobra? He that went away just now said nothing. He was hunting."

"It was another."

"Hast thou many dealings with the Poison People? I give them their own path. They carry death in the fore-tooth, and that is not good—for they are so small. But what hood is this thou hast spoken with?"

Kaa rolled slowly in the water like a steamer in a beam sea. "Three or four moons since," said he, "I hunted in Cold Lairs, which place thou hast not forgotten. And the thing I hunted fled shrieking past the tanks and to that house whose side I once broke for thy sake, and ran into the ground."

"But the people of Cold Lairs do not live in burrows." Mowgli knew that Kaa was telling of the Monkey People.

"This thing was not living, but seeking to live," Kaa replied, with a quiver of his tongue. "He ran into a burrow that led very far. I followed, and having killed, I slept. When I waked I went forward."

"Under the earth?"

"Even so, coming at last upon a White Hood [a white cobra], who spoke of things beyond my knowledge, and showed me many things I had never before seen."

"New game? Was it good hunting?" Mowgli turned quickly on his side.

"It was no game, and would have broken all my teeth; but the White Hood said that a man—he spoke as one that knew the breed—that a man would give the breath under his ribs for only the sight of those things."

"We will look," said Mowgli. "I now remember that I was once a man."

"Slowly—slowly. It was haste killed the Yellow Snake that ate the sun. We two spoke together under the earth, and I spoke of thee, naming thee as a man. Said the White Hood (and he is indeed as old as the Jungle): 'It is long since I have seen a man. Let him come, and he shall see all these things, for the least of which very many men would die.'"

"That MUST be new game. And yet the Poison People do not tell us when game is afoot. They are an unfriendly folk."

"It is NOT game. It is—it is—I cannot say what it is."

"We will go there. I have never seen a White Hood, and I wish to see the other things. Did he kill them?"

"They are all dead things. He says he is the keeper of them all."

"Ah! As a wolf stands above meat he has taken to his own lair. Let us go."

Mowgli swam to bank, rolled on the grass to dry himself, and the two set off for Cold Lairs, the deserted city of which you may have heard. Mowgli was not the least afraid of the Monkey People in those days, but the Monkey People had the liveliest horror of Mowgli. Their tribes, however, were raiding in the Jungle, and so Cold Lairs stood empty and silent in the moonlight. Kaa led up to the ruins of the queens' pavilion that stood on the terrace, slipped over the rubbish, and dived down the half-choked staircase that went underground from the centre of the pavilion. Mowgli gave the snake-call,—"We be of one blood, ye and I,"—and followed on his hands and knees. They crawled a long distance down a sloping passage that turned and twisted several times, and at last came to where the root of some great tree, growing thirty feet overhead, had forced out a solid stone in the wall. They crept through the gap, and found themselves in a large vault, whose domed roof had been also broken away by tree-roots so that a few streaks of light dropped down into the darkness.

"A safe lair," said Mowgli, rising to his firm feet, "but over-far to visit daily. And now what do we see?"

"Am I nothing?" said a voice in the middle of the vault; and Mowgli saw something white move till, little by little, there stood up the hugest cobra he had ever set eyes on—a creature nearly eight feet long, and bleached by being in darkness to an old ivory-white. Even the spectacle-marks of his spread hood had faded to faint yellow. His eyes were as red as rubies, and altogether he was most wonderful.

"Good hunting!" said Mowgli, who carried his manners with his knife, and that never left him.

"What of the city?" said the White Cobra, without answering the greeting. "What of the great, the walled city— the city of a hundred elephants and twenty thousand horses, and cattle past counting—the city of the King of Twenty Kings? I grow deaf here, and it is long since I heard their war-gongs."

"The Jungle is above our heads," said Mowgli. "I know only Hathi and his sons among elephants. Bagheera has slain all the horses in one village, and—what is a King?"

"I told thee," said Kaa softly to the Cobra,—"I told thee, four moons ago, that thy city was not."

"The city—the great city of the forest whose gates are guarded by the King's towers—can never pass. They builded it before my father's father came from the egg, and it shall endure when my son's sons are as white as I! Salomdhi, son of Chandrabija, son of Viyeja, son of Yegasuri, made it in the days of Bappa Rawal. Whose cattle are YE?"

"It is a lost trail," said Mowgli, turning to Kaa. "I know not his talk."

"Nor I. He is very old. Father of Cobras, there is only the Jungle here, as it has been since the beginning."

"Then who is HE," said the White Cobra, "sitting down before me, unafraid, knowing not the name of the King, talking our talk through a man's lips? Who is he with the knife and the snake's tongue?"

"Mowgli they call me," was the answer. "I am of the Jungle. The wolves are my people, and Kaa here is my brother. Father of Cobras, who art thou?"

"I am the Warden of the King's Treasure. Kurrun Raja builded the stone above me, in the days when my skin was dark, that I might teach death to those who came to steal. Then they let down the treasure through the stone, and I heard the song of the Brahmins my masters."

"Umm!" said Mowgli to himself. "I have dealt with one Brahmin already, in the Man-Pack, and—I know what I know. Evil comes here in a little."

"Five times since I came here has the stone been lifted, but always to let down more, and never to take away. There are no riches like these riches—the treasures of a hundred kings. But it is long and long since the stone was last moved, and I think that my city has forgotten."

"There is no city. Look up. Yonder are roots of the great trees tearing the stones apart. Trees and men do not grow together," Kaa insisted.

"Twice and thrice have men found their way here," the White Cobra answered savagely; "but they never spoke till I came upon them groping in the dark, and then they cried only a little time. But ye come with lies, Man and Snake both, and would have me believe the city is not, and that my wardship ends. Little do men change in the years. But I change never! Till the stone is lifted, and the Brahmins come down singing the songs that I know, and feed me with warm milk, and take me to the light again, I—I—_I_, and no other, am the Warden of the King's Treasure! The city is dead, ye say, and here are the roots of the trees? Stoop down, then, and take what ye will. Earth has no treasure like to these. Man with the snake's tongue, if thou canst go alive by the way that thou hast entered it, the lesser Kings will be thy servants!"

"Again the trail is lost," said Mowgli coolly. "Can any jackal have burrowed so deep and bitten this great White Hood? He is surely mad. Father of Cobras, I see nothing here to take away."

"By the Gods of the Sun and Moon, it is the madness of death upon the boy!" hissed the Cobra. "Before thine eyes close I will allow thee this favour. Look thou, and see what man has never seen before!"

"They do not well in the Jungle who speak to Mowgli of favours," said the boy, between his teeth; "but the dark changes all, as I know. I will look, if that please thee."

He stared with puckered-up eyes round the vault, and then lifted up from the floor a handful of something that glittered.

"Oho!" said he, "this is like the stuff they play with in the Man-Pack: only this is yellow and the other was brown."

He let the gold pieces fall, and move forward. The floor of the vault was buried some five or six feet deep in coined gold and silver that had burst from the sacks it had been originally stored in, and, in the long years, the metal had packed and settled as sand packs at low tide. On it and in it and rising through it, as wrecks lift through the sand, were jewelled elephant-howdahs of embossed silver, studded with plates of hammered gold, and adorned with carbuncles and turquoises. There were palanquins and litters for carrying queens, framed and braced with silver and enamel, with jade-handled poles and amber curtain-rings; there were golden candlesticks hung with pierced emeralds that quivered on the branches; there were studded images, five feet high, of forgotten gods, silver with jewelled eyes; there were coats of mail, gold inlaid on steel, and fringed with rotted and blackened seed-pearls; there were helmets, crested and beaded with pigeon's-blood rubies; there were shields of lacquer, of tortoise-shell and rhinoceros-hide, strapped and bossed with red gold and set with emeralds at the edge; there were sheaves of diamond-hilted swords, daggers, and hunting-knives; there were golden sacrificial bowls and ladles, and portable altars of a shape that never sees the light of day; there were jade cups and bracelets; there were incense-burners, combs, and pots for perfume, henna, and eye-powder, all in embossed gold; there were nose-rings, armlets, head-bands, finger-rings, and girdles past any counting; there were belts, seven fingers broad, of square-cut diamonds and rubies, and wooden boxes, trebly clamped with iron, from which the wood had fallen away in powder, showing the pile of uncut star-sapphires, opals, cat's-eyes, sapphires, rubies, diamonds, emeralds, and garnets within.

The White Cobra was right. No mere money would begin to pay the value of this treasure, the sifted pickings of centuries of war, plunder, trade, and taxation. The coins alone were priceless, leaving out of count all the precious stones; and the dead weight of the gold and silver alone might be two or three hundred tons. Every native ruler in India to-day, however poor, has a hoard to which he is always adding; and though, once in a long while, some enlightened prince may send off forty or fifty bullock-cart loads of silver to be exchanged for Government securities, the bulk of them keep their treasure and the knowledge of it very closely to themselves.

But Mowgli naturally did not understand what these things meant. The knives interested him a little, but they did not balance so well as his own, and so he dropped them. At last he found something really fascinating laid on the front of a howdah half buried in the coins. It was a three-foot ankus, or elephant-goad—something like a small boat-hook. The top was one round, shining ruby, and eight inches of the handle below it were studded with rough turquoises close together, giving a most satisfactory grip. Below them was a rim of jade with a flower-pattern running round it—only the leaves were emeralds, and the blossoms were rubies sunk in the cool, green stone. The rest of the handle was a shaft of pure ivory, while the point—the spike and hook—was gold-inlaid steel with pictures of elephant-catching; and the pictures attracted Mowgli, who saw that they had something to do with his friend Hathi the Silent.

The White Cobra had been following him closely.

"Is this not worth dying to behold?" he said. "Have I not done thee a great favour?"

"I do not understand," said Mowgli. "The things are hard and cold, and by no means good to eat. But this"—he lifted the ankus—"I desire to take away, that I may see it in the sun. Thou sayest they are all thine? Wilt thou give it to me, and I will bring thee frogs to eat?"

The White Cobra fairly shook with evil delight. "Assuredly I will give it," he said. "All that is here I will give thee—till thou goest away."

"But I go now. This place is dark and cold, and I wish to take the thorn-pointed thing to the Jungle."

"Look by thy foot! What is that there?" Mowgli picked up something white and smooth. "It is the bone of a man's head," he said quietly. "And here are two more."

"They came to take the treasure away many years ago. I spoke to them in the dark, and they lay still."

"But what do I need of this that is called treasure? If thou wilt give me the ankus to take away, it is good hunting. If not, it is good hunting none the less. I do not fight with the Poison People, and I was also taught the Master-word of thy tribe."

"There is but one Master-word here. It is mine!"

Kaa flung himself forward with blazing eyes. "Who bade me bring the Man?" he hissed.

"I surely," the old Cobra lisped. "It is long since I have seen Man, and this Man speaks our tongue."

"But there was no talk of killing. How can I go to the Jungle and say that I have led him to his death?" said Kaa.

"I talk not of killing till the time. And as to thy going or not going, there is the hole in the wall. Peace, now, thou fat monkey-killer! I have but to touch thy neck, and the Jungle will know thee no longer. Never Man came here that went away with the breath under his ribs. I am the Warden of the Treasure of the King's City!"

"But, thou white worm of the dark, I tell thee there is neither king nor city! The Jungle is all about us!" cried Kaa.

"There is still the Treasure. But this can be done. Wait awhile, Kaa of the Rocks, and see the boy run. There is room for great sport here. Life is good. Run to and fro awhile, and make sport, boy!"

Mowgli put his hand on Kaa's head quietly.

"The white thing has dealt with men of the Man-Pack until now. He does not know me," he whispered. "He has asked for this hunting. Let him have it." Mowgli had been standing with the ankus held point down. He flung it from him quickly and it dropped crossways just behind the great snake's hood, pinning him to the floor. In a flash, Kaa's weight was upon the writhing body, paralysing it from hood to tail. The red eyes burned, and the six spare inches of the head struck furiously right and left.

"Kill!" said Kaa, as Mowgli's hand went to his knife.

"No," he said, as he drew the blade; "I will never kill again save for food. But look you, Kaa!" He caught the snake behind the hood, forced the mouth open with the blade of the knife, and showed the terrible poison-fangs of the upper jaw lying black and withered in the gum. The White Cobra had outlived his poison, as a snake will.

"THUU" ("It is dried up"—Literally, a rotted out tree-stump), said Mowgli; and motioning Kaa away, he picked up the ankus, setting the White Cobra free.

"The King's Treasure needs a new Warden," he said gravely. "Thuu, thou hast not done well. Run to and fro and make sport, Thuu!"

"I am ashamed. Kill me!" hissed the White Cobra.

"There has been too much talk of killing. We will go now. I take the thorn-pointed thing, Thuu, because I have fought and worsted thee."

"See, then, that the thing does not kill thee at last. It is Death! Remember, it is Death! There is enough in that thing to kill the men of all my city. Not long wilt thou hold it, Jungle Man, nor he who takes it from thee. They will kill, and kill, and kill for its sake! My strength is dried up, but the ankus will do my work. It is Death! It is Death! It is Death!"

Mowgli crawled out through the hole into the passage again, and the last that he saw was the White Cobra striking furiously with his harmless fangs at the stolid golden faces of the gods that lay on the floor, and hissing, "It is Death!"

They were glad to get to the light of day once more; and when they were back in their own Jungle and Mowgli made the ankus glitter in the morning light, he was almost as pleased as though he had found a bunch of new flowers to stick in his hair.

"This is brighter than Bagheera's eyes," he said delightedly, as he twirled the ruby. "I will show it to him; but what did the Thuu mean when he talked of death?"

"I cannot say. I am sorrowful to my tail's tail that he felt not thy knife. There is always evil at Cold Lairs—above ground or below. But now I am hungry. Dost thou hunt with me this dawn?" said Kaa.

"No; Bagheera must see this thing. Good hunting!" Mowgli danced off, flourishing the great ankus, and stopping from time to time to admire it, till he came to that part of the Jungle Bagheera chiefly used, and found him drinking after a heavy kill. Mowgli told him all his adventures from beginning to end, and Bagheera sniffed at the ankus between whiles. When Mowgli came to the White Cobra's last words, the Panther purred approvingly.

"Then the White Hood spoke the thing which is?" Mowgli asked quickly.

"I was born in the King's cages at Oodeypore, and it is in my stomach that I know some little of Man. Very many men would kill thrice in a night for the sake of that one big red stone alone."

"But the stone makes it heavy to the hand. My little bright knife is better; and—see! the red stone is not good to eat. Then WHY would they kill?"

"Mowgli, go thou and sleep. Thou hast lived among men, and——"

"I remember. Men kill because they are not hunting;—for idleness and pleasure. Wake again, Bagheera. For what use was this thorn-pointed thing made?"

Bagheera half opened his eyes—he was very sleepy—with a malicious twinkle.

"It was made by men to thrust into the head of the sons of Hathi, so that the blood should pour out. I have seen the like in the street of Oodeypore, before our cages. That thing has tasted the blood of many such as Hathi."

"But why do they thrust into the heads of elephants?"

"To teach them Man's Law. Having neither claws nor teeth, men make these things—and worse."

"Always more blood when I come near, even to the things the Man-Pack have made," said Mowgli disgustedly. He was getting a little tired of the weight of the ankus. "If I had known this, I would not have taken it. First it was Messua's blood on the thongs, and now it is Hathi's. I will use it no more. Look!"

The ankus flew sparkling, and buried itself point down thirty yards away, between the trees. "So my hands are clean of Death," said Mowgli, rubbing his palms on the fresh, moist earth. "The Thuu said Death would follow me. He is old and white and mad."

"White or black, or death or life, _I_ am going to sleep, Little Brother. I cannot hunt all night and howl all day, as do some folk."

Bagheera went off to a hunting-lair that he knew, about two miles off. Mowgli made an easy way for himself up a convenient tree, knotted three or four creepers together, and in less time than it takes to tell was swinging in a hammock fifty feet above ground. Though he had no positive objection to strong daylight, Mowgli followed the custom of his friends, and used it as little as he could. When he waked among the very loud-voiced peoples that live in the trees, it was twilight once more, and he had been dreaming of the beautiful pebbles he had thrown away.

"At least I will look at the thing again," he said, and slid down a creeper to the earth; but Bagheera was before him. Mowgli could hear him snuffing in the half light.

"Where is the thorn-pointed thing?" cried Mowgli.

"A man has taken it. Here is the trail."

"Now we shall see whether the Thuu spoke truth. If the pointed thing is Death, that man will die. Let us follow."

"Kill first," said Bagheera. "An empty stomach makes a careless eye. Men go very slowly, and the Jungle is wet enough to hold the lightest mark."

They killed as soon as they could, but it was nearly three hours before they finished their meat and drink and buckled down to the trail. The Jungle People know that nothing makes up for being hurried over your meals.

"Think you the pointed thing will turn in the man's hand and kill him?" Mowgli asked. "The Thuu said it was Death."

"We shall see when we find," said Bagheera, trotting with his head low. "It is single-foot" (he meant that there was only one man), "and the weight of the thing has pressed his heel far into the ground."

"Hai! This is as clear as summer lightning," Mowgli answered; and they fell into the quick, choppy trail-trot in and out through the checkers of the moonlight, following the marks of those two bare feet.

"Now he runs swiftly," said Mowgli. "The toes are spread apart." They went on over some wet ground. "Now why does he turn aside here?"

"Wait!" said Bagheera, and flung himself forward with one superb bound as far as ever he could. The first thing to do when a trail ceases to explain itself is to cast forward without leaving, your own confusing foot-marks on the ground. Bagheera turned as he landed, and faced Mowgli, crying, "Here comes another trail to meet him. It is a smaller foot, this second trail, and the toes turn inward."

Then Mowgli ran up and looked. "It is the foot of a Gond hunter," he said. "Look! Here he dragged his bow on the grass. That is why the first trail turned aside so quickly. Big Foot hid from Little Foot."

"That is true," said Bagheera. "Now, lest by crossing each other's tracks we foul the signs, let each take one trail. I am Big Foot, Little Brother, and thou art Little Foot, the Gond."

Bagheera leaped back to the original trail, leaving Mowgli stooping above the curious narrow track of the wild little man of the woods.

"Now," said Bagheera, moving step by step along the chain of footprints, "I, Big Foot, turn aside here. Now I hide me behind a rock and stand still, not daring to shift my feet. Cry thy trail, Little Brother."

"Now, I, Little Foot, come to the rock," said Mowgli, running up his trail. "Now, I sit down under the rock, leaning upon my right hand, and resting my bow between my toes. I wait long, for the mark of my feet is deep here."

"I also," said Bagheera, hidden behind the rock. "I wait, resting the end of the thorn-pointed thing upon a stone. It slips, for here is a scratch upon the stone. Cry thy trail, Little Brother."

"One, two twigs and a big branch are broken here," said Mowgli, in an undertone. "Now, how shall I cry THAT? Ah! It is plain now. I, Little Foot, go away making noises and tramplings so that Big Foot may hear me." He moved away from the rock pace by pace among the trees, his voice rising in the distance as he approached a little cascade. "I—go, far— away—to—where—the—noise—of—falling-water— covers—my—noise; and—here—I—wait. Cry thy trail, Bagheera, Big Foot!"

The panther had been casting in every direction to see how Big Foot's trail led away from behind the rock. Then he gave tongue:

"I come from behind the rock upon my knees, dragging the thorn-pointed thing. Seeing no one, I run. I, Big Foot, run swiftly. The trail is clear. Let each follow his own. I run!"

Bagheera swept on along the clearly-marked trail, and Mowgli followed the steps of the Gond. For some time there was silence in the Jungle.

"Where art thou, Little Foot?" cried Bagheera. Mowgli's voice answered him not fifty yards to the right.

"Um!" said the Panther, with a deep cough. "The two run side by side, drawing nearer!"

They raced on another half-mile, always keeping about the same distance, till Mowgli, whose head was not so close to the ground as Bagheera's, cried: "They have met. Good hunting—look! Here stood Little Foot, with his knee on a rock—and yonder is Big Foot indeed!"

Not ten yards in front of them, stretched across a pile of broken rocks, lay the body of a villager of the district, a long, small-feathered Gond arrow through his back and breast.

"Was the Thuu so old and so mad, Little Brother?" said Bagheera gently. "Here is one death, at least."

"Follow on. But where is the drinker of elephant's blood— the red-eyed thorn?"

"Little Foot has it—perhaps. It is single-foot again now."

The single trail of a light man who had been running quickly and bearing a burden on his left shoulder held on round a long, low spur of dried grass, where each footfall seemed, to the sharp eyes of the trackers, marked in hot iron.

Neither spoke till the trail ran up to the ashes of a camp-fire hidden in a ravine.

"Again!" said Bagheera, checking as though he had been turned into stone.

The body of a little wizened Gond lay with its feet in the ashes, and Bagheera looked inquiringly at Mowgli.

"That was done with a bamboo," said the boy, after one glance. "I have used such a thing among the buffaloes when I served in the Man-Pack. The Father of Cobras—I am sorrowful that I made a jest of him—knew the breed well, as I might have known. Said I not that men kill for idleness?"

"Indeed, they killed for the sake of the red and blue stones," Bagheera answered. "Remember, I was in the King's cages at Oodeypore."

"One, two, three, four tracks," said Mowgli, stooping over the ashes. "Four tracks of men with shod feet. They do not go so quickly as Gonds. Now, what evil had the little woodman done to them? See, they talked together, all five, standing up, before they killed him. Bagheera, let us go back. My stomach is heavy in me, and yet it heaves up and down like an oriole's nest at the end of a branch."

"It is not good hunting to leave game afoot. Follow!" said the panther. "Those eight shod feet have not gone far."

No more was said for fully an hour, as they worked up the broad trail of the four men with shod feet.

It was clear, hot daylight now, and Bagheera said, "I smell smoke."

Men are always more ready to eat than to run, Mowgli answered, trotting in and out between the low scrub bushes of the new Jungle they were exploring. Bagheera, a little to his left, made an indescribable noise in his throat.

"Here is one that has done with feeding," said he. A tumbled bundle of gay-coloured clothes lay under a bush, and round it was some spilt flour.

"That was done by the bamboo again," said Mowgli. "See! that white dust is what men eat. They have taken the kill from this one,—he carried their food,—and given him for a kill to Chil, the Kite."

"It is the third," said Bagheera.

"I will go with new, big frogs to the Father of Cobras, and feed him fat," said Mowgli to himself. "The drinker of elephant's blood is Death himself—but still I do not understand!"

"Follow!" said Bagheera.

They had not gone half a mile farther when they heard Ko, the Crow, singing the death-song in the top of a tamarisk under whose shade three men were lying. A half-dead fire smoked in the centre of the circle, under an iron plate which held a blackened and burned cake of unleavened bread. Close to the fire, and blazing in the sunshine, lay the ruby-and-turquoise ankus.

"The thing works quickly; all ends here," said Bagheera. "How did THESE die, Mowgli? There is no mark on any."

A Jungle-dweller gets to learn by experience as much as many doctors know of poisonous plants and berries. Mowgli sniffed the smoke that came up from the fire, broke off a morsel of the blackened bread, tasted it, and spat it out again.

"Apple of Death," he coughed. "The first must have made it ready in the food for THESE, who killed him, having first killed the Gond."

"Good hunting, indeed! The kills follow close," said Bagheera.

"Apple of Death" is what the Jungle call thorn-apple or dhatura, the readiest poison in all India.

"What now?" said the panther. "Must thou and I kill each other for yonder red-eyed slayer?"

"Can it speak?" said Mowgli in a whisper. "Did I do it a wrong when I threw it away? Between us two it can do no wrong, for we do not desire what men desire. If it be left here, it will assuredly continue to kill men one after another as fast as nuts fall in a high wind. I have no love to men, but even I would not have them die six in a night."

"What matter? They are only men. They killed one another, and were well pleased," said Bagheera. "That first little woodman hunted well."

"They are cubs none the less; and a cub will drown himself to bite the moon's light on the water. The fault was mine," said Mowgli, who spoke as though he knew all about everything. "I will never again bring into the Jungle strange things—not though they be as beautiful as flowers. This"—he handled the ankus gingerly—"goes back to the Father of Cobras. But first we must sleep, and we cannot sleep near these sleepers. Also we must bury HIM, lest he run away and kill another six. Dig me a hole under that tree."

"But, Little Brother," said Bagheera, moving off to the spot, "I tell thee it is no fault of the blood-drinker. The trouble is with the men."

"All one," said Mowgli. "Dig the hole deep. When we wake I will take him up and carry him back."

*****

Two nights later, as the White Cobra sat mourning in the darkness of the vault, ashamed, and robbed, and alone, the turquoise ankus whirled through the hole in the wall, and clashed on the floor of golden coins.

"Father of Cobras," said Mowgli (he was careful to keep the other side of the wall), "get thee a young and ripe one of thine own people to help thee guard the King's Treasure, so that no man may come away alive any more."

"Ah-ha! It returns, then. I said the thing was Death. How comes it that thou art still alive?" the old Cobra mumbled, twining lovingly round the ankus-haft.

"By the Bull that bought me, I do not know! That thing has killed six times in a night. Let him go out no more."

THE SONG OF THE LITTLE HUNTER

Ere Mor the Peacock flutters, ere the Monkey People cry,
Ere Chil the Kite swoops down a furlong sheer,
Through the Jungle very softly flits a shadow and a sigh--
He is Fear, O Little Hunter, he is Fear!
Very softly down the glade runs a waiting, watching shade,
And the whisper spreads and widens far and near;
And the sweat is on thy brow, for he passes even now--
He is Fear, O Little Hunter, he is Fear!
Ere the moon has climbed the mountain, ere the rocks
are ribbed with light,
When the downward-dipping trails are dank and drear,
Comes a breathing hard behind thee--snuffle-snuffle
through the night--
It is Fear, O Little Hunter, it is Fear!
On thy knees and draw the bow; bid the shrilling arrow go;
In the empty, mocking thicket plunge the spear;
But thy hands are loosed and weak, and the blood has left
thy cheek--
It is Fear, O Little Hunter, it is Fear!
When the heat-cloud sucks the tempest, when the slivered
pine-trees fall,
When the blinding, blaring rain-squalls lash and veer;

Through the war-gongs of the thunder rings a voice more
loud than all--
It is Fear, O Little Hunter, it is Fear!
Now the spates are banked and deep; now the footless
boulders leap--
Now the lightning shows each littlest leaf-rib clear--
But thy throat is shut and dried, and thy heart against
thy side
Hammers: Fear, O Little Hunter--this is Fear!

QUIQUERN

Translation.

"He has opened his eyes. Look!"

"Put him in the skin again. He will be a strong dog. On the fourth month we will name him."

"For whom?" said Amoraq.

Kadlu's eye rolled round the skin-lined snow-house till it fell on fourteen-year-old Kotuko sitting on the sleeping-bench, making a button out of walrus ivory. "Name him for me," said Kotuko, with a grin. "I shall need him one day."

Kadlu grinned back till his eyes were almost buried in the fat of his flat cheeks, and nodded to Amoraq, while the puppy's fierce mother whined to see her baby wriggling far out of reach in the little sealskin pouch hung above the warmth of the blubber-lamp. Kotuko went on with his carving, and Kadlu threw a rolled bundle of leather dog-harnesses into a tiny little room that opened from one side of the house, slipped off his heavy deerskin hunting-suit, put it into a whalebone-net that hung above another lamp, and dropped down on the sleeping-bench to whittle at a piece of frozen seal-meat till Amoraq, his wife, should bring the regular dinner of boiled meat and blood-soup. He had been out since early dawn at the seal-holes, eight miles away, and had come home with three big seal. Half-way down the long, low snow passage or tunnel that led to the inner door of the house you could hear snappings and yelpings, as the dogs of his sleigh-team, released from the day's work, scuffled for warm places.

When the yelpings grew too loud Kotuko lazily rolled off the sleeping-bench, and picked up a whip with an eighteen-inch handle of springy whalebone, and twenty-five feet of heavy, plaited thong. He dived into the passage, where it sounded as though all the dogs were eating him alive; but that was no more than their regular grace before meals. When he crawled out at the far end, half a dozen furry heads followed him with their eyes as he went to a sort of gallows of whale-jawbones, from which the dog's meat was hung; split off the frozen stuff in big lumps with a broad-headed spear; and stood, his whip in one hand and the meat in the other. Each beast was called by name, the weakest first, and woe betide any dog that moved out of his turn; for the tapering lash would shoot out like thonged lightning, and flick away an inch or so of hair and hide. Each beast growled, snapped, choked once over his portion, and hurried back to the protection of the passage, while the boy stood upon the snow under the blazing Northern Lights and dealt out justice. The last to be served was the big black leader of the team, who kept order when the dogs were harnessed; and to him Kotuko gave a double allowance of meat as well as an extra crack of the whip.

"Ah!" said Kotuko, coiling up the lash, "I have a little one over the lamp that will make a great many howlings. SARPOK! Get in!"

He crawled back over the huddled dogs, dusted the dry snow from his furs with the whalebone beater that Amoraq kept by the door, tapped the skin-lined roof of the house to shake off any icicles that might have fallen from the dome of snow above, and curled up on the bench. The dogs in the passage snored and whined in their sleep, the boy-baby in Amoraq's deep fur hood kicked and choked and gurgled, and the mother of the newly-named puppy lay at Kotuko's side, her eyes fixed on the bundle of sealskin, warm and safe above the broad yellow flame of the lamp.

And all this happened far away to the north, beyond Labrador, beyond Hudson's Strait, where the great tides heave the ice about, north of Melville Peninsula—north even of the narrow Fury and Hecla Straits—on the north shore of Baffin Land, where Bylot's Island stands above the ice of Lancaster Sound like a pudding-bowl wrong side up. North of Lancaster Sound there is little we know anything about, except North Devon and Ellesmere Land; but even there live a few scattered people, next door, as it were, to the very Pole.

Kadlu was an Inuit,—what you call an Esquimau,—and his tribe, some thirty persons all told, belonged to the Tununirmiut—"the country lying at the back of something." In the maps that desolate coast is written Navy Board Inlet, but the Inuit name is best, because the country lies at the very back of everything in the world. For nine months of the year there is only ice and snow, and gale after gale, with a cold that no one can realise who has never seen the thermometer even at zero. For six months of those nine it is dark; and that is what makes it so horrible. In the three months of the summer it only freezes every other day and every night, and then the snow begins to weep off on the southerly slopes, and a few ground-willows put out their woolly buds, a tiny stonecrop or so makes believe to blossom, beaches of fine gravel and rounded stones run down to the open sea, and polished boulders and streaked rocks lift up above the granulated snow. But all that is gone in a few weeks, and the wild winter locks down again on the land; while at sea the ice tears up and down the offing, jamming and ramming, and splitting and hitting, and pounding and grounding, till it all freezes together, ten feet thick, from the land outward to deep water.

In the winter Kadlu would follow the seal to the edge of this land-ice, and spear them as they came up to breathe at their blow-holes. The seal must have open water to live and catch fish in, and in the deep of winter the ice would sometimes run eighty miles without a break from the nearest shore. In the spring he and his people retreated from the floes to the rocky mainland, where they put up tents of skins, and snared the sea-birds, or speared the young seal basking on the beaches. Later, they would go south into Baffin Land after the reindeer, and to get their year's store of salmon from the hundreds of streams and lakes of the interior; coming back north in September or October for the musk-ox hunting and the regular winter sealery. This travelling was done with dog-sleighs, twenty and thirty miles a day, or sometimes down the coast in big skin "woman-boats," when the dogs and the babies lay among the feet of the rowers, and the women sang songs as they glided from cape to cape over the glassy, cold waters. All the luxuries that the Tununirmiut knew came from the south— driftwood for sleigh-runners, rod-iron for harpoon-tips, steel knives, tin kettles that cooked food much better than the old soap-stone affairs, flint and steel, and even matches, as well as coloured ribbons for the women's hair, little cheap mirrors, and red cloth for the edging of deerskin dress-jackets. Kadlu traded the rich, creamy, twisted narwhal horn and musk-ox teeth (these are just as valuable as pearls) to the Southern Inuit, and they, in turn, traded with the whalers and the missionary-posts of Exeter and Cumberland Sounds; and so the chain went on, till a kettle picked up by a ship's cook in the Bhendy Bazaar might end its days over a blubber-lamp somewhere on the cool side of the Arctic Circle.

Kadlu, being a good hunter, was rich in iron harpoons, snow-knives, bird-darts, and all the other things that make life easy up there in the great cold; and he was the head of his tribe, or, as they say, "the man who knows all about it by practice." This did not give him any authority, except now and then he could advise his friends to change their hunting-grounds; but Kotuko used it to domineer a little, in the lazy, fat Inuit fashion, over the other boys, when they came out at night to play ball in the moonlight, or to sing the Child's Song to the Aurora Borealis.

But at fourteen an Inuit feels himself a man, and Kotuko was tired of making snares for wild-fowl and kit-foxes, and most tired of all of helping the women to chew seal-and deer-skins (that supples them as nothing else can) the long day through, while the men were out hunting. He wanted to go into the quaggi, the Singing-House, when the hunters gathered there for their mysteries, and the angekok, the sorcerer, frightened them into the most delightful fits after the lamps were put out, and you could hear the Spirit of the Reindeer stamping on the roof; and when a spear was thrust out into the open black night it came back covered with hot blood. He wanted to throw his big boots into the net with the tired air of the head of a family, and to gamble with the hunters when they dropped in of an evening and played a sort of home-made roulette with a tin pot and a nail. There were hundreds of things that he wanted to do, but the grown men laughed at him and said, "Wait till you have been in the buckle, Kotuko. Hunting is not ALL catching."

Now that his father had named a puppy for him, things looked brighter. An Inuit does not waste a good dog on his son till the boy knows something of dog-driving; and Kotuko was more than sure that he knew more than everything.

If the puppy had not had an iron constitution he would have died from over-stuffing and over-handling. Kotuko made him a tiny harness with a trace to it, and hauled him all over the house-floor, shouting: "Aua! Ja aua!" (Go to the right). "Choiachoi! Ja choiachoi!" (Go to the left). "Ohaha!" (Stop). The puppy did not like it at all, but being fished for in this way was pure happiness beside being put to the sleigh for the first time. He just sat down on the snow, and played with the seal-hide trace that ran from his harness to the pitu, the big thong in the bows of the sleigh. Then the team started, and the puppy found the heavy ten-foot sleigh running up his back, and dragging him along the snow, while Kotuko laughed till the tears ran down his face. There followed days and days of the cruel whip that hisses like the wind over ice, and his companions all bit him because he did not know his work, and the harness chafed him, and he was dot allowed to sleep with Kotuko any more, but had to take the coldest place in the passage. It was a sad time for the puppy.

The boy learned, too, as fast as the dog; though a dog-sleigh is a heart-breaking thing to manage. Each beast is harnessed, the weakest nearest to the driver, by his own separate trace, which runs under his left fore-leg to the main thong, where it is fastened by a sort of button and loop which can be slipped by a turn of the wrist, thus freeing one dog at a time. This is very necessary, because young dogs often get the trace between their hind legs, where it cuts to the bone. And they one and all WILL go visiting their friends as they run, jumping in and out among the traces. Then they fight, and the result is more mixed than a wet fishing-line next morning. A great deal of trouble can be avoided by scientific use of the whip. Every Inuit boy prides himself as being a master of the long lash; but it is easy to flick at a mark on the ground, and difficult to lean forward and catch a shirking dog just behind the shoulders when the sleigh is going at full speed. If you call one dog's name for "visiting," and accidentally lash another, the two will fight it out at once, and stop all the others. Again, if you travel with a companion and begin to talk, or by yourself and sing, the dogs will halt, turn round, and sit down to hear what you have to say. Kotuko was run away from once or twice through forgetting to block the sleigh when he stopped; and he broke many lashings, and ruined a few thongs before he could be trusted with a full team of eight and the light sleigh. Then he felt himself a person of consequence, and on smooth, black ice, with a bold heart and a quick elbow, he smoked along over the levels as fast as a pack in full cry. He would go ten miles to the seal-holes, and when he was on the hunting-grounds he would twitch a trace loose from the pitu, and free the big black leader, who was the cleverest dog in the team. As soon as the dog had scented a breathing-hole, Kotuko would reverse the sleigh, driving a couple of sawed-off antlers, that stuck up like perambulator-handles from the back-rest, deep into the snow, so that the team could not get away. Then he would crawl forward inch by inch, and wait till the seal came up to breathe. Then he would stab down swiftly with his spear and running-line, and presently would haul his seal up to the lip of the ice, while the black leader came up and helped to pull the carcass across the ice to the sleigh. That was the time when the harnessed dogs yelled and foamed with excitement, and Kotuko laid the long lash like a red-hot bar across all their faces, till the carcass froze stiff. Going home was the heavy work. The loaded sleigh had to be humoured among the rough ice, and the dogs sat down and looked hungrily at the seal instead of pulling. At last they would strike the well-worn sleigh-road to the village, and toodle-kiyi along the ringing ice, heads down and tails up, while Kotuko struck up the "An-gutivaun tai-na tau-na-ne taina" (The Song of the Returning Hunter), and voices hailed him from house to house under all that dim, star-littern sky.

When Kotuko the dog came to his full growth he enjoyed himself too. He fought his way up the team steadily, fight after fight, till one fine evening, over their food, he tackled the big, black leader (Kotuko the boy saw fair play), and made second dog of him, as they say. So he was promoted to the long thong of the leading dog, running five feet in advance of all the others: it was his bounden duty to stop all fighting, in harness or out of it, and he wore a collar of copper wire, very thick and heavy. On special occasions he was fed with cooked food inside the house, and sometimes was allowed to sleep on the bench with Kotuko. He was a good seal-dog, and would keep a musk-ox at bay by running round him and snapping at his heels. He would even—and this for a sleigh-dog is the last proof of bravery—he would even stand up to the gaunt Arctic wolf, whom all dogs of the North, as a rule, fear beyond anything that walks the snow. He and his master—they did not count the team of ordinary dogs as company—hunted together, day after day and night after night, fur-wrapped boy and savage, long-haired, narrow-eyed, white-fanged, yellow brute. All an Inuit has to do is to get food and skins for himself and his family. The women-folk make the skins into clothing, and occasionally help in trapping small game; but the bulk of the food—and they eat enormously—must be found by the men. If the supply fails there is no one up there to buy or beg or borrow from. The people must die.

An Inuit does not think of these chances till he is forced to. Kadlu, Kotuko, Amoraq, and the boy-baby who kicked about in Amoraq's fur hood and chewed pieces of blubber all day, were as happy together as any family in the world. They came of a very gentle race—an Inuit seldom loses his temper, and almost never strikes a child—who did not know exactly what telling a real lie meant, still less how to steal. They were content to spear their living out of the heart of the bitter, hopeless cold; to smile oily smiles, and tell queer ghost and fairy tales of evenings, and eat till they could eat no more, and sing the endless woman's song: "Amna aya, aya amna, ah! ah!" through the long lamp-lighted days as they mended their clothes and their hunting-gear.

But one terrible winter everything betrayed them. The Tununirmiut returned from the yearly salmon-fishing, and made their houses on the early ice to the north of Bylot's Island, ready to go after the seal as soon as the sea froze. But it was an early and savage autumn. All through September there were continuous gales that broke up the smooth seal-ice when it was only four or five feet thick, and forced it inland, and piled a great barrier, some twenty miles broad, of lumped and ragged and needly ice, over which it was impossible to draw the dog-sleighs. The edge of the floe off which the seal were used to fish in winter lay perhaps twenty miles beyond this barrier, and out of reach of the Tununirmiut. Even so, they might have managed to scrape through the winter on their stock of frozen salmon and stored blubber, and what the traps gave them, but in December one of their hunters came across a tupik (a skin-tent) of three women and a girl nearly dead, whose men had come down from the far North and been crushed in their little skin hunting-boats while they were out after the long-horned narwhal. Kadlu, of course, could only distribute the women among the huts of the winter village, for no Inuit dare refuse a meal to a stranger. He never knows when his own turn may come to beg. Amoraq took the girl, who was about fourteen, into her own house as a sort of servant. From the cut of her sharp-pointed hood, and the long diamond pattern of her white deer-skin leggings, they supposed she came from Ellesmere Land. She had never seen tin cooking-pots or wooden-shod sleighs before; but Kotuko the boy and Kotuko the dog were rather fond of her.

Then all the foxes went south, and even the wolverine, that growling, blunt-headed little thief of the snow, did not take the trouble to follow the line of empty traps that Kotuko set. The tribe lost a couple of their best hunters, who were badly crippled in a fight with a musk-ox, and this threw more work on the others. Kotuko went out, day after day, with a light hunting-sleigh and six or seven of the strongest dogs, looking till his eyes ached for some patch of clear ice where a seal might perhaps have scratched a breathing-hole. Kotuko the dog ranged far and wide, and in the dead stillness of the ice-fields Kotuko the boy could hear his half-choked whine of excitement, above a seal-hole three miles away, as plainly as though he were at his elbow. When the dog found a hole the boy would build himself a little, low snow wall to keep off the worst of the bitter wind, and there he would wait ten, twelve, twenty hours for the seal to come up to breathe, his eyes glued to the tiny mark he had made above the hole to guide the downward thrust of his harpoon, a little seal-skin mat under his feet, and his legs tied together in the tutareang (the buckle that the old hunters had talked about). This helps to keep a man's legs from twitching as he waits and waits and waits for the quick-eared seal to rise. Though there is no excitement in it, you can easily believe that the sitting still in the buckle with the thermometer perhaps forty degrees below zero is the hardest work an Inuit knows. When a seal was caught, Kotuko the dog would bound forward, his trace trailing behind him, and help to pull the body to the sleigh, where the tired and hungry dogs lay sullenly under the lee of the broken ice.

A seal did not go very far, for each mouth in the little village had a right to be filled, and neither bone, hide, nor sinew was wasted. The dogs' meat was taken for human use, and Amoraq fed the team with pieces of old summer skin-tents raked out from under the sleeping-bench, and they howled and howled again, and waked to howl hungrily. One could tell by the soap-stone lamps in the huts that famine was near. In good seasons, when blubber was plentiful, the light in the boat-shaped lamps would be two feet high—cheerful, oily, and yellow. Now it was a bare six inches: Amoraq carefully pricked down the moss wick, when an unwatched flame brightened for a moment, and the eyes of all the family followed her hand. The horror of famine up there in the great cold is not so much dying, as dying in the dark. All the Inuit dread the dark that presses on them without a break for six months in each year; and when the lamps are low in the houses the minds of people begin to be shaken and confused.

But worse was to come.

The underfed dogs snapped and growled in the passages, glaring at the cold stars, and snuffing into the bitter wind, night after night. When they stopped howling the silence fell down again as solid and heavy as a snowdrift against a door, and men could hear the beating of their blood in the thin passages of the ear, and the thumping of their own hearts, that sounded as loud as the noise of sorcerers' drums beaten across the snow. One night Kotuko the dog, who had been unusually sullen in harness, leaped up and pushed his head against Kotuko's knee. Kotuko patted him, but the dog still pushed blindly forward, fawning. Then Kadlu waked, and gripped the heavy wolf-like head, and stared into the glassy eyes. The dog whimpered and shivered between Kadlu's knees. The hair rose about his neck, and he growled as though a stranger were at the door; then he barked joyously, and rolled on the ground, and bit at Kotuko's boot like a puppy.

"What is it?" said Kotuko; for he was beginning to be afraid.

"The sickness," Kadlu answered. "It is the dog sickness." Kotuko the dog lifted his nose and howled and howled again.

"I have not seen this before. What will he do?" said Kotuko.

Kadlu shrugged one shoulder a little, and crossed the hut for his short stabbing-harpoon. The big dog looked at him, howled again, and slunk away down the passage, while the other dogs drew aside right and left to give him ample room. When he was out on the snow he barked furiously, as though on the trail of a musk-ox, and, barking and leaping and frisking, passed out of sight. His trouble was not hydrophobia, but simple, plain madness. The cold and the hunger, and, above all, the dark, had turned his head; and when the terrible dog-sickness once shows itself in a team, it spreads like wild-fire. Next hunting-day another dog sickened, and was killed then and there by Kotuko as he bit and struggled among the traces. Then the black second dog, who had been the leader in the old days, suddenly gave tongue on an imaginary reindeer-track, and when they slipped him from the pitu he flew at the throat of an ice-cliff, and ran away as his leader had done, his harness on his back. After that no one would take the dogs out again. They needed them for something else, and the dogs knew it; and though they were tied down and fed by hand, their eyes were full of despair and fear. To make things worse, the old women began to tell ghost-tales, and to say that they had met the spirits of the dead hunters lost that autumn, who prophesied all sorts of horrible things.

Kotuko grieved more for the loss of his dog than anything else; for though an Inuit eats enormously he also knows how to starve. But the hunger, the darkness, the cold, and the exposure told on his strength, and he began to hear voices inside his head, and to see people who were not there, out of the tail of his eye. One night—he had unbuckled himself after ten hours' waiting above a "blind" seal-hole, and was staggering back to the village faint and dizzy—he halted to lean his back against a boulder which happened to be supported like a rocking-stone on a single jutting point of ice. His weight disturbed the balance of the thing, it rolled over ponderously, and as Kotuko sprang aside to avoid it, slid after him, squeaking and hissing on the ice-slope.

That was enough for Kotuko. He had been brought up to believe that every rock and boulder had its owner (its inua), who was generally a one-eyed kind of a Woman-Thing called a tornaq, and that when a tornaq meant to help a man she rolled after him inside her stone house, and asked him whether he would take her for a guardian spirit. (In summer thaws the ice-propped rocks and boulders roll and slip all over the face of the land, so you can easily see how the idea of live stones arose.) Kotuko heard the blood beating in his ears as he had heard it all day, and he thought that was the tornaq of the stone speaking to him. Before he reached home he was quite certain that he had held a long conversation with her, and as all his people believed that this was quite possible, no one contradicted him.

"She said to me, 'I jump down, I jump down from my place on the snow,'" cried Kotuko, with hollow eyes, leaning forward in the half-lighted hut. "She said, 'I will be a guide.' She said, 'I will guide you to the good seal-holes.' To-morrow I go out, and the tornaq will guide me."

Then the angekok, the village sorcerer, came in, and Kotuko told him the tale a second time. It lost nothing in the telling.

"Follow the tornait [the spirits of the stones], and they will bring us food again," said the angekok.

Now the girl from the North had been lying near the lamp, eating very little and saying less for days past; but when Amoraq and Kadlu next morning packed and lashed a little hand-sleigh for Kotuko, and loaded it with his hunting-gear and as much blubber and frozen seal-meat as they could spare, she took the pulling-rope, and stepped out boldly at the boy's side.

"Your house is my house," she said, as the little bone-shod sleigh squeaked and bumped behind them in the awful Arctic night.

"My house is your house," said Kotuko; "but I think that we shall both go to Sedna together."

Now Sedna is the Mistress of the Underworld, and the Inuit believe that every one who dies must spend a year in her horrible country before going to Quadliparmiut, the Happy

Place, where it never freezes and the fat reindeer trot up when you call.

Through the village people were shouting: "The tornait have spoken to Kotuko. They will show him open ice. He will bring us the seal again!" Their voices were soon swallowed up by the cold, empty dark, and Kotuko and the girl shouldered close together as they strained on the pulling-rope or humoured the sleigh through the ice in the direction of the Polar Sea. Kotuko insisted that the tornaq of the stone had told him to go north, and north they went under Tuktuqdjung the Reindeer—those stars that we call the Great Bear.

No European could have made five miles a day over the ice-rubbish and the sharp-edged drifts; but those two knew exactly the turn of the wrist that coaxes a sleigh round a hummock, the jerk that nearly lifts it out of an ice-crack, and the exact strength that goes to the few quiet strokes of the spear-head that make a path possible when everything looks hopeless.

The girl said nothing, but bowed her head, and the long wolverine-fur fringe of her ermine hood blew across her broad, dark face. The sky above them was an intense velvety black, changing to bands of Indian red on the horizon, where the great stars burned like street-lamps. From time to time a greenish wave of the Northern Lights would roll across the hollow of the high heavens, flick like a flag, and disappear; or a meteor would crackle from darkness to darkness, trailing a shower of sparks behind. Then they could see the ridged and furrowed surface of the floe tipped and laced with strange colours—red, copper, and bluish; but in the ordinary starlight everything turned to one frost-bitten gray. The floe, as you will remember, had been battered and tormented by the autumn gales till it was one frozen earthquake. There were gullies and ravines, and holes like gravel-pits, cut in ice; lumps and scattered pieces frozen down to the original floor of the floe; blotches of old black ice that had been thrust under the floe in some gale and heaved up again; roundish boulders of ice; saw-like edges of ice carved by the snow that flies before the wind; and sunken pits where thirty or forty acres lay below the level of the rest of the field. From a little distance you might have taken the lumps for seal or walrus, overturned sleighs or men on a hunting expedition, or even the great Ten-legged White Spirit-Bear himself; but in spite of these fantastic shapes, all on the very edge of starting into life, there was neither sound nor the least faint echo of sound. And through this silence and through this waste, where the sudden lights flapped and went out again, the sleigh and the two that pulled it crawled like things in a nightmare—a nightmare of the end of the world at the end of the world.

When they were tired Kotuko would make what the hunters call a "half-house," a very small snow hut, into which they would huddle with the travelling-lamp, and try to thaw out the frozen seal-meat. When they had slept, the march began again—thirty miles a day to get ten miles northward. The girl was always very silent, but Kotuko muttered to himself and broke out into songs he had learned in the Singing-House— summer songs, and reindeer and salmon songs—all horribly out of place at that season. He would declare that he heard the tornaq growling to him, and would run wildly up a hummock, tossing his arms and speaking in loud, threatening tones. To tell the truth, Kotuko was very nearly crazy for the time being; but the girl was sure that he was being guided by his guardian spirit, and that everything would come right. She was not surprised, therefore, when at the end of the fourth march Kotuko, whose eyes were burning like fire-balls in his head, told her that his tornaq was following them across the snow in the shape of a two-headed dog. The girl looked where Kotuko pointed, and something seemed to slip into a ravine. It was certainly not human, but everybody knew that the tornait preferred to appear in the shape of bear and seal, and such like.

It might have been the Ten-legged White Spirit-Bear himself, or it might have been anything, for Kotuko and the girl were so starved that their eyes were untrustworthy. They had trapped nothing, and seen no trace of game since they had left the village; their food would not hold out for another week, and there was a gale coming. A Polar storm can blow for ten days without a break, and all that while it is certain death to be abroad. Kotuko laid up a snow-house large enough to take in the hand-sleigh (never be separated from your meat), and while he was shaping the last irregular block of ice that makes the key-stone of the roof, he saw a Thing looking at him from a little cliff of ice half a mile away. The air was hazy, and the Thing seemed to be forty feet long and ten feet high, with twenty feet of tail and a shape that quivered all along the outlines. The girl saw it too, but instead of crying aloud with terror, said quietly, "That is Quiquern. What comes after?"

"He will speak to me," said Kotuko; but the snow-knife trembled in his hand as he spoke, because however much a man may believe that he is a friend of strange and ugly spirits, he seldom likes to be taken quite at his word. Quiquern, too, is the phantom of a gigantic toothless dog without any hair, who is supposed to live in the far North, and to wander about the country just before things are going to happen. They may be pleasant or unpleasant things, but not even the sorcerers care to speak about Quiquern. He makes the dogs go mad. Like the Spirit-Bear, he has several extra pairs of legs,—six or eight,—and this Thing jumping up and down in the haze had more legs than any real dog needed. Kotuko and the girl huddled into their hut quickly. Of course if Quiquern had wanted them, he could have torn it to pieces above their heads, but the sense of a foot-thick snow-wall between themselves and the wicked dark was great comfort. The gale broke with a shriek of wind like the shriek of a train, and for three days and three nights it held, never varying one point, and never lulling even for a minute. They fed the stone lamp between their knees, and nibbled at the half-warm seal-meat, and watched the black soot gather on the roof for seventy-two long hours. The girl counted up the food in the sleigh; there was not more than two days' supply, and Kotuko looked over the iron heads and the deer-sinew fastenings of his harpoon and his seal-lance and his bird-dart. There was nothing else to do.

"We shall go to Sedna soon—very soon," the girl whispered. "In three days we shall lie down and go. Will your tornaq do nothing? Sing her an angekok's song to make her come here."

He began to sing in the high-pitched howl of the magic songs, and the gale went down slowly. In the middle of his song the girl started, laid her mittened hand and then her head to the ice floor of the hut. Kotuko followed her example, and the two kneeled, staring into each other's eyes, and listening with every nerve. He ripped a thin sliver of whalebone from the rim of a bird-snare that lay on the sleigh, and, after straightening, set it upright in a little hole in the ice, firming it down with his mitten. It was almost as delicately adjusted as a compass-needle, and now instead of listening they watched. The thin rod quivered a little—the least little jar in the world; then it vibrated steadily for a few seconds, came to rest, and vibrated again, this time nodding to another point of the compass.

"Too soon!" said Kotuko. "Some big floe has broken far away outside."

The girl pointed at the rod, and shook her head. "It is the big breaking," she said. "Listen to the ground-ice. It knocks."

When they kneeled this time they heard the most curious muffled grunts and knockings, apparently under their feet. Sometimes it sounded as though a blind puppy were squeaking above the lamp; then as if a stone were being ground on hard ice; and again, like muffled blows on a drum; but all dragged out and made small, as though they travelled through a little horn a weary distance away.

"We shall not go to Sedna lying down," said Kotuko. "It is the breaking. The tornaq has cheated us. We shall die."

All this may sound absurd enough, but the two were face to face with a very real danger. The three days' gale had driven the deep water of Baffin's Bay southerly, and piled it on to the edge of the far-reaching land-ice that stretches from Bylot's Island to the west. Also, the strong current which sets east out of Lancaster Sound carried with it mile upon mile of what they call pack-ice—rough ice that has not frozen into fields; and this pack was bombarding the floe at the same time that the swell and heave of the storm-worked sea was weakening and undermining it. What Kotuko and the girl had been listening to were the faint echoes of that fight thirty or forty miles away, and the little tell-tale rod quivered to the shock of it.

Now, as the Inuit say, when the ice once wakes after its long winter sleep, there is no knowing what may happen, for solid floe-ice changes shape almost as quickly as a cloud. The gale was evidently a spring gale sent out of time, and anything was possible.

Yet the two were happier in their minds than before. If

the floe broke up there would be no more waiting and suffering. Spirits, goblins, and witch-people were moving about on the racking ice, and they might find themselves stepping into Sedna's country side by side with all sorts of wild Things, the flush of excitement still on them. When they left the hut after the gale, the noise on the horizon was steadily growing, and the tough ice moaned and buzzed all round them.

"It is still waiting," said Kotuko.

On the top of a hummock sat or crouched the eight-legged Thing that they had seen three days before—and it howled horribly.

"Let us follow," said the girl. "It may know some way that does not lead to Sedna"; but she reeled from weakness as she took the pulling-rope. The Thing moved off slowly and clumsily across the ridges, heading always toward the westward and the land, and they followed, while the growling thunder at the edge of the floe rolled nearer and nearer. The floe's lip was split and cracked in every direction for three or four miles inland, and great pans of ten-foot-thick ice, from a few yards to twenty acres square, were jolting and ducking and surging into one another, and into the yet unbroken floe, as the heavy swell took and shook and spouted between them. This battering-ram ice was, so to speak, the first army that the sea was flinging against the floe. The incessant crash and jar of these cakes almost drowned the ripping sound of sheets of pack-ice driven bodily under the floe as cards are hastily pushed under a tablecloth. Where the water was shallow these sheets would be piled one atop of the other till the bottommost touched mud fifty feet down, and the discoloured sea banked behind the muddy ice till the increasing pressure drove all forward again. In addition to the floe and the pack-ice, the gale and the currents were bringing down true bergs, sailing mountains of ice, snapped off from the Greenland side of the water or the north shore of Melville Bay. They pounded in solemnly, the waves breaking white round them, and advanced on the floe like an old-time fleet under full sail. A berg that seemed ready to carry the world before it would ground helplessly in deep water, reel over, and wallow in a lather of foam and mud and flying frozen spray, while a much smaller and lower one would rip and ride into the flat floe, flinging tons of ice on either side, and cutting a track half a mile long before it was stopped. Some fell like swords, shearing a raw-edged canal; and others splintered into a shower of blocks, weighing scores of tons apiece, that whirled and skirted among the hummocks. Others, again, rose up bodily out of the water when they shoaled, twisted as though in pain, and fell solidly on their sides, while the sea threshed over their shoulders. This trampling and crowding and bending and buckling and arching of the ice into every possible shape was going on as far as the eye could reach all along the north line of the floe. From where Kotuko and the girl were, the confusion looked no more than an uneasy, rippling, crawling movement under the horizon; but it came toward them each moment, and they could hear, far away to landward a heavy booming, as it might have been the boom of artillery through a fog. That showed that the floe was being jammed home against the iron cliffs of Bylot's Island, the land to the southward behind them.

"This has never been before," said Kotuko, staring stupidly. "This is not the time. How can the floe break NOW?"

"Follow THAT!" the girl cried, pointing to the Thing half limping, half running distractedly before them. They followed, tugging at the hand-sleigh, while nearer and nearer came the roaring march of the ice. At last the fields round them cracked and starred in every direction, and the cracks opened and snapped like the teeth of wolves. But where the Thing rested, on a mound of old and scattered ice-blocks some fifty feet high, there was no motion. Kotuko leaped forward wildly, dragging the girl after him, and crawled to the bottom of the mound. The talking of the ice grew louder and louder round them, but the mound stayed fast, and, as the girl looked at him, he threw his right elbow upward and outward, making the Inuit sign for land in the shape of an island. And land it was that the eight-legged, limping Thing had led them to—some granite-tipped, sand-beached islet off the coast, shod and sheathed and masked with ice so that no man could have told it from the floe, but at the bottom solid earth, and not shifting ice! The smashing and rebound of the floes as they grounded and splintered marked the borders of it, and a friendly shoal ran out to the northward, and turned aside the rush of the heaviest ice, exactly as a ploughshare turns over loam. There was danger, of course, that some heavily squeezed ice-field might shoot up the beach, and plane off the top of the islet bodily; but that did not trouble Kotuko and the girl when they made their snow-house and began to eat, and heard the ice hammer and skid along the beach. The Thing had disappeared, and Kotuko was talking excitedly about his power over spirits as he crouched round the lamp. In the middle of his wild sayings the girl began to laugh, and rock herself backward and forward.

Behind her shoulder, crawling into the hut crawl by crawl, there were two heads, one yellow and one black, that belonged to two of the most sorrowful and ashamed dogs that ever you saw. Kotuko the dog was one, and the black leader was the other. Both were now fat, well-looking, and quite restored to their proper minds, but coupled to each other in an extraordinary fashion. When the black leader ran off, you remember, his harness was still on him. He must have met Kotuko the dog, and played or fought with him, for his shoulder-loop had caught in the plaited copper wire of Kotuko's collar, and had drawn tight, so that neither could get at the trace to gnaw it apart, but each was fastened sidelong to his neighbour's neck. That, with the freedom of hunting on their own account, must have helped to cure their madness. They were very sober.

The girl pushed the two shamefaced creatures towards Kotuko, and, sobbing with laughter, cried, "That is Quiquern, who led us to safe ground. Look at his eight legs and double head!"

Kotuko cut them free, and they fell into his arms, yellow and black together, trying to explain how they had got their senses back again. Kotuko ran a hand down their ribs, which were round and well clothed. "They have found food," he said, with a grin. "I do not think we shall go to Sedna so soon. My tornaq sent these. The sickness has left them."

As soon as they had greeted Kotuko, these two, who had been forced to sleep and eat and hunt together for the past few weeks, flew at each other's throat, and there was a beautiful battle in the snow-house. "Empty dogs do not fight," Kotuko said. "They have found the seal. Let us sleep. We shall find food."

When they waked there was open water on the north beach of the island, and all the loosened ice had been driven landward. The first sound of the surf is one of the most delightful that the Inuit can hear, for it means that spring is on the road. Kotuko and the girl took hold of hands and smiled, for the clear, full roar of the surge among the ice reminded them of salmon and reindeer time and the smell of blossoming ground-willows. Even as they looked, the sea began to skim over between the floating cakes of ice, so intense was the cold; but on the horizon there was a vast red glare, and that was the light of the sunken sun. It was more like hearing him yawn in his sleep than seeing him rise, and the glare lasted for only a few minutes, but it marked the turn of the year. Nothing, they felt, could alter that.

Kotuko found the dogs fighting over a fresh-killed seal who was following the fish that a gale always disturbs. He was the first of some twenty or thirty seal that landed on the island in the course of the day, and till the sea froze hard there were hundreds of keen black heads rejoicing in the shallow free water and floating about with the floating ice.

It was good to eat seal-liver again; to fill the lamps recklessly with blubber, and watch the flame blaze three feet in the air; but as soon as the new sea-ice bore, Kotuko and the girl loaded the hand-sleigh, and made the two dogs pull as they had never pulled in their lives, for they feared what might have happened in their village. The weather was as pitiless as usual; but it is easier to draw a sleigh loaded with good food than to hunt starving. They left five-and-twenty seal carcasses buried in the ice of the beach, all ready for use, and hurried back to their people. The dogs showed them the way as soon as Kotuko told them what was expected, and though there was no sign of a landmark, in two days they were giving tongue outside Kadlu's house. Only three dogs answered them; the others had been eaten, and the houses were all dark. But when Kotuko shouted, "Ojo!" (boiled meat), weak voices replied, and when he called the muster of the village name by name, very distinctly, there were no gaps in it.

An hour later the lamps blazed in Kadlu's house; snow-water was heating; the pots were beginning to simmer, and the snow was dripping from the roof, as Amoraq made ready a meal for all the village, and the boy-baby in the hood chewed at a strip of rich nutty blubber, and the hunters slowly and methodically filled themselves to the very brim with seal-meat.

Kotuko and the girl told their tale. The two dogs sat between them, and whenever their names came in, they cocked an ear apiece and looked most thoroughly ashamed of themselves. A dog who has once gone mad and recovered, the Inuit say, is safe against all further attacks.

"So the tornaq did not forget us," said Kotuko. "The storm blew, the ice broke, and the seal swam in behind the fish that were frightened by the storm. Now the new seal-holes are not two days distant. Let the good hunters go to-morrow and bring back the seal I have speared—twenty-five seal buried in the ice. When we have eaten those we will all follow the seal on the floe."

"What do YOU do?" said the sorcerer in the same sort of voice as he used to Kadlu, richest of the Tununirmiut.

Kadlu looked at the girl from the North, and said quietly, "WE build a house." He pointed to the north-west side of Kadlu's house, for that is the side on which the married son or daughter always lives.

The girl turned her hands palm upward, with a little despairing shake of her head. She was a foreigner, picked up starving, and could bring nothing to the housekeeping.

Amoraq jumped from the bench where she sat, and began to sweep things into the girl's lap—stone lamps, iron skin-scrapers, tin kettles, deer-skins embroidered with musk-ox teeth, and real canvas-needles such as sailors use—the finest dowry that has ever been given on the far edge of the Arctic Circle, and the girl from the North bowed her head down to the very floor.

"Also these!" said Kotuko, laughing and signing to the dogs, who thrust their cold muzzles into the girl's face.

"Ah," said the angekok, with an important cough, as though

he had been thinking it all over. "As soon as Kotuko left the village I went to the Singing-House and sang magic. I sang all the long nights, and called upon the Spirit of the Reindeer. MY singing made the gale blow that broke the ice and drew the two dogs toward Kotuko when the ice would have crushed his bones. MY song drew the seal in behind the broken ice. My body lay still in the quaggi, but my spirit ran about on the ice, and guided Kotuko and the dogs in all the things they did. I did it."

Everybody was full and sleepy, so no one contradicted; and the angekok, by virtue of his office, helped himself to yet another lump of boiled meat, and lay down to sleep with the others in the warm, well-lighted, oil-smelling home.

*****

Now Kotuko, who drew very well in the Inuit fashion, scratched pictures of all these adventures on a long, flat piece of ivory with a hole at one end. When he and the girl went north to Ellesmere Land in the year of the Wonderful Open Winter, he left the picture-story with Kadlu, who lost it in the shingle when his dog-sleigh broke down one summer on the beach of Lake Netilling at Nikosiring, and there a Lake Inuit found it next spring and sold it to a man at Imigen who was interpreter on a Cumberland Sound whaler, and he sold it to Hans Olsen, who was afterward a quartermaster on board a big steamer that took tourists to the North Cape in Norway. When the tourist season was over, the steamer ran between London and Australia, stopping at Ceylon, and there Olsen sold the ivory to a Cingalese jeweller for two imitation sapphires. I found it under some rubbish in a house at Colombo, and have translated it from one end to the other.

'ANGUTIVAUN TAINA'

[This is a very free translation of the Song of the Returning
Hunter, as the men used to sing it after seal-spearing. The
Inuit always repeat things over and over again.]

Our gloves are stiff with the frozen blood,
Our furs with the drifted snow,
As we come in with the seal--the seal!
In from the edge of the floe.
Au jana! Aua! Oha! Haq!
And the yelping dog-teams go,
And the long whips crack, and the men come back,
Back from the edge of the floe!
We tracked our seal to his secret place,
We heard him scratch below,
We made our mark, and we watched beside,
Out on the edge of the floe.
We raised our lance when he rose to breathe,
We drove it downward--so!
And we played him thus, and we killed him thus,
Out on the edge of the floe.
Our gloves are glued with the frozen blood,
Our eyes with the drifting snow;
But we come back to our wives again,
Back from the edge of the floe!
Au jana! Aua! Oha! Haq!
And the loaded dog-teams go,
And the wives can hear their men come back.
Back from the edge of the floe!

RED DOG

For our white and our excellent nights---for the nights
of swift running.
Fair ranging, far seeing, good hunting, sure cunning!
For the smells of the dawning, untainted, ere dew has
departed!
For the rush through the mist, and the quarry blind-started!
For the cry of our mates when the sambhur has wheeled and
is standing at bay,
For the risk and the riot of night!
For the sleep at the lair-mouth by day,
It is met, and we go to the fight.

Bay! O Bay!

It was after the letting in of the Jungle that the pleasantest part of Mowgli's life began. He had the good conscience that comes from paying debts; all the Jungle was his friend, and just a little afraid of him. The things that he did and saw and heard when he was wandering from one people to another, with or without his four companions, would make many many stories, each as long as this one. So you will never be told how he met the Mad Elephant of Mandla, who killed two-and-twenty bullocks drawing eleven carts of coined silver to the

Government Treasury, and scattered the shiny rupees in the dust; how he fought Jacala, the Crocodile, all one long night in the Marshes of the North, and broke his skinning-knife on the brute's back-plates; how he found a new and longer knife round the neck of a man who had been killed by a wild boar, and how he tracked that boar and killed him as a fair price for the knife; how he was caught up once in the Great Famine, by the moving of the deer, and nearly crushed to death in the swaying hot herds; how he saved Hathi the Silent from being once more trapped in a pit with a stake at the bottom, and how, next day, he himself fell into a very cunning leopard-trap, and how Hathi broke the thick wooden bars to pieces above him; how he milked the wild buffaloes in the swamp, and how—

But we must tell one tale at a time. Father and Mother Wolf died, and Mowgli rolled a big boulder against the mouth of their cave, and cried the Death Song over them; Baloo grew very old and stiff, and even Bagheera, whose nerves were steel and whose muscles were iron, was a shade slower on the kill than he had been. Akela turned from gray to milky white with pure age; his ribs stuck out, and he walked as though he had been made of wood, and Mowgli killed for him. But the young wolves, the children of the disbanded Seeonee Pack, throve and increased, and when there were about forty of them, masterless, full-voiced, clean-footed five-year-olds, Akela told them that they ought to gather themselves together and follow the Law, and run under one head, as befitted the Free People.

This was not a question in which Mowgli concerned himself, for, as he said, he had eaten sour fruit, and he knew the tree it hung from; but when Phao, son of Phaona (his father was the Gray Tracker in the days of Akela's headship), fought his way to the leadership of the Pack, according to the Jungle Law, and the old calls and songs began to ring under the stars once more, Mowgli came to the Council Rock for memory's sake. When he chose to speak the Pack waited till he had finished, and he sat at Akela's side on the rock above Phao. Those were days of good hunting and good sleeping. No stranger cared to break into the jungles that belonged to Mowgli's people, as they called the Pack, and the young wolves grew fat and strong, and there were many cubs to bring to the Looking-over. Mowgli always attended a Looking-over, remembering the night when a black panther bought a naked brown baby into the pack, and the long call, "Look, look well, O Wolves," made his heart flutter. Otherwise, he would be far away in the Jungle with his four brothers, tasting, touching, seeing, and feeling new things.

One twilight when he was trotting leisurely across the ranges to give Akela the half of a buck that he had killed, while the Four jogged behind him, sparring a little, and tumbling one another over for joy of being alive, he heard a cry that had never been heard since the bad days of Shere Khan. It was what they call in the Jungle the pheeal, a hideous kind of shriek that the jackal gives when he is hunting behind a tiger, or when there is a big killing afoot. If you can imagine a mixture of hate, triumph, fear, and despair, with a kind of leer running through it, you will get some notion of the pheeal that rose and sank and wavered and quavered far away across the Waingunga. The Four stopped at once, bristling and growling. Mowgli's hand went to his knife, and he checked, the blood in his face, his eyebrows knotted.

"There is no Striped One dare kill here," he said.

"That is not the cry of the Forerunner," answered Gray Brother. "It is some great killing. Listen!"

It broke out again, half sobbing and half chuckling, just as though the jackal had soft human lips. Then Mowgli drew deep breath, and ran to the Council Rock, overtaking on his way hurrying wolves of the Pack. Phao and Akela were on the Rock together, and below them, every nerve strained, sat the others. The mothers and the cubs were cantering off to their lairs; for when the pheeal cries it is no time for weak things to be abroad.

They could hear nothing except the Waingunga rushing and gurgling in the dark, and the light evening winds among the tree-tops, till suddenly across the river a wolf called. It was no wolf of the Pack, for they were all at the Rock. The note changed to a long, despairing bay; and "Dhole!" it said, "Dhole! dhole! dhole!" They heard tired feet on the rocks, and a gaunt wolf, streaked with red on his flanks, his right fore-paw useless, and his jaws white with foam, flung himself into the circle and lay gasping at Mowgli's feet.

"Good hunting! Under whose Headship?" said Phao gravely.

"Good hunting! Won-tolla am I," was the answer. He meant that he was a solitary wolf, fending for himself, his mate, and his cubs in some lonely lair, as do many wolves in the south. Won-tolla means an Outlier—one who lies out from any Pack. Then he panted, and they could see his heart-beats shake him backward and forward.

"What moves?" said Phao, for that is the question all the Jungle asks after the pheeal cries.

"The dhole, the dhole of the Dekkan—Red Dog, the Killer! They came north from the south saying the Dekkan was empty and killing out by the way. When this moon was new there were four to me—my mate and three cubs. She would teach them to kill on the grass plains, hiding to drive the buck, as we do who are of the open. At midnight I heard them together, full tongue on the trail. At the dawn-wind I found them stiff in the grass—four, Free People, four when this moon was new. Then sought I my Blood-Right and found the dhole."

"How many?" said Mowgli quickly; the Pack growled deep in their throats.

"I do not know. Three of them will kill no more, but at the last they drove me like the buck; on my three legs they drove me. Look, Free People!"

He thrust out his mangled fore-foot, all dark with dried blood. There were cruel bites low down on his side, and his throat was torn and worried.

"Eat," said Akela, rising up from the meat Mowgli had brought him, and the Outlier flung himself on it.

"This shall be no loss," he said humbly, when he had taken off the first edge of his hunger. "Give me a little strength, Free People, and I also will kill. My lair is empty that was full when this moon was new, and the Blood Debt is not all paid."

Phao heard his teeth crack on a haunch-bone and grunted approvingly.

"We shall need those jaws," said he. "Were there cubs with the dhole?"

"Nay, nay. Red Hunters all: grown dogs of their Pack, heavy and strong for all that they eat lizards in the Dekkan."

What Won-tolla had said meant that the dhole, the red hunting-dog of the Dekkan, was moving to kill, and the Pack knew well that even the tiger will surrender a new kill to the dhole. They drive straight through the Jungle, and what they meet they pull down and tear to pieces. Though they are not as big nor half as cunning as the wolf, they are very strong and very numerous. The dhole, for instance, do not begin to call themselves a pack till they are a hundred strong; whereas forty wolves make a very fair pack indeed. Mowgli's wanderings had taken him to the edge of the high grassy downs of the Dekkan, and he had seen the fearless dholes sleeping and playing and scratching themselves in the little hollows and tussocks that they use for lairs. He despised and hated them because they did not smell like the Free People, because they did not live in caves, and, above all, because they had hair between their toes while he and his friends were clean-footed. But he knew, for Hathi had told him, what a terrible thing a dhole hunting-pack was. Even Hathi moves aside from their line, and until they are killed, or till game is scarce, they will go forward.

Akela knew something of the dholes, too, for he said to Mowgli quietly, "It is better to die in a Full Pack than leaderless and alone. This is good hunting, and—my last. But, as men live, thou hast very many more nights and days, Little Brother. Go north and lie down, and if any live after the dhole has gone by he shall bring thee word of the fight."

"Ah," said Mowgli, quite gravely, "must I go to the marshes and catch little fish and sleep in a tree, or must I ask help of the Bandar-log and crack nuts, while the Pack fight below?"

"It is to the death," said Akela. "Thou hast never met the dhole—the Red Killer. Even the Striped One——"

"Aowa! Aowa!" said Mowgli pettingly. "I have killed one striped ape, and sure am I in my stomach that Shere Khan would have left his own mate for meat to the dhole if he had winded a pack across three ranges. Listen now: There was a wolf, my father, and there was a wolf, my mother, and there was an old gray wolf (not too wise: he is white now) was my father and my mother. Therefore I—" he raised his voice, "I say that when the dhole come, and if the dhole come, Mowgli and the Free People are of one skin for that hunting; and I say, by the Bull that bought me—by the Bull Bagheera paid for me in the old days which ye of the Pack do not remember— _I_ say, that the Trees and the River may hear and hold fast if I forget; _I_ say that this my knife shall be as a tooth to the Pack—and I do not think it is so blunt. This is my Word which has gone from me."

"Thou dost not know the dhole, man with a wolf's tongue," said Won-tolla. "I look only to clear the Blood Debt against them ere they have me in many pieces. They move slowly, killing out as they go, but in two days a little strength will come back to me and I turn again for the Blood Debt. But for YE, Free People, my word is that ye go north and eat but little for a while till the dhole are gone. There is no meat in this hunting."

"Hear the Outlier!" said Mowgli with a laugh. "Free People, we must go north and dig lizards and rats from the bank, lest by any chance we meet the dhole. He must kill out our hunting-grounds, while we lie hid in the north till it please him to give us our own again. He is a dog—and the pup of a dog—red, yellow-bellied, lairless, and haired between every toe! He counts his cubs six and eight at the litter, as though he were Chikai, the little leaping rat. Surely we must run away, Free People, and beg leave of the peoples of the north for the offal of dead cattle! Ye know the saying: 'North are the vermin; south are the lice. WE are the Jungle.' Choose ye, O choose. It is good hunting! For the Pack—for the Full Pack—for the lair and the litter; for the in-kill and the out-kill; for the mate that drives the doe and the little, little cub within the cave; it is met!—it is met!—it is met!"

The Pack answered with one deep, crashing bark that sounded in the night like a big tree falling. "It is met!" they cried. "Stay with these," said Mowgli to the Four. "We shall need every tooth. Phao and Akela must make ready the battle. I go to count the dogs."

"It is death!" Won-tolla cried, half rising. "What can such a hairless one do against the Red Dog? Even the Striped One, remember——"

"Thou art indeed an Outlier," Mowgli called back; "but we will speak when the dholes are dead. Good hunting all!"

He hurried off into the darkness, wild with excitement, hardly looking where he set foot, and the natural consequence was that he tripped full length over Kaa's great coils where the python lay watching a deer-path near the river.

"Kssha!" said Kaa angrily. "Is this jungle-work, to stamp and tramp and undo a night's hunting—when the game are moving so well, too?"

"The fault was mine," said Mowgli, picking himself up. "Indeed I was seeking thee, Flathead, but each time we meet thou art longer and broader by the length of my arm. There is none like thee in the Jungle, wise, old, strong, and most beautiful Kaa."

"Now whither does THIS trail lead?" Kaa's voice was gentler. "Not a moon since there was a Manling with a knife threw stones at my head and called me bad little tree-cat names, because I lay asleep in the open."

"Ay, and turned every driven deer to all the winds, and Mowgli was hunting, and this same Flathead was too deaf to hear his whistle, and leave the deer-roads free," Mowgli answered composedly, sitting down among the painted coils.

"Now this same Manling comes with soft, tickling words

to this same Flathead, telling him that he is wise and strong and beautiful, and this same old Flathead believes and makes a place, thus, for this same stone-throwing Manling, and—Art thou at ease now? Could Bagheera give thee so good a resting-place?"

Kaa had, as usual, made a sort of soft half-hammock of himself under Mowgli's weight. The boy reached out in the darkness, and gathered in the supple cable-like neck till Kaa's head rested on his shoulder, and then he told him all that had happened in the Jungle that night.

"Wise I may be," said Kaa at the end; "but deaf I surely am. Else I should have heard the *pheeal.* Small wonder the Eaters of Grass are uneasy. How many be the dhole?"

"I have not yet seen. I came hot-foot to thee. Thou art older than Hathi. But oh, Kaa,"—here Mowgli wriggled with sheerjoy,—"it will be good hunting. Few of us will see another moon."

"Dost THOU strike in this? Remember thou art a Man; and remember what Pack cast thee out. Let the Wolf look to the Dog. THOU art a Man."

"Last year's nuts are this year's black earth," said Mowgli. "It is true that I am a Man, but it is in my stomach that this night I have said that I am a Wolf. I called the River and the Trees to remember. I am of the Free People, Kaa, till the dhole has gone by."

"Free People," Kaa grunted. "Free thieves! And thou hast tied thyself into the death-knot for the sake of the memory of the dead wolves? This is no good hunting."

"It is my Word which I have spoken. The Trees know, the River knows. Till the dhole have gone by my Word comes not back to me."

"Ngssh! This changes all trails. I had thought to take thee away with me to the northern marshes, but the Word—even the Word of a little, naked, hairless Manling—is the Word. Now I, Kaa, say——"

"Think well, Flathead, lest thou tie thyself into the death-knot also. I need no Word from thee, for well I know——"

"Be it so, then," said Kaa. "I will give no Word; but what is in thy stomach to do when the dhole come?"

"They must swim the Waingunga. I thought to meet them with my knife in the shallows, the Pack behind me; and so stabbing and thrusting, we a little might turn them down-stream, or cool their throats."

"The dhole do not turn and their throats are hot," said Kaa. "There will be neither Manling nor Wolf-cub when that hunting is done, but only dry bones."

"Alala! If we die, we die. It will be most good hunting. But my stomach is young, and I have not seen many Rains. I am not wise nor strong. Hast thou a better plan, Kaa?"

"I have seen a hundred and a hundred Rains. Ere Hathi cast his milk-tushes my trail was big in the dust. By the First Egg, I am older than many trees, and I have seen all that the Jungle has done."

"But THIS is new hunting," said Mowgli. "Never before have the dhole crossed our trail."

"What is has been. What will be is no more than a forgotten year striking backward. Be still while I count those my years."

For a long hour Mowgli lay back among the coils, while Kaa, his head motionless on the ground, thought of all that he had seen and known since the day he came from the egg. The light seemed to go out of his eyes and leave them like stale opals, and now and again he made little stiff passes with his head, right and left, as though he were hunting in his sleep. Mowgli dozed quietly, for he knew that there is nothing like sleep before hunting, and he was trained to take it at any hour of the day or night.

Then he felt Kaa's back grow bigger and broader below him as the huge python puffed himself out, hissing with the noise of a sword drawn from a steel scabbard.

"I have seen all the dead seasons," Kaa said at last, "and the great trees and the old elephants, and the rocks that were bare and sharp-pointed ere the moss grew. Art THOU still alive, Manling?"

"It is only a little after moonset," said Mowgli. "I do not understand———"

"Hssh! I am again Kaa. I knew it was but a little time. Now we will go to the river, and I will show thee what is to be done against the dhole."

He turned, straight as an arrow, for the main stream of the Waingunga, plunging in a little above the pool that hid the Peace Rock, Mowgli at his side.

"Nay, do not swim. I go swiftly. My back, Little Brother."

Mowgli tucked his left arm round Kaa's neck, dropped his right close to his body, and straightened his feet. Then Kaa breasted the current as he alone could, and the ripple of the checked water stood up in a frill round Mowgli's neck, and his feet were waved to and fro in the eddy under the python's lashing sides. A mile or two above the Peace Rock the Waingunga narrows between a gorge of marble rocks from eighty to a hundred feet high, and the current runs like a mill-race between and over all manner of ugly stones. But Mowgli did not trouble his head about the water; little water in the world could have given him a moment's fear. He was looking at the gorge on either side and sniffing uneasily, for there was a sweetish-sourish smell in the air, very like the smell of a big ant-hill on a hot day. Instinctively he lowered himself in the water, only raising his head to breathe from time to time, and Kaa came to anchor with a double twist of his tail round a sunken rock, holding Mowgli in the hollow of a coil, while the water raced on.

"This is the Place of Death," said the boy. "Why do we come here?"

"They sleep," said Kaa. "Hathi will not turn aside for the Striped One. Yet Hathi and the Striped One together turn aside for the dhole, and the dhole they say turn aside for nothing. And yet for whom do the Little People of the Rocks turn aside? Tell me, Master of the Jungle, who is the Master of the Jungle?"

"These," Mowgli whispered. "It is the Place of Death. Let us go."

"Nay, look well, for they are asleep. It is as it was when I was not the length of thy arm."

The split and weatherworn rocks of the gorge of the Waingunga had been used since the beginning of the Jungle by the Little People of the Rocks—the busy, furious, black wild bees of India; and, as Mowgli knew well, all trails turned off half a mile before they reached the gorge. For centuries the Little People had hived and swarmed from cleft to cleft, and swarmed again, staining the white marble with stale honey, and made their combs tall and deep in the dark of the inner caves, where neither man nor beast nor fire nor water had ever touched them. The length of the gorge on both siaes was hung as it were with black shimmery velvet curtains, and

Mowgli sank as he looked, for those were the clotted millions of the sleeping bees. There were other lumps and festoons and things like decayed tree-trunks studded on the face of the rock, the old combs of past years, or new cities built in the shadow of the windless gorge, and huge masses of spongy, rotten trash had rolled down and stuck among the trees and creepers that clung to the rock-face. As he listened he heard more than once the rustle and slide of a honey-loaded comb turning over or failing away somewhere in the dark galleries; then a booming of angry wings, and the sullen drip, drip, drip, of the wasted honey, guttering along till it lipped over some ledge in the open air and sluggishly trickled down on the twigs. There was a tiny little beach, not five feet broad, on one side of the river, and that was piled high with the rubbish of uncounted years. There were dead bees, drones, sweepings, and stale combs, and wings of marauding moths that had strayed in after honey, all tumbled in smooth piles of the finest black dust. The mere sharp smell of it was enough to frighten anything that had no wings, and knew what the Little People were.

Kaa moved up-stream again till he came to a sandy bar at the head of the gorge.

"Here is this season's kill," said he. "Look!" On the bank lay the skeletons of a couple of young deer and a buffalo. Mowgli could see that neither wolf nor jackal had touched the hones, which were laid out naturally.

"They came beyond the line; they did not know the Law," murmured Mowgli, "and the Little People killed them. Let us go ere they wake."

"They do not wake till the dawn," said Kaa. "Now I will tell thee. A hunted buck from the south, many, many Rains ago, came hither from the south, not knowing the Jungle, a

Pack on his trail. Being made blind by fear, he leaped from above, the Pack running by sight, for they were hot and blind on the trail. The sun was high, and the Little People were many and very angry. Many, too, were those of the Pack who leaped into the Waingunga, but they were dead ere they took water. Those who did not leap died also in the rocks above. But the buck lived."

"How?"

"Because he came first, running for his life, leaping ere the Little People were aware, and was in the river when they gathered to kill. The Pack, following, was altogether lost under the weight of the Little People."

"The buck lived?" Mowgli repeated slowly.

"At least he did not die THEN, though none waited his coming down with a strong body to hold him safe against the water, as a certain old fat, deaf, yellow Flathead would wait for a Manling—yea, though there were all the dholes of the Dekkan on his trail. What is in thy stomach?" Kaa's head was close to Mowgli's ear; and it was a little time before the boy answered.

"It is to pull the very whiskers of Death, but—Kaa, thou art, indeed, the wisest of all the Jungle."

"So many have said. Look now, if the dhole follow thee—"

"As surely they will follow. Ho! ho! I have many little thorns under my tongue to prick into their hides."

"If they follow thee hot and blind, looking only at thy shoulders, those who do not die up above will take water either here or lower down, for the Little People will rise up and cover them. Now the Waingunga is hungry water, and they will have no Kaa to hold them, but will go down, such as live, to the shallows by the Seeonee Lairs, and there thy Pack may meet them by the throat."

"Ahai! Eowawa! Better could not be till the Rains fall in the dry season. There is now only the little matter of the run and the leap. I will make me known to the dholes, so that they shall follow me very closely."

"Hast thou seen the rocks above thee? From the landward side?"

"Indeed, no. That I had forgotten."

"Go look. It is all rotten ground, cut and full of holes. One of thy clumsy feet set down without seeing would end the hunt. See, I leave thee here, and for thy sake only I will carry word to the Pack that they may know where to look for the dhole. For myself, I am not of one skin with ANY wolf."

When Kaa disliked an acquaintance he could be more unpleasant than any of the Jungle People, except perhaps Bagheera. He swam down-stream, and opposite the Rock he came on Phao and Akela listening to the night noises.

"Hssh! Dogs," he said cheerfully. "The dholes will come down-stream. If ye be not afraid ye can kill them in the shallows."

"When come they?" said Phao. "And where is my Man-cub?" said Akela.

"They come when they come," said Kaa. "Wait and see. As for THY Man-cub, from whom thou hast taken a Word and so laid him open to Death, THY Man-cub is with ME, and if he be not already dead the fault is none of thine, bleached dog! Wait here for the dhole, and be glad that the Man-cub and I strike on thy side."

Kaa flashed up-stream again, and moored himself in the

middle of the gorge, looking upward at the line of the cliff. Presently he saw Mowgli's head move against the stars, and then there was a whizz in the air, the keen, clean schloop of a body falling feet first, and next minute the boy was at rest again in the loop of Kaa's body.

"It is no leap by night," said Mowgli quietly. "I have jumped twice as far for sport; but that is an evil place above—low bushes and gullies that go down very deep, all full of the Little People. I have put big stones one above the other by the side of three gullies. These I shall throw down with my feet in running, and the Little People will rise up behind me, very angry."

"That is Man's talk and Man's cunning," said Kaa. "Thou art wise, but the Little People are always angry."

"Nay, at twilight all wings near and far rest for a while. I will play with the dhole at twilight, for the dhole hunts best by day. He follows now Won-tolla's blood-trail."

"Chil does not leave a dead ox, nor the dhole the blood-trail," said Kaa.

"Then I will make him a new blood-trail, of his own blood, if I can, and give him dirt to eat. Thou wilt stay here, Kaa, till I come again with my dholes?"

"Ay, but what if they kill thee in the Jungle, or the Little People kill thee before thou canst leap down to the river?"

"When to-morrow comes we will kill for to-morrow," said Mowgli, quoting a Jungle saying; and again, "When I am dead it is time to sing the Death Song. Good hunting, Kaa!"

He loosed his arm from the python's neck and went down the gorge like a log in a freshet, paddling toward the far bank, where he found slack-water, and laughing aloud from sheer happiness. There was nothing Mowgli liked better than, as he himself said, "to pull the whiskers of Death," and make the Jungle know that he was their overlord. He had often, with Baloo's help, robbed bees' nests in single trees, and he knew that the Little People hated the smell of wild garlic. So he gathered a small bundle of it, tied it up with a bark string, and then followed Won-tolla's blood-trail, as it ran southerly from the Lairs, for some five miles, looking at the trees with his head on one side, and chuckling as he looked.

"Mowgli the Frog have I been," said he to himself; "Mowgli the Wolf have I said that I am. Now Mowgli the Ape must I be before I am Mowgli the Buck. At the end I shall be Mowgli the Man. Ho!" and he slid his thumb along the eighteen-inch blade of his knife.

Won-tolla's trail, all rank with dark blood-spots, ran under a forest of thick trees that grew close together and stretched away north-eastward, gradually growing thinner and thinner to within two miles of the Bee Rocks. From the last tree to the low scrub of the Bee Rocks was open country, where there was hardly cover enough to hide a wolf. Mowgli trotted along under the trees, judging distances between branch and branch, occasionally climbing up a trunk and taking a trial leap from one tree to another till he came to the open ground, which he studied very carefully for an hour. Then he turned, picked up Won-tolla's trail where he had left it, settled himself in a tree with an outrunning branch some eight feet from the ground, and sat still, sharpening his knife on the sole of his foot and singing to himself.

A little before mid-day, when the sun was very warm, he heard the patter of feet and smelt the abominable smell of the dhole-pack as they trotted pitilessly along Won-tolla's trail. Seen from above, the red dhole does not look half the size of a wolf, but Mowgli knew how strong his feet and jaws were. He watched the sharp bay head of the leader snuffing along the trail, and gave him "Good hunting!"

The brute looked up, and his companions halted behind him, scores and scores of red dogs with low-hung tails, heavy shoulders, weak quarters, and bloody mouths. The dholes are a very silent people as a rule, and they have no manners even in their own Jungle. Fully two hundred must have gathered below him, but he could see that the leaders sniffed hungrily on Won-tolla's trail, and tried to drag the Pack forward. That would never do, or they would be at the Lairs in broad daylight, and Mowgli meant to hold them under his tree till dusk.

"By whose leave do ye come here?" said Mowgli.

"All Jungles are our Jungle," was the reply, and the dhole that gave it bared his white teeth. Mowgli looked down with a smile, and imitated perfectly the sharp chitter-chatter of Chikai, the leaping rat of the Dekkan, meaning the dholes to understand that he considered them no better than Chikai. The Pack closed up round the tree-trunk and the leader bayed savagely, calling Mowgli a tree-ape. For an answer Mowgli stretched down one naked leg and wriggled his bare toes just above the leader's head. That was enough, and more than enough, to wake the Pack to stupid rage. Those who have hair between their toes do not care to be reminded of it. Mowgli caught his foot away as the leader leaped up, and said sweetly: "Dog, red dog! Go back to the Dekkan and eat lizards. Go to Chikai thy brother—dog, dog—red, red dog! There is hair between every toe!" He twiddled his toes a second time.

"Come down ere we starve thee out, hairless ape!" yelled the Pack, and this was exactly what Mowgli wanted. He laid himself down along the branch, his cheek to the bark, his right arm free, and there he told the Pack what he thought and knew about them, their manners, their customs, their mates, and their puppies. There is no speech in the world so rancorous and so stinging as the language the Jungle People use to show scorn and contempt. When you come to think of it you will see how this must be so. As Mowgli told Kaa, he had many little thorns under his tongue, and slowly and deliberately he drove the dholes from silence to growls, from growls to yells, and from yells to hoarse slavery ravings. They tried to answer his taunts, but a cub might as well have tried to answer Kaa in a rage; and all the while Mowgli's right hand lay crooked at his side, ready for action, his feet locked round the branch. The big bay leader had leaped many times in the air, but Mowgli dared not risk a false blow. At last, made furious beyond his natural strength, he bounded up seven or eight feet clear of the ground. Then Mowgli's hand shot out like the head of a tree-snake, and gripped him by the scruff of his neck, and the branch shook with the jar as his weight fell back, almost wrenching Mowgli to the ground. But he never loosed his grip, and inch by inch he hauled the beast, hanging like a drowned jackal, up on the branch. With his left hand he reached for his knife and cut off the red, bushy tail, flinging the dhole back to earth again. That was all he needed. The Pack would not go forward on Won-tolla's trail now till they had killed Mowgli or Mowgli had killed them. He saw them settle down in circles with a quiver of the haunches that meant they were going to stay, and so he climbed to a higher crotch, settled his back comfortably, and went to sleep.

After three or four hours he waked and counted the Pack. They were all there, silent, husky, and dry, with eyes of steel. The sun was beginning to sink. In half an hour the Little People of the Rocks would be ending their labours, and, as you know, the dhole does not fight best in the twilight.

"I did not need such faithful watchers," he said politely, standing up on a branch, "but I will remember this. Ye be true dholes, but to my thinking over much of one kind. For that reason I do not give the big lizard-eater his tail again. Art thou not pleased, Red Dog?"

"I myself will tear out thy stomach!" yelled the leader, scratching at the foot of the tree.

"Nay, but consider, wise rat of the Dekkan. There will now be many litters of little tailless red dogs, yea, with raw red stumps that sting when the sand is hot. Go home, Red Dog, and cry that an ape has done this. Ye will not go? Come, then, with me, and I will make you very wise!"

He moved, Bandar-log fashion, into the next tree, and so on into the next and the next, the Pack following with lifted hungry heads. Now and then he would pretend to fall, and the Pack would tumble one over the other in their haste to be at the death. It was a curious sight—the boy with the knife that shone in the low sunlight as it sifted through the upper branches, and the silent Pack with their red coats all aflame, huddling and following below. When he came to the last tree he took the garlic and rubbed himself all over carefully, and the dholes yelled with scorn. "Ape with a wolf's tongue, dost thou think to cover thy scent?" they said. "We follow to the death."

"Take thy tail," said Mowgli, flinging it back along the course he had taken. The Pack instinctively rushed after it. "And follow now—to the death."

He had slipped down the tree-trunk, and headed like the wind in bare feet for the Bee Rocks, before the dholes saw what he would do.

They gave one deep howl, and settled down to the long,

lobbing canter that can at the last run down anything that runs. Mowgli knew their pack-pace to be much slower than that of the wolves, or he would never have risked a two-mile run in full sight. They were sure that the boy was theirs at last, and he was sure that he held them to play with as he pleased. All his trouble was to keep them sufficiently hot behind him to prevent their turning off too soon. He ran cleanly, evenly, and springily; the tailless leader not five yards behind him; and the Pack tailing out over perhaps a quarter of a mile of ground, crazy and blind with the rage of slaughter. So he kept his distance by ear, reserving his last effort for the rush across the Bee Rocks.

The Little People had gone to sleep in the early twilight, for it was not the season of late blossoming flowers; but as Mowgli's first foot-falls rang hollow on the hollow ground he heard a sound as though all the earth were humming. Then he ran as he had never run in his life before, spurned aside one—two—three of the piles of stones into the dark, sweet-smelling gullies; heard a roar like the roar of the sea in a cave; saw with the tail of his eye the air grow dark behind him; saw the current of the Waingunga far below, and a flat, diamond-shaped head in the water; leaped outward with all his strength, the tailless dhole snapping at his shoulder in mid-air, and dropped feet first to the safety of the river, breathless and triumphant. There was not a sting upon him, for the smell of the garlic had checked the Little People for just the few seconds that he was among them. When he rose Kaa's coils were steadying him and things were bounding over the edge of the cliff—great lumps, it seemed, of clustered bees falling like plummets; but before any lump touched water the bees flew upward and the body of a dhole whirled down-stream. Overhead they could hear furious short yells that were drowned in a roar like breakers—the roar of the wings of the Little People of the Rocks. Some of the dholes, too, had fallen into the gullies that communicated with the underground caves, and there choked and fought and snapped among the tumbled honeycombs, and at last, borne up, even when they were dead, on the heaving waves of bees beneath them, shot out of some hole in the river-face, to roll over on the black rubbish-heaps. There were dholes who had leaped short into the trees on the cliffs, and the bees blotted out their shapes; but the greater number of them, maddened by the stings, had flung themselves into the river; and, as Kaa said, the Waingunga was hungry water.

Kaa held Mowgli fast till the boy had recovered his breath.

"We may not stay here," he said. "The Little People are roused indeed. Come!"

Swimming low and diving as often as he could, Mowgli went down the river, knife in hand.

"Slowly, slowly," said Kaa. "One tooth does not kill a hundred unless it be a cobra's, and many of the dholes took water swiftly when they saw the Little People rise."

"The more work for my knife, then. Phai! How the Little People follow!" Mowgli sank again. The face of the water was blanketed with wild bees, buzzing sullenly and stinging all they found.

"Nothing was ever yet lost by silence," said Kaa—no sting could penetrate his scales—"and thou hast all the long night for the hunting. Hear them howl!"

Nearly half the pack had seen the trap their fellows rushed into, and turning sharp aside had flung themselves into the water where the gorge broke down in steep banks. Their cries of rage and their threats against the "tree-ape" who had brought them to their shame mixed with the yells and growls of those who had been punished by the Little People. To remain ashore was death, and every dhole knew it. Their pack was swept along the current, down to the deep eddies of the Peace Pool, but even there the angry Little People followed and forced them to the water again. Mowgli could hear the voice of the tailless leader bidding his people hold on and kill out every wolf in Seeonee. But he did not waste his time in listening.

"One kills in the dark behind us!" snapped a dhole. "Here is tainted water!"

Mowgli had dived forward like an otter, twitched a struggling dhole under water before he could open his mouth, and dark rings rose as the body plopped up, turning on its side. The dholes tried to turn, but the current prevented them, and the Little People darted at the heads and ears, and they could hear the challenge of the Seeonee Pack growing louder and deeper in the gathering darkness. Again Mowgli dived, and again a dhole went under, and rose dead, and again the clamour broke out at the rear of the pack; some howling that it was best to go ashore, others calling on their leader to lead them back to the Dekkan, and others bidding Mowgli show himself and be killed.

"They come to the fight with two stomachs and several voices," said Kaa. "The rest is with thy brethren below yonder, The Little People go back to sleep. They have chased us far. Now I, too, turn back, for I am not of one skin with any wolf. Good hunting, Little Brother, and remember the dhole bites low."

A wolf came running along the bank on three legs, leaping up and down, laying his head sideways close to the ground, hunching his back, and breaking high into the air, as though he were playing with his cubs. It was Won-tolla, the Outlier, and he said never a word, but continued his horrible sport beside the dholes. They had been long in the water now, and were swimming wearily, their coats drenched and heavy, their bushy tails dragging like sponges, so tired and shaken that they, too, were silent, watching the pair of blazing eyes that moved abreast.

"This is no good hunting," said one, panting.

"Good hunting!" said Mowgli, as he rose boldly at the brute's side, and sent the long knife home behind the shoulder, pushing hard to avoid his dying snap.

"Art thou there, Man-cub?" said Won-tolla across the water.

"Ask of the dead, Outlier," Mowgli replied. "Have none come down-stream? I have filled these dogs' mouths with dirt; I have tricked them in the broad daylight, and their leader lacks his tail, but here be some few for thee still. Whither shall I drive them?"

"I will wait," said Won-tolla. "The night is before me."

Nearer and nearer came the bay of the Seeonee wolves. "For the Pack, for the Full Pack it is met!" and a bend in the river drove the dholes forward among the sands and shoals opposite the Lairs.

Then they saw their mistake. They should have landed half a mile higher up, and rushed the wolves on dry ground. Now it was too late. The bank was lined with burning eyes, and except for the horrible pheeal that had never stopped since sundown, there was no sound in the Jungle. It seemed as though Won-tolla were fawning on them to come ashore; and "Turn and take hold!" said the leader of the dholes. The entire Pack flung themselves at the shore, threshing and squattering through the shoal water, till the face of the Waingunga was all white and torn, and the great ripples went from side to side, like bow-waves from a boat. Mowgli followed the rush, stabbing and slicing as the dholes, huddled together, rushed up the river-beach in one wave.

Then the long fight began, heaving and straining and splitting and scattering and narrowing and broadening along the red, wet sands, and over and between the tangled tree-roots, and through and among the bushes, and in and out of the grass clumps; for even now the dholes were two to one. But they met wolves fighting for all that made the Pack, and not only the short, high, deep-chested, white-tusked hunters of the Pack, but the anxious-eyed lahinis—the she-wolves of the lair, as the saying is—fighting for their litters, with here and there a yearling wolf, his first coat still half woolly, tugging and grappling by their sides. A wolf, you must know, flies at the throat or snaps at the flank, while a dhole, by preference, bites at the belly; so when the dholes were struggling out of the water and had to raise their heads, the odds were with the wolves. On dry land the wolves suffered; but in the water or ashore, Mowgli's knife came and went without ceasing. The Four had worried their way to his side. Gray Brother, crouched between the boy's knees, was protecting his stomach, while the others guarded his back and either side, or stood over him when the shock of a leaping, yelling dhole who had thrown himself full on the steady blade bore him down. For the rest, it was one tangled confusion—a locked and swaying mob that moved from right to left and from left to right along the bank; and also ground round and round slowly on its own centre. Here would be a heaving mound, like a water-blister in a whirlpool, which would break like a water-blister, and throw up four or five mangled dogs, each striving to get back to the centre; here would be a single wolf borne down by two or three dholes, laboriously dragging them forward, and sinking the while; here a yearling cub would be held up by the pressure round him, though he had been killed early, while his mother, crazed with dumb rage, rolled over and over, snapping, and passing on; and in the middle of the thickest press, perhaps, one wolf and one dhole, forgetting everything else, would be manoeuvring for first hold till they were whirled away by a rush of furious fighters. Once Mowgli passed Akela, a dhole on either flank, and his all but toothless jaws closed over the loins of a third; and once he saw Phao, his teeth set in the throat of a dhole, tugging the unwilling beast forward till the yearlings could finish him. But the bulk of the fight was blind flurry and smother in the dark; hit, trip, and tumble, yelp, groan, and worry-worry-worry, round him and behind him and above him. As the night wore on, the quick, giddy-go-round motion increased. The dholes were cowed and afraid to attack the stronger wolves, but did not yet dare to run away. Mowgli felt that the end was coming soon, and contented himself with striking merely to cripple. The yearlings were growing bolder; there was time now and again to breathe, and pass a word to a friend, and the mere flicker of the knife would sometimes turn a dog aside.

"The meat is very near the bone," Gray Brother yelled. He was bleeding from a score of flesh-wounds.

"But the bone is yet to be cracked," said Mowgli. "Eowawa! THUS do we do in the Jungle!" The red blade ran like a flame along the side of a dhole whose hind-quarters were hidden by the weight of a clinging wolf.

"My kill!" snorted the wolf through his wrinkled nostrils. "Leave him to me."

"Is thy stomach still empty, Outlier?" said Mowgli. Wontolla was fearfully punished, but his grip had paralysed the dhole, who could not turn round and reach him.

"By the Bull that bought me," said Mowgli, with a bitter laugh, "it is the tailless one!" And indeed it was the big bay-coloured leader.

"It is not wise to kill cubs and lahinis," Mowgli went on philosophically, wiping the blood out of his eyes, "unless one has also killed the Outlier; and it is in my stomach that this Won-tolla kills thee."

A dhole leaped to his leader's aid; but before his teeth had found Won-tolla's flank, Mowgli's knife was in his throat, and Gray Brother took what was left.

"And thus do we do in the Jungle," said Mowgli.

Won-tolla said not a word, only his jaws were closing and closing on the backbone as his life ebbed. The dhole shuddered, his head dropped, and he lay still, and Won-tolla dropped above him.

"Huh! The Blood Debt is paid," said Mowgli. "Sing the song, Won-tolla."

"He hunts no more," said Gray Brother; "and Akela, too, is silent this long time."

"The bone is cracked!" thundered Phao, son of Phaona. "They go! Kill, kill out, O hunters of the Free People!"

Dhole after dhole was slinking away from those dark and bloody sands to the river, to the thick Jungle, up-stream or down-stream as he saw the road clear.

"The debt! The debt!" shouted Mowgli. "Pay the debt! They have slain the Lone Wolf! Let not a dog go!"

He was flying to the river, knife in hand, to check any dhole who dared to take water, when, from under a mound of nine dead, rose Akela's head and fore-quarters, and Mowgli dropped on his knees beside the Lone Wolf.

"Said I not it would be my last fight?" Akela gasped. "It is good hunting. And thou, Little Brother?"

"I live, having killed many."

"Even so. I die, and I would—I would die by thee, Little Brother."

Mowgli took the terrible scarred head on his knees, and put his arms round the torn neck.

"It is long since the old days of Shere Khan, and a Man-cub that rolled naked in the dust."

"Nay, nay, I am a wolf. I am of one skin with the Free People," Mowgli cried. "It is no will of mine that I am a man."

"Thou art a man, Little Brother, wolfling of my watching. Thou art a man, or else the Pack had fled before the dhole. My life I owe to thee, and to-day thou hast saved the Pack even as once I saved thee. Hast thou forgotten? All debts are paid now. Go to thine own people. I tell thee again, eye of my eye, this hunting is ended. Go to thine own people."

"I will never go. I will hunt alone in the Jungle. I have said it."

"After the summer come the Rains, and after the Rains comes the spring. Go back before thou art driven."

"Who will drive me?"

"Mowgli will drive Mowgli. Go back to thy people. Go to Man."

"When Mowgli drives Mowgli I will go," Mowgli answered.

"There is no more to say," said Akela. "Little Brother, canst thou raise me to my feet? I also was a leader of the Free People."

Very carefully and gently Mowgli lifted the bodies aside,

and raised Akela to his feet, both arms round him, and the Lone Wolf drew a long breath, and began the Death Song that a leader of the Pack should sing when he dies. It gathered strength as he went on, lifting and lifting, and ringing far across the river, till it came to the last "Good hunting!" and Akela shook himself clear of Mowgli for an instant, and, leaping into the air, fell backward dead upon his last and most terrible kill.

Mowgli sat with his head on his knees, careless of anything else, while the remnant of the flying dholes were being overtaken and run down by the merciless lahinis. Little by little the cries died away, and the wolves returned limping, as their wounds stiffened, to take stock of the losses. Fifteen of the Pack, as well as half a dozen lahinis, lay dead by the river, and of the others not one was unmarked. And Mowgli sat through it all till the cold daybreak, when Phao's wet, red muzzle was dropped in his hand, and Mowgli drew back to show the gaunt body of Akela.

"Good hunting!" said Phao, as though Akela were still alive, and then over his bitten shoulder to the others: "Howl, dogs! A Wolf has died to-night!"

But of all the Pack of two hundred fighting dholes, whose boast was that all jungles were their Jungle, and that no living thing could stand before them, not one returned to the Dekkan to carry that word.

CHIL'S SONG

[This is the song that Chil sang as the kites dropped down one after another to the river-bed, when the great fight was finished. Chil is good friends with everybody, but he is a cold-blooded kind of creature at heart, because he knows that almost everybody in the Jungle comes to him in the long-run.]

These were my companions going forth by night--
(For Chil! Look you, for Chil!)
Now come I to whistle them the ending of the fight.
(Chil! Vanguards of Chil!)
Word they gave me overhead of quarry newly slain,
Word I gave them underfoot of buck upon the plain.
Here's an end of every trail--they shall not speak again!
They that called the hunting-cry--they that followed fast--
(For Chil! Look you, for Chil!)
They that bade the sambhur wheel, or pinned him as he
passed--
(Chil! Vanguards of Chil!)
They that lagged behind the scent--they that ran before,
They that shunned the level horn--they that overbore.
Here's an end of every trail--they shall not follow more.
These were my companions. Pity 'twas they died!
(For Chil! Look you, for Chil!)
Now come I to comfort them that knew them in their pride.
(Chil! Vanguards of Chil!)
Tattered flank and sunken eye, open mouth and red,
Locked and lank and lone they lie, the dead upon their dead.
Here's an end of every trail--and here my hosts are fed.

THE SPRING RUNNING

Man goes to Man! Cry the challenge through the Jungle!
He that was our Brother goes away.
Hear, now, and judge, O ye People of the Jungle,--
Answer, who shall turn him--who shall stay?

Man goes to Man! He is weeping in the Jungle:
He that was our Brother sorrows sore!
Man goes to Man! (Oh, we loved him in the Jungle!)
To the Man-Trail where we may not follow more.

The second year after the great fight with Red Dog and the death of Akela, Mowgli must have been nearly seventeen years old. He looked older, for hard exercise, the best of good eating, and baths whenever he felt in the least hot or dusty, had given him strength and growth far beyond his age. He could swing by one hand from a top branch for half an hour at a time, when he had occasion to look along the tree-roads. He could stop a young buck in mid-gallop and throw him sideways by the head. He could even jerk over the big, blue wild boars that lived in the Marshes of the North. The Jungle People who used to fear him for his wits feared him now for his strength, and when he moved quietly on his own affairs the mere whisper of his coming cleared the wood-paths. And yet the look in his eyes was always gentle. Even when he fought, his eyes never blazed as Bagheera's did. They only grew more and more interested and excited; and that was one of the things that Bagheera himself did not understand.

He asked Mowgli about it, and the boy laughed and said. "When I miss the kill I am angry. When I must go empty for two days I am very angry. Do not my eyes talk then?"

"The mouth is hungry," said Bagheera, "but the eyes say nothing. Hunting, eating, or swimming, it is all one—like a stone in wet or dry weather." Mowgli looked at him lazily from under his long eyelashes, and, as usual, the panther's head dropped. Bagheera knew his master.

They were lying out far up the side of a hill overlooking the Waingunga, and the morning mists hung below them in bands of white and green. As the sun rose it changed into bubbling seas of red gold, churned off, and let the low rays stripe the dried grass on which Mowgli and Bagheera were resting. It was the end of the cold weather, the leaves and the trees looked worn and faded, and there was a dry, ticking rustle everywhere when the wind blew. A little leaf tap-tap-tapped furiously against a twig, as a single leaf caught in a current will. It roused Bagheera, for he snuffed the morning air with a deep, hollow cough, threw himself on his back, and struck with his fore-paws at the nodding leaf above.

"The year turns," he said. "The Jungle goes forward. The Time of New Talk is near. That leaf knows. It is very good."

"The grass is dry," Mowgli answered, pulling up a tuft. "Even Eye-of-the-Spring [that is a little trumpet-shaped, waxy red flower that runs in and out among the grasses]—even Eye-of-the Spring is shut, and... Bagheera, IS it well for the Black Panther so to lie on his back and beat with his paws in the air, as though he were the tree-cat?"

"Aowh?" said Bagheera. He seemed to be thinking of other things.

"I say, IS it well for the Black Panther so to mouth and cough, and howl and roll? Remember, we be the Masters of the Jungle, thou and I."

"Indeed, yes; I hear, Man-cub." Bagheera rolled over hurriedly and sat up, the dust on his ragged black flanks. (He was just casting his winter coat.) "We be surely the Masters of the Jungle! Who is so strong as Mowgli? Who so wise?" There was a curious drawl in the voice that made Mowgli turn to see whether by any chance the Black Panther were making fun of him, for the Jungle is full of words that sound like one thing, but mean another. "I said we be beyond question the Masters of the Jungle," Bagheera repeated. "Have I done wrong? I did not know that the Man-cub no longer lay upon the ground. Does he fly, then?"

Mowgli sat with his elbows on his knees, looking out across the valley at the daylight. Somewhere down in the woods below a bird was trying over in a husky, reedy voice the first few notes of his spring song. It was no more than a shadow of the liquid, tumbling call he would be pouring later, but Bagheera heard it.

"I said the Time of New Talk is near," growled the panther, switching his tail.

"I hear," Mowgli answered. "Bagheera, why dost thou shake all over? The sun is warm."

"That is Ferao, the scarlet woodpecker," said Bagheera. "HE has not forgotten. Now I, too, must remember my song," and he began purring and crooning to himself, harking back dissatisfied again and again.

"There is no game afoot," said Mowgli.

"Little Brother, are BOTH thine ears stopped? That is no killing-word, but my song that I make ready against the need."

"I had forgotten. I shall know when the Time of New Talk is here, because then thou and the others all run away and leave me alone." Mowgli spoke rather savagely.

"But, indeed, Little Brother," Bagheera began, "we do not always——"

"I say ye do," said Mowgli, shooting out his forefinger angrily. "Ye DO run away, and I, who am the Master of the Jungle, must needs walk alone. How was it last season, when I would gather sugar-cane from the fields of a Man-Pack? I sent a runner—I sent thee!—to Hathi, bidding him to come upon such a night and pluck the sweet grass for me with his trunk."

"He came only two nights later," said Bagheera, cowering a little; "and of that long, sweet grass that pleased thee so he gathered more than any Man-cub could eat in all the nights of the Rains. That was no fault of mine."

"He did not come upon the night when I sent him the word. No, he was trumpeting and running and roaring through the valleys in the moonlight. His trail was like the trail of three elephants, for he would not hide among the trees. He danced in the moonlight before the houses of the Man-Pack. I saw him, and yet he would not come to me; and _I_ am the Master of the Jungle!"

"It was the Time of New Talk," said the panther, always very humble. "Perhaps, Little Brother, thou didst not that time call him by a Master-word? Listen to Ferao, and be glad!"

Mowgli's bad temper seemed to have boiled itself away. He lay back with his head on his arms, his eyes shut. "I do not know—nor do I care," he said sleepily. "Let us sleep,

Bagheera. My stomach is heavy in me. Make me a rest for my head."

The panther lay down again with a sigh, because he could hear Ferao practising and repractising his song against the Springtime of New Talk, as they say.

In an Indian Jungle the seasons slide one into the other almost without division. There seem to be only two—the wet and the dry; but if you look closely below the torrents of rain and the clouds of char and dust you will find all four going round in their regular ring. Spring is the most wonderful, because she has not to cover a clean, bare field with new leaves and flowers, but to drive before her and to put away the hanging-on, over-surviving raffle of half-green things which the gentle winter has suffered to live, and to make the partly-dressed stale earth feel new and young once more. And this she does so well that there is no spring in the world like the Jungle spring.

There is one day when all things are tired, and the very smells, as they drift on the heavy air, are old and used. One cannot explain this, but it feels so. Then there is another day— to the eye nothing whatever has changed—when all the smells are new and delightful, and the whiskers of the Jungle People quiver to their roots, and the winter hair comes away from their sides in long, draggled locks. Then, perhaps, a little rain falls, and all the trees and the bushes and the bamboos and the mosses and the juicy-leaved plants wake with a noise of growing that you can almost hear, and under this noise runs, day and night, a deep hum. THAT is the noise of the spring—a vibrating boom which is neither bees, nor falling water, nor the wind in tree-tops, but the purring of the warm, happy world.

Up to this year Mowgli had always delighted in the turn of the seasons. It was he who generally saw the first Eye-of-the-

Spring deep down among the grasses, and the first bank of spring clouds, which are like nothing else in the Jungle. His voice could be heard in all sorts of wet, star-lighted, blossoming places, helping the big frogs through their choruses, or mocking the little upside-down owls that hoot through the white nights. Like all his people, spring was the season he chose for his flittings—moving, for the mere joy of rushing through the warm air, thirty, forty, or fifty miles between twilight and the morning star, and coming back panting and laughing and wreathed with strange flowers. The Four did not follow him on these wild ringings of the Jungle, but went off to sing songs with other wolves. The Jungle People are very busy in the spring, and Mowgli could hear them grunting and screaming and whistling according to their kind. Their voices then are different from their voices at other times of the year, and that is one of the reasons why spring in the Jungle is called the Time of New Talk.

But that spring, as he told Bagheera, his stomach was changed in him. Ever since the bamboo shoots turned spotty-brown he had been looking forward to the morning when the smells should change. But when the morning came, and Mor the Peacock, blazing in bronze and blue and gold, cried it aloud all along the misty woods, and Mowgli opened his mouth to send on the cry, the words choked between his teeth, and a feeling came over him that began at his toes and ended in his hair—a feeling of pure unhappiness, so that he looked himself over to be sure that he had not trod on a thorn. Mor cried the new smells, the other birds took it over, and from the rocks by the Waingunga he heard Bagheera's hoarse scream—something between the scream of an eagle and the neighing of a horse. There was a yelling and scattering of Bandar-log in the new-budding branches above, and there stood Mowgli, his chest, filled to answer Mor, sinking in little gasps as the breath was driven out of it by this unhappiness.

He stared all round him, but he could see no more than the mocking Bandar-log scudding through the trees, and Mor, his tail spread in full splendour, dancing on the slopes below.

"The smells have changed," screamed Mor. "Good hunting, Little Brother! Where is thy answer?"

"Little Brother, good hunting!" whistled Chil the Kite and his mate, swooping down together. The two baffed under Mowgli's nose so close that a pinch of downy white feathers brushed away.

A light spring rain—elephant-rain they call it—drove across the Jungle in a belt half a mile wide, left the new leaves wet and nodding behind, and died out in a double rainbow and a light roll of thunder. The spring hum broke out for a minute, and was silent, but all the Jungle Folk seemed to be giving tongue at once. All except Mowgli.

"I have eaten good food," he said to himself. "I have drunk good water. Nor does my throat burn and grow small, as it did when I bit the blue-spotted root that Oo the Turtle said was clean food. But my stomach is heavy, and I have given very bad talk to Bagheera and others, people of the Jungle and my people. Now, too, I am hot and now I am cold, and now I am neither hot nor cold, but angry with that which I cannot see. Huhu! It is time to make a running! To-night I will cross the ranges; yes, I will make a spring running to the Marshes of the North, and back again. I have hunted too easily too long. The Four shall come with me, for they grow as fat as white grubs."

He called, but never one of the Four answered. They were far beyond earshot, singing over the spring songs—the Moon and Sambhur Songs—with the wolves of the pack; for in the spring-time the Jungle People make very little difference between the day and the night. He gave the sharp, barking note, but his only answer was the mocking maiou of the little spotted tree-cat winding in and out among the branches for early birds' nests. At this he shook all over with rage, and half drew his knife. Then he became very haughty, though there was no one to see him, and stalked severely down the hillside, chin up and eyebrows down. But never a single one of his people asked him a question, for they were all too busy with their own affairs.

"Yes," said Mowgli to himself, though in his heart he knew that he had no reason. "Let the Red Dhole come from the Dekkan, or the Red Flower dance among the bamboos, and all the Jungle runs whining to Mowgli, calling him great elephant-names. But now, because Eye-of-the-Spring is red, and Mor, forsooth, must show his naked legs in some spring dance, the Jungle goes mad as Tabaqui.... By the Bull that bought me! am I the Master of the Jungle, or am I not? Be silent! What do ye here?"

A couple of young wolves of the Pack were cantering down a path, looking for open ground in which to fight. (You will remember that the Law of the Jungle forbids fighting where the Pack can see.) Their neck-bristles were as stiff as wire, and they bayed furiously, crouching for the first grapple. Mowgli leaped forward, caught one outstretched throat in either hand, expecting to fling the creatures backward as he had often done in games or Pack hunts. But he had never before interfered with a spring fight. The two leaped forward and dashed him aside, and without word to waste rolled over and over close locked.

Mowgli was on his feet almost before he fell, his knife and

his white teeth were bared, and at that minute he would have killed both for no reason but that they were fighting when he wished them to be quiet, although every wolf has full right under the Law to fight. He danced round them with lowered shoulders and quivering hand, ready to send in a double blow when the first flurry of the scuffle should be over; but while he waited the strength seemed to ebb from his body, the knife-point lowered, and he sheathed the knife and watched.

"I have surely eaten poison," he sighed at last. "Since I broke up the Council with the Red Flower—since I killed Shere Khan—none of the Pack could fling me aside. And these be only tail-wolves in the Pack, little hunters! My strength is gone from me, and presently I shall die. Oh, Mowgli, why dost thou not kill them both?"

The fight went on till one wolf ran away, and Mowgli was left alone on the torn and bloody ground, looking now at his knife, and now at his legs and arms, while the feeling of unhappiness he had never known before covered him as water covers a log.

He killed early that evening and ate but little, so as to be in good fettle for his spring running, and he ate alone because all the Jungle People were away singing or fighting. It was a perfect white night, as they call it. All green things seemed to have made a month's growth since the morning. The branch that was yellow-leaved the day before dripped sap when Mowgli broke it. The mosses curled deep and warm over his feet, the young grass had no cutting edges, and all the voices of the Jungle boomed like one deep harp-string touched by the moon—the Moon of New Talk, who splashed her light full on rock and pool, slipped it between trunk and creeper, and sifted it through a million leaves. Forgetting his unhappiness, Mowgli sang aloud with pure delight as he settled into his stride. It was more like flying than anything else, for he had chosen the long downward slope that leads to the Northern Marshes through the heart of the main Jungle, where the springy ground deadened the fall of his feet. A man-taught man would have picked his way with many stumbles through the cheating moonlight, but Mowgli's muscles, trained by years of experience, bore him up as though he were a feather. When a rotten log or a hidden stone turned under his foot he saved himself, never checking his pace, without effort and without thought. When he tired of ground-going he threw up his hands monkey-fashion to the nearest creeper, and seemed to float rather than to climb up into the thin branches, whence he would follow a tree-road till his mood changed, and he shot downward in a long, leafy curve to the levels again. There were still, hot hollows surrounded by wet rocks where he could hardly breathe for the heavy scents of the night flowers and the bloom along the creeper buds; dark avenues where the moonlight lay in belts as regular as checkered marbles in a church aisle; thickets where the wet young growth stood breast-high about him and threw its arms round his waist; and hilltops crowned with broken rock, where he leaped from stone to stone above the lairs of the frightened little foxes. He would hear, very faint and far off, the chug-drug of a boar sharpening his tusks on a bole; and would come across the great gray brute all alone, scribing and rending the bark of a tall tree, his mouth dripping with foam, and his eyes blazing like fire. Or he would turn aside to the sound of clashing horns and hissing grunts, and dash past a couple of furious sambhur, staggering to and fro with lowered heads, striped with blood that showed black in the moonlight. Or at some rushing ford he would hear Jacala the Crocodile bellowing like a bull, or disturb a twined knot of the Poison People, but before they could strike he would be away and across the glistening shingle, and deep in the Jungle again.

So he ran, sometimes shouting, sometimes singing to himself, the happiest thing in all the Jungle that night, till the smell of the flowers warned him that he was near the marshes, and those lay far beyond his farthest hunting-grounds.

Here, again, a man-trained man would have sunk overhead in three strides, but Mowgli's feet had eyes in them, and they passed him from tussock to tussock and clump to quaking clump without asking help from the eyes in his head. He ran out to the middle of the swamp, disturbing the duck as he ran, and sat down on a moss-coated tree-trunk lapped in the black water. The marsh was awake all round him, for in the spring the Bird People sleep very lightly, and companies of them were coming or going the night through. But no one took any notice of Mowgli sitting among the tall reeds humming songs without words, and looking at the soles of his hard brown feet in case of neglected thorns. All his unhappiness seemed to have been left behind in his own Jungle, and he was just beginning a full-throat song when it came back again—ten times worse than before.

This time Mowgli was frightened. "It is here also!" he said half aloud. "It has followed me," and he looked over his shoulder to see whether the It were not standing behind him. "There is no one here." The night noises of the marsh went on, but never a bird or beast spoke to him, and the new feeling of misery grew.

"I have surely eaten poison," he said in an awe-stricken voice. "It must be that carelessly I have eaten poison, and my strength is going from me. I was afraid—and yet it was not _I_ that was afraid—Mowgli was afraid when the two wolves fought. Akela, or even Phao, would have silenced them; yet Mowgli was afraid. That is true sign I have eaten poison.... But what do they care in the Jungle? They sing and howl and fight, and run in companies under the moon, and I—Hai-mai!—I am dying in the marshes, of that poison which I have eaten." He was so sorry for himself that he nearly wept. "And after," he went on, "they will find me lying in the black water. Nay, I will go back to my own Jungle, and I will die upon the Council Rock, and Bagheera, whom I love, if he is not screaming in the valley—Bagheera, perhaps, may watch by what is left for a little, lest Chil use me as he used Akela."

A large, warm tear splashed down on his knee, and, miserable as he was, Mowgli felt happy that he was so miserable, if you can understand that upside-down sort of happiness. "As Chil the Kite used Akela," he repeated, "on the night I saved the Pack from Red Dog." He was quiet for a little, thinking of the last words of the Lone Wolf, which you, of course, remember. "Now Akela said to me many foolish things before he died, for when we die our stomachs change. He said... None the less, I AM of the Jungle!"

In his excitement, as he remembered the fight on Waingunga bank, he shouted the last words aloud, and a wild buffalo-cow among the reeds sprang to her knees, snorting, "Man!"

"Uhh!" said Mysa the Wild Buffalo (Mowgli could hear him turn in his wallow), "THAT is no man. It is only the hairless wolf of the Seeonee Pack. On such nights runs he to and fro."

"Uhh!" said the cow, dropping her head again to graze, "I thought it was Man."

"I say no. Oh, Mowgli, is it danger?" lowed Mysa.

"Oh, Mowgli, is it danger?" the boy called back mockingly. "That is all Mysa thinks for: Is it danger? But for Mowgli, who goes to and fro in the Jungle by night, watching, what do ye care?"

"How loud he cries!" said the cow. "Thus do they cry," Mysa answered contemptuously, "who, having torn up the grass, know not how to eat it."

"For less than this," Mowgli groaned to himself, "for less than this even last Rains I had pricked Mysa out of his wallow, and ridden him through the swamp on a rush halter." He stretched a hand to break one of the feathery reeds, but drew it back with a sigh. Mysa went on steadily chewing the cud, and the long grass ripped where the cow grazed. "I will not die HERE," he said angrily. "Mysa, who is of one blood with Jacala and the pig, would see me. Let us go beyond the swamp and see what comes. Never have I run such a spring running— hot and cold together. Up, Mowgli!"

He could not resist the temptation of stealing across the reeds to Mysa and pricking him with the point of his knife. The great dripping bull broke out of his wallow like a shell exploding, while Mowgli laughed till he sat down.

"Say now that the hairless wolf of the Seeonee Pack once herded thee, Mysa," he called.

"Wolf! THOU?" the bull snorted, stamping in the mud. "All the jungle knows thou wast a herder of tame cattle— such a man's brat as shouts in the dust by the crops yonder. THOU of the Jungle! What hunter would have crawled like a snake among the leeches, and for a muddy jest—a jackal's jest—have shamed me before my cow? Come to firm ground, and I will—I will..." Mysa frothed at the mouth, for Mysa has nearly the worst temper of any one in the Jungle.

Mowgli watched him puff and blow with eyes that never changed. When he could make himself heard through the pattering mud, he said: "What Man-Pack lair here by the marshes, Mysa? This is new Jungle to me."

"Go north, then," roared the angry bull, for Mowgli had pricked him rather sharply. "It was a naked cow-herd's jest. Go and tell them at the village at the foot of the marsh."

"The Man-Pack do not love jungle-tales, nor do I think, Mysa, that a scratch more or less on thy hide is any matter for a council. But I will go and look at this village. Yes, I will go. Softly now. It is not every night that the Master of the Jungle comes to herd thee."

He stepped out to the shivering ground on the edge of the marsh, well knowing that Mysa would never charge over it and laughed, as he ran, to think of the bull's anger.

"My strength is not altogether gone," he said. "It may be that the poison is not to the bone. There is a star sitting low yonder." He looked at it between his half-shut hands. "By the Bull that bought me, it is the Red Flower—the Red Flower that I lay beside before—before I came even to the first Seeonee Pack! Now that I have seen, I will finish the running."

The marsh ended in a broad plain where a light twinkled. It was a long time since Mowgli had concerned himself with the doings of men, but this night the glimmer of the Red Flower drew him forward.

"I will look," said he, "as I did in the old days, and I will see how far the Man-Pack has changed."

Forgetting that he was no longer in his own Jungle, where he could do what he pleased, he trod carelessly through the dew-loaded grasses till he came to the hut where the light stood. Three or four yelping dogs gave tongue, for he was on the outskirts of a village.

"Ho!" said Mowgli, sitting down noiselessly, after sending back a deep wolf-growl that silenced the curs. "What comes will come. Mowgli, what hast thou to do any more with the lairs of the Man-Pack?" He rubbed his mouth, remembering where a stone had struck it years ago when the other Man-Pack had cast him out.

The door of the hut opened, and a woman stood peering out into the darkness. A child cried, and the woman said over her shoulder, "Sleep. It was but a jackal that waked the dogs. In a little time morning comes."

Mowgli in the grass began to shake as though he had fever. He knew that voice well, but to make sure he cried softly, surprised to find how man's talk came back, "Messua! O Messua!"

"Who calls?" said the woman, a quiver in her voice.

"Hast thou forgotten?" said Mowgli. His throat was dry as he spoke.

"If it be THOU, what name did I give thee? Say!" She had half shut the door, and her hand was clutching at her breast.

"Nathoo! Ohe, Nathoo!" said Mowgli, for, as you remember, that was the name Messua gave him when he first came to the Man-Pack.

"Come, my son," she called, and Mowgli stepped into the light, and looked full at Messua, the woman who had been good to him, and whose life he had saved from the Man-Pack so long before. She was older, and her hair was gray, but her eyes and her voice had not changed. Woman-like, she expected to find Mowgli where she had left him, and her eyes travelled upward in a puzzled way from his chest to his head, that touched the top of the door.

"My son," she stammered; and then, sinking to his feet: "But it is no longer my son. It is a Godling of the Woods! Ahai!"

As he stood in the red light of the oil-lamp, strong, tall, and beautiful, his long black hair sweeping over his shoulders, the knife swinging at his neck, and his head crowned with a wreath of white jasmine, he might easily have been mistaken for some wild god of a jungle legend. The child half asleep on a cot sprang up and shrieked aloud with terror. Messua turned to soothe him, while Mowgli stood still, looking in at the water-jars and the cooking-pots, the grain-bin, and all the other human belongings that he found himself remembering so well.

"What wilt thou eat or drink?" Messua murmured. "This is all thine. We owe our lives to thee. But art thou him I called Nathoo, or a Godling, indeed?"

"I am Nathoo," said Mowgli, "I am very far from my own place. I saw this light, and came hither. I did not know thou wast here."

"After we came to Khanhiwara," Messua said timidly, "the English would have helped us against those villagers that sought to burn us. Rememberest thou?"

"Indeed, I have not forgotten."

"But when the English Law was made ready, we went to the village of those evil people, and it was no more to be found."

"That also I remember," said Mowgli, with a quiver of his nostril.

"My man, therefore, took service in the fields, and at last— for, indeed, he was a strong man—we held a little land here. It is not so rich as the old village, but we do not need much— we two."

"Where is he the man that dug in the dirt when he was afraid on that night?"

"He is dead—a year."

"And he?" Mowgli pointed to the child.

"My son that was born two Rains ago. If thou art a Godling, give him the Favour of the Jungle, that he may be safe among thy—thy people, as we were safe on that night."

She lifted up the child, who, forgetting his fright, reached out to play with the knife that hung on Mowgli's chest, and Mowgli put the little fingers aside very carefully.

"And if thou art Nathoo whom the tiger carried away," Messua went on, choking, "he is then thy younger brother. Give him an elder brother's blessing."

"Hai-mai! What do I know of the thing called a blessing? I am neither a Godling nor his brother, and—O mother, mother, my heart is heavy in me." He shivered as he set down the child.

"Like enough," said Messua, bustling among the cooking-pots. "This comes of running about the marshes by night. Beyond question, the fever had soaked thee to the marrow." Mowgli smiled a little at the idea of anything in the Jungle hurting him. "I will make a fire, and thou shalt drink warm milk. Put away the jasmine wreath: the smell is heavy in so small a place."

Mowgli sat down, muttering, with his face in his hands. All manner of strange feelings that he had never felt before were running over him, exactly as though he had been poisoned, and he felt dizzy and a little sick. He drank the warm milk in long gulps, Messua patting him on the shoulder from time to time, not quite sure whether he were her son Nathoo of the long ago days, or some wonderful Jungle being, but glad to feel that he was at least flesh and blood.

"Son," she said at last,—her eyes were full of pride,—"have any told thee that thou art beautiful beyond all men?"

"Hah?" said Mowgli, for naturally he had never heard anything of the kind. Messua laughed softly and happily. The look in his face was enough for her.

"I am the first, then? It is right, though it comes seldom, that a mother should tell her son these good things. Thou art very beautiful. Never have I looked upon such a man."

Mowgli twisted his head and tried to see over his own hard shoulder, and Messua laughed again so long that Mowgli, not knowing why, was forced to laugh with her, and the child ran from one to the other, laughing too.

"Nay, thou must not mock thy brother," said Messua, catching him to her breast. "When thou art one-half as fair we will marry thee to the youngest daughter of a king, and thou shalt ride great elephants."

Mowgli could not understand one word in three of the talk here; the warm milk was taking effect on him after his long run, so he curled up and in a minute was deep asleep, and Messua put the hair back from his eyes, threw a cloth over him, and was happy. Jungle-fashion, he slept out the rest of that night and all the next day; for his instincts, which never wholly slept, warned him there was nothing to fear. He waked at last with a bound that shook the hut, for the cloth over his face made him dream of traps; and there he stood, his hand on his knife, the sleep all heavy in his rolling eyes, ready for any fight.

Messua laughed, and set the evening meal before him. There were only a few coarse cakes baked over the smoky fire, some rice, and a lump of sour preserved tamarinds—just enough to go on with till he could get to his evening kill. The smell of the dew in the marshes made him hungry and restless. He wanted to finish his spring running, but the child insisted on sitting in his arms, and Messua would have it that his long, blue-black hair must be combed out. So she sang, as she combed, foolish little baby-songs, now calling Mowgli her son, and now begging him to give some of his jungle power to the child. The hut door was closed, but Mowgli heard a sound he knew well, and saw Messua's jaw drop with horror as a great gray paw came under the bottom of the door, and Gray Brother outside whined a muffled and penitent whine of anxiety and fear.

"Out and wait! Ye would not come when I called," said Mowgli in Jungle-talk, without turning his head, and the great gray paw disappeared.

"Do not—do not bring thy—thy servants with thee," said Messua. "I—we have always lived at peace with the Jungle."

"It is peace," said Mowgli, rising. "Think of that night on the road to Khanhiwara. There were scores of such folk before thee and behind thee. But I see that even in springtime the Jungle People do not always forget. Mother, I go."

Messua drew aside humbly—he was indeed a wood-god, she thought; but as his hand was on the door the mother in her made her throw her arms round Mowgli's neck again and again.

"Come back!" she whispered. "Son or no son, come back, for I love thee—Look, he too grieves."

The child was crying because the man with the shiny knife was going away.

"Come back again," Messua repeated. "By night or by day this door is never shut to thee."

Mowgli's throat worked as though the cords in it were being pulled, and his voice seemed to be dragged from it as he answered, "I will surely come back."

"And now," he said, as he put by the head of the fawning wolf on the threshold, "I have a little cry against thee, Gray

Brother. Why came ye not all four when I called so long ago?"

"So long ago? It was but last night. I—we—were singing in the Jungle the new songs, for this is the Time of New Talk. Rememberest thou?"

"Truly, truly."

"And as soon as the songs were sung," Gray Brother went on earnestly, "I followed thy trail. I ran from all the others and followed hot-foot. But, O Little Brother, what hast THOU done, eating and sleeping with the Man-Pack?"

"If ye had come when I called, this had never been," said Mowgli, running much faster.

"And now what is to be?" said Gray Brother. Mowgli was going to answer when a girl in a white cloth came down some path that led from the outskirts of the village. Gray Brother dropped out of sight at once, and Mowgli backed noiselessly into a field of high-springing crops. He could almost have touched her with his hand when the warm, green stalks closed before his face and he disappeared like a ghost. The girl screamed, for she thought she had seen a spirit, and then she gave a deep sigh. Mowgli parted the stalks with his hands and watched her till she was out of sight.

"And now I do not know," he said, sighing in his turn. "WHY did ye not come when I called?"

"We follow thee—we follow thee," Gray Brother mumbled, licking at Mowgli's heel. "We follow thee always, except in the Time of the New Talk."

"And would ye follow me to the Man-Pack?" Mowgli whispered.

"Did I not follow thee on the night our old Pack cast thee out? Who waked thee lying among the crops?"

"Ay, but again?"

"Have I not followed thee to-night?"

"Ay, but again and again, and it may be again, Gray Brother?"

Gray Brother was silent. When he spoke he growled to himself, "The Black One spoke truth."

"And he said?"

"Man goes to Man at the last. Raksha, our mother, said—"

"So also said Akela on the night of Red Dog," Mowgli muttered.

"So also says Kaa, who is wiser than us all."

"What dost thou say, Gray Brother?"

"They cast thee out once, with bad talk. They cut thy mouth with stones. They sent Buldeo to slay thee. They would have thrown thee into the Red Flower. Thou, and not I, hast said that they are evil and senseless. Thou, and not I—I follow my own people—didst let in the Jungle upon them. Thou, and not I, didst make song against them more bitter even than our song against Red Dog."

"I ask thee what THOU sayest?"

They were talking as they ran. Gray Brother cantered on a while without replying, and then he said,—between bound and bound as it were,—"Man-cub—Master of the Jungle—Son of Raksha, Lair-brother to me—though I forget for a little while in the spring, thy trail is my trail, thy lair is my lair, thy kill is my kill, and thy death-fight is my death-fight. I speak for the Three. But what wilt thou say to the Jungle?"

"That is well thought. Between the sight and the kill it is not good to wait. Go before and cry them all to the Council Rock, and I will tell them what is in my stomach. But they may not come—in the Time of New Talk they may forget me."

"Hast thou, then, forgotten nothing?" snapped Gray Brother over his shoulder, as he laid himself down to gallop, and Mowgli followed, thinking.

At any other season the news would have called all the Jungle together with bristling necks, but now they were busy hunting and fighting and killing and singing. From one to another Gray Brother ran, crying, "The Master of the Jungle goes back to Man! Come to the Council Rock." And the happy, eager People only answered, "He will return in the summer heats. The Rains will drive him to lair. Run and sing with us, Gray Brother."

"But the Master of the Jungle goes back to Man," Gray Brother would repeat.

"Eee—Yoawa? Is the Time of New Talk any less sweet for that?" they would reply. So when Mowgli, heavy-hearted, came up through the well-remembered rocks to the place where he had been brought into the Council, he found only the Four, Baloo, who was nearly blind with age, and the heavy, cold-blooded Kaa coiled around Akela's empty seat.

"Thy trail ends here, then, Manling?" said Kaa, as Mowgli threw himself down, his face in his hands. "Cry thy cry. We be of one blood, thou and I—man and snake together."

"Why did I not die under Red Dog?" the boy moaned. "My strength is gone from me, and it is not any poison. By night and by day I hear a double step upon my trail. When I turn my head it is as though one had hidden himself from me that instant. I go to look behind the trees and he is not there. I call and none cry again; but it is as though one listened and kept back the answer. I lie down, but I do not rest. I run the spring running, but I am not made still. I bathe, but I am not made cool. The kill sickens me, but I have no heart to fight except I kill. The Red Flower is in my body, my bones are water—and—I know not what I know.”

“What need of talk?” said Baloo slowly, turning his head to where Mowgli lay. “Akela by the river said it, that Mowgli should drive Mowgli back to the Man-Pack. I said it. But who listens now to Baloo? Bagheera—where is Bagheera this night?—he knows also. It is the Law.”

“When we met at Cold Lairs, Manling, I knew it,” said Kaa, turning a little in his mighty coils. “Man goes to Man at the last, though the Jungle does not cast him out.”

The Four looked at one another and at Mowgli, puzzled but obedient.

“The Jungle does not cast me out, then?” Mowgli stammered.

Gray Brother and the Three growled furiously, beginning, “So long as we live none shall dare——” But Baloo checked them.

“I taught thee the Law. It is for me to speak,” he said; “and, though I cannot now see the rocks before me, I see far. Little Frog, take thine own trail; make thy lair with thine own blood and pack and people; but when there is need of foot or tooth or eye, or a word carried swiftly by night, remember, Master of the Jungle, the Jungle is thine at call.”

“The Middle Jungle is thine also,” said Kaa. “I speak for no small people.”

“Hai-mai, my brothers,” cried Mowgli, throwing up his arms with a sob. “I know not what I know! I would not go; but I am drawn by both feet. How shall I leave these nights?”

“Nay, look up, Little Brother,” Baloo repeated. “There is

no shame in this hunting. When the honey is eaten we leave the empty hive."

"Having cast the skin," said Kaa, "we may not creep into it afresh. It is the Law."

"Listen, dearest of all to me," said Baloo. There is neither word nor will here to hold thee back. Look up! Who may question the Master of the Jungle? I saw thee playing among the white pebbles yonder when thou wast a little frog; and Bagheera, that bought thee for the price of a young bull newly killed, saw thee also. Of that Looking Over we two only remain; for Raksha, thy lair-mother, is dead with thy lair-father; the old Wolf-Pack is long since dead; thou knowest whither Shere Khan went, and Akela died among the dholes, where, but for thy wisdom and strength, the second Seeonee Pack would also have died. There remains nothing but old bones. It is no longer the Man-cub that asks leave of his Pack, but the Master of the Jungle that changes his trail. Who shall question Man in his ways?"

"But Bagheera and the Bull that bought me," said Mowgli. "I would not——"

His words were cut short by a roar and a crash in the thicket below, and Bagheera, light, strong, and terrible as always, stood before him.

"Therefore," he said, stretching out a dripping right paw, "I did not come. It was a long hunt, but he lies dead in the bushes now—a bull in his second year—the Bull that frees thee, Little Brother. All debts are paid now. For the rest, my word is Baloo's word." He licked Mowgli's foot. "Remember, Bagheera loved thee," he cried, and bounded away. At the foot of the hill he cried again long and loud, "Good hunting on a new trail, Master of the Jungle! Remember, Bagheera loved thee."

"Thou hast heard," said Baloo. "There is no more. Go now; but first come to me. O wise Little Frog, come to me!"

"It is hard to cast the skin," said Kaa as Mowgli sobbed and sobbed, with his head on the blind bear's side and his arms round his neck, while Baloo tried feebly to lick his feet.

"The stars are thin," said Gray Brother, snuffing at the dawn wind. "Where shall we lair to-day? for from now, we follow new trails."

*****

And this is the last of the Mowgli stories.

THE OUT SONG

[This is the song that Mowgli heard behind him in the Jungle till he came to Messua's door again.]

Baloo

For the sake of him who showed
One wise Frog the Jungle-Road,
Keep the Law the Man-Pack make--
For thy blind old Baloo's sake!
Clean or tainted, hot or stale,
Hold it as it were the Trail,
Through the day and through the night,
Questing neither left nor right.
For the sake of him who loves
Thee beyond all else that moves,
When thy Pack would make thee pain,
Say: "Tabaqui sings again."
When thy Pack would work thee ill,
Say: "Shere Khan is yet to kill."
When the knife is drawn to slay,
Keep the Law and go thy way.
(Root and honey, palm and spathe,
Guard a cub from harm and scathe!)

Wood and Water, Wind and Tree,
Jungle-Favour go with thee!

Kaa

Anger is the egg of Fear--
Only lidless eyes are clear.
Cobra-poison none may leech.
Even so with Cobra-speech.
Open talk shall call to thee
Strength, whose mate is Courtesy.
Send no lunge beyond thy length;
Lend no rotten bough thy strength.
Gauge thy gape with buck or goat,
Lest thine eye should choke thy throat,
After gorging, wouldst thou sleep?
Look thy den is hid and deep,
Lest a wrong, by thee forgot,
Draw thy killer to the spot.
East and West and North and South,
Wash thy hide and close thy mouth.
(Pit and rift and blue pool-brim,
Middle-Jungle follow him!)
Wood and Water, Wind and Tree,
Jungle-Favour go with thee!

Bagheera

In the cage my life began;
Well I know the worth of Man.
By the Broken Lock that freed--
Man-cub, 'ware the Man-cub's breed!
Scenting-dew or starlight pale,
Choose no tangled tree-cat trail.
Pack or council, hunt or den,

Cry no truce with Jackal-Men.
Feed them silence when they say:
"Come with us an easy way."
Feed them silence when they seek
Help of thine to hurt the weak.
Make no banaar's boast of skill;
Hold thy peace above the kill.
Let nor call nor song nor sign
Turn thee from thy hunting-line.
(Morning mist or twilight clear,
Serve him, Wardens of the Deer!)
Wood and Water, Wind and Tree,
Jungle-Favour go with thee!

The Three

On the trail that thou must tread
To the thresholds of our dread,
Where the Flower blossoms red;
Through the nights when thou shalt lie
Prisoned from our Mother-sky,
Hearing us, thy loves, go by;
In the dawns when thou shalt wake
To the toil thou canst not break,
Heartsick for the Jungle's sake:
Wood and Water, Wind and Tree,
Wisdom, Strength, and Courtesy,
Jungle-Favour go with thee!

JUST SO STORIES

HOW THE WHALE GOT HIS THROAT

IN the sea, once upon a time, O my Best Beloved, there was a Whale, and he ate fishes. He ate the starfish and the garfish, and the crab and the dab, and the plaice and the dace, and the skate and his mate, and the mackereel and the pickereel, and the really truly twirly-whirly eel. All the fishes he could find in all the sea he ate with his mouth—so! Till at last there was only one small fish left in all the sea, and he was a small 'Stute Fish, and he swam a little behind the Whale's right ear, so as to be out of harm's way. Then the Whale stood up on his tail and said, 'I'm hungry.' And the small 'Stute Fish said in a small 'stute voice, 'Noble and generous Cetacean, have you ever tasted Man?'

'No,' said the Whale. 'What is it like?'

'Nice,' said the small 'Stute Fish. 'Nice but nubbly.'

'Then fetch me some,' said the Whale, and he made the sea froth up with his tail.

'One at a time is enough,' said the 'Stute Fish. 'If you swim to latitude Fifty North, longitude Forty West (that is magic), you will find, sitting _on_ a raft, _in_ the middle of the sea, with nothing on but a pair of blue canvas breeches, a pair of suspenders (you must _not_ forget the suspenders, Best

Beloved), and a jack-knife, one ship-wrecked Mariner, who, it is only fair to tell you, is a man of infinite-resource-and-sagacity.'

So the Whale swam and swam to latitude Fifty North, longitude Forty West, as fast as he could swim, and _on_ a raft, _in_ the middle of the sea, _with_ nothing to wear except a pair of blue canvas breeches, a pair of suspenders (you must particularly remember the suspenders, Best Beloved), _and_ a jack-knife, he found one single, solitary shipwrecked Mariner, trailing his toes in the water. (He had his mummy's leave to paddle, or else he would never have done it, because he was a man of infinite-resource-and-sagacity.)

Then the Whale opened his mouth back and back and back till it nearly touched his tail, and he swallowed the shipwrecked Mariner, and the raft he was sitting on, and his blue canvas breeches, and the suspenders (which you _must_ not forget), _and_ the jack-knife—He swallowed them all down into his warm, dark, inside cup-boards, and then he smacked his lips—so, and turned round three times on his tail.

But as soon as the Mariner, who was a man of infinite-resource-and-sagacity, found himself truly inside the Whale's warm, dark, inside cup-boards, he stumped and he jumped and he thumped and he bumped, and he pranced and he danced, and he banged and he clanged, and he hit and he bit, and he leaped and he creeped, and he prowled and he howled, and he hopped and he dropped, and he cried and he sighed, and he crawled and he bawled, and he stepped and he lepped, and he danced hornpipes where he shouldn't, and the Whale felt most unhappy indeed. (_Have_ you forgotten the suspenders?)

So he said to the 'Stute Fish, 'This man is very nubbly, and besides he is making me hiccough. What shall I do?'

'Tell him to come out,' said the 'Stute Fish.

So the Whale called down his own throat to the shipwrecked Mariner, 'Come out and behave yourself. I've got the hiccoughs.'

'Nay, nay!' said the Mariner. 'Not so, but far otherwise. Take me to my natal-shore and the white-cliffs-of-Albion, and I'll think about it.' And he began to dance more than ever.

'You had better take him home,' said the 'Stute Fish to the Whale. 'I ought to have warned you that he is a man of infinite-resource-and-sagacity.'

So the Whale swam and swam and swam, with both flippers and his tail, as hard as he could for the hiccoughs; and at last he saw the Mariner's natal-shore and the white-cliffs-of-Albion, and he rushed half-way up the beach, and opened his mouth wide and wide and wide, and said, 'Change here for Winchester, Ashuelot, Nashua, Keene, and stations on the _Fitch_burg Road;' and just as he said 'Fitch' the Mariner walked out of his mouth. But while the Whale had been swimming, the Mariner, who was indeed a person of infinite-resource-and-sagacity, had taken his jack-knife and cut up the raft into a little square grating all running criss-cross, and he had tied it firm with his suspenders (_now_, you know why you were not to forget the suspenders!), and he dragged that grating good and tight into the Whale's throat, and there it stuck! Then he recited the following _Sloka_, which, as you have not heard it, I will now proceed to relate—

By means of a grating I have stopped your ating.

For the Mariner he was also an Hi-ber-ni-an. And he stepped out on the shingle, and went home to his mother, who had given him leave to trail his toes in the water; and he married and lived happily ever afterward. So did the Whale. But from that day on, the grating in his throat, which he could neither cough up nor swallow down, prevented him eating anything except very, very small fish; and that is the reason why whales nowadays never eat men or boys or little girls.

The small 'Stute Fish went and hid himself in the mud under the Door-sills of the Equator. He was afraid that the Whale might be angry with him.

The Sailor took the jack-knife home. He was wearing the blue canvas breeches when he walked out on the shingle. The suspenders were left behind, you see, to tie the grating with; and that is the end of _that_ tale.

WHEN the cabin port-holes are dark and green

Because of the seas outside;

When the ship goes _wop_ (with a wiggle between)

And the steward falls into the soup-tureen,

And the trunks begin to slide;

When Nursey lies on the floor in a heap,

And Mummy tells you to let her sleep,

And you aren't waked or washed or dressed,

Why, then you will know (if you haven't guessed)

You're 'Fifty North and Forty West!'

HOW THE CAMEL GOT HIS HUMP

NOW this is the next tale, and it tells how the Camel got his big hump.

In the beginning of years, when the world was so new and all, and the Animals were just beginning to work for Man, there was a Camel, and he lived in the middle of a Howling Desert because he did not want to work; and besides, he was a Howler himself. So he ate sticks and thorns and tamarisks and milkweed and prickles, most 'scruciating idle; and when anybody spoke to him he said 'Humph!' Just 'Humph!' and no more.

Presently the Horse came to him on Monday morning, with a saddle on his back and a bit in his mouth, and said, 'Camel, O Camel, come out and trot like the rest of us.'

'Humph!' said the Camel; and the Horse went away and told the Man.

Presently the Dog came to him, with a stick in his mouth, and said, 'Camel, O Camel, come and fetch and carry like the rest of us.'

'Humph!' said the Camel; and the Dog went away and told the Man.

Presently the Ox came to him, with the yoke on his neck and said, 'Camel, O Camel, come and plough like the rest of us.'

'Humph!' said the Camel; and the Ox went away and told the Man.

At the end of the day the Man called the Horse and the Dog and the Ox together, and said, 'Three, O Three, I'm very sorry for you (with the world so new-and-all); but that Humph-thing in the Desert can't work, or he would have been here by now, so I am going to leave him alone, and you must work double-time to make up for it.'

That made the Three very angry (with the world so new-and-all), and they held a palaver, and an _indaba_, and a _punchayet_, and a pow-wow on the edge of the Desert; and the Camel came chewing on milkweed _most_ 'scruciating idle, and laughed at them. Then he said 'Humph!' and went away again.

Presently there came along the Djinn in charge of All Deserts, rolling in a cloud of dust (Djinns always travel that way because it is Magic), and he stopped to palaver and pow-pow with the Three.

'Djinn of All Deserts,' said the Horse, 'is it right for any one to be idle, with the world so new-and-all?'

'Certainly not,' said the Djinn.

'Well,' said the Horse, 'there's a thing in the middle of your Howling Desert (and he's a Howler himself) with a long neck and long legs, and he hasn't done a stroke of work since Monday morning. He won't trot.'

'Whew!' said the Djinn, whistling, 'that's my Camel, for all the gold in Arabia! What does he say about it?'

'He says "Humph!"' said the Dog; 'and he won't fetch and carry.'

'Does he say anything else?'

'Only "Humph!"; and he won't plough,' said the Ox.

'Very good,' said the Djinn. 'I'll humph him if you will kindly wait a minute.'

The Djinn rolled himself up in his dust-cloak, and took a bearing across the desert, and found the Camel most 'scruciatingly idle, looking at his own reflection in a pool of water.

'My long and bubbling friend,' said the Djinn, 'what's this I hear of your doing no work, with the world so new-and-all?'

'Humph!' said the Camel.

The Djinn sat down, with his chin in his hand, and began to think a Great Magic, while the Camel looked at his own reflection in the pool of water.

'You've given the Three extra work ever since Monday morning, all on account of your 'scruciating idleness,' said the Djinn; and he went on thinking Magics, with his chin in his hand.

'Humph!' said the Camel.

'I shouldn't say that again if I were you,' said the Djinn; you might say it once too often. Bubbles, I want you to work.'

And the Camel said 'Humph!' again; but no sooner had he said it than he saw his back, that he was so proud of, puffing up and puffing up into a great big lolloping humph.

'Do you see that?' said the Djinn. 'That's your very own humph that you've brought upon your very own self by not working. To-day is Thursday, and you've done no work since Monday, when the work began. Now you are going to work.'

'How can I,' said the Camel, 'with this humph on my back?'

'That's made a-purpose,' said the Djinn, 'all because you missed those three days. You will be able to work now for three days without eating, because you can live on your humph; and don't you ever say I never did anything for you. Come out of the Desert and go to the Three, and behave. Humph yourself!'

And the Camel humphed himself, humph and all, and went away to join the Three. And from that day to this the Camel always wears a humph (we call it 'hump' now, not to hurt his feelings); but he has never yet caught up with the three days that he missed at the beginning of the world, and he has never yet learned how to behave.

THE Camel's hump is an ugly lump
Which well you may see at the Zoo;
But uglier yet is the hump we get
From having too little to do.

Kiddies and grown-ups too-oo-oo,
If we haven't enough to do-oo-oo,
We get the hump--
Cameelious hump--
The hump that is black and blue!
We climb out of bed with a frouzly head

And a snarly-yarly voice.
We shiver and scowl and we grunt and we growl
At our bath and our boots and our toys;
And there ought to be a corner for me
(And I know there is one for you)
When we get the hump--
Cameelious hump--
The hump that is black and blue!

The cure for this ill is not to sit still,
Or frowst with a book by the fire;
But to take a large hoe and a shovel also,

And dig till you gently perspire;

And then you will find that the sun and the wind.

And the Djinn of the Garden too,
Have lifted the hump--
The horrible hump--
The hump that is black and blue!

I get it as well as you-oo-oo--
If I haven't enough to do-oo-oo--
We all get hump--
Cameelious hump--
Kiddies and grown-ups too!

HOW THE RHINOCEROS
GOT HIS SKIN

ONCE upon a time, on an uninhabited island on the shores of the Red Sea, there lived a Parsee from whose hat the rays of the sun were reflected in more-than-oriental splendour. And the Parsee lived by the Red Sea with nothing but his hat and his knife and a cooking-stove of the kind that you must particularly never touch. And one day he took flour and water and currants and plums and sugar and things, and made himself one cake which was two feet across and three feet thick. It was indeed a Superior Comestible (that's magic), and he put it on stove because he was allowed to cook on the stove, and he baked it and he baked it till it was all done brown and smelt most sentimental. But just as he was going to eat it there came down to the beach from the Altogether Uninhabited Interior one Rhinoceros with a horn on his nose, two piggy eyes, and few manners. In those days the Rhinoceros's skin fitted him quite tight. There were no wrinkles in it anywhere. He looked exactly like a Noah's Ark Rhinoceros, but of course much bigger. All the same, he had no manners then, and he has no manners now, and he never will have any manners. He said, 'How!' and the Parsee left that cake and climbed to the top of a palm tree with nothing on but his hat, from which the rays of the sun were always reflected in more-than-oriental splendour. And the Rhinoceros upset the oil-stove with his nose, and the cake rolled on the sand, and he spiked that cake on the horn of his nose, and he ate it, and he went away, waving his tail, to the desolate and Exclusively Uninhabited Interior which abuts on the islands of Mazanderan, Socotra, and Promontories of the Larger Equinox. Then the Parsee came down from his palm-tree and put the stove on its legs and recited the following Sloka, which, as you have not heard, I will now proceed to relate:—

> *Them that takes cakes*
> *Which the Parsee-man bakes*
> *Makes dreadful mistakes.*

And there was a great deal more in that than you would think.

Because, five weeks later, there was a heat wave in the Red Sea, and everybody took off all the clothes they had. The Parsee took off his hat; but the Rhinoceros took off his skin and carried it over his shoulder as he came down to the beach to bathe. In those days it buttoned underneath with three buttons and looked like a waterproof. He said nothing whatever about the Parsee's cake, because he had eaten it all; and he never had any manners, then, since, or henceforward. He waddled straight into the water and blew bubbles through his nose, leaving his skin on the beach.

Presently the Parsee came by and found the skin, and he smiled one smile that ran all round his face two times. Then he danced three times round the skin and rubbed his hands. Then he went to his camp and filled his hat with cake-crumbs, for the Parsee never ate anything but cake, and never swept out his camp. He took that skin, and he shook that skin, and he scrubbed that skin, and he rubbed that skin just as full of old, dry, stale, tickly cake-crumbs and some burned currants as ever it could possibly hold. Then he climbed to the top of his palm-tree and waited for the Rhinoceros to come out of the water and put it on.

And the Rhinoceros did. He buttoned it up with the three buttons, and it tickled like cake crumbs in bed. Then he wanted to scratch, but that made it worse; and then he lay down on the sands and rolled and rolled and rolled, and every time he rolled the cake crumbs tickled him worse and worse and worse. Then he ran to the palm-tree and rubbed and rubbed and rubbed himself against it. He rubbed so much and so hard that he rubbed his skin into a great fold over his shoulders, and another fold underneath, where the buttons used to be (but he rubbed the buttons off), and he rubbed some more folds over his legs. And it spoiled his temper, but it didn't make the least difference to the cake-crumbs. They were inside his skin and they tickled. So he went home, very angry indeed and horribly scratchy; and from that day to this every rhinoceros has great folds in his skin and a very bad temper, all on account of the cake-crumbs inside.

But the Parsee came down from his palm-tree, wearing his hat, from which the rays of the sun were reflected in more-than-oriental splendour, packed up his cooking-stove, and went away in the direction of Orotavo, Amygdala, the Upland Meadows of Anantarivo, and the Marshes of Sonaput.

THIS Uninhabited Island

Is off Cape Gardafui,

By the Beaches of Socotra

And the Pink Arabian Sea:

But it's hot--too hot from Suez

For the likes of you and me

Ever to go

In a P. and O.

And call on the Cake-Parsee!

HOW THE LEOPARD
GOT HIS SPOTS

IN the days when everybody started fair, Best Beloved, the Leopard lived in a place called the High Veldt. 'Member it wasn't the Low Veldt, or the Bush Veldt, or the Sour Veldt, but the 'sclusively bare, hot, shiny High Veldt, where there was sand and sandy-coloured rock and 'sclusively tufts of sandy-yellowish grass. The Giraffe and the Zebra and the Eland and the Koodoo and the Hartebeest lived there; and they were 'sclusively sandy-yellow-brownish all over; but the Leopard, he was the 'sclusivest sandiest-yellowish-brownest of them all—a greyish-yellowish catty-shaped kind of beast, and he matched the 'sclusively yellowish-greyish-brownish colour of the High Veldt to one hair. This was very bad for the Giraffe and the Zebra and the rest of them; for he would lie down by a 'sclusively yellowish-greyish-brownish stone or clump of grass, and when the Giraffe or the Zebra or the Eland or the Koodoo or the Bush-Buck or the Bonte-Buck came by he would surprise them out of their jumpsome lives. He would indeed! And, also, there was an Ethiopian with bows and arrows (a 'sclusively greyish-brownish-yellowish man he was then), who lived on the High Veldt with the Leopard; and the two used to hunt together—the Ethiopian with his bows and arrows, and the Leopard 'sclusively with his teeth and claws—till the Giraffe and the Eland and the Koodoo and the

Quagga and all the rest of them didn't know which way to jump, Best Beloved. They didn't indeed!

After a long time—things lived for ever so long in those days—they learned to avoid anything that looked like a Leopard or an Ethiopian; and bit by bit—the Giraffe began it, because his legs were the longest—they went away from the High Veldt. They scuttled for days and days and days till they came to a great forest, 'sclusively full of trees and bushes and stripy, speckly, patchy-blatchy shadows, and there they hid: and after another long time, what with standing half in the shade and half out of it, and what with the slippery-slidy shadows of the trees falling on them, the Giraffe grew blotchy, and the Zebra grew stripy, and the Eland and the Koodoo grew darker, with little wavy grey lines on their backs like bark on a tree trunk; and so, though you could hear them and smell them, you could very seldom see them, and then only when you knew precisely where to look. They had a beautiful time in the 'sclusively speckly-spickly shadows of the forest, while the Leopard and the Ethiopian ran about over the 'sclusively greyish-yellowish-reddish High Veldt outside, wondering where all their breakfasts and their dinners and their teas had gone. At last they were so hungry that they ate rats and beetles and rock-rabbits, the Leopard and the Ethiopian, and then they had the Big Tummy-ache, both together; and then they met Baviaan—the dog-headed, barking Baboon, who is Quite the Wisest Animal in All South Africa.

Said Leopard to Baviaan (and it was a very hot day), 'Where has all the game gone?'

And Baviaan winked. He knew.

Said the Ethiopian to Baviaan, 'Can you tell me the present habitat of the aboriginal Fauna?' (That meant just the same thing, but the Ethiopian always used long words. He was a grown-up.)

And Baviaan winked. He knew.

Then said Baviaan, 'The game has gone into other spots; and my advice to you, Leopard, is to go into other spots as soon as you can.'

And the Ethiopian said, 'That is all very fine, but I wish to know whither the aboriginal Fauna has migrated.'

Then said Baviaan, 'The aboriginal Fauna has joined the aboriginal Flora because it was high time for a change; and my advice to you, Ethiopian, is to change as soon as you can.'

That puzzled the Leopard and the Ethiopian, but they set off to look for the aboriginal Flora, and presently, after ever so many days, they saw a great, high, tall forest full of tree trunks all 'sclusively speckled and sprottled and spottled, dotted and splashed and slashed and hatched and cross-hatched with shadows. (Say that quickly aloud, and you will see how very shadowy the forest must have been.)

'What is this,' said the Leopard, 'that is so 'sclusively dark, and yet so full of little pieces of light?'

'I don't know, said the Ethiopian, 'but it ought to be the aboriginal Flora. I can smell Giraffe, and I can hear Giraffe, but I can't see Giraffe.'

'That's curious,' said the Leopard. 'I suppose it is because we have just come in out of the sunshine. I can smell Zebra, and I can hear Zebra, but I can't see Zebra.'

'Wait a bit, said the Ethiopian. 'It's a long time since we've hunted 'em. Perhaps we've forgotten what they were like.'

'Fiddle!' said the Leopard. 'I remember them perfectly on the High Veldt, especially their marrow-bones. Giraffe is about seventeen feet high, of a 'sclusively fulvous golden-yellow from head to heel; and Zebra is about four and a half feet high, of a'sclusively grey-fawn colour from head to heel.'

'Umm, said the Ethiopian, looking into the speckly-spickly shadows of the aboriginal Flora-forest. 'Then they ought to show up in this dark place like ripe bananas in a smokehouse.'

But they didn't. The Leopard and the Ethiopian hunted all day; and though they could smell them and hear them, they never saw one of them.

'For goodness' sake,' said the Leopard at tea-time, 'let us wait till it gets dark. This daylight hunting is a perfect scandal.'

So they waited till dark, and then the Leopard heard something breathing sniffily in the starlight that fell all stripy through the branches, and he jumped at the noise, and it smelt like Zebra, and it felt like Zebra, and when he knocked it down it kicked like Zebra, but he couldn't see it. So he said, 'Be quiet, O you person without any form. I am going to sit on your head till morning, because there is something about you that I don't understand.'

Presently he heard a grunt and a crash and a scramble, and the Ethiopian called out, 'I've caught a thing that I can't see. It smells like Giraffe, and it kicks like Giraffe, but it hasn't any form.'

'Don't you trust it,' said the Leopard. 'Sit on its head till the morning—same as me. They haven't any form—any of 'em.'

So they sat down on them hard till bright morning-time, and then Leopard said, 'What have you at your end of the table, Brother?'

The Ethiopian scratched his head and said, 'It ought to be 'sclusively a rich fulvous orange-tawny from head to heel, and it ought to be Giraffe; but it is covered all over with chestnut blotches. What have you at your end of the table, Brother?'

And the Leopard scratched his head and said, 'It ought to be 'sclusively a delicate greyish-fawn, and it ought to be Zebra; but it is covered all over with black and purple stripes. What

in the world have you been doing to yourself, Zebra? Don't
you know that if you were on the High Veldt I could see you
ten miles off? You haven't any form.'

'Yes,' said the Zebra, 'but this isn't the High Veldt. Can't
you see?'

'I can now,' said the Leopard. 'But I couldn't all yesterday.
How is it done?'

'Let us up,' said the Zebra, 'and we will show you.'

They let the Zebra and the Giraffe get up; and Zebra moved
away to some little thorn-bushes where the sunlight fell all
stripy, and Giraffe moved off to some tallish trees where the
shadows fell all blotchy.

'Now watch,' said the Zebra and the Giraffe. 'This is the
way it's done. One—two—three! And where's your breakfast?'

Leopard stared, and Ethiopian stared, but all they could
see were stripy shadows and blotched shadows in the forest,
but never a sign of Zebra and Giraffe. They had just walked
off and hidden themselves in the shadowy forest.

'Hi! Hi!' said the Ethiopian. 'That's a trick worth learning.
Take a lesson by it, Leopard. You show up in this dark place
like a bar of soap in a coal-scuttle.'

'Ho! Ho!' said the Leopard. 'Would it surprise you very
much to know that you show up in this dark place like a
mustard-plaster on a sack of coals?'

'Well, calling names won't catch dinner, said the Ethiopian.
'The long and the little of it is that we don't match our
backgrounds. I'm going to take Baviaan's advice. He told me
I ought to change; and as I've nothing to change except my
skin I'm going to change that.'

'What to?' said the Leopard, tremendously excited.

To a nice working blackish-brownish colour, with a little
purple in it, and touches of slaty-blue. It will be the very thing for
hiding in hollows and behind trees.'

So he changed his skin then and there, and the Leopard was more excited than ever; he had never seen a man change his skin before.

'But what about me?' he said, when the Ethiopian had worked his last little finger into his fine new black skin.

'You take Baviaan's advice too. He told you to go into spots.'

'So I did,' said the Leopard. I went into other spots as fast as I could. I went into this spot with you, and a lot of good it has done me.'

'Oh,' said the Ethiopian, 'Baviaan didn't mean spots in South Africa. He meant spots on your skin.'

'What's the use of that?' said the Leopard.

'Think of Giraffe,' said the Ethiopian. 'Or if you prefer stripes, think of Zebra. They find their spots and stripes give them per-feet satisfaction.'

'Umm,' said the Leopard. 'I wouldn't look like Zebra—not for ever so.'

'Well, make up your mind,' said the Ethiopian, 'because I'd hate to go hunting without you, but I must if you insist on looking like a sun-flower against a tarred fence.'

'I'll take spots, then,' said the Leopard; 'but don't make 'em too vulgar-big. I wouldn't look like Giraffe—not for ever so.'

'I'll make 'em with the tips of my fingers,' said the Ethiopian. 'There's plenty of black left on my skin still. Stand over!'

Then the Ethiopian put his five fingers close together (there was plenty of black left on his new skin still) and pressed them all over the Leopard, and wherever the five fingers touched they left five little black marks, all close together. You can see them on any Leopard's skin you like, Best Beloved. Sometimes the fingers slipped and the marks got a little blurred; but if you look closely at any Leopard now you will see that there are always five spots—off five fat black finger-tips.

'Now you are a beauty!' said the Ethiopian. 'You can lie out on the bare ground and look like a heap of pebbles. You can lie out on the naked rocks and look like a piece of pudding-stone. You can lie out on a leafy branch and look like sunshine sifting through the leaves; and you can lie right across the centre of a path and look like nothing in particular. Think of that and purr!'

'But if I'm all this,' said the Leopard, 'why didn't you go spotty too?'

'Oh, plain black's best for a nigger,' said the Ethiopian. 'Now come along and we'll see if we can't get even with Mr. One-Two-Three Where's your Breakfast!'

So they went away and lived happily ever afterward, Best Beloved. That is all.

Oh, now and then you will hear grown-ups say, 'Can the Ethiopian change his skin or the Leopard his spots?' I don't think even grown-ups would keep on saying such a silly thing if the Leopard and the Ethiopian hadn't done it once—do you? But they will never do it again, Best Beloved. They are quite contented as they are.

I AM the Most Wise Baviaan, saying in most wise tones,

'Let us melt into the landscape--just us two by our lones.'

People have come--in a carriage--calling. But Mummy is
there....

Yes, I can go if you take me--Nurse says she don't care.

Let's go up to the pig-sties and sit on the farmyard rails!

Let's say things to the bunnies, and watch 'em skitter their
tails!
Let's--oh, anything, daddy, so long as it's you and me,
And going truly exploring, and not being in till tea!
Here's your boots (I've brought 'em), and here's your cap and
stick,
And here's your pipe and tobacco. Oh, come along out of it--
quick.

THE ELEPHANT'S CHILD

IN the High and Far-Off Times the Elephant, O Best Beloved, had no trunk. He had only a blackish, bulgy nose, as big as a boot, that he could wriggle about from side to side; but he couldn't pick up things with it. But there was one Elephant— a new Elephant—an Elephant's Child—who was full of 'satiable curtiosity, and that means he asked ever so many questions. And he lived in Africa, and he filled all Africa with his 'satiable curtiosities. He asked his tall aunt, the Ostrich, why her tail-feathers grew just so, and his tall aunt the Ostrich spanked him with her hard, hard claw. He asked his tall uncle, the Giraffe, what made his skin spotty, and his tall uncle, the Giraffe, spanked him with his hard, hard hoof. And still he was full of 'satiable curtiosity! He asked his broad aunt, the Hippopotamus, why her eyes were red, and his broad aunt, the Hippopotamus, spanked him with her broad, broad hoof; and he asked his hairy uncle, the Baboon, why melons tasted just so, and his hairy uncle, the Baboon, spanked him with his hairy, hairy paw. And still he was full of 'satiable curtiosity! He asked questions about everything that he saw, or heard, or felt, or smelt, or touched, and all his uncles and his aunts spanked him. And still he was full of 'satiable curtiosity!

One fine morning in the middle of the Precession of the Equinoxes this 'satiable Elephant's Child asked a new fine question that he had never asked before. He asked, 'What does the Crocodile have for dinner?' Then everybody said, 'Hush!' in a loud and dretful tone, and they spanked him immediately and directly, without stopping, for a long time.

By and by, when that was finished, he came upon Kolokolo Bird sitting in the middle of a wait-a-bit thorn-bush, and he said, 'My father has spanked me, and my mother has spanked me; all my aunts and uncles have spanked me for my 'satiable curtiosity; and still I want to know what the Crocodile has for dinner!'

Then Kolokolo Bird said, with a mournful cry, 'Go to the banks of the great grey-green, greasy Limpopo River, all set about with fever-trees, and find out.'

That very next morning, when there was nothing left of the Equinoxes, because the Precession had preceded according to precedent, this 'satiable Elephant's Child took a hundred pounds of bananas (the little short red kind), and a hundred pounds of sugar-cane (the long purple kind), and seventeen melons (the greeny-crackly kind), and said to all his dear families, 'Goodbye. I am going to the great grey-green, greasy Limpopo River, all set about with fever-trees, to find out what the Crocodile has for dinner.' And they all spanked him once more for luck, though he asked them most politely to stop.

Then he went away, a little warm, but not at all astonished, eating melons, and throwing the rind about, because he could not pick it up.

He went from Graham's Town to Kimberley, and from Kimberley to Khama's Country, and from Khama's Country he went east by north, eating melons all the time, till at last he came to the banks of the great grey-green, greasy Limpopo River, all set about with fever-trees, precisely as Kolokolo Bird had said.

Now you must know and understand, O Best Beloved, that till that very week, and day, and hour, and minute, this 'satiable Elephant's Child had never seen a Crocodile, and did not know what one was like. It was all his 'satiable curtiosity.

The first thing that he found was a Bi-Coloured-Python-Rock-Snake curled round a rock.

''Scuse me,' said the Elephant's Child most politely, 'but have you seen such a thing as a Crocodile in these promiscuous parts?'

'Have I seen a Crocodile?' said the Bi-Coloured-Python-Rock-Snake, in a voice of dretful scorn. 'What will you ask me next?'

''Scuse me,' said the Elephant's Child, 'but could you kindly tell me what he has for dinner?'

Then the Bi-Coloured-Python-Rock-Snake uncoiled himself very quickly from the rock, and spanked the Elephant's Child with his scalesome, flailsome tail.

'That is odd,' said the Elephant's Child, 'because my father and my mother, and my uncle and my aunt, not to mention my other aunt, the Hippopotamus, and my other uncle, the Baboon, have all spanked me for my 'satiable curtiosity—and I suppose this is the same thing.

So he said good-bye very politely to the Bi-Coloured-Python-Rock-Snake, and helped to coil him up on the rock again, and went on, a little warm, but not at all astonished, eating melons, and throwing the rind about, because he could not pick it up, till he trod on what he thought was a log of wood at the very edge of the great grey-green, greasy Limpopo River, all set about with fever-trees.

But it was really the Crocodile, O Best Beloved, and the Crocodile winked one eye—like this!

''Scuse me,' said the Elephant's Child most politely, 'but do you happen to have seen a Crocodile in these promiscuous parts?'

Then the Crocodile winked the other eye, and lifted half his tail out of the mud; and the Elephant's Child stepped back most politely, because he did not wish to be spanked again.

'Come hither, Little One,' said the Crocodile. 'Why do you ask such things?'

''Scuse me,' said the Elephant's Child most politely, 'but my father has spanked me, my mother has spanked me, not to mention my tall aunt, the Ostrich, and my tall uncle, the Giraffe, who can kick ever so hard, as well as my broad aunt, the Hippopotamus, and my hairy uncle, the Baboon, and including the Bi-Coloured-Python-Rock-Snake, with the scalesome, flailsome tail, just up the bank, who spanks harder than any of them; and so, if it's quite all the same to you, I don't want to be spanked any more.'

'Come hither, Little One,' said the Crocodile, 'for I am the Crocodile,' and he wept crocodile-tears to show it was quite true.

Then the Elephant's Child grew all breathless, and panted, and kneeled down on the bank and said, 'You are the very person I have been looking for all these long days. Will you please tell me what you have for dinner?'

'Come hither, Little One,' said the Crocodile, 'and I'll whisper.'

Then the Elephant's Child put his head down close to the Crocodile's musky, tusky mouth, and the Crocodile caught him by his little nose, which up to that very week, day, hour, and minute, had been no bigger than a boot, though much more useful.

'I think, said the Crocodile—and he said it between his teeth, like this—'I think to-day I will begin with Elephant's Child!'

At this, O Best Beloved, the Elephant's Child was much annoyed, and he said, speaking through his nose, like this, 'Led go! You are hurtig be!'

Then the Bi-Coloured-Python-Rock-Snake scuffled down from the bank and said, 'My young friend, if you do not now, immediately and instantly, pull as hard as ever you can, it is my opinion that your acquaintance in the large-pattern leather ulster' (and by this he meant the Crocodile) 'will jerk you into yonder limpid stream before you can say Jack Robinson.'

This is the way Bi-Coloured-Python-Rock-Snakes always talk.

Then the Elephant's Child sat back on his little haunches, and pulled, and pulled, and pulled, and his nose began to stretch. And the Crocodile floundered into the water, making it all creamy with great sweeps of his tail, and he pulled, and pulled, and pulled.

And the Elephant's Child's nose kept on stretching; and the Elephant's Child spread all his little four legs and pulled, and pulled, and pulled, and his nose kept on stretching; and the Crocodile threshed his tail like an oar, and he pulled, and pulled, and pulled, and at each pull the Elephant's Child's nose grew longer and longer—and it hurt him hijjus!

Then the Elephant's Child felt his legs slipping, and he said through his nose, which was now nearly five feet long, 'This is too butch for be!'

Then the Bi-Coloured-Python-Rock-Snake came down from the bank, and knotted himself in a double-clove-hitch round the Elephant's Child's hind legs, and said, 'Rash and inexperienced traveller, we will now seriously devote ourselves to a little high tension, because if we do not, it is my impression that yonder self-propelling man-of-war with the armour-plated upper deck' (and by this, O Best Beloved, he meant the Crocodile), 'will permanently vitiate your future career.

That is the way all Bi-Coloured-Python-Rock-Snakes always talk.

So he pulled, and the Elephant's Child pulled, and the Crocodile pulled; but the Elephant's Child and the Bi-Coloured-Python-Rock-Snake pulled hardest; and at last the Crocodile let go of the Elephant's Child's nose with a plop that you could hear all up and down the Limpopo.

Then the Elephant's Child sat down most hard and sudden; but first he was careful to say 'Thank you' to the Bi-Coloured-Python-Rock-Snake; and next he was kind to his poor pulled nose, and wrapped it all up in cool banana leaves, and hung it in the great grey-green, greasy Limpopo to cool.

'What are you doing that for?' said the Bi-Coloured-Python-Rock-Snake.

''Scuse me,' said the Elephant's Child, 'but my nose is badly out of shape, and I am waiting for it to shrink.

'Then you will have to wait a long time, said the Bi-Coloured-Python-Rock-Snake. 'Some people do not know what is good for them.'

The Elephant's Child sat there for three days waiting for his nose to shrink. But it never grew any shorter, and, besides, it made him squint. For, O Best Beloved, you will see and understand that the Crocodile had pulled it out into a really truly trunk same as all Elephants have to-day.

At the end of the third day a fly came and stung him on the shoulder, and before he knew what he was doing he lifted up his trunk and hit that fly dead with the end of it.

''Vantage number one!' said the Bi-Coloured-Python-Rock-Snake. 'You couldn't have done that with a mere-smear nose. Try and eat a little now.'

Before he thought what he was doing the Elephant's Child put out his trunk and plucked a large bundle of grass, dusted it clean against his fore-legs, and stuffed it into his own mouth.

'Vantage number two!' said the Bi-Coloured-Python-Rock-Snake. 'You couldn't have done that with a mear-smear nose. Don't you think the sun is very hot here?'

'It is,' said the Elephant's Child, and before he thought what he was doing he schlooped up a schloop of mud from the banks of the great grey-green, greasy Limpopo, and slapped it on his head, where it made a cool schloopy-sloshy mud-cap all trickly behind his ears.

'Vantage number three!' said the Bi-Coloured-Python-Rock-Snake. 'You couldn't have done that with a mere-smear nose. Now how do you feel about being spanked again?'

''Scuse me,' said the Elephant's Child, 'but I should not like it at all.'

'How would you like to spank somebody?' said the Bi-Coloured-Python-Rock-Snake.

'I should like it very much indeed,' said the Elephant's Child.

'Well,' said the Bi-Coloured-Python-Rock-Snake, 'you will find that new nose of yours very useful to spank people with.'

'Thank you,' said the Elephant's Child, 'I'll remember that; and now I think I'll go home to all my dear families and try.'

So the Elephant's Child went home across Africa frisking and whisking his trunk. When he wanted fruit to eat he pulled fruit down from a tree, instead of waiting for it to fall as he used to do. When he wanted grass he plucked grass up from the ground, instead of going on his knees as he used to do. When the flies bit him he broke off the branch of a tree and used it as fly-whisk; and he made himself a new, cool, slushy-squshy mud-cap whenever the sun was hot. When he felt lonely walking through Africa he sang to himself down his trunk, and the noise was louder than several brass bands.

He went especially out of his way to find a broad Hippopotamus (she was no relation of his), and he spanked her very hard, to make sure that the Bi-Coloured-Python-Rock-Snake had spoken the truth about his new trunk. The rest of the time he picked up the melon rinds that he had dropped on his way to the Limpopo—for he was a Tidy Pachyderm.

One dark evening he came back to all his dear families, and he coiled up his trunk and said, 'How do you do?' They were very glad to see him, and immediately said, 'Come here and be spanked for your 'satiable curtiosity.'

'Pooh,' said the Elephant's Child. 'I don't think you peoples know anything about spanking; but I do, and I'll show you.' Then he uncurled his trunk and knocked two of his dear brothers head over heels.

'O Bananas!' said they, 'where did you learn that trick, and what have you done to your nose?'

'I got a new one from the Crocodile on the banks of the great grey-green, greasy Limpopo River,' said the Elephant's Child. 'I asked him what he had for dinner, and he gave me this to keep.'

'It looks very ugly,' said his hairy uncle, the Baboon.

'It does,' said the Elephant's Child. 'But it's very useful,' and he picked up his hairy uncle, the Baboon, by one hairy leg, and hove him into a hornet's nest.

Then that bad Elephant's Child spanked all his dear families for a long time, till they were very warm and greatly astonished. He pulled out his tall Ostrich aunt's tail-feathers; and he caught his tall uncle, the Giraffe, by the hind-leg, and dragged him through a thorn-bush; and he shouted at his broad aunt, the Hippopotamus, and blew bubbles into her ear when she was sleeping in the water after meals; but he never let any one touch Kolokolo Bird.

At last things grew so exciting that his dear families went off one by one in a hurry to the banks of the great grey-green, greasy Limpopo River, all set about with fever-trees, to borrow new noses from the Crocodile. When they came back nobody spanked anybody any more; and ever since that day, O Best Beloved, all the Elephants you will ever see, besides all those that you won't, have trunks precisely like the trunk of the 'satiable Elephant's Child.

I Keep six honest serving-men:
(They taught me all I knew)
Their names are What and Where and When
And How and Why and Who.
I send them over land and sea,
I send them east and west;
But after they have worked for me,
I give them all a rest.

I let them rest from nine till five.
For I am busy then,
As well as breakfast, lunch, and tea,
For they are hungry men:
But different folk have different views:
I know a person small--

 Rudyard Kipling

She keeps ten million serving-men,
Who get no rest at all!
She sends 'em abroad on her own affairs,
From the second she opens her eyes--
One million Hows, two million Wheres,
And seven million Whys!

THE SING-SONG OF OLD MAN KANGAROO

NOT always was the Kangaroo as now we do behold him, but a Different Animal with four short legs. He was grey and he was woolly, and his pride was inordinate: he danced on an outcrop in the middle of Australia, and he went to the Little God Nqa.

He went to Nqa at six before breakfast, saying, 'Make me different from all other animals by five this afternoon.'

Up jumped Nqa from his seat on the sandflat and shouted, 'Go away!'

He was grey and he was woolly, and his pride was inordinate: he danced on a rock-ledge in the middle of Australia, and he went to the Middle God Nquing.

He went to Nquing at eight after breakfast, saying, 'Make me different from all other animals; make me, also, wonderfully popular by five this afternoon.'

Up jumped Nquing from his burrow in the spinifex and shouted, 'Go away!'

He was grey and he was woolly, and his pride was inordinate: he danced on a sandbank in the middle of Australia, and he went to the Big God Nqong.

He went to Nqong at ten before dinner-time, saying, 'Make me different from all other animals; make me popular and wonderfully run after by five this afternoon.'

Up jumped Nqong from his bath in the salt-pan and shouted, 'Yes, I will!'

Nqong called Dingo—Yellow-Dog Dingo—always hungry, dusty in the sunshine, and showed him Kangaroo. Nqong said, 'Dingo! Wake up, Dingo! Do you see that gentleman dancing on an ashpit? He wants to be popular and very truly run after. Dingo, make him SO!'

Up jumped Dingo—Yellow-Dog Dingo—and said, 'What, that cat-rabbit?'

Off ran Dingo—Yellow-Dog Dingo—always hungry, grinning like a coal-scuttle,—ran after Kangaroo.

Off went the proud Kangaroo on his four little legs like a bunny.

This, O Beloved of mine, ends the first part of the tale!

He ran through the desert; he ran through the mountains; he ran through the salt-pans; he ran through the reed-beds; he ran through the blue gums; he ran through the spinifex; he ran till his front legs ached.

He had to!

Still ran Dingo—Yellow-Dog Dingo—always hungry, grinning like a rat-trap, never getting nearer, never getting farther,—ran after Kangaroo.

He had to!

Still ran Kangaroo—Old Man Kangaroo. He ran through the ti-trees; he ran through the mulga; he ran through the long grass; he ran through the short grass; he ran through the Tropics of Capricorn and Cancer; he ran till his hind legs ached.

He had to!

He had to!

Still ran Dingo—Yellow-Dog Dingo—hungrier and hungrier, grinning like a horse-collar, never getting nearer, never getting farther; and they came to the Wollgong River.

Now, there wasn't any bridge, and there wasn't any ferry-boat, and Kangaroo didn't know how to get over; so he stood on his legs and hopped.

He had to!

He hopped through the Flinders; he hopped through the Cinders; he hopped through the deserts in the middle of Australia. He hopped like a Kangaroo.

First he hopped one yard; then he hopped three yards; then he hopped five yards; his legs growing stronger; his legs growing longer. He hadn't any time for rest or refreshment, and he wanted them very much.

Still ran Dingo—Yellow-Dog Dingo—very much bewildered, very much hungry, and wondering what in the world or out of it made Old Man Kangaroo hop.

For he hopped like a cricket; like a pea in a saucepan; or a new rubber ball on a nursery floor.

He had to!

He tucked up his front legs; he hopped on his hind legs; he stuck out his tail for a balance-weight behind him; and he hopped through the Darling Downs.

He had to!

Still ran Dingo—Tired-Dog Dingo—hungrier and hungrier, very much bewildered, and wondering when in the world or out of it would Old Man Kangaroo stop.

Then came Nqong from his bath in the salt-pans, and said, 'It's five o'clock.'

Down sat Dingo—Poor Dog Dingo—always hungry, dusky in the sunshine; hung out his tongue and howled.

Down sat Kangaroo—Old Man Kangaroo—stuck out his tail like a milking-stool behind him, and said, 'Thank goodness that's finished!'

Then said Nqong, who is always a gentleman, 'Why aren't you grateful to Yellow-Dog Dingo? Why don't you thank him for all he has done for you?'

Then said Kangaroo—Tired Old Kangaroo—He's chased me out of the homes of my childhood; he's chased me out of my regular meal-times; he's altered my shape so I'll never get it back; and he's played Old Scratch with my legs.'

Then said Nqong, 'Perhaps I'm mistaken, but didn't you ask me to make you different from all other animals, as well as to make you very truly sought after? And now it is five o'clock.'

'Yes,' said Kangaroo. 'I wish that I hadn't. I thought you would do it by charms and incantations, but this is a practical joke.'

'Joke!' said Nqong from his bath in the blue gums. 'Say that again and I'll whistle up Dingo and run your hind legs off.'

'No,' said the Kangaroo. 'I must apologise. Legs are legs, and you needn't alter 'em so far as I am concerned. I only meant to explain to Your Lordliness that I've had nothing to eat since morning, and I'm very empty indeed.'

'Yes,' said Dingo—Yellow-Dog Dingo,—'I am just in the same situation. I've made him different from all other animals; but what may I have for my tea?'

Then said Nqong from his bath in the salt-pan, 'Come and ask me about it tomorrow, because I'm going to wash.'

So they were left in the middle of Australia, Old Man Kangaroo and Yellow-Dog Dingo, and each said, 'That's your fault.'

THIS is the mouth-filling song
Of the race that was run by a Boomer,
Run in a single burst--only event of its kind--
Started by big God Nqong from Warrigaborrigarooma,
Old Man Kangaroo first: Yellow-Dog Dingo behind.

Kangaroo bounded away,
His back-legs working like pistons--
Bounded from morning till dark,
Twenty-five feet to a bound.
Yellow-Dog Dingo lay
Like a yellow cloud in the distance--
Much too busy to bark.
My! but they covered the ground!

Nobody knows where they went,
Or followed the track that they flew in,
For that Continent
Hadn't been given a name.
They ran thirty degrees,
From Torres Straits to the Leeuwin
(Look at the Atlas, please),
And they ran back as they came.

S'posing you could trot
From Adelaide to the Pacific,

For an afternoon's run
Half what these gentlemen did
You would feel rather hot,
But your legs would develop terrific--
Yes, my importunate son,
You'd be a Marvellous Kid!

THE BEGINNING OF THE ARMADILLOS

THIS, O Best Beloved, is another story of the High and Far-Off Times. In the very middle of those times was a Stickly-Prickly Hedgehog, and he lived on the banks of the turbid Amazon, eating shelly snails and things. And he had a friend, a Slow-Solid Tortoise, who lived on the banks of the turbid Amazon, eating green lettuces and things. And so that was all right, Best Beloved. Do you see?

But also, and at the same time, in those High and Far-Off Times, there was a Painted Jaguar, and he lived on the banks of the turbid Amazon too; and he ate everything that he could catch. When he could not catch deer or monkeys he would eat frogs and beetles; and when he could not catch frogs and beetles he went to his Mother Jaguar, and she told him how to eat hedgehogs and tortoises.

She said to him ever so many times, graciously waving her tail, 'My son, when you find a Hedgehog you must drop him into the water and then he will uncoil, and when you catch a Tortoise you must scoop him out of his shell with your paw.' And so that was all right, Best Beloved.

One beautiful night on the banks of the turbid Amazon, Painted Jaguar found Stickly-Prickly Hedgehog and Slow-Solid

Tortoise sitting under the trunk of a fallen tree. They could not run away, and so Stickly-Prickly curled himself up into a ball, because he was a Hedgehog, and Slow-Solid Tortoise drew in his head and feet into his shell as far as they would go, because he was a Tortoise; and so that was all right, Best Beloved. Do you see?

'Now attend to me,' said Painted Jaguar, 'because this is very important. My mother said that when I meet a Hedgehog I am to drop him into the water and then he will uncoil, and when I meet a Tortoise I am to scoop him out of his shell with my paw. Now which of you is Hedgehog and which is Tortoise? because, to save my spots, I can't tell.'

'Are you sure of what your Mummy told you?' said Stickly-Prickly Hedgehog. 'Are you quite sure? Perhaps she said that when you uncoil a Tortoise you must shell him out the water with a scoop, and when you paw a Hedgehog you must drop him on the shell.'

'Are you sure of what your Mummy told you?' said Slow-and-Solid Tortoise. 'Are you quite sure? Perhaps she said that when you water a Hedgehog you must drop him into your paw, and when you meet a Tortoise you must shell him till he uncoils.'

'I don't think it was at all like that,' said Painted Jaguar, but he felt a little puzzled; 'but, please, say it again more distinctly.'

'When you scoop water with your paw you uncoil it with a Hedgehog,' said Stickly-Prickly. 'Remember that, because it's important.'

'But,' said the Tortoise, 'when you paw your meat you drop it into a Tortoise with a scoop. Why can't you understand?'

'You are making my spots ache,' said Painted Jaguar; 'and besides, I didn't want your advice at all. I only wanted to know which of you is Hedgehog and which is Tortoise.'

'I shan't tell you,' said Stickly-Prickly, 'but you can scoop me out of my shell if you like.'

'Aha!' said Painted Jaguar. 'Now I know you're Tortoise. You thought I wouldn't! Now I will.' Painted Jaguar darted out his paddy-paw just as Stickly-Prickly curled himself up, and of course Jaguar's paddy-paw was just filled with prickles. Worse than that, he knocked Stickly-Prickly away and away into the woods and the bushes, where it was too dark to find him. Then he put his paddy-paw into his mouth, and of course the prickles hurt him worse than ever. As soon as he could speak he said, 'Now I know he isn't Tortoise at all. But'—and then he scratched his head with his un-prickly paw—'how do I know that this other is Tortoise?'

'But I am Tortoise,' said Slow-and-Solid. Your mother was quite right. She said that you were to scoop me out of my shell with your paw. Begin.'

'You didn't say she said that a minute ago, said Painted Jaguar, sucking the prickles out of his paddy-paw. 'You said she said something quite different.'

'Well, suppose you say that I said that she said something quite different, I don't see that it makes any difference; because if she said what you said I said she said, it's just the same as if I said what she said she said. On the other hand, if you think she said that you were to uncoil me with a scoop, instead of pawing me into drops with a shell, I can't help that, can I?'

'But you said you wanted to be scooped out of your shell with my paw,' said Painted Jaguar.

'If you'll think again you'll find that I didn't say anything of the kind. I said that your mother said that you were to scoop me out of my shell,' said Slow-and-Solid.

'What will happen if I do?' said the Jaguar most sniffily and most cautious.

'I don't know, because I've never been scooped out of my shell before; but I tell you truly, if you want to see me swim away you've only got to drop me into the water.'

'I don't believe it,' said Painted Jaguar. 'You've mixed up all the things my mother told me to do with the things that you asked me whether I was sure that she didn't say, till I don't know whether I'm on my head or my painted tail; and now you come and tell me something I can understand, and it makes me more mixy than before. My mother told me that I was to drop one of you two into the water, and as you seem so anxious to be dropped I think you don't want to be dropped. So jump into the turbid Amazon and be quick about it.'

'I warn you that your Mummy won't be pleased. Don't tell her I didn't tell you,' said Slow-Solid.

'If you say another word about what my mother said—' the Jaguar answered, but he had not finished the sentence before Slow-and-Solid quietly dived into the turbid Amazon, swam under water for a long way, and came out on the bank where Stickly-Prickly was waiting for him.

'That was a very narrow escape,' said Stickly-Prickly. 'I don't rib Painted Jaguar. What did you tell him that you were?'

'I told him truthfully that I was a truthful Tortoise, but he wouldn't believe it, and he made me jump into the river to see if I was, and I was, and he is surprised. Now he's gone to tell his Mummy. Listen to him!'

They could hear Painted Jaguar roaring up and down among the trees and the bushes by the side of the turbid Amazon, till his Mummy came.

'Son, son!' said his mother ever so many times, graciously waving her tail, 'what have you been doing that you shouldn't have done?'

'I tried to scoop something that said it wanted to be scooped out of its shell with my paw, and my paw is full of per-ickles,' said Painted Jaguar.

'Son, son!' said his mother ever so many times, graciously waving her tail, 'by the prickles in your paddy-paw I see that that must have been a Hedgehog. You should have dropped him into the water.

'I did that to the other thing; and he said he was a Tortoise, and I didn't believe him, and it was quite true, and he has dived under the turbid Amazon, and he won't come up again, and I haven't anything at all to eat, and I think we had better find lodgings somewhere else. They are too clever on the turbid Amazon for poor me!'

'Son, son!' said his mother ever so many times, graciously waving her tail, 'now attend to me and remember what I say. A Hedgehog curls himself up into a ball and his prickles stick out every which way at once. By this you may know the Hedgehog.'

'I don't like this old lady one little bit,' said Stickly-Prickly, under the shadow of a large leaf. 'I wonder what else she knows?'

'A Tortoise can't curl himself up,' Mother Jaguar went on, ever so many times, graciously waving her tail. 'He only draws his head and legs into his shell. By this you may know the tortoise.'

'I don't like this old lady at all—at all,' said Slow-and-Solid Tortoise. 'Even Painted Jaguar can't forget those directions. It's a great pity that you can't swim, Stickly-Prickly.'

'Don't talk to me,' said Stickly-Prickly. 'Just think how much better it would be if you could curl up. This is a mess! Listen to Painted Jaguar.'

Painted Jaguar was sitting on the banks of the turbid Amazon sucking prickles out of his Paws and saying to himself—

> *'Can't curl, but can swim—*
> *Slow-Solid, that's him!*
> *Curls up, but can't swim—*
> *Stickly-Prickly, that's him!'*

'He'll never forget that this month of Sundays,' said Stickly-Prickly. 'Hold up my chin, Slow-and-Solid. I'm going to try to learn to swim. It may be useful.'

'Excellent!' said Slow-and-Solid; and he held up Stickly-Prickly's chin, while Stickly-Prickly kicked in the waters of the turbid Amazon.

'You'll make a fine swimmer yet,' said Slow-and-Solid. 'Now, if you can unlace my back-plates a little, I'll see what I can do towards curling up. It may be useful.'

Stickly-Prickly helped to unlace Tortoise's back-plates, so that by twisting and straining Slow-and-Solid actually managed to curl up a tiddy wee bit.

'Excellent!' said Stickly-Prickly; 'but I shouldn't do any more just now. It's making you black in the face. Kindly lead me into the water once again and I'll practice that side-stroke which you say is so easy.' And so Stickly-Prickly practiced, and Slow-Solid swam alongside.

'Excellent!' said Slow-and-Solid. 'A little more practice will make you a regular whale. Now, if I may trouble you to unlace my back and front plates two holes more, I'll try that fascinating bend that you say is so easy. Won't Painted Jaguar be surprised!'

'Excellent!' said Stickly-Prickly, all wet from the turbid Amazon. 'I declare, I shouldn't know you from one of my own family. Two holes, I think, you said? A little more expression, please, and don't grunt quite so much, or Painted Jaguar may hear us. When you've finished, I want to try that long dive which you say is so easy. Won't Painted Jaguar be surprised!'

And so Stickly-Prickly dived, and Slow-and-Solid dived alongside.

'Excellent!' said Slow-and-Solid. 'A leetle more attention to holding your breath and you will be able to keep house at the bottom of the turbid Amazon. Now I'll try that exercise of putting my hind legs round my ears which you say is so peculiarly comfortable. Won't Painted Jaguar be surprised!'

'Excellent!' said Stickly-Prickly. 'But it's straining your back-plates a little. They are all overlapping now, instead of lying side by side.'

'Oh, that's the result of exercise,' said Slow-and-Solid. 'I've noticed that your prickles seem to be melting into one another, and that you're growing to look rather more like a pinecone, and less like a chestnut-burr, than you used to.'

'Am I?' said Stickly-Prickly. 'That comes from my soaking in the water. Oh, won't Painted Jaguar be surprised!'

They went on with their exercises, each helping the other, till morning came; and when the sun was high they rested and dried themselves. Then they saw that they were both of them quite different from what they had been.

'Stickly-Prickly,' said Tortoise after breakfast, 'I am not what I was yesterday; but I think that I may yet amuse Painted Jaguar.

'That was the very thing I was thinking just now,' said Stickly-Prickly. 'I think scales are a tremendous improvement on prickles—to say nothing of being able to swim. Oh, won't Painted Jaguar be surprised! Let's go and find him.'

By and by they found Painted Jaguar, still nursing his paddy-paw that had been hurt the night before. He was so astonished that he fell three times backward over his own painted tail without stopping.

'Good morning!' said Stickly-Prickly. 'And how is your dear gracious Mummy this morning?'

'She is quite well, thank you,' said Painted Jaguar; 'but you must forgive me if I do not at this precise moment recall your name.'

'That's unkind of you,' said Stickly-Prickly, 'seeing that this time yesterday you tried to scoop me out of my shell with your paw.'

'But you hadn't any shell. It was all prickles,' said Painted Jaguar. 'I know it was. Just look at my paw!'

'You told me to drop into the turbid Amazon and be drowned,' said Slow-Solid. 'Why are you so rude and forgetful to-day?'

'Don't you remember what your mother told you?' said Stickly-Prickly,—

> *'Can't curl, but can swim—*
> *Stickly-Prickly, that's him!*
> *Curls up, but can't swim—*
> *Slow-Solid, that's him!'*

Then they both curled themselves up and rolled round and round Painted Jaguar till his eyes turned truly cart-wheels in his head.

Then he went to fetch his mother.

'Mother,' he said, 'there are two new animals in the woods to-day, and the one that you said couldn't swim, swims, and the one that you said couldn't curl up, curls; and they've gone shares in their prickles, I think, because both of them are scaly all over, instead of one being smooth and the other very prickly; and, besides that, they are rolling round and round in circles, and I don't feel comfy.'

'Son, son!' said Mother Jaguar ever so many times, graciously waving her tail, 'a Hedgehog is a Hedgehog, and can't be anything but a Hedgehog; and a Tortoise is a Tortoise, and can never be anything else.'

'But it isn't a Hedgehog, and it isn't a Tortoise. It's a little bit of both, and I don't know its proper name.'

'Nonsense!' said Mother Jaguar. 'Everything has its proper name. I should call it "Armadillo" till I found out the real one. And I should leave it alone.'

So Painted Jaguar did as he was told, especially about leaving them alone; but the curious thing is that from that day to this, O Best Beloved, no one on the banks of the turbid Amazon has ever called Stickly-Prickly and Slow-Solid anything except Armadillo. There are Hedgehogs and Tortoises in other places, of course (there are some in my garden); but the real old and clever kind, with their scales lying lippety-lappety one over the other, like pine-cone scales, that lived on the banks of the turbid Amazon in the High and Far-Off Days, are always called Armadillos, because they were so clever.

So that; all right, Best Beloved. Do you see?

I'VE never sailed the Amazon,

I've never reached Brazil;

But the Don and Magdelana,

They can go there when they will!

Yes, weekly from Southampton,

Great steamers, white and gold,

Go rolling down to Rio
(Roll down--roll down to Rio!)
And I'd like to roll to Rio
Some day before I'm old!

I've never seen a Jaguar,

Nor yet an Armadill
O dilloing in his armour,
And I s'pose I never will,

Unless I go to Rio
These wonders to behold--
Roll down--roll down to Rio--
Roll really down to Rio!
Oh, I'd love to roll to Rio
Some day before I'm old!

HOW THE FIRST LETTER WAS WRITTEN

ONCE upon a most early time was a Neolithic man. He was not a Jute or an Angle, or even a Dravidian, which he might well have been, Best Beloved, but never mind why. He was a Primitive, and he lived cavily in a Cave, and he wore very few clothes, and he couldn't read and he couldn't write and he didn't want to, and except when he was hungry he was quite happy. His name was Tegumai Bopsulai, and that means, 'Man-who-does-not-put-his-foot-forward-in-a-hurry'; but we, O Best Beloved, will call him Tegumai, for short. And his wife's name was Teshumai Tewindrow, and that means, 'Lady-who-asks-a-very-many-questions'; but we, O Best Beloved, will call her Teshumai, for short. And his little girl-daughter's name was Taffimai Metallumai, and that means, 'Small-person-without-any-manners-who-ought-to-be-spanked'; but I'm going to call her Taffy. And she was Tegumai Bopsulai's Best Beloved and her own Mummy's Best Beloved, and she was not spanked half as much as was good for her; and they were all three very happy. As soon as Taffy could run about she went everywhere with her Daddy Tegumai, and sometimes they would not come home to the Cave till they were hungry, and then Teshumai Tewindrow would say, 'Where in the world have you two been to, to get so shocking dirty? Really, my Tegumai, you're no better than my Taffy.'

Now attend and listen!

One day Tegumai Bopsulai went down through the beaver-swamp to the Wagai river to spear carp-fish for dinner, and Taffy went too. Tegumai's spear was made of wood with shark's teeth at the end, and before he had caught any fish at all he accidentally broke it clean across by jabbing it down too hard on the bottom of the river. They were miles and miles from home (of course they had their lunch with them in a little bag), and Tegumai had forgotten to bring any extra spears.

'Here's a pretty kettle of fish!' said Tegumai. 'It will take me half the day to mend this.'

'There's your big black spear at home,' said Taffy. 'Let me run back to the Cave and ask Mummy to give it me.'

'It's too far for your little fat legs,' said Tegumai. 'Besides, you might fall into the beaver-swamp and be drowned. We must make the best of a bad job.' He sat down and took out a little leather mendy-bag, full of reindeer-sinews and strips of leather, and lumps of bee's-wax and resin, and began to mend the spear.

Taffy sat down too, with her toes in the water and her chin in her hand, and thought very hard. Then she said—'I say, Daddy, it's an awful nuisance that you and I don't know how to write, isn't it? If we did we could send a message for the new spear.'

'Taffy,' said Tegumai, 'how often have I told you not to use slang? "Awful" isn't a pretty word, but it could be a convenience, now you mention it, if we could write home.'

Just then a Stranger-man came along the river, but he belonged to a far tribe, the Tewaras, and he did not understand one word of Tegumai's language. He stood on the bank and smiled at Taffy, because he had a little girl-daughter Of his own at home. Tegumai drew a hank of deer-sinews from his mendy-bag and began to mend his spear.

'Come here, said Taffy. 'Do you know where my Mummy lives?' And the Stranger-man said 'Um!' being, as you know, a Tewara.

'Silly!' said Taffy, and she stamped her foot, because she saw a shoal of very big carp going up the river just when her Daddy couldn't use his spear.

'Don't bother grown-ups,' said Tegumai, so busy with his spear-mending that he did not turn round.

'I aren't, said Taffy. 'I only want him to do what I want him to do, and he won't understand.'

'Then don't bother me, said Tegumai, and he went on pulling and straining at the deer-sinews with his mouth full of loose ends. The Stranger-man—a genuine Tewara he was— sat down on the grass, and Taffy showed him what her Daddy was doing. The Stranger-man thought, this is a very wonderful child. She stamps her foot at me and she makes faces. She must be the daughter of that noble Chief who is so great that he won't take any notice of me.' So he smiled more politely than ever.

'Now,' said Taffy, 'I want you to go to my Mummy, because your legs are longer than mine, and you won't fall into the beaver-swamp, and ask for Daddy's other spear—the one with the black handle that hangs over our fireplace.'

The Stranger-man (and he was a Tewara) thought, 'This is a very, very wonderful child. She waves her arms and she shouts at me, but I don't understand a word of what she says. But if I don't do what she wants, I greatly fear that that haughty Chief, Man-who-turns-his-back-on-callers, will be angry.' He got up and twisted a big flat piece of bark off a birch-tree and gave it to Taffy. He did this, Best Beloved, to show that his heart was as white as the birch-bark and that he meant no harm; but Taffy didn't quite understand.

'Oh!' said she. 'Now I see! You want my Mummy's living-address? Of course I can't write, but I can draw pictures if I've anything sharp to scratch with. Please lend me the shark's tooth off your necklace.'

The Stranger-man (and he was a Tewara) didn't say anything, So Taffy put up her little hand and pulled at the beautiful bead and seed and shark-tooth necklace round his neck.

The Stranger-man (and he was a Tewara) thought, 'This is a very, very, very wonderful child. The shark's tooth on my necklace is a magic shark's tooth, and I was always told that if anybody touched it without my leave they would immediately swell up or burst, but this child doesn't swell up or burst, and that important Chief, Man-who-attends-strictly-to-his-business, who has not yet taken any notice of me at all, doesn't seem to be afraid that she will swell up or burst. I had better be more polite.'

So he gave Taffy the shark's tooth, and she lay down flat on her tummy with her legs in the air, like some people on the drawing-room floor when they want to draw pictures, and she said, 'Now I'll draw you some beautiful pictures! You can look over my shoulder, but you mustn't joggle. First I'll draw Daddy fishing. It isn't very like him; but Mummy will know, because I've drawn his spear all broken. Well, now I'll draw the other spear that he wants, the black-handled spear. It looks as if it was sticking in Daddy's back, but that's because the shark's tooth slipped and this piece of bark isn't big enough. That's the spear I want you to fetch; so I'll draw a picture of me myself 'splaining to you. My hair doesn't stand up like

I've drawn, but it's easier to draw that way. Now I'll draw you. I think you're very nice really, but I can't make you pretty in the picture, so you mustn't be 'fended. Are you 'fended?'

The Stranger-man (and he was a Tewara) smiled. He thought, 'There must be a big battle going to be fought somewhere, and this extraordinary child, who takes my magic shark's tooth but who does not swell up or burst, is telling me to call all the great Chief's tribe to help him. He is a great Chief, or he would have noticed me.

'Look,' said Taffy, drawing very hard and rather scratchily, 'now I've drawn you, and I've put the spear that Daddy wants into your hand, just to remind you that you're to bring it. Now I'll show you how to find my Mummy's living-address. You go along till you come to two trees (those are trees), and then you go over a hill (that's a hill), and then you come into a beaver-swamp all full of beavers. I haven't put in all the beavers, because I can't draw beavers, but I've drawn their heads, and that's all you'll see of them when you cross the swamp. Mind you don't fall in! Then our Cave is just beyond the beaver-swamp. It isn't as high as the hills really, but I can't draw things very small. That's my Mummy outside. She is beautiful. She is the most beautifullest Mummy there ever was, but she won't be 'fended when she sees I've drawn her so plain. She'll be pleased of me because I can draw. Now, in case you forget, I've drawn the spear that Daddy wants outside our Cave. It's inside really, but you show the picture to my Mummy and she'll give it you. I've made her holding up her hands, because I know she'll be so pleased to see you. Isn't it a beautiful picture? And do you quite understand, or shall I 'splain again?'

The Stranger-man (and he was a Tewara) looked at the picture and nodded very hard. He said to himself,' If I do not fetch this great Chief's tribe to help him, he will be slain by his enemies who are coming up on all sides with spears. Now I see why the great Chief pretended not to notice me! He feared that his enemies were hiding in the bushes and would see him. Therefore he turned to me his back, and let the wise and wonderful child draw the terrible picture showing me his difficulties. I will away and get help for him from his tribe.' He did not even ask Taffy the road, but raced off into the bushes like the wind, with the birch-bark in his hand, and Taffy sat down most pleased.

Now this is the picture that Taffy had drawn for him!

'What have you been doing, Taffy?' said Tegumai. He had mended his spear and was carefully waving it to and fro.

'It's a little berangement of my own, Daddy dear,' said Taffy. 'If you won't ask me questions, you'll know all about it in a little time, and you'll be surprised. You don't know how surprised you'll be, Daddy! Promise you'll be surprised.'

'Very well,' said Tegumai, and went on fishing.

The Stranger-man—did you know he was a Tewara?—hurried away with the picture and ran for some miles, till quite by accident he found Teshumai Tewindrow at the door of her Cave, talking to some other Neolithic ladies who had come in to a Primitive lunch. Taffy was very like Teshumai, especially about the upper part of the face and the eyes, so the Stranger-man—always a pure Tewara—smiled politely and handed Teshumai the birch-bark. He had run hard, so that he panted, and his legs were scratched with brambles, but he still tried to be polite.

As soon as Teshumai saw the picture she screamed like anything and flew at the Stranger-man. The other Neolithic ladies at once knocked him down and sat on him in a long line of six, while Teshumai pulled his hair.

'It's as plain as the nose on this Stranger-man's face,' she said. 'He has stuck my Tegumai all full of spears, and frightened poor Taffy so that her hair stands all on end; and not content with that, he brings me a horrid picture of how it was done. Look!' She showed the picture to all the Neolithic ladies sitting patiently on the Stranger-man. 'Here is my Tegumai with his arm broken; here is a spear sticking into his back; here is a man with a spear ready to throw; here is another man throwing a spear from a Cave, and here are a whole pack of people' (they were Taffy's beavers really, but they did look rather like people) 'coming up behind Tegumai. Isn't it shocking!'

'Most shocking!' said the Neolithic ladies, and they filled the Stranger-man's hair with mud (at which he was surprised), and they beat upon the Reverberating Tribal Drums, and called together all the chiefs of the Tribe of Tegumai, with their Hetmans and Dolmans, all Neguses, Woons, and Akhoonds of the organisation, in addition to the Warlocks, Angekoks, Juju-men, Bonzes, and the rest, who decided that before they chopped the Stranger-man's head off he should instantly lead them down to the river and show them where he had hidden poor Taffy.

By this time the Stranger-man (in spite of being a Tewara) was really annoyed. They had filled his hair quite solid with mud; they had rolled him up and down on knobby pebbles; they had sat upon him in a long line of six; they had thumped him and bumped him till he could hardly breathe; and though he did not understand their language, he was almost sure that the names the Neolithic ladies called him were not ladylike. However, he said nothing till all the Tribe of Tegumai were assembled, and then he led them back to the bank of the Wagai river, and there they found Taffy making daisy-chains, and Tegumai carefully spearing small carp with his mended spear.

'Well, you have been quick!' said Taffy. 'But why did you bring so many people? Daddy dear, this is my surprise. Are you surprised, Daddy?'

'Very,' said Tegumai; 'but it has ruined all my fishing for the day. Why, the whole dear, kind, nice, clean, quiet Tribe is here, Taffy.'

And so they were. First of all walked Teshumai Tewindrow and the Neolithic ladies, tightly holding on to the Stranger-man, whose hair was full of mud (although he was a Tewara). Behind them came the Head Chief, the Vice-Chief, the Deputy and Assistant Chiefs (all armed to the upper teeth), the Hetmans and Heads of Hundreds, Platoffs with their Platoons, and Dolmans with their Detachments; Woons, Neguses, and Akhoonds ranking in the rear (still armed to the teeth). Behind them was the Tribe in hierarchical order, from owners of four caves (one for each season), a private reindeer-run, and two salmon-leaps, to feudal and prognathous Villeins, semi-entitled to half a bearskin of winter nights, seven yards from the fire, and adscript serfs, holding the reversion of a scraped marrow-bone under heriot (Aren't those beautiful words, Best Beloved?). They were all there, prancing and shouting, and they frightened every fish for twenty miles, and Tegumai thanked them in a fluid Neolithic oration.

Then Teshumai Tewindrow ran down and kissed and hugged Taffy very much indeed; but the Head Chief of the Tribe of Tegumai took Tegumai by the top-knot feathers and shook him severely.

'Explain! Explain! Explain!' cried all the Tribe of Tegumai.

'Goodness' sakes alive!' said Tegumai. 'Let go of my top-knot. Can't a man break his carp-spear without the whole countryside descending on him? You're a very interfering people.'

'I don't believe you've brought my Daddy's black-handled spear after all,' said Taffy. 'And what are you doing to my nice Stranger-man?'

They were thumping him by twos and threes and tens till his eyes turned round and round. He could only gasp and point at Taffy.

'Where are the bad people who speared you, my darling?' said Teshumai Tewindrow.

'There weren't any,' said Tegumai. 'My only visitor this morning was the poor fellow that you are trying to choke. Aren't you well, or are you ill, O Tribe of Tegumai?'

'He came with a horrible picture,' said the Head Chief,—'a picture that showed you were full of spears.'

'Er-um-Pr'aps I'd better 'splain that I gave him that picture,' said Taffy, but she did not feel quite comfy.

'You!' said the Tribe of Tegumai all together. 'Small-person-with-no-manners-who-ought-to-be-spanked! You?'

'Taffy dear, I'm afraid we're in for a little trouble,' said her Daddy, and put his arm round her, so she didn't care.

'Explain! Explain! Explain!' said the Head Chief of the Tribe of Tegumai, and he hopped on one foot.

'I wanted the Stranger-man to fetch Daddy's spear, so I drawded it,' said Taffy. 'There wasn't lots of spears. There was only one spear. I drawded it three times to make sure. I couldn't help it looking as if it stuck into Daddy's head—there wasn't room on the birch-bark; and those things that Mummy called bad people are my beavers. I drawded them to show him the way through the swamp; and I drawded Mummy at the mouth of the Cave looking pleased because he is a nice Stranger-man, and I think you are just the stupidest people in the world,' said Taffy. 'He is a very nice man. Why have you filled his hair with mud? Wash him!'

Nobody said anything at all for a longtime, till the Head Chief laughed; then the Stranger-man (who was at least a Tewara) laughed; then Tegumai laughed till he fell down flat on the bank; then all the Tribe laughed more and worse and louder. The only people who did not laugh were Teshumai Tewindrow and all the Neolithic ladies. They were very polite to all their husbands, and said 'Idiot!' ever so often.

hen the Head Chief of the Tribe of Tegumai cried and said and sang, 'O Small-person-with-out-any-manners-who-ought-to-be-spanked, you've hit upon a great invention!'

'I didn't intend to; I only wanted Daddy's black-handled spear,' said Taffy.

'Never mind. It is a great invention, and some day men will call it writing. At present it is only pictures, and, as we have seen to-day, pictures are not always properly understood. But a time will come, O Babe of Tegumai, when we shall make letters—all twenty-six of 'em,—and when we shall be able to read as well as to write, and then we shall always say exactly what we mean without any mistakes. Let the Neolithic ladies wash the mud out of the stranger's hair.'

'I shall be glad of that,' said Taffy, 'because, after all, though you've brought every single other spear in the Tribe of Tegumai, you've forgotten my Daddy's black-handled spear.'

Then the Head Chief cried and said and sang, 'Taffy dear, the next time you write a picture-letter, you'd better send a man who can talk our language with it, to explain what it means. I don't mind it myself, because I am a Head Chief, but it's very bad for the rest of the Tribe of Tegumai, and, as you can see, it surprises the stranger.'

Then they adopted the Stranger-man (a genuine Tewara of Tewar) into the Tribe of Tegumai, because he was a gentleman and did not make a fuss about the mud that the Neolithic ladies had put into his hair. But from that day to this (and I suppose it is all Taffy's fault), very few little girls have ever liked learning to read or write. Most of them prefer to draw pictures and play about with their Daddies—just like Taffy.

THERE runs a road by Merrow Down--
A grassy track to-day it is
An hour out of Guildford town,
Above the river Wey it is.

Here, when they heard the horse-bells ring,
The ancient Britons dressed and rode
To watch the dark Phoenicians bring
Their goods along the Western Road.

And here, or hereabouts, they met
To hold their racial talks and such--
To barter beads for Whitby jet,
And tin for gay shell torques and such.

But long and long before that time
(When bison used to roam on it)
Did Taffy and her Daddy climb
That down, and had their home on it.

Then beavers built in Broadstone brook
And made a swamp where Bramley stands:
And hears from Shere would come and look
For Taffimai where Shamley stands.

The Wey, that Taffy called Wagai,
Was more than six times bigger then;
And all the Tribe of Tegumai
They cut a noble figure then!

HOW THE ALPHABET WAS MADE

THE week after Taffimai Metallumai (we will still call her Taffy, Best Beloved) made that little mistake about her Daddy's spear and the Stranger-man and the picture-letter and all, she went carp-fishing again with her Daddy. Her Mummy wanted her to stay at home and help hang up hides to dry on the big drying-poles outside their Neolithic Cave, but Taffy slipped away down to her Daddy quite early, and they fished. Presently she began to giggle, and her Daddy said, 'Don't be silly, child.'

'But wasn't it inciting!' said Taffy. 'Don't you remember how the Head Chief puffed out his cheeks, and how funny the nice Stranger-man looked with the mud in his hair?'

'Well do I,' said Tegumai. 'I had to pay two deerskins—soft ones with fringes—to the Stranger-man for the things we did to him.'

'We didn't do anything,' said Taffy. 'It was Mummy and the other Neolithic ladies—and the mud.'

'We won't talk about that,' said her Daddy, 'Let's have lunch.'

Taffy took a marrow-bone and sat mousy-quiet for ten whole minutes, while her Daddy scratched on pieces of birch-bark with a shark's tooth. Then she said, 'Daddy, I've thinked of a secret surprise. You make a noise—any sort of noise.'

'Ah!' said Tegumai. 'Will that do to begin with?'

'Yes,' said Taffy. 'You look just like a carp-fish with its mouth open. Say it again, please.'

'Ah! ah! ah!' said her Daddy. 'Don't be rude, my daughter.'

'I'm not meaning rude, really and truly,' said Taffy. 'It's part of my secret-surprise-think. Do say ah, Daddy, and keep your mouth open at the end, and lend me that tooth. I'm going to draw a carp-fish's mouth wide-open.'

'What for?' said her Daddy.

'Don't you see?' said Taffy, scratching away on the bark. 'That will be our little secret s'prise. When I draw a carp-fish with his mouth open in the smoke at the back of our Cave—if Mummy doesn't mind—it will remind you of that ah-noise. Then we can play that it was me jumped out of the dark and s'prised you with that noise—same as I did in the beaver-swamp last winter.'

'Really?' said her Daddy, in the voice that grown-ups use when they are truly attending. 'Go on, Taffy.'

'Oh bother!' she said. 'I can't draw all of a carp-fish, but I can draw something that means a carp-fish's mouth. Don't you know how they stand on their heads rooting in the mud? Well, here's a pretence carp-fish (we can play that the rest of him is drawn). Here's just his mouth, and that means ah.' And she drew this. (1.)

'That's not bad,' said Tegumai, and scratched on his own piece of bark for himself; but you've forgotten the feeler that hangs across his mouth.'

'But I can't draw, Daddy.'

'You needn't draw anything of him except just the opening of his mouth and the feeler across. Then we'll know he's a carp-fish, 'cause the perches and trouts haven't got feelers. Look here, Taffy.' And he drew this. (2.)

'Now I'll copy it.' said Taffy. 'Will you understand this when you see it?'

'Perfectly,' said her Daddy.

And she drew this. (3.) 'And I'll be quite as s'prised when I see it anywhere, as if you had jumped out from behind a tree and said '"Ah!"'

'Now, make another noise,' said Taffy, very proud.

'Yah!' said her Daddy, very loud.

'H'm,' said Taffy. 'That's a mixy noise. The end part is ah-carp-fish-mouth; but what can we do about the front part? Yer-yer-yer and ah! Ya!'

'It's very like the carp-fish-mouth noise. Let's draw another bit of the carp-fish and join 'em,' said her Daddy. He was quite incited too.

'No. If they're joined, I'll forget. Draw it separate. Draw his tail. If he's standing on his head the tail will come first. 'Sides, I think I can draw tails easiest,' said Taffy.

'A good notion,' said Tegumai. 'Here's a carp-fish tail for the yer-noise.' And he drew this. (4.)

'I'll try now,' said Taffy. ''Member I can't draw like you, Daddy. Will it do if I just draw the split part of the tail, and the sticky-down line for where it joins?' And she drew this. (5.)

Her Daddy nodded, and his eyes were shiny bright with 'citement.

'That's beautiful,' she said. 'Now make another noise, Daddy.'

'Oh!' said her Daddy, very loud.

'That's quite easy,' said Taffy. 'You make your mouth all around like an egg or a stone. So an egg or a stone will do for that.'

'You can't always find eggs or stones. We'll have to scratch a round something like one.' And he drew this. (6.)

'My gracious!' said Taffy, 'what a lot of noise-pictures we've made,—carp-mouth, carp-tail, and egg! Now, make another noise, Daddy.'

'Ssh!' said her Daddy, and frowned to himself, but Taffy was too incited to notice.

'That's quite easy,' she said, scratching on the bark.

'Eh, what?' said her Daddy. 'I meant I was thinking, and didn't want to be disturbed.'

'It's a noise just the same. It's the noise a snake makes, Daddy, when it is thinking and doesn't want to be disturbed. Let's make the ssh-noise a snake. Will this do?' And she drew this. (7.)

'There,' she said. 'That's another s'prise-secret. When you draw a hissy-snake by the door of your little back-cave where you mend the spears, I'll know you're thinking hard; and I'll come in most mousy-quiet. And if you draw it on a tree by the river when you are fishing, I'll know you want me to walk most most mousy-quiet, so as not to shake the banks.'

'Perfectly true,' said Tegumai. And there's more in this game than you think. Taffy, dear, I've a notion that your Daddy's daughter has hit upon the finest thing that there ever was since the Tribe of Tegumai took to using shark's teeth instead of flints for their spear-heads. I believe we've found out the big secret of the world.'

'Why?' said Taffy, and her eyes shone too with incitement.

'I'll show,' said her Daddy. 'What's water in the Tegumai language?'

'Ya, of course, and it means river too—like Wagai-ya— the Wagai river.'

'What is bad water that gives you fever if you drink it—black water—swamp-water?'

'Yo, of course.'

'Now look,' said her Daddy. 'S'pose you saw this scratched by the side of a pool in the beaver-swamp?' And he drew this. (8.)

'Carp-tail and round egg. Two noises mixed! Yo, bad water,' said Taffy. ''Course I wouldn't drink that water because I'd know you said it was bad.'

'But I needn't be near the water at all. I might be miles away, hunting, and still—'

'And still it would be just the same as if you stood there and said, "G'way, Taffy, or you'll get fever." All that in a carp-fish-tail and a round egg! O Daddy, we must tell Mummy, quick!' and Taffy danced all round him.

'Not yet,' said Tegumai; 'not till we've gone a little further. Let's see. Yo is bad water, but So is food cooked on the fire, isn't it?' And he drew this. (9.)

'Yes. Snake and egg,' said Taffy 'So that means dinner's ready. If you saw that scratched on a tree you'd know it was time to come to the Cave. So'd I.'

'My Winkie!' said Tegumai. 'That's true too. But wait a minute. I see a difficulty. SO means "come and have dinner," but sho means the drying-poles where we hang our hides.'

'Horrid old drying-poles!' said Taffy. 'I hate helping to hang heavy, hot, hairy hides on them. If you drew the snake and egg, and I thought it meant dinner, and I came in from the wood and found that it meant I was to help Mummy hang the two hides on the drying-poles, what would I do?'

'You'd be cross. So'd Mummy. We must make a new picture for sho. We must draw a spotty snake that hisses sh-sh, and we'll play that the plain snake only hisses ssss.'

'I couldn't be sure how to put in the spots,' said Taffy. 'And p'raps if you were in a hurry you might leave them out, and I'd think it was so when it was sho, and then Mummy would catch me just the same. No! I think we'd better draw a picture of the horrid high drying-poles their very selves, and make quite sure. I'll put them in just after the hissy-snake. Look!' And she drew this. (10.)

'P'raps that's safest. It's very like our drying-poles, anyhow,' said her Daddy, laughing. 'Now I'll make a new noise with a snake and drying-pole sound in it. I'll say shi. That's Tegumai for spear, Taffy.' And he laughed.

'Don't make fun of me,' said Taffy, as she thought of her picture-letter and the mud in the Stranger-man's hair. 'You draw it, Daddy.'

'We won't have beavers or hills this time, eh?' said her Daddy, 'I'll just draw a straight line for my spear.' and he drew this. (11.)

'Even Mummy couldn't mistake that for me being killed.'

'Please don't, Daddy. It makes me uncomfy. Do some more noises. We're getting on beautifully.'

'Er-hm!' said Tegumai, looking up. 'We'll say shu. That means sky.'

Taffy drew the snake and the drying-pole. Then she stopped. 'We must make a new picture for that end sound, mustn't we?'

'Shu-shu-u-u-u!' said her Daddy. 'Why, it's just like the round-egg-sound made thin.'

'Then s'pose we draw a thin round egg, and pretend it's a frog that hasn't eaten anything for years.'

'N-no,' said her Daddy. 'If we drew that in a hurry we might mistake it for the round egg itself. Shu-shu-shu! 'I tell you what we'll do. We'll open a little hole at the end of the round egg to show how the O-noise runs out all thin, ooo-oo-oo. Like this.' And he drew this. (12.)

'Oh, that's lovely! Much better than a thin frog. Go on,' said Taffy, using her shark's tooth. Her Daddy went on drawing, and his hand shook with incitement. He went on till he had drawn this. (13.)

'Don't look up, Taffy,' he said. 'Try if you can make out what that means in the Tegumai language. If you can, we've found the Secret.'

'Snake—pole—broken—egg—carp—tail and carp-mouth,' said Taffy. 'Shu-ya. Sky-water (rain).' Just then a drop fell on her hand, for the day had clouded over. 'Why, Daddy, it's raining. Was that what you meant to tell me?'

'Of course,' said her Daddy. 'And I told it you without saying a word, didn't I?'

'Well, I think I would have known it in a minute, but that raindrop made me quite sure. I'll always remember now. Shu-ya means rain, or "it is going to rain." Why, Daddy!' She got up and danced round him. 'S'pose you went out before I was awake, and drawed shu-ya in the smoke on the wall, I'd know it was going to rain and I'd take my beaver-skin hood. Wouldn't Mummy be surprised?'

Tegumai got up and danced. (Daddies didn't mind doing those things in those days.) 'More than that! More than that!' he said. 'S'pose I wanted to tell you it wasn't going to rain much and you must come down to the river, what would we draw? Say the words in Tegumai-talk first.'

'Shu-ya-las, ya maru. (Sky-water ending. River come to.) what a lot of new sounds! I don't see how we can draw them.'

'But I do—but I do!' said Tegumai. 'Just attend a minute, Taffy, and we won't do any more to-day. We've got shu-ya all right, haven't we? But this las is a teaser. La-la-la' and he waved his shark-tooth.

'There's the hissy-snake at the end and the carp-mouth before the snake—as-as-as. We only want la-la,' said Taffy.

'I know it, but we have to make la-la. And we're the first people in all the world who've ever tried to do it, Taffimai!'

'Well,' said Taffy, yawning, for she was rather tired. 'Las means breaking or finishing as well as ending, doesn't it?'

'So it does,' said Tegumai. 'To-las means that there's no water in the tank for Mummy to cook with—just when I'm going hunting, too.'

'And shi-las means that your spear is broken. If I'd only thought of that instead of drawing silly beaver pictures for the Stranger!'

'La! La! La!' said Tegumai, waiving his stick and frowning. 'Oh bother!'

'I could have drawn shi quite easily,' Taffy went on. 'Then I'd have drawn your spear all broken—this way!' And she drew. (14.)

'The very thing,' said Tegumai. 'That's la all over. It isn't like any of the other marks either.' And he drew this. (15.)

'Now for ya. Oh, we've done that before. Now for maru. Mum-mum-mum. Mum shuts one's mouth up, doesn't it? We'll draw a shut mouth like this.' And he drew. (16.)

'Then the carp-mouth open. That makes Ma-ma-ma! But what about this rrrrr-thing, Taffy?'

'It sounds all rough and edgy, like your shark-tooth saw when you're cutting out a plank for the canoe,' said Taffy.

'You mean all sharp at the edges, like this?' said Tegumai. And he drew. (17.)

''Xactly,' said Taffy. 'But we don't want all those teeth: only put two.'

'I'll only put in one,' said Tegumai. 'If this game of ours is going to be what I think it will, the easier we make our sound-pictures the better for everybody.' And he drew. (18.)

'Now, we've got it,' said Tegumai, standing on one leg. 'I'll draw 'em all in a string like fish.'

'Hadn't we better put a little bit of stick or something between each word, so's they won't rub up against each other and jostle, same as if they were carps?'

'Oh, I'll leave a space for that,' said her Daddy. And very incitedly he drew them all without stopping, on a big new bit of birch-bark. (19.)

'Shu-ya-las ya-maru,' said Taffy, reading it out sound by sound.

'That's enough for to-day,' said Tegumai. 'Besides, you're getting tired, Taffy. Never mind, dear. We'll finish it all to-morrow, and then we'll be remembered for years and years after the biggest trees you can see are all chopped up for firewood.'

So they went home, and all that evening Tegumai sat on one side of the fire and Taffy on the other, drawing ya's and yo's and shu's and shi's in the smoke on the wall and giggling together till her Mummy said, 'Really, Tegumai, you're worse than my Taffy.'

'Please don't mind,' said Taffy. 'It's only our secret-s'prise, Mummy dear, and we'll tell you all about it the very minute it's done; but please don't ask me what it is now, or else I'll have to tell.'

So her Mummy most carefully didn't; and bright and early next morning Tegumai went down to the river to think about new sound pictures, and when Taffy got up she saw Ya-las (water is ending or running out) chalked on the side of the big stone water-tank, outside the Cave.

'Um,' said Taffy. 'These picture-sounds are rather a bother! Daddy's just as good as come here himself and told me to get more water for Mummy to cook with.' She went to the spring at the back of the house and filled the tank from a bark bucket, and then she ran down to the river and pulled her Daddy's left ear—the one that belonged to her to pull when she was good.

'Now come along and we'll draw all the left-over sound-pictures,' said her Daddy, and they had a most inciting day of it, and a beautiful lunch in the middle, and two games of romps. When they came to T, Taffy said that as her name, and her Daddy's, and her Mummy's all began with that sound, they should draw a sort of family group of themselves holding hands. That was all very well to draw once or twice; but when it came to drawing it six or seven times, Taffy and Tegumai drew it scratchier and scratchier, till at last the T-sound was only a thin long Tegumai with his arms out to hold Taffy and Teshumai. You can see from these three pictures partly how it happened. (20, 21, 22.)

Many of the other pictures were much too beautiful to begin with, especially before lunch, but as they were drawn over and over again on birch-bark, they became plainer and easier, till at last even Tegumai said he could find no fault with them. They turned the hissy-snake the other way round for the Z-sound, to show it was hissing backwards in a soft and gentle way (23); and they just made a twiddle for E, because it came into the pictures so often (24); and they drew pictures of the sacred Beaver of the Tegumais for the B-sound (25, 26, 27, 28); and because it was a nasty, nosy noise, they just drew noses for the N-sound, till they were tired (29); and they drew a picture of the big lake-pike's mouth for the greedy Ga-sound (30); and they drew the pike's mouth again with a spear behind it for the scratchy, hurty Ka-sound (31); and they drew pictures of a little bit of the winding Wagai river for the nice windy-windy Wa-sound (32, 33); and so on and so forth and so following till they had done and drawn all the sound-pictures that they wanted, and there was the Alphabet, all complete.

And after thousands and thousands and thousands of years, and after Hieroglyphics and Demotics, and Nilotics, and Cryptics, and Cufics, and Runics, and Dorics, and Ionics, and all sorts of other ricks and tricks (because the Woons, and the Neguses, and the Akhoonds, and the Repositories of Tradition would never leave a good thing alone when they saw it), the fine old easy, understandable Alphabet—A, B, C, D, E, and the rest of 'em—got back into its proper shape again for all Best Beloveds to learn when they are old enough.

But I remember Tegumai Bopsulai, and Taffimai Metallumai and Teshumai Tewindrow, her dear Mummy, and all the days gone by. And it was so—just so—a little time ago—on the banks of the big Wagai!

OF all the Tribe of Tegumai
Who cut that figure, none remain,--
On Merrow Down the cuckoos cry
The silence and the sun remain.

But as the faithful years return
And hearts unwounded sing again,
Comes Taffy dancing through the fern
To lead the Surrey spring again.

Her brows are bound with bracken-fronds,
And golden elf-locks fly above;
Her eyes are bright as diamonds
And bluer than the skies above.

In mocassins and deer-skin cloak,
Unfearing, free and fair she flits,
And lights her little damp-wood smoke
To show her Daddy where she flits.

For far--oh, very far behind,
So far she cannot call to him,
Comes Tegumai alone to find
The daughter that was all to him.

THE CRAB THAT PLAYED WITH THE SEA

EFORE the High and Far-Off Times, O my Best Beloved, came the Time of the Very Beginnings; and that was in the days when the Eldest Magician was getting Things ready. First he got the Earth ready; then he got the Sea ready; and then he told all the Animals that they could come out and play. And the Animals said, 'O Eldest Magician, what shall we play at?' and he said, 'I will show you. He took the Elephant—All-the-Elephant-there-was—and said, 'Play at being an Elephant,' and All-the-Elephant-there-was played. He took the Beaver—All-the-Beaver-there-was and said, 'Play at being a Beaver,' and All-the Beaver-there-was played. He took the Cow—All-the Cow-there-was—and said, 'Play at being a Cow,' and All-the-Cow-there-was played. He took the Turtle—All-the-Turtle there-was and said, 'Play at being a Turtle,' and All-the-Turtle-there-was played. One by one he took all the beasts and birds and fishes and told them what to play at.

But towards evening, when people and things grow restless and tired, there came up the Man (With his own little girl-daughter?)—Yes, with his own best beloved little girl-daughter sitting upon his shoulder, and he said, 'What is this play, Eldest Magician?' And the Eldest Magician said, 'Ho, Son of Adam, this is the play of the Very Beginning; but you are too wise for this play.' And the Man saluted and said, 'Yes, I am too wise for this play; but see that you make all the Animals obedient to me.'

Now, while the two were talking together, Pau Amma the Crab, who was next in the game, scuttled off sideways and stepped into the sea, saying to himself, 'I will play my play alone in the deep waters, and I will never be obedient to this son of Adam.' Nobody saw him go away except the little girl-daughter where she leaned on the Man's shoulder. And the play went on till there were no more Animals left without orders; and the Eldest Magician wiped the fine dust off his hands and walked about the world to see how the Animals were playing.

He went North, Best Beloved, and he found All-the-Elephant-there-was digging with his tusks and stamping with his feet in the nice new clean earth that had been made ready for him.

'Kun?' said All-the-Elephant-there-was, meaning, 'Is this right?'

'Payah kun,' said the Eldest Magician, meaning, 'That is quite right'; and he breathed upon the great rocks and lumps of earth that All-the-Elephant-there-was had thrown up, and they became the great Himalayan Mountains, and you can look them out on the map.

He went East, and he found All-the-Cow there-was feeding in the field that had been made ready for her, and she licked her tongue round a whole forest at a time, and swallowed it and sat down to chew her cud.

'Kun?' said All-the-Cow-there-was.

'Payah kun,' said the Eldest Magician; and he breathed upon the bare patch where she had eaten, and upon the place where she had sat down, and one became the great Indian

Desert, and the other became the Desert of Sahara, and you can look them out on the map.

He went West, and he found All-the-Beaver-there-was making a beaver-dam across the mouths of broad rivers that had been got ready for him.

'Kun?' said All-the-Beaver-there-was.

'Payah kun,' said the Eldest Magician; and he breathed upon the fallen trees and the still water, and they became the Everglades in Florida, and you may look them out on the map.

Then he went South and found All-the-Turtle-there-was scratching with his flippers in the sand that had been got ready for him, and the sand and the rocks whirled through the air and fell far off into the sea.

'Kun?' said All-the-Turtle-there-was.

'Payah kun,' said the Eldest Magician; and he breathed upon the sand and the rocks, where they had fallen in the sea, and they became the most beautiful islands of Borneo, Celebes, Sumatra, Java, and the rest of the Malay Archipelago, and you can look them out on the map!

By and by the Eldest Magician met the Man on the banks of the Perak river, and said, 'Ho! Son of Adam, are all the Animals obedient to you?'

'Yes,' said the Man.

'Is all the Earth obedient to you?'

'Yes,' said the Man.

'Is all the Sea obedient to you?'

'No,' said the Man. 'Once a day and once a night the Sea runs up the Perak river and drives the sweet-water back into the forest, so that my house is made wet; once a day and once a night it runs down the river and draws all the water after it, so that there is nothing left but mud, and my canoe is upset. Is that the play you told it to play?'

'No,' said the Eldest Magician. 'That is a new and a bad play.'

'Look!' said the Man, and as he spoke the great Sea came up the mouth of the Perak river, driving the river backwards till it overflowed all the dark forests for miles and miles, and flooded the Man's house.

'This is wrong. Launch your canoe and we will find out who is playing with the Sea,' said the Eldest Magician. They stepped into the canoe; the little girl-daughter came with them; and the Man took his kris—a curving, wavy dagger with a blade like a flame,—and they pushed out on the Perak river. Then the sea began to run back and back, and the canoe was sucked out of the mouth of the Perak river, past Selangor, past Malacca, past Singapore, out and out to the Island of Bingtang, as though it had been pulled by a string.

Then the Eldest Magician stood up and shouted, 'Ho! beasts, birds, and fishes, that I took between my hands at the Very Beginning and taught the play that you should play, which one of you is playing with the Sea?'

Then all the beasts, birds, and fishes said together, 'Eldest Magician, we play the plays that you taught us to play—we and our children's children. But not one of us plays with the Sea.'

Then the Moon rose big and full over the water, and the Eldest Magician said to the hunchbacked old man who sits in the Moon spinning a fishing-line with which he hopes one day to catch the world, 'Ho! Fisher of the Moon, are you playing with the Sea?'

'No,' said the Fisherman, 'I am spinning a line with which I shall some day catch the world; but I do not play with the Sea.' And he went on spinning his line.

Now there is also a Rat up in the Moon who always bites the old Fisherman's line as fast as it is made, and the Eldest Magician said to him, 'Ho! Rat of the Moon, are you playing with the Sea?'

And the Rat said, 'I am too busy biting through the line that this old Fisherman is spinning. I do not play with the Sea.' And he went on biting the line.

Then the little girl-daughter put up her little soft brown arms with the beautiful white shell bracelets and said, 'O Eldest Magician! when my father here talked to you at the Very Beginning, and I leaned upon his shoulder while the beasts were being taught their plays, one beast went away naughtily into the Sea before you had taught him his play.

And the Eldest Magician said, 'How wise are little children who see and are silent! What was the beast like?'

And the little girl-daughter said, 'He was round and he was flat; and his eyes grew upon stalks; and he walked sideways like this; and he was covered with strong armour upon his back.'

And the Eldest Magician said, 'How wise are little children who speak truth! Now I know where Pau Amma went. Give me the paddle!'

So he took the paddle; but there was no need to paddle, for the water flowed steadily past all the islands till they came to the place called Pusat Tasek—the Heart of the Sea—where the great hollow is that leads down to the heart of the world, and in that hollow grows the Wonderful Tree, Pauh Janggi, that bears the magic twin nuts. Then the Eldest Magician slid his arm up to the shoulder through the deep warm water, and under the roots of the Wonderful Tree he touched the broad back of Pau Amma the Crab. And Pau Amma settled down at the touch, and all the Sea rose up as water rises in a basin when you put your hand into it.

'Ah!' said the Eldest Magician. 'Now I know who has been playing with the Sea;' and he called out, 'What are you doing, Pau Amma?'

And Pau Amma, deep down below, answered, 'Once a day and once a night I go out to look for my food. Once a day and once a night I return. Leave me alone.'

Then the Eldest Magician said, 'Listen, Pau Amma. When you go out from your cave the waters of the Sea pour down into Pusat Tasek, and all the beaches of all the islands are left bare, and the little fish die, and Raja Moyang Kaban, the King of the Elephants, his legs are made muddy. When you come back and sit in Pusat Tasek, the waters of the Sea rise, and half the little islands are drowned, and the Man's house is flooded, and Raja Abdullah, the King of the Crocodiles, his mouth is filled with the salt water.

Then Pau Amma, deep down below, laughed and said, 'I did not know I was so important. Henceforward I will go out seven times a day, and the waters shall never be still.'

And the Eldest Magician said, 'I cannot make you play the play you were meant to play, Pau Amma, because you escaped me at the Very Beginning; but if you are not afraid, come up and we will talk about it.'

'I am not afraid,' said Pau Amma, and he rose to the top of the sea in the moonlight. There was nobody in the world so big as Pau Amma—for he was the King Crab of all Crabs. Not a common Crab, but a King Crab. One side of his great shell touched the beach at Sarawak; the other touched the beach at Pahang; and he was taller than the smoke of three volcanoes! As he rose up through the branches of the Wonderful Tree he tore off one of the great twin fruits—the magic double kernelled nuts that make people young,—and the little girl-daughter saw it bobbing alongside the canoe, and pulled it in and began to pick out the soft eyes of it with her little golden scissors.

'Now,' said the Magician, 'make a Magic, Pau Amma, to show that you are really important.'

Pau Amma rolled his eyes and waved his legs, but he could only stir up the Sea, because, though he was a King Crab, he was nothing more than a Crab, and the Eldest Magician laughed.

'You are not so important after all, Pau Amma,' he said. 'Now, let me try,' and he made a Magic with his left hand—with just the little finger of his left hand—and—lo and behold, Best Beloved, Pau Amma's hard, blue-green-black shell fell off him as a husk falls off a cocoa-nut, and Pau Amma was left all soft—soft as the little crabs that you sometimes find on the beach, Best Beloved.

'Indeed, you are very important,' said the Eldest Magician. 'Shall I ask the Man here to cut you with kris? Shall I send for Raja Moyang Kaban, the King of the Elephants, to pierce you with his tusks, or shall I call Raja Abdullah, the King of the Crocodiles, to bite you?'

And Pau Amma said, 'I am ashamed! Give me back my hard shell and let me go back to Pusat Tasek, and I will only stir out once a day and once a night to get my food.'

And the Eldest Magician said, 'No, Pau Amma, I will not give you back your shell, for you will grow bigger and prouder and stronger, and perhaps you will forget your promise, and you will play with the Sea once more.

Then Pau Amma said, 'What shall I do? I am so big that I can only hide in Pusat Tasek, and if I go anywhere else, all soft as I am now, the sharks and the dogfish will eat me. And if I go to Pusat Tasek, all soft as I am now, though I may be safe, I can never stir out to get my food, and so I shall die.' Then he waved his legs and lamented.

'Listen, Pau Amma,' said the Eldest Magician. 'I cannot make you play the play you were meant to play, because you escaped me at the Very Beginning; but if you choose, I can make every stone and every hole and every bunch of weed in all the seas a safe Pusat Tasek for you and your children for always.'

Then Pau Amma said, 'That is good, but I do not choose yet. Look! there is that Man who talked to you at the Very Beginning. If he had not taken up your attention I should not have grown tired of waiting and run away, and all this would never have happened. What will he do for me?'

And the Man said, 'If you choose, I will make a Magic, so that both the deep water and the dry ground will be a home for you and your children—so that you shall be able to hide both on the land and in the sea.'

And Pau Amma said, 'I do not choose yet. Look! there is that girl who saw me running away at the Very Beginning. If she had spoken then, the Eldest Magician would have called me back, and all this would never have happened. What will she do for me?'

And the little girl-daughter said, 'This is a good nut that I am eating. If you choose, I will make a Magic and I will give you this pair of scissors, very sharp and strong, so that you and your children can eat cocoa-nuts like this all day long when you come up from the Sea to the land; or you can dig a Pusat Tasek for yourself with the scissors that belong to you when there is no stone or hole near by; and when the earth is too hard, by the help of these same scissors you can run up a tree.'

And Pau Amma said, 'I do not choose yet, for, all soft as I am, these gifts would not help me. Give me back my shell, O Eldest Magician, and then I will play your play.'

And the Eldest Magician said, 'I will give it back, Pau Amma, for eleven months of the year; but on the twelfth month of every year it shall grow soft again, to remind you and all your children that I can make magics, and to keep you humble, Pau Amma; for I see that if you can run both under the water and on land, you will grow too bold; and if you can climb trees and crack nuts and dig holes with your scissors, you will grow too greedy, Pau Amma.'

Then Pau Amma thought a little and said, 'I have made my choice. I will take all the gifts.'

Then the Eldest Magician made a Magic with the right hand, with all five fingers of his right hand, and lo and behold, Best Beloved, Pau Amma grew smaller and smaller and smaller, till at last there was only a little green crab swimming in the water alongside the canoe, crying in a very small voice, 'Give me the scissors!'

And the girl-daughter picked him up on the palm of her little brown hand, and sat him in the bottom of the canoe and gave him her scissors, and he waved them in his little arms, and opened them and shut them and snapped them, and said, 'I can eat nuts. I can crack shells. I can dig holes. I can climb trees. I can breathe in the dry air, and I can find a safe Pusat Tasek under every stone. I did not know I was so important. Kun?' (Is this right?)

'Payah-kun,' said the Eldest Magician, and he laughed and gave him his blessing; and little Pau Amma scuttled over the side of the canoe into the water; and he was so tiny that he could have hidden under the shadow of a dry leaf on land or of a dead shell at the bottom of the sea.

'Was that well done?' said the Eldest Magician.

'Yes,' said the Man. 'But now we must go back to Perak, and that is a weary way to paddle. If we had waited till Pau

Amma had gone out of Pusat Tasek and come home, the water would have carried us there by itself.'

'You are lazy,' said the Eldest Magician. 'So your children shall be lazy. They shall be the laziest people in the world. They shall be called the Malazy—the lazy people;' and he held up his finger to the Moon and said, 'O Fisherman, here is the Man too lazy to row home. Pull his canoe home with your line, Fisherman.'

'No,' said the Man. 'If I am to be lazy all my days, let the Sea work for me twice a day for ever. That will save paddling.'

And the Eldest Magician laughed and said, 'Payah kun' (That is right).

And the Rat of the Moon stopped biting the line; and the Fisherman let his line down till it touched the Sea, and he pulled the whole deep Sea along, past the Island of Bintang, past Singapore, past Malacca, past Selangor, till the canoe whirled into the mouth of the Perak River again. Kun?' said the Fisherman of the Moon.

'Payah kun,' said the Eldest Magician. 'See now that you pull the Sea twice a day and twice a night for ever, so that the Malazy fishermen may be saved paddling. But be careful not to do it too hard, or I shall make a magic on you as I did to Pau Amma.'

Then they all went up the Perak River and went to bed, Best Beloved.

Now listen and attend!

From that day to this the Moon has always pulled the sea up and down and made what we call the tides. Sometimes the Fisher of the Sea pulls a little too hard, and then we get spring tides; and sometimes he pulls a little too softly, and then we get what are called neap-tides; but nearly always he is careful, because of the Eldest Magician.

And Pau Amma? You can see when you go to the beach, how all Pau Amma's babies make little Pusat Taseks for themselves under every stone and bunch of weed on the sands; you can see them waving their little scissors; and in some parts of the world they truly live on the dry land and run up the palm trees and eat cocoa-nuts, exactly as the girl-daughter promised. But once a year all Pau Ammas must shake off their hard armour and be soft—to remind them of what the Eldest Magician could do. And so it isn't fair to kill or hunt Pau Amma's babies just because old Pau Amma was stupidly rude a very long time ago.

Oh yes! And Pau Amma's babies hate being taken out of their little Pusat Taseks and brought home in pickle-bottles. That is why they nip you with their scissors, and it serves you right!

> *CHINA-GOING P's and O's*
> *Pass Pau Amma's playground close,*
> *And his Pusat Tasek lies*
> *Near the track of most B.I.'s.*
> *U.Y.K. and N.D.L.*
> *Know Pau Amma's home as well*
> *As the fisher of the Sea knows*
> *'Bens,' M.M.'s, and Rubattinos.*
> *But (and this is rather queer)*
> *A.T.L.'s can not come here;*
> *O. and O. and D.O.A.*
> *Must go round another way.*
> *Orient, Anchor, Bibby, Hall,*
> *Never go that way at all.*

U.C.S. would have a fit

If it found itself on it.

And if 'Beavers' took their cargoes

To Penang instead of Lagos,

Or a fat Shaw-Savill bore

Passengers to Singapore,

Or a White Star were to try a

Little trip to Sourabaya,

Or a B.S.A. went on

Past Natal to Cheribon,

Then great Mr. Lloyds would come

With a wire and drag them home!

You'll know what my riddle means

When you've eaten mangosteens.

You'll know what my riddle means

When you've eaten mangosteens.

Or if you can't wait till then, ask them to let you have the outside page of the Times; turn over to page 2 where it is marked 'Shipping' on the top left hand; then take the Atlas (and that is the finest picture-book in the world) and see how the names of the places that the steamers go to fit into the names of the places on the map. Any steamer-kiddy ought to be able to do that; but if you can't read, ask some one to show it you.

THE CAT THAT WALKED BY HIMSELF

HEAR and attend and listen; for this befell and behappened and became and was, O my Best Beloved, when the Tame animals were wild. The Dog was wild, and the Horse was wild, and the Cow was wild, and the Sheep was wild, and the Pig was wild—as wild as wild could be—and they walked in the Wet Wild Woods by their wild lones. But the wildest of all the wild animals was the Cat. He walked by himself, and all places were alike to him.

Of course the Man was wild too. He was dreadfully wild. He didn't even begin to be tame till he met the Woman, and she told him that she did not like living in his wild ways. She picked out a nice dry Cave, instead of a heap of wet leaves, to lie down in; and she strewed clean sand on the floor; and she lit a nice fire of wood at the back of the Cave; and she hung a dried wild-horse skin, tail-down, across the opening of the Cave; and she said, 'Wipe you feet, dear, when you come in, and now we'll keep house.'

That night, Best Beloved, they ate wild sheep roasted on the hot stones, and flavoured with wild garlic and wild pepper; and wild duck stuffed with wild rice and wild fenugreek and wild coriander; and marrow-bones of wild oxen; and wild cherries, and wild grenadillas. Then the Man went to sleep in front of the fire ever so happy; but the Woman sat up, combing her hair. She took the bone of the shoulder of mutton—the big fat blade-bone—and she looked at the wonderful marks on it, and she threw more wood on the fire, and she made a Magic. She made the First Singing Magic in the world.

Out in the Wet Wild Woods all the wild animals gathered together where they could see the light of the fire a long way off, and they wondered what it meant.

Then Wild Horse stamped with his wild foot and said, 'O my Friends and O my Enemies, why have the Man and the Woman made that great light in that great Cave, and what harm will it do us?'

Wild Dog lifted up his wild nose and smelled the smell of roast mutton, and said, 'I will go up and see and look, and say; for I think it is good. Cat, come with me.'

'Nenni!' said the Cat. 'I am the Cat who walks by himself, and all places are alike to me. I will not come.'

'Then we can never be friends again,' said Wild Dog, and he trotted off to the Cave. But when he had gone a little way the Cat said to himself, 'All places are alike to me. Why should I not go too and see and look and come away at my own liking.' So he slipped after Wild Dog softly, very softly, and hid himself where he could hear everything.

When Wild Dog reached the mouth of the Cave he lifted up the dried horse-skin with his nose and sniffed the beautiful smell of the roast mutton, and the Woman, looking at the blade-bone, heard him, and laughed, and said, 'Here comes the first. Wild Thing out of the Wild Woods, what do you want?'

Wild Dog said, 'O my Enemy and Wife of my Enemy, what is this that smells so good in the Wild Woods?'

Then the Woman picked up a roasted mutton-bone and threw it to Wild Dog, and said, 'Wild Thing out of the Wild Woods, taste and try.' Wild Dog gnawed the bone, and it was more delicious than anything he had ever tasted, and he said, 'O my Enemy and Wife of my Enemy, give me another.'

The Woman said, 'Wild Thing out of the Wild Woods, help my Man to hunt through the day and guard this Cave at night, and I will give you as many roast bones as you need.'

'Ah!' said the Cat, listening. 'This is a very wise Woman, but she is not so wise as I am.'

Wild Dog crawled into the Cave and laid his head on the Woman's lap, and said, 'O my Friend and Wife of my Friend, I will help Your Man to hunt through the day, and at night I will guard your Cave.'

'Ah!' said the Cat, listening. 'That is a very foolish Dog.' And he went back through the Wet Wild Woods waving his wild tail, and walking by his wild lone. But he never told anybody.

When the Man waked up he said, 'What is Wild Dog doing here?' And the Woman said, 'His name is not Wild Dog any more, but the First Friend, because he will be our friend for always and always and always. Take him with you when you go hunting.'

Next night the Woman cut great green armfuls of fresh grass from the water-meadows, and dried it before the fire, so that it smelt like new-mown hay, and she sat at the mouth of the Cave and plaited a halter out of horse-hide, and she looked at the shoulder of mutton-bone—at the big broad blade-bone—and she made a Magic. She made the Second Singing Magic in the world.

Out in the Wild Woods all the wild animals wondered what had happened to Wild Dog, and at last Wild Horse stamped with his foot and said, 'I will go and see and say why Wild Dog has not returned. Cat, come with me.'

'Nenni!' said the Cat. 'I am the Cat who walks by himself, and all places are alike to me. I will not come.' But all the same he followed Wild Horse softly, very softly, and hid himself where he could hear everything.

When the Woman heard Wild Horse tripping and stumbling on his long mane, she laughed and said, 'Here comes the second. Wild Thing out of the Wild Woods what do you want?'

Wild Horse said, 'O my Enemy and Wife of my Enemy, where is Wild Dog?'

The Woman laughed, and picked up the blade-bone and looked at it, and said, 'Wild Thing out of the Wild Woods, you did not come here for Wild Dog, but for the sake of this good grass.'

And Wild Horse, tripping and stumbling on his long mane, said, 'That is true; give it me to eat.'

The Woman said, 'Wild Thing out of the Wild Woods, bend your wild head and wear what I give you, and you shall eat the wonderful grass three times a day.'

'Ah,' said the Cat, listening, 'this is a clever Woman, but she is not so clever as I am.' Wild Horse bent his wild head, and the Woman slipped the plaited hide halter over it, and Wild Horse breathed on the Woman's feet and said, 'O my Mistress, and Wife of my Master, I will be your servant for the sake of the wonderful grass.'

'Ah,' said the Cat, listening, 'that is a very foolish Horse.' And he went back through the Wet Wild Woods, waving his wild tail and walking by his wild lone. But he never told anybody.

When the Man and the Dog came back from hunting, the Man said, 'What is Wild Horse doing here?' And the Woman said, 'His name is not Wild Horse any more, but the First Servant, because he will carry us from place to place for always and always and always. Ride on his back when you go hunting.

Next day, holding her wild head high that her wild horns should not catch in the wild trees, Wild Cow came up to the Cave, and the Cat followed, and hid himself just the same as before; and everything happened just the same as before; and the Cat said the same things as before, and when Wild Cow had promised to give her milk to the Woman every day in exchange for the wonderful grass, the Cat went back through the Wet Wild Woods waving his wild tail and walking by his wild lone, just the same as before. But he never told anybody. And when the Man and the Horse and the Dog came home from hunting and asked the same questions same as before, the Woman said, 'Her name is not Wild Cow any more, but the Giver of Good Food. She will give us the warm white milk for always and always and always, and I will take care of her while you and the First Friend and the First Servant go hunting.

Next day the Cat waited to see if any other Wild thing would go up to the Cave, but no one moved in the Wet Wild Woods, so the Cat walked there by himself; and he saw the Woman milking the Cow, and he saw the light of the fire in the Cave, and he smelt the smell of the warm white milk.

Cat said, 'O my Enemy and Wife of my Enemy, where did Wild Cow go?'

The Woman laughed and said, 'Wild Thing out of the Wild Woods, go back to the Woods again, for I have braided up my hair, and I have put away the magic blade-bone, and we have no more need of either friends or servants in our Cave.

Cat said, 'I am not a friend, and I am not a servant. I am the Cat who walks by himself, and I wish to come into your cave.'

Woman said, 'Then why did you not come with First Friend on the first night?'

Cat grew very angry and said, 'Has Wild Dog told tales of me?'

Then the Woman laughed and said, 'You are the Cat who walks by himself, and all places are alike to you. Your are neither a friend nor a servant. You have said it yourself. Go away and walk by yourself in all places alike.'

Then Cat pretended to be sorry and said, 'Must I never come into the Cave? Must I never sit by the warm fire? Must I never drink the warm white milk? You are very wise and very beautiful. You should not be cruel even to a Cat.'

Woman said, 'I knew I was wise, but I did not know I was beautiful. So I will make a bargain with you. If ever I say one word in your praise you may come into the Cave.'

'And if you say two words in my praise?' said the Cat.

'I never shall,' said the Woman, 'but if I say two words in your praise, you may sit by the fire in the Cave.'

'And if you say three words?' said the Cat.

'I never shall,' said the Woman, 'but if I say three words in your praise, you may drink the warm white milk three times a day for always and always and always.'

Then the Cat arched his back and said, 'Now let the Curtain at the mouth of the Cave, and the Fire at the back of the Cave, and the Milk-pots that stand beside the Fire, remember what my Enemy and the Wife of my Enemy has said.' And he went away through the Wet Wild Woods waving his wild tail and walking by his wild lone.

That night when the Man and the Horse and the Dog came home from hunting, the Woman did not tell them of the bargain that she had made with the Cat, because she was afraid that they might not like it.

Cat went far and far away and hid himself in the Wet Wild Woods by his wild lone for a long time till the Woman forgot all about him. Only the Bat—the little upside-down Bat— that hung inside the Cave, knew where Cat hid; and every evening Bat would fly to Cat with news of what was happening.

One evening Bat said, 'There is a Baby in the Cave. He is new and pink and fat and small, and the Woman is very fond of him.'

'Ah,' said the Cat, listening, 'but what is the Baby fond of?'

'He is fond of things that are soft and tickle,' said the Bat. 'He is fond of warm things to hold in his arms when he goes to sleep. He is fond of being played with. He is fond of all those things.'

'Ah,' said the Cat, listening, 'then my time has come.'

Next night Cat walked through the Wet Wild Woods and hid very near the Cave till morning-time, and Man and Dog and Horse went hunting. The Woman was busy cooking that morning, and the Baby cried and interrupted. So she carried him outside the Cave and gave him a handful of pebbles to play with. But still the Baby cried.

Then the Cat put out his paddy paw and patted the Baby on the cheek, and it cooed; and the Cat rubbed against its fat knees and tickled it under its fat chin with his tail. And the Baby laughed; and the Woman heard him and smiled.

Then the Bat—the little upside-down bat—that hung in the mouth of the Cave said, 'O my Hostess and Wife of my

Host and Mother of my Host's Son, a Wild Thing from the Wild Woods is most beautifully playing with your Baby.'

'A blessing on that Wild Thing whoever he may be,' said the Woman, straightening her back, 'for I was a busy woman this morning and he has done me a service.'

That very minute and second, Best Beloved, the dried horse-skin Curtain that was stretched tail-down at the mouth of the Cave fell down—whoosh!—because it remembered the bargain she had made with the Cat, and when the Woman went to pick it up—lo and behold!—the Cat was sitting quite comfy inside the Cave.

'O my Enemy and Wife of my Enemy and Mother of my Enemy,' said the Cat, 'it is I: for you have spoken a word in my praise, and now I can sit within the Cave for always and always and always. But still I am the Cat who walks by himself, and all places are alike to me.'

The Woman was very angry, and shut her lips tight and took up her spinning-wheel and began to spin. But the Baby cried because the Cat had gone away, and the Woman could not hush it, for it struggled and kicked and grew black in the face.

'O my Enemy and Wife of my Enemy and Mother of my Enemy,' said the Cat, 'take a strand of the wire that you are spinning and tie it to your spinning-whorl and drag it along the floor, and I will show you a magic that shall make your Baby laugh as loudly as he is now crying.'

'I will do so,' said the Woman, 'because I am at my wits' end; but I will not thank you for it.'

She tied the thread to the little clay spindle whorl and drew it across the floor, and the Cat ran after it and patted it with his paws and rolled head over heels, and tossed it backward over his shoulder and chased it between his hind-legs and pretended to lose it, and pounced down upon it again, till the Baby laughed as loudly as it had been crying, and scrambled after the Cat and frolicked all over the Cave till it grew tired and settled down to sleep with the Cat in its arms.

'Now,' said the Cat, 'I will sing the Baby a song that shall keep him asleep for an hour. And he began to purr, loud and low, low and loud, till the Baby fell fast asleep. The Woman smiled as she looked down upon the two of them and said, 'That was wonderfully done. No question but you are very clever, O Cat.'

That very minute and second, Best Beloved, the smoke of the fire at the back of the Cave came down in clouds from the roof—puff!—because it remembered the bargain she had made with the Cat, and when it had cleared away—lo and behold!—the Cat was sitting quite comfy close to the fire.

'O my Enemy and Wife of my Enemy and Mother of My Enemy,' said the Cat, 'it is I, for you have spoken a second word in my praise, and now I can sit by the warm fire at the back of the Cave for always and always and always. But still I am the Cat who walks by himself, and all places are alike to me.'

Then the Woman was very very angry, and let down her hair and put more wood on the fire and brought out the broad blade-bone of the shoulder of mutton and began to make a Magic that should prevent her from saying a third word in praise of the Cat. It was not a Singing Magic, Best Beloved, it was a Still Magic; and by and by the Cave grew so still that a little wee-wee mouse crept out of a corner and ran across the floor.

'O my Enemy and Wife of my Enemy and Mother of my Enemy,' said the Cat, 'is that little mouse part of your magic?'

'Ouh! Chee! No indeed!' said the Woman, and she dropped the blade-bone and jumped upon the footstool in front of the fire and braided up her hair very quick for fear that the mouse should run up it.

'Ah,' said the Cat, watching, 'then the mouse will do me no harm if I eat it?'

'No,' said the Woman, braiding up her hair, 'eat it quickly and I will ever be grateful to you.'

Cat made one jump and caught the little mouse, and the Woman said, 'A hundred thanks. Even the First Friend is not quick enough to catch little mice as you have done. You must be very wise.'

That very moment and second, O Best Beloved, the Milk-pot that stood by the fire cracked in two pieces—ffft—because it remembered the bargain she had made with the Cat, and when the Woman jumped down from the footstool—lo and behold!—the Cat was lapping up the warm white milk that lay in one of the broken pieces.

'O my Enemy and Wife of my Enemy and Mother of my Enemy,' said the Cat, 'it is I; for you have spoken three words in my praise, and now I can drink the warm white milk three times a day for always and always and always. But still I am the Cat who walks by himself, and all places are alike to me.'

Then the Woman laughed and set the Cat a bowl of the warm white milk and said, 'O Cat, you are as clever as a man, but remember that your bargain was not made with the Man or the Dog, and I do not know what they will do when they come home.'

'What is that to me?' said the Cat. 'If I have my place in the Cave by the fire and my warm white milk three times a day I do not care what the Man or the Dog can do.'

That evening when the Man and the Dog came into the Cave, the Woman told them all the story of the bargain while the Cat sat by the fire and smiled. Then the Man said, 'Yes, but he has not made a bargain with me or with all proper Men after me.' Then he took off his two leather boots and he took up his little stone axe (that makes three) and he fetched a piece of wood and a hatchet (that is five altogether), and he set them out in a row and he said, 'Now we will make our bargain. If you do not catch mice when you are in the Cave for always and always and always, I will throw these five things at you whenever I see you, and so shall all proper Men do after me.'

'Ah,' said the Woman, listening, 'this is a very clever Cat, but he is not so clever as my Man.'

The Cat counted the five things (and they looked very knobby) and he said, 'I will catch mice when I am in the Cave for always and always and always; but still I am the Cat who walks by himself, and all places are alike to me.'

'Not when I am near,' said the Man. 'If you had not said that last I would have put all these things away for always and always and always; but I am now going to throw my two boots and my little stone axe (that makes three) at you whenever I meet you. And so shall all proper Men do after me!'

Then the Dog said, 'Wait a minute. He has not made a bargain with me or with all proper Dogs after me.' And he showed his teeth and said, 'If you are not kind to the Baby while I am in the Cave for always and always and always, I will hunt you till I catch you, and when I catch you I will bite you. And so shall all proper Dogs do after me.'

'Ah,' said the Woman, listening, 'this is a very clever Cat, but he is not so clever as the Dog.'

Cat counted the Dog's teeth (and they looked very pointed) and he said, 'I will be kind to the Baby while I am in the Cave, as long as he does not pull my tail too hard, for always and always and always. But still I am the Cat that walks by himself, and all places are alike to me.'

'Not when I am near,' said the Dog. 'If you had not said that last I would have shut my mouth for always and always and always; but now I am going to hunt you up a tree whenever I meet you. And so shall all proper Dogs do after me.'

Then the Man threw his two boots and his little stone axe (that makes three) at the Cat, and the Cat ran out of the Cave and the Dog chased him up a tree; and from that day to this, Best Beloved, three proper Men out of five will always throw things at a Cat whenever they meet him, and all proper Dogs will chase him up a tree. But the Cat keeps his side of the bargain too. He will kill mice and he will be kind to Babies when he is in the house, just as long as they do not pull his tail too hard. But when he has done that, and between times, and when the moon gets up and night comes, he is the Cat that walks by himself, and all places are alike to him. Then he goes out to the Wet Wild Woods or up the Wet Wild Trees or on the Wet Wild Roofs, waving his wild tail and walking by his wild lone.

> *PUSSY can sit by the fire and sing,*
>
> *Pussy can climb a tree,*
>
> *Or play with a silly old cork and string*
>
> *To'muse herself, not me.*
>
> *But I like Binkie my dog, because*
>
> *He Lnows how to behave;*
>
> *So, Binkie's the same as the First Friend was,*
>
> *And I am the Man in the Cave.*

> *Pussy will play man-Friday till*
>
> *It's time to wet her paw*
>
> *And make her walk on the window-sill*

(For the footprint Crusoe saw);
Then she fluffles her tail and mews,
And scratches and won't attend.
But Binkie will play whatever I choose,
And he is my true First Friend.

Pussy will rub my knees with her head
Pretending she loves me hard;
But the very minute I go to my bed
Pussy runs out in the yard,
And there she stays till the morning-light;
So I know it is only pretend;
But Binkie, he snores at my feet all night,
And he is my Firstest Friend!

THE BUTTERFLY THAT STAMPED

THIS, O my Best Beloved, is a story—a new and a wonderful story—a story quite different from the other stories—a story about The Most Wise Sovereign Suleiman-bin-Daoud—Solomon the Son of David.

There are three hundred and fifty-five stories about Suleiman-bin-Daoud; but this is not one of them. It is not the story of the Lapwing who found the Water; or the Hoopoe who shaded Suleimanbin-Daoud from the heat. It is not the story of the Glass Pavement, or the Ruby with the Crooked Hole, or the Gold Bars of Balkis. It is the story of the Butterfly that Stamped.

Now attend all over again and listen!

Suleiman-bin-Daoud was wise. He understood what the beasts said, what the birds said, what the fishes said, and what the insects said. He understood what the rocks said deep under the earth when they bowed in towards each other and groaned; and he understood what the trees said when they rustled in the middle of the morning. He understood everything, from the bishop on the bench to the hyssop on the wall, and Balkis, his Head Queen, the Most Beautiful Queen Balkis, was nearly as wise as he was.

Suleiman-bin-Daoud was strong. Upon the third finger of the right hand he wore a ring. When he turned it once, Afrits and Djinns came Out of the earth to do whatever he told them. When he turned it twice, Fairies came down from the sky to do whatever he told them; and when he turned it three times, the very great angel Azrael of the Sword came dressed as a water-carrier, and told him the news of the three worlds, Above—Below—and Here.

And yet Suleiman-bin-Daoud was not proud. He very seldom showed off, and when he did he was sorry for it. Once he tried to feed all the animals in all the world in one day, but when the food was ready an Animal came out of the deep sea and ate it up in three mouthfuls. Suleiman-bin-Daoud was very surprised and said, 'O Animal, who are you?' And the Animal said, 'O King, live for ever! I am the smallest of thirty thousand brothers, and our home is at the bottom of the sea. We heard that you were going to feed all the animals in all the world, and my brothers sent me to ask when dinner would be ready.' Suleiman-bin-Daoud was more surprised than ever and said, 'O Animal, you have eaten all the dinner that I made ready for all the animals in the world.' And the Animal said, 'O King, live for ever, but do you really call that a dinner? Where I come from we each eat twice as much as that between meals.' Then Suleiman-bin-Daoud fell flat on his face and said, 'O Animal! I gave that dinner to show what a great and rich king I was, and not because I really wanted to be kind to the animals. Now I am ashamed, and it serves me right. Suleiman-bin-Daoud was a really truly wise man, Best Beloved. After that he never forgot that it was silly to show off; and now the real story part of my story begins.

He married ever so many wifes. He married nine hundred and ninety-nine wives, besides the Most Beautiful Balkis; and they all lived in a great golden palace in the middle of a lovely garden with fountains. He didn't really want nine-hundred and ninety-nine wives, but in those days everybody married ever so many wives, and of course the King had to marry ever so many more just to show that he was the King.

Some of the wives were nice, but some were simply horrid, and the horrid ones quarrelled with the nice ones and made them horrid too, and then they would all quarrel with Suleiman-bin-Daoud, and that was horrid for him. But Balkis the Most Beautiful never quarrelled with Suleiman-bin-Daoud. She loved him too much. She sat in her rooms in the Golden Palace, or walked in the Palace garden, and was truly sorry for him.

Of course if he had chosen to turn his ring on his finger and call up the Djinns and the Afrits they would have magicked all those nine hundred and ninety-nine quarrelsome wives into white mules of the desert or greyhounds or pomegranate seeds; but Suleiman-bin-Daoud thought that that would be showing off. So, when they quarrelled too much, he only walked by himself in one part of the beautiful Palace gardens and wished he had never been born.

One day, when they had quarrelled for three weeks—all nine hundred and ninety-nine wives together—Suleiman-bin-Daoud went out for peace and quiet as usual; and among the orange trees he met Balkis the Most Beautiful, very sorrowful because Suleiman-bin-Daoud was so worried. And she said to him, 'O my Lord and Light of my Eyes, turn the ring upon your finger and show these Queens of Egypt and Mesopotamia and Persia and China that you are the great and terrible King.' But Suleiman-bin-Daoud shook his head and said, 'O my Lady and Delight of my Life, remember the Animal that came out of the sea and made me ashamed before all the animals in all the world because I showed off. Now, if I showed off before these Queens of Persia and Egypt and Abyssinia and China, merely because they worry me, I might be made even more ashamed than I have been.'

And Balkis the Most Beautiful said, 'O my Lord and Treasure of my Soul, what will you do?'

And Suleiman-bin-Daoud said, 'O my Lady and Content of my Heart, I shall continue to endure my fate at the hands of these nine hundred and ninety-nine Queens who vex me with their continual quarrelling.'

So he went on between the lilies and the loquats and the roses and the cannas and the heavy-scented ginger-plants that grew in the garden, till he came to the great camphor-tree that was called the Camphor Tree of Suleiman-bin-Daoud. But Balkis hid among the tall irises and the spotted bamboos and the red lillies behind the camphor-tree, so as to be near her own true love, Suleiman-bin-Daoud.

Presently two Butterflies flew under the tree, quarrelling.

Suleiman-bin-Daoud heard one say to the other, 'I wonder at your presumption in talking like this to me. Don't you know that if I stamped with my foot all Suleiman-bin-Daoud's Palace and this garden here would immediately vanish in a clap of thunder.'

Then Suleiman-bin-Daoud forgot his nine hundred and ninety-nine bothersome wives, and laughed, till the camphor-tree shook, at the Butterfly's boast. And he held out his finger and said, 'Little man, come here.'

The Butterfly was dreadfully frightened, but he managed to fly up to the hand of Suleiman-bin-Daoud, and clung there, fanning himself. Suleiman-bin-Daoud bent his head and whispered very softly, 'Little man, you know that all your stamping wouldn't bend one blade of grass. What made you tell that awful fib to your wife?—for doubtless she is your wife.'

The Butterfly looked at Suleiman-bin-Daoud and saw the most wise King's eye twinkle like stars on a frosty night, and he picked up his courage with both wings, and he put his head on one side and said, 'O King, live for ever. She is my wife; and you know what wives are like.

Suleiman-bin-Daoud smiled in his beard and said, 'Yes, I know, little brother.

'One must keep them in order somehow, said the Butterfly, and she has been quarrelling with me all the morning. I said that to quiet her.'

And Suleiman-bin-Daoud said, 'May it quiet her. Go back to your wife, little brother, and let me hear what you say.'

Back flew the Butterfly to his wife, who was all of a twitter behind a leaf, and she said, 'He heard you! Suleiman-bin-Daoud himself heard you!'

'Heard me!' said the Butterfly. 'Of course he did. I meant him to hear me.'

'And what did he say? Oh, what did he say?'

'Well,' said the Butterfly, fanning himself most importantly, 'between you and me, my dear—of course I don't blame him, because his Palace must have cost a great deal and the oranges are just ripening,—he asked me not to stamp, and I promised I wouldn't.'

'Gracious!' said his wife, and sat quite quiet; but Suleiman-bin-Daoud laughed till the tears ran down his face at the impudence of the bad little Butterfly.

Balkis the Most Beautiful stood up behind the tree among the red lilies and smiled to herself, for she had heard all this talk. She thought, 'If I am wise I can yet save my Lord from the persecutions of these quarrelsome Queens,' and she held out her finger and whispered softly to the Butterfly's Wife, 'Little woman, come here.' Up flew the Butterfly's Wife, very frightened, and clung to Balkis's white hand.

Balkis bent her beautiful head down and whispered, 'Little woman, do you believe what your husband has just said?'

The Butterfly's Wife looked at Balkis, and saw the most beautiful Queen's eyes shining like deep pools with starlight on them, and she picked up her courage with both wings and said, 'O Queen, be lovely for ever. You know what men-folk are like.'

And the Queen Balkis, the Wise Balkis of Sheba, put her hand to her lips to hide a smile and said, 'Little sister, I know.'

'They get angry,' said the Butterfly's Wife, fanning herself quickly, 'over nothing at all, but we must humour them, O Queen. They never mean half they say. If it pleases my husband to believe that I believe he can make Suleiman-bin-Daoud's Palace disappear by stamping his foot, I'm sure I don't care. He'll forget all about it to-morrow.'

'Little sister,' said Balkis, 'you are quite right; but next time he begins to boast, take him at his word. Ask him to stamp, and see what will happen. We know what men-folk are like, don't we? He'll be very much ashamed.'

Away flew the Butterfly's Wife to her husband, and in five minutes they were quarrelling worse than ever.

'Remember!' said the Butterfly. 'Remember what I can do if I stamp my foot.'

'I don't believe you one little bit,' said the Butterfly's Wife. 'I should very much like to see it done. Suppose you stamp now.'

'I promised Suleiman-bin-Daoud that I wouldn't,' said the Butterfly, 'and I don't want to break my promise.'

'It wouldn't matter if you did,' said his wife. 'You couldn't bend a blade of grass with your stamping. I dare you to do it,' she said. Stamp! Stamp! Stamp!'

Suleiman-bin-Daoud, sitting under the camphor-tree, heard every word of this, and he laughed as he had never laughed in his life before. He forgot all about his Queens; he forgot all about the Animal that came out of the sea; he forgot about showing off. He just laughed with joy, and Balkis, on the other side of the tree, smiled because her own true love was so joyful.

Presently the Butterfly, very hot and puffy, came whirling back under the shadow of the camphor-tree and said to Suleiman, 'She wants me to stamp! She wants to see what will happen, O Suleiman-bin-Daoud! You know I can't do it, and now she'll never believe a word I say. She'll laugh at me to the end of my days!'

'No, little brother,' said Suleiman-bin-Daoud, 'she will never laugh at you again,' and he turned the ring on his finger—just for the little Butterfly's sake, not for the sake of showing off,—and, lo and behold, four huge Djinns came out of the earth!

'Slaves,' said Suleiman-bin-Daoud, 'when this gentleman on my finger' (that was where the impudent Butterfly was sitting) 'stamps his left front forefoot you will make my Palace and these gardens disappear in a clap of thunder. When he stamps again you will bring them back carefully.'

'Now, little brother,' he said, 'go back to your wife and stamp all you've a mind to.'

Away flew the Butterfly to his wife, who was crying, 'I dare you to do it! I dare you to do it! Stamp! Stamp now! Stamp!' Balkis saw the four vast Djinns stoop down to the four corners of the gardens with the Palace in the middle, and she clapped her hands softly and said, 'At last Suleiman-bin-Daoud will do for the sake of a Butterfly what he ought to have done long ago for his own sake, and the quarrelsome Queens will be frightened!'

The the butterfly stamped. The Djinns jerked the Palace and the gardens a thousand miles into the air: there was a most awful thunder-clap, and everything grew inky-black. The

Butterfly's Wife fluttered about in the dark, crying, 'Oh, I'll be good! I'm so sorry I spoke. Only bring the gardens back, my dear darling husband, and I'll never contradict again.'

The Butterfly was nearly as frightened as his wife, and Suleiman-bin-Daoud laughed so much that it was several minutes before he found breath enough to whisper to the Butterfly, 'Stamp again, little brother. Give me back my Palace, most great magician.'

'Yes, give him back his Palace,' said the Butterfly's Wife, still flying about in the dark like a moth. 'Give him back his Palace, and don't let's have any more horrid.magic.'

'Well, my dear,' said the Butterfly as bravely as he could, 'you see what your nagging has led to. Of course it doesn't make any difference to me—I'm used to this kind of thing— but as a favour to you and to Suleiman-bin-Daoud I don't mind putting things right.'

So he stamped once more, and that instant the Djinns let down the Palace and the gardens, without even a bump. The sun shone on the dark-green orange leaves; the fountains played among the pink Egyptian lilies; the birds went on singing, and the Butterfly's Wife lay on her side under the camphor-tree waggling her wings and panting, 'Oh, I'll be good! I'll be good!'

Suleiman-bin-Daolld could hardly speak for laughing. He leaned back all weak and hiccoughy, and shook his finger at the Butterfly and said, 'O great wizard, what is the sense of returning to me my Palace if at the same time you slay me with mirth!'

Then came a terrible noise, for all the nine hundred and ninety-nine Queens ran out of the Palace shrieking and shouting and calling for their babies. They hurried down the great marble steps below the fountain, one hundred abreast, and the Most Wise Balkis went statelily forward to meet them and said, 'What is your trouble, O Queens?'

They stood on the marble steps one hundred abreast and shouted, 'What is our trouble? We were living peacefully in our golden palace, as is our custom, when upon a sudden the Palace disappeared, and we were left sitting in a thick and noisome darkness; and it thundered, and Djinns and Afrits moved about in the darkness! That is our trouble, O Head Queen, and we are most extremely troubled on account of that trouble, for it was a troublesome trouble, unlike any trouble we have known.'

Then Balkis the Most Beautiful Queen—Suleiman-bin-Daoud's Very Best Beloved—Queen that was of Sheba and Sable and the Rivers of the Gold of the South—from the Desert of Zinn to the Towers of Zimbabwe—Balkis, almost as wise as the Most Wise Suleiman-bin-Daoud himself, said, 'It is nothing, O Queens! A Butterfly has made complaint against his wife because she quarrelled with him, and it has pleased our Lord Suleiman-bin-Daoud to teach her a lesson in low-speaking and humbleness, for that is counted a virtue among the wives of the butterflies.'

Then up and spoke an Egyptian Queen—the daughter of a Pharoah—and she said, 'Our Palace cannot be plucked up by the roots like a leek for the sake of a little insect. No! Suleiman-bin-Daoud must be dead, and what we heard and saw was the earth thundering and darkening at the news.'

Then Balkis beckoned that bold Queen without looking at her, and said to her and to the others, 'Come and see.'

They came down the marble steps, one hundred abreast, and beneath his camphor-tree, still weak with laughing, they saw the Most Wise King Suleiman-bin-Daoud rocking back and forth with a Butterfly on either hand, and they heard him say, 'O wife of my brother in the air, remember after this, to please your husband in all things, lest he be provoked to stamp his foot yet again; for he has said that he is used to this magic, and he is most eminently a great magician—one who steals away the very Palace of Suleirnan-bin-Daoud himself. Go in peace, little folk!' And he kissed them on the wings, and they flew away.

Then all the Queens except Balkis—the Most Beautiful and Splendid Balkis, who stood apart smiling—fell flat on their faces, for they said, 'If these things are done when a Butterfly is displeased with his wife, what shall be done to us who have vexed our King with our loud-speaking and open quarrelling through many days?'

Then they put their veils over their heads, and they put their hands over their mouths, and they tiptoed back to the Palace most mousy-quiet.

Then Balkis—The Most Beautiful and Excellent Balkis— went forward through the red lilies into the shade of the camphor-tree and laid her hand upon Suleiman-bin-Daoud's shoulder and said, 'O my Lord and Treasure of my Soul, rejoice, for we have taught the Queens of Egypt and Ethiopia and Abyssinia and Persia and India and China with a great and a memorable teaching.'

And Suleiman-bin-Daoud, still looking after the Butterflies where they played in the sunlight, said, 'O my Lady and Jewel of my Felicity, when did this happen? For I have been jesting with a Butterfly ever since I came into the garden.' And he told Balkis what he had done.

Balkis—The tender and Most Lovely Balkis—said, 'O my Lord and Regent of my Existence, I hid behind the camphor-tree and saw it all. It was I who told the Butterfly's Wife to ask the Butterfly to stamp, because I hoped that for the sake of the jest my Lord would make some great magic and that the Queens would see it and be frightened.' And she told him what the Queens had said and seen and thought.

Then Suleiman-bin-Daoud rose up from his seat under the camphor-tree, and stretched his arms and rejoiced and said, 'O my Lady and Sweetener of my Days, know that if I had made a magic against my Queens for the sake of pride or anger, as I made that feast for all the animals, I should certainly have been put to shame. But by means of your wisdom I made the magic for the sake of a jest and for the sake of a little Butterfly, and—behold—it has also delivered me from the vexations of my vexatious wives! Tell me, therefore, O my Lady and Heart of my Heart, how did you come to be so wise?' And Balkis the Queen, beautiful and tall, looked up into Suleiman-bin-Daoud's eyes and put her head a little on one side, just like the Butterfly, and said, 'First, O my Lord, because I loved you; and secondly, O my Lord, because I know what women-folk are.'

Then they went up to the Palace and lived happily ever afterwards.

But wasn't it clever of Balkis?

THERE was never a Queen like Balkis,
From here to the wide world's end;
But Balkis tailed to a butterfly
As you would talk to a friend.

There was never a King like Solomon,
Not since the world began;
But Solomon talked to a butterfly
As a man would talk to a man.

She was Queen of Sabaea--
And he was Asia's Lord--
But they both of 'em ta lked to butterflies
When they took their walks abroad!

THE EYES OF ASIA

A RETIRED GENTLEMAN

From Bishen Singh Saktawut, Subedar Major, 215th Indurgurh [Todd's] Rajputs, now at Lyndhurst, Hampshire, England, this letter is sent to Madhu Singh, Sawant, Risaldar Major [retired] 146th [Dublana] Horse, on his fief which he holds under the Thakore Sahib of Pech at Bukani by the River, near Chiturkaira, Kotah, Rajputana, written in the fifth month of the year 1916, English count.

Having experienced five months of this war, I became infected with fever and a strong coldness of the stomach [rupture]. The doctor ordered me out of it altogether. They have also cut me with knives for a wound on my leg. It is now healed but the strength is gone, and it is very frightened of the ground. I have been in many hospitals for a long time. At this present I am living in a hospital for Indian troops in a forest-reservation called "New," which was established by a King's order in ages past. There is no order for my return to India. I do not desire it. My Regiment has now gone out of France—to Egypt, or Africa. My officer Sahibs are for the most part dead or in hospitals. During a railway journey when two people sit side by side for two hours one feels the absence of the other when he alights. How great then was my anguish at being severed from my Regiment after thirty-three years!

Now, however, I am finished. If I return to India I cannot drill the new men between my two crutches. I should subsist in my village on my wound-pension among old and young who have never seen war. Here I have great consideration. Though I am useless they are patient with me.

Having knowledge of the English tongue, I am sometimes invited to interpret between those in the hospital for the Indian troops and visitors of high position. I advance eminent visitors, such as relatives of Kings and Princes into the presence of the Colonel Doctor Sahib. I enjoy a small room apart from the hospital wards. I have a servant. The Colonel Doctor Sahib examines my body at certain times. I am forbidden to stoop even for my crutches. They are instantly restored to me by orderlies and my friends among the English. I come and go at my pleasure where I will, and my presence is solicited by the honourable.

You say I made a mistake to join the war at the end of my service? I have endured five months of it. Come you out and endure two and a half. You are three years younger than I. Why do you sit at home and drill new men? Remember:

The Brahman who steals,

The widow who wears ornaments,

The Rajput who avoids the battle,

Are only fit for crows' meat.

You write me that this is a war for young men? The old are not entirely useless. The Badshah [the King] himself gave me the medal for fetching in my captain from out of the wires upon my back. That work caused me the coldness in my stomach. Old men should not do coolie-work. Your cavalry were useless in France. Infantry can fight in this war—not cavalry. It is as impossible for us to get out of our trenches and exterminate the enemy as it is for the enemy to attack us. Doubtless the cavalry brigades will show what they are made of in Egypt or Persia. This business in France is all Artillery work and mines. The blowing up of the Chitoree Bastion when Arjoon went to Heaven waving his sword, as the song says, would not be noticed in the noise of this war.

The nature of the enemy is to go to earth and flood us with artillery of large weight. When we were in the trenches it was a burden. When we rested in the villages we found great ease. As to our food, it was like a bunnia's marriage-feast. Everything given, nothing counted. Some of us—especially among your cavalry—grew so fat that they were compelled to wrestle to keep thin. This is because there was no marching.

The nature of the enemy is to commit shame upon women and children, and to defile the shrines of his own faith with his own dung. It is done by him as a drill. We believed till then they were some sort of caste apart from the rest. We did not know they were outcaste. Now it is established by the evidence of our senses. They attack on all fours running like apes. They are specially careful for their faces. When death is certain to them they offer gifts and repeat the number of their children. They are very good single shots from cover.

It is the nature of the enemy to shower seductions from out of their air-machines on our troops in the lines. They promised such as would desert that they would become Rajahs among them. Some of the men went over to see if this were true. No report came back. In this way we cleaned out five bad characters from our Company exactly as it used to be in the little wars on the Border. May the enemy be pleased with them! No man of any caste disgraced our Regiment.

The nature of the enemy in this war is like the Nat [juggler] who is compelled to climb a pole for his belly's sake. If he does not climb he starves. If he stops he falls down. This is my thought concerning the enemy.

Now that our troops have gone out of France, the war is entirely between the enemy and the English, etc., etc. Both sides accordingly increased the number and the size of their guns. The new wounded officers in the English hospital say that the battles of even yesterday are not to be compared with the battle of to-day. Tell this to those who have returned and who boast. Only fools will desire more war when this war is ended. Their reward will be an instant extinction on account of the innumerable quantity of arms, munitions, etc., etc., which will be left in the hands of the experts. Those who make war henceforward will be as small jackals fighting beneath the feet of elephants. This Government has abundance of material, and fresh strength is added every hour. Let there be no mistake. The foolish have been greatly deceived in these matters by the nature of the English which is in the highest degree deceptive. Everything is done and spoken upside-down in this country of the English. He who has a thousand says: "It is but a scant hundred." The possessor of palaces says: "It is a hut," and the rest in proportion. Their boast is not to boast. Their greatness is to make themselves very small. They draw a curtain in front of all they do. It is as difficult to look upon the naked face of their achievements as in our country upon the faces of women.

It is not true there is no caste in England. The mark of the high castes, such as Ul or Baharun [Earl or Baron] is that they can perform any office, such as handling the dead, wounds, blood, etc., without loss of caste. The Maharanee of the Nurses in the English Hospital which is near our Hospital is by caste Baharanee [Baroness]. I resort thither daily for society and enlightenment on the habits of this people. The high castes are forbidden to show curiosity, appetite, or fear in public places. In this respect they resemble troops on parade. Their male children are beaten from their ninth year to their seventeenth year, by men with sticks. Their women are counted equal with their men. It is reckoned as disgraceful for a Baharanee to show fear when lights are extinguished in the hospital on account of bomb-dropping air-ships, as for an Ul to avoid battle. They do not blacken each other's faces by loud abuse, but by jests spoken in a small voice.

The nature of the young men of high caste is as the nature of us Rajputs. They do not use opium, but they delight in horses, and sport and women, and are perpetually in debt to the moneylender. They shoot partridge and they are forced to ride foxes because there are no wild pig here. They know nothing of hawking or quail-fighting, but they gamble up to the hilt on all occasions and bear losses laughing. Their card-play is called Baraich [Bridge?]. They belittle their own and the achievements of their friends, so long as that friend faces them. In his absence they extol his deeds. They are of cheerful countenance. When they jest, they respect honour. It is so also with their women. The Nurses in the Hospital of my Baharanee where I resort for society jest with me as daughters with a father. They say that they will be stricken with grief if I return to India. They call me Dada which is father also in their tongue. Though I am utterly useless they are unwearied of me. They themselves hasten to restore me my crutches when I let them fall. None of these women lament their dead openly. The eldest son of my Baharanee at the English Hospital where I am made welcome, was slain in battle. The next morning after the news my Baharanee let loose the plate-pianos [turned on the gramophones] for the delectation of the wounded. It comes into my mind to suggest to you that our women are unable to stand by themselves.

When the Badshah commanded me to his Palace to receive the medal, I saw all the wonders and entertainments of the city of London. There was neither trouble nor expense. My Baharanee gave orders I should inhabit her own house in that city. It was in reality a palace filled with carpets, gilt furniture, marbles, mirrors, silks, velvets, carvings, etc., etc. Hot water ran in silver pipes to my very bedside. The perfumed baths were perpetually renewed. When it rained daily I walked in a glass pavilion filled with scented flowers. I inhabited here ten days. Though I was utterly useless they were unwearied of me. A companion was found me. He was a Risaldar of Dekkani Horse, a man of family, wounded in the arms. We two received our medals together. We saw the King's Palace, and the custom of the Guard Mount in the mornings daily. Their drill is like stone walls, but the nature of the English music is without any meaning. We two saw the great temple, Seyn Pol [St. Paul's?], where their dead are. It is as a country enclosed in a house. My companion ascended to the very roof-top and saw all the city. We are nothing beside these people. We two also saw the Bird Garden [Zoological Gardens] where they studiously preserve all sorts of wild animals, even down to jackals and green parrots. It is the nature of the English to consider all created beings as equal. The Badshah himself wears khaki. His son the Shahzada is a young man who inhabits the trenches except when he is forbidden. He is a keen son of the sword.

It is true that trains run underneath the city in all directions. We descended into the earth upon a falling platform [lift] and travelled. The stopping-places are as close as beads on a thread. The doors of the carriages are guarded with gates that strike out sideways like cobras. Each sitter is allowed a space upon a divan of yellow canework. When the divans are full the surplus hang from the roof by leathers. Though our carriage was full, place was made for us. At the end of our journey the train was halted beyond its lawful time that we might come forth at ease. The trains were full of English soldiers. All castes of the English are now soldiers. They are become like us Rajputs—as many people so many soldiers.

We two saw houses, shops, carriages, and crowds till our souls were broken. The succeeding days were as the first, without intermission. We begged at last to be excused from the sight of the multitudes and the height of the houses.

We two agreed that understanding is most needful in this present age. We in India must get education before all things. Hereafter we Rajputs must seriously consider our arrangements in all respects—in our houses as well as in our fields, etc., etc. Otherwise we become nothing. We have been deceived by the nature of the English. They have not at any time shown us anything of their possessions or their performances. We are not even children beside them. They have dealt with us as though they were themselves children talking _chotee boli_ [little talk]. In this manner the ill-informed have been misled. Nothing is known in India of the great strength of this people. Make that perfectly clear to all fools. Why should we who serve the Government have the blood of the misinformed on our heads when they behave foolishly? This people have all the strength. There is no reason except the nature of the English that anything in their dominions should stand up which has been ordered to lie down. It is only their soft nature which saves evil from destruction. As the saying is, "We thought it was only an armed horseman. Behold, it is an elephant bearing a tower!"

It is in my mind that the glory of us Rajputs has become diminished since the old days. In the old days, our Princesses charged in battle beside their men, and the name of the clans was great. Then all Rajputs were brothers and sisters. How has this come about? What man of us now relies upon the advice of his womenkind in any matter outside? In this country and in France the women understand perfectly what is needful in the day of trial. They say to their men: "Add to the renown of your race. We will attend to the rest through the excellent education which this just Government has caused us to receive." Thus the men's hearts are lightened when they go to the war. They confide securely in their well educated women. How is it with our horses? Shape and size from the sire: temper and virtue from the dam. If the mare endures thirst, the colt can run without water. Man's nature also draws from the spindle-side. Why have we allowed forgetfulness to impair our memory? This was well known in the old days. In this country arrangements for washing clothes exist in almost every house, such as tubs, boards, and irons, and there is a machine to squeeze water out of the washed clothes. They do not conceal their astonishment at our methods. Our women should be taught. Only by knowledge is anything achieved. Otherwise we are as children running about naked under the feet of grown men and women.

See what our women have already accomplished by education! The Thakore Sahib of Philawat was refused leave from the Government to go to the war, on account of his youth. Yet his sister, who wedded the Rana of Haliana had prepared a contingent of infantry out of her own dower-villages. They were set down in the roll of the Princes' contingents as stretcher-bearers: they being armed men out of the desert. She sent a telegram to her brother, commissioning him to go with them as Captain of stretcher-bearers: he being a son of the Sword for seventy generations. Thus cleverly he received permission from the Government to go. When they reached France he stole them out of the camp, every one of his sister's men, and joined himself to the Rajah of Kandesur's contingent. Those two boys together made their name bright in the trenches. The Philawat boy was hit twice and came to hospital here. The Government sent him a sealed letter by messenger where he lay. He had great fear of it, because what he and Kandesur had done was without orders. He expected a reprimand from the Government and also from his uncle because of the succession. But the letter was an announcement of decoration from the Shahzada himself, and when he had read it, the child hid his face beneath the sheets and wept for joy. I saw and heard this from my very bed in the hospital. So his Military Cross and the rest was due to the Maharanee of Haliana, his sister. Before her marriage she attended instruction in England at the great school for maidens called Ghatun [Girton?]. She goes unveiled among Englishmen, laying hold upon her husband's right arm in public assemblies in open daylight. And Haliana is sunborn.[1] Consider it! Consider it!

Do not be concerned if I do not return. I have seen all the reports of all the arrangements made for burial, etc., etc., in this country. They are entirely in accordance with our faith. My youth and old age have been given to the service of the Government, and if the Government can be served with the dust of my bones it is theirs, Now that my boy is dead in Arabia I have also withdrawn my petition to the Government for a land-grant. What use? The house is empty.

Man does not remain in the world

But his name remains.

[1] The royal clans of the Rajputs derive their descent from the Sun.

Though Jam and Suliman are gone
Their names are not lost.

When that arrives, my Maharanee Baharanee will despatch
to you _posh-free par parshel-posh_ [post-free per parcel-post]
my Cross that the Badshah gave me, and a letter from my
Captain Sahib's Mother with whose brother I served when I
was a man. As for my debts, it does not trouble me in the
least that the moneylenders should be so troubled about them.
But for the Army and the Police the people would have killed
all moneylenders. Give my duty to the Rana of Pech, for his
line were my father's overlords from the first. He can hang
up my sword beside my father's.

Do not be concerned for whatever overtakes me. I have
sifted the sands of France: now I sift those of England. Here
I am held in the greatest kindness and honour imaginable by
all whom I meet. Though I am useless as a child yet they are
unwearied of me. The nurses in my Maharanee Baharanee's
Hospital, which is by day a home and a house to me, minister
to me as daughters to a father. They run after me and rebuke
me if I do not wear a certain coat when it rains daily. I am
like a dying tree in a garden of flowers.

THE FUMES OF THE HEART

Scene._ Pavilion and Dome Hospital, Brighton—1915.

What talk is this, Doctor Sahib? This Sahib says he will be my letter-writer? Just as though he were a bazar letter-writer at home?... What are the Sahib's charges? Two annas? Too much! I give one.... No. No! Sahib. You shouldn't have come down so quickly. You've forgotten, we Sikhs always bargain.... Well; one anna be it. I will give a bond to pay it out of my wound-pension when I get home. Sit by the side of my bed....

This is the trouble, Sahib. My brother who holds his land and works mine, outside Amritsar City, is a fool. He is older than I. He has done his service and got one wound out of it in what they used to call war—that child's play in the Tirah years ago. He thinks himself a soldier! But that is not his offence. He sends me postcards, Sahib—scores of postcards—whining about the drouth or the taxes, or the crops, or our servants' pilferings or some such trouble. He doesn't know what trouble means. I want to tell him he is a fool.... What? True! True! One can get money and land but never a new brother. But for all that, he is a fool.... Is he a good farmer? Sa-heeb! _If an Amritsar Sikh isn't a good farmer, a hen doesn't know an egg.... Is he honest? As my own pet yoke of bullocks. He is only a fool. My belly is on fire now with knowledge I never had before, and I wish to impart it to him—to the village elders—to all people. Yes, that is true, too. If I keep calling him a fool, he will not gain any knowledge.... Let me think it over on all sides! Aha! Now that I have a bazar-writer of my own I will write a book—a very book of a letter to my fool of a brother.... And now we will begin. Take down my words from my lips to my foolish old farmer-brother:—_

     *   *   *   *   *

"You will have received the notification of my wounds which I took in Franceville. Now that I am better of my wounds, I have leisure to write with a long hand. Here we have paper and ink at command. Thus it is easy to let off the fumes of our hearts. Send me all the news of all the crops and what is being done in our village. This poor parrot is always thinking of Kashmir.

"As to my own concerns, the trench in which I sat was broken by a _bomb-golee_ as large as our smallest grain-chest." [_He'll go off and measure it at once!_] "It dropped out of the air. It burst, the ground was opened and replaced upon seven of us. I and two others took wounds. Sweetmeats are not distributed in war-time. God permitted my soul to live, by means of the doctors' strong medicines. I have inhabited six hospitals before I came here to England. This hospital is like a temple. It is set in a garden beside the sea. We lie on iron cots beneath a dome of gold and colours and glittering glass work, with pillars." [_You know that's true, Sahib. We can see it—but d'you think_ he'll _believe? Never! Never!_] "Our food is cooked for us according to our creeds—Sikh, or Brahmin, or Mussulman and all the rest—When a man dies he is also buried according to his creed. Though he has been a groom or a sweeper, he is buried like some great land-owner. Do not let such matters trouble you henceforth.

Living or dying, all is done in accordance with the ordinance of our faiths. Some low-caste men, such as sweepers, counting upon the ignorance of the doctors here make a claim to be of reputable caste in order that they may get consideration. If a sweeper in this hospital says he is forbidden by his caste to do certain things he is believed. He is not beaten." [_Now, why is that, Sahib? They ought to be beaten for pretending to have caste, and making a mock of the doctors._ I _should slipper them publicly—but—I'm not the Government. We will go on._]

"The English do not despise any sort of work. They are of many castes, but they are all one kind in this. On account of my wounds, I have not yet gone abroad to see English fields or towns." [_It is true I have been out twice in a motor-carriage, Sahib, but that goes too quickly for a man to see shops, let alone faces. We will not tell him that. He does not like motor-cars._] "The French in Franceville work continually without rest. The French and the Phlahamahnds [Flamands] who are a caste of French, are Kings among cultivators. As to cultivation—" [_Now, I pray, Sahib, write quickly for I am as full of this matter as a buffalo of water_] "their fields are larger than ours, without any divisions, and they do not waste anything except the width of the footpath. Their land descends securely from father to son upon payment of tax to the Government, just as in civilized countries. I have observed that they have their land always at their hearts and in their mouths, just as in civilized countries. They do not grow more than one crop a year, but this is recompensed to them because their fields do not need irrigation. The rain in Franceville is always sure and abundant and in excess. They grow all that we grow such as peas, onions, garlic, spinach, beans, cabbages and wheat. They do not grow small grains or millet, and their only spice is mustard. They do not drink water, but the juice of apples which they squeeze into barrels for that purpose. A full bottle is sold for two pice. They do not drink milk but there is abundance of it. It is all cows' milk, of which they make butter in a churn which is turned by a dog." [_Now, how shall we make my brother believe that? Write it large._] "In Franceville, the dogs are both courteous and industrious. They play with the cat, they tend the sheep, they churn the butter, they draw a cart and guard it too. When a regiment meets a flock, the dogs of their own wisdom order the sheep to step to one side of the road. I have often seen this." [_Not one word of this will he or anyone in the villages believe, Sahib. What can you expect? They have never even seen Lahore City! We will tell him what he can understand._] "Ploughs and carts are drawn by horses. Oxen are not used for these purposes in these villages. The field work is wholly done by old men and women and children, who can all read and write. The young men are all at the war. The war comes also to the people in the villages, but they do not regard the war because they are cultivators. I have a friend among the French—an old man in the village where the Regiment was established, who daily fills in the holes made in his fields by the enemy's shells with dirt from a long-handled spade. I begged him once to desist when we were together on this work, but he said that idleness would cause him double work for the day following. His grandchild, a very small maiden, grazed a cow behind a wood where the shells fell, and was killed in that manner. Our Regiment was told the news and they took an account of it, for she was often among them, begging buttons from their uniforms. She was small and full of laughter, and she had learned a little of our tongue." [_Yes. That was a very great shame, Sahib. She was the child of us all. We exacted a payment, but she was slain—slain like a calf for no fault. A black shame!... We will write about other matters._]

"As to cultivation, there are no words for its excellence or for the industry of the cultivators. They esteem manure most highly. They have no need to burn cow-dung for fuel. There is abundance of charcoal. Thus, not irrigating nor burning dung for fuel, their wealth increases of itself. They build their houses from ancient times round about mountainous dung-heaps, upon which they throw all things in season. It is a possession from father to son, and increase comes forth. Owing to the number of Army horses in certain places there arises very much horse-dung. When it is excessive, the officers cause a little straw to be lit near the heaps. The French and the Phlahamahnds seeing the smoke, assemble with carts, crying:—'What waste is this?' The officers reply:—'None will carry away this dung. Therefore, we burn it.' All the cultivators then entreat for leave to carry it away in their carts, be it only as much as two dogs can draw. By this device horse-lines are cleaned.

"Listen to one little thing. The women and the girls cultivate as well as the men in all respects." [_That is a true tale, Sahib. We know—but my brother knows nothing except the road to market._] "They plough with two and four horses as great as hills. The women of Franceville also keep the accounts and the bills. They make one price for everything. No second price is to be obtained by _any_ talking. They cannot be cheated over the value of one grain. Yet of their own will they are generous beyond belief. When we come back from our work in the trenches, they arise at any hour and make us warm drinks of hot coffee and milk and bread and butter. May God reward these ladies a thousand times for their kindness!

"But do not throw everything upon God. I desire you will get me in Amritsar City a carpet, at the shop of Davee Sahai and Chumba Mall—one yard in width and one yard and a half in length, of good colour and quality to the value of forty rupees. The shop must send it with _all_ charges paid, to the address which I have had written in English character on the edge of this paper. She is the lady of the house in which I was billeted in a village for three months. Though she was advanced in years and belonged to a high family, yet in the whole of those three months I never saw this old lady sit idle. Her three sons had gone to the war. One had been killed; one was in hospital, and a third, at that time, was in the trenches. She did not weep nor wail at the death or the sickness but accepted the dispensation. During the time I was in her house, she ministered to me to such an extent that I cannot adequately describe her kindness. Of her own free-will she washed my clothes, arranged my bed, and polished my boots daily for three months. She washed down my bedroom daily with hot water, having herself heated it. Each morning she prepared me a tray with bread, butter, milk and coffee. When we had to leave that village that old lady wept on my shoulder. It is strange that I had never seen her weep for her dead son, but she wept for me. Moreover, at parting she would have had me take a _fi-farang_ [five franc] note for expenses on the road." [_What a woman! What a woman! I had never believed such women existed in this Black Age._]

"If there be any doubt of the quality or the colour of the carpet, ask for an audience of the Doctor Linley Sahib if he be still in Amritsar. He knows carpets. Tell him all I have written concerning this old lady—may God keep her and her remaining household!—and he will advise. I do not know the Doctor Sahib, but this he will overlook in war-time. If the carpet is even fifty rupees, I can securely pay out of the monies which our lands owe me. She is an old lady. It must be soft to her feet, and not inclined to slide upon the wooden floor. She is well-born and educated." [_And now we will begin to enlighten him and the elders!_]

"We must cause our children to be educated in the future. That is the opinion of all the Regiment, for by education, even women accomplish marvels, like the women of Franceville. Get the boys and girls taught to read and write well. Here teaching is by Government order. The men go to the war daily. It is the women who do all the work at home, having been well taught in their childhood. We have only yoked one buffalo to the plough up till now. It is now time to yoke up the milch-buffaloes. Tell the village elders this and exercise influence." [_Write that down strongly, Sahib. We who have seen Franceville_ all _know it is true._]

"But as to cultivation. The methods in Franceville are good. All tools are of iron. They do not break. A man keeps the tools he needs for his work and his repairs in his house under his own hand. He has not to go back to the village a mile away if anything breaks. We never thought, as these people do, that all repairs to tools and ploughs can be done on the very spot. All that is needed when a strap breaks, is that each ploughman should have an awl and a leather-cutter to stitch the leather. How is it with us in our country? If leather breaks, we farmers say that leather is unclean, and we go back from the fields into the village to the village cobbler that he may mend it. Unclean? Do not we handle that same thing with the leather on it after it has been repaired? Do we not even drink water all day with the very hand that has sweated into the leather? Meantime, we have surely lost an hour or two in coming and going from the fields." [_He will understand_ that. _He chatters like a monkey when the men waste time.

But the village cobbler will be very angry with me!_] "The people of Franceville are astonished to learn that all our land is full of dogs which do no work—not even to keep the cattle out of the tilled fields. Among the French, both men and women and little children occupy themselves with work at all times on the land. The children wear no jewelry, but they are more beautiful than I can say. It is a country where the women are not veiled. Their marriage is at their own choice, and takes place between their twentieth and twenty-fifth year. They seldom quarrel or shout out. They do not pilfer from each other. They do not tell lies at all. When calamity overtakes them there is no ceremonial of grief such as tearing the hair or the like. They swallow it down and endure silently. Doubtless, this is the fruit of learning in youth."

[_Now we will have a word for our Guru at home. He is a very holy man. Write this carefully, Sahib._] "It is said that the French worship idols. I have spoken of this with my old lady and her _guru_ [priest]. It is _not_ true in any way. There are certainly images in their shrines and _deotas_ [local gods] to whom they present petitions as we do in our home affairs, but the prayer of the heart goes to the God Himself. I have been assured this by the old priests. All the young priests are fighting in the war. The French men uncover the head but do not take off the shoes at prayer. They do not speak of their religion to strangers, and they do not go about to make converts. The old priest in the village where I was billeted so long, said that all roads, at such times as these, return to God." [_Our Guru at home says that himself; so he cannot be surprised if there are others who think it._] "The old priest gave me a little medal which he wished me to wear round my neck. Such medals are reckoned holy among the French. He was a very holy man and it averts the Evil Eye. The Women also carry holy beads to help keep count of their prayers.

"Certain men of our Regiment divided among themselves as many as they could pick up of the string of such beads that used to be carried by the small maiden whom the shell slew. It was found forty yards distant from the hands. It was that small maiden who begged us for our buttons and had no fear. The Regiment made an account of it, reckoning one life of the enemy for each bead. They deposited the beads as a pledge with the regimental clerk. When a man of the guarantors became killed, the number of his beads which remained unredeemed was added to the obligation of the other guarantors, or they elected an inheritor of the debt in his place." [_He will understand that. It was all very correct and business-like, Sahib. Our Pathan Company arranged it._] "It was seven weeks before all her beads were redeemed because the weather was bad and our guns were strong and the enemy did not stir abroad after dark. When all the account was cleared, the beads were taken out of pawn and returned to her grandfather, with a certificate, and he wept.

"This war is not a war. It is a world-destroying battle. All that has gone before this war in this world till now has been only boys throwing coloured powder at each other. No man could conceive it! What do you or the Mohmunds or anyone who has not been here know of war? When the ignorant in future speak of war, I shall laugh, even though they be my elder brethren. Consider what things are done here and for what reasons.

"A little before I took my wounds, I was on duty near an officer who worked in wire and wood and earth to make traps for the enemy. He had acquired a tent of green cloth upon sticks, with a window of soft glass that could not be broken. All coveted the tent. It was three paces long and two wide. Among the covetous was an Officer of Artillery, in charge of a gun that shook mountains. It gave out a shell of ten maunds or more [eight hundred pounds]. But those who have never seen even a rivulet cannot imagine the Indus. He offered many rupees to purchase the tent. He would come at all hours increasing his offer. He overwhelmed the owner with talk about it." [_I heard them often, Sahib._] "At last, and I heard this also, that tent-owner said to that Artillery Officer:—'I am wearied with your importunity. Destroy to-day a certain house that I shall show you, and I will give you the tent for a gift. Otherwise, have no more talk.' He showed him the roof of a certain white house which stood back three _kos_ [six miles] in the enemy country, a little underneath a hill with woods on each side. Consider this, measuring three _kos_ in your mind along the Amritsar Road. The Gunner Officer said:—'By God, I accept this bargain.' He issued orders and estimated the distance. I saw him going back and forth as swiftly as a lover. Then fire was delivered and at the fourth discharge the watchers through their glasses saw the house spring high and spread abroad and lie upon its face. It was as a tooth taken out by a barber. Seeing this, the Gunner Officer sprang into the tent and looked through the window and smiled because the tent was now his. But the enemy did not understand the reasons. There was a great gunfire all that night, as well as many enemy-regiments moving about. The prisoners taken afterwards told us their commanders were disturbed at the fall of the house, ascribing it to some great design on our part, so that their men had no rest for a week. Yet it was all done for a little green tent's sake!

"I tell you this that you may understand the meaning of things. This is a world where the very hills are turned upside down, with the cities upon them. He who comes alive out of this business will forever after be as a giant. If anyone wishes to see it let him come here or remain disappointed all his life."

[_We will finish with affection and sweet words. After all, a brother is a brother._] "As for myself, why do you write to me so many complaints? Are _you_ fighting in this war or I? You know the saying: 'A soldier's life is for his family: his death is for his country: his discomforts are for himself alone.' I joined to fight when I was young. I have eaten the Government's salt till I am old. I am discharging my obligation. When all is at an end, the memory of our parting will be but a dream.

"I pray the Guru to bring together those who are separated.

"God alone is true. Everything else is but a shadow."

[_That is poetry. Oh—and add this, Sahib._]

"Let there be no delay about the carpet. She would not accept anything else."

THE PRIVATE ACCOUNT

Scene: Three and a half miles across the Border—Kohat way. _Time_: The edge of sunset. Single room in a stone built tower house reached by a ladder from the ground. An Afghan woman, wrapped in a red cotton quilt, squats on the floor trimming a small kerosene lamp. Her husband, an elderly Afghan with a purple dyed beard, lies on a native cot, covered by a striped blue and white cloth. He is wounded in the knee and hip. A Government rifle leans against the cot. Their son, aged twenty, kneels beside him, unfolding a letter. As the mother places the lighted lamp in a recess in the wall, the son picks up the rifle and pushes the half-opened door home with the butt. The wife passes her husband a filled pipe of tobacco, blowing on the charcoal ball in the bowl.

SON [_as he unfolds letter_]. It is from France. His Regiment is still there.

FATHER. What does he say about the money?

SON [_reading_]. He says: "I am made easy by the news that you are now receiving my pay-allotment regularly. You may depend upon its coming every month henceforward. I have also sent eleven rupees over and above the allotment. It is a gift towards the purchase of the machine needed in your business."

FATHER [_drawing a cheap nickel-plated revolver from

his breast_]. It is a good machine, and he is a good son. What else.

SON. He says: "You tell me our enemies have killed my uncle and my brother, beside wounding our father. I am very far away and can give no help whatever. It is a matter for great regret. Our enemies are now two lives to the good against us in the account. We must take our revenge quickly. The responsibility, I suppose, is altogether on the head of my youngest brother."

FATHER.But I am still good for sitting-shots.

MOTHER[_soothingly_]. Ah! But he means, to think over all the arrangements. Wounded men cannot think clearly till the fever is out of the wound.

SON [_reading_]. "My youngest brother said he would enlist after me when the harvest was gathered. That is now out of the question. Tell him he must attend to the work in hand." (That is true, I cannot enlist now.) "Tell him not to wander about after the people who did the actual killing. They will probably have taken refuge on the Government side of the Border." (That is true, too. It is exactly what they did.) "Even up the account from the nearest household of our enemies. This will force the murderers for their honour's sake to return and attend to their proper business when—God willing—they can be added as a bonus. Take our revenge quickly."

FATHER [_stroking beard_]. This is all wisdom. I have a man for a son. What else does he say, Akbar?

SON. He says: "I have a letter from Kohat telling me that a certain man of a family that we know is coming out here with a draft in order to settle with me for an account which he says I opened."

MOTHER [_quickly_]. Would that be Gul Shere Khan—about that Peshawari girl?

SON. Perhaps. But Ahmed is not afraid. Listen! He says: "If that man or even his brothers wish to come to France after me I shall be very pleased. If, in fact, anyone wishes to kill me, let them by all means come out. I am here present in the field of battle. I have placed my life on a tray. The people in our country who talk about killing are children. They have not seen the reality of things. _We_ do not turn our heads when forty are killed at a breath. Men are swallowed up or blown apart here as one divides meat. When we are in the trenches, there is no time to strike a blow on the private account. When we are at rest in the villages, one's lust for killing has been satisfied. Two men joined us in the draft last month to look after a close friend of mine with whom they had a private account. They were great swash-bucklers at first. They even volunteered to go into the trenches though it was not their turn of duty. They expected that their private account could be settled during some battle. Since that turn of duty they have become quite meek. They had, till then, only seen men killed by ones and twos, half a mile separating them. _This_ business was like killing flies on sugar. Have no fear for me, therefore, no matter who joins the Regiment. It needs a very fierce stomach to add anything to our Government rations."

MOTHER. He writes like a poet, my son. That is wonderful writing.

FATHER. All the young men write the same with regard to the war. It _quite_ satisfies all desires. What else does he say?

SON [_summarizing_]. He says that he is well fed and has learned to drink the French coffee. He says there are two sorts of French tobacco—one yellow, one blue. The blue, he says, is the best. They are named for the papers they are wrapped in. He says that on no account must we send him any opium or drugs, because the punishment for drugging is severe and the doctors are quick to discover. He desires to be sent to him some strong hair-dye of the sort that our father uses.

MOTHER [_with a gesture_]. Hair-dye! He is a child. What's he been doing?

SON. He says he wishes to win favour from his native officer whose white hairs are showing and who has no proper dye. He says he will repay the cost and that no charges are made for the parcel. It must be very strong henna-dye.

MOTHER [_laughing_]. It shall be. I will make it myself. A start it gave me to hear _him_ ask for dyes! They are not due for another twenty years.

FATHER [_fretfully_]. Read it. Read it all as it is written, word for word. What else does he say?

SON. He speaks of the country of the French. Listen! He says: "This country is full of precious objects, such as grain, ploughs, and implements, and sheep which lie about the fields by day with none to guard them. The French are a virtuous people and do not steal from each other. If a man merely approaches towards anything there are eyes watching him. To take one chicken is to loosen the tongues of fifty old women. I was warned on joining that the testimony of one such would outweigh the testimony of six honourable Pathans. It is true. Money and valuables are, therefore, left openly in houses. None dare even to look at them with a covetous eye. I have seen two hundred rupees' worth of clothing hung up on a nail. None knew the owner, yet it remained till her return."

MOTHER. That is the country for me! Dresses worth two hundred rupees hanging on nails! Princesses all they must be.

SON [_continuing_]. Listen to these fresh marvels. He says: "We reside in brick houses with painted walls of flowers and birds; we sit upon chairs covered with silks. We sleep on high beds that cost a hundred rupees each. There is glass in all the doors and windows; the abundance of iron and brass, pottery, and copper kitchen-utensils is not to be estimated. Every house is a palace of entertainment filled with clocks, lamps, candlesticks, gildings, and images."

FATHER. What a country! What a country! How much will he be able to bring back of it all?

SON. He says: "The inhabitants defend their possessions to the uttermost—even down to the value of half a chicken or a sheep's kidney. They do not keep their money in their houses, but send it away on loan. Their rates of interest are very low. They talk among themselves of loans and pledges and the gaining of money, just as we do. We Indian troops are esteemed and honoured by all, by the children specially. These children wear no jewelry. Therefore, there are no murders committed for the sake of ornaments except by the enemy. These children resemble small moons. They make mud figures in their play of men and horses. He who can add figures of oxen, elephants and palanquins is highly praised. Do you remember when I used to make them?"

MOTHER. Do I remember? Am I a block of wood or an old churn? Go on, Akbar? What of my child?

SON. He says: "When the children are not in the school they are at work in the fields from their earliest years. They soon lose all fear of us soldiers, and drill us up and down the streets of the villages. The smallest salute on all occasions.

They suffer little from sickness. The old women here are skilful in medicines. They dry the leaves of trees and give them for a drink against diseases. One old woman gave me an herb to chew for a worm in my tooth [toothache] which cured me in an hour."

MOTHER. God reward that woman! I wonder what she used.

SON. He says: "She is my French mother."

MOTHER. What-t! How many mothers has a man? But God reward her none the less! It must have been that old double-tooth at the back on the left lower side, for I remember——

FATHER. Let it wait. It is cured now. What else does he write?

SON. He writes, making excuses for not having written. He says: "I have been so occupied and sent from one place to another that on several occasions I have missed the post. I know you must have experienced anxiety. But do not be displeased. Let my mother remember that I can only write when I have opportunity, and the only remedy for helplessness is patience."

FATHER [_groaning_]. Ah! He has not yet been wounded, and he sets himself up for a physician.

MOTHER. He speaks wisely and beautifully. But what of his "French mother"—burn her!

SON. He says: "Moreover, this French mother of mine in France is displeased with me if I do not write to her about my welfare. My mother, like you, my French mother does all she can for my welfare. I cannot write sufficiently in praise of what she does for me. When I was in the village behind the trench if, on any day, by reason of duty, I did not return till evening, she, herself, would come in search of me and lead me back to the house.

MOTHER. Aha! _She_ knew! I wish I could have caught him by the other ear!

SON. He says: "And when I was sent away on duty to another village, and so could not find time to write either to you or to her, she came close to the place where I was and where no one is permitted to come and asked to see her boy. She brought with her a great parcel of things for me to eat. What more am I to say for the concern she has for my welfare?"

MOTHER. Fools all old women are! May God reward that Kafir woman for her kindness, and her children after her.... As though any orders could keep out a mother! Does he say what she resembles in the face?

SON. No. He goes on to speak more about the customs of the French. He says: "The new men who join us come believing they are in the country of the Rakshas [Demons]. They are told this by the ignorant on their departure. It is always cold here. Many clothes are worn. The sun is absent. The wet is present. Yet this France is a country created by Allah, and its people are manifestly a reasonable people with reason for all they do. The windows of their houses are well barred. The doors are strong, with locks of a sort I have never before tried. Their dogs are faithful. They gather in and keep their kine and their asses and their hens under their hands at night. Their cattle graze and return at the proper hour in charge of the children. They prune their fruit trees as carefully as our barbers attend to men's nostrils and ears. The old women spin, walking up and down. Scissors, needles, threads, and buttons are exposed for sale on stalls in a market. They carry hens by the feet. Butchers sell dressed portions of fowls and sheep ready to be cooked. There is aniseed, coriander, and very good garlic."

MOTHER. But all this—but all this is our very own way—

SON. He says so. He says: "Seeing these things, the new men are relieved in their minds. Do not be anxious for me. These people precisely resemble all mankind. They are, however, idolators. They do not speak to any of us about their religion. Their Imams [priests] are old men of pious appearance, living in poverty. They go about their religious offices, even while the shells fall. Their God is called Bandoo [Bon Dieu?]. There is also the Bibbee Miriam [the Virgin Mary]. She is worshipped on account of the intelligence and capacity of the women."

FATHER. Hmm! Ah! This travelling about is bad for the young. Women are women—world over. What else, Akbar?

SON [_reading_]. "There are holy women in this country, dressed in black who wear horns of white cloth on their heads. They too, are without any sort of fear of death from the falling shells. I am acquainted with one such who often commands me to carry vegetables from the market to the house which they inhabit. It is filled with the fatherless. She is very old, very highborn, and of irascible temper. All men call her Mother. The Colonel himself salutes her. Thus are all sorts mingled in this country of France."

MOTHER. Ha! Well, at least that holy woman was well-born, but she is too free with her tongue. Go on!

SON. He says: "Through my skill with my rifle, I have been made a sharp-shooter. A special place is given to me to shoot at the enemy singly. This was old work to me. This country was flat and open at the beginning. In time it became all _kandari-kauderi_—cut up—with trenches, _sungars_ and bye-ways in the earth. Their faces show well behind the loop-holes of their _sungars_. The distance was less than three hundred yards. Great cunning was needed. Before they grew careful, I accounted for nine in five days. It is more difficult by night. They then send up fireballs which light all the ground. This is a good arrangement to reveal one's enemy, but the expense would be too great for poor people."

FATHER. He thinks of everything—everything! Even of the terrible cost for us poor people.

SON [_reading_]. "I attended the funeral of a certain French child. She was known to us all by the name of 'Marri' which is Miriam. She would openly claim the Regiment for her own regiment in the face of the Colonel walking in the street. She was slain by a shell while grazing cattle. What remained was carried upon a litter precisely after our custom. There were no hired mourners. All mourners walked slowly behind the litter, the women with the men. It is not their custom to scream or beat the breast. They recite all prayers above the grave itself for they reckon the burial-ground to be holy. The prayers are recited by the Imam of the village. The grave is not bricked and there is no recess. They do not know that the Two Angels visit the dead. They say at the end, 'Peace and Mercy be on you'."

MOTHER. One sees as he writes! He would have made a great priest, this son of ours. So they pray over their dead, out yonder, those foreigners?

FATHER. Even a Kafir may pray, but—they are manifestly Kafirs or they would not pray in a grave-yard. Go on!

SON. "When their prayers were done, our Havildar-Major, who is orthodox, recited the appropriate verse from the Koran, and cast a little mud into the grave. The Imam of the village then embraced him. I do not know if this is the custom. The French weep very little. The French women are small-handed and small-footed. They bear themselves in walking as though they were of birth and descent. They commune with themselves, walking up and down. Their lips move. This is on account of their dead. They are never abashed or at a loss for words. They forget nothing. Nothing either do they forgive."

MOTHER. Good. Very good. That is the right honour.

SON. Listen! He says: "Each village keeps a written account of all that the enemy has done against it. If a life—a life, whether it be man or priest, or hostage, or woman or babe. Every horn driven off; and every feather; all bricks and tiles broken, all things burned, and their price, are written in the account. The shames and the insults are also written. There is no price set against them."

FATHER. This is without flaw! This is a people! There is never any price for shame offered. And they write it all down. Marvellous!

SON. Yes. He says: "Each village keeps its own tally and all tallies go to their Government to be filed. The whole of the country of France is in one great account against the enemy—for the loss, for the lives, and for the shames done. It has been kept from the first. The women keep it with the men. All French women read, write, and cast accounts from youth. By this they are able to keep the great account against the enemy. I think that it is good that our girls should get schooling like this. Then we shall have no more confusion in our accounts. It is only to add up the sums lost and the lives. We should teach our girls. We are fools compared with these people."

MOTHER. But a Pathani girl remembers without all this book-work. It is waste. Who of any decent descent ever forgot a blood-debt? He must be sickening for illness to write thus.

FATHER. One should not forget. Yet we depend on songs and tales. It is more secure—certainly, it is more business-like—that a written account should be kept. Since it is the men who must pay off the debt, why should not the women keep it?

MOTHER. They can keep tally on a stick or a distaff. It is unnecessary for a girl to scribble in books. They never come to good ends. They end by——

SON. Sometimes, my mother, sometimes. On the Government side of the Border, women are taught to read, and write, and cast accounts, and—

MOTHER [_with intention_]. Far be the day when such an one is brought to _my_ house as a bride. For _I_ say——

FATHER. No matter. What does _he_ say about those French women?

SON. He says: "They are not divided in opinion as to which of their enemies shall be sought after first. They say: 'Let us even the account every day and night out of the nearest assembly of the enemy and when we have brought all the enemy into the right way of thinking we can demand the very people who did the shame and offences. In the meantime, let it be any life.' This is good counsel for _us_ in our account, oh my mother."

FATHER [_after a pause_]. True! True! It is good advice. Let it be any life.... Is that all?

SON. That is all. He says: "Let it be _any_ life." And I think so too.

MOTHER. "_Any_ life." Even so! And then we can write to him quickly that we have taken our revenge quickly. [_She reaches for her husband's rifle which she passes over to her son, who stretches his hand towards it with a glance at his father._]

FATHER. On your head, Akbar, our account must lie—at least till I am better. Do you try to-night?

SON. May be! I wish we had the high-priced illuminating fireballs he spoke of. [_Half rises._]

MOTHER. Wait a little. There is the call for the Ishr [the evening prayer].

MUEZZIN [_in the village mosque without as the first stars show_]. God is great! God is great! God is great! I bear witness, etc.

[_The family compose themselves for evening prayer._]

A TROOPER OF HORSE

To the sister of the pensioned Risaldar Major Abdul Qadr Khan, at her own house behind the shrine of Gulu Shah near by the village of Korake in the Pasrur Tehsil of the Sialkot District in the Province of the Punjab. Sent out of the country of France on the 23rd of August, 1916, by Duffadar Abdul Rahman of the 132nd (Pakpattan) Cavalry—late Lambart's Horse.

Mother! The news is that once only in five months I have not received a letter from you. My thoughts are always with you. Mother, put your ear down and listen to me. Do not fret; I will soon be with you again. Imagine that I have merely gone to Lyallpur [the big recruiting-depot in India]; think that I have been delayed there by an officer's order, or that I am not yet ready to come back. Mother, think of me always as though I were sitting near by, just as I imagine you always beside me. Be of good cheer, Mother, there is nothing that I have done which is hidden from you. I tell you truly, Mother, I will salute you again. Do not grieve. I tell you confidently I shall bow before you again in salutation. It will be thus, Mother. I shall come in the dead of the night and knock at your door. Then I will call loudly that you may wake and open the door to me. With great delight you will open the door and fold me to your breast, my Mother. Then I will sit down beside you and tell you what has happened to me—good and evil. Then having rested the night in comfort I will go out after the day has come and I will salute all my brethren at the mosque and in the village. Then I will return and eat my bread in pleasure and happiness. You, Mother, will say to me: "Shall I give you some _ghi_?" [native butter]. I will say at first proudly, like one who has travelled:—"No, I want none." You will press me, and I will softly push my plate over to you and you will fill it with _ghi_, and I shall dip my cake in it with delight. Believe me, Mother, this homecoming will take place just as I have described it. I see you before me always. It seems to me only yesterday that I bent to your feet when I made salutation and you put your hand upon my head.

Mother, put your trust in God to guard my head. If my grave lies in France it can never be in the Punjab, though we try for a thousand years. If it be in the Punjab then I shall certainly return to it to that very place. Meantime, Mother, consider what I have to eat. This is the true list. I eat daily sugar and ghi and flour, salt, meat, red peppers, some almonds and dates, sweets of various kinds as well as raisins and cardamoms. In the morning I eat tea and white biscuits. An hour after, halwa and puri [native dishes]. At noon, tea and bread; at seven o'clock of the evening, vegetable curry. At bedtime I drink milk. There is abundance of milk in this country. I am more comfortable here, I swear it to you, Mother, than any high officer in India. As for our clothing, there is no account kept of it. You would cry out, Mother, to see the thick cloth expended. So I beg you, Mother, to take comfort concerning your son. Do not tear my heart by telling me your years. Though we both lived to be as old as elephants I am your son who will come asking for you as I said, at your door.

As to the risk of death, who is free from it anywhere? Certainly not in the Punjab. I hear that all those religious mendicants at Zilabad have proclaimed a holy fair this summer in order that pious people may feed them, and now, having collected in thousands beside the river in hot weather, they have spread cholera all over the district. There is trouble raging throughout all the world, Mother, and yet these sons of mean fathers must proclaim a beggars' festival in order to add to it! There should be an order of the Government to take all those lazy rascals out of India into France and put them in our front-line that their bodies may be sieves for the machine guns. Why cannot they blacken their faces and lie in a corner with a crust of bread? It is certainly right to feed the family priests, Mother, but when the idle assemble in thousands begging and making sickness and polluting the drinking-water, punishment should be administered.

Very much sickness, such as cholera and dysentery, is caused by drinking foul water. Therefore, it is best to have it boiled, Mother, no matter what is said. When clothes are washed in foul water, sickness also spreads. You will say, Mother, that I am no longer a trooper but a washer-woman or an apothecary, but I swear to you, my Mother, what I have said is true. Now, I have two charges to deliver to you as to the household under you. I beg you, my Mother, to give order that my son drink water which is boiled, at least from the beginning of the hot weather till after the Rains. That is one charge. The second is that when I was going down to the sea with the Regiment from home, the Lady Doctor Sahiba in the Civil Lines asked of our Colonel's lady whether any of us desired that their households should take the charm against the small-pox [be vaccinated]. I was then busy with my work and I made no reply. Now let that Doctor Sahiba know that I desire by her favour that my son take the charm as soon as may be. I charge you, Mother, upon _his_ head that it is done soon. I beg you respectfully to take this charge upon you.

Oh, my Mother, if I could now see you for but half of one watch in the night or at evening preparing food! I remember the old days in my dreamings but when I awake—there is the sleeper and there is the bedding and it is more far off than Delhi. But God will accomplish the meetings and surely arrange the return.

Mother, before going out to the attack the other day, I had a dream. I dreamed that a great snake appeared in our trenches in France and at the same time our Pir Murshid [our family priest] whose face I saw quite clearly, appeared with a stick and destroyed it. Well then, Mother, our lot went in to the attack and returned from it safely. Those who were fated to be the victims of death were taken and those who were fated to be wounded were wounded; and all our party returned safely. At the same time, the Government secured a victory and the Regiment obtained renown. It was _our_ horse that went out over the trenches, Mother, and the Germans, being alarmed, fled. We were forbidden to pursue because of hidden guns. This was trouble to us. We owed them much blood on our brethren's account. Tell the Murshid my dream and ask him for a full interpretation. I have also seen our Murshid twice before in my dreams. Ask him why he comes to me thus. I am not conscious of any wrong-doing, and if it is a sign of favour to me, then the shape should speak.

I am quite aware how God rewards the unwilling. He is all powerful. Look at the case of that man of our own family who was ordered to the front with a higher rank. He refused promotion in order to stay behind, and in a month's time he died of the plague in his own village. If he had gone to the front his family would have received the war pension. An atheist never achieves honour, Mother. He is always unsettled and has no consolations. Do we Mussulmans think that the Prophet will spend all his time in asking God to forgive our transgressions? Tell the Pir Murshid what I have written.

Mother, put down your ear and listen to me in this matter, my Mother. There is one thing I wish to impress earnestly on you. You must know that among recruits for the Regiment there are too few of our kind of Mussulmans. They are sending recruits from the Punjab who were formerly labourers and common workmen. The consequence of this is, in the Regiment, that we Mussulmans are completely outnumbered by these low people, and the promotions go accordingly. Each of our troops, my Mother, has been divided into two; that is to say there are four troops to a squadron. We Mussulmans should have at least two troops out of the four, but owing to the lack of recruits we have not sufficient men of our faith to form more than one. Now, Mother, as it was in our fathers' time, he who supplies the men gets the promotion. Therefore, if our friends at home, and especially our Pir Murshid, would exert themselves to supply fifteen or twenty recruits, I could approach my Colonel Sahib in regard to promotion. If my Colonel received my request favourably then you at home would only have the trouble to provide the men. But I do not think, Mother, there would be any trouble if our Pir Murshid exerted himself in the matter and if my father's brother also exerted himself. A family is a family even [if it be] scattered to the ends of the earth, Mother. My father's brother's name is still remembered in the Regiment on account of his long service and his great deeds of old. Tell him, my Mother, that the men talk of him daily as though he had only resigned yesterday. If he rides out among the villages with his medals he will certainly fetch in many of our class. If it were fifty it would mean much more influence for me with my Colonel. He is very greedy for our class of Mahommedans.

Mother, our Pir Murshid too, is a very holy man. If he preached to them after harvest he would fetch in many and I should be promoted, and the pensions go with the promotion. In a short time by God's assistance, I might command a troop if sufficient recruits were attained by the exertions of my friends and well-wishers. The honour of one is the honour of all. Lay all this before the Murshid and my uncle.

None of the Cavalry have yet done anything to compare with our Regiment. This may be because of fate or that their nature is not equal to ours. There is great honour to be got out of a lance before long. The war has become loosened and cavalry patrols are being sent forward. We have driven Mama Lumra [a nickname for the enemy] several miles across country. He has planted his feet again but it is not the same Mama Lumra. His arrogance is gone. Our guns turn the earth upside down upon him. He has made himself houses underground which are in all respects fortresses with beds, chairs and lights. Our guns break these in. There is little to see because Mama Lumra is buried underneath. These days are altogether different from the days when all our Army was here and Mama Lumra's guns overwhelmed us by day and by night. Now Mama Lumra eats his own stick. Fighting goes on in the sky, on earth and under earth. Such a fighting is rarely vouchsafed any one to behold. Yet if one reflects upon God it is no more than rain on a roof. Mother, once I was reported "missing, killed or believed taken prisoner." I went with a patrol to a certain place beyond which we went forward to a place which had recently been taken by the English infantry. Suddenly the enemy's fire fell upon us and behind us like water. Seeing we could not go back, we lay down in the holes made by the shells. The enemy exerted himself to the utmost, but our guns having found him bombarded him and he ceased. In the evening we retired out of our shell-holes. We had to walk; it was fasting time and we suffered from thirst. So our hearts were relieved when we returned to the Regiment. We had all been reported to Divisional Headquarters as lost. This false report was then cancelled. The shell-holes in the ground are the size of our goat-pen and as deep as my height with the arm raised. They are more in number than can be counted, and of all colours. It is like small-pox upon the ground.

We have no small-pox or diseases here. Our doctors are strict, and refuse is burned by the sweepers. It is said there is no physician like fire. He leaves nothing to the flies. It is said that flies produce sicknesses, especially when they are allowed to sit on the nostrils and the corners of the eyes of the children or to fall into their milk-pots. The young children of this country of France are beautiful and do not suffer from sickness. Their women do not die in childbed. This is on account of physicians and midwives who abound in knowledge. It is a Government order, Mother, that none can establish as a midwife till she has shown her ability. These people are idolators. When there is a death which is not caused by war, they instantly ascribe it to some fault in eating or drinking or the conduct of life on the part of the dead. If one dies without manifest cause the physicians at once mutilate the body to ascertain what evil was hidden inside it. If anything is discovered there is a criminal trial. Thus the women-folk do not traffic in poisons and wives have no suspicion one against the other. Truly, Mother, people are only defective on account of ignorance. Learning and knowledge are the important things.

Your letters come to me with every mail exactly as if we were at headquarters. This is accomplished solely by knowledge. There are hundreds of women behind our lines who make clean and repair the dirty clothes of the troops. Afterwards, they are baked in very hot ovens which utterly destroy the vermin and also, it is said, diseases. We have, too, been issued iron helmets to protect the head against falling shots. It was asked of us all if any had an objection. The Sikhs reported that they had not found any permission in their Law to wear such things. They, therefore, go uncovered. It was reported by our priests for us Mahommedans that our Law neither forbids nor enjoins. It is a thing indifferent. They are heavier than the pagri [turban], but they turn falling iron. Doubtless, it is Allah's will that the lives of His Faithful should be prolonged by these hats. The sons of mothers who go to foreign parts are specially kept under His Eye.

We know very well how the world is made. To earn a living and bear trouble is the duty of man. If I send you a report that I have won promotion in the Regiment, do not forget to distribute alms to the extent of fifteen rupees and to feed the poor.

Mother, put down your ear and listen to me. There is no danger whatever in box-pictures [snapshot-photographs]. Anyone submitted to them is in all respects as he was before. Nothing is taken out of his spirit. I, myself, Mother, have submitted myself to many box-pictures, both mounted and standing beside my horse. If at any time again the Zenana Doctor Sahiba desires to make a box-picture of _him_ do not snatch the child away but send the picture to me. I cannot see him in my dreams because at his age he changes with each month. When I went away he was still on all fours. Now you tell me he stands up holding by the skirts. I wish to see a box-picture of this very greatly indeed. I can read box-pictures now as perfectly as the French. When I was new to this country I could not understand their meaning in the least. This is on account of knowledge which comes by foreign travel and experience. Mother, this world abounds in marvels beyond belief. We in India are but stones compared to these people. They do not litigate among themselves; they speak truth at first answer; their weddings are not [performed] till both sides are at least eighteen, and no man has authority here to beat his wife.

I have resided in billets with an old man and his wife, who possess seven hens, an ass, and a small field of onions. They collect dung from our horse-lines upon their backs, a very little at a time but continuously. They are without means of maintenance, yet they do not lay a finger upon any food except through invitation. They exhibit courtesy to each other in all things.

They call me _Sia_ [monsieur?] which is Mian [Mahommedan title of respect] and also _man barah_ [mon brave?] which signifies hero. I have spoken to them many times of you, my Mother, and they desire I send you their salutations. She calls me to account strictly for my doings each day. At evening tide I am fetched in with the hens. My clothes are then inspected and repaired when there is need. She turns me back and forth between her hands. If I exhibit impatience, she hits me upon the side of the head, and I say to my heart it is your hands.

Now this is the French language, Mother.

(1) _Zuur mononfahn._ The morning salutation.

(2) _Wasi lakafeh._ Coffee is prepared.

(3) _Abil towah mononfahn._ Rise and go to parade.

(4) _Dormeh beeahn mon fiz nublieh pahleh Bondihu._

This is their dismissal at night, invoking the blessing of their God. They use a _Tasbih_ [rosary] in form like ours but of more beads. They recite prayers both sitting and walking. Having seen my _Tasbih_ these old people become curious concerning the Faith. Certainly they are idolators. I have seen the images by the roadside which they worship. Yet they are certainly not Kafirs, who hide the truth and the mercy of Allah is illimitable. They two send you their salutations thus:— _Onvoyeh no zalutazioun zempresseh ar zmadam vot mair._ It is their form of blessing.

She has borne three sons. Two are already dead in this war and of the third no information since the spring-time. There remains in the house the son of the eldest son. He is three years old. His name is Pir, which in their language also means a holy man. He runs barefoot in summer and wears only one garment. He eats all foods and specially dates. In this country it is not allowed to give children pepper or cardamoms. He has learned to speak our tongue and bears a wooden sword which was made for him and a turban of our sort. When he is weary he repairs to the centre of my bed which is forbidden to him by his grandmother of whom he has no fear. He fears nothing. My Mother, he is almost the same sort as my own. He sends his salutations to him. He calls him "My brother who is in India." He also prays for him aloud before an idol which he is taken to worship. On account of his fatness he cannot yet kneel long, but falls over sideways. The idol is of Bibbee Miriam [the Virgin Mary] whom they, in this country, believe to watch over children. He has also a small idol of his own above his bed which represents a certain saint called Pir. He rides upon the ass and says he will become a trooper. I take delight in his presence and his conversation.

The children in this country are learned from their very birth. They go to the schools even when the shells fall near by. They know all the countries in the world, and to read and write in their language and to cast accounts. Even the girls of eight years can cast accounts and those that are marriageable have complete knowledge of cookery, accounts, and governments, and washing of clothes, agriculture and the manufacture of garments and all other offices: otherwise they are reckoned infirm-minded. Each girl is given a dowry to which she adds with her own hands. No man molests any woman here on any occasion. They come and go at their pleasure upon their business. There is one thing I should like to see, Mother. I should like to see all the men of India with all their wives brought to France in order to see the country and profit by their experiences. Here are no quarrels or contentions, and there is no dishonesty. All day long men do their work and the women do theirs. Compared with these people the people of India do not work at all, but all day long are occupied with evil thoughts and our women all day long they do nothing but quarrel. Now I see this. The blame for this state of affairs, Mother, lies upon the men of India, for if the men were to educate the women they would give up quarrelling.

When a man goes out into the world his understanding is enlarged and he becomes proficient in different kinds of work. All that is needed is to show courage. At the present time, one's bravery or one's cowardice is apparent. The opportunities for advancement come quickly. Such opportunities will not occur again.

As for any marriage proposed [for me?] when I return, those things can wait till I return. It is no gain to take into the house a child or a sickly one who, through no fault of her own, dies in bringing forth. If there be any talk between our house and any other family upon this subject they should understand that I desire knowledge more than dowry. There are schools where girls are educated by English ladies. I am not of the sort to make a wedding outside my clan or country, but if I fight to keep Mama Lumra out of the Punjab I will choose my wives out of the Punjab. I desire nothing that is contrary to the Faith, Mother, but what was ample yesterday does not cover even the palm of the hand to-day. This is owing to the spread of enlightenment among all men coming and going and observing matters which they had never before known to exist.

In this country when one of them dies, the tomb is marked and named and kept like a garden so that the others may go to mourn over her. Nor do they believe a burial-ground to be inhabited by evil spirits or ghouls. When I was upon a certain duty last month, I lay three nights in a grave-yard. None troubled me, even though the dead had been removed from their graves by the violence of shells bursting. One was a woman of this country, newly dead, whom we reburied for the sake of the Pity of Allah, and made the prayer. Tell the Pir Murshid this, and that I performed _Tayamummum_ [the shorter purification with sand or dust] afterwards. There was no time for the full purification.

Oh, my Mother, my Mother, I am your son, your son; and as I have said at the beginning I will return to your arms from out of this country, when God shall permit!

THE STORY OF GADSBY

Preface

TO THE ADDRESS OF
CAPTAIN J. MAFFLIN,
Duke of Derry's (Pink) Hussars.

DEAR MAFFLIN,—You will remember that I wrote this story as an Awful Warning. None the less you have seen fit to disregard it and have followed Gadsby's example—as I betted you would. I acknowledge that you paid the money at once, but you have prejudiced the mind of Mrs. Mafflin against myself, for though I am almost the only respectable friend of your bachelor days, she has been darwaza band to me throughout the season. Further, she caused you to invite me to dinner at the Club, where you called me "a wild ass of the desert," and went home at half-past ten, after discoursing for twenty minutes on the responsibilities of housekeeping. You now drive a mail-phaeton and sit under a Church of England clergyman. I am not angry, Jack. It is your kismet, as it was Gaddy's, and his kismet who can avoid? Do not think that I am moved by a spirit of revenge as I write, thus publicly, that you and you alone are responsible for this book. In other and more expansive days, when you could look at a magnum without flushing and at a cheroot without turning white, you supplied me with most of the material. Take it back again—would that I could have preserved your fatherless speech in the telling—take it back, and by your slippered hearth read it to the late Miss Deercourt. She will not be any the more willing to receive my cards, but she will admire you immensely, and you, I feel sure, will love me. You may even invite me to another very bad dinner—at the Club, which, as you and your wife know, is a safe neutral ground for the entertainment of wild asses. Then, my very dear hypocrite, we shall be quits.

Yours always,

RUDYARD KIPLING.

P. S.—On second thoughts I should recommend you to keep the book away from Mrs. Mafflin.

POOR DEAR MAMMA

The wild hawk to the wind-swept sky, The deer to the wholesome wold, And the heart of a man to the heart of a maid, As it was in the days of old. Gypsy Song.

SCENE.—Interior of Miss MINNIE THREEGAN'S Bedroom at Simla. Miss THREEGAN, in window-seat, turning over a drawerful of things. Miss EMMA DEERCOURT, bosom—friend, who has come to spend the day, sitting on the bed, manipulating the bodice of a ballroom frock, and a bunch of artificial lilies of the valley. Time, 5:30 P. M. on a hot May afternoon.

Miss DEERCOURT. And he said: "I shall never forget this dance," and, of course, I said: "Oh, how can you be so silly!" Do you think he meant anything, dear?

Miss THREEGAN. (Extracting long lavender silk stocking from the rubbish.) You know him better than I do.

Miss D. Oh, do be sympathetic, Minnie! I'm sure he does. At least I would be sure if he wasn't always riding with that odious Mrs. Hagan.

Miss T. I suppose so. How does one manage to dance through one's heels first? Look at this—isn't it shameful? (Spreads stocking—heel on open hand for inspection.)

Miss D. Never mind that! You can't mend it. Help me

with this hateful bodice. I've run the string so, and I've run the string so, and I can't make the fulness come right. Where would you put this? (Waves lilies of the valley.)

Miss T. As high up on the shoulder as possible.

Miss D. Am I quite tall enough? I know it makes May Older look lopsided.

Miss T. Yes, but May hasn't your shoulders. Hers are like a hock-bottle.

BEARER. (Rapping at door.) Captain Sahib aya.

Miss D. (Jumping up wildly, and hunting for bodice, which she has discarded owing to the heat of the day.) Captain Sahib! What Captain Sahib? Oh, good gracious, and I'm only half dressed! Well, I sha'n't bother.

Miss T. (Calmly.) You needn't. It isn't for us. That's Captain Gadsby. He is going for a ride with Mamma. He generally comes five days out of the seven.

AGONIZED VOICE. (Prom an inner apartment.) Minnie, run out and give Captain Gadsby some tea, and tell him I shall be ready in ten minutes; and, O Minnie, come to me an instant, there's a dear girl!

Miss T. Oh, bother! (Aloud.) Very well, Mamma.

Exit, and reappears, after five minutes, flushed, and rubbing her fingers.

Miss D. You look pink. What has happened?

Miss T. (In a stage whisper.) A twenty-four-inch waist, and she won't let it out. Where are my bangles? (Rummager on the toilet-table, and dabs at her hair with a brush in the interval.)

Miss D. Who is this Captain Gadsby? I don't think I've met him.

Miss T. You must have. He belongs to the Harrar set. I've danced with him, but I've never talked to him. He's a big yellow man, just like a newly-hatched chicken, with an enormous moustache. He walks like this (imitates Cavalry swagger), and he goes "Ha—Hmmm!" deep down in his throat when he can't think of anything to say. Mamma likes him. I don't.

Miss D. (Abstractedly.) Does he wax that moustache?

Miss T. (Busy with Powder-puff.) Yes, I think so. Why?

Miss D. (Bending over the bodice and sewing furiously.) Oh, nothing—only—Miss T. (Sternly.) Only what? Out with it, Emma.

Miss D. Well, May Olger—she's engaged to Mr. Charteris, you know—said—Promise you won't repeat this?

Miss T. Yes, I promise. What did she say?

Miss D. That—that being kissed (with a rush) with a man who didn't wax his moustache was—like eating an egg without salt.

Miss T. (At her full height, with crushing scorn.) May Olger is a horrid, nasty Thing, and you can tell her I said so. I'm glad she doesn't belong to my set—I must go and feed this man! Do I look presentable?

Miss D. Yes, perfectly. Be quick and hand him over to your Mother, and then we can talk. I shall listen at the door to hear what you say to him.

Miss T. 'Sure I don't care. I'm not afraid of Captain Gadsby.

In proof of this swings into the drawing-room with a mannish stride followed by two short steps, which Produces the effect of a restive horse entering. Misses CAPTAIN GADSBY, who is sitting in the shadow of the window-curtain, and gazes round helplessly.

CAPTAIN GADSBY. (Aside.) The filly, by Jove! 'Must ha' picked up that action from the sire. (Aloud, rising.) Good evening, Miss Threegan.

Miss T. (Conscious that she is flushing.) Good evening, Captain Gadsby. Mamma told me to say that she will be ready in a few minutes. Won't you have some tea? (Aside.) I hope Mamma will be quick. What am I to say to the creature? (Aloud and abruptly.) Milk and sugar?

CAPT. G. No sugar, tha-anks, and very little milk. Ha—Hmmm.

Miss T. (Aside.) If he's going to do that, I'm lost. I shall laugh. I know I shall!

CAPT. G. (Pulling at his moustache and watching it sideways down his nose.) Ha—Hamm. (Aside.) 'Wonder what the little beast can talk about. 'Must make a shot at it.

Miss T. (Aside.) Oh, this is agonizing. I must say something.

Both Together. Have you Been—CAPT. G. I beg your pardon. You were going to say—Miss T. (Who has been watching the moustache with awed fascination.) Won't you have some eggs?

CAPT. G. (Looking bewilderedly at the tea-table.) Eggs! (Aside.) O Hades! She must have a nursery-tea at this hour. S'pose they've wiped her mouth and sent her to me while the Mother is getting on her duds. (Aloud.) No, thanks.

Miss T. (Crimson with confusion.) Oh! I didn't mean that. I wasn't thinking of mou—eggs for an instant. I mean salt. Won't you have some sa—sweets? (Aside.) He'll think me a raving lunatic. I wish Mamma would come.

CAPT. G. (Aside.) It was a nursery-tea and she's ashamed of it. By Jove! She doesn't look half bad when she colors up like that. (Aloud, helping himself from the dish.) Have you seen those new chocolates at Peliti's?

Miss T. No, I made these myself. What are they like?

CAPT. G. These! De-licious. (Aside.) And that's a fact.

Miss T. (Aside.) Oh, bother! he'll think I'm fishing for compliments. (Aloud.) No, Peliti's of course.

CAPT. G. (Enthusiastically.) Not to compare with these. How d'you make them? I can't get my khansamah to understand the simplest thing beyond mutton and fowl.

Miss T. Yes? I'm not a khansamah, you know. Perhaps you frighten him. You should never frighten a servant. He loses his head. It's very bad policy.

CAPT. G. He's so awf'ly stupid.

Miss T. (Folding her hands in her Zap.) You should call him quietly and say: "O khansamah jee!"

CAPT. G. (Getting interested.) Yes? (Aside.) Fancy that little featherweight saying, "O khansamah jee" to my bloodthirsty Mir Khan!

Miss T Then you should explain the dinner, dish by dish.

CAPT. G. But I can't speak the vernacular.

Miss T. (Patronizingly.) You should pass the Higher Standard and try.

CAPT. G. I have, but I don't seem to be any the wiser. Are you?

Miss T. I never passed the Higher Standard. But the khansamah is very patient with me. He doesn't get angry when I talk about sheep's topees, or order maunds of grain when I mean seers.

CAPT. G. (Aside with intense indignation.) I'd like to see Mir Khan being rude to that girl! Hullo! Steady the Buffs! (Aloud.) And do you understand about horses, too?

Miss T. A little—not very much. I can't doctor them, but I know what they ought to eat, and I am in charge of our stable.

CAPT. G. Indeed! You might help me then. What ought a man to give his sais in the Hills? My ruffian says eight rupees, because everything is so dear.

Miss T. Six rupees a month, and one rupee Simla allowance—neither more nor less. And a grass-cut gets six rupees. That's better than buying grass in the bazar.

CAPT. G. (Admiringly.) How do you know?

Miss T. I have tried both ways.

CAPT. G. Do you ride much, then? I've never seen you on the Mall.

Miss T. (Aside.) I haven't passed him more than fifty times. (Aloud.) Nearly every day.

CAPT. G. By Jove! I didn't know that. Ha—Hamm (Pulls at his moustache and is silent for forty seconds.) Miss T. (Desperately, and wondering what will happen next.) It looks beautiful. I shouldn't touch it if I were you. (Aside.) It's all Mamma's fault for not coming before. I will be rude!

CAPT. G. (Bronzing under the tan and bringing down his hand very quickly.) Eh! What-at! Oh, yes! Ha! Ha! (Laughs uneasily.) (Aside.) Well, of all the dashed cheek! I never had a woman say that to me yet. She must be a cool hand or else— Ah! that nursery-tea!

VOICE PROM THE UNKNOWN. Tchk! Tchk! Tchk!

CAPT. G. Good gracious! What's that?

Miss T. The dog, I think. (Aside.) Emma has been listening, and I'll never forgive her!

CAPT. G. (Aside.) They don't keep dogs here. (Aloud.) 'Didn't sound like a dog, did it?

Miss T. Then it must have been the cat. Let's go into the veranda. What a lovely evening it is!

Steps into veranda and looks out across the hills into sunset. The CAPTAIN follows.

CAPT. G. (Aside.) Superb eyes! I wonder that I never noticed them before! (Aloud.) There's going to be a dance at Viceregal Lodge on Wednesday. Can you spare me one?

Miss T. (Shortly.) No! I don't want any of your charity-dances. You only ask me because Mamma told you to. I hop and I bump. You know I do!

CAPT. G. (Aside.) That's true, but little girls shouldn't understand these things. (Aloud.) No, on my word, I don't. You dance beautifully.

Miss T. Then why do you always stand out after half a dozen turns? I thought officers in the Army didn't tell fibs.

CAPT. G. It wasn't a fib, believe me. I really do want the pleasure of a dance with you.

Miss T. (Wickedly.) Why? Won't Mamma dance with you any more?

CAPT. G. (More earnestly than the necessity demands.) I wasn't thinking of your Mother. (Aside.) You little vixen!

Miss T. (Still looking out of the window.) Eh? Oh, I beg your par don. I was thinking of something else.

CAPT. G. (Aside.) Well! I wonder what she'll say next. I've never known a woman treat me like this before. I might be—Dash it, I might be an Infantry subaltern! (Aloud.) Oh, please don't trouble. I'm not worth thinking about. Isn't your Mother ready yet?

Miss T. I should think so; but promise me, Captain Gadsby, you won't take poor dear Mamma twice round Jakko any more. It tires her so.

CAPT. G. She says that no exercise tires her.

Miss T. Yes, but she suffers afterward. You don't know what rheumatism is, and you oughtn't to keep her out so late, when it gets chill in the evenings.

CAPT. G. (Aside.) Rheumatism. I thought she came off her horse rather in a bunch. Whew! One lives and learns. (Aloud.) I'm sorry to hear that. She hasn't mentioned it to me.

Miss T. (Flurried.) Of course not! Poor dear Mamma never would. And you mustn't say that I told you either. Promise me that you won't. Oh, CAPTAIN Gadsby, promise me you won't!

CAPT. G. I am dumb, or—I shall be as soon as you've given me that dance, and another—if you can trouble yourself to think about me for a minute.

Miss T. But you won't like it one little bit. You'll be awfully sorry afterward.

CAPT. G. I shall like it above all things, and I shall only be sorry that I didn't get more. (Aside.) Now what in the world am I saying?

Miss T. Very well. You will have only yourself to thank if your toes are trodden on. Shall we say Seven?

CAPT. G. And Eleven. (Aside.) She can't be more than eight stone, but, even then, it's an absurdly small foot. (Looks at his own riding boots.)

Miss T. They're beautifully shiny. I can almost see my face in them.

CAPT. G. I was thinking whether I should have to go on crutches for the rest of my life if you trod on my toes.

Miss T. Very likely. Why not change Eleven for a square?

CAPT. G. No, please! I want them both waltzes. Won't you write them down?

Miss T. J don't get so many dances that I shall confuse them. You will be the offender.

CAPT. G. Wait and see! (Aside.) She doesn't dance perfectly, perhaps, but—

Miss T. Your tea must have got cold by this time. Won't you have another cup?

CAPT. G. No, thanks. Don't you think it's pleasanter out in the veranda? (Aside.) I never saw hair take that color in the sunshine before. (Aloud.) It's like one of Dicksee's pictures.

Miss T. Yes I It's a wonderful sunset, isn't it? (Bluntly.) But what do you know about Dicksee's pictures?

CAPT. G. I go Home occasionally. And I used to know the Galleries. (Nervously.) You mustn't think me only a Philistine with—a moustache.

Miss T. Don't! Please don't. I'm so sorry for what I said then. I was horribly rude. It slipped out before I thought. Don't you know the temptation to say frightful and shocking things just for the mere sake of saying them? I'm afraid I gave way to it.

CAPT. G. (Watching the girl as she flushes.) I think I know the feeling. It would be terrible if we all yielded to it, wouldn't it? For instance, I might say—POOR DEAR MAMMA. (Entering, habited, hatted, and booted.) Ah, Captain Gadsby? 'Sorry to keep you waiting. 'Hope you haven't been bored. 'My little girl been talking to you?

Miss T. (Aside.) I'm not sorry I spoke about the rheumatism. I'm not! I'm NOT! I only wished I'd mentioned the corns too.

CAPT. G. (Aside.) What a shame! I wonder how old she is. It never occurred to me before. (Aloud.) We've been discussing "Shakespeare and the musical glasses" in the veranda.

Miss T. (Aside.) Nice man! He knows that quotation. He isn't a Philistine with a moustache. (Aloud.) Good-bye, Captain Gadsby. (Aside.) What a huge hand and what a squeeze! I don't suppose he meant it, but he has driven the rings into my fingers.

POOR DEAR MAMMA. Has Vermillion come round yet? Oh, yes! Captain Gadsby, don't you think that the saddle is too far forward? (They pass into the front veranda.)

CAPT. G. (Aside.) How the dickens should I know what she prefers? She told me that she doted on horses. (Aloud.) I think it is.

Miss T. (Coming out into front veranda.) Oh! Bad Buldoo! I must speak to him for this. He has taken up the curb two links, and Vermillion bates that. (Passes out and to horse's head.)

CAPT. G. Let me do it!

Miss. T. No, Vermillion understands me. Don't you, old man? (Looses curb-chain skilfully, and pats horse on nose and throttle.) Poor Vermillion! Did they want to cut his chin off? There!

Captain Gadsby watches the interlude with undisguised admiration.

POOR DEAR MAMMA. (Tartly to Miss T.) You've forgotten your guest, I think, dear.

Miss T. Good gracious! So I have! Good-bye. (Retreats indoors hastily.)

POOR DEAR MAMMA. (Bunching reins in fingers hampered by too tight gauntlets.) CAPTAIN Gadsby!

CAPTAIN GADSBY stoops and makes the foot-rest. POOR DEAR MAMMA blunders, halts too long, and breaks through it.

CAPT. G. (Aside.) Can't hold up even stone forever. It's all your rheumatism. (Aloud.) Can't imagine why I was so clumsy. (Aside.) Now Little Featherweight would have gone up like a bird.

They ride oat of the garden. The Captain falls back.

CAPT. G. (Aside.) How that habit catches her under the arms! Ugh!

POOR DEAR MAMMA. (With the worn smile of sixteen seasons, the worse for exchange.) You're dull this afternoon, CAPTAIN Gadsby.

CAPT. G. (Spurring up wearily.) Why did you keep me waiting so long?

Et cetera, et cetera, et cetera.

(AN INTERVAL OF THREE WEEKS.)

GILDED YOUTH. (Sitting on railings opposite Town Hall.) Hullo, Gandy! 'Been trotting out the Gorgonzola! We all thought it was the Gorgan you're mashing.

CAPT. G. (With withering emphasis.) You young cub! What the—does it matter to you?

Proceeds to read GILDED YOUTH a lecture on discretion and deportment, which crumbles latter like a Chinese Lantern. Departs fuming.

(FURTHER INTERVAL OF FIVE WEEKS.) SCENE.—

Exterior of New Simla Library on a foggy evening. Miss THREECAN and Miss DEERCOURT meet among the 'rickshaws. Miss T. is carrying a bundle of books under her left arm.

Miss D. (Level intonation.) Well?

Miss 'I'. (Ascending intonation.) Well?

Miss D. (Capturing her friend's left arm, taking away all the books, placing books in 'rickshaw, returning to arm, securing hand by third finger and investigating.) Well! You bad girl! And you never told me.

Miss T. (Demurely.) He—he—he only spoke yesterday afternoon.

Miss D. Bless you, dear! And I'm to be bridesmaid, aren't I? You know you promised ever so long ago.

Miss T. Of course. I'll tell you all about it to-morrow. (Gets into 'rickshaw.) O Emma!

Miss D. (With intense interest.) Yes, dear?

Miss T. (Piano.) It's quite true—— about—the—egg.

Miss D. What egg?

Miss T. (Pianissimo prestissimo.) The egg without the salt. (Porte.) Chalo ghar ko jaldi, jhampani! (Go home, jhampani.)

THE WORLD WITHOUT

Certain people of importance.

SCENE.—Smoking-room of the Degchi Club. Time, 10.30 P. M. of a stuffy night in the Rains. Four men dispersed in picturesque attitudes and easy-chairs. To these enter BLAYNE of the Irregular Moguls, in evening dress.

BLAYNE. Phew! The Judge ought to be hanged in his own store-godown. Hi, khitmatgarl Poora whiskey-peg, to take the taste out of my mouth.

CURTISS. (Royal Artillery.) That's it, is it? What the deuce made you dine at the Judge's? You know his bandobust.

BLAYNE. 'Thought it couldn't be worse than the Club, but I'll swear he buys ullaged liquor and doctors it with gin and ink (looking round the room.) Is this all of you to-night?

DOONE. (P.W.D.) Anthony was called out at dinner. Mingle had a pain in his tummy.

CURTISS. Miggy dies of cholera once a week in the Rains, and gets drunk on chlorodyne in between. 'Good little chap, though. Any one at the Judge's, Blayne?

BLAYNE. Cockley and his memsahib looking awfully white and fagged. Female—girl—couldn't catch the name—on her way to the Hills, under the Cockleys' charge—the Judge, and Markyn fresh from Simla—disgustingly fit.

CURTISS. Good Lord, how truly magnificent! Was there enough ice? When I mangled garbage there I got one whole lump—nearly as big as a walnut. What had Markyn to say for himself?

BLAYNE. 'Seems that every one is having a fairly good time up there in spite of the rain. By Jove, that reminds me! I know I hadn't come across just for the pleasure of your society. News! Great news! Markyn told me.

DOONE. Who's dead now?

BLAYNE. No one that I know of; but Gandy's hooked at last!

DROPPING CHORUS. How much? The Devil! Markyn was pulling your leg. Not GANDY!

BLAYNE. (Humming.) "Yea, verily, verily, verily! Verily, verily, I say unto thee." Theodore, the gift o' God! Our Phillup! It's been given out up above.

MACKESY. (Barrister-at-Law.) Huh! Women will give out anything. What does accused say?

BLAYNE. Markyn told me that he congratulated him warily—one hand held out, t'other ready to guard. Gandy turned pink and said it was so.

CURTISS. Poor old Caddy! They all do it. Who's she? Let's hear the details.

BLAYNE. She's a girl—daughter of a Colonel Somebody.

DOONE. Simla's stiff with Colonels' daughters. Be more explicit.

BLAYNE. Wait a shake. What was her name? Thresomething. Three—

CURTISS. Stars, perhaps. Caddy knows that brand.

BLAYNE. Threegan—Minnie Threegan.

MACKESY. Threegan Isn't she a little bit of a girl with red hair?

BLAYNE. 'Bout that—from what from what Markyn said.

MACKESY. Then I've met her. She was at Lucknow last season. 'Owned a permanently juvenile Mamma, and danced damnably. I say, Jervoise, you knew the Threegans, didn't you?

JERVOISE. (Civilian of twenty-five years' service, waking up from his doze.) Eh? What's that? Knew who? How? I thought I was at Home, confound you!

MACKESY. The Threegan girl's engaged, so Blayne says.

JERVOISE. (Slowly.) Engaged—en-gaged! Bless my soul! I'm getting an old man! Little Minnie Threegan engaged. It was only the other day I went home with them in the Surat—no, the Massilia—and she was crawling about on her hands and knees among the ayahs. 'Used to call me the "Tick Tack Sahib" because I showed her my watch. And that was in Sixty—Seven-no, Seventy. Good God, how time flies! I'm an old man. I remember when Threegan married Miss Derwent—daughter of old Hooky Derwent—but that was before your time. And so the little baby's engaged to have a little baby of her own! Who's the other fool?

MACKESY. Gadsby of the Pink Hussars.

JERVOISE. 'Never met him. Threegan lived in debt, married in debt, and 'll die in debt. 'Must be glad to get the girl off his hands.

BLAYNE. Caddy has money—lucky devil. Place at Home, too.

DOONE. He comes of first-class stock. 'Can't quite understand his being caught by a Colonel's daughter, and (looking cautiously round room.) Black Infantry at that! No offence to you, Blayne.

BLAYNE. (Stiffly.) Not much, thaanks.

CURTISS. (Quoting motto of Irregular Moguls.) "We are what we are," eh, old man? But Gandy was such a superior animal as a rule. Why didn't he go Home and pick his wife there?

MACKESY. They are all alike when they come to the turn into the straight. About thirty a man begins to get sick of living alone.

CURTISS. And of the eternal muttony-chop in the morning.

DOONE. It's a dead goat as a rule, but go on, Mackesy.

MACKESY. If a man's once taken that way nothing will hold him, Do you remember Benoit of your service, Doone? They transferred him to Tharanda when his time came, and he married a platelayer's daughter, or something of that kind. She was the only female about the place.

DONE. Yes, poor brute. That smashed Benoit's chances of promotion altogether. Mrs. Benoit used to ask "Was you gem' to the dance this evenin'?"

CURTISS. Hang it all! Gandy hasn't married beneath him. There's no tarbrush in the family, I suppose.

JERVOISE. Tar-brush! Not an anna. You young fellows talk as though the man was doing the girl an honor in marrying her. You're all too conceited—nothing's good enough for you.

BLAYNE. Not even an empty Club, a dam' bad dinner at the Judge's, and a Station as sickly as a hospital. You're quite right. We're a set of Sybarites.

DOONE. Luxurious dogs, wallowing in—

CURTISS. Prickly heat between the shoulders. I'm covered with it. Let's hope Beora will be cooler.

BLAYNE. Whew! Are you ordered into camp, too? I thought the Gunners had a clean sheet.

CURTISS. No, worse luck. Two cases yesterday—one died—and if we have a third, out we go. Is there any shooting at Beora, Doone?

DOONE. The country's under water, except the patch by the Grand Trunk Road. I was there yesterday, looking at a bund, and came across four poor devils in their last stage. It's rather bad from here to Kuchara.

CURTISS. Then we're pretty certain to have a heavy go of it. Heigho! I shouldn't mind changing places with Gaddy for a while. 'Sport with Amaryllis in the shade of the Town Hall, and all that. Oh, why doesn't somebody come and marry me, instead of letting me go into cholera-camp?

MACKESY. Ask the Committee.

CURTISS. You ruffian! You'll stand me another peg for that. Blayne, what will you take? Mackesy is fine on moral grounds. Done, have you any preference?

DONE. Small glass Kummel, please. Excellent carminative, these days. Anthony told me so.

MACKESY. (Signing voucher for four drinks.) Most unfair punishment. I only thought of Curtiss as Actaeon being chivied round the billiard tables by the nymphs of Diana.

BLAYNE. Curtiss would have to import his nymphs by train. Mrs. Cockley's the only woman in the Station. She won't leave Cockley, and he's doing his best to get her to go.

CURTISS. Good, indeed! Here's Mrs. Cockley's health. To the only wife in the Station and a damned brave woman!

OMNES. (Drinking.) A damned brave woman

BLAYNE. I suppose Gandy will bring his wife here at the end of the cold weather. They are going to be married almost immediately, I believe.

CURTISS. Gandy may thank his luck that the Pink Hussars are all detachment and no headquarters this hot weather, or he'd be torn from the arms of his love as sure as death. Have you ever noticed the thorough-minded way British Cavalry take to cholera? It's because they are so expensive. If the Pinks had stood fast here, they would have been out in camp a. month ago. Yes, I should decidedly like to be Gandy.

MACKESY. He'll go Home after he's married, and send in his papers—see if he doesn't.

BLAYNE. Why shouldn't he? Hasn't he money? Would any one of us be here if we weren't paupers?

DONE. Poor old pauper! What has become of the six hundred you rooked from our table last month?

BLAYNE. It took unto itself wings. I think an enterprising tradesman got some of it, and a shroff gobbled the rest—or else I spent it.

CURTISS. Gandy never had dealings with a shroff in his life.

DONE. Virtuous Gandy! If I had three thousand a month, paid from England, I don't think I'd deal with a shroff either.

MACKESY. (Yawning.) Oh, it's a sweet life! I wonder whether matrimony would make it sweeter.

CURTISS. Ask Cockley—with his wife dying by inches!

BLAYNE. Go home and get a fool of a girl to come out to—what is it Thackeray says?-"the splendid palace of an Indian pro-consul."

DOONE. Which reminds me. My quarters leak like a sieve. I had fever last night from sleeping in a swamp. And the worst of it is, one can't do anything to a roof till the Rains are over.

CURTISS. What's wrong with you? You haven't eighty rotting Tommies to take into a running stream.

DONE. No: but I'm mixed boils and bad language. I'm a regular Job all over my body. It's sheer poverty of blood, and I don't see any chance of getting richer—either way.

BLAYNE. Can't you take leave? DONE. That's the pull you Army men have over us. Ten days are nothing in your sight. I'm so important that Government can't find a substitute if I go away. Ye-es, I'd like to be Gandy, whoever his wife may be.

CURTISS. You've passed the turn of life that Mackesy was speaking of.

DONE. Indeed I have, but I never yet had the brutality to ask a woman to share my life out here.

BLAYNE. On my soul I believe you're right. I'm thinking of Mrs. Cockley. The woman's an absolute wreck.

DONE. Exactly. Because she stays down here. The only way to keep her fit would be to send her to the Hills for eight months—and the same with any woman. I fancy I see myself taking a wife on those terms.

MACKESY. With the rupee at one and sixpence. The little Doones would be little Debra Doones, with a fine Mussoorie chi-chi anent to bring home for the holidays.

CURTISS. And a pair of be-ewtiful sambhur-horns for Done to wear, free of expense, presented by—DONE. Yes, it's an enchanting prospect. By the way, the rupee hasn't done falling yet. The time will come when we shall think ourselves lucky if we only lose half our pay.

CURTISS. Surely a third's loss enough. Who gains by the arrangement? That's what I want to know.

BLAYNE. The Silver Question! I'm going to bed if you begin squabbling Thank Goodness, here's Anthony—looking like a ghost.

Enter ANTHONY, Indian Medical Staff, very white and tired.

ANTHONY. 'Evening, Blayne. It's raining in sheets. Whiskey peg lao, khitmatgar. The roads are something ghastly.

CURTISS. How's Mingle?

ANTHONY. Very bad, and more frightened. I handed him over to Few-ton. Mingle might just as well have called him in the first place, instead of bothering me.

BLAYNE. He's a nervous little chap. What has he got, this time?

ANTHONY. 'Can't quite say. A very bad tummy and a blue funk so far. He asked me at once if it was cholera, and I told him not to be a fool. That soothed him.

CURTIS. Poor devil! The funk does half the business in a man of that build.

ANTHONY. (Lighting a cheroot.) I firmly believe the funk will kill him if he stays down. You know the amount of trouble he's been giving Fewton for the last three weeks. He's doing his very best to frighten himself into the grave.

GENERAL CHORUS. Poor little devil! Why doesn't he get away?

ANTHONY. 'Can't. He has his leave all right, but he's so dipped he can't take it, and I don't think his name on paper would raise four annas. That's in confidence, though.

MACKESY. All the Station knows it.

ANTHONY. "I suppose I shall have to die here," he said, squirming all across the bed. He's quite made up his mind to Kingdom Come. And I know he has nothing more than a wet-weather tummy if he could only keep a hand on himself.

BLAYNE. That's bad. That's very bad. Poor little Miggy. Good little chap, too. I say—

ANTHONY. What do you say?

BLAYNE. Well, look here—anyhow. If it's like that—as you say—I say fifty.

CURTISS. I say fifty.

MACKESY. I go twenty better.

DONE. Bloated Croesus of the Bar! I say fifty. Jervoise, what do you say? Hi! Wake up!

JERVOISE. Eh? What's that? What's that?

CURTISS. We want a hundred rupees from you. You're a bachelor drawing a gigantic income, and there's a man in a hole.

JERVOISE. What man? Any one dead?

BLAYNE. No, but he'll die if you don't give the hundred. Here! Here's a peg-voucher. You can see what we've signed for, and Anthony's man will come round to-morrow to collect it. So there will be no trouble.

JERVOISE. (Signing.) One hundred, E. M. J. There you are (feebly). It isn't one of your jokes, is it?

BLAYNE. No, it really is wanted. Anthony, you were the biggest poker-winner last week, and you've defrauded the tax-collector too long. Sign!

ANTHONY. Let's see. Three fifties and a seventy-two twenty-three twenty-say four hundred and twenty. That'll give him a month clear at the Hills. Many thanks, you men. I'll send round the chaprassi to-morrow.

CURTISS. You must engineer his taking the stuff, and of course you mustn't—

ANTHONY. Of course. It would never do. He'd weep with gratitude over his evening drink.

BLAYNE. That's just what he would do, damn him. Oh! I say, Anthony, you pretend to know everything. Have you heard about Gandy?

ANTHONY. No. Divorce Court at last?

BLAYNE. Worse. He's engaged!

ANTHONY. How much? He can't be!

BLAYNE. He is. He's going to be married in a few weeks. Markyn told me at the Judge's this evening. It's pukka.

ANTHONY. You don't say so? Holy Moses! There'll be a shine in the tents of Kedar.

CURTISS. 'Regiment cut up rough, think you?

ANTHONY. 'Don't know anything about the Regiment.

MACKESY. It is bigamy, then?

ANTHONY. Maybe. Do you mean to say that you men have forgotten, or is there more charity in the world than I thought?

DONE. You don't look pretty when you are trying to keep a secret. You bloat. Explain.

ANTHONY. Mrs. Herriott!

BLAYNE. (After a long pause, to the room generally.) It's my notion that we are a set of fools.

MACKESY. Nonsense. That business was knocked on the head last season. Why, young Mallard—

ANTHONY. Mallard was a candlestick, paraded as such. Think awhile. Recollect last season and the talk then. Mallard or no Mallard, did Gandy ever talk to any other woman?

CURTISS. There's something in that. It was slightly noticeable now you come to mention it. But she's at Naini Tat and he's at Simla.

ANTHONY. He had to go to Simla to look after a globe-trotter relative of his—a person with a title. Uncle or aunt.

BLAYNE And there he got engaged. No law prevents a man growing tired of a woman.

ANTHONY. Except that he mustn't do it till the woman is tired of him. And the Herriott woman was not that.

CURTISS. She may be now. Two months of Naini Tal works wonders.

DONE. Curious thing how some women carry a Fate with them. There was a Mrs. Deegie in the Central Provinces whose men invariably fell away and got married. It became a regular proverb with us when I was down there. I remember three men desperately devoted to her, and they all, one after another, took wives.

CURTISS. That's odd. Now I should have thought that Mrs. Deegie's influence would have led them to take other men's wives. It ought to have made them afraid of the judgment of Providence.

ANTHONY. Mrs. Herriott will make Gandy afraid of something more than the judgment of Providence, I fancy.

BLAYNE. Supposing things are as you say, he'll be a fool to face her. He'll sit tight at Simla.

ANTHONY. 'Shouldn't be a bit surprised if he went off to Naini to explain. He's an unaccountable sort of man, and she's likely to be a more than unaccountable woman.

DONE. What makes you take her character away so confidently?

ANTHONY. Primum tern pus. Caddy was her first and a woman doesn't allow her first man to drop away without expostulation. She justifies the first transfer of affection to herself by swearing that it is forever and ever. Consequently—

BLAYNE. Consequently, we are sitting here till past one o'clock, talking scandal like a set of Station cats. Anthony, it's all your fault. We were perfectly respectable till you came in Go to bed. I'm off, Good-night all.

CURTISS. Past one! It's past two by Jove, and here's the khit coming for the late charge. Just Heavens! One, two, three, four, five rupees to pay for the pleasure of saying that a poor little beast of a woman is no better than she should be. I'm ashamed of myself. Go to bed, you slanderous villains, and if I'm sent to Beora to-morrow, be prepared to hear I'm dead before paying my card account!

THE TENTS OF KEDAR

Only why should it be with pain at all Why must I 'twix the leaves of corona! Put any kiss of pardon on thy brow? Why should the other women know so much, And talk together—Such the look and such The smile he used to love with, then as now.—*Any Wife to any Husband.*

CENE—A Naini Tal dinner for thirty-four. Plate, wines, crockery, and khitmatgars carefully calculated to scale of Rs. 6000 per mensem, less Exchange. Table split lengthways by bank of flowers.

RS. HERRIOTT. (After conversation has risen to proper pitch.) Ah! 'Didn't see you in the crush in the drawing-room. (Sotto voce.) Where have you been all this while, Pip?

CAPTAIN GADSBY. (Turning from regularly ordained dinner partner and settling hock glasses.) Good evening. (Sotto voce.) Not quite so loud another time. You've no notion how your voice carries. (Aside.) So much for shirking the written explanation. It'll have to be a verbal one now. Sweet prospect! How on earth am I to tell her that I am a respectable, engaged member of society and it's all over between us?

MRS. H. I've a heavy score against you. Where were you at the Monday Pop? Where were you on Tuesday? Where were you at the Lamonts' tennis? I was looking everywhere.

CAPT. G. For me! Oh, I was alive somewhere, I suppose.

(Aside.) It's for Minnie's sake, but it's going to be dashed unpleasant.

MRS. H. Have I done anything to offend you? I never meant it if I have. I couldn't help going for a ride with the Vaynor man. It was promised a week before you came up.

CAPT. G. I didn't know—

MRS. H. It really was.

CAPT. G. Anything about it, I mean.

MRS. H. What has upset you today? All these days? You haven't been near me for four whole days—nearly one hundred hours. Was it kind of you, Pip? And I've been looking forward so much to your coming.

CAPT. G. Have you?

MRS. H. You know I have! I've been as foolish as a schoolgirl about it. I made a little calendar and put it in my card-case, and every time the twelve o'clock gun went off I scratched out a square and said: "That brings me nearer to Pip. My Pip!"

CAPT. G. (With an uneasy laugh). What will Mackler think if you neglect him so?

MRS. H. And it hasn't brought you nearer. You seem farther away than ever. Are you sulking about something? I know your temper.

CAPT. G. No.

MRS. H. Have I grown old in' the last few months, then? (Reaches forward to bank of flowers for menu-card.)

PARTNER ON LEFT. Allow me. (Hands menu-card. MRS. H. keeps her arm at full stretch for three seconds.)

MRS. H. (To partner.) Oh, thanks. I didn't see. (Turns right again.) Is anything in me changed at all?

CAPT. G. For Goodness's sake go on with your dinner!

You must eat something. Try one of those cutlet arrangements. (Aside.) And I fancied she had good shoulders, once upon a time! What an ass a man can make of himself!

MRS. H. (Helping herself to a paper frill, seven peas, some stamped carrots and a spoonful of gravy.) That isn't an answer. Tell me whether I have done anything.

CAPT. G. (Aside.) If it isn't ended here there will be a ghastly scene somewhere else. If only I'd written to her and stood the racket—at long range! (To Khitmatgar.) Han! Simpkin do. (Aloud.) I'll tell you later on.

MRS. H. Tell me now. It must be some foolish misunderstanding, and you know that there was to be nothing of that sort between us. We, of all people in the world, can't afford it. Is it the Vaynor man, and don't you like to say so? On my honor—

CAPT. G. I haven't given the Vaynor man a thought.

MRS. H. But how d'you know that I haven't?

CAPT. G. (Aside.) Here's my chance and may the Devil help me through with it. (Aloud and measuredly.) Believe me, I do not care how often or how tenderly you think of the Vaynor man.

MRS. H. I wonder if you mean that! Oh, what is the good of squabbling and pretending to misunderstand when you are only up for so short a time? Pip, don't be a stupid!

Follows a pause, during which he crosses his left leg over his right and continues his dinner.

CAPT. G. (In answer to the thunderstorm in her eyes.) Corns—my worst.

MRS. H. Upon my word, you are the very rudest man in the world! I'll never do it again.

CAPT. G. (Aside.) No, I don't think you will; but I wonder

what you will do before it's all over. (To Khitmatgar.) Thorah ur Simpkin do.

MRS. H. Well! Haven't you the grace to apologize, bad man?

CAPT. G. (Aside.) I mustn't let it drift back now. Trust a woman for being as blind as a bat when she won't see.

MRS. H. I'm waiting; or would you like me to dictate a form of apology?

CAPT. G. (Desperately.) By all means dictate.

MRS. H. (Lightly.) Very well. Rehearse your several Christian names after me and go on: "Profess my sincere repentance."

CAPT. G. "Sincere repentance."

MRS. H. "For having behaved"—

CAPT. G. (Aside.) At last! I wish to Goodness she'd look away. "For having behaved"—as I have behaved, and declare that I am thoroughly and heartily sick of the whole business, and take this opportunity of making clear my intention of ending it, now, henceforward, and forever. (Aside.) If any one had told me I should be such a blackguard—!

MRS. H. (Shaking a spoonful of potato chips into her plate.) That's not a pretty joke.

CAPT. G. No. It's a reality. (Aside.) I wonder if smashes of this kind are always so raw.

MRS. H. Really, Pip, you're getting more absurd every day.

CAPT. G. I don't think you quite understand me. Shall I repeat it?

MRS. H. No! For pity's sake don't do that. It's too terrible, even in fur.

CAPT. G. I'll let her think it over for a while. But I ought to be horsewhipped.

MRS. H. I want to know what you meant by what you said just now.

CAPT. G. Exactly what I said. No less.

MRS. H. But what have I done to deserve it? What have I done?

CAPT. G. (Aside.) If she only wouldn't look at me. (Aloud and very slowly, his eyes on his plate.) D'you remember that evening in July, before the Rains broke, when you said that the end would have to come sooner or later—and you wondered for which of US it would come first?

MRS. H. Yes! I was only joking. And you swore that, as long as there was breath in your body, it should never come. And I believed you.

CAPT. G. (Fingering menu-card.) Well, it has. That's all.

A long pause, during which MRS. H. bows her head and rolls the bread-twist into little pellets; G. stares at the oleanders.

MRS. H. (Throwing back her head and laughing naturally.) They train us women well, don't they, Pip?

CAPT. G. (Brutally, touching shirt-stud.) So far as the expression goes. (Aside.) It isn't in her nature to take things quietly. There'll be an explosion yet.

MRS. H. (With a shudder.) Thank you. B-but even Red Indians allow people to wriggle when they're being tortured, I believe. (Slips fan from girdle and fans slowly: rim of fan level with chin.)

PARTNER ON LEFT. Very close tonight, isn't it? 'You find it too much for you?

MRS. H. Oh, no, not in the least. But they really ought to have punkahs, even in your cool Naini Tal, oughtn't they? (Turns, dropping fan and raising eyebrows.)

CAPT. G. It's all right. (Aside.) Here comes the storm!

MRS. H. (Her eyes on the tablecloth: fan ready in right hand.) It was very cleverly managed, Pip, and I congratulate you. You swore—you never contented yourself with merely Saying a thing—you swore that, as far as lay in your power, you'd make my wretched life pleasant for me. And you've denied me the consolation of breaking down. I should have done it—indeed I should. A woman would hardly have thought of this refinement, my kind, considerate friend. (Fan-guard as before.) You have explained things so tenderly and truthfully, too! You haven't spoken or written a word of warning, and you have let me believe in you till the last minute. You haven't condescended to give me your reason yet. No! A woman could not have managed it half so well. Are there many men like you in the world?

CAPT. G. I'm sure I don't know. (To Khitmatgar.) Ohe! Simpkin do.

MRS. H. You call yourself a man of the world, don't you? Do men of the world behave like Devils when they a woman the honor to get tired of her?

CAPT. G. I'm sure I don't know. Don't speak so loud!

MRS. H. Keep us respectable, O Lord, whatever happens. Don't be afraid of my compromising you. You've chosen your ground far too well, and I've been properly brought up. (Lowering fan.) Haven't you any pity, Pip, except for yourself?

CAPT. G. Wouldn't it be rather impertinent of me to say that I'm sorry for you?

MRS. H. I think you have said it once or twice before. You're growing very careful of my feelings. My God, Pip, I was a good woman once! You said I was. You've made me what I am. What are you going to do with me? What are you going to do with me? Won't you say that you are sorry? (Helps herself to iced asparagus.)

CAPT. G. I am sorry for you, if you Want the pity of such a brute as I am. I'm awf'ly sorry for you.

MRS. H. Rather tame for a man of the world. Do you think that that admission clears you?

CAPT. G. What can I do? I can only tell you what I think of myself. You can't think worse than that?

MRS. H. Oh, yes, I can! And now, will you tell me the reason of all this? Remorse? Has Bayard been suddenly conscience-stricken?

CAPT. G. (Angrily, his eyes still lowered.) No! The thing has come to an end on my side. That's all. Mafisch!

MRS. H. "That's all. Mafisch!" As though I were a Cairene Dragoman. You used to make prettier speeches. D'you remember when you said?—

CAPT. G. For Heaven's sake don't bring that back! Call me anything you like and I'll admit it—

MRS. H. But you don't care to be reminded of old lies? If I could hope to hurt you one-tenth as much as you have hurt me to-night—No, I wouldn't—I couldn't do it—liar though you are.

CAPT. G. I've spoken the truth.

MRS. H. My dear Sir, you flatter yourself. You have lied over the reason. Pip, remember that I know you as you don't know yourself. You have been everything to me, though you are—(Fan-guard.) Oh, what a contemptible Thing it is! And so you are merely tired of me?

CAPT. G. Since you insist upon my repeating it—Yes.

MRS. H. Lie the first. I wish I knew a coarser word. Lie seems so in-effectual in your case. The fire has just died out and there is no fresh one? Think for a minute, Pip, if you care whether I despise you more than I do. Simply Mafisch, is it?

CAPT. G. Yes. (Aside.) I think I deserve this.

MRS. H. Lie number two. Before the next glass chokes you, tell me her name.

CAPT. G. (Aside.) I'll make her pay for dragging Minnie into the business! (Aloud.) Is it likely?

MRS. H. Very likely if you thought that it would flatter your vanity. You'd cry my name on the house-tops to make people turn round.

CAPT. G. I wish I had. There would have been an end to this business.

MRS. H. Oh, no, there would not—And so you were going to be virtuous and blase', were you? To come to me and say: "I've done with you. The incident is clo-osed." I ought to be proud of having kept such a man so long.

CAPT. G. (Aside.) It only remains to pray for the end of the dinner. (Aloud.) You know what I think of myself.

MRS. H. As it's the only person in he world you ever do think of, and as I know your mind thoroughly, I do. You want to get it all over and—Oh, I can't keep you back! And you're going—think of it, Pip—to throw me over for another woman. And you swore that all other women were—Pip, my Pip! She can't care for you as I do. Believe me, she can't. Is it any one that I know?

CAPT. G. Thank Goodness it isn't. (Aside.) I expected a cyclone, but not an earthquake.

MRS. H. She can't! Is there anything that I wouldn't do for you—or haven't done? And to think that I should take this trouble over you, knowing what you are! Do you despise me for it?

CAPT. G. (Wiping his mouth to hide a smile.) Again? It's entirely a work of charity on your part.

MRS. H. Ahhh! But I have no right to resent it.—Is she better-looking than I? Who was it said?—

CAPT. G. No—not that!

MRS. H. I'll be more merciful than you were. Don't you know that all women are alike?

CAPT. G. (Aside.) Then this is the exception that proves the rule.

MRS. H. All of them! I'll tell you anything you like. I will, upon my word! They only want the admiration—from anybody—no matter who—anybody! But there is always one man that they care for more than any one else in the world, and would sacrifice all the others to. Oh, do listen! I've kept the Vaynor man trotting after me like a poodle, and he believes that he is the only man I am interested in. I'll tell you what he said to me.

CAPT. G. Spare him. (Aside.) I wonder what his version is.

MRS. H. He's been waiting for me to look at him all through dinner. Shall I do it, and you can see what an idiot he looks?

CAPT. G. "But what imports the nomination of this gentleman?"

MRS. H. Watch! (Sends a glance to the Vaynor man, who tries vainly to combine a mouthful of ice pudding, a smirk of self-satisfaction, a glare of intense devotion, and the stolidity of a British dining countenance.)

CAPT. G. (Critically.) He doesn't look pretty. Why didn't you wait till the spoon was out of his mouth?

MRS. H. To amuse you. She'll make an exhibition of you as I've made of him; and people will laugh at you. Oh, Pip, can't you see that? It's as plain as the noonday Sun. You'll be trotted about and told lies, and made a fool of like the others. I never made a fool of you, did I?

CAPT. G. (Aside.) What a clever little woman it is!

MRS. H. Well, what have you to say?

CAPT. G. I feel better.

MRS. H. Yes, I suppose so, after I have come down to your level. I couldn't have done it if I hadn't cared for you so much. I have spoken the truth.

CAPT. G. It doesn't alter the situation.

MRS. H. (Passionately.) Then she has said that she cares for you! Don't believe her, Pip. It's a lie—as bad as yours to me!

CAPT. G. Ssssteady! I've a notion that a friend of yours is looking at you.

MRS. H. He! I hate him. He introduced you to me.

CAPT. G. (Aside.) And some people would like women to assist in making the laws. Introduction to imply condonement. (Aloud.) Well, you see, if you can remember so far back as that, I couldn't, in' common politeness, refuse the offer.

MRS. H. In common politeness I We have got beyond that!

CAPT. G. (Aside.) Old ground means fresh trouble. (Aloud.) On my honor

MRS. H. Your what? Ha, ha!

CAPT. G. Dishonor, then. She's not what you imagine. I meant to—

MRS. H. Don't tell me anything about her! She won't care for you, and when you come back, after having made an exhibition of yourself, you'll find me occupied with—

CAPT. G. (Insolently.) You couldn't while I am alive.

(Aside.) If that doesn't bring her pride to her rescue, nothing will.

MRS. H. (Drawing herself up.) Couldn't do it? I' (Softening.) You're right. I don't believe I could—though you are what you are—a coward and a liar in grain.

CAPT. G. It doesn't hurt so much after your little lecture—with demonstrations.

MRS. H. One mass of vanity! Will nothing ever touch you in this life? There must be a Hereafter if it's only for the benefit of—But you will have it all to yourself.

CAPT. G. (Under his eyebrows.) Are you certain of that?

MRS. H. I shall have had mine in this life; and it will serve me right.

CAPT. G. But the admiration that you insisted on so strongly a moment ago? (Aside.) Oh, I am a brute!

MRS. H. (Fiercely.) Will that con-sole me for knowing that you will go to her with the same words, the same arguments, and the—the same pet names you used to me? And if she cares for you, you two will laugh over my story. Won't that be punishment heavy enough even for me—even for me?—And it's all useless. That's another punishment.

CAPT. G. (Feebly.) Oh, come! I'm not so low as you think.

MRS. H. Not now, perhaps, but you will be. Oh, Pip, if a woman flatters your vanity, there's nothing on earth that you would not tell her; and no meanness that you would not do. Have I known you so long without knowing that?

CAPT. G. If you can trust me in nothing else—and I don't see why I should be trusted—you can count upon my holding my tongue.

MRS. H. If you denied everything you've said this evening and declared it was all in' fun (a long pause), I'd trust you.

Not otherwise. All I ask is, don't tell her my name. Please don't. A man might forget: a woman never would. (Looks up table and sees hostess beginning to collect eyes.) So it's all ended, through no fault of mine—Haven't I behaved beautifully? I've accepted your dismissal, and you managed it as cruelly as you could, and I have made you respect my sex, haven't I? (Arranging gloves and fan.) I only pray that she'll know you some day as I know you now. I wouldn't be you then, for I think even your conceit will be hurt. I hope she'll pay you back the humiliation you've brought on me. I hope— No. I don't! I can't give you up! I must have something to look forward to or I shall go crazy. When it's all over, come back to me, come back to me, and you'll find that you're my Pip still!

CAPT. G. (Very clearly.) False move, and you pay for it. It's a girl!

MRS. H. (Rising.) Then it was true! They said—but I wouldn't insult you by asking. A girl! I was a girl not very long ago. Be good to her, Pip. I daresay she believes in' you.

Goes out with an uncertain smile. He watches her through the door, and settles into a chair as the men redistribute themselves.

CAPT. G. Now, if there is any Power who looks after this world, will He kindly tell me what I have done? (Reaching out for the claret, and half aloud.) What have I done?

WITH ANY AMAZEMENT

And are not afraid with any amazement.—Marriage Service.

SCENE.—A bachelor's bedroom-toilet-table arranged with unnatural neatness. CAPTAIN GADSBY asleep and snoring heavily. Time, 10:30 A. M.—a glorious autumn day at Simla. Enter delicately Captain MAFFLIN of GADSBY's regiment. Looks at sleeper, and shakes his head murmuring "Poor Gaddy." Performs violent fantasia with hair-brushes on chairback.

CAPT. M. Wake up, my sleeping beauty! (Roars.)

"Uprouse ye, then, my merry merry men! It is our opening day! It is our opening da-ay!"

Gaddy, the little dicky-birds have been billing and cooing for ever so long; and I'm here!

CAPT. G. (Sitting up and yawning.) 'Mornin'. This is awf'ly good of you, old fellow. Most awf'ly good of you. 'Don't know what I should do without you. 'Pon my soul, I don't. 'Haven't slept a wink all night.

CAPT. M. I didn't get in till half-past eleven. 'Had a look at you then, and you seemed to be sleeping as soundly as a condemned criminal.

CAPT. G. Jack, if you want to make those disgustingly

worn-out jokes, you'd better go away. (With portentous gravity.) It's the happiest day in my life.

CAPT. M. (Chuckling grimly.) Not by a very long chalk, my son. You're going through some of the most refined torture you've ever known. But be calm. I am with you. 'Shun! Dress!

CAPT. G. Eh! Wha-at?

CAPT. M. Do you suppose that you are your own master for the next twelve hours? If you do, of course-(Makes for the door.)

CAPT. G. No! For Goodness' sake, old man, don't do that! You'll see through, won't you? I've been mugging up that beastly drill, and can't remember a line of it.

CAPT. M. (Overturning G.'s uniform.) Go and tub. Don't bother me. I'll give you ten minutes to dress in. (Interval, filled by the noise as of one splashing in the bath-room.)

CAPT. G. (Emerging from dressing-room.) What time is it?

CAPT. M. Nearly eleven.

CAPT. G. Five hours more. O Lord!

CAPT. M. (Aside.) 'First sign of funk, that. 'Wonder if it's going to spread. (Aloud.) Come along to breakfast.

CAPT. G. I can't eat anything. I don't want any breakfast.

CAPT. M. (Aside.) So early! (Aloud) CAPTAIN Gadsby, I order you to eat breakfast, and a dashed good breakfast, too. None of your bridal airs and graces with me! Leads G. downstairs and stands over him while he eats two chops.

CAPT. G. (Who has looked at his watch thrice in the last five minutes.) What time is it?

CAPT. M. Time to come for a walk. Light up.

CAPT. G. I haven't smoked for ten days, and I won't now.

(Takes cheroot which M. has cut for him, and blows smoke through his nose luxuriously.) We aren't going down the Mall, are we?

CAPT. M. (Aside.) They're all alike in these stages. (Aloud.) No, my Vestal. We're going along the quietest road we can find.

CAPT. G. Any chance of seeing Her? CAPT. M. Innocent! No! Come along, and, if you want me for the final obsequies, don't cut my eye out with your stick.

CAPT. G. (Spinning round.) I say, isn't She the dearest creature that ever walked? What's the time? What comes after "wilt thou take this woman"?

CAPT. M. You go for the ring. R'clect it'll be on the top of my right-hand little finger, and just be careful how you draw it off, because I shall have the Verger's fees somewhere in my glove.

CAPT. G. (Walking forward hastily.) D—— the Verger! Come along! It's past twelve and I haven't seen Her since yesterday evening. (Spinning round again.) She's an absolute angel, Jack, and She's a dashed deal too good for me. Look here, does She come up the aisle on my arm, or how?

CAPT. M. If I thought that there was the least chance of your remembering anything for two consecutive minutes, I'd tell you. Stop passaging about like that!

CAPT. G. (Halting in the middle of the road.) I say, Jack.

CAPT. M. Keep quiet for another ten minutes if you can, you lunatic; and walk! The two tramp at five miles an hour for fifteen minutes.

CAPT. G. What's the time? How about the cursed wedding-cake and the slippers? They don't throw 'em about in church, do they?

CAPT. M. In-variably. The Padre leads off with his boots.

CAPT. G. Confound your silly soul! Don't make fun of me. I can't stand it, and I won't!

CAPT. M. (Untroubled.) So-ooo, old horse You'll have to sleep for a couple of hours this afternoon.

CAPT. G. (Spinning round.) I'm not going to be treated like a dashed child. Understand that!

CAPT. M. (Aside.) Nerves gone to fiddle-strings. What a day we're having! (Tenderly putting his hand on G.'s shoulder.) My David, how long have you known this Jonathan? Would I come up here to make a fool of you—after all these years?

CAPT. G. (Penitently.) I know, I know, Jack—but I'm as upset as I can be. Don't mind what I say. Just hear me run through the drill and see if I've got it all right:-"To have and to hold for better or worse, as it was in the beginning, is now, and ever shall be, world without end, so help me God. Amen."

CAPT. M. (Suffocating with suppressed laughter.) Yes. That's about the gist of it. I'll prompt if you get into a hat.

CAPT. G. (Earnestly.) Yes, you'll stick by me, Jack, won't you? I'm awfully happy, but I don't mind telling you that I'm in a blue funk!

CAPT. M. (Gravely.) Are you? I should never have noticed it. You don't look like it.

CAPT. G. Don't I? That's all right. (Spinning round.) On my soul and honor, Jack, She's the sweetest little angel that ever came down from the sky. There isn't a woman on earth fit to speak to Her.

CAPT. M. (Aside.) And this is old Gandy! (Aloud.) Go on if it relieves you.

CAPT. G. You can laugh! That's all you wild asses of bachelors are fit for.

CAPT. M. (Drawling.) You never would wait for the troop to come up. You aren't quite married yet, y'know.

CAPT. G. Ugh! That reminds me. I don't believe I shall be able to get into any boots Let's go home and try 'em on (Hurries forward.)

CAPT. M. 'Wouldn't be in your shoes for anything that Asia has to offer.

CAPT. G. (Spinning round.) That just shows your hideous blackness of soul—your dense stupidity—your brutal narrow-mindedness. There's only one fault about you. You're the best of good fellows, and I don't know what I should have done without you, but—you aren't married. (Wags his head gravely.) Take a wife, Jack.

CAPT. M. (With a face like a wall.) Va-as. Whose for choice?

CAPT. G. If you're going to be a blackguard, I'm going on—What's the time?

CAPT. M. (Hums.)—

> "An' since 'twas very clear we drank only ginger-beer,
>
> Faith, there must ha' been some stingo in the ginger."

Come back, you maniac. I'm going to take you home, and you're going to lie down.

CAPT. G. What on earth do I want to lie down for?

CAPT. M. Give me a light from your cheroot and see.

CAPT. G. (Watching cheroot-butt quiver like a tuning-fork.) Sweet state I'm in!

CAPT. M. You are. I'll get you a peg and you'll go to sleep. They return and M. compounds a four-finger peg.

CAPT. G. O bus! bus! It'll make me as drunk as an owl.

CAPT. M. 'Curious thing, 'twon't have the slightest effect on you. Drink it off, chuck yourself down there, and go to bye-bye.

CAPT. G. It's absurd. I sha'n't sleep, I know I sha'n't!

(Falls into heavy doze at end of seven minutes. CAPT. M. watches him tenderly.)

CAPT. M. Poor old Gandy! I've seen a few turned off before, but never one who went to the gallows in this condition. 'Can't tell how it affects 'em, though. It's the thoroughbreds that sweat when they're backed into double-harness.—And that's the man who went through the guns at Amdheran like a devil possessed of devils. (Leans over G.) But this is worse than the guns, old pal—worse than the guns, isn't it? (G. turns in his sleep, and M. touches him clumsily on the forehead.) Poor, dear old Gaddy I Going like the rest of 'em—going like the rest of 'em—Friend that sticketh closer than a brother—eight years. Dashed bit of a slip of a girl—eight weeks! And—where's your friend? (Smokes disconsolately till church clock strikes three.)

CAPT. M. Up with you! Get into your kit.

CAPT. C. Already? Isn't it too soon? Hadn't I better have a shave?

CAPT. M. No! You're all right. (Aside.) He'd chip his chin to pieces.

CAPT. C. What's the hurry?

CAPT. M. You've got to be there first.

CAPT. C. To be stared at?

CAPT. M. Exactly. You're part of the show. Where's the burnisher? Your spurs are in a shameful state.

CAPT. G. (Gruffly.) Jack, I be damned if you shall do that for me.

CAPT. M. (More gruffly.) Dry' up and get dressed! If I choose to clean your spurs, you're under my orders.

CAPT. G. dresses. M. follows suit.

CAPT. M. (Critically, walking round.) M'yes, you'll do. Only don't look so like a criminal. Ring, gloves, fees—that's all right for me. Let your moustache alone. Now, if the ponies are ready, we'll go.

CAPT. G. (Nervously.) It's much too soon. Let's light up! Let's have a peg! Let's—CAPT. M. Let's make bally asses of ourselves!

BELLS. (Without.)—

"Good-peo-ple-all To prayers-we call."

CAPT. M. There go the bells! Come an—unless you'd rather not. (They ride off.)

BELLS.—

"We honor the King And Brides joy do bring—Good tidings we tell, And ring the Dead's knell."

CAPT. G. (Dismounting at the door of the Church.) I say, aren't we much too soon? There are no end of people inside. I say, aren't we much too late? Stick by me, Jack! What the devil do I do?

CAPT. M. Strike an attitude at the head of the aisle and wait for Her. (G. groans as M. wheels him into position before three hundred eyes.)

CAPT. M. (Imploringly.) Gaddy, if you love me, for pity's sake, for the Honor of the Regiment, stand up! Chuck yourself into your uniform! Look like a man! I've got to speak to the Padre a minute. (G. breaks into a gentle Perspiration.) your face I'll never man again. Stand up! (Visibly.) If you wipe your face I'll never be your best man again. Stand up! (G. Trembles visibly.)

CAPT. M. (Returning.) She's coming now. Look out when the music starts. There's the organ beginning to clack.

(Bride steps out of 'rickshaw at Church door. G. catches a glimpse of her and takes heart.)

ORGAN.—

> *"The Voice that breathed o'er Eden,*
> *That earliest marriage day,*
> *The primal marriage-blessing,*
> *It hath not passed away."*

CAPT. M. (Watching G.) By Jove! He is looking well. 'Didn't think he had it in him.

CAPT. G. How long does this hymn go on for?

CAPT. M. It will be over directly. (Anxiously.) Beginning to beltch and gulp. Hold on, Gabby, and think o' the Regiment.

CAPT. G. (Measuredly.) I say there's a big brown lizard crawling up that wall.

CAPT. M. My Sainted Mother! The last stage of collapse!

Bride comes Up to left of altar, lifts her eyes once to G., who is suddenly smitten mad.

CAPT. G. (TO himself again and again.) Little Featherweight's a woman—a woman! And I thought she was a little girl.

CAPT. M. (In a whisper.) Form the halt—inward wheel.

CAPT. G. obeys mechanically and the ceremony proceeds.

PADRE.... only unto her as ye both shall live?

CAPT. G. (His throat useless.) Ha—hmmm!

CAPT. M. Say you will or you won't. There's no second deal here. Bride gives response with perfect calmness, and is given away by the father.

CAPT. G. (Thinking to show his learning.) Jack give me away now, quick!

CAPT. M. You've given yourself away quite enough. Her right hand, man! Repeat! Repeat! "Theodore Philip." Have you forgotten your own name?

CAPT. G. stumbles through Affirmation, which Bride repeats without a tremor.

CAPT. M. Now the ring! Follow the Padre! Don't pull off my glove! Here it is! Great Cupid, he's found his voice.

CAPT. G. repeats Troth in a voice to be heard to the end of the Church and turns on his heel.

CAPT. M. (Desperately.) Rein back! Back to your troop! 'Tisn't half legal yet.

PADRE.... joined together let no man put asunder.

CAPT. G. paralyzed with fear jibs after Blessing.

CAPT. M. (Quickly.) On your own front—one length. Take her with you. I don't come. You've nothing to say. (CAPT. G. jingles up to altar.)

CAPT. M. (In a piercing rattle meant to be a whisper.) Kneel, you stiff-necked ruffian! Kneel!

PADRE... whose daughters are ye so long as ye do well and are not afraid with any amazement.

CAPT. M. Dismiss! Break off! Left wheel!

All troop to vestry. They sign.

CAPT. M. Kiss Her, Gaddy.

CAPT. G. (Rubbing the ink into his glove.) Eh! Wha-at?

CAPT. M. (Taking one pace to Bride.) If you don't, I shall.

CAPT. G. (Interposing an arm.) Not this journey!

General kissing, in which CAPT. G. is pursued by unknown female.

CAPT. G. (Faintly to M.) This is Hades! Can I wipe my face now?

CAPT. M. My responsibility has ended. Better ask Misses GADSBY.

CAPT. G. winces as though shot and procession is Mendelssohned out of Church to house, where usual tortures take place over the wedding-cake.

CAPT. M. (At table.) Up with you, Gaddy. They expect a speech.

CAPT. G. (After three minutes' agony.) Ha-hmmm. (Thunders Of applause.)

CAPT. M. Doocid good, for a first attempt. Now go and change your kit while Mamma is weeping over "the Missus." (CAPT. G. disappears. CAPT. M. starts up tearing his hair.) It'senot half legal. Where are the shoes? Get an ayah.

AYAH. Missie Captain Sahib done gone band karo all the jutis.

CAPT. M. (Brandishing scab larded sword.) Woman, produce those shoes Some one lend me a bread-knife. We mustn't crack Gaddy's head more than it is. (Slices heel off white satin slipper and puts slipper up his sleeve.)

Where is the Bride? (To the company at large.) Be tender with that rice. It's a heathen custom. Give me the big bag.

* * * * * *

Bride slips out quietly into 'rickshaw and departs toward the sunset.

CAPT. M. (In the open.) Stole away, by Jove! So much the worse for Gaddy! Here he is. Now Gaddy, this'll be livelier than Amdberan! Where's your horse?

CAPT. G. (Furiously, seeing that the women are out of an earshot.) Where the—is my Wife?

CAPT. M. Half-way to Mahasu by this time. You'll have to ride like Young Lochinvar.

Horse comes round on his hind legs; refuses to let G. handle him.

CAPT. G. Oh you will, will you? Get 'round, you brute—you hog—you beast! Get round!

Wrenches horse's head over, nearly breaking lower jaw: swings himself into saddle, and sends home both spurs in the midst of a spattering gale of Best Patna.

CAPT. M. For your life and your love-ride, Gaddy—And God bless you!

Throws half a pound of rice at G. who disappears, bowed forward on the saddle, in a cloud of sunlit dust.

CAPT. M. I've lost old Gaddy. (Lights cigarette and strolls off, singing absently):—

"You may carve it on his tombstone, you may cut it on his card, That a young man married is a young man marred!"

Miss DEERCOURT. (From her horse.) Really, Captain Mafflin! You are more plain spoken than polite!

CAPT. M. (Aside.) They say marriage is like cholera. 'Wonder who'll be the next victim.

White satin slipper slides from his sleeve and falls at his feet. Left wondering.

THE GARDEN OF EDEN AND YE SHALL BE AS—GODS!

SCENE.—Thymy grass-plot at back of t!'e Mahasu dak-bungalow, overlooking little wooded valley. On the left, glimpse of the Dead Forest of Fagoo; on the right, Simla Hills. In background, line of the Snows. CAPTAIN GADSBY, now three weeks a husband, is smoking the pipe of peace on a rug in the sunshine. Banjo and tobacco-pouch on rug. Overhead the Fagoo eagles. MRS. G. comes out of bungalow.

MRS. G. My husband! CAPT. G. (Lazily, with intense enjoyment.) Eb, wha-at? Say that again.

MRS. G. I've written to Mamma and told her that we shall be back on the 17th.

CAPT. G. Did you give her my love?

MRS. G. No, I kept all that for myself. (Sitting down by his side.) I thought you wouldn't mind.

CAPT. G. (With mock sternness.) I object awf'ly. How did you know that it was yours to keep?

MRS. G. I guessed, Phil.

CAPT. G. (Rapturously.) Lit-tle Featherweight!

MRS. G. I won' t be called those sporting pet names, bad boy.

CAPT. G. You'll be called anything I choose. Has it ever occurred to you, Madam, that you are my Wife?

MRS. G. It has. I haven't ceased wondering at it yet.

CAPT. G. Nor I. It seems so strange; and yet, somehow, it doesn't. (Confidently.) You see, it could have been no one else.

MRS. G. (Softly.) No. No one else—for me or for you. It must have been all arranged from the beginning. Phil, tell me again what made you care for me.

CAPT. G. How could I help it? You were you, you know.

MRS. G. Did you ever want to help it? Speak the truth!

CAPT. G. (A twinkle in his eye.) I did, darling, just at the first. Rut only at the very first. (Chuckles.) I called you—stoop low and I'll whisper—"a little beast." Ho! Ho! Ho!

MRS. G. (Taking him by the moustache and making him sit up.) "A—little—beast!" Stop laughing over your crime! And yet you had the—the—awful cheek to propose to me!

CAPT. C. I'd changed my mind then. And you weren't a little beast any more.

MRS. G. Thank you, sir! And when was I ever?

CAPT. G. Never! But that first day, when you gave me tea in that peach-colored muslin gown thing, you looked—you did indeed, dear—such an absurd little mite. And I didn't know what to say to you.

MRS. G. (Twisting moustache.) So you said "little beast." Upon my word, Sir! I called you a "Crrrreature," but I wish now I had called you something worse.

CAPT. G. (Very meekly.) I apologize, but you're hurting me awf'ly. (Interlude.) You're welcome to torture me again on those terms.

MRS. G. Oh, why did you let me do it?

CAPT. G. (Looking across valley.) No reason in particular, but—if it amused you or did you any good—you might—wipe those dear little boots of yours on me.

MRS. G. (Stretching out her hands.) Don't! Oh, don't! Philip, my King, please don't talk like that. It's how I feel. You're so much too good for me. So much too good!

CAPT. G. Me! I'm not fit to put my arm around you. (Puts it round.)

MRS. C. Yes, you are. But I—what have I ever done?

CAPT. G. Given me a wee bit of your heart, haven't you, my Queen!

MRS. G. That's nothing. Any one would do that. They cou-couldn't help it.

CAPT. G. Pussy, you'll make me horribly conceited. Just when I was beginning to feel so humble, too.

MRS. G. Humble! I don't believe it's in your character.

CAPT. G. What do you know of my character, Impertinence?

MRS. G. Ah, but I shall, shan't I, Phil? I shall have time in all the years and years to come, to know everything about you; and there will be no secrets between us.

CAPT. G. Little witch! I believe you know me thoroughly already.

MRS. G. I think I can guess. You're selfish?

CAPT. G. Yes.

MRS. G. Foolish?

CAPT. G. Very.

MRS. G. And a dear?

CAPT. G. That is as my lady pleases.

MRS. G. Then your lady is pleased. (A pause.) D'you know that we're two solemn, serious, grown-up people—CAPT. G. (Tilting her straw hat over her eyes.) You grown-up! Pooh! You're a baby.

MRS. G. And we're talking nonsense.

CAPT. G. Then let's go on talking nonsense. I rather like it. Pussy, I'll tell you a secret. Promise not to repeat?

MRS. G. Ye-es. Only to you.

CAPT. G. I love you.

MRS. G. Re-ally! For how long?

CAPT. G. Forever and ever.

MRS. G. That's a long time.

CAPT. G. 'Think so? It's the shortest I can do with.

MRS. G. You're getting quite clever.

CAPT. G. I'm talking to you.

MRS. G. Prettily turned. Hold up your stupid old head and I'll pay you for it.

CAPT. G. (Affecting supreme contempt.) Take it yourself if you want it.

MRS. G. I've a great mind to—and I will! (Takes it and is repaid with interest.)

CAPT. G, Little Featherweight, it's my opinion that we are a couple of idiots.

MRS. G. We're the only two sensible people in the world. Ask the eagle. He's coming by.

CAPT. G. Ah! I dare say he's seen a good many sensible people at Mahasu. They say that those birds live for ever so long.

MRS. G. How long?

CAPT. G. A hundred and twenty years.

MRS. G. A hundred and twenty years! O-oh! And in a hundred and twenty years where will these two sensible people be?

CAPT. G. What does it matter so long as we are together now?

MRS. G. (Looking round the horizon.) Yes. Only you and I—I and you—in the whole wide, wide world until the end. (Sees the line of the Snows.) How big and quiet the hills look! D'you think they care for us?

CAPT. G. 'Can't say I've consulted em particularly. I care, and that's enough for me.

MRS. G. (Drawing nearer to him.) Yes, now—but afterward. What's that little black blur on the Snows?

CAPT. G. A snowstorm, forty miles away. You'll see it move, as the wind carries it across the face of that spur and then it will be all gone.

MRS. G. And then it will be all gone. (Shivers.)

CAPT. G. (Anxiously.) Not chilled, pet, are you? Better let me get your cloak.

MRS. G. No. Don't leave me, Phil. Stay here. I believe I am afraid. Oh, why are the hills so horrid! Phil, promise me that you'll always love me.

CAPT. G. What's the trouble, darling? I can't promise any more than I have; but I'll promise that again and again if you like.

MRs. G. (Her head on his shoulder.) Say it, then—say it! N-no—don't! The—the—eagles would laugh. (Recovering.) My husband, you've married a little goose.

CAPT. G. (Very tenderly.) Have I? I am content whatever she is, so long as she is mine.

MRS. G. (Quickly.) Because she is yours or because she is me mineself?

CAPT. G. Because she is both. (Piteously.) I'm not clever, dear, and I don't think I can make myself understood properly.

MRS. G. I understand. Pip, will you tell me something?

CAPT. G. Anything you like. (Aside.) I wonder what's coming now.

MRS. G. (Haltingly, her eyes 'owered.) You told me once in the old days—centuries and centuries ago—that you had been engaged before. I didn't say anything—then.

CAPT. G. (Innocently.) Why not?

MRS. G. (Raising her eyes to his.) Because—because I was afraid of losing you, my heart. But now—tell about it—please.

CAPT. G. There's nothing to tell. I was awf'ly old then— nearly two and twenty—and she was quite that.

MRS. G. That means she was older than you. I shouldn't like her to have been younger. Well?

CAPT. G. Well, I fancied myself in love and raved about a bit, and—oh, yes, by Jove! I made up poetry. Ha! Ha!

MRS. G. You never wrote any for me! What happened?

CAPT. G. I came out here, and the whole thing went phut. She wrote to say that there had been a mistake, and then she married.

MRS. G. Did she care for you much?

CAPT. G. No. At least she didn't show it as far as I remember.

MRS. G. As far as you remember! Do you remember her name? (Hears it and bows her head.) Thank you, my husband.

CAPT. G. Who but you had the right? Now, Little Featherweight, have you ever been mixed up in any dark and dismal tragedy?

MRS. G. If you call me Mrs. Gadsby, p'raps I'll tell.

CAPT. G. (Throwing Parade rasp into his voice.) Mrs. Gadsby, confess!

MRS. G. Good Heavens, Phil! I never knew that you could speak in that terrible voice.

CAPT. G. You don't know half my accomplishments yet. Wait till we are settled in the Plains, and I'll show you how I bark at my troop. You were going to say, darling?

MRS. G. I—I don't like to, after that voice. (Tremulously.) Phil, never you dare to speak to me in that tone, whatever I may do!

CAPT. G. My poor little love! Why, you're shaking all over. I am so sorry. Of course I never meant to upset you Don't tell me anything, I'm a brute.

MRS. G. No, you aren't, and I will tell—There was a man.

CAPT. G. (Lightly.) Was there? Lucky man!

MRS. G. (In a whisper.) And I thought I cared for him.

CAPT. G. Still luckier man! Well?

MRS. G. And I thought I cared for him—and I didn't— and then you came—and I cared for you very, very much indeed. That's all. (Face hidden.) You aren't angry, are you?

CAPT. G. Angry? Not in the least. (Aside.) Good Lord, what have I done to deserve this angel?

MRS. G. (Aside.) And he never asked for the name! How funny men are! But perhaps it's as well.

CAPT. G. That man will go to heaven because you once thought you cared for him. 'Wonder if you'll ever drag me up there?

MRS. G. (Firmly.) 'Sha'n't go if you don't.

CAPT. G. Thanks. I say, Pussy, I don't know much about your religious beliefs. You were brought up to believe in a heaven and all that, weren't you?

MRS. G. Yes. But it was a pincushion heaven, with hymn-books in all the pews.

CAPT. G. (Wagging his head with intense conviction.) Never mind. There is a pukka heaven.

MRS. G. Where do you bring that message from, my prophet?

CAPT. G. Here! Because we care for each other. So it's all right.

Mrs. G. (As a troop of langurs crash through the branches.) So it's all right. But Darwin says that we came from those!

CAPT. G. (Placidly.) Ah! Darwin was never in love with an angel. That settles it. Sstt, you brutes! Monkeys, indeed! You shouldn't read those books.

MRS. G. (Folding her hands.) If it pleases my Lord the King to issue proclamation.

CAPT. G. Don't, dear one. There are no orders between us. Only I'd rather you didn't. They lead to nothing, and bother people's heads.

MRS. G. Like your first engagement.

CAPT. G. (With an immense calm.) That was a necessary evil and led to you. Are you nothing?

MRS. G. Not so very much, am I?

CAPT. G. All this world and the next to me.

MRS. G. (Very softly.) My boy of boys! Shall I tell you something?

CAPT. G. Yes, if it's not dreadful—about other men.

MRS. G. It's about my own bad little self.

CAPT. G. Then it must be good. Go on, dear.

MRS. G. (Slowly.) I don't know why I'm telling you, Pip; but if ever you marry again-(Interlude.) Take your hand from my mouth or I'll bite! In the future, then remember—I don't know quite how to put it!

CAPT. G. (Snorting indignantly.) Don't try. "Marry again," indeed!

MRS. G. I must. Listen, my husband. Never, never, never tell your wife anything that you do not wish her to remember and think over all her life. Because a woman—yes, I am a woman—can't forget.

CAPT. G. By Jove, how do you know that?

MRS. G. (Confusedly.) I don't. I'm only guessing. I am— I was—a silly little girl; but I feel that I know so much, oh, so very much more than you, dearest. To begin with, I'm your wife.

CAPT. G. So I have been led to believe.

MRS. G. And I shall want to know every one of your secrets—to share everything you know with you. (Stares round desperately.)

CAPT. G. So you shall, dear, so you shall—but don't look like that.

MRS. G. For your own sake don't stop me, Phil. I shall never talk to you in this way again. You must not tell me! At least, not now. Later on, when I'm an old matron it won't matter, but if you love me, be very good to me now; for this part of my life I shall never forget! Have I made you understand?

CAPT. G. I think so, child. Have I said anything yet that you disapprove of?

MRS. G. Will you be very angry? That—that voice, and what you said about the engagement—

CAPT. G. But you asked to be told that, darling.

MRS. G. And that's why you shouldn't have told me! You

must be the Judge, and, oh, Pip, dearly as I love you, I shan't be able to help you! I shall hinder you, and you must judge in spite of me!

CAPT. G. (Meditatively.) We have a great many things to find out together, God help us both—say so, Pussy—but we shall understand each other better every day; and I think I'm beginning to see now. How in the world did you come to know just the importance of giving me just that lead?

MRS. G. I've told you that I don't know. Only somehow it seemed that, in all this new life, I was being guided for your sake as well as my own.

CAPT. G. (Aside.) Then Mafilin was right! They know, and we—we're blind all of us. (Lightly.) 'Getting a little beyond our depth, dear, aren't we? I'll remember, and, if I fail, let me be punished as I deserve.

MRS. G. There shall be no punishment. We'll start into life together from here—you and I—and no one else.

CAPT. G. And no one else. (A pause.) Your eyelashes are all wet, Sweet? Was there ever such a quaint little Absurdity?

MRS. G. Was there ever such nonsense talked before?

CAPT. G. (Knocking the ashes out of his pipe.) 'Tisn't what we say, it's what we don't say, that helps. And it's all the profoundest philosophy. But no one would understand—even if it were put into a book.

MRS. G. The idea! No—only we ourselves, or people like ourselves—if there are any people like us.

CAPT. G. (Magisterially.) All people, not like ourselves, are blind idiots.

MRS. G. (Wiping her eyes.) Do you think, then, that there are any people as happy as we are?

CAPT. G. 'Must be—unless we've appropriated all the happiness in the world.

MRS. G. (Looking toward Simla.) Poor dears! Just fancy if we have!

CAPT. G. Then we'll hang on to the whole show, for it's a great deal too jolly to lose—eh, wife o' mine?

MRS. G. O Pip! Pip! How much of you is a solemn, married man and how much a horrid slangy schoolboy?

CAPT. G. When you tell me how much of you was eighteen last birthday and how much is as old as the Sphinx and twice as mysterious, perhaps I'll attend to you. Lend me that banjo. The spirit moveth me to jowl at the sunset.

MRS. G. Mind! It's not tuned. Ah! How that jars!

CAPT G. (Turning pegs.) It's amazingly different to keep a banjo to proper pitch.

MRS. G. It's the same with all musical instruments, What shall it be?

CAPT. G. "Vanity," and let the hills hear. (Sings through the first and hal' of the second verse. Turning to MRS. G.) Now, chorus! Sing, Pussy!

BOTH TOGETHER. (Con brio, to the horror of the monkeys who are settling for the night.)—

> *"Vanity, all is Vanity," said Wisdom, scorning me—*
> *I clasped my true Love's tender hand and answered frank and free-ee*
> *"If this be Vanity who'd be wise? If this be Vanity who'd be wise?*
> *If this be Vanity who'd be wi-ise (Crescendo.) Vanity let it be!"*

MRS. G. (Defiantly to the grey of the evening sky.) "Vanity let it be!"

ECHO. (Prom the Fagoo spur.) Let it be!

FATIMA

And you may go in every room of the house and see everything that is there, but into the Blue Room you must not go.—The Story of Blue Beard.

SCENE.—The GADSBYS' bungalow in the Plains. Time, 11 A. M. on a Sunday morning. Captain GADSBY, in his shirt-sleeves, is bending over a complete set of Hussar's equipment, from saddle to picketing-rope, which is neatly spread over the floor of his study. He is smoking an unclean briar, and his forehead is puckered with thought.

CAPT. G. (To himself, fingering a headstall.) Jack's an ass. There's enough brass on this to load a mule—and, if the Americans know anything about anything, it can be cut down to a bit only. 'Don't want the watering-bridle, either. Humbug!-Half a dozen sets of chains and pulleys for one horse! Rot! (Scratching his head.) Now, let's consider it all over from the be-ginning. By Jove, I've forgotten the scale of weights! Ne'er mind. 'Keep the bit only, and eliminate every boss from the crupper to breastplate. No breastplate at all. Simple leather strap across the breast-like the Russians. Hi! Jack never thought of that!

MRS. G. (Entering hastily, her hand bound in a cloth.) Oh, Pip, I've scalded my hand over that horrid, horrid Tiparee jam!

CAPT. G. (Absently.) Eh! Wha-at?

MRS. G. (With round-eyed reproach.) I've scalded it awfully! Aren't you sorry? And I did so want that jam to jam properly.

CAPT. G. Poor little woman! Let me kiss the place and make it well. (Unrolling bandage.) You small sinner! Where's that scald? I can't see it.

MRS. G. On the top of the little finger. There!—It's a most 'normous big burn!

CAPT. G. (Kissing little finger.) Baby! Let Hyder look after the jam. You know I don't care for sweets.

MRS. G. In-deed?—Pip!

CAPT. G. Not of that kind, anyhow. And now run along, Minnie, and leave me to my own base devices. I'm busy.

MRS. G. (Calmly settling herself in long chair.) So I see. What a mess you're making! Why have you brought all that smelly leather stuff into the house?

CAPT. G. To play with. Do you mind, dear?

MRS. G. Let me play too. I'd like it.

CAPT. G. I'm afraid you wouldn't. Pussy—Don't you think that jam will burn, or whatever it is that jam does when it's not looked after by a clever little housekeeper?

MRS. G. I thought you said Hyder could attend to it. I left him in the veranda, stirring—when I hurt myself so.

CAPT. G. (His eye returning to the equipment.) Po-oor little woman!—Three pounds four and seven is three eleven, and that can be cut down to two eight, with just a lee-tle care, without weakening anything. Farriery is all rot in incompetent hands. What's the use of a shoe-case when a man's scouting? He can't stick it on with a lick-like a stamp—the shoe! Skittles—

MRS. G. What's skittles? Pah! What is this leather cleaned with?

CAPT. G. Cream and champagne and—Look here, dear, do you really want to talk to me about anything important?

MRS. G. No. I've done my accounts, and I thought I'd like to see what you're doing.

CAPT. G. Well, love, now you've seen and—Would you mind?—That is to say—Minnie, I really am busy.

MRS. G. You want me to go?

CAPT. G, Yes, dear, for a little while. This tobacco will hang in your dress, and saddlery doesn't interest you.

MRS. G. Everything you do interests me, Pip.

CAPT. G. Yes, I know, I know, dear. I'll tell you all about it some day when I've put a head on this thing. In the meantime—

MRS. G. I'm to be turned out of the room like a troublesome child?

CAPT. G. No-o. I don't mean that exactly. But, you see, I shall be tramping up and down, shifting these things to and fro, and I shall be in your way. Don't you think so?

MRS. G. Can't I lift them about? Let me try. (Reaches forward to trooper's saddle.)

CAPT. G. Good gracious, child, don't touch it. You'll hurt yourself. (Picking up saddle.) Little girls aren't expected to handle numdahs. Now, where would you like it put? (Holds saddle above his head.)

MRS. G. (A break in her voice.) Nowhere. Pip, how good you are—and how strong! Oh, what's that ugly red streak inside your arm?

CAPT. G. (Lowering saddle quickly.) Nothing. It's a mark of sorts. (Aside.) And Jack's coming to tiffin with his notions all cut and dried!

MRS. G. I know it's a mark, but I've never seen it before. It runs all up the arm. What is it?

CAPT. G. A cut—if you want to know.

MRS. G. Want to know! Of course I do! I can't have my husband cut to pieces in this way. How did it come? Was it an accident? Tell me, Pip.

CAPT. G. (Grimly.) No. 'Twasn't an accident. I got it—from a man—in Afghanistan.

MRS. G. In action? Oh, Pip, and you never told me!

CAPT. G. I'd forgotten all about it.

MRS. G. Hold up your arm! What a horrid, ugly scar! Are you sure it doesn't hurt now! How did the man give it you?

CAPT. G. (Desperately looking at his watch.) With a knife. I came down—old Van Loo did, that's to say—and fell on my leg, so I couldn't run. And then this man came up and began chopping at me as I sprawled.

MRS. G. Oh, don't, don't! That's enough!—Well, what happened?

CAPT. G. I couldn't get to my holster, and Mafflin came round the corner and stopped the performance.

MRS. G. How? He's such a lazy man, I don't believe he did.

CAPT. G. Don't you? I don't think the man had much doubt about it. Jack cut his head off.

MRS. G. Cut-his-head-off! "With one blow," as they say in the books?

CAPT. G. I'm not sure. I was too interested in myself to know much about it. Anyhow, the head was off, and Jack was punching old Van Loo in the ribs to make him get up. Now you know all about it, dear, and now—

MRS. G. You want me to go, of course. You never told me about this, though I've been married to you for ever so long; and you never would have told me if I hadn't found out; and you never do tell me anything about yourself, or what you do, or what you take an interest in.

CAPT. G. Darling, I'm always with you, aren't I?

MRS. G. Always in my pocket, you were going to say. I know you are; but you are always thinking away from me.

CAPT. G. (Trying to hide a smile.) Am I? I wasn't aware of it. I'm awf'ly sorry.

MRS. G. (Piteously.) Oh, don't make fun of me! Pip, you know what I mean. When you are reading one of those things about Cavalry, by that idiotic Prince—why doesn't he be a Prince instead of a stable-boy?

CAPT. G. Prince Kraft a stable-boy—Oh, my Aunt! Never mind, dear. You were going to say?

MRS. G. It doesn't matter; you don't care for what I say. Only—only you get up and walk about the room, staring in front of you, and then Mafflin comes in to dinner, and after I'm in the drawing-room I can hear you and him talking, and talking, and talking, about things I can't understand, and— oh, I get so tired and feel so lonely!—I don't want to complain and be a trouble, Pip; but I do indeed I do!

CAPT. G. My poor darling! I never thought of that. Why don't you ask some nice people in to dinner?

MRS. G. Nice people! Where am I to find them? Horrid frumps! And if I did, I shouldn't be amused. You know I only want you.

CAPT, G. And you have me surely, Sweetheart?

MRS. G. I have not! Pip why don't you take me into your life?

CAPT. G. More than I do? That would be difficult, dear.

MRS. G. Yes, I suppose it would—to you. I'm no help to you—no companion to you; and you like to have it so.

CAPT. G. Aren't you a little unreasonable, Pussy?

MRS. G. (Stamping her foot.) I'm the most reasonable woman in the world—when I'm treated properly.

CAPT. G. And since when have I been treating you improperly?

MRS. G. Always—and since the beginning. You know you have.

CAPT. G. I don't; but I'm willing to be convinced.

MRS. G. (Pointing to saddlery.) There!

CAPT. G. How do you mean?

MRS. G. What does all that mean? Why am I not to be told? Is it so precious?

CAPT. G. I forget its exact Government value just at present. It means that it is a great deal too heavy.

MRS. G. Then why do you touch it?

CAPT. G. To make it lighter. See here, little love, I've one notion and Jack has another, but we are both agreed that all this equipment is about thirty pounds too heavy. The thing is how to cut it down without weakening any part of it, and, at the same time, allowing the trooper to carry everything he wants for his own comfort-socks and shirts and things of that kind.

MRS. G. Why doesn't he pack them in a little trunk?

CAPT. G. (Kissing her.) Oh, you darling! Pack them in a little trunk, indeed! Hussars don't carry trunks, and it's a most important thing to make the horse do all the carrying.

MRS. G. But why need you bother about it? You're not a trooper.

CAPT. G. No; but I command a few score of him; and equipment is nearly everything in these days.

MRS. G. More than me?

CAPT. G. Stupid! Of course not; but it's a matter that I'm tremendously interested in, because if I or Jack, or I and Jack, work out some sort of lighter saddlery and all that, it's possible that we may get it adopted.

MRS. G. How?

CAPT. G. Sanctioned at Home, where they will make a sealed pattern—a pattern that all the saddlers must copy— and so it will be used by all the regiments.

MRS. G. And that interests you?

CAPT. G. It's part of my profession, y'know, and my profession is a good deal to me. Everything in a soldier's equipment is important, and if we can improve that equipment, so much the better for the soldiers and for us.

MRS. G. Who's "us"?

CAPT. G. Jack and I; only Jack's notions are too radical. What's that big sigh for, Minnie?

MRS. G. Oh, nothing—and you've kept all this a secret from me! Why?

CAPT. G. Not a secret, exactly, dear. I didn't say anything about it to you because I didn't think it would amuse you.

MRS. G. And am I only made to be amused?

CAPT. G. No, of course. I merely mean that it couldn't interest you.

MRS. G. It's your work and—and if you'd let me, I'd count all these things up. If they are too heavy, you know by how much they are too heavy, and you must have a list of things made out to your scale of lightness, and—

CAPT. G. I have got both scales somewhere in my head; but it's hard to tell how light you can make a head-stall, for instance, until you've actually had a model made.

MRS. G. But if you read out the list, I could copy it down, and pin it up there just above your table. Wouldn't that do?

CAPT. G. It would be awf'ly nice, dear, but it would be giving you trouble for nothing. I can't work that way. I go by rule of thumb. I know the present scale of weights, and the other one—the one that I'm trying to work to—will shift and vary so much that I couldn't be certain, even if I wrote it down.

MRS. G. I'm so sorry. I thought I might help. Is there anything else that I could be of use in?

CAPT. G. (Looking round the room.) I can't think of anything. You're always helping me you know.

MRS. G. Am I? How?

CAPT. G. You are of course, and as long as you're near me—I can't explain exactly, but it's in the air.

MRS. G. And that's why you wanted to send me away?

CAPT. G. That's only when I'm trying to do work—grubby work like this.

MRS. G. Mafflin's better, then, isn't he?

CAPT. G. (Rashly.) Of course he is. Jack and I have been thinking along the same groove for two or three years about this equipment. It's our hobby, and it may really be useful some day.

MRS. G. (After a pause.) And that's all that you have away from me?

CAPT. G. It isn't very far away from you now. Take care the oil on that bit doesn't come off on your dress.

MRS. G. I wish—I wish so much that I could really help you. I believe I could—if I left the room. But that's not what I mean.

CAPT. G. (Aside.) Give me patience! I wish she would go. (Aloud.) I as-sure you you can't do anything for me, Minnie, and I must really settle down to this. Where's my pouch?

MRS. G. (Crossing to writing-table.) Here you are, Bear. What a mess you keep your table in!

CAPT. G. Don't touch it. There's a method in my madness, though you mightn't think of it.

MRS. G. (At table.) I want to look—Do you keep accounts, Pip?

CAPT. G. (Bending over saddlery.) Of a sort. Are you rummaging among the Troop papers? Be careful.

MRs. G. Why? I sha'n't disturb anything. Good gracious! I had no idea that you had anything to do with so many sick horses.

CAPT. G. 'Wish I hadn't, but they insist on falling sick. Minnie, if I were you I really should not investigate those papers. You may come across something that you won't like.

MRS. G. Why will you always treat me like a child? I know I'm not displacing the horrid things.

CAPT. G. (Resignedly.) Very well, then. Don't blame me if anything happens. Play with the table and let me go on with the saddlery. (Slipping hand into trousers-pocket.) Oh, the deuce!

MRS. G. (Her back to G.) What's that for?

CAPT. G. Nothing. (Aside.) There's not much in it, but I wish I'd torn it up.

MRS. G. (Turning over contents of table.) I know you'll hate me for this; but I do want to see what your work is like. (A pause.) Pip, what are "farcybuds"?

CAPT. G. Hah! Would you really like to know? They aren't pretty things.

MRS. G. This Journal of Veterinary Science says they are of "absorbing interest." Tell me.

CAPT. G. (Aside.) It may turn her attention.

Gives a long and designedly loathsome account of glanders and farcy.

MRS. G. Oh, that's enough. Don't go on!

CAPT. G. But you wanted to know—Then these things suppurate and matterate and spread—

MRS. G. Pin, you're making me sick! You're a horrid, disgusting schoolboy.

CAPT. G. (On his knees among the bridles.) You asked to be told. It's not my fault if you worry me into talking about horrors.

MRS. G. Why didn't you say—No?

CAPT. G. Good Heavens, child! Have you come in here simply to bully me?

MRS. G. I bully you? How could I! You're so strong. (Hysterically.) Strong enough to pick me up and put me outside the door and leave me there to cry. Aren't you?

CAPT. G. It seems to me that you're an irrational little baby. Are you quite well?

MRS. G. Do I look ill? (Returning to table). Who is your lady friend with the big grey envelope and the fat monogram outside?

CAPT. G. (Aside.) Then it wasn't locked up, confound it. (Aloud.) "God made her, therefore let her pass for a woman." You remember what farcybuds are like?

MRS. G. (Showing envelope.) This has nothing to do with them. I'm going to open it. May I?

CAPT. G. Certainly, if you want to. I'd sooner you didn't though. I don't ask to look at your letters to the Deer-court girl.

MRS. G. You'd better not, Sir! (Takes letter from envelope.) Now, may I look? If you say no, I shall cry.

CAPT. G. You've never cried in my knowledge of you, and I don't believe you could.

MRS. G. I feel very like it to-day, Pip. Don't be hard on me. (Reads letter.) It begins in the middle, without any "Dear Captain Gadsby," or anything. How funny!

CAPT. G. (Aside.) No, it's not Dear Captain Gadsby, or anything, now. How funny!

MRS. G. What a strange letter! (Reads.) "And so the moth has come too near the candle at last, and has been singed into—shall I say Respectability? I congratulate him, and hope he will be as happy as he deserves to be." What does that mean? Is she congratulating you about our marriage?

CAPT. G. Yes, I suppose so.

MRS. G. (Still reading letter.) She seems to be a particular friend of yours.

CAPT. G. Yes. She was an excellent matron of sorts—a Mrs. Herriott—wife of a Colonel Herriott. I used to know some of her people at Home long ago—before I came out.

MRS. G. Some Colonel's wives are young—as young as me. I knew one who was younger.

CAPT. G. Then it couldn't have been Mrs. Herriott. She was old enough to have been your mother, dear.

MRS. G. I remember now. Mrs. Scargill was talking about her at the Dutfins' tennis, before you came for me, on Tuesday. Captain Mafflin said she was a "dear old woman." Do you know, I think Mafilin is a very c lumsy man with his feet.

CAPT. G. (Aside.) Good old Jack! (Aloud.) Why, dear?

MRS. G. He had put his cup down on the ground then, and he literally stepped into it. Some of the tea spirted over my dress—the grey one. I meant to tell you about it before.

CAPT. G. (Aside.) There are the makings of a strategist about Jack though his methods are coarse. (Aloud.) You'd better get a new dress, then. (Aside.) Let us pray that that will turn her.

MRS. G. Oh, it isn't stained in the least. I only thought that I'd tell you. (Returning to letter.) What an extraordinary person! (Reads.) "But need I remind you that you have taken upon yourself a charge of wardship"—what in the world is a charge of wardship?—"which as you yourself know, may end in Consequences"—

CAPT. G. (Aside.) It's safest to let em see everything as they come across it; but 'seems to me that there are exceptions to the rule. (Aloud.) I told you that there was nothing to be gained from rearranging my table.

MRS. G. (Absently.) What does the woman mean? She goes on talking about Consequences—"almost inevitable Consequences" with a capital C— for half a page. (Flushing scarlet.) Oh, good gracious! How abominable!

CAPT. G. (Promptly.) Do you think so? Doesn't it show a sort of motherly interest in us? (Aside.) Thank Heaven. Harry always wrapped her meaning up safely! (Aloud.) Is it absolutely necessary to go on with the letter, darling?

MRS. G. It's impertinent—it's simply horrid. What right has this woman to write in this way to you? She oughtn't to.

CAPT. G. When you write to the Deercourt girl, I notice that you generally fill three or four sheets. Can't you let an old woman babble on paper once in a way? She means well.

MRS. G. I don't care. She shouldn't write, and if she did, you ought to have shown me her letter.

CAPT. G. Can't you understand why I kept it to myself, or must I explain at length—as I explained the farcybuds?

MRS. G. (Furiously.) Pip I hate you! This is as bad as those idiotic saddle-bags on the floor. Never mind whether it would please me or not, you ought to have given it to me to read.

CAPT. G. It comes to the same thing. You took it yourself.

MRS. G. Yes, but if I hadn't taken it, you wouldn't have said a word. I think this Harriet Herriott—it's like a name in a book—is an interfering old Thing.

CAPT. G. (Aside.) So long as you thoroughly understand that she is old, I don't much care what you think. (Aloud.) Very good, dear. Would you like to write and tell her so? She's seven thousand miles away.

MRS. G. I don't want to have anything to do with her, but you ought to have told me. (Turning to last page of letter.) And she patronizes me, too. I've never seen her! (Reads.) "I do not know how the world stands with you; in all human probability I shall never know; but whatever I may have said before, I pray for her sake more than for yours that all may be well. I have learned what misery means, and I dare not wish that any one dear to you should share my knowledge."

CAPT. G. Good God! Can't you leave that letter alone, or, at least, can't you refrain from reading it aloud? I've been through it once. Put it back on 'he desk. Do you hear me?

MRS. G. (Irresolutely.) I sh-sha'n't! (Looks at G.'s eyes.) Oh, Pip, please! I didn't mean to make you angry—'Deed, I didn't. Pip, I'm so sorry. I know I've wasted your time—

CAPT. G. (Grimly.) You have. Now, will you be good enough

to go—if there is nothing more in my room that you are anxious to pry into?

MRS. G. (Putting out her hands.) Oh, Pip, don't look at me like that! I've never seen you look like that before and it hu-urts me! I'm sorry. I oughtn't to have been here at all, and—and—and—(sobbing.) Oh, be good to me! Be good to me! There's only you—anywhere! Breaks down in long chair, hiding face in cushions.

CAPT. G. (Aside.) She doesn't know how she flicked me on the raw. (Aloud, bending over chair.) I didn't mean to be harsh, dear—I didn't really. You can stay here as long as you please, and do what you please. Don't cry like that. You'll make yourself sick. (Aside.) What on earth has come over her? (Aloud.) Darling, what's the matter with you?

Mrs. G. (Her face still hidden.) Let me go—let me go to my own room. Only—only say you aren't angry with me.

CAPT. G. Angry with you, love! Of course not. I was angry with myself. I'd lost my temper over the saddlery—Don't hide your face, Pussy. I want to kiss it.

Bends lower, MRS. G. slides right arm round his neck. Several interludes and much sobbing.

MRS. G. (In a whisper.) I didn't mean about the jam when I came in to tell you—

CAPT'. G. Bother the jam and the equipment! (Interlude.)

MRS. G. (Still more faintly.) My finger wasn't scalded at all. I—wanted to speak to you about—about—something else, and—I didn't know how.

CAPT. G. Speak away, then. (Looking into her eyes.) Eh! Wha-at? Minnie! Here, don't go away! You don't mean?

MRS. G. (Hysterically, backing to portiere and hiding her face in its fold's.) The—the Almost Inevitable Consequences!

(Flits through portiere as G. attempts to catch her, and bolts her self in her own room.)

CAPT. G. (His arms full of portiere.) Oh! (Sitting down heavily in chair.) I'm a brute—a pig—a bully, and a blackguard. My poor, poor little darling! "Made to be amused only?"—

THE VALLEY OF THE SHADOW

Knowing Good and Evil.

SCENE.--The GADSBYS' bungalow in the Plains, in June. Punkah--coolies asleep in veranda where Captain GADSBY is walking up and down. DOCTOR'S trap in porch. JUNIOR CHAPLAIN drifting generally and uneasily through the house. Time, 3:40 A. M. Heat 94 degrees in veranda.

DOCTOR. (Coming into veranda and touching G. on the shoulder.) You had better go in and see her now.

CAPT. G. (The color of good cigar-ash.) Eh, wha-at? Oh, yes, of course. What did you say?

DOCTOR. (Syllable by syllable.) Go--in--to--the--room--and--see--her. She wants to speak to you. (Aside, testily.) I shall have him on my hands next.

JUNIOR CHAPLAIN. (In half-lighted dining room.) Isn't there any?--

DOCTOR. (Savagely.) Hsh, you little fool!

JUNIOR CHAPLAIN. Let me do my work. Gadsby, stop a minute! (Edges after G.)

DOCTOR. Wait till she sends for you at least--at least. Man alive, he'll kill you if you go in there! What are you bothering him for?

JUNIOR CHAPLAIN. (Coming into veranda.) I've given him a stiff brandy-peg. He wants it. You've forgotten him for the last ten hours and--forgotten yourself too.

CAPT. G. enters bedroom, which is lit by one night-lamp. Ayak on the floor pretending to be asleep.

VOICE. (From the bed.) All down the street--such bonfires! Ayah, go and put them out! (Appealingly.) How can I sleep with an installation of the C.I.E. in my room? No--not C.I.E. Something else. What was it?

CAPT. G. (Trying to control his voice.) Minnie, I'm here. (Bending over bed.) Don't you know me, Minnie? It's me-- it's Phil--it's your husband.

VOICE. (Mechanically.) It's me--it's Phil--it's your husband.

CAPT. G. She doesn't know mel--It's your own husband, darling.

VOICE. Your own husband, darling. AYAH. (With an inspiration.) Memsahib understanding all I saying.

CAPT. G. Make her understand me then--quick!

AYAH. (Hand on MRS. G.'s forehead.) Memsahib! Captain Sahib here.

VOICE. Salaem do. (Fretfully.) I know I'm not fit to be seen.

AYAH. (Aside to G.) Say "marneen" same as breakfash.

CAPT. G. Good-morning, little woman. How are we to-day?

VOICE. That's Phil. Poor old Phil. (Viciously.) Phil, you fool, I can't see you. Come nearer.

CAPT. G. Minnie! Minnie! It's me--you know me?

VOICE. (Mockingly.) Of course I do. Who does not know the man who was so cruel to his wife--almost the only one he ever had?

CAPT. G. Yes, dear. Yes--of course, of course. But won't you speak to him? He wants to speak to you so much.

VOICE. They'd never let him in. The Doctor would give darwaza bund even if he were in the house. He'll never come. (Despairingly.) O Judas! Judas! Judas!

CAPT. G. (Putting out his arms.) They have let him in, and he always was in the house Oh, my love--don't you know me?

VOICE. (In a half chant.) "And it came to pass at the eleventh hour that this poor soul repented." It knocked at the gates, but they were shut--tight as a plaster--a great, burning plaster They had pasted our marriage certificate all across the door, and it was made of red-hot iron--people really ought to be more careful, you know.

CAPT. G. What am I to do? (Taking her in his arms.) Minnie! speak to me--to Phil.

VOICE. What shall I say? Oh, tell me what to say before it's too late! They are all going away and I can't say anything.

CAPT. G. Say you know me! Only say you know me!

DOCTOR. (Who has entered quietly.) For pity's sake don't take it too much to heart, Gadsby. It's this way sometimes. They won't recognize. They say all sorts of queer things-- don't you see?

CAPT. G. All right! All right! Go away now; she'll recognize me; you're bothering her. She must--mustn't she?

DOCTOR. She will before--Have I your leave to try?--

CAPT. G. Anything you please, so long as she'll know me. It's only a question of--hours, isn't it?

DOCTOR. (Professionally.) While there's life there's hope y'know. But don't build on it.

CAPT. G. I don't. Pull her together if it's possible. (Aside.)

What have I done to deserve this?

DOCTOR. (Bending over bed.) Now, Mrs. Gadsby! We shall be all right tomorrow. You must take it, or I sha'n't let Phil see you. It isn't nasty, is it?

Voice. Medicines! Always more medicines! Can't you leave me alone?

CAPT. G. Oh, leave her in peace, Doc!

DOCTOR. (Stepping back,--aside.) May I be forgiven if I've none wrong. (Aloud.) In a few minutes she ought to be sensible; but I daren't tell you to look for anything. It's only-

CAPT. G. What? Go on, man.

DOCTOR. (In a whisper.) Forcing the last rally.

CAPT. G. Then leave us alone.

DOCTOR. Don't mind what she says at first, if you can. They--they-they turn against those they love most sometimes in this.--It's hard, but--

CAPT. G. Am I her husband or are you? Leave us alone for what time we have together.

VOICE. (Confidentially.) And we were engaged quite suddenly, Emma. I assure you that I never thought of it for a moment; but, oh, my little Me!--I don't know what I should have done if he hadn't proposed.

CAPT. G. She thinks of that Deercourt girl before she thinks of me. (Aloud.) Minnie!

VOICE. Not from the shops, Mummy dear. You can get the real leaves from Kaintu, and (laughing weakly) never mind about the blossoms--Dead white silk is only fit for widows, and I won't wear it. It's as bad as a winding sheet. (A long pause.)

CAPT. G. I never asked a favor yet. If there is anybody to listen to me, let her know me--even if I die too!

VOICE. (Very faintly.) Pip, Pip dear.

CAPT. G. I'm here, darling.

VOICE. What has happened? They've been bothering me so with medicines and things, and they wouldn't let you come and see me. I was never ill before. Am I ill now?

CAPT. G. You--you aren't quite well.

VOICE. How funny! Have I been ill long?

CAPT. G. Some day; but you'll be all right in a little time.

VOICE. Do you think so, Pip? I don't feel well and--Oh! what have they done to my hair?

CAPT. G. I d-d-on't know.

VOICE. They've cut it off. What a shame!

CAPT. G. It must have been to make your head cooler.

VOICE. Just like a boy's wig. Don't I look horrid?

CAPT. G. Never looked prettier in your life, dear. (Aside.) How am I to ask her to say good-bye?

VOICE. I don't feel pretty. I feel very ill. My heart won't work. It's nearly dead inside me, and there's a funny feeling in my eyes. Everything seems the same distance--you and the almirah and the table inside my eyes or miles away. What does it mean, Pip?

CAPT. G. You're a little feverish, Sweetheart--very feverish. (Breaking down.) My love! my love! How can I let you go?

VOICE. I thought so. Why didn't you tell me that at first?

CAPT. G. What?

VOICE. That I am going to--die.

CAPT. G. But you aren't! You sha'n't.

AYAH to punkah-coolie. (Stepping into veranda after a glance at the bed.). Punkah chor do! (Stop pulling the punkah.)

VOICE. It's hard, Pip. So very, very hard after one year--just one year.

(Wailing.) And I'm only twenty. Most girls aren't even married at twenty. Can't they do anything to help me? I don't want to die.

CAPT. G. Hush, dear. You won't.

VOICE. What's the use of talking? Help me! You've never failed me yet. Oh, Phil, help me to keep alive. (Feverishly.) I don't believe you wish me to live. You weren't a bit sorry when that horrid Baby thing died. I wish I'd killed it!

CAPT. G. (Drawing his hand across his forehead.) It's more than a man's meant to bear--it's not right. (Aloud.) Minnie, love, I'd die for you if it would help.

VOICE. No more death. There's enough already. Pip, don't you die too.

CAPT. G. I wish I dared.

VOICE. It says: "Till Death do us part." Nothing after that--and so it would be no use. It stops at the dying. Why does it stop there? Only such a very short life, too. Pip, I'm sorry we married.

CAPT. G. No! Anything but that, Mm!

VOICE. Because you'll forget and I'll forget. Oh, Pip, don't forget! I always loved you, though I was cross sometimes. If I ever did anything that you didn't like, say you forgive me now.

CAPT. G. You never did, darling. On my soul and honor you never did. I haven't a thing to forgive you.

VOICE. I sulked for a whole week about those petunias. (With a laugh.) What a little wretch I was, and how grieved you were! Forgive me that, Pp.

CAPT. G. There's nothing to forgive. It was my fault. They were too near the drive. For God's sake don't talk so, Minnie! There's such a lot to say and so little time to say it in.

VOICE. Say that you'll always love me--until the end.

CAPT. G. Until the end. (Carried away.) It's a lie. It must be, because we've loved each other. This isn't the end.

VOICE. (Relapsing into semi-delirium.) My Church-service has an ivory-cross on the back, and it says so, so it must be true. "Till Death do us part."--but that's a lie. (With a parody of G.'s manner.) A damned lie! (Recklessly.) Yes, I can swear as well as a Trooper, Pip. I can't make my head think, though. That's because they cut off my hair. How can one think with one's head all fuzzy? (Pleadingly.) Hold me, Pip! Keep me with you always and always. (Relapsing.) But if you marry the Thorniss girl when I'm dead, I'll come back and howl under our bedroom window all night. Oh, bother! You'll think I'm a jackall. Pip, what time is it?

CAPT. G. A little before the dawn, dear.

VOICE. I wonder where I shall be this time to-morrow?

CAPT. G. Would you like to see the Padre?

VOICE. Why should I? He'd tell me that I am going to heaven; and that wouldn't be true, because you are here. Do you recollect when he upset the cream-ice all over his trousers at the Gassers' tennis?

CAPT. G. Yes, dear.

VOICE. I often wondered whether he got another pair of trousers; but then his are so shiny all over that you really couldn't tell unless you were told. Let's call him in and ask.

CAPT. G. (Gravely.) No. I don't think he'd like that. 'Your head comfy, Sweetheart?'

VOICE. (Faintly with a sigh of contentment.) Yeth! Gracious, Pip, when did you shave last? Your chin's worse than the barrel of a musical box.--No, don't lift it up. I like it. (A pause.) You said you've never cried at all. You're crying all over my cheek.

CAPT. G. I--I--I can't help it, dear.

VOICE. How funny! I couldn't cry now to save my life. (G. shivers.) I want to sing.

CAPT. G. Won't it tire you? 'Better not, perhaps.

VOICE. Why? I won't be bothered about. (Begins in a hoarse quaver)

"Minnie bakes oaten cake, Minnie brews ale, All because her Johnnie's coming home from the sea. (That's parade, Pip.) And she grows red as a rose, who was so pale; And 'Are you sure the church--clock goes?' says she."

(Pettishly.) I knew I couldn't take the last note. How do the bass chords run? (Puts out her hands and begins playing piano on the sheet.)

CAPT. G. (Catching up hands.) Ahh! Don't do that, Pussy, if you love me.

VOICE. Love you? Of course I do. Who else should it be? (A pause.)

VOICE. (Very clearly.) Pip, I'm going now. Something's choking me cruelly. (Indistinctly.) Into the dark--without you, my heart--But it's a lie, dear--we mustn't believe it.--Forever and ever, living or dead. Don't let me go, my husband--hold me tight.--They can't--whatever happens. (A cough.) Pip--my Pip! Not for always--and--so--soon! (Voice ceases.)

Pause of ten minutes. G. buries his face in the side of the bed while AYAH bends over bed from opposite side and feels MRS. G.'s breast and forehead.

CAPT. G. (Rising.) Doctor Sahib ko salaam do.

AYAH. (Still by bedside, with a shriek.) Ail Ail Tuta-phuta! My Memsahib! Not getting--not have got!--Pusseena agyal (The sweat has come.) (Fiercely to G.) TUM jao Doctor Sahib ko jaldi! (You go to the doctor.) Oh, my Memsahib!

DOCTOR. (Entering hastily.) Come away, Gadsby. (Bends over bed.) Eh! The Dev--What inspired you to stop the punkab?

Get out, man--go away--wait outside! Go! Here, Ayah! (Over his shoulder to G.) Mind I promise nothing.

The dawn breaks as G. stumbles into the garden.

CAPT. M. (Rehung up at the gate on his way to parade and very soberly.) Old man, how goes?

CAPT. G. (Dazed.) I don't quite know. Stay a bit. Have a drink or something. Don't run away. You're just getting amusing. Ha! ha!

CAPT. M. (Aside.) What am I let in for? Gaddy has aged ten years in the night.

CAPT. G. (Slowly, fingering charger's headstall.) Your curb's too loose.

CAPT. M. So it is. Put it straight, will you? (Aside.) I shall be late for parade. Poor Gaddy.

CAPT. G. links and unlinks curb-chain aimlessly, and finally stands staring toward the veranda. The day brightens.

DOCTOR. (Knocked out of professional gravity, tramping across flower-beds and shaking G's hands.) It'--it's--it's!-- Gadsby, there's a fair chance--a dashed fair chance. The flicker, y'know. The sweat, y'know I saw how it would be. The punkab, y'know. Deuced clever woman that Ayah of yours. Stopped the punkab just at the right time. A dashed good chance! No--you don't go in. We'll pull her through yet I promise on my reputation--under Providence. Send a man with this note to Bingle. Two heads better than one. 'Specially the Ayah! We'll pull her round. (Retreats hastily to house.)

CAPT. G. (His head on neck of M.'s charger.) Jack! I bub- -bu--believe, I'm going to make a bu-bub-bloody exhibit of byself.

CAPT. M. (Sniffing openly and feeling in his left cuff.) I b- b-believe, I'b doing it already. Old bad, what cad I say? I'b as pleased as--Cod dab you, Gaddy! You're one big idiot and I'b adother. (Pulling himself together.) Sit tight! Here comes the Devil-dodger.

JUNIOR CHAPLAIN. (Who is not in the Doctor's confidence.) We--we are only men in these things, Gadsby. I know that I can say nothing now to help.

CAPT. M. (jealously.) Then don't say it Leave him alone. It's not bad enough to croak over. Here, Gaddy, take the chit to Bingle and ride hell-for-leather. It'll do you good. I can't go.

JUNIOR CHAPLAIN. Do him good! (Smiling.) Give me the chit and I'll drive. Let him lie down. Your horse is blocking my cart--please!

CAPT. M. (Slowly without reining back.) I beg your pardon--I'll apologize. On paper if you like.

JUNIOR CHAPLAIN. (Flicking M.'s charger.) That'll do, thanks. Turn in, Gadsby, and I'll bring Bingle back--ahem--"hell-for-leather."

CAPT. M. (Solus.) It would have served me right if he'd cut me across the face. He can drive too. I shouldn't care to go that pace in a bamboo cart. What a faith he must have in his Maker--of harness! Come hup, you brute! (Gallops off to parade, blowing his nose, as the sun rises.)

(INTERVAL OF' FIVE WEEKS.)

MRS. G. (Very white and pinched, in morning wrapper at break fast table.) How big and strange the room looks, and how glad I am to see it again! What dust, though! I must talk to the servants. Sugar, Pip? I've almost forgotten. (Seriously.) Wasn't I very ill?

CAPT. G. Iller than I liked. (Tenderly.) Oh, you bad little Pussy, what a start you gave me.

MRS. G. I'll never do it again.

CAPT. G. You'd better not. And now get those poor pale

cheeks pink again, or I shall be angry. Don't try to lift the urn. You'll upset it. Wait. (Comes round to head of table and lifts urn.)

MRS. G. (Quickly.) Khitmatgar, howarchikhana see kettly lao. Butler, get a kettle from the cook-house. (Drawing down G.'s face to her own.) Pip dear, I remember.

CAPT. G. What?

MRS. G. That last terrible night.

CAPT'. G. Then just you forget all about it.

MRS. G. (Softly, her eyes filling.) Never. It has brought us very close together, my husband. There! (Interlude.) I'm going to give Junda a saree.

CAPT. G. I gave her fifty dibs.

MRS. G. So she told me. It was a 'normous reward. Was I worth it? (Several interludes.) Don't! Here's the khitmatgar.--Two lumps or one Sir?

THE SWELLING OF JORDAN

If thou hast run with the footmen and they have wearied thee, then how canst thou contend with horses? And if in the land of peace wherein thou trustedst they wearied thee, then how wilt thou do in the swelling of Jordan?

SCENE.--The GADSBYS' bungalow in the Plains, on a January morning. MRS. G. arguing with bearer in back veranda.

CAPT. M. rides up.

CAPT. M. 'Mornin', Mrs. Gadsby. How's the Infant Phenomenon and the Proud Proprietor?

MRS. G. You'll find them in the front veranda; go through the house. I'm Martha just now.

CAPT. M, 'Cumbered about with cares of Khitmatgars? I fly.

Passes into front veranda, where GADSBY is watching GADSBY JUNIOR, aged ten months, crawling about the matting.

CAPT. M. What's the trouble, Gaddy--spoiling an honest man's Europe morning this way? (Seeing G. JUNIOR.) By Jove, that yearling's comm' on amazingly! Any amount of bone below the knee there.

CAPT. G. Yes, he's a healthy little scoundrel. Don't you think his hair's growing?

CAPT. M. Let's have a look. Hi! Hst Come here, General Luck, and we'll report on you.

MRS. G. (Within.) What absurd name will you give him next? Why do you call him that?

CAPT. M. Isn't he our Inspector--General of Cavalry? Doesn't he come down in his seventeen-two perambulator every morning the Pink Hussars parade? Don't wriggle, Brigadier. Give us your private opinion on the way the third squadron went past. 'Trifle ragged, weren't they?

CAPT. G. A bigger set of tailors than the new draft I don't wish to see. They've given me more than my fair share-- knocking the squadron out of shape. It's sickening!

CAPT. M. When you're in command, you'll do better, young 'un. Can't you walk yet? Grip my finger and try. (To G.) 'Twon't hurt his hocks, will it?

CAPT. G. Oh, no. Don't let him99 flop, though, or he'll lick all the blacking off your boots.

MRS. G. (Within.) Who's destroying my son's character?

CAPT. M. And my Godson's. I'm ashamed of you, Gaddy. Punch your father in the eye, Jack! Don't you stand it! Hit him again!

CAPT. G. (Sotto voce.) Put The Butcha down and come to the end of the veranda. I'd rather the Wife didn't hear--just now.

CAPT. M. You look awf'ly serious. Anything wrong?

CAPT. G. 'Depends on your view entirely. I say, Jack, you won't think more hardly of me than you can help, will you? Come further this way.--The fact of the matter is, that I've made up my mind--at least I'm thinking seriously of--cutting the Service.

CAPT. M. Hwhatt?

CAPT. G. Don't shout. I'm going to send in my papers.

CAPT. M. You! Are you mad?

CAPT. G. No--only married.

CAPT. M. Look here! What's the meaning of it all? You never intend to leave us. You can't. Isn't the best squadron of the best regiment of the best cavalry in all the world good enough for you?

CAPT. G. (Jerking his head over his shoulder.) She doesn't seem to thrive in this God-forsaken country, and there's The Butcha to be considered and all that, you know.

CAPT. M. Does she say that she doesn't like India?

CAPT. G. That's the worst of it. She won't for fear of leaving me.

CAPT. M. What are the Hills made for?

CAPT. G. Not for my wife, at any rate.

CAPT. M. You know too much, Gaddy, and--I don't like you any the better for it!

CAPT. G. Never mind that. She wants England, and The Butcha would be all the better for it. I'm going to chuck. You don't understand.

CAPT. M. (Hotly.) I understand this One hundred and thirty-seven new horse to be licked into shape somehow before Luck comes round again; a hairy-heeled draft who'll give more trouble than the horses; a camp next cold weather for a certainty; ourselves the first on the roster; the Russian shindy ready to come to a head at five minutes' notice, and you, the best of us all, backing out of it all! Think a little, Gaddy. You won't do it.

CAPT. G. Hang it, a man has some duties toward his family, I suppose.

CAPT. M. I remember a man, though, who told me, the night after Amdheran, when we were picketed under Jagai, and he'd left his sword--by the way, did you ever pay Ranken for that sword?--in an Utmanzai's head--that man told me that he'd stick by me and the Pinks as long as he lived. I don't blame him for not sticking by me--I'm not much of a man-- but I do blame him for not sticking by the Pink Hussars.

CAPT. G. (Uneasily.) We were little more than boys then. Can't you see, Jack, how things stand? 'Tisn't as if we were serving for our bread. We've all of us, more or less, got the filthy lucre. I'm luckier than some, perhaps. There's no call for me to serve on.

CAPT. M. None in the world for you or for us, except the Regimental. If you don't choose to answer to that, of course–

CAPT. G. Don't be too hard on a man. You know that a lot of us only take up the thing for a few years and then go back to Town and catch on with the rest.

CAPT. M. Not lots, and they aren't some of Us.

CAPT. G. And then there are one's affairs at Home to be considered--my place and the rents, and all that. I don't suppose my father can last much longer, and that means the title, and so on.

CAPT. M. 'Fraid you won't be entered in the Stud Book correctly unless you go Home? Take six months, then, and come out in October. If I could slay off a brother or two, I s'pose I should be a Marquis of sorts. Any fool can be that; but it needs men, Gaddy--men like you--to lead flanking squadrons properly. Don't you delude yourself into the belief that you're going Home to take your place and prance about among pink-nosed Kabuli dowagers. You aren't built that way. I know better.

CAPT. G. A man has a right to live his life as happily as he can. You aren't married.

CAPT. M. No--praise be to Providence and the one or two women who have had the good sense to jawab me.

CAPT. G. Then you don't know what it is to go into your own room and see your wife's head on the pillow, and when everything else is safe and the house shut up for the night, to wonder whether the roof-beams won't give and kill her.

CAPT. M. (Aside.) Revelations first and second! (Aloud.) So-o! I knew a man who got squiffy at our Mess once and confided to me that he never helped his wife on to her horse without praying that she'd break her neck before she came back. All husbands aren't alike, you see.

CAPT. G. What on earth has that to do with my case? The man must ha' been mad, or his wife as bad as they make 'em.

CAPT. M. (Aside.) 'No fault of yours if either weren't all you say. You've forgotten the time when you were insane about the Herriott woman. You always were a good hand at forgetting. (Aloud.) Not more mad than men who go to the other extreme. Be reasonable, Gaddy. Your roof-beams are sound enough.

CAPT. G. That was only a way of speaking. I've been uneasy and worried about the Wife ever since that awful business three years ago--when--I nearly lost her. Can you wonder?

CAPT. M. Oh, a shell never falls twice in the same place. You've paid your toll to misfortune--why should your Wife be picked out more than anybody else's?

CAPT. G. I can talk just as reasonably as you can, but you don't understand--you don't understand. And then there's The Butcha. Deuce knows where the Ayah takes him to sit in the evening! He has a bit of a cough. Haven't you noticed it?

CAPT. M. Bosh! The Brigadier's jumping out of his skin with pure condition. He's got a muzzle like a rose-leaf and the chest of a two-year-old. What's demoralized you?

CAPT. G. Funk. That's the long and the short of it. Funk!

CAPT. M. But what is there to funk?

CAPT. G. Everything. It's ghastly.

CAPT. M. Ah! I see.

You don't want to fight, And by Jingo when we do, You've got the kid, you've got the Wife, You've got the money, too.

That's about the case, eh?

CAPT. G. I suppose that's it. But it's not br myself. It's because of them. At least I think it is.

CAPT. M. Are you sure? Looking at the matter in a cold-blooded light, the Wife is provided for even if you were wiped out tonight. She has an ancestral home to go to, money and the Brigadier to carry on the illustrious name.

CAPT. G. Then it is for myself or because they are part of me. You don't see it. My life's so good, so pleasant, as it is, that I want to make it quite safe. Can't you understand?

CAPT. M. Perfectly. "Shelter-pit for the Off'cer's charger," as they say in the Line.

CAPT. G. And I have everything to my hand to make it so. I'm sick of the strain and the worry for their sakes out here; and there isn't a single real difficulty to prevent my dropping it altogether. It'll only cost me--Jack, I hope you'll never know the shame that I've been going through for the past six months.

CAPT. M. Hold on there! I don't wish to be told. Every man has his moods and tenses sometimes.

CAPT. G. (Laughing bitterly.) Has he? What do you call craning over to see where your near-fore lands?

CAPT. M. In my case it means that I have been on the Considerable Bend, and have come to parade with a Head and a Hand. It passes in three strides.

CAPT. G. (Lowering voice.) It never passes with me, Jack.

I'm always thinking about it. Phil Gadsby funking a fall on parade! Sweet picture, isn't it! Draw it for me.

CAPT. M. (Gravely.) Heaven forbid! A man like you can't be as bad as that. A fall is no nice thing, but one never gives it a thought.

CAPT. G. Doesn't one? Wait till you've got a wife and a youngster of your own, and then you'll know how the roar of the squadron behind you turns you cold all up the back.

CAPT. M. (Aside.) And this man led at Amdheran after Bagal Deasin went under, and we were all mixed up together, and he came out of the snow dripping like a butcher. (Aloud.) Skittles! The men can always open out, and you can always pick your way more or less. We haven't the dust to bother us, as the men have, and whoever heard of a horse stepping on a man?

CAPT. G. Never-as long as he can see. But did they open out for poor 'Errington?

CAPT. M. Oh, this is childish!

CAPT. G. I know it is, worse than that. I don't care. You've ridden Van Loo. Is he the sort of brute to pick his way-'specially when we're coming up in column of troop with any pace on?

CAPT. M. Once in a Blue Moon do we gallop in column of troop, and then only to save time. Aren't three lengths enough for you?

CAPT. G. Yes--quite enough. They just allow for the full development of the smash. I'm talking like a cur, I know: but I tell you that, for the past three months, I've felt every hoof of the squadron in the small of my back every time that I've led.

CAPT. M. But, Gaddy, this is awful!

CAPT. G. Isn't it lovely? Isn't it royal? A Captain of the ink Hussars watering up his charger before parade like the blasted boozing Colonel of a Black Regiment!

CAPT. M. You never did!

CAPT. G. Once Only. He squelched like a mussuck, and the Troop--Sergeant-Major cocked his eye at me. You know old Haffy's eye. I was afraid to do it again.

CAPT. M. I should think so. That was the best way to rupture old Van Loo's tummy, and make him crumple you up. You knew that.

CAPT. G. I didn't care. It took the edge off him.

CAPT. M. "Took the edge off him"? Gaddy, you--you--you mustn't, you know! Think of the men.

CAPT. G. That's another thing I am afraid of. D'you s'pose they know?

CAPT. M. Let's hope not; but they're deadly quick to spot skirm--little things of that kind. See here, old man, send the Wife Home for the hot weather and come to Kashmir with me. We'll start a boat on the Dal or cross the Rhotang--shoot ibex or loaf--which you please. Only come! You're a bit off your oats and you're talking nonsense. Look at the Colonel--swag-bellied rascal that he is. He has a wife and no end of a bow-window of his own. Can any one of us ride round him--chalkstones and all? I can't, and I think I can shove a crock along a bit.

CAPT. G. Some men are different. I haven't any nerve. Lord help me, I haven't the nerve! I've taken up a hole and a half to get my knees well under the wallets. I can't help it. I'm so afraid of anything happening to me. On my soul, I ought to be broke in front of the squadron, for cowardice.

CAPT. M. Ugly word, that. I should never have the courage to own up.

CAPT. G. I meant to lie about my reasons when I began, but--I've got out of the habit of lying to you, old man. Jack, you won't?--But I know you won't.

CAPT. M. Of course not. (Half aloud.) The Pinks are paying dearly for their Pride.

CAPT. G. Eb! What-at?

CAPT. M. Don't you know? The men have called Mrs. Gadsby the Pride of the Pink Hussars ever since she came to us.

CAPT. G. 'Tisn't her fault. Don't think that. It's all mine.

CAPT. M. What does she say?

CAPT. G. I haven't exactly put it before her. She's the best little woman in the world, Jack, and all that--but she wouldn't counsel a man to stick to his calling if it came between him and her. At least, I think--

CAPT. M. Never mind. Don't tell her what you told me. Go on the Peerage and Landed-Gentry tack.

CAPT. G. She'd see through it. She's five times cleverer than I am.

CAPT. M. (Aside.) Then she'll accept the sacrifice and think a little bit worse of him for the rest of her days.

CAPT. G. (Absently.) I say, do you despise me?

CAPT. M. 'Queer way of putting it. Have you ever been asked that question? Think a minute. What answer used you to give?

CAPT. G. So bad as that? I'm not entitled to expect anything more, butit's a bit hard when one's best friend turns round and--

CAPT. M. So! have found But you will have consolations--Bailiffs and Drains and Liquid Manure and the Primrose League, and, perhaps, if you're lucky, the Colonelcy of a Yeomanry Cav-al-ry Regiment--all uniform and no riding, I believe. How old are you?

CAPT. G. Thirty-three. I know it's--

CAPT. M. At forty you'll be a fool of a J. P. landlord. At fifty you'll own a bath-chair, and The Brigadier, if he takes after you, will be fluttering the dovecotes of--what's the particular dunghill you're going to? Also, Mrs. Gadsby will be fat.

CAPT. G. (Limply.) This is rather more than a joke.

CAPT. M. D'you think so? Isn't cutting the Service a joke? It generally takes a man fifty years to arrive at it. You're quite right, though. It is more than a joke. You've managed it in thirty-three.

CAPT. G. Don't make me feel worse than I do. Will it satisfy you if I own that I am a shirker, a skrim-shanker, and a coward?

CAPT. M. It wil! not, because I'm the only man in the world who can talk to you like this without being knocked down. You mustn't take all that I've said to heart in this way. I only spoke--a lot of it at least--out of pure selfishness, because, because--Oh, damn it all, old man,--I don't know what I shall do without you. Of course, you've got the money and the place and all that--and there are two very good reasons why you should take care of yourself.

CAPT. G. 'Doesn't make it any sweeter. I'm backing out--I know I am. I always had a soft drop in me somewhere--and I daren't risk any danger to them.

CAPT. M. Why in the world should you? You're bound to think of your family-bound to think. Er--hmm. If I wasn't a younger son I'd go too--be shot if I wouldn't!

CAPT. G. Thank you, Jack. It's a kind lie, but it's the blackest you've told for some time. I know what I'm doing, and I'm going into it with my eyes open. Old man, I can't help it. What would you do if you were in my place?

CAPT. M. (Aside.) 'Couldn't conceive any woman getting

permanently between me and the Regiment. (Aloud.) 'Can't say. 'Very likely I should do no better. I'm sorry for you--awf'ly sorry--but "if them's your sentiments," I believe, I really do, that you are acting wisely.

CAPT. G. Do you? I hope you do. (In a whisper.) Jack, be very sure of yourself before you marry. I'm an ungrateful ruffian to say this, but marriage--even as good a marriage as mine has been--hampers a man's work, it cripples his sword-arm, and oh, it plays Hell with his notions of duty. Sometimes--good and sweet as she is--sometimes I could wish that I had kept my freedom--No, I don't mean that exactly.

MRS. G. (Coming down veranda.) What are you wagging your head over, Pip?

CAPT. M. (Turning quickly.) Me, as usual. The old sermon. Your husband is recommending me to get married. 'Never saw such a one-ideaed man.

MRS. G. Well, why don't you? I dare say you would make some woman very happy.

CAPT. G. There's the Law and the Prophets, Jack. Never mind the Regiment. Make a woman happy. (Aside.) O Lord!

CAPT. M. We'll see. I must be off to make a Troop Cook desperately unhappy. I won't have the wily Hussar fed on Government Bullock Train shinbones--(Hastily.) Surely black ants can't be good for The Brigadier. He's picking em off the matting and eating 'em. Here, Senor Comandante Don Grubbynuse, come and talk to me. (Lifts G. JUNIOR in his arms.) 'Want my watch? You won't be able to put it into your mouth, but you can try. (G. JUNIOR drops watch, breaking dial and hands.)

MRS. G. Oh, Captain Mafflin, I am so sorry! Jack, you bad, bad little villain. Ahhh!

CAPT. M. It's not the least consequence, I assure you.

He'd treat the world in the same way if he could get it into his hands. Everything's made to be played, with and broken, isn't it, young 'un?

* * * *

MRS. G. Mafflin didn't at all like his watch being broken, though he was too polite to say so. It was entirely his fault for giving it to the child. Dem little puds are werry, werry feeble, aren't dey, by Jack-in-de-box? (To G.) What did he want to see you for?

CAPT. G. Regimental shop as usual.

MRS. G. The Regiment! Always the Regiment. On my word, I sometimes feel jealous of Mafflin.

CAPT. G. (Wearily.) Poor old Jack? I don't think you need. Isn't it time for The Butcha to have his nap? Bring a chair out here, dear. I've got some thing to talk over with you.

www.ingramcontent.com/pod-product-compliance
Lightning Source LLC
Chambersburg PA
CBHW031924110726

47902CB00001B/28